❧ Bear Ridge ❧

BEAR RIDGE

A NOVEL

ELAINE LONG

University of New Mexico Press
Albuquerque

Library of Congress Cataloging-in-Publication Data

Long, Elaine.
Bear ridge / Elaine Long.
p. cm.
ISBN-13: 978-0-8263-3742-9 (cloth : alk. paper)
ISBN-10: 0-8263-3742-2 (cloth : alk. paper)
1. Bears—Fiction.
2. Biologists—Fiction.
3. Utah—Fiction. I. Title.

PS3562.O4937B43 2006
813'.54—dc22
2005031378

DESIGN AND COMPOSITION: *Mina Yamashita*

⟡ For the Bears ⟡

For: Hal Black and Dianna Black, Scott Richardson
and Kendra Richardson, Brett Hill

With Special Thanks To: Annetta Hiatt, Janene Auger,
Sylvia and Martin Bingham, Paul Bingham, DVM, Bob Bernhardt,
Butch Propernick, John Mueller, Brenda Troudt

With appreciation and love: To my daughter Mary K. Long
for constant, loving support and courageous critical reviews.
To my granddaughter Angela Moreno-Long (T. & T. & F. & E.).
To my generous and caring son-in-law Rafael Moreno-Sanchez

In loving memory of Arthur W. Long

✢

Acknowledgments

I could never have written this book without the help of the people named in the dedication. I bless them all.

Now, to correct past omissions: I want to thank Natalie Hill and Paul Whyman for help with the research on Bittersweet Country. My thanks as well to Hy Cohen for his part in the publication of earlier novels.

I deeply appreciate Richard Wheeler's intelligent reading and helpful advice about Bear Ridge. And I thank Carl Donner for his reading of the manuscript and for gifts with a bear motif.

I am especially grateful to Luther Wilson for his support and interest. ∾

Author's Note

When one does research in the field, as I do, the people one meets are the best part of the research. All over the West, there are fascinating men and women doing interesting, unusual work.

It is my custom to create my characters before going into the field. When I introduce the characters to the experts who have agreed to help me, we have a lot of fun as they make suggestions about the plot and the problems.

There is an ongoing bear study out of Brigham Young University in Utah. The members of the project were generous with their knowledge. They hauled me around on their four-wheelers and let me slow down their work as I had "hands-on" experience with the bears. (None of them was ever as ungracious as some of the characters in this book.) I was cherished and cared for while I was at the project. The professors and members of the crews took the time to read the manuscript to be sure the technical information was correct. I will always be grateful.

The other people to whom this book is dedicated were also generous with time and information. They showed me the Ruger Redhawk, allowed me to sit in a bear stand, described hunting from a stand, and showed me the bear carcass after a hunt.

The parts of the Honor Code that are included in Bear Ridge are authentic. Although thousands of students sign the Honor Code, live by it, and graduate from BYU having honored it, the Honor Code itself is a subject of fierce debate on the BYU campus, a debate too complicated for inclusion in Kelly's story. I am grateful to Sybil Downing and Jerrie Hurd for their consideration of this aspect of the book and for their valuable comments. ❧

Chapter One

Kelly Jones paused on the steps of the Widstoe Building on the Brigham Young University campus to knock snow from her boots. As she bent to free a scrap of soggy paper from her heel, Rick Santini came up behind her and swatted her smartly on her jeans-clad rear with the flat of his hand. Kelly jerked upward, but Santini bounded up the stairs and into the building.

Kelly gritted her teeth and stood still, attempting to regain her poise. Rick Santini didn't want her on the project. She already knew that. This was just another way—though a new and especially distasteful one—of trying to intimidate her. For a moment she was tempted to abort the lab session she had scheduled for herself, but she took a deep breath and straightened her shoulders. No point in giving Santini the satisfaction of knowing he had rattled her. She moved into the building and to the bear lab in the basement. As she stepped inside the empty lab, Kelly's nose prickled. The odor of warm bear scat seeped from the laboratory oven.

She smiled thinking of Matt's early morning phone call. She had declined his invitation to go skiing and had mentioned her lab work.

"Great," Matt said. "My girl turns me down so she can study bear shit."

"We call it scat."

"Nice neutral term," Matt said. "What in hell can you learn poking around in . . . scat?"

"You'd be surprised how much I know about a bear by the time I've analyzed a sample." Kelly put the phone against her shoulder and talked as she finished dressing. "I know the variety of things the bear has eaten—acorns, berries, ants. I can even tell the season of the year."

"Well, I can tell you're too—uh—deeply involved to go skiing today, but when am I going to see you?"

Kelly hesitated. "I've got a lot of studying to do."

"Tell me something new." He sounded sulky.

"Darn it, Matt," Kelly said. "Will you back off? Did I ever want to be anything but a biologist?" Between her classes and study schedule and her weekend work in the store, finding moments to see Matt was a constant problem. But it wasn't his fault. She softened her tone. "You know it takes time."

"Yeah, but I didn't know it was going to take you off into the woods with a couple of horny intellectuals."

He's jealous! For a moment she was furious. Matt didn't seem to think she would have any control over the situation. She said, "I wish I were as certain as you are that I'm heading for the woods. I haven't heard from Dr. Andrews. Maybe they won't let me on the project."

"How can they keep you off the project? You've earned the right to go."

Matt was back on her side. Kelly took a deep breath. "Rick Santini is field leader, and he doesn't want me on the project."

"What did you ever do to Santini?"

Kelly gathered her notebooks and stuffed them into her day pack. "I don't know, Matt. He came into the program as a totally funded, hotshot brain. I guess he was used to being alone at the top of the academic heap. He wasn't gracious when I moved into 'his' territory this year, and he thinks all the bears on that mountain belong to him."

"Well, don't let him get you down," Matt said. "Hey, I'll call you when I'm off the slopes."

Kelly selected several dried scat samples and moved into her study area at the back of the lab. She had set up a microscope on a desk behind the file cabinets where she enjoyed relative privacy and the chance for total concentration. She reached for a stack of blank data sheets, sat down, and focused the microscope on the first sample.

∾

"I knew I'd find you here."

Kelly looked up. Her sister Peggy smiled at her from the doorway. "Hi, Peg. I thought you undergraduates didn't believe in Saturday classes."

"Heavens, girl, I'm not on campus to study." Peggy rolled her blue eyes upward. "I came to drag you away for lunch. I bet you don't even know what time it is."

Kelly could never resist her younger sister's Irish grin. "You got me," she said. "What time is it?"

"Three o'clock."

"Really?" Kelly stood and reached for her jacket.

After Kelly and Peggy had settled into a booth in the Cougareat, Peggy said, "I haven't seen you at home for a week. Are you always in that lab?"

"Lab, library, or hardware store." Kelly poured a puddle of ketchup on her plate and swirled a french fry around in it. Then she looked at her sister. "Oh, Peg, I want this bear project more than I ever wanted anything. It's perfect field research, and I can get a significant thesis out of it. Something solid—covering new ground—at least in Utah."

Peggy said, "You've seen Rick Santini today haven't you?"

Kelly blinked. "How can you tell?"

"You're always hyper after a run-in with him."

Kelly told Peggy about the incident on the steps.

"Is he coming on to you?"

Kelly shook her head. "The tension between us isn't sexual."

Peggy grinned around the tuna-fish sandwich she had lifted to her mouth. "Kelly, you crack me up. All tension between males and females is sexual—and especially when the male is Rick Santini. Haven't you ever looked at him?"

Kelly laughed. "Sure. I've done a data sheet on him. Height—six foot two. Weight—hundred and seventy-five pounds. Pelage—dark brown, excellent condition. Estimated age—twenty-seven years. No visible snare wounds."

Peggy added to Kelly's list. "No collar, no ear tags. But nice tight buns." She peered at Kelly. "'Fess up. Aren't you ever tempted to pat him on the butt?"

Kelly laughed again. "I made some rules for myself when I started grad school," she said. "I never attend late-night social sessions. I never date grad students in my department and . . ." She jabbed a french fry toward her sister in emphasis. "I absolutely never look upon master's candidates as sex objects."

Peggy giggled and then asked, "How are the rest of them treating you this semester?"

Kelly said, "We're all more relaxed. I was so scared last fall—starting the graduate program and being the only female in this particular group—that I took every unfriendly action as being hostile to me as a woman. I never noticed how nervous the men were." She paused, thinking about how much easier this semester had been. "Now that we all know each other, they give me some measure of respect. They don't interrupt me as often as they used to when I speak up in class."

"Negative progress," Peggy said.

Kelly ignored her sister's comment and continued, "But it always amazes me how much they interrupt each other. Their never-ending need to dominate keeps group tension high."

"You seem to thrive on that kind of tension," Peggy said.

Kelly nodded. "There's something to be said for having a Santini heading the pack." She reached across to squeeze her sister's hand. "It's nice to see you on campus, and you're good for me. This morning, I felt like murdering Rick Santini, but you've got me complimenting him."

"Don't tell Matt," Peggy said.

Kelly met her eyes. "Has Matt been crying on your shoulder?"

Peggy drained her glass and wiped away a milky mustache. "He says that every time you mention this big-deal, government-sponsored bear project, he's more aware that he drives a logging truck."

"Oh . . . scat," Kelly said. "He's a logging contractor; he owns his own company; he's got a hundred skills I wish I had. Why does he have to do that to himself? He didn't act that way when I was an undergrad."

"Maybe because you're not seeing him as a sex object these days, either."

Kelly waved an impatient hand. "Did he send you to the lab to talk to me?"

"It was my own idea. Cross my heart." Peggy solemnly sketched an X on her chest, looking more like nine years old than nineteen until she said, "Matt wouldn't put me in a bind with you."

"Matt didn't used to put me in a bind either, but ever since I applied for this field program, he's been different."

"Different how?"

"Suddenly, he is trying to own me."

"Maybe he just thinks it's time to get more serious. You've known each other forever." Peggy smiled at a student who greeted her from another booth. "Maybe he's going to propose."

"I hope not," Kelly said. "It was always fun—learning to ski, learning to drive his jeep, shooting his twenty-two, but I don't think that leads to a wedding."

"Don't you want to get married?"

"Well, sure, someday. But I want to marry somebody who includes my mind on his data sheet."

"You're kind of hard on Matt."

"You like him, don't you?"

"Well shoot, Kelly, he's been around our place a long time, acting like my big brother."

Kelly felt a flicker of annoyance. "Matt's enlisted everyone," she said.

"Except Dad," Peggy said. "He thinks he kept Mom from getting her degree. He doesn't want Matt to do that to you."

Kelly had started to rise, but she sat back down. "Am I missing something at home?"

"Now that I'm on campus, Mom seems more restless than usual."

"Do you think she wants to go back to school?"

"She says she can't because Dad needs her to clerk in the store, but she's just scared she'll fail, and she won't admit it."

Kelly felt a surge of sympathy for her mother. "You're not being fair. Dad can't afford another clerk, and since Mom is also his bookkeeper, she knows that."

Peggy tossed her head. "If you really want to do something, you can always find a way."

What way will I find if Dr. Andrews turns me down for the bear project? Kelly stood. "I've got to get back to the lab."

Peggy left her at the steps of the zoology building, and Kelly returned to the scat samples in her small room, relieved to escape the family gossip and the unhappy rumblings from Matt.

She had been working for an hour when she heard voices just outside the door. She recognized Rick Santini's deep baritone, but not the other male voice. They were talking about the perpetual problem of finding bear bait. She listened to the discussion of dead cows, but focused most of her attention on the microscope until she heard Santini mention Dr. Andrews.

"Sure, Jerry knows how I feel about dumping Kelly Jones into the project. I told him this morning that I'm not hot about spending the summer babysitting."

Kelly's pulse leaped, and she clenched her fists. "Come on, Santini," the other voice said. "She's not dumb and not bad-looking if you like the type."

"Well I don't like the type. It's a bad cross between a female grad student and an earth muffin."

He knows I'm in here, Kelly thought. He's set this up on purpose. She didn't know the men's description of a female grad student, but she had heard one of them define an earth muffin: long stringy hair, long cotton skirt, chunky leather sandals. Attends readings of esoteric poetry and weeps over obscure endangered species. Damn you, Rick Santini, I'm every bit as good, every bit as objective a scientist as you are, and you've never seen me weep over anything.

She couldn't stay in the lab. She replaced the samples and filed her data sheets. On her way out of the building, she checked her box, and her chest felt suddenly tight. Dr. Andrews had left a note asking her to drop in and see him on Monday morning. ∽

Chapter Two

Kelly wriggled away from the impatient finger that poked her shoulder. "Kelly, are you awake?"

"I am now, Ryan," she said as her brother pulled the covers from her head. "Sunday is my only morning to sleep in. Go pester Peggy." She nodded toward the hump in the bed across the room.

Ryan grinned. "Peggy's out in Matt's truck. We talked him into taking us skiing at Alta."

"Well, go. Go!" Kelly said, tugging unsuccessfully at the blanket in Ryan's hand.

"Can I borrow the gloves Matt gave you for your birthday?"

"They're in the bottom drawer of my dresser."

"I know," Ryan said, "but I didn't think I should just take them."

Kelly captured her blanket and the twelve-year-old in a bear hug. "You're a good kid."

Ryan squirmed away and said, "I almost forgot. Matt says he'll pick you up at six."

Bundling in the blanket, she tried to go back to sleep, but instead she began a review of the notes she'd studied until midnight. It was vital to find a focus for her field study—if Rick Santini didn't foul up her chances for getting into the field. As her thoughts veered toward Santini, she groaned and got up to take a shower. She made her bed, and then attacking the lump of bedclothes, began making Peggy's bed.

"That's nice of you."

Kelly looked up. Her mother stood just outside the doorway. "Not really. Peggy's housekeeping makes me feel itchy." She regretted her words immediately. Peggy and her mother kept house in the same way, and she could tell by the way her mother pulled back that she felt criticized. Kelly said, "Come in and talk."

Her mother sidled in and sat on the edge of Kelly's bed. "Didn't you want to go skiing?"

"I wasn't invited. But anyway, I'd rather spend the day getting ready for my interview with Dr. Andrews."

"About this bear thing." Her mother shifted her position on the bed. "I know you're an adult, but . . ." She plucked a piece of lint from the bedspread and leaned to put it into the wastebasket. She's thinner than usual, Kelly thought. Her mother was small, sparse, dark-haired with intelligent brown eyes in a tight-lipped face. She was an indifferent cook and a haphazard housekeeper, but she had been a wonderful tutor, especially for Kelly's math homework. The closest moments they had ever shared were over tough trigonometry problems, her mother patiently explaining in as many ways as it took until Kelly understood. Kelly felt sympathy for her mother as she waited for her to find a way to say what she really meant. Sympathy followed by irritation, because her mother was never going to say what she meant.

Kelly moved to the dressing table and began to replace the lids on Peggy's cosmetics jars. Her mother perched tensely on the edge of the bed. Kelly glanced into the mirror and studied her mother's closed face; then she looked at her own reflection. Rick Santini was wrong about her. She was not an earth muffin. Her blonde hair was straight, but never stringy. It fell smoothly to her shoulders, staying easily in place. She didn't own a long cotton skirt or a pair of chunky leather sandals. Most of the time, she wore sneakers and jeans with tailored shirts and cardigans.

"Will you have a room of your own this summer?"

Kelly turned from the mirror. "I don't know. They're moving to a new location on the mountain. The Forest Service will probably donate the use of a cabin."

"I hope it's adequate." Kelly looked around the small room. Like every house they had ever lived in, this one was too small for the family—definitely not adequate. Her mother rose. "I'd better see to breakfast. Your father wants you to help him unload the van this morning." She paused at the door. "You will be careful on this project won't you, Kelly?"

"Don't worry. I'm only interested in bears."

Her mother said, "Did you know that some Indian tribes wouldn't let the women eat bear meat? They reserved its power for the men." In its strange way—as was so often true with her mother's odd comments— the remark was to the point. Rick Santini wanted the power of the bear project for himself.

The old khaki-colored delivery van sat in the store parking lot. Kelly fingered the gear-shift rod through its temperamental dance into reverse and, dragging the steering wheel around, angled the van into the alley and lined it up with the rear doors of the store. After she set the brake and slid out of the van, her father handed her a carton of nails. She lugged it into the store and deposited it next to the nail bin. He followed with another box, setting it by the first, and then turned to Kelly. "Before you make a final decision about this summer plan of yours," he said, "we need to talk about money."

"I'll get a small paycheck," Kelly said. "Not right away, maybe, but the project will eventually pay for my summer expenses."

But her father was thinking about his expenses. "I'll have to replace you, and I can't afford to pay another delivery driver and still give you money in the fall."

"Well, there's some of Grandma's money left. It will pay for part of my tuition, and if I do okay this summer, Dr. Andrews might get me on as a guaranteed student in the fall."

Kelly's father opened a box of ten-penny nails and began to fill the metal bins. "It's a shame my mother didn't see fit to leave money for Peggy's tuition, too."

Kelly did not wish to talk about her grandmother's bequest again. Her grief about her grandmother's death and her joy in knowing that there was money for college had both been tainted by a sense of guilt. "She knew I wanted to be a biologist," Kelly said, because she didn't know what else to say.

Kelly's father grinned at her, and grinning, looked like Peggy, who had inherited his red hair and blue eyes. "Your grandmother always knew what everyone wanted." Despite the grin, the bitterness in the remark came through.

"Didn't you want the hardware store?"

Her father stepped out to the van, and she thought he was going to evade her question, but when he came back, he set a bolt box in the next aisle and said, "It was time to settle down, I guess, but you know Kel, there's nothing like being on the road—tracking your customers, sizing them up, getting them in your clutches, and selling them. It's a great gamble, every time." He looked around the store and added, "It stirs up your blood a lot more than restocking for the same group of do-it-yourselfers every Sunday for seven years."

Kelly was quiet, waiting, unwilling to interrupt the unusual confidence. "I suppose my mother was still hoping to reform me when she set us up in Provo." He pried the lid from the box. "But nothing repays you for leaving your own path," he said. He pointed a thick finger at her. "So if your path has to take you into bear country, we'll manage without you for the summer."

Kelly turned back to unloading, shaken by the insight into her father's unhappiness. It was a family given that her mother was unhappy, but the bleakness in her father's eyes made her stomach hurt. They finished in silence and afterward, Kelly asked her father to drop her off at the lab. It would be a relief to return to the well-ordered data sheets. "Tell Matt I'll be on the south side of the Widstoe Building at six."

❦

Matt had double-parked his red Dodge pickup in the small parking lot. Kelly hurried to climb in. He smiled at her, teeth pearly in a face burnished by the wind and sun. His blonde hair was sun-bleached almost white. Kelly returned his smile, enjoying the way his blue eyes sparkled. Matt maneuvered the pickup out of the lot. "Dink's okay?" Dink's was a noisy truck stop. She wasn't in the mood for one of Matt's places, but she nodded. It was easier than discussing restaurants they could agree on.

The cafe was neon-lighted with yellow-painted cinder block walls. As Matt opened the door for her, a blast of music from the jukebox drowned out her "thank you." She followed Matt toward a booth knowing that by the time they left, her hair would smell of smoke. They ordered, and as they ate, Matt launched into a report of his bidding for summer logging jobs. Kelly ate quietly, nodding occasionally, but thinking about the odd exchange she'd had with her father. She realized suddenly that Matt had stopped talking and was looking at her. He said, "I don't think you've heard a damned word I've been saying. Something go wrong with your bear shit today?"

"I'm just tired, Matt. I helped Dad unload a whole vanload of bolts and nails before I went to the lab." She hesitated and then, because she needed to talk about it, she said, "And I had an upsetting conversation with him."

"Did he say you can't go to that bear project?"

There was such a hopeful tone to Matt's comment that Kelly was annoyed. "No, he's all for my going, although he's worried about money as usual." She watched as Matt moved his steak to the front of his plate, and then she said, "I never realized how much my father hates what he's doing. If my grandmother hadn't bought the store, I don't think we'd have settled in Provo."

"Yeah, Peggy's told me about your grandmother." Matt cut a large chunk from his steak. "She was a meddlesome old biddy."

Meddlesome! Peggy had called Grandma a meddler? Kelly couldn't answer for a moment. Then she picked her words carefully. "I guess some people might have seen it that way," she said, "but I think she was truly concerned for us. We were just drifting from town to town. Peggy and I had been to seven different schools by the time I was a junior in high school. I'm glad Grandma helped us to settle in Provo."

"But your dad was doing okay. And your mom always seems to go along."

Kelly felt a rush of resentment. He didn't have a clue to her mother's unhappiness. The only necessary thing, apparently, was that her mother should give in to her father's wishes. She said, "I owe a lot to Grandma. She gave me my first plant-identification book."

"Not to mention enough money for four years of college and her old Buick," Matt said, "leaving Peggy and Ryan out in the cold."

Kelly tried to lead the conversation in a different direction. "If we hadn't settled in Provo, you and I would never have met."

Matt was wiping steak juice from his plate with a piece of bread. He looked up. "So what good did that do us? You're going to take off and live with the bears."

Her hand tightened on her fork. He was still sulking. "You have projects every summer," she said.

"That's different. That's my job," he said. He didn't give her a chance to respond, but gestured at her half-empty plate. "You finished with that? You want dessert?" She shook her head and rose from the booth when he did. The noisy music had given her a headache.

Matt drove away from town and took a side road that led to a clearing on the hill, an open place where they parked from time to time. "Matt, I can't stay out late."

"You don't have a curfew like some high school kid."

"No, but I have an important meeting tomorrow."

Matt reached for her and said, "Well, come on, just look at the moon for a while."

She slid into the familiar circle of his arm and looked out at the dark sky where a tiny cuticle of moon gleamed, not giving enough light to illuminate the clearing, let alone the shadowy depths under the trees at its edge. "Not much of a moon."

"Picky, picky," he said, pulling her closer to him. She leaned her head against his shoulder, and they were silent.

Then she stirred. "I really do need to get home. I have a meeting with Dr. Andrews at nine o'clock in the morning." Matt's hand tightened on her shoulder. *He could at least wish me good luck.* But without saying anything at all, Matt turned and grasped her chin with his left hand, tilted her mouth upward, and kissed her thoroughly and for a long time.

At first she responded, enjoying his mouth, but when Matt didn't pull away, Kelly tried to. Matt hardened the circle of his arm into a restraint. She twisted her head sideways, but he put his hand on her face and lowered his mouth again for a hard, hurting kiss. She moved her head and began to struggle as Matt's right hand gripped her, and his left hand moved inside her coat, exploring her body. "Stop it, Matt." She grabbed the roving hand. He jerked it free and pushed it down between her legs. What was he doing? He'd never tried to force her before. "Stop it, stop it." She hammered her free hand against his shoulder, but Matt was bending her steadily backward with his body.

"I didn't sign any damned code," he said.

"Well, I did, and even if I hadn't signed the Honor Code, I wouldn't want . . ." Matt stopped her words with his mouth. He was almost on top of her. His belt buckle poked her stomach. Kelly jerked her head upward sharply, hitting Matt's chin. As soon as he reared back, she slid to the door and grabbed the handle. She clung to it as the door opened outward, pulling her with it. As she sagged toward the ground, she swung her legs around and stood up. Slamming the door behind her, she ran toward the shadowy grove of trees.

Well into the darkness, she stopped and leaned against a tree to catch her breath. Damn him. Her breathing gradually became quiet, and her heartbeat slowed. There was no sound from the truck. It was cold and dark under the trees. She shivered, wondering what she should do. It was a long walk to the other side of town. She straightened her clothes. Matt had actually unzipped her jeans a couple of inches. She pulled her coat closer around her, but as she heard the truck door open, she stopped moving and stood completely still. Matt's footsteps crunched through the dried leaves. "Kelly?" His voice was subdued. "Kelly, where are you?" She didn't answer, and when he spoke again, his voice was closer. "Kelly, damn it, you know I'm not going to hurt you. Where are you?"

She buttoned her coat slowly. She could hear him breathing, but he didn't move. Finally, she said, "Over here, Matt."

When his fingers brushed her face as he groped in the dark, she stepped farther into the trees. He didn't follow, but said, "Kelly, I didn't mean to get carried away. But, if you loved me, I'd think you'd want to . . ."

He paused, and despite her anger at his attempt to force her, she felt his pain. She simply could not say what he waited to hear. They'd had good times, been good friends in their way, and now Matt was going to push her until she hurt him. Then he said, "You wouldn't have to worry about getting pregnant or anything. I'm not that dumb. I came prepared."

Her sympathy was swept away. He had planned this. She stepped behind the tree she was leaning on and waited until she could control her voice. "Matt, this is not about my getting pregnant or getting a disease. First of all, I did sign the Honor Code, and my honor matters to me. But even if there weren't a code, I have things to do and plans for my life. I don't want to complicate them with sex. I'm just not ready."

"Well, if you're not ready at twenty-four, when are you going to be ready? You can't be that under-sexed."

She gritted her teeth. "That's stupid, Matt. I'm not some animal that matures and goes into estrus."

"Well, you're sure as hell not living in the modern world."

"Don't be ridiculous. My world is just as much the modern world as anyone else's. If sexual freedom doesn't give me the right to say no, as well as the right to say yes, it isn't freedom. I've heard all these arguments before, Matt, and I've always been grateful that you didn't use them."

"Well, I've spent a hell of a lot of time and money on you."

Kelly gripped the tree to keep from hitting him. "And so I owe you sex? You know what that's called? That's called prostitution." Kelly heard Matt take in a deep breath. *I hate this. I wish we'd just gone home.*

Matt moved in the leaves, and she stepped back, but he didn't touch her. He said, "I love you, Kelly." But there was no tenderness in the phrase. It sounded like blackmail: I love you, so you have to give me what I want.

She said, "I don't think tonight has anything to do with love. I think this is all about power. You are determined to mark me as your possession before I leave for the bear project. You don't want *me*, you want some sort of trophy."

She started toward the edge of the grove, but the ice in Matt's tone stopped her. "Maybe this is *not* about power," he said. "Maybe this is about generosity and caring, if you have any idea what that means. You won't give anything, any time. You talk polite and sweet, but you're as tight and selfish as those damned ugly shirts you wear buttoned clear up to your neck."

Kelly broke and ran for the truck. She climbed in and huddled on the cold seat, hugging her knees, her head buried in her arms. "Tight and selfish. Tight and selfish." The words ricocheted in her head. Matt got into the truck. She did not look at him. He shut the door, and they sat silently in the dark. Finally Kelly said, "If you really think I'm like that, why do you keep asking me to go places?"

Matt laid a hand on her bent head, caressed her hair for a moment, and said, "You always want to learn. You always ask me to teach you what I know, and it's fun to teach you."

Kelly opened her door so the dome light would come on. She needed to make an honest reply, and she wanted to see Matt's face. "You've taught me a lot, Matt, and I've enjoyed learning from you, but are you aware that never once in all these years have you asked me to teach *you* anything?"

Matt's face flushed and for a moment, she thought he would deal with her question—give *her* an honest reply, a reply that might leave them with something. But then Matt grinned and said, "Hell, Kelly, what do I need to learn from you? I've already seen bear scat in the woods." ❧

Chapter Three

"I heard your guitar last night," Peggy said on Monday morning, reaching around Kelly to snatch her makeup from the dressing table.

"I'm sorry if I kept you awake," Kelly said, scooting sideways to give her sister a share of the mirror.

Peggy grinned at her in the glass. "It wasn't the music; it was my curiosity. You haven't sung yourself to sleep for months. Did you and Matt have a fight?"

Kelly studied the pale green shirt and teal blue sweater she had chosen, She didn't want to tell Peggy about last night. "What do you think? Does this outfit look right for an interview with a professor? Should I unbutton the top shirt button? Does it look too . . . tight . . . too uptight?"

Peggy turned. "The color's nice," she said. "Makes your eyes greener. You might wear slacks instead of jeans if you're trying to look dressed up." She picked up her lipstick and leaned toward the mirror. "But I thought you wanted to look tough enough to handle bears."

Kelly slid past her toward the closet. "I guess this outfit is okay." She took a jacket from the hanger, but when she turned, Peggy blocked her way.

"What happened between you and Matt?"

"I told him I thought we should stop seeing each other."

Peggy stared at her for a moment, her eyes darkening to an opaque blue. Finally she said with only the hint of a smile, "The time to break up with Matt is *after* he puts new spark plugs in that creaky old Buick, not before." Peggy paused, and Kelly waited. Her sister seemed to be struggling with some new feelings. But she let it go. Even if she asked, Peggy would just make a joke.

Kelly left the house and turned toward campus, running her hand lightly across the top of her parked car as she passed, leaving dark green lines where her fingers trailed through the dust. Maybe Peggy had a point. The Buick had 67,000 miles on it, and it definitely needed a tune-up.

Dr. Andrews's office door was open, but Kelly paused in the doorway.

Dr. Andrews lounged in his chair, laughing. When he saw Kelly, he sat up straight and said, "Come in, Kelly. These two were just leaving." He nodded toward Rick Santini who sat in a chair by the desk, and when Kelly glanced at him, she couldn't keep from staring.

Rick was wearing gray slacks and a dark blue blazer with a light blue shirt and a maroon tie. As he bent to pick up a black briefcase, she could see the shine of his dark well-cut hair. She had never seen him dressed up before. He was only three years older than she, but he looked ten years older right now, and he also looked totally, thoroughly, absolutely professional. Why hadn't Dr. Andrews warned her that this was a formal meeting? She owned a suit, too. She glanced at the other student.

Standing near the bookcase, with elbows resting behind him on the shelves and one thick-soled boot propped on the edge of the wastebasket, was Adam Wainwright, an undergraduate she'd met on a December weekend at the bear project. He was wearing jeans and a red-and-white-checked flannel shirt. His brown hair was tousled, and when he grinned, he looked as young as Ryan. He had a dimple on his right cheek, which gave his smile a sort of lopsided charm.

Adam smiled at her now, his brown eyes friendly. "Hi, Kelly. Looks like we passed Dr. Andrews's test by rain, hail, sleet, snow, and mechanical insult."

Kelly thought of the miserable weekend that she, Dr. Andrews, Adam, and two other undergraduate volunteers had spent trying to get to a bear's den. The weather had been blustery, neither the snowmobile nor the four-wheeler had run properly, and Dr. Andrews had cancelled the trip after several cold hours on the mountain. She returned Adam's smile and said, "It was fun, wasn't it?"

Adam laughed. Dr. Andrews smiled, but said to Rick and Adam, "Out, you two. Go down to the lab and do something useful, but be back here in half an hour because I want to talk to all three of you together." Kelly swallowed. Adam winked at her as he left. Rick gave her a slight nod. Kelly stepped aside to let him pass, and he closed the door behind him.

Dr. Andrews half rose from his desk, his long thin body bending awkwardly. "Sit down, Kelly." He nodded toward the chair Rick Santini had vacated. Kelly sat down, and Dr. Andrews folded himself into the desk chair. He seemed nervous. He tapped his long fingers on the desk blotter for a moment and then, reaching toward a pack of gum on the desk, he pulled out a stick. He held the pack toward Kelly.

She shook her head, and he unwrapped the gum, dropping the foil wrapping into a large seashell that overflowed with gum wrappers. His cheeks dipped in under his high cheekbones, increasing the gaunt look of his long face. His hair was reddish brown, streaked with gray at the temples; his bristly eyebrows were white. Chewing gum, he looked less formidable. Kelly relaxed a little. She realized she'd been sitting on the edge of her chair.

Dr. Andrews said, "This was planned to be a fairly routine meeting, but something has come up—a difficulty, or at least an unpleasantness." He paused and picked up a pencil that he rolled between his fingers.

Kelly took a deep breath and said, "Would it help if I told you that I already know that Rick Santini has protested my being on the project?"

The professor's face lost some of its gauntness. "Well, thank you, Kelly. Rick does seem to have some strong objections." He smiled at her. "We'll get back to him a little later, and I'll give you a chance to answer them."

Kelly's mouth and throat were dry. She sat up straighter again, trying to think of a reply. But Dr. Andrews, having said that much, was ready to go on to other things. "You have a fine academic record, Kelly. You've done well in the lab, and . . ." The professor met her eyes and smiled. "You even survived our little jaunt in the snow."

"You were testing us!" Kelly said, thinking of the hike through deep snowdrifts and scrubby bushes. She had carried the same size pack as the three guys.

Dr. Andrews nodded. He pointed the eraser end of the pencil her way. "I'd never take an untried student onto a project, even a straight-A student. Not everyone who can pass an exam and do lab work is suited to the field." Kelly thought of the undergraduate who had complained steadily on the long hike down the mountain after the snowmobile had stalled. She would hate to spend a summer with him.

"It's a shame you had to work summers for your dad instead of being an undergraduate volunteer. You could have used the field experience." Dr. Andrews frowned slightly. "But you held up well on that denning trip and you have another quality for which I've been looking, and of which this project is in great need—discretion."

He leaned back, his long legs extending all the way under the desk. "You know that we were hired by the Utah Division of Wildlife Resources and the U.S. Forest Service to provide them with information about bears." Kelly nodded, and he continued. "The biggest challenge for the DWR and the federal people today is that they must try to please everyone. You probably know from the outset, that is impossible."

Holding up his left hand, Dr. Andrews raised the pointer finger. "You have the nonconsumptive users—people who simply want to view wildlife. This group includes those people who want hunting totally abolished on public range lands—hunting of anything."

Dr. Andrews raised a second finger. "And then there are the hunters—deer, elk, bear. But let's just talk about bear hunters. You've got people who get a big kick out of chasing and treeing a bear, looking at it, and walking away. Other houndsmen use their dogs to tree bears so they can shoot them. Some want a spring hunt; others, a fall hunt. Some hunt with a bow, considering a rifle unfair; and the bow hunters themselves are split between those who lure bears with bait and those who hunt from a blind, willing to wait a long time for a bear."

Dr. Andrews took a breath and held up a third finger. Kelly was amused. Maybe she should take notes before he ran out of fingers. Dr. Andrews continued his lecture. "And then you've got the livestock people who are afraid that the division *will* limit the number of hunting permits given here in Utah, and they'll suffer increased stock loss. They're asking, 'Are you killing *enough* bears, *enough* mountain lions?'" Kelly nodded. She had read about some of this.

The professor held up a fourth finger. "There are campers, bikers, and hikers to be considered, too." He raised his thumb. "And the Forest Service is interested in the management of logging."

Dr. Andrews raised his whole hand, fingers extended, and met Kelly's eyes. "Your job, if you go on this project" (Kelly hated the *if*, but she swallowed it and continued to listen.) "—the graduate students' job—is to get the scientific data without alienating these interest groups."

"Will we be dealing with any of them?"

Dr. Andrews nodded his head slowly, looking a little grim. "From time to time, you'll probably have representatives from every group visiting the project. You'll have to feed them and show them around. And if more than one faction arrives at the same time, I'm counting on you to prevent conflict, especially dissension that jeopardizes any aspect of the project—the funding, the data recording, the actual work—whatever."

Kelly leaned back against the chair. *What if the dissension is among the graduate students?* She only thought the question, but Dr. Andrews seemed to address it.

"I like the way you handle yourself in class," he said. "You've got a good sense of humor, and you're always polite and professional." Kelly remembered Matt's assessment: You talk polite and sweet, but you're tight and selfish. Dr. Andrews's words eased that pain a little.

"And now," Dr. Andrews said, "I need to touch on another aspect of your life. I hope you won't find it uncomfortable. If I'm counting on you to man the bear project . . ." He paused and grinned at her. "You aren't going to require that I say 'woman' the bear project?" Kelly laughed and brushed her fingers across the air between them. "As I was saying, if I'm counting on your total attention up there on the mountain, I don't want you to be worrying about some family problem. So tell me, what do your folks think about your plans for the summer?"

Kelly considered a moment before answering. "I think my mother envies me the chance. She didn't finish college. And my father . . . well, yesterday, he said that nothing is as important as following your own path." The half-truths made a nice story. She added another. "And my boyfriend is usually gone in the summer anyway."

Dr. Andrews was nodding his head. *Do we all deal in half-truths?* Kelly thought. *We may try to be honest in what we say, but do we all pick the words carefully out of a huge complicated lie? What if I told him: My mother is lost in misery. My father is on the end of a fraying string. My boyfriend thinks I'm both frigid and rigid. And I'm scared to death that you'll turn me down after Rick Santini grills me.*

But Kelly said nothing. She sat still. She did not move her hands to check her hair; she did not grip her notebook. She simply waited for Dr. Andrews's response.

Dr. Andrews picked up the seashell and leaned to dump the gum wrappers into his wastebasket, and then he rose from the desk. "Let's get Rick and Adam back in here and see if you three will make a team." ∾

Chapter Four

Dr. Andrews and Adam brought chairs from another office, and as soon as everyone was seated, the professor said, "Now, Rick, I know you have a paper to present, so we'll get right down to business." Kelly was relieved to hear that Rick was speaking elsewhere and wasn't dressed up specifically for this interview. Dr. Andrews said, "I want you to outline for Kelly your objections to her being on the project."

Rick blinked his eyes and a flush deepened the olive tint of his skin. Kelly could tell that he had not expected this. She glanced at Dr. Andrews and caught the briefest twinkle.

Rick recovered quickly. "I have two concerns. First, of course, for the project." He turned toward Kelly. "Fieldwork requires more than reading. It's the real thing, not just an easily controlled lab project. Data collection often involves hard physical effort. We weigh the bears while they are tranquilized, and from time to time we snare a male who weighs as much as three hundred pounds. A team member needs the strength to carry his part of the load."

Kelly had to admire his response. His tone was professional, his manner polite. There was no hint of the smart alec who had smacked her on the rear. Rick continued without waiting for her to reply. "In addition to strength, many project tasks require mechanical ability. We build our own snares, maintain the four-wheelers, keep the trailer working smoothly, and do field repairs." He paused.

Kelly decided to answer him before his list of impossibles grew any longer. "I appreciate your concern for the project." She could be as professional, as cool, as Santini. "There are, however, ways to augment physical strength. Deer and elk hunters regularly use a come-along . . ." She paused and then, allowing herself the pleasure of it, she explained the term to Rick. "A small hand winch." He nodded, and she continued, "With rope or chain and a couple of cable clamps, one can devise a way to hoist a heavier animal."

She thought briefly about naming her own skill in driving Matt's jeep and her father's van and about telling Rick how often she lugged boxes of bolts and nails, but she decided to keep her answers impersonal. "The four-wheelers are probably no harder to drive than a jeep or a four-wheel drive pickup, and the ties and hitches used in logging would serve when weighing a bear or pulling a bear from the den." She glanced at Adam who was doodling on the paper on his clipboard as he listened to the exchange.

Rick had changed topics. He spoke now of the primitive living conditions and the isolation, loneliness, and boredom. Kelly turned this topic back to Rick. "How do *you* deal with these conditions?" she asked. Rick's skin flushed to a muddy color. She could tell that he did not like it when a conversation took a turn he hadn't directed. But it was stupid to imply that outdoor toilets, woodstoves, and lack of radio reception were gender-based problems.

"The project work comes first," Rick said, "preparing bear bait, snaring, collecting scat samples, and keeping data sheets up to date. Woodcutting and ash hauling are done in spare moments."

Adam continued to doodle. Kelly could see that he had drawn a box, at the top of which he had lettered SCOREBOARD. Underneath he had labeled two columns—one JONES, the other SANTINI. Beneath the name JONES there was a mark. As Rick finished dealing with the question about the remote camp, Adam made another mark under JONES. Kelly smiled, but Rick was launching a new missile, and she shifted her attention to him, studying his face. She had no idea what emotions lay behind that cold exterior.

As Rick raised his next objection, it seemed to be colored with strong feeling. "The major problem in having a woman associated with the field aspect of the bear study is the difficulty a female's presence creates in public relations. It is vital to the project that we work smoothly with all factions involved in the study. There are prejudices against women in the field."

Kelly thought of the weekend she had gone with the denning crew. Perhaps the men had been a little surprised at first, and they had seemed to glance her way fairly often, but they had not objected in any way to her presence. *This prejudice he's talking about comes mostly from Rick Santini,* Kelly thought, but Santini was still talking. "Many bear trappers believe strongly that women are totally out of place in wild-animal work and especially with bears."

Suddenly Kelly was furious. In icy tones, she said, "I understand the importance of smooth interaction between the Forest Service, the Division of Wildlife, and the project personnel. However, times have changed. There are capable women in every field of endeavor, and few officials find it unusual or remarkable. As for the bear trappers," Kelly felt a flush rise to her face, and she could not keep all emotion from her reply, "I have a job to do, and I am not responsible for other people's prejudices."

She saw Rick's mouth tighten, and she knew she had made a mistake. She glanced at Adam's scoreboard just as he made a mark under the name SANTINI. Adam was right. The score was now Jones–2, Santini–1. Her last remarks had increased Rick Santini's antagonism toward her. Dr. Andrews had picked up a new stick of gum. As he unwrapped it, he nodded his head toward Adam. "What do you think, Adam? Can you work with these two?"

Adam stopped doodling and grinned his lopsided grin. "Sure, I can work with them, but I have an idea that by the end of the summer, I'll wish I were living with the bears."

Dr. Andrews laughed out loud, tossed the gum wrapper in the vicinity of the wastebasket, and stood up. "Well, let's give it a try." Kelly could feel her relief in the pit of her stomach—she was on the project. But Dr. Andrews wasn't quite finished with the interview. He picked up three copies of a small blue brochure from his desk and handed one to each of them. "You'll recognize this, of course, but the department head has asked me to make sure that you review it."

The front of the brochure contained three words in black—On Your Honor. Inside were the principles of the Honor Code. Kelly looked at Dr. Andrews who met her eyes without a smile. She perused the brochure:

> The Church of Jesus Christ of Latter-day Saints sponsors colleges and a university in order to provide an education in an atmosphere consistent with the ideals and principles of the Church. The maintenance of high standards of personal behavior and appearance is essential to the preservation of that atmosphere and to the development of men and women who personify these ideals and principles. By enrolling or accepting employment at a Church college or university, a person signifies his willingness to live in accordance with the following principles, whether on or off campus.

Kelly glanced at Rick and Adam, but they were looking at the brochure. She continued her review, skimming the list of twelve items: Observe high principles of honor, integrity, and morality. Be honest in all behavior—including not cheating, plagiarizing, or knowingly giving false information. Respect personal rights—not physically or verbally abusing any person . . . not obstructing or disrupting the functions of the college or university. Respect property rights. Obey, honor, and sustain the law. Avoid drug abuse. Comply with all college and university regulations. Observe the Word of Wisdom—including abstinence from alcoholic beverages, tobacco, tea, and coffee. Live the law of chastity—including abstinence from all sexual relations outside the bonds of marriage. Observe high standards of taste and decency. Help others fulfill their responsibilities under this code.

Kelly read quickly through the grooming and dress-code paragraphs and kept herself from grinning. What was modest, neat, and dignified attire for collecting bear scat? She closed the brochure, and looking again at Dr. Andrews, caught his slight frown as Rick returned the brochure to the desk without comment or change of expression. Adam had clipped his copy to his clipboard. She tucked hers into her jeans pocket. Dr. Andrews turned his attention back to the bear project. "We want to have the snares all set by the end of the first full week in May. That gives us a couple of weeks to get ready here." He looked at Kelly. "Can you haul groceries in your car if the fellows go for bear bait in the pickup?"

"Is it a two-wheel drive road?"

"The Forest Service guy who arranged for the cabin said it was." He turned to Rick. "You get hold of him and get some directions for your crew."

Rick said, "Okay, Jerry." Whatever his feelings about Dr. Andrews's decision to include her on the crew, he wasn't showing them. Kelly gathered up her books, feeling nervous instead of elated. It would be so much easier if they really were a team—but she needed more than a data sheet on Rick Santini. She needed a whole field manual. ❧

Chapter Five

The Buick labored under its load as Kelly shifted down and began the climb out of the wide valley near Spanish Fork. The highway fit bench-like against the rock walls of the canyon. The back seat was crammed with household goods, sleeping bags, and suitcases—Rick's and Adam's as well as her own. Her guitar case blocked part of the back window. The trunk held groceries and canned goods, plus meat and cheese in a cooler with dry ice.

Rick and Adam had left before Kelly to pick up some dead sheep from a farmer. They had already loaded the two four-wheelers—one in the pickup bed, the other in a small trailer hitched to the pickup— and tools, cable, scat-drying boxes, fuel, and an empty fifty-five gallon oil drum for a bait barrel. Kelly glanced at the clipboard on the pile of books beside her. Rick had given her a piece of paper with neatly penned directions to the cabin. It was just ten-thirty. She should be at the project area in four hours.

She sighed. Four hours of her own company was not a pleasant prospect. She was leaving too much unfinished business and carrying too much anger. She felt diminished as she thought for the hundredth time of Matt's condescending words, "That's different. It's my *job*." *Does he think my master's program is just a hobby?*

Down in the bottom of the canyon, a freight train, coal cars loaded, wound its way toward the west. Kelly braked briefly heading into a curve and then accelerated out of it, the way Matt had taught her to do in mountain driving. Confusion washed against her anger, eroding it like waves on sand. Matt had given her so much. Hadn't he gotten anything in return? Wasn't she worth something without bartering her body?

She looked away from the questions in her mind. Patches of old snow hung on the north-facing road banks and under the evergreens in the shadowed gulches. "Be sure you've got warm clothes," her father had said when she was packing. "The month of May can be damn cold in the high country." But thinking of her father brought no comfort either. Nothing could have been colder than her family's farewell. She blinked. *I will not think about anything in Provo.*

A truck groaned up the mountain behind her. Her radio was erratic, bursting with music on one curve, drowning in static around the next. She turned it down a little. The road crested, and she could hear the impatient driver of the semi behind her shift up as they started the downhill run. Kelly pulled into a turn-out and let the truck pass.

As she eased the Buick around the curves and onto a straighter stretch, road signs flipped by: Sheep Creek, Strawberry Reservoir, The Narrows, and one more pertinent that said, Rest Area, One Mile Ahead. She parked in the roadside rest stop, got out of the Buick, and stretched. An old Indian woman was sitting on the sidewalk. Bead earrings, bracelets, and necklaces were scattered on a printed cloth. Kelly paused to look at the display, smiling at the woman, who wore a down jacket over a long cotton skirt. "Did you make the jewelry?"

"No. My twelve-year-old grandson, he made it. His school wants some money."

Kelly went on up the sidewalk to the restrooms where the water she ran into the stainless steel sink was icy and the air in the hand-drying machine not much warmer. She hated to walk past the Indian woman again without buying something—the cold sidewalk must be uncomfortable—so she stopped and chose a pair of blue bead earrings that dangled from a silver thread. As she tucked the earrings into her purse, she could hear Peggy saying, "And where do you plan to wear those? Wrestling bears or skinning dead things?" The old Peggy. The Peggy she'd left in Provo this morning was not making jokes.

Back in her car, Kelly blurred her thoughts by listening to country-and-western music as she climbed toward Soldier Summit where the wind was blowing the ribbons on the tall snow markers. A Utah State Highway Patrolman with the beehive insignia on the side of his car raised a hand in greeting as they met and passed. As she came down into level country, she disturbed a group of magpies that rose squawking from a road-killed deer.

She crossed the Price River several times as it wound through a valley. The canyons were changing. The rocky peaks of the Wasatch Range near Provo and Salt Lake had given way to fantastic red castle-shaped formations. But she was just an hour out and there were miles yet to travel. Kelly rubbed the back of her neck.

The land grew more arid away from the mountains—mounds of parched earth with humped leathery surfaces. On the horizon, only dusty mesas. Road signs announced "Eagles on the highway," but she saw no eagles and no deer, no antelope, no rabbits. A small poodle at the edge of the street of a one-street town considered darting across the highway and then changed its mind and trotted into the borrow pit. The radio station was scratchier. The jangly music and the disk jockey's shallow comments seemed totally unrelated to the vast land and the sky and the hypnotic motion of the wind. Kelly shut the radio off, and the inner silence of the car settled down around her.

She dropped her speed to create some space between herself and the truck ahead. When she reached the junction indicated on Rick's direction sheet, she was glad to see that most of the trucks took the other road. In a few moments she was the only traveler on the long straight stretch of highway. She passed mile markers and a few scrawny cattle, but no other cars. She checked the gauges on the dashboard, and then looked once more across the land. She could not possibly walk to where she wanted to go. Her car became a dear thing, and she felt comforted by the steady purr of the engine.

But as the road claimed less of her attention, uncomfortable thoughts of Provo seeped back into her mind. She hadn't a clue to her parents' current situation; she was worried about Peggy; and Dr. Andrews's parting words had settled on her like a heavy pack.

The day after Kelly had been accepted for the bear project, Kelly's parents had begun a long-lasting argument, which they carried on in their bedroom at night. The words were not audible, but the bitter tones drilled through the thin walls into Kelly and Peggy's bedroom; and Kelly could tell by Ryan's face each morning that the walls of his room on the porch were no barrier to the twisting anguish in the voices.

The tones of the argument were painful enough, but sometimes after the voices had stopped for the night, the walls conveyed more disturbing sounds: Despite the ongoing disagreement, her parents made love with intensity—the rhythmic pounding of their bed allowed no other interpretation. Kelly's mother often cried out—thin, yowling noises like the nighttime cries of a cat. Finally, as the sound continued to cut through the darkness, Peggy and Kelly talked to keep from listening.

"We shouldn't be living at home anymore," Peggy said. "Can you imagine trying to have a decent sex life with grown kids in the house? At least when we were little, we didn't know what it was all about."

Kelly had known. She thought of the year she was twelve, living in a different thin-walled house. While seven-year-old Peggy slept deeply in the bed beside her, Kelly had listened night after night to the insistent pounding of her parents' bed, staring into the darkness until the sounds stopped. "I think sex has always been a problem for Mother," she said. "Because she and Dad have this strong thing between them, she gave up her own dreams. She might have been happier if there had been an Honor Code at her college and someone back then to help her combine education with marriage."

"Just signing a paper saying that you won't drink, smoke, cheat, or have sex doesn't necessarily guarantee anything," Peggy said, and Kelly wondered if Peggy was trying to share some problem.

She waited, but Peggy didn't add to her statement, so Kelly said, "But the code helps. There are enough pressures in college. The Honor Code helps to establish some standards."

"I think you hide behind the code," Peggy said. "It's easier to throw the code up to Matt than to tell him honestly how you feel."

Kelly's face grew hot. "Matt doesn't listen when I tell him how I feel, or why I feel that way."

"Well, why do you?" Peggy's tone showed sharp interest.

"In the years we traveled from town to town, and I started over and over again at different junior high and high schools, every new guy I dated assumed that I was hot and ready for sex." Kelly was silent for a moment, remembering, and then said, "I'd go on a date, end up in a backseat struggle, and come home furious and miserable because the guy called me old-fashioned or uptight just because I said no."

"But don't you ever feel like saying yes?"

Again Kelly sensed that there was more to Peggy's question than she was saying. She tried to give a totally honest answer, "My thoughts about sex are complicated—I am put off by the idea that a sexual need is just some itch that can be scratched. My body isn't dead, but I'm not just a body."

"Well, whatever you are, I don't think some list of rules should run your life . . . and lots of my friends feel the same way. That's almost all we talk about. That dumb code could force you to live a lie." Peggy's voice came strained and miserable from the darkness.

Kelly hesitated. *What's the right thing to say? I've known her all my life, but at this moment, I have no idea what her problem is or how to make her tell me about it.* "I can only speak for myself," she said finally, "and I'm *not* living a lie. I've been on this campus for four years, and I've heard all those discussions about the Honor Code, but so far I haven't met a guy who could change the way I look at it."

"Don't you have any feelings for Matt at all?"

Kelly was suddenly tired of the conversation. She had enjoyed dating Matt when they skied and hiked and hunted, but at other times, being with him had made her feel lonely and restless. "I don't want to talk about Matt." She turned on her side and pulled the covers over her head.

The family came out the next morning to tell her goodbye. "Have you got the tool kit we made up?" her father asked. Kelly nodded. "And the hand saw and the come-along?"

"They're right behind the front seat on the floor."

Her mother said, "Be careful, Kelly."

Ryan said, "Remember, you promised that I could see a bear."

Peggy walked around the car and stood while Kelly got into the driver's seat and fastened the seat belt. "Peg," Kelly said, "about the Honor Code. If you've got problems with it, why don't you talk to someone? I know it's hard to talk to Mother, but maybe someone on campus."

Peggy shrugged. "I'll figure things out."

Kelly was at a loss. All she could do was borrow her mother's inadequate phrase: "Be careful," she said and put the Buick in gear. No one had hugged her; no one had wished her good luck.

But Kelly hadn't had time then to worry about her family. As she and Rick Santini and Adam Wainwright finished loading, Dr. Andrews came out of the building. He cleared his throat and said, "Some of my colleagues think I may be taking a chance on you three, considering the fact that there has been some dissension." He looked from Rick to Kelly. "But I believe you two care enough about this project to set personal differences aside. I hope I'm not wrong in my estimation of your intelligence and common sense." Kelly left Provo feeling burdened by things over which she had no control.

She focused now on road signs because it was time to leave the interstate. She headed south away from the dry plains and into a green valley. The cliffs above the valley were red, shading to mauve in the shadows, and softening to pink where the afternoon sun touched them. She passed through Moab getting a fleeting impression of motels, cafes, and Indian art galleries; she was glad to see a large grocery store on the south edge of town.

On the horizon, a strange, almost exotic island of forested mountains with high, pointed peaks rose out of the surrounding desert and flat sandstone mesas. The mountain group was a laccolith. Kelly retreated from emotional thoughts about her family and reviewed facts from her geology class about the formation of the mountain. As she pictured the thick magma pushing itself up through the cracks and continuing to build until it raised the highest peak to 12,000 feet, she felt calmer. It was a pleasure to know something about the hills where the bear project was centered. She took the turnoff marked on Rick's map and after several more miles of empty highway, began to look for the gravel road that would take her to the cabin. ❧

Chapter Six

Turning where a sign pointed the way to several creeks and a reservoir, she stopped briefly to reread Rick's directions, noting as she did so that he had written "Kelly Jones" in small letters at the top of the sheet. After going two or three miles, she was to "take the first major left-hand turn."

On the narrow road there seemed nothing one could call "major"—no houses, ranches, driveways, mailboxes, not even power poles, but eventually the road did reach an ill-defined junction, and the left-hand turn seemed to lead along a trail less rocky than the one to the right. Kelly swung the car onto the new track, searching the hump along the center for rocks or stumps high enough to hit the oil pan. The track leveled out, and she breathed a sigh of relief. Perhaps the forest ranger who had called this a two-wheel-drive road had not been exaggerating. The Buick wheezed a little as the grade became steeper, but she shifted down, the engine speeded up, and the car settled into a steady pull.

The car slowed to a crawl as the trail got steeper; she shifted to the lowest gear. Then the trail disappeared. *This is crazy. This is no two-wheel-drive road.* She looked again at the clipboard, and for the first time she wondered if Rick had misled her. The thought made her grit her teeth. *He couldn't be that mean.* But why had he written her name at the top of the sheet? Was there some reason she should get this particular set of directions? She rejected the idea quickly. *That's absolutely paranoid.*

Kelly stopped and got out of the car. Thoughts like that were stupid, and they weren't going to get her to the cabin before dark. She walked back along the road. She couldn't go forward; maybe she'd missed a turn. But there was no other track. When she came to a small stretch of meadow, she decided to back down to it, park the car, and continue uphill on foot. She couldn't risk damage to the Buick—it was her only way back to civilization.

She forced all thoughts of civilization and Rick's possible incivility out of her mind. Her safety right now depended on her own mental focus, her own steady nerves. Slowly, carefully, she backed the car between, around, and over the obstacles and eased it onto the meadow grass. She slung her canteen strap over her shoulder, locked the car, and walked up the trail, searching for sign that someone else had recently driven there.

Occasionally, the scant dirt seemed to show that it had been disturbed, but as she progressed up the steep slope, the ground became so rocky that no tracks could have registered. The only sign that humans had passed near was a dirt-encrusted beer can under a bush. By the time she had walked for half an hour, she was sweaty and tired and totally discouraged. She sat down and took a few sips of water from her canteen. Fatigue settled over her, and with it came renewed suspicion of Rick Santini. If he *had* sent her on this wild goose chase, how could they ever work as a team?

Sitting on the ground, miserable and uncertain, Kelly was eight years old again, huddled in the dirt of a scrubby schoolyard. It was her first day at a remote school where most of the students were related to each other or had known each other all their lives. The other girls had stared at her when the teacher introduced her and had only grudgingly made room for her at one of the scarred wooden tables.

During the noon recess, several girls had approached her. "You want to play hide-and-seek?" a grinning, freckled redhead asked. Surprised and pleased, Kelly nodded her head and followed the girls to a far corner of the playground where there were small trees and bushes, perfect for hiding.

"You get to hide first," the redheaded girl said, "'cause you're new. We'll turn our backs, and you go hide and stay there until we find you."

Kelly had never played the game that way before, but she didn't want to question these new friends, so she slipped away to hide while they shaded their eyes. She crawled deep amongst the roots of a large bush and waited. She heard the other girls giggling and chatting as they seemed to look for her close by, and then their sounds moved farther away, and then there was silence.

Kelly crouched in the bush until her legs were numb. Finally, she crawled from under the scratchy branches and looked toward the schoolhouse. The tail-end of a line of children was just disappearing through the door. The bell must have rung. She walked slowly back to the building, knowing that there would be no friends at that school.

Kelly shook her head to clear away the memory that, even now, caused her stomach to tighten. She put the cap back on the canteen and, looking around, saw a sand lily at the edge of the road. Several white star-shaped blossoms crowded the center, the long slender leaves raying out around them. *Leucocrinum montanum.* Saying the scientific name aloud, she remembered the day her grandmother had pointed out to her that there were some things that were always the same, and once you learned their names, you had something familiar to count on.

Kelly had spent each summer of her childhood on her grandparents' small ranch in the foothills. She helped to feed the goats and the chickens, learned to milk the cow, and rode her grandfather's fat horse. She also carried wood for the cookstove where her grandmother baked bread and cinnamon rolls.

One summer, speaking of familiar plants, Grandma had taken a dog-eared book about plant identification from her shelf and given it to Kelly. Together they had walked the meadows and hills, finding and naming the flowers, plants, and trees.

It had made so much difference. Kelly hand-carried the book when her family moved to the next small town, and as soon as she could slip away, she found plants she knew in the woods and fields. They were always there, not all of them on every hillside, but enough of them so that she never again felt totally alien in a new place.

And after that, going to a strange school was not nearly so frightening. Gradually, by watching and listening, Kelly developed ways of joining in that shielded her from ridicule. She allowed herself to blend with the new "foliage" of each school—never showing her loneliness, learning how to laugh instead of cry. She had learned the discretion that Dr. Andrews seemed to value so much.

Kelly leaned over and touched a leaf of the sand lily. She looked around. The white-barked aspens to the side of the track were huge. The sun filtered through their lime-green leaves and spangled the grasses in the open area beneath the trees. *A good place to put a snare.* The bears would be eating grass now as they shook off the heaviness of hibernation.

Kelly stood and shouldered her canteen. There was no road, no cabin on this slope, and whether or not Rick had misled her didn't matter at the moment. It was important to the project that they get settled in, start snaring bears in their early post-hibernation condition, and collect some of the early scat so they could have information about the entire season.

Returning to her car, she eased it down the steep road, and just as she reached the junction again, she met a blue pickup driven by a man wearing a tired-looking Stetson. She waved him to a stop and went to his window. The rancher smiled at her. The lined face under the old hat showed a day's growth of whiskers, but his eyes were friendly as he waited for her to speak.

"I wonder if you could tell me how to get to the Forest Service guard station that's supposed to be somewhere near here."

The man's eyes widened a little. "Are *you* one of those bear people, too?"

"Yes. I'm a biologist with the bear project."

The rancher grinned. "I think you're going to surprise a few people around here."

Kelly felt the warmth of his humor. There was nothing in his gaze or his comments to indicate that he disapproved of a woman on the project. She smiled at him. "My name's Kelly Jones, and I'd really like to get to that cabin before the other team members show up."

"Well, you're too late already then." Kelly bit her lip, but the rancher went on. "I showed a couple of young fellows with a truckload of dead sheep to that cabin, not twenty minutes ago."

"You mean they were lost, too?"

"Yup."

Kelly felt a huge sense of relief. She looked at the friendly old rancher. "Do you suppose you could just tell me how to get to that cabin, without taking me there?"

He laughed. "You don't want them to know you got lost."

Kelly felt herself flush, but she laughed and said, "They have enough doubts about me already."

"How far did you go up that old road?"

"A lot farther than I should have with this car."

"Did you see any livestock up there? I'm missing a cow and a calf."

"No. I didn't see any animals, and I didn't see any fresh sign either. I was probably about two miles up."

"That far?" His eyes twinkled. "You must be a good driver."

"I'm a good walker. I parked the Buick in one of your meadows." Kelly felt at ease with the man. His matter-of-fact country speech was lightened by his humor. He reminded her of her grandmother.

"Well now, you want to get to that cabin." The man put his truck in gear. "Just follow me."

In a few minutes, the blue pickup stopped near a barbed-wire gate that blocked a narrow track. The man stepped down from his truck and approached her car. He was dressed in jeans, a faded denim jacket, and a blue chambray shirt with snap fasteners. "There's your turnoff," he said.

Kelly laughed. "The directions said it was a major left-hand turn."

The rancher smiled and said, "Good luck with those bears . . . and those boys." He walked to the barbed-wire gate, opened it, and dragged it back so Kelly could pass through. She waved at him, and he returned the wave before he closed the gate and latched it with the wire loop.

Kelly drove slowly along the track, thinking, *I wasted a lot of emotion today. From now on, I am not going to let Rick Santini upset me. I'm here to learn how to run this bear project.* The thought startled her. When had she moved from simply hoping to be accepted on the project to wanting to run it?

It was the truth. Next year, when Rick Santini had finished his master's study and gone on, Kelly Jones wanted to be the field leader of the bear project. But she would have to prove to Dr. Andrews that she was capable first of being part of a team, and then of being able to lead a team. Just ahead, Kelly spotted Rick and Adam standing next to the pickup. *I will keep my eyes and ears open*, Kelly vowed to herself as she drew nearer, and *I will keep my mouth shut.* ❧

Chapter Seven

Kelly pulled alongside the pickup and watched Rick and Adam, who were bent over a dead ewe, sawing at the carcass. Rick stood up as a chunk of meat came free. He dropped it into the bait barrel, which they had unloaded in a clearing a few feet from the road, then came toward her car, the dirty skinning knife in his right hand. Kelly rolled down her window.

"You made it," Rick said. He shifted the knife to his left hand and dug in the pocket of his jeans. Handing her a key ring, he said, "We didn't open the cabin. You'll want to get your kitchen stuff unpacked and your pantry set up."

Kelly blinked. MY *kitchen stuff?* MY *pantry? This is 1990, not 1890.* She took a deep breath and reminded herself of what she had decided, not five minutes ago. *Keep your mouth shut.* Reaching for the key, she glanced at Adam who grinned and waved a chunk of meat, wisps of dirty wool still clinging to it. Setting up the kitchen would be preferable to the job they were doing. She waved back at Adam and drove past them to the cabin, which was around a bend a quarter of a mile up the road.

The cabin stood at the base of a hillside covered with scrub oak. The faded brown paint on the siding blended with the dead leaves in the yard. At the back of the yard, a three-sided woodshed sagged toward a pole fence. At the other side of the yard was an outhouse. Kelly got out of the car and went around the cabin to the outhouse. She opened the door and laughed out loud. A two-holer! She used the facility and made her way back to the cabin, immensely cheered by her mental picture of two forest rangers sitting side by side on the elaborate toilet seat.

As she stepped up on the concrete slab that served as a front porch, the sound of running water drew her eyes to the left. At the corner of the cabin, on the woodshed side—*uphill from the toilet, thank goodness*— a small spring bubbled into a rough concrete trough.

Unlocking the door, Kelly entered a large, dimly lit room. She released the spring-loaded shade on the front window to her right, and, as the afternoon sun lighted the room, turned to survey her summer home. The first thing she saw, backed up to the front wall in the corner to the left side of the door, was her grandmother's stove.

Of course, it couldn't be the exact stove, but it looked exactly like it: a black-iron range with chrome trim on the warming oven and on the oven door, its chrome legs sitting squarely on a brown tin mat. The stove even had the same type of hot-water reservoir with hinged lid. Feeling warmed and welcomed although the stove was cold, Kelly continued her survey.

Across from the stove, walls of rough planking separated a small storeroom from the larger room. Attached to the wall to the right of the storeroom door was a wooden counter, made of boards and covered with a piece of wildly flowered vinyl floor material. A water bucket and dipper, a granite washbasin chipped around the rim, and a dented aluminum dishpan sat on the counter. Above the counter, two shelves were nailed to the outside of the storeroom wall.

The vinyl was awful, and the countertop didn't mark the end of it. The floor of the large room was covered with vinyl of the same design: huge maroon flowers trapped in masses of olive-green leaves and wound about with yellowish vines that trailed along a drab beige background. But at least the vinyl was clean and not badly marred.

A square wooden table and four chairs filled the space near the front window, which had no curtain now that the roller shade had rewound. Underneath the other window, on the right hand wall, was an empty metal bookcase. Three cots stood close together along the back wall, bare mattresses sagging. Kelly frowned as she looked at the cots. She had hoped for more privacy. She stepped to the storeroom door seeking something with which to screen her cot.

On the left side of the storeroom, a set of shallow shelves, six inches deep, stretched from floor to ceiling. The shelves to the right of the door were three feet deep, three feet wide and four feet high. Above them, filling the space to the ceiling was a cupboard with doors, closed with tongue and hasp. The storeroom floor had been left bare; the wide planks, scrubbed clean. Behind the deep shelves stood several empty cardboard boxes, none big enough to screen a cot. Kelly eyed the space where the boxes sat and went to her car for the measure from her tool kit. She moved the boxes into the kitchen, measured the space behind the deep shelves and then measured one of the cots. It would just fit into the space. The idea of creating her own private nook in the storeroom gave Kelly a burst of energy.

She decided to heat some water first. Rick and Adam would certainly want to wash away the residue of their bait work. She placed one of the empty cartons against the wall for a wood box, brought wood and kindling from the woodshed, and after checking the ash pan behind the small door at the bottom of the stove, she built a fire.

Initially, just as her grandmother's stove had done, the little range began to smoke. "Oh, no you don't," Kelly said out loud. She opened the air hole on the ash door and turned the damper knob in the chimney. In a moment or two, the stove was drawing well. The fire crackled cheerfully as Kelly carried buckets of water from the spring, filling the reservoir and, after setting them on the stove, the dishpan and the washbasin. She filled the water bucket a last time and put it on the counter. Then she dragged the cot to the storeroom door, and tipping it on its side, angled it through the doorway, set it on its feet and pushed it carefully into place. Perfect. She stepped outside the storeroom. From the kitchen, only a narrow edge of the cot was visible.

She leaned her guitar in the corner near the small window at the back of the storeroom. She retrieved her sleeping bag from the car and spread it on the cot. Then opening her suitcase, she took out the quilt her grandmother had made for her birthday when she was fifteen. Grateful that there was no clashing vinyl on the floor, she tucked the quilt around her sleeping bag and stood for a moment admiring the soft greens and blues of the hand-sewn squares.

She shoved the suitcase under her bed, and hurrying now as the sunlight faded a little, she moved one of the other cots to the far wall near the cabin window and put Rick's sleeping bags and luggage on it. She placed Adam's belongings on the cot nearer the kitchen.

Setting the glass-globed lamp provided by the university on the table, she filled it with fuel and trimmed the wick. Kerosene would make dim light. She wished she had brought a Coleman lantern from the store.

She went to the car for the tool kit, her six-volt flashlight, the come-along, some small tools Rick had put in her car, and the small ice chest that kept the tranquilizing drugs cold. She stowed them in the deep shelves and went back for the canned food and the large ice chest that was heavy with meat. She was lining up cans on the narrow storeroom shelves when Rick and Adam drove up.

The two men came into the house and the stench of dead animals came with them. Adam looked around the cabin, grinned at her and said, "A veritable castle." Rick also glanced around the room. She saw him search the gear near his bed.

Turning to her, he said, "Where are the drugs?"

Kelly led the way to the storeroom and showed Rick the small ice chest. He moved it from the shelves to the cupboard above them. "We'll get a padlock for that hasp and keep the drugs locked up when we're not here."

Adam peered around Kelly's shoulder. "Aha, I see where Cinderella sleeps."

Kelly stepped away from the two and indicated the hot water that steamed on the stove. She had unwrapped a bar of soap and put it on a saucer on the counter. They were supposed to have brought their own towels. "Would you like to wash?"

Adam grinned at her. "Is that a polite way of suggesting that we're rank?"

"Rank and vile," Kelly said. Adam laughed at her pun, and as he and Rick dug into their packs for towels, Kelly lit the kerosene lamp. Working at the table, she made a stack of ham sandwiches and set out canned pineapple and mugs for the hot cocoa, which she heated in a small pan.

She had brought three cheap aluminum pans from the hardware store, and they hung now on the wall beside the stove. After stacking the dishes on the shelves above the counter, she had cut down a cardboard box for a utensil tray, which she had set on the counter away from the water bucket.

Reaching around Rick, who was bent over the wash basin splashing water onto his face, she took spoons and knives from the box and placed them on the table with paper napkins and three plates. She added a jar of mustard and a bag of chips. Not a great meal.

The men made no comment as they sat down at the table. They had scrubbed, but still carried the scent of putrefied flesh. Rick was dressed in a light khaki shirt that complimented the olive tint of his skin. Adam looked like a lumberjack in his blue-and-white-checked shirt. He took two sandwiches and piled his plate high with chips. Rick took one sandwich and began talking to Adam.

"The sheep will be enough bait for the first day's trail sets. What worked best last summer on the other side of the mountain was to choose a drainage and then to set several snares, each a quarter- to a half-mile apart."

"Will all the snares be in the aspen?" Kelly asked.

Rick flicked a glance her way; the light from the kerosene lamp did not reach his eyes and his voice was cold. "No. If we can find some obvious trails in the conifer forest, we'll set snares there too."

The conifer forest, Kelly knew, was made up of firs and pines that grew so close together that little sunlight reached the forest floor. Beneath them were none of the lush meadows that grew beneath the aspen.

"Did you get large containers of peanut butter?" Rick asked.

Kelly nodded. "Generic, five-pound jars. They're in the storeroom."

Rick turned back to Adam. "We'll build a snare, set out a chunk of meat, and smear it with peanut butter. Then we'll sear the whole thing with a propane torch."

Adam was spooning up pineapple. He looked at Rick. "Burn the bait? Why?"

"Just singe it a little to broadcast the scent."

Rick finished his sandwich and fruit and drained his cocoa. "We need to clear this stuff away so we can spread the map out on the table," he said. But since he didn't take his dishes with him as he rose to get the map, Kelly assumed that "we" did not include him.

Kelly dipped water from the reservoir into the dishpan. To her surprise, Adam stacked the dishes and carried them to the counter. He put the mustard and chips on a storeroom shelf and, taking the sponge from her hand, wiped the wooden tabletop.

After moving the lamp to the back of the table, Rick opened a large Forest Service map and spread it out. Kelly stood at the dishpan for only a moment, then dried her hands on her jeans and joined Rick and Adam at the table. Rick ignored her, but as she continued to crowd close and bent to look at the map, he shifted away from her and gave her room to stand near the table.

But no matter how near they got, they could not see the tiny lines indicating the gullies and creeks. The light from the lamp did not extend far enough to illuminate more than a small part of the map. Outside its circle, the map was in shadow.

Adam said, "If we're going to study this thing at night, we've got to get a different system."

Kelly said, "Maybe we could tack it to the wall and use a flashlight. I've got an assortment of nails in my tool kit."

They chose the wall between the men's cots, stretched the map, and nailed it. Then while Adam held Kelly's large flashlight so that it lighted the general area, Rick pointed out the specific drainage he had in mind for the next day.

Kelly was not about to tell him that she found the detailed map confusing, so she studied it as closely as she could, resolving to memorize it by daylight. Adam seemed to be having the same problems she was. In an exasperated tone, he said, "Come on, Rick. We can't see the details. Let's call it a night. We can study this thing in the morning." Kelly was surprised. Adam had so far handled everything with humor.

Rick took the flashlight and studied the map alone for a while, and then he sat down on his cot and began unpacking a box of equipment. Adam unzipped his sleeping bag, pulled out two pillows, and fluffed them up. He propped them against the wall and, stretching out on the bed, he leaned back into the pillows. "That man is a veritable slave driver," he said with a grin.

"You like that word veritable, don't you?" Kelly said.

"Veritably," Adam said, stretching his arms out and then folding them behind his head.

It was obvious that if the dishes were to be finished tonight, it was up to Kelly. She picked up the flashlight and took it to the kitchen counter. She washed, rinsed, and dried the dishes and put them on the shelf. As she stepped toward the door with the dirty dishwater, Rick looked up.

"Be sure to throw that on the down side of the cabin so you don't pollute the spring."

Kelly felt her whole body stiffen, and the water in the pan bounced as she clutched the rim in tight fists. He was insufferable! Smug, condescending, and infuriating. But she was not going to let him know that it bothered her. She took a breath, said lightly, "Aye, aye, captain," and stepped with relief into the sweet-smelling night.

She dumped the dishpan and stood in the dark, grateful that the bait barrel was around the bend. Above her, the sky shimmered with stars. She studied the bright points of light, glad to be alone. When she stepped back into the cabin, Adam looked up with a grin. "Well done, thou good and faithful servant."

"Veritably," Kelly said with a sour smile. She put the dishpan on the counter and ladling hot water into the washbasin, carried it and the flashlight into the storeroom where she took a quick sponge bath, nervous about the lack of a door. The best she could do for her hair was to brush it. She changed into an old sweat suit she'd brought for pajamas and went outside again. The outhouse was rather peaceful. She sat with the door open and enjoyed the spring night wondering what small animals were about—each searching for food and being sought for the same purpose.

"Kelly?" It was Rick's voice. Kelly stood quickly and pulled her clothes up. *What in the world?*

She hurried back to the cabin. Rick stood on the steps peering into the darkness.

"Did you want something?"

"I'm about ready to shut things down for the night and put out the light. Everyone should be safely inside."

And what if she needed to go out in the middle of the night? Was she supposed to wake him up and ask for his permission? She slipped quickly past him and went to her room. Was it possible that he really did feel burdened by having a woman on the project, more responsible somehow for her safety than for Adam's? She hadn't a clue. She burrowed into her sleeping bag, sighed deeply, and let it go. She was simply too tired to think about Rick Santini. ❧

Chapter Eight

Kelly woke coughing. The storeroom was filled with smoke. She struggled from the sleeping bag and headed for the kitchen. Adam was fiddling with the damper on the chimney. Smoke poured out around the stove lids. "For gosh sake, are you trying to suffocate us?" She pushed Adam aside and bent to open the lower damper. Then she adjusted the damper on the chimney, and the stove ceased to smoke. It was scarcely dawn. Kelly rubbed her eyes and peered at Adam. He was fully dressed in the same blue-and-white-checked shirt and jeans. "Why are you up so early?"

He looked scrubbed and wide awake. His brown eyes were bright. "I always get up early."

From his cot, Rick groaned, and for once Kelly completely agreed with him. "Well, why were you building a fire?" she asked. "It's not that cold."

Adam said plaintively, "I wanted a cup of cocoa."

Kelly had to laugh. He seemed no older than Ryan. She stepped into the storeroom and opened the small window. Adam took the water bucket and went out. Kelly dressed and brushed her hair, wishing she had thought to bring a mirror. *We take so many modern things for granted,* she thought, as she scrunched through the oak leaves to the outhouse.

"Please," she said to Adam when she reached the front step again, "pour some over my hands." Adam tipped the bucket, splashing icy water and grinning as she winced. She wiped her hands on her jeans and followed him into the cabin. She moved to the map.

Rick came in. He, too, was dressed in the same clothes he'd worn the day before—light khaki shirt and khaki pants. He didn't speak, but stood beside her studying the map. Kelly traced the lines indicating creek beds and drainages, trying to fix in her mind the direction they would travel from the cabin. Adam brought each of them a cup of cocoa and then pointed to a section on the map where the elevation lines were closely spaced. "Is that the ridge where your bears denned?"

"Just a couple of them. The others stayed up north, nearer to the area where we were snaring last summer." Rick turned to the boxes at the foot of his bed and pulled out a green folder. He flipped through it and took out two sheets of paper.

"Marie and Jenny denned up on the ridge. We picked up their signals when we flew over in October. We managed to find Marie when we were denning in mid-March. She has new cubs. We lost Jenny's signal." He frowned. "I wanted to find Jenny."

"Marie . . . Jenny," Adam said. "Where did you get those names?"

"Marie is named for Dr. Andrews's wife," Rick said, "and Jenny is named for the wife of a guy who donated money to buy a radio collar."

"I thought the project was funded by the Forest Service and the DWR," Kelly said.

"Under-funded," Rick said. "Dr. Andrews is always looking for private donors."

"Why did you particularly want to find Jenny?"

"She was young when we collared her last year. Young bears grow quickly. I need to snare her and make sure the collar's not too tight. That's one reason I chose Warren Gulch. It leads down from the ridge." He put the data sheets back in the folder. "As long as we're up, we might as well get going." He looked sleepy, but when he started giving orders he was well organized, thorough, and self-contained. He turned to Adam. "Check the fuel in those four-wheelers; I'll be out in a minute and help hook up the trailer." Adam went obediently out the door, and Rick said to Kelly, "We'll need breakfast and some sandwiches to carry."

Kelly took a breath, but said only, "What do you want in the sandwiches?"

Rick's nose wrinkled. "Anything but peanut butter." He picked up his gloves and stepped outside. Kelly added wood to the fire and set the skillet to heat, depressed by her new kitchen assignment. *If he's determined that's where I belong, how am I going to learn anything?*

The noisy engine of a four-wheeler spurred her to action. She made ham-and-cheese sandwiches, then cut up the rest of the ham and put it in the heated skillet. *I wish I'd stuck with Matt and had him teach me to drive a four-wheeler.* Breaking and stirring four eggs, she added them to the ham, but the skillet was too hot, and the eggs cooked quickly into a mass of lumps. When Rick and Adam entered, they dumped a pile of chains and cable on Rick's bed and sat down at the table. Kelly set the scrambled eggs and ham on the table. Adam grinned at her and said, "What horrendous calamity befell the omelet?"

Kelly refused to let his comment get to her. She answered his smile and asked, "Don't you know any one- and two-syllable words?"

"Sure do. Where's the ketchup?"

Rick was silent, though he, too, smothered his eggs with the ketchup she brought from the storeroom. A sense of panic made her stomach tighten. *I don't want to cook for them all summer.* But when Rick rose, she cleared the table and began to wash the dishes.

Rick spread the equipment on the bed. "We'll start out with eight snares. We probably won't get that many set up, but we'll take them along."

"How long will it take us to set up a snare?" Adam asked.

"We'll have to find a site and clear it. After we've prepared the site, it takes forty-five minutes to an hour." Kelly stepped closer with the plate she was drying as Rick picked up a loop of cable. It was secured by a cable clamp. "We're using an Aldrich foot snare. It's basically a two-part snare, not counting the chain that holds it to the tree." He indicated a steel spring that looked like a huge safety pin with a tongue. "This is the throw arm—the trigger mechanism."

Rick spread the cable loop and stepped his hand through it onto the tongue of the spring. "If a bear stepped through the loop, the bear's weight would release the spring, and the cable would pull close around the bear's wrist."

"Does it pull tight enough to hold the bear?" Adam asked.

Rick gave a short laugh. "The bear does the pulling," he said. "He jerks that cable around his wrist and tightens it as he fights to free himself."

"What happens if he doesn't get his paw clear through the loop?"

Rick glanced up. "A bear can be caught by just a couple of toes."

"Can he pull free?"

"They do sometimes, but we might have to work with them that way, caught by just the toes." Adam and Kelly exchanged glances but Rick was gathering the snares and putting them into a large metal box. He added a knife and said to Adam, "We need the torches and the axe and that little shovel that's behind the front seat of the truck," and turning to Kelly, he said, "Pack the sandwiches in your fanny pack."

She took the compass from her toolbox and slipped it into her jeans pocket and then packed the lunch as Rick had directed. He looked up from filling his own backpack and said, "Get us three sodas and some extra sandwich bags. We may find some scat." He turned away and then back. "Oh, and we'll need one of those large jars of peanut butter."

Determined to remember everything he asked for so that he wouldn't have to ask the next time, Kelly began to make a mental list. The only way not to feel like a stupid child around him was to learn everything that he could teach. She handed the peanut butter jar to Rick.

They strapped the equipment box on the rack of the four-wheeler in the truck. The four-wheeler in the back of the trailer had an ice chest strapped to its rack. "The bait box," Rick said when Adam asked about the chest. He got into the cab of the truck, and Adam and Kelly followed. Pulling the trailer around the curve to the clearing, Rick fiddled with the radio receiver that rested in its leather case on the dash. "I want to see if Jenny is up and about," he said.

When they reached the bait barrel, Rick fished under the seat of the truck for a pair of long rubber gloves. He turned, and with the closest thing to a real smile that Kelly had seen from him, asked, "Which one of you two wants to fill the bait box?"

Kelly reached for the gloves. "I will." If she was one of the crew, she could not gag and shrink from the smell of the bait.

Rick's eyelids flickered as if he were surprised, but he said only, "We'll need two chunks for each set." He picked up a bundle in the bottom of the truck and handing it to Adam said, "If you'll put the antenna together, we'll try to locate Marie and Jenny while Kelly loads the bait."

Flies swarmed around the lid of the barrel. Kelly donned the rubber gloves, removed the lid, and stretched to retrieve a chunk of bait. The stinking meat was a dark bruised color with an overlay of greenish film. The first piece she grasped slithered from her hand. She reached in with two hands and gripped the slippery flesh. The chunk probably weighed fifteen pounds. Holding the bait away from her body, she climbed awkwardly into the trailer, and resting the meat on the rack to free one hand, she opened the bait box. Depositing the putrid meat into the chest, she turned away for a deep breath of air and went back to the barrel.

Rick and Adam were walking up the road with the antenna and receiver. They never looked her way. Holding her breath often and for as long as she could, Kelly hauled chunks of slimy meat until she had crammed the bait box full. She shut and latched the lid and pulled the straps over the chest, securing the hooks to the metal rack of the four-wheeler.

When Rick and Adam returned, Rick stowed the receiver and antenna, went to the bait box, and looked in it. He restrapped it without a word and climbed into the truck.

"Marie is moving about," Adam said to Kelly.

"She's hungry," Rick said.

"There's nothing to eat," Adam said.

"No, not much but grass right now, and bears don't really digest grass well."

Adam said, "How do they get anything out of grass then? How do they survive?"

Kelly turned to him. "By eating large volumes of it." She was surprised at Adam's questions, but she realized that though he was a zoology major, he was an undergraduate and had probably studied bears only generally.

"When do they feed?" he asked her, shifting his body to look at her and placing his arm behind her on the back of the seat.

"Bears are crepuscular," she said.

"Sounds nasty."

She smiled at him. "That just means that they are active in the evenings and early mornings. During the middle of the night and during the day, they bed down somewhere and sleep."

"But towards fall," Rick said, "when they need to be putting on fat for hibernation, they'll stay active into the day, just feeding." He pointed to the side of the road as a deer bounded away from the truck and into the trees.

Kelly relaxed. They seemed to be focusing on the project with none of the undercurrents she'd felt in the cabin. For the first time since she had overheard Rick's description of her as an earth muffin, she felt some hope about being a real part of the team.

They turned onto a steeper road that curved around the side of the mountain. As they approached a broad meadow, Rick said, "We'll leave the truck and trailer here." He glanced at Kelly and then said to Adam, "I guess you'll have to unload both those four-wheelers." Kelly stepped down and studied the machine Adam was unloading from the trailer. The handlebars, saddle seat, and four, deeply grooved, fat tires made it look like a cross between a motorcycle and a dune buggy.

Rick spread a small map on the hood of the truck. "We're here." Kelly stepped forward to look. Rick pointed to a spot on the map. "We'll take the four-wheelers up there," he said as he ran his finger along a broken line that angled northwest, "and we'll set the first snares in Warren Gulch—here."

Kelly recognized the lines they had studied on the big map on the cabin wall. She looked around the area to get the directions set in her mind. "Did you pick up Jenny's signal?" she asked with a glance toward the ridge.

"No. But silence is better than a mortality beep." Kelly nodded. She knew that the pulse rate of a collar's signal changed, became faster, if the bear stayed motionless for four hours.

Adam said to Kelly, "If I unhitch the trailer, will you pull the truck forward so I can unload the other four-wheeler?" Rick picked up his map and stepped back. Kelly moved the truck slowly away from the trailer and stopped at Adam's signal. Adam pulled the ramps from the bed and backed the four-wheeler to the ground.

Rick said, "You haul Kelly. And don't get any hot-dog ideas about driving that machine. We're going to set snares where there's little disturbance from on-road vehicles. We'll be taking obscure roads and narrow trails, and they're going to be rough."

Rick climbed onto one four-wheeler and Adam got on the other, but remained standing so that Kelly could climb on behind him, just in front of the bait box. As they settled onto the seat, Kelly felt something poke her leg; she glanced down. Adam was wearing a gun belt. The lower end of the holster pushed against her thigh. She hadn't noticed the gun belt before. She looked over at Rick, and he, too, was wearing a gun. "What are the guns for?" Kelly asked.

"Just for ornament, I hope," Adam said. "He told me to wear mine every time we go out."

"Can you shoot that thing?"

Adam turned his head and grinned at her. "Like a veritable pro."

The tenacious little four-wheeler took them over rocks and small branches and into washes and out again, bouncing them around on the hard seat. Rick had told Adam not to be reckless, but it was almost impossible to keep up with Rick without pushing the machine to its limit. Kelly could hear the engine labor as Adam changed gears and moved up a steep rise. They stopped in a meadow where Rick had stopped near a small stream. "Look at that," Rick yelled over the sounds of the engines, "damn cows are making a bog out of this and destroying food and cover."

The bank of the stream was broken, the grasses along it, trampled. The water was muddy, and where the cows had dropped a pile, the manure disintegrated slowly in the water, turning it slightly green. Rick shook his head, gunned his engine, and went on across the stream. Kelly started to fish her compass from her pocket, but Adam hit a large bump, and she grabbed the sides of the rack as they roared upward along a faint trail through the trees.

Finally Rick halted on a high flat spot. "We'll walk from here," he said. He opened the equipment box on the back of his machine and handed the hatchet and shovel to Adam. He stuck tools in his back and side pockets and picked up the axe, a length of chain, and one of the snares with its spring and cable. As Rick and Adam started down slope through the meadow, Rick said over his shoulder, "Kelly, after you haul two chunks of meat to the site, come back and get the peanut butter." ❧

Chapter Nine

Kelly dumped the bait near the low spot Rick had chosen where four aspens stood in a line. "We'll set the snare between the two middle trees and build barricades on each side," Rick said, "but first we'll clear the brush around the center. If a bear caught his snared foot in the brush, he might break his leg."

They took turns with the axe and hatchet. "We'll need some longer poles to work the short branches into," Rick said. "You bring those up, while I start setting the snare."

The four trees created three spaces. Kelly and Adam leaned large limbs against the trees in one of the side spaces and started weaving the smaller branches in and out to create the barrier. In the center of the middle space, Rick began digging a small hole, but Adam and Kelly had only worked for a few moments before Rick left his shovel and came to the barricade. He rearranged the branches they had secured. "The barrier has to be high enough so that the bear won't feel like going over it and wide enough so that he won't go around."

Kelly and Adam tried to follow Rick's instructions, but he was up every moment or two making adjustments to their work. Finally, Adam walked away. Kelly hesitated and then followed him. She didn't say anything as they tugged limbs away from a tangle of grass and twigs. If she and Adam joined forces against Rick, it wouldn't help them to operate as a team. Adam and Kelly dragged the poles to the other side space, but didn't start the second barricade.

Rick was on his hands and knees. He fastened the chain around one of the center aspens and secured the snare to the chain. They watched as he settled the trigger mechanism into the hole. Then Rick moved to the steel spring and with a grunt of effort closed it, setting the throw arm and putting tension on the trigger mechanism. Seeing the muscles of his arm bulge, Kelly felt concern. *Can I do that? Am I strong enough?*

"We'll cover the trigger with a light coating of grass to hide it, but we won't use anything big," Rick said. "If the throw arm hits something, the cable won't throw all the way." Adam reached to smooth the dirt under the cable. Rick releveled the dirt after Adam had finished.

I don't know why he even bothers to say "we," Kelly thought. *He won't let us do anything on our own.* She looked at Rick, wondering what Peggy saw in that face to call it handsome. The features were even and well-balanced, but the square jaw was tight, the mouth was a grim slit, and the dark eyes focused like laser beams. Rick was far too cold to be sexy.

Rick said, "Go ahead with that other barricade."

"You think we can do it without help?" Adam asked.

Rick flushed, but didn't respond. He spoke to Kelly. "Sharpen some sticks for me." He gave her a knife. "Cut them about eighteen inches long and make a point on one end."

Kelly had read everything she could about setting snares, and she knew that he would use the sticks to direct the bear's steps. But when she asked, "Shall I position them in the ground?" he said, "No. Just stack them near me." He glanced often at the barricade Adam was building and twice got up to change what Adam had done, making little difference as far as Kelly could see. She didn't know Adam well enough to know what he was feeling, and he said nothing, but the relaxed atmosphere she'd felt in the truck had been replaced with tension.

Kelly moved around so that she could see better as Rick spread and camouflaged the cable loop and placed the upright sticks. When he finished, the structure looked like a haphazard fort, enclosing the snare almost casually.

But Kelly knew that it was neither a haphazard nor a casual placement. Rick had left a gap on the front and back side of the "fort." From either side of the snare, the sticks on the left stood as a barrier; the sticks on the right leaned slightly sideways, leaving a convenient gate, as if in invitation to the bear's right front paw. Rick turned to Adam. "You want to go get one of those propane torches?" Adam nodded and headed through the meadow toward the four-wheelers. Rick said to Kelly, "Put one piece of bait five feet from the snare on this side and the other piece directly across on the other side." Kelly donned the gloves and placed the putrid meat where Rick indicated. Adam returned with the propane torch—just a propane bottle with a slender curving gas jet attached to the top. Rick spread peanut butter liberally over the top of each piece of bait, lit the torch, and seared the peanut butter and the meat. Then he surveyed the trail set and smoothed the dirt.

"Do you have to remove our footprints?" Adam asked.

"It's not our footprints I'm interested in," Rick said. "The smooth dirt will show the footprints of any animals who pass by."

They returned to the four-wheelers and stowed the tools. Rick gave Kelly a roll of blue surveyor's tape. "Tie a piece of this on a bush in line with the set."

Back on the four-wheelers, they moved up the mountain, found a new cluster of aspens, cleared the area, and went to work setting the second snare. Rick continued to check and redo Adam and Kelly's work. The changes he made were scarcely noticeable, but each time Rick redid something, Adam was quieter, and Kelly felt more fatigue and frustration. *He's not a leader; he's a loner. He just pushes us ahead of him, as if we were in the way.*

By the time they completed the second set, it was nearly noon. They ate the ham sandwiches quickly and then worked all afternoon, but by five o'clock, they had only finished two more trail sets. Rick was silent as they returned to the truck and loaded the four-wheelers.

Adam and Kelly were quiet too until they neared the clearing where the bait barrel stood, then Adam said, "Let's unhook the trailer here and keep that stinking bait box away from the house." Rick stopped the truck, and the two men unhooked the trailer. Kelly slid over into the driver's seat and pulled the truck forward.

When they parked by the cabin, Rick said, "We'll have to get going earlier in the morning. We're behind schedule."

Kelly said, "Maybe if you'd let us do more of the work, we'd get more done."

Rick's face flushed. "If the sets aren't right, we won't catch bears. We're here to catch bears."

Kelly said quietly, "We won't learn to build the sets right unless we do it ourselves."

Rick said, "Dr. Andrews will be here Friday. He'll expect the snares to be set and the work to be in full swing." He opened the truck door and stepped down. As he started for the outhouse, he said, "I haven't got time to teach amateurs and women."

Adam got out of the truck, but Kelly just sat there, seething, until Rick strode toward the cabin. Then she went to the outhouse and closed the door behind her. Sitting on the smooth wood of the broad seat, she tried to sort out her emotions.

Why am I so angry because Rick's acting like a jerk? What would Peggy say? For a moment, Kelly was washed with homesickness, but she didn't have time for it. She had to figure this out now.

I'm mad because I'm scared. I am afraid that when Dr. Andrews comes, he'll see that we aren't working together, and he'll make me go home. But if this crew is going to work together, I'll have to learn more about Rick. She had no idea what he was feeling. Where should she start? *We're too tired, dirty, and hungry for a confrontation.* With food. That was how to start.

Adam was carrying a bucket of water up the steps. She held the door open for him and went into the cabin, which was filled with smoke. "Oh damn," Adam said. Kelly stepped to the stove and adjusted the dampers. The stove stopped smoking. "How do you do that?" Adam said, sounding plaintive.

Kelly laughed. "I have magic fingers." She washed her hands then took the hamburger from the ice chest and moved the skillet over the firebox.

Coming near to her at the stove, Adam draped an arm across Kelly's shoulder. His hand did not touch her body, but it hung in front of her breast, and she could feel its heat. Her body tightened. Adam's face was close to hers. "What gastronomical extravaganza are you planning for dinner?" he asked.

Kelly was irritated by his familiarity, but grateful for any sort of warmth, and additionally irritated by her own gratitude. *What am I, some orphaned puppy?* She was also aware that her hair smelled of bear bait and smoke. She pulled away from him. "We're having spaghetti and meatballs."

"Wow! I'm impressed. I guess I'd better dress for dinner."

Kelly laughed and said, "I'll bet that just means another blue-and-white checked shirt."

"You wound me deeply," Adam said. "It's red-and-white checked."

Feeling hypocritical because her purpose was manipulation, not beauty, Kelly folded place mats, using flowered paper towels, and set the table carefully. She cooked spaghetti sauce. She even managed to toast some bread on the back stove plate and, mixing garlic salt with margarine, produced garlic toast to go with the spaghetti. As she worked, she refined her plan for approaching Rick, who had washed at the counter and was now marking the four snare locations in Warren Gulch on the large map.

Rick and Adam gobbled up the spaghetti and meatballs. They ate seconds and wiped their plates clean with the toast. As Rick started up from the table, Kelly said, "Rick, could we talk?"

Rick frowned. Kelly kept looking at him until he sat back down in his chair. She took a breath and began the speech she'd been rehearsing. "I think that Adam and I have been holding you back." The frown disappeared, and Rick's eyes softened a little. *He thought I was going to criticize him.* Kelly stored the data point for future use as she continued, "So I have a suggestion." Rick shifted in his chair, but looked at her without speaking.

"We have twelve more snares to set before Dr. Andrews gets here. Why don't we choose six spaces tomorrow and clear them first, and then Adam and I can build some of the trail sets while you go ahead with the others." Rick started to speak, but Kelly hurried on. "It will take less time for you to check our mistakes if you do all our sets at once."

"Do you think you really know how to build a trail set?"

Kelly suppressed her rise of anger and said calmly, "I knew the theory before we came up here, and I watched you today." She pushed a little. "If we do six tomorrow and six Friday, we'll finish by the time Dr. Andrews arrives unless we catch a bear. If we catch a bear, Dr. Andrews will understand why the sets aren't finished."

Rick's skin had darkened slightly each time she mentioned the professor. *He's afraid of what Dr. Andrews will say.*

Rick said, "Do you think you two can really handle all this?"

"We can do the work, and you can check it," Kelly said, forcing herself to sound pleasant. "It's bound to take less time that way."

"Well, we *have* to be set up by Friday," Rick said. "I guess we can give it a try." He rose from the table and Adam followed. Neither picked up their dishes. *At this rate, I'm liable to bite my tongue in two before Friday.* Kelly stacked the plates and carried them to the counter.

By the time she washed the dishes, most of the hot water was gone. She took the basin into her room, stripped, and sponged herself with what water there was and then put on her nightclothes. The smell of bear bait hung like mist around her.

Kelly woke to the sound of someone banging stove lids. She sat up and said, "Adam?"

He stuck his head into the storeroom. "Didn't mean to wake you."

"It's okay, but before you start the fire, you should empty the ash pan. It's behind that little door."

Rick was awake, too. He said, "Be sure the ashes aren't hot, and don't dump them near the cabin."

The three of them swung into the morning work. Rick sent Adam to check the gas in the four-wheeler on the trailer near the bait barrel. He went to the truck. Kelly fried bacon and pushed the skillet back from the fire to cool before she scrambled the eggs, which were fluffier than the eggs she'd cooked on Wednesday. She was aware that Adam had left a gritty layer of ashes on the floor around the stove, but she didn't have time to sweep.

She reviewed her mental list and supplied everything Rick had asked for the day before. More supplies would be needed today. If they had snared a bear, they'd want the drugs, the medical kit, and the jab stick. They'd also need collars and ear tags. Rick came in for the supplies Kelly had packed. He took the extra items without a word.

When Rick and Adam sat down for breakfast, Adam launched into the meal, saying to Kelly with a full-mouthed grin, "Maybe we'll keep you on as chuck wagon cook. You're getting the hang of it."

It was a sore subject, so Kelly changed the direction of the conversation. "Before I ride another day with that gun, do you mind telling me if it's loaded?"

"Well, of course it's loaded. What good is an empty gun?"

Kelly kept her voice light. "And what assurance can you give me as we bounce around on the mountain, that it's not going to shoot my leg off?"

Adam wiped his plate with a piece of bread, rose from his chair, and picked up the gun belt. Taking the gun from the holster, he said, "This is a Ruger Redhawk. Rugers have a unique feature: instead of having the firing pin attached to the hammer, the hammer's a free hammer, and in between the hammer and the firing pin is what they call a transfer bar." Adam touched the hammer. "The transfer bar keeps the hammer from hitting the firing pin unless it's cocked. So, don't worry. When we're bouncing around on the mountain, the gun won't fire."

Kelly said, "Well, I might get back on that four-wheeler then." She looked at Rick. "Why do you carry the guns?"

"For protection. In case we got between a sow and her cubs and she charged us; or for some reason a bear got loose from a snare." Rick got up from the table.

Kelly did the dishes and joined them in the truck. By eight-thirty, they were at Warren Gulch. "The first thing we have to do is check the snares we set yesterday." Rick was on his four-wheeler. "Can you two find the first ones?"

"Sure," Adam said. Kelly wasn't quite so certain, but thinking of the blue ribbons tied to specific bushes on the trail, she nodded.

"If there's a bear in the snare, don't even go near it," Rick said. "Come and get me."

None of the snares held bears, although one piece of meat had been chewed a little. When Kelly told Rick, he said, "Probably a coyote.

They sometimes come in and worry the bait." They cleared four new sites in Warren Gulch.

"After we each finish our sets," Rick said, "we'll go back to the lower road and cut across to Chase Creek." He repeated the set-building instructions in a tone that suggested that Adam and Kelly were mentally deficient. But, finally, he went down the trail and left them alone. ∾

Chapter Ten

"What do you want to build first?" Kelly asked. "Snare set or barricade?"

"Barricade," Adam said. "So we can leave the bait in the box until the last minute." He wrinkled his nose. Kelly thought of how close his nose had been to her hair the evening before. She moved away from him and began to drag limbs from the meadow.

Using logs, limbs, and sticks, they created a barricade that looked like a natural pile of brush, totally blocking the space between the two side trees. Adam stood back to admire it.

"It looks great," he said. "You can't tell it's been touched by human hands."

Kelly studied the barricade. "Do you think it will suit Rick?"

"Probably not." Adam grinned at her. "Kelly, you have to accept the facts. Rick isn't going to be any happier when you do it right than when you do it wrong. I'll bet you he'll change something on every set we build."

Kelly laughed. Adam reminded her of Peggy—the way Peggy used to be—joking about everything. Kelly stood in the sun for a moment, chilled by concern for Peggy.

"Is there something wrong with the barricade?"

Kelly looked at Adam. "No, I was just thinking about my sister—worrying actually."

"You're the oldest, right?"

"How did you know that?"

"You and Rick both have that first-born, run-the-world way about you."

"I'm not like Rick."

Adam said, "You want to manage this project, don't you?"

Kelly stared at him and could not answer for a moment. Finally, she said, "Is it that obvious?"

"Maybe not to Rick, but to us mortals who are just trying to get along, the seesaw ride is dizzying."

"Seesaw ride?"

"He delivers a learned pronouncement—he's up, you're down. You quote from the book—he's down, you're up. It's hard to breathe when the air is so thick with frustrated ambition."

Kelly could not accept that view of herself. She walked toward a tangle of downed branches and began tugging on a limb. Adam joined her. They built the second barricade in silence.

Finally Kelly said, "You're right, Adam, I do want to run the project, but not this year. I want to learn enough to run it next year."

"You've got plenty of time. This is only our second day in the field."

It seemed like she had been on the project a lot longer than two days. Kelly smiled at him and said, "I can't believe this is just our second day. My hair has been dirty for at least two weeks."

Adam laughed and picked up the shovel. He knelt to dig the hole for the trigger. Kelly began cutting and sharpening sticks. "What do you want from this project?" she asked him.

Adam glanced up. "I'm not sure what I want. I don't know that I'm really into fieldwork. I decided to try a few things I've never done." He seemed at ease with himself.

"Doesn't Rick make you angry?"

"I don't particularly like to be followed around with a tape measure and magnifying glass, but he is what he is. No point in all three of us trying to be boss."

"I take it you are not a first-born child," Kelly said.

Adam flashed his grin at her. "Last-born and grateful."

"How many siblings do you have?"

"Two older sisters and an older brother. All of them movers and shakers."

"What do your parents do?"

"My dad's a doctor. My mother worked as a pharmacist until she started having children."

"Was she unhappy because she had to give up working?"

"Nope," Adam said. "She likes us. She says every wheel has to have a hub. We're all spokes aiming different directions. She holds us together." He moved back from the hole, saying, "There, will that pass inspection?"

Kelly looked at his work and turned to smile at him. "Mine, anyway."

They set the trigger in the hole and concealed it with grass and small twigs. "Let me try," Kelly said when it was time to load the spring. "If I can't do it, I need to know."

The steel spring was powerful. As Kelly struggled with it, it slued sideways, disturbing the cable. She finally knelt and secured the spring with her knees and then used the weight of her upper body to augment the strength in her arms.

Adam watched without comment. When she finished, he moved quietly to arrange the cable loop on top—open wide and lying flat. He straightened the rest of the cable; Kelly smoothed and releveled the soil underneath the cable; Adam concealed it with grass.

Placing the stepping sticks, they checked the angle. Kelly took a few deep breaths and went to the four-wheeler for the bait. They spread the peanut butter and burnt the surface with the torch.

They were removing the traces of their work when Rick came across the meadow.

"Have you already done two snares?" Kelly asked.

"No, just one, but I thought I'd better see how things were going here." Kelly felt a rise of irritation. *He doesn't think we can do it without him.*

Rick looked at their work. Then he knelt by the snare and slightly rearranged the stepping sticks. Adam caught Kelly's eyes and winked. Her irritation dissipated. She stepped to Adam's side to watch as Rick added a few twigs to the pile in front of the snare, straightened the cable, and checked the spring.

"We'll head up to the next site," Adam said. "Come on, Kelly."

"Is first-born bossiness catching?" she asked him as she followed him obediently, carrying the tools.

"Just thought I'd see how it feels," he said.

Kelly and Adam finished the next set in forty-five minutes, working in silence. Adam's comments had rubbed a sore spot in Kelly's mind, and she kept returning to them, hating to see herself the way he pictured her. Matt had called her selfish, uncaring, uptight. Adam's adjectives seemed to be *competitive* and *bossy*.

But, if she hadn't insisted, Rick would still be trying to do everything himself. As it was, working separately, they would set as many snares before lunch today as they'd done in the entire day, yesterday. And she had managed the arrangement without making Rick lose face. Adam just didn't see the whole picture.

Kelly took a break to find a bathroom bush. She was tired, but not totally from the work. It was a strain dealing with strangers. She wished she could run the whole business herself. That thought made her grin. Maybe Adam was right about her.

When she came back to the snare, Adam was leaning a stick over the throw arm. He knew better than that. "What are you doing?"

He looked up, his eyes sparkling. "I read a story about a portrait painter who always painted a dark blotch in one corner of a finished picture just before he delivered it. The client immediately focused on the blotch instead of the portrait. The painter would then agree to remove the blotch and the client would declare himself totally satisfied." Adam added another small stick to the arm. "I'm just making a blotch for Santini."

Kelly had to laugh. Adam was as much like Ryan as he was like Peggy. As she watched Rick come toward them and stop in front of the trail set, she felt less strain than before.

"Not bad," Rick said after a moment's survey, "except for these." He stooped to remove the sticks from the throw arm, repeating the instructions he'd given the day before. "If the throw arm comes up and hits a stick, the cable won't throw all the way."

"Well, Santini. Have we earned our lunch?" Adam did not look toward Kelly, and she was glad, because she was struggling to suppress her giggles.

"Let's move over to Chase Creek before we eat," Rick said.

It took them two hours to move, choose new sites, and clear the area. Chopping shrubs, hauling branches, and digging holes in the ground was hot, dirty work, but Rick was finally satisfied with the clearings. They ate a late lunch, and he left them with a reminder to keep the line of sight clear between the two pieces of bait.

Kelly and Adam reviewed every step of the work as they built the sets. Adam asked a lot of questions, not seeming to care that Kelly was female and that she had the answers.

"You really enjoy learning stuff, don't you?" he said.

"My mind gets to feeling thinned and empty if there's not some new challenge."

"Is your mind a separate entity? You make it sound like you're talking about somebody else."

"My mind is a friend of mine."

"You're a little weird, Kelly Jones." Adam knelt and deliberately pushed a few of the stepping sticks until they leaned too close to the gap in the snare.

Santini's Blotch, as Adam called it, worked to the purpose on that set and again on the second set along Chase Creek, which they finished building late in the day. Each time he checked their sets, Rick removed the obvious blunders and approved the rest of the work.

Kelly knew that they had built the sets well, so she didn't feel guilty directing Rick's attention away. But as they marked the trail with blue ribbons and got on the four-wheelers, she was glad that Dr. Andrews did not know about her conspiring with Adam to get Rick off their backs. She did not think he would consider it real teamwork.

Bouncing along the trail with the gun holster hitting the sore spot on her leg, she directed cranky mental questions toward Dr. Andrews. *What makes a group of strangers turn into a team? How can I focus on the project if the others get their egos in the way?*

She considered that thought a minute. Was it fair to Adam to say that his ego was in the way? She decided that it was. Adam was quite willing to treat her as an equal when they were alone together, but he was different when they were all three together in the cabin. He had picked up his dishes the first night, but Rick hadn't cleared his dishes. After that Adam didn't do it again. Santini obviously thought dishes were women's work. Adam was trying to be as much a man as Santini. He was on his own seesaw.

Her thoughts were interrupted by Rick's shout of disgust from the creek. "Those damn cattle have been in here, too," he said, when Adam and Kelly stopped near him. "If they're up this high already, eating grass, how can the bears compete for food?" On the drive to the cabin, Rick continued fuming. "In the western states, bears have been considered only as predators. Ranchers used to shoot them on sight." Rick slowed the truck near the bait barrel. "Sometimes I'd like to start shooting cows."

Rick and Adam unhooked the trailer near the bait barrel, and then they drove on. As they rounded the curve, they saw a blue pickup sitting in front of the cabin. Kelly recognized the rancher who had shown her the turnoff. Rick swung in behind the pickup. "What in the hell is he doing here?" ∾

Chapter Eleven

Kelly followed Rick to the rancher's truck. The rancher said, "I brought you a couple of dead calves. Thought you could use them as bait." Rick flushed. Kelly added another data point to her file. Santini knew when he had been ungracious.

She stepped forward and held out her hand as the rancher got down from his truck. "Hi, I'm Kelly Jones. It's nice of you to think of the project. We can always use bear bait."

The rancher's eyes twinkled. He took her hand, acting as if they'd never met. "I'm Jim McCarthy." Adam and Rick moved to the side of the truck and looked at the stiff dead calves. Rick said, "If you want to drive back to the bait barrel, we'll unload 'em there." He added, a little stiffly, "Thanks, Jim."

Kelly felt she owed this man more than that. "Would you come back and eat supper with us, Mr. McCarthy?"

The rancher turned to her. "I'd like that. Ever since I've been a widower, I jump at a chance to ride the grub line."

The three men left in the blue truck. Kelly washed and put on a clean shirt, frowning slightly as she saw that the dirty-clothes pile beneath her bed was growing. She set the table nicely again—this time because she felt gracious.

Supper went smoothly at first. The men talked generally about the area. Then, as they were finishing their dessert, Rick said, "Are those your cattle up on Chase Creek?"

Mr. McCarthy's eyes narrowed at Rick's tone. He nodded and said, "Some of my cattle are up there. Why do you ask?"

"It's damned early to push them into higher pasture. There's scarcely enough forage for the wildlife."

"I have permits." The rancher's tone was cold, his face, stony. Kelly didn't know what to do. She glanced at Adam, who shrugged. Before she could say a word to smooth things over, Mr. McCarthy rose from the table. "I've got to check my stock tanks." He smiled at Kelly, his face softening. "Thanks for supper."

Kelly walked with the rancher to his pickup. She said, "I'm sorry about that. Rick was upset this afternoon because the water was fouled and the vegetation trampled."

"Not your fault." His face was somber. "I'm hearing more and more complaints about my cattle. If they push this—and ranchers lose their permits to graze on federal land—we'll go on hard times." With a nod of his head toward the cabin, he said, "Did you hire on as cook and dishwasher for those two?"

Kelly felt herself flush. "No, I came here to do fieldwork."

"Well, don't let them keep you in the kitchen."

He was nice. Kelly said, "I don't know how to get out."

He grinned at her. "You're out now. Why don't you leave the dishes and ride with me while I check my water tanks? I'd be glad of the company."

"Okay," Kelly said, "but I'd better tell them where I'm going." She ran up the steps and stuck her head inside the door. "I'll be back in a little while. I'm going with Mr. McCarthy to check his tanks."

Rick had pushed his plate aside so that he could spread his papers under the glow of the kerosene lamp. He looked up from the data sheets he was reading. "What about the dishes?"

What about the dishes? she thought, feeling a scratchy irritation. But she answered in a light tone. "Go ahead and do them. Just save me enough hot water to wash my hair." Savoring the look on Rick's face, she let the screen door slam behind her.

It was pleasant to ride across the pastures in the dusk, and she was glad to talk with someone besides Rick and Adam. "How long have you been a widower, Mr. McCarthy?"

He glanced at her. "Do you have to mister me? Call me Jim . . . or Jamie. That's what my wife called me." He answered her question. "She's been dead almost three years now."

"I'm sorry."

"I'm sorry, too, but not so much for myself. I'm sorry that she died before she got to do what she really wanted to do."

"And what was that?"

"She wanted to write. But me and the kids and the ranch got in her way."

There was so much pain in the man's voice that Kelly was silent for a moment. Then she asked, "Did your wife tell you that?"

"No." He looked her way again, and his face was tight. "She never told me, but she wrote it in her journals." He turned onto a rutted trail across the pasture toward a windmill. He pulled up beside the water tank and killed the engine, but he didn't get out. He turned toward Kelly. "I've been reading those journals, nights since she died. She talked a lot about focus and priorities." He shook his head slightly. "She talked about never having any time." His eyes looked old and misty now. Kelly didn't know what to say, so she stayed silent, waiting through the man's battle with his pain, aware that she was a stranger. He finally stirred and reached for the door handle. "I'd better turn the windmill on. This tank's getting low."

When they got back to the cabin, Kelly said, "Thanks for the outing, Jamie."

"We'll do it again," he said. His smile was friendly, but Kelly went inside feeling tense and sorry. He had shared something out of his loneliness, and she had done nothing to ease his hurt.

The dishes had been washed and returned to the shelves; the dishpan lay upside down on the counter. Rick and Adam were reading. The water in the reservoir was still warm. Silently Kelly filled the dishpan and shampooed her hair. Then she put on her sweat suit and opened her guitar case. Sitting on her cot with her back against the wall, she sang "When You and I Were Young, Maggie" and "In the Gloaming" and "I'll Take You Home Again, Kathleen" and several more sad old songs. At last, the tight pain eased, dissolving the knot that had gathered in her chest as Jamie McCarthy had talked about his wife. Kelly put the guitar back in its case and went to bed.

She woke early with a plan that made her smile, and she knew that it would make the rancher smile, too. Taking up her notebook, Kelly wrote out three neat schedules labeled Week One, Week Two, and Week Three. Under Week One, she wrote, "Cook—Kelly," "Dishwasher—Rick," "Wood and Ash Hauler—Adam." Under Week Two, she arranged the names so that Rick was cook and Adam was dishwasher. And for Week Three, she rearranged the names again, making Adam the cook. Underneath the schedules, she wrote, "Repeat, beginning with Week One." She slipped into the kitchen and fastened the schedules to the wall above the washbasin. By the time Rick and Adam were up, Kelly had breakfast ready and the sandwiches made. She hummed as she worked.

Adam said, "Wow. We ought to give you a night on the town more often. You must have had a good time with that old rancher."

Kelly looked his way, but didn't answer. She didn't understand why the rancher had confided in her, but she thought it had something to do with his wife's words about focus. And the idea of focusing on her goals had given Kelly a steady, happy feeling.

Adam was still studying her. "I just don't understand this. You were out with me all day yesterday, and you didn't sing."

Kelly laughed. "Well, Mr. McCarthy smells better than you do."

"Cow manure smells better than bear bait?"

"Veritably," Kelly said.

Rick spoke for the first time. "Speaking of bear bait, Adam. We'll have to cut up those calves as soon as we can. We should get them into the barrel before the maggots take over completely."

"Bears like maggots, don't they?" Adam said, but Kelly could tell by his anemic laugh that he didn't like the idea of more butchering.

"Doesn't the smell bother you?" she asked Rick.

"You get used to it," he said.

Though both men had washed at the counter, neither had mentioned the schedules Kelly had posted above it. Kelly left the dishes on the table and went out to the truck. As she climbed up and checked the equipment box, her heart beat a little faster. Maybe today they would find a bear in one of the twelve snares they had already set. She ran her mental checklist. The equipment for placing new trail sets and processing a bear was complete. She went back to the cabin for the fanny pack with their lunch in it. The dishes had been washed and stacked on the shelf. Rick went out and rechecked the equipment box. *Win one, lose one,* Kelly thought as she climbed into the truck beside Adam.

There were no bears. Rick fussed over each of the eight snares in Warren Gulch, checking and rechecking, before he gave it up and went with them to Chase Creek. No bears had triggered the Chase Creek snares either. Rick stopped at the lower sites, sending Adam and Kelly higher up the creek to begin building sets. When they finished their first set of the day, and Adam started to add the Santini Blotch, Kelly said, "Let's allow our work to stand on its merits, Adam. It's possible that we've done it right, and Rick will recognize the fact."

After they finished the second set, Kelly took a bathroom break and walked down the other side of the hill away from Chase Creek and the four-wheeler. Choosing a game trail, she walked slowly into the gully, which was shadowed by conifers. Suddenly, she saw a dark deposit on the trail ahead, and her pulse quickened. It had to be bear scat. It was too big for coyote.

Digging into her pocket for a plastic bag, she gathered some of the scat. It wasn't old—as last summer's scat would be—but it wasn't completely fresh. It had dried a little. She pulled it apart with her fingers and studied the grass it held. Then she ran back up the hill, carrying the bag in her hand. Rick had just finished checking their second snare, but she didn't have time to worry about the set. She held out the scat and said, "I found this back there in the conifer stand."

Rick took the bag and studied it briefly, then looked up at her with a light in his eyes. "Let's go see where you found it." Kelly guided them to the spot. A little farther down the trail, Rick found the track of a bear's paw. "It's a fairly big bear." Rick was still businesslike, but Kelly could feel an undercurrent of excitement as he turned and hurried up the trail to the equipment box. "We'll set a snare in the conifers."

"Before lunch?" Adam asked.

It was past noon, but Kelly wasn't hungry. She shared Rick's excitement about the bear sign. "Before lunch," she said to Adam.

They set the snare in the bottom of the draw. Kelly looked into the shaded depths of the forest that climbed the slope. "That will be a good area for day beds when the weather gets hotter," she said to Rick.

He nodded. "I hope we can collar a bear in this area and follow her for some habitat data."

Rick was much more relaxed now that all the sets were finished, and they had seen fresh sign. "We have to be careful with labeling," Rick said to Adam, showing him how he had marked the bag to identify the area and time of year. "Losing the label on a scat sample makes the sample less valuable. Every data point is important."

"Especially when you're working with large animals," Kelly said. "If we were working with mice, and we could get hundreds or thousands of samples, the loss of a data point wouldn't be a big deal. But there are fewer bears than mice, and every data point is essential." Adam looked at her with a suggestion of a grin and seesawed his head from side to side. Kelly didn't offer any more information.

They ate lunch and made some notes about grasses and forbs in the area. Then Rick said, "Well, those calves aren't getting any sweeter. We'd better head back."

Adam said, "Are we going to have to cut up meat all summer?"

"I hope so," Rick said. "If we don't get new supplies of bait, the project will be shot down."

"How much bait are we going to need?" Kelly asked.

"We'll be snaring for eight weeks, so we'll need a couple of tons of bait before we're done."

"That's a lot of meat," Adam said. "What if we can't get that many animals?"

"Then Dr. Andrews will go scrounging at the meat-packing plants for scraps, but that takes money, and Jerry Andrews *hates* to buy bait." Kelly enjoyed the sun on her back as she walked toward the four-wheelers listening to Rick. *When a perfectionist has things under control, he can actually sound quite human.* "Spring's the worst time for bears," Rick said, "and it's especially hard on last year's cubs. The yearlings are nothing but bones right now and, pretty soon, they'll be kicked off from their mothers to fend for themselves. They haven't learned yet how to find the good places to eat." Kelly turned to study Rick. He spoke almost tenderly of the yearling bears. She'd never heard that tone in his voice before.

When they pulled up by the bait barrel, the calves were no longer there. There were new chunks of bait in the barrel. Kelly pointed at a small bit of litter. "That's a gum wrapper. I'll bet Dr. Andrews has been here."

At the cabin, Dr. Andrews and two young men were just getting out of a van. *Two more for supper,* Kelly thought. *There aren't enough pork chops for everyone.* Dr. Andrews introduced the young men as Kevin and Jonathan. As they all went inside, Kelly was swiftly revising her evening menu. Dr. Andrews stopped inside the door and looked around. "Well, you've settled right in." Kelly tried to see the cabin through his eyes. Adam's corner was a little too casually arranged—piled might be a better word—but the rest of the cabin was tidy. The map on the wall was decorative, as well as useful.

Dr. Andrews looked into the storeroom and said to Kelly, "Your sister sent you a care package." He glanced at the schedules over the counter without comment. Rick had stepped to the map to mark the new trail sets. Dr. Andrews said, "Kevin, you and Jonathan want to bring in the groceries and the package for Kelly?" He joined Rick at the map, where Kelly heard them discussing Jenny.

Kevin said to Kelly, "Could I wash my hands first? I helped cut up those calves."

The cabin seemed suddenly crowded. Kelly built a fire, moving around the two young men who first washed at the counter and then unloaded groceries onto it. Adam washed at one end of the stove. Rick and Dr. Andrews pulled two chairs from the table and sat down to look at some periodicals Dr. Andrews had brought. To set the table, she had to sidle past the back of Rick's chair.

Kelly put the large package from Peggy on her bed. She yearned to open the letter that was taped to the top, but she didn't have time. When Adam brought in an armload of wood, she smiled at him. With "new" strangers in the cabin, Adam seemed more like an old friend.

During dinner, Rick explained the trail sets, describing what they would see on Saturday, while Kelly worried, *How are we going to get everyone up there with just two four-wheelers?* At the end of the meal, Dr. Andrews rose and picked up his plate. "Well, Rick, I see that you're the dishwasher. I'll help you clear up. Before we go to bed, I want to explain to Kevin and Jonathan how we put the bears down."

Rick glanced at the table. The darkening of his skin showed his emotion. *He can hardly refuse to do dishes since Dr. Andrews is helping.* Kelly followed his glance toward Kevin and Jonathan. *But he hates to do them in front of these two.* She happened to look up just then and found that Dr. Andrews was studying her as closely as she had been studying Rick. She felt her own face flush. She turned and went outside to regain her poise in the quiet of the outhouse.

When she started back toward the cabin, she saw Adam at the woodshed, chopping more wood. She joined him. "You're kind of overdoing the chore-boy bit tonight, aren't you?"

He set the axe against the chopping block and said, "There's no room for me in the cabin." Kelly had the feeling that he wasn't speaking of physical space.

"Dr. Andrews wants to talk about the drugs," Kelly said. "Why don't you join us?"

Adam grinned at her. "Are you activities coordinator at this boys camp?" He draped an arm across her shoulder as they walked to the cabin, adding, "Or are you my mama?"

Embarrassed, Kelly shrugged out from under his arm. "Sorry. I didn't mean to be so obvious."

Adam patted her shoulder. "That's okay. I need to learn one end of the jab stick from the other. I'm glad you ordered me inside." Kelly smiled as she held the door open for him. Adam had a way of making everything seem less serious. ༄

Chapter Twelve

Dr. Andrews and Rick were setting up a display on the table. The jab stick, which was usually in three parts in the cylinder, had been assembled so that it was now a slender metal pole, eight feet long. The drugs had been taken from the ice chest in the cupboard. Dr. Andrews started his explanation by speaking of money.

"The drugs are an expensive and absolutely necessary part of this project. Without them, we couldn't do the work." Dr. Andrews picked up one of the small bottles. "This bottle alone cost over fifty dollars."

"Wow," Jonathan said. He and Kevin were sitting on the edge of Rick's cot. Kelly and Adam had taken two of the chairs. Rick tipped back against the wall in another.

"The scientific name of this drug is ketamine hydrochloride," the professor said.

Jonathan said, "What does it do?" Kelly noticed that Kevin was yawning.

"It's not an anesthetic," Dr. Andrews said with a slight frown as he also glanced at Kevin. "It works on the nervous system."

"Does it put them to sleep?"

"It numbs the whole nervous system in such a way that the bear is out of it, but not asleep." He glanced again at Kevin. "Its eyes are open, but it can't move or react."

Dr. Andrews continued. "There are some drawbacks to just using the ketamine. The bear goes stiff as a board. You can imagine trying to pull a huge stiff bear around."

Rick set his chair down on four legs and said, "Another drawback is that if the bear is aware of what's happening, it may be undergoing considerable stress."

He even takes over from Dr. Andrews.

Dr. Andrews took the lecture back into his control. "In combination with the ketamine, we use xylazine hydrochloride. It's called Rompun and works on the muscles to relax them." He indicated the syringe at one end of the jab stick. "We combine one cc of Rompun per hundredweight of bear with two cc's of ketamine per hundredweight of bear."

He fished in his pocket for a package of gum, unwrapped a stick, and dropped the wrapper on the table. He grinned around the gum. "One problem for beginners lies in estimating the size of the bear."

Rick said, "Yeah, the first bear you see looks a lot bigger than he really is." They all laughed.

"How do we tell if the bear has gotten enough of the drug?" Adam asked. "And how do we know if the anesthetic is working?"

"Maybe we'll get a chance to see the signs tomorrow," Dr. Andrews said. "Usually, the bear starts panting and licking its lips and proceeds to blinking its eyes. Then the head begins to droop; the bear acts drowsy and suddenly goes down."

The two students came alive with interest as Dr. Andrews spoke of seeing a bear, but Kelly felt a surge of concern. If there were a bear in one of the snares tomorrow, would more people cause it more stress? Rick seemed to think that bears were aware of people, even under the drug.

Dr. Andrews finished answering questions and said, "Well, if we're going to process bears, we'd better get to bed." He pushed his chair under the table and went outside. The young men spread their sleeping bags on the floor between the table and the cots.

Kelly went to her room, turned on her flashlight, and was about to open Peggy's letter when Rick came in with the drug chest and the other equipment. Adam followed him into the storeroom. "Can I sleep in your room tonight, Kelly?" he asked softly, adding with a grin, "The dormitory is too crowded."

Kelly laughed and said, also very softly, "You have to be polite to your little visitors, Adam."

Adam saw the package. "Hey, can we open your present?"

Kelly was surprised to see that Rick had lingered. He didn't speak, but he seemed interested in her package, too. She set Peggy's letter aside, sat down on the bed, and pulled away the tape and paper. Peggy had sent a shaggy throw rug and a large fat pillow, both of a shade of green that complemented the colors in her quilt. Adam took the pillow and joining Kelly on the bed tucked it behind him. He leaned back and said, "No fair. You have nicer stuff than we do."

Dr. Andrews stuck his head into the storeroom. "Are you about ready for us to blow out the light?"

"No," said Kelly, "not until these two find their way out of my room." Adam clutched the pillow. Kelly snatched it away and said, "Out!"

After the light was extinguished in the other room, Kelly aimed the flashlight beam at Peggy's letter.

Dear Kelly,

It seems like you've been gone a whole month, and it's only been four days. I miss you, and I'm sorry I was so stupid the day you left. The house is still filled with nighttime rumblings. Sometimes I'm tempted to move out. I hope you like the "I'm sorry" present I'm sending you. (You'd better; it took a major portion of the money I got from selling last semester's books.) Ryan is really serious about visiting you. I may borrow Dad's car and drive him down one of these days just to see how you're getting along with the Fabulous Santini.

Love, Peggy

Smiling, Kelly folded the letter and shut out the light. It did seem longer than four days, and it was nice to feel close to Peggy again. She thought about her parents. It was selfish, but she was simply glad to be away.

In the morning, Dr. Andrews took care of breakfast. He set dishes, cereal boxes, milk, and oranges on the table. "Wash up your own stuff when you're through," he said, "and don't get in Kelly's way." Kelly was surprised, but grateful. She started the lunches and, with everyone doing something, they were soon on their way.

Adam and the other two undergraduates rode in the back of the truck to the bait barrel. Kevin flatly refused to fill the bait box. Jonathan took the gloves and did the job quickly. Kelly began to think about a crew for next year as she watched him. She definitely did not want someone like Kevin, but Jonathan might be all right. She caught Adam's eye, and he winked as if he knew that she was choosing a crew for "her" project.

After they parked in the meadow and unloaded the four-wheelers, Dr. Andrews and Rick took Kevin and Jonathan up Warren Gulch to check the snares. As the noisy machines went up the hill, Adam said, "I hope they don't find any bears."

Kelly laughed out loud. "Are you always so honest? I feel the same way, but I'd never have told you that."

"Well, *we* built those trail-sets. Why should they get to see our bears first?"

"Rick won't be happy if there aren't any bears."

"I didn't come to this project to make Santini happy," Adam said. He grinned. "Although I grant you, that it is better for us peons when the great lord is content."

Kelly said, "Let's see if we can find some scat for the newcomers to poke through."

Adam laughed and said, "*Fresh* scat."

The four-wheelers returned sooner than Kelly had expected. She looked at Rick. He shook his head. "No bears."

Kevin decided not to go to Chase Creek. Kelly stayed behind so that Adam could go. Kevin immediately crawled in the truck and sacked out. When the four-wheelers returned, Kelly could tell at once that the other sets had also been empty.

"Wasted morning," Rick said tersely as Kelly began to unpack their lunch. They ate in the meadow. Rick was grim. He and Dr. Andrews discussed the trail sets, the bait, the area. "I think we're high enough for spring snaring," Rick said. "But maybe we're in the wrong area. We'll have wasted a lot of time and work if the bears aren't ranging to this side of the mountain."

"I think it's more likely that we're a bit early," Dr. Andrews said. "The bears are still sleepy and may not be moving a lot."

Jonathan was studying the scat samples she and Adam had collected. Kelly grinned when she heard Adam say, "Don't lose the labels. The samples are less valuable without the labels." Adam wasn't above showing off a little himself.

After dinner on Saturday evening, Dr. Andrews said to the two students, "We'd better head back to Provo. Why don't you get our stuff together while I go gas up?"

After Dr. Andrews had left for the small general store and service station, which was out on the highway and up a mile or two, Kelly joined Rick and Adam, who were studying data sheets from the year before. Rick said, "I don't think we're too early. We snared a bear this time last year. We're going to go over each of those sets tomorrow and see what we've done wrong."

When Dr. Andrews returned, he directed the loading of the gear. Rick, Adam, and Kelly came out to the porch with him. Kevin and Jonathan had already climbed into the van. "I ran into Jim McCarthy at the store," Dr. Andrews said.

Standing next to Rick, Kelly heard his soft intake of breath. Had

Jim McCarthy mentioned the discussion about his cattle? The three of them exchanged a quick glance, and Kelly was certain that Dr. Andrews caught the exchange, but all he said was, "It was a good idea to invite him to dinner. He seemed to enjoy himself." He went down the steps.

As the van bumped off toward the main road, Adam said, "I owe my mother an apology."

Kelly raised her eyebrows. "What brought that on?"

"I used to drag home overnight guests all the time. Never thought anything of it."

Rick said, "We could use fewer guests and more bears." He turned and went back inside the cabin to pull material from the files. The kerosene lamp burned for a long time after Kelly and Adam went to bed.

With just three of them in the cabin Sunday morning, it seemed easy to get their gear together and head for Warren Gulch. Adam said, "I'm glad we don't have to stop at the bait barrel."

Rick scowled. "When we don't need bait, it means that we haven't been doing our job." He was fiddling with the receiver. "Damn it, Jenny, where are you? Do you want to choke on that collar?" His mood infected them all, and they were silent and separate as they rode along.

When they reached the meadow, Kelly said, "Shall we go to the Warren Gulch sets with you or go ahead and check out Chase Creek?"

"Go to Chase Creek and check for bears. But if the snares are empty, don't touch the sets until I get a chance to look them over." Kelly sighed. He didn't have to be so rude. She and Adam wanted to snare a bear as much as he did, and she was sure their sets were done correctly.

While they were unloading the four-wheelers, they heard the sound of a truck. Rick said, "Damn. I hope that's not a logging truck. Jerry mentioned rumors that the Forest Service had let a new logging contract up here, but I didn't think they'd hire us and then let a logger in."

But it was a logging truck. They stood in dismay as the noisy vehicle chugged past them, throwing up a trail of dust that powdered the roadside vegetation. The truck took a right-hand fork and moved out of sight, but they could hear it for a long time after it disappeared.

"That's going to shoot down our chances for bears in the lower sets," Rick said. He climbed on his four-wheeler. "Let's really get with it and check the sets we've got. If we haven't snared a bear, we'll have time to move a couple of sets up higher." He seemed more tuned in to Adam and Kelly.

"It's odd," Kelly said to Adam as they started up the road to the Chase Creek turnoff, "how we unite when some outsider shows up."

As Kelly and Adam checked sets and each snare proved to be

undisturbed, she began to share Rick's worries. What had they done wrong? She and Adam discussed each set, and even though Rick had told them not to touch anything, they fussed with the barricades and the stepping sticks until finally, unable to see other possible changes, they fired up the torch, researed the meat to broadcast new scent, and went on—bouncing farther up the rough trail, walking hopefully across the meadows—to each of the aspen sets. All were empty, undisturbed. They headed toward the conifer forest.

Adam seemed moody. "How come you aren't your usual smiling self?" Kelly asked, leaning forward so her voice would carry over the sound of the four-wheeler's engine.

He looked over his shoulder. "Do you realize what a boring, miserable summer this is going to be if we don't start snaring some bears?"

"We will," Kelly said. "We will. You reminded me just a day or so ago that we haven't even been here a week yet."

"But if we don't?" Adam's voice was loud. "Do you want to ride these trails over and over again, burning that stinking bait, washing your hair in a dish pan, for no purpose?"

Kelly laughed. "Adam, you've got to be more scientific. Don't you know that even the lack of a data point is a data point? We could write a whole paper about the fact that there were bears on the other side of the mountain, but none on this side of the mountain."

Adam kept his head turned toward her, but he didn't respond. Kelly continued, "We could launch a comparative study of habitat, or we might map logging locations with relation to their nearness to known bear cover—any number of things. We don't need to sit around and get on each other's nerves."

Adam pulled the four-wheeler to a stop and shut it off just above the gully where the last set was located. He turned to her with a grin. "Next you'll be telling me that patience is a virtue. Well, I'm not impressed with fieldwork to date, and I'm not convinced that *anything* can keep us from getting on each other's nerves, but thanks for the pep talk."

Adam and Kelly started down toward the set. Suddenly, Adam stopped. "Kelly, we have a bear."

Kelly's heart lurched. She looked where Adam pointed. In the bottom of the shadowy gully, almost lost in the shadows itself, was a large dark brown bear. ❧

Chapter Thirteen

The bear was standing quietly on all fours with its head and nose down.

But it was obvious that it had not been quiet all the time. "Look," whispered Kelly, "look at the tree where the snare is chained." Adam whistled softly. The fir tree was battle-scarred. The bark had been chewed and clawed entirely off one side to a height of at least ten feet.

"How could it get up that high?" Adam asked with awe in his voice.

"It must have climbed and dragged the chain up with it," Kelly said. "The bear's probably been in that snare all night."

The barricades were totally destroyed—just piles of shattered sticks. The ground around the tree was torn and clawed. Kelly couldn't see the bait or the snare in the shadows below the trees, but what she could see told her plainly of the bear's panic.

As Kelly looked at the tired bear, she was suddenly, unexpectedly, overwhelmed with regret. She bit her lip as she pictured the bear's battle with the foot snare and chain. *I'm supposed to be objective, and I just told Adam to be more scientific.* The thought didn't help. *I wish we had met on equal terms. If we had met in the woods, we would each have acknowledged the other's presence and gone our separate ways, freely.* She felt slightly nauseated, hating the snare, loathing the necessity to dominate the bear in order to study it.

She glanced at Adam, who was studying *her.* "What's the matter, Kelly? Are you afraid?"

Kelly met his eyes. "No, Adam, I am not afraid; I am ashamed." She turned to head up the slope. "We'd better go get Rick, so we can get that bear out of the snare as soon as possible."

They met Rick halfway down Chase Creek. He stopped his four-wheeler. "Any luck?" Kelly could tell by the tension in his face that the Warren Gulch snares were empty.

Adam said, "We've got a fair-sized brown bear in the conifers." Rick smiled, and the light in his eyes changed his whole face.

"Do you think it's Jenny?" Kelly asked.

Rick shook his head. "Jenny is cinnamon colored, not brown."

As Adam turned the machine and they headed back toward the bear in the forest, Kelly tried to find a way to deal with her anguish over the bear. She was a poor scientist if she couldn't be objective. She had known they would be trapping—holding bears against their will. That was the only way you could do a study, and ultimately, it was for the bears' own good. If their research could prove that there was a certain number of bears needing space on this mountain, the Forest Service could reroute those logging trucks, limit clear-cutting, and make the bears' habitat more peaceful. She began to review the steps for anesthetizing and gathering data. The smoother the operation, the sooner that bear would be up and on its way to freedom and privacy.

When they were once more standing on the slope above the bear, Rick said, "Well, Adam, how much do you think that bear weighs?"

"At least a hundred and fifty pounds."

Rick nodded and began to gather equipment. "We'll get a little closer and unload our gear. Then I'll put the bear down and see how close your estimate is."

They took the cylinder with the jab stick in it, the drug case, needles, and syringes, the collar and ear tags, the clipboard for the data sheets, the measuring tools, and the pliers. Rick stopped about halfway down the slope and said to Adam, "When we get near the bottom, be sure your gun is ready, just in case that bear charges and the snare doesn't hold."

"What do you want me to do?" Kelly asked, ready to cooperate, to do anything to get the bear processing on its way.

Rick frowned slightly. "Stay out of the way, Kelly. You have no gun and you couldn't shoot it if you did have one. Until I am certain the bear is firmly snared, you are a liability." Kelly could feel the flush that rose along her throat and over her face. Rick continued. "We'll leave the gear here for the moment. When it's safe, you can start hauling some of it down."

Feeling as if she had been named camp burro, Kelly stood on the slope and watched as Adam and Rick worked their way slowly toward the bear. She hated being considered so useless. She thought of Kevin, who had yawned in the midst of the discussion about drugs. *What if I were project leader? If I got stuck with Kevin, I'd have to protect him and still get the work done. But damn it, Rick, I'm not a Kevin. You're wrong about me.*

Rick turned and said, "The snare is secure. Bring the drugs and the jab stick."

Kelly pasted a smile on her face, picked up the requested equipment, and went down the hill. Rick took the cylinder and, slipping the parts of the jab stick from it, swiftly put the jab stick together. He surprised Kelly by asking, "Can you figure out how much ketamine you're supposed to use for a hundred and fifty-pound bear?"

"Two cc's per hundred weight," Kelly said. "So this bear would require 3 cc's of ketamine."

"And the Rompun?" Rick looked at Adam, who shrugged and said nothing.

"One cc per hundredweight," Kelly said. "One and a half cc's for this bear."

"Right," Rick said. He put appropriate amounts of each drug in the syringe in the long tube at the end of the jab stick, then screwed in the needle and pushed enough drug through the tip of the needle to guarantee that there were no air bubbles. Kelly knew about that precaution, and she watched closely. The bear moved around in the bottom of the gully fighting the cable on its leg.

"Now, Adam," Rick said, "go around to the front of that bear, but be sure you're at a safe distance and plan an escape route." Adam swallowed and his face flushed. He nodded without speaking. "When I get down there with the jab stick, I'll give you a signal. When you see my signal, you yell 'hey, bear!' loud enough to attract its attention."

Adam moved along the slope and then downward toward the bear, which watched him, making huffing sounds. When the bear began to clack its teeth together, Adam moved up the slope a few steps. Rick stepped quietly toward the bear, and when he was about eight feet away, he said, "Now!"

Adam raised both arms and tried to yell. His first "Hey, bear!" came out muffled and scratchy sounding. He cleared his throat and this time yelled loudly, "Hey, bear!"

The bear lifted its head, its full attention on Adam. At the same moment, Rick moved in, the jab stick in his right hand. With a quick thrust he jabbed the needle into the bear's rump, and then he was backing away. The entire action was smooth and efficient. The bear had turned toward Rick, but Rick had already moved to safety.

Kelly followed as Rick walked back up the hill before stopping to check the syringe.

"The follow-through is important," he said. "You break the skin with the needle, but you've got to push that syringe down and deliver all the drug."

Adam joined them on the slope. They watched the bear. It began to pant and lick its lips. It blinked its eyes, and the head drooped a little, but after ten minutes, the bear was still standing. Rick said, "It's not going down fast enough. Maybe I ought to give it an extra dose."

Kelly was immediately concerned. "The field guide says it takes at least fifteen minutes."

Rick said, "The field guide deals with a hypothetical bear. I'm dealing with a real one. This bear's a fighter. It fought the snare, and it's fighting the drug." He began to refill the syringe. "I'll give it another half dose."

Kelly didn't say anything else, although she worried about the bear. Adam had the same concerns. "Won't you overdose the bear?"

"These drugs are safe for the bears," Rick said. "You could overdose the bear several times." He grinned at Adam. "But if you stuck yourself with even one dose of that Rompun, it would kill you."

"Thanks a lot," Adam said.

Rick checked the drug at the end of the needle and said, "You ready to distract that bear again?"

The bear was standing on four feet, not moving. Adam went around toward its head, but the bear didn't react, except to blink its eyes when he approached. Rick stepped behind the bear and delivered the second dose.

While they waited, Rick took the jab stick apart. He showed them the needle. "The jab stick needle is smooth. If I used a dart gun, the needle would have a collar to catch in the bear's skin."

"When would we use the dart gun?"

"I don't like to use it at all because of the force with which it impacts the bear's flesh," Rick said, keeping his eyes on the bear in the gully, "but sometimes I have to use it in dens. The bends and turns in some of those tight places make the jab stick unwieldy."

When he used *I* that way, Rick made it sound as if he did the bear work all by himself. Kelly felt irritated with him again. Suddenly, the bear collapsed onto the ground.

Kelly could feel Rick's relief. The tension left his face, his body relaxed, and he turned with a real smile and said to Kelly and Adam. "Now we can get this project going."

She relaxed too, as he used the term *we*. She would have to think about his use of *I* and *we*. It was another clue to getting along with him, but she didn't have time right now to figure him out. She picked up the collar, tags, and data board and followed Rick and Adam down to the bear. ❧

Chapter Fourteen

Collapsed onto the ground with the cable stretched from the tree to its leg, the bear did not seem so big. Flies buzzed loudly around the mangled bait and the large flops of scat. The smell of rotten meat and fresh manure rose in the narrow gully, mingling with the odor of moist soil and dead leaves. It was chilly in the shadows under the tree. Kelly shivered, still fighting her feelings of regret.

She glanced at the other two. Adam was remote, his face closed. But Rick was totally focused. He seemed so alive that she just stared at him a moment, fascinated by the difference in him when things were going well. When the tension left his face, and the muddy flush that accompanied his anger and frustration faded, his olive-toned skin took on a clear golden look. His eyes were wider, and Kelly could see little sparks of light in the gleaming dark color. As he looked at the bear, his interest and pleasure were obvious—and contagious.

Kelly felt a renewed surge of excitement about the bear project. Their first bear was lying asleep at their feet, offering her a chance to learn so much.

"First thing we need to do," Rick said, "is to get the cable off the leg. If the bear wakes up too soon, we wouldn't want to have to drug it again to release it from the snare." Adam remained motionless and silent until Rick said, "You want to give me a hand here, Adam?" The bear was totally "down"—completely under the anesthetic. Adam and Rick grunted as they shifted the heavy animal so that the taut cable eased. Rick loosened the clamp.

As they pulled the loop over the bear's right front paw, Adam said, "This bear's been hurt!" Alarmed by the strong note of concern in Adam's voice, Kelly stepped forward to see what he was talking about.

Rick had stretched the foreleg out and was looking at a deep cable cut in the wrist. "We'll have to use the sulfa spray on that."

Kelly was about to ask a question, but Adam interrupted. "How in hell can you be so casual, Santini? This bear's been injured by that damn cable." Kelly turned in surprise. Adam's face was bright red. His tone was angry. "I thought we were supposed to be helping these bears."

And suddenly Adam, too, was alive and vital. In his concern for the bear, he had abandoned his earlier sulky mood. His jaw had firmed, his eyes had focused. Kelly was, for the first time, aware of Adam as a man. He was much more attractive in his anger, but he was also much more dangerous to the project.

Kelly glanced at Rick. The muddy flush had returned to his skin. She looked down at the bear. There wasn't time for a battle between the two males. Before Rick could reply, she said, "We'd better cover the eyes." Rick shook his head slightly and then glanced at Kelly and nodded. She dug into the supplies.

Rick said, "We need to stretch the bear out so we can work with it." Kelly looked up to watch Adam's reaction. His face was still red, but he shrugged and stepped forward. They turned the bear on its belly, front legs stretched forward, back legs extended to the back.

Kelly found the ointment used to protect the eyes. Rick reached into his pack and brought out a piece of yellow cloth. "Here, we can shade the eyes with this."

"Are bears extremely susceptible to pain?" Kelly asked. The cable burn was deep, and Adam was studying it again.

"They feel pain," Rick said, "but I don't think it's to the extent that humans do. Bears have an amazing capacity to heal themselves. One bear we saw had broken its leg, but it healed right up with no problems. Another bear that we found had suffered broken ribs, and they had healed over, too. She was doing just fine."

Rick checked the bear's rear end. "This is a female," he said. "We'll put a radio collar on her." As he took the collar and checked the bolts that would fasten it, he said, "One of the reasons I want to check Jenny again is that she only has three good legs."

"Did you scientists break one of her legs?" Adam said, still sounding hostile.

Rick lost his temper. "Damn it, Wainwright, back off. We're careful, and there's usually not a mark on the bear." His voice calmed a little, and he answered Adam's question. "Jenny had a withered foot when we first caught her. Who knows what happened to her?"

The tension between the two men was slowing the work. Kelly was not certain how to intervene. There were too many layers of feeling involved. Adam was obviously upset by the injury to the bear, but the intensity of his reactions implied something more. She glanced at her watch. Rick seemed to catch the look because he set the collar aside to retrieve the antiseptic spray and the vet wrap from the pack. "Here, Adam, why don't you fix up the leg while I get the collar ready." Adam took the supplies.

"That spray will disinfect the wound," Rick said. "We usually give a shot of penicillin, as well, just to insure against infection." Rick sounded conciliatory.

"Won't this wrap cause more problems for the bear?" Adam sounded calmer, too.

"No, it's made so that it sticks only to itself. She'll pull it off after awhile."

Kelly waited, looking at the scattered remains of the barricade, the tattered bark, and the claw marks on the trees, aware of the power that they had subdued for a short while. And thinking of that power, she realized that she had been foolish to think of meeting this bear on equal terms. No way was she equal to a bear. She was sure that all three of them felt something of the same awe. Even drugged and quiet, the brown-colored bear was a vital presence among them.

She remembered her mother's comment about Indians refusing to let women eat bear meat because they didn't want the women to have the bear's power. Except for other adult male bears and mankind, the adult bear was without enemies. *Do Rick and Adam feel threatened by the bear's power?* If she were ever to be field leader, she would have to try to understand what her team members were feeling. She had thought that she was beginning to know Adam a little, but his anger was something new. Rick was still a mystery. She respected his mind and was increasingly aware of skills that she envied, but aside from his resenting her presence on the project, she wasn't certain of anything about him.

She breathed a sigh of relief as Rick picked up the collar and knelt by the bear's head. He began to attach the collar, explaining as he went. "The collar is fitted close enough so that it will stay on and allow for growth but not choke the bear. You cut the collar to length, but be careful not to cut the antenna or there's no point in putting the collar on at all." Rick continued to demonstrate the collar to Adam. "See this cotton rot-tab between the end clamps? It's a safety measure for the bear. In two years, it will rot away and the collar will fall off."

"Well why do you worry so much about Jenny, then?"

"She's younger than this bear, and she's growing fast. We didn't find her den, so we couldn't change the collar. I worry that she'll choke herself before the cotton rots." Rick worked as he talked. Kelly noticed that he glanced frequently at the bear. She knew that they had a lot to do in a short time.

Rick turned to her and said, "Fill out the data sheet as I give you the numbers." She picked up the clipboard. "Be sure to record the time of the injections and the time the bear went down." Rick turned back to Adam. "When you're finished with the vet wrap, will you do the measuring?" Kelly felt a flicker of dissatisfaction. She wanted to get her hands on that bear, too.

But Rick said to her, "Date the top of the sheet and put the time now. Fill in our names under 'Personnel.' This is bear number one for us, but for the whole project, this is bear sixty-three." Adam had extended the bear's broad front leg and was wrapping the cable wound. Rick said, "What's your mother's name, Adam?"

Adam glanced up, a frown wrinkle in his forehead. "It's Samantha; my dad calls her Sam. Why?"

Rick nodded toward Kelly. "We'll call this bear Samantha." Kelly wrote the name under the number, amused by Rick's obvious attempt to soothe Adam's feelings. Maybe Adam didn't want a bear named after his mother.

Kelly filled in the drainage name next. "What about specific location?"

"We'll get the numbers from the map when we get back."

"Habitat is aspen/conifer isn't it?"

Rick finished attaching the collar and then turned to Kelly. "Yeah, aspen/conifer. This is a Telonics collar, number two-nine-six-nine-seven, with a radio frequency of eighty-twenty, with a single rot tab." Kelly wrote the collar information as Rick picked up the ear tags. "We tag both ears," he said to Adam, "so in case she pulls one out, we have an extra way to identify the bear."

Adam asked, "Why are some tags yellow and some white?"

"The yellow is for females. It helps us to tell the sexes apart at a distance." Rick looked up. "Get me one of those vials out of the drug kit, will you?" he said to Kelly, and turning again to Adam, he explained what they were doing. "We'll save the flesh plug from the ear and send it in for DNA analysis."

Using a small tagging tool, Rich inserted the ear tag and gave Kelly the tiny roll of flesh that was pushed out as the tag went in. She put it in the vial and labeled it. Taking a syringe and another vial from the drug kit, Rick extracted a sample of blood, labeled the vial, and returned it to the chest. "We need to get some more ice to keep these samples good," he said. He glanced at Kelly. "Don't forget to fill in the medication and injection information. Along with the tranquilizer, I've given her three cc's of penicillin."

Kelly felt the joy that she always experienced when she was learning. The field manual was no substitute for field experience. She recorded the dosage for each drug, first and second injection. Adam was helping with the second ear tag. He ran his hand down Samantha's face. "Hey, she's got porcupine quills in her nose."

Rick said, "You can do her a favor and remove them, but let me pull a tooth first."

Adam said, "This bear is going to hate the day she came near that bait."

"It's just a small tooth," Kelly said. "A tiny little tooth behind the canine. She won't miss it, and it will be a great help to us. There's a lab where the technicians study the growth rings and verify our estimate of the bear's age."

Rick nodded at Kelly and suddenly, for some reason, the three of them began to work as a team. Rick pulled the tooth, then gave the pliers to Adam who started removing the porcupine quills, while Kelly put the tooth in a small envelope and labeled it. Since Adam was busy, Rick said, "Help me with the measurements, Kelly," and she felt like crowing with pleasure as she knelt beside the bear. She was at last involved, hands-on, with the bear project.

Samantha looked soft because her coat—her pelage—was in such good shape: thick, dark chocolate brown on the surface with a lighter-colored matting of dense hair underneath. But Samantha was *not* soft. Her muscles were hard. Kelly lifted the huge front leg and the weight of it—the broad, muscled weight of it—was startling.

Adam looked up from where he held the bear's strong jaw in his hand as he pulled the quills. "She's no teddy bear. Look at these teeth."

Rick was measuring the shoulder height. He laughed. "Those teeth should erase any lingering impression you have that bears are cuddly playmates." He handed the measure to Kelly as he turned to write on the data sheet. "Go ahead and measure the width and length of the pad, and the length of the foot and the claws."

The front foot was four-and-a-fourth inches in length; the claw itself was one-and-seven-eighths inches. Kelly shuddered, thinking of the damage the claws could do, backed by the power in the forearm. She repeated the figures, and Rick wrote them on the data sheet. She measured the left rear paw and gave Rick those figures, too.

Adam placed the long porcupine quills on the data sheet. "Well, at least these won't cause her any more pain."

"Record them," Rick said. "We record everything about each bear." He gave Adam the pencil. "Write down the location of the snare wound, too."

Rick took the tape and measured the neck girth, then the chest girth. Adam recorded the figures while Kelly and Rick measured the bear from head to base of tail and then clear to the end of the tail. The bear was fifty-two inches long, fifty-seven inches with the tail.

They estimated the fat level and noted breeding condition. She hadn't had cubs, and it was too early in the year for estrus, but Rick said, "I think she's about four years old. She'll probably breed this year." He glanced at the bear's head. "Let's keep at it. We don't want her to wake up on us."

He picked up a rope and pulling the bear over on her side, he tied the front legs together and looped the rope round the rear legs, tying all four legs together with a final loop. Picking up the field scale, he secured the hook in the rope. He stood, and glancing toward Adam, said, "Let's lift her off the ground and find out if your weight estimate was close."

Before Adam could move, Kelly bent and took hold of one section of the rope. Rick's eyes flickered, but he just shrugged and grasped the other section. "Ready?"

Kelly nodded and on the count of three, they lifted the bear. As she felt the dead weight of the bear, Kelly was glad for every box of nails she'd hefted in the hardware store, and she resolved to add the come-along to the equipment box on the four-wheeler in case they came upon a heavier bear.

Adam checked the scale. "I was way off. She only weighs one hundred and thirty pounds."

Rick laughed. "Didn't I tell you that your first bear looks bigger than she really is?" Kelly noticed that Rick seemed to smile or laugh most often when one of them was uncomfortable about something. Otherwise, he seldom laughed or joked. The idea tainted the feeling of teamwork that she had felt, and she was suddenly aware of being tired.

They lowered the bear. Removing the ropes, they stretched Samantha on her stomach again with the protective cloth over her eyes. She was still fully down. Rick picked up the data sheet and checked it over; then he studied the bear. "Since we don't have any other bears to process, we'll stay here and rebuild the set. I'd like to see that she comes up okay."

"Isn't there a chance she'll wake up and blunder into the snare again?" Kelly asked. She was ready to eat lunch, to go home—to get away from the odd tensions that being with the bear had caused.

"We usually rebuild the set the day after we snare a bear to keep that from happening, but if we're here when she wakes, she'll head away from us." Rick nodded toward the remnant of bait on one side of the set. "We'll need to replace that. Adam, you go get us another chunk of bait." He turned to Kelly. "And before you clear the area and start on the barricade, collect that scat. Since we know the age, sex, and location of the bear, her scat can give us important information."

Kelly was chagrined. Involved with her emotions about the bear, she hadn't even thought about the scat except to be aware of its odor. She began to collect the scat, resolving to pay more attention to scientific details of the project.

After Adam returned, he and Kelly went up and down the gully, retrieving branches to redo the barricade, while Rick reset the snare. Kelly noticed that Rick's eyes flicked to the bear every few moments. Kelly watched Samantha too, but she must have missed some sign that Rick saw, because all of a sudden, Rick said, "Climb the hill. She's coming up."

They paused and turned to watch as Samantha stirred and raised her head. She tried to move away from them, out of the gully and up the opposite hillside. But she staggered, and when she got to the slope, she lost her balance and rolled backward. "Damn," Rick said softly.

Samantha rested a moment before moving slowly up the slope again. She crawled over a log and paused there, shaking her head slightly from side to side. Adam said, "She's thinking, 'what in hell happened to me? I just went down to check out a good smell.'"

The brown bear scrambled over a rock, leaned briefly against it, and then went on up the hill. They watched until she was lost in the brown shadows of the forest. Despite her resolve, Kelly felt renewed regret. *I wish I had seen her in the wild instead of snared and drugged.*

"Well," Adam said. "I suppose we have to move those lower sets before we get anything to eat."

"Nope," Rick said. "We've done a pretty good day's work. Why don't we eat lunch, then go load our dirty clothes and head for town? We'll wash clothes, get some ice, eat supper, and be back before dark."

Adam cheered, and Kelly set aside her thoughts of Samantha. A trip to town was what they needed. Rick had picked the perfect way to ease the strain of trapping their first bear. ∾

Chapter Fifteen

Riding between the men on the road to Moab, Kelly was aware of something unusual. They smelled good. She leaned toward Adam and inhaled. "You're wearing something besides Eau de Bear."

Adam touched Kelly's hair, which was still damp. "And I feel my grand passion for you waning since you washed away the haunting aroma of bait."

Kelly laughed. "Something else just occurred to me," she said. "You've both been clean shaven every day. How do you shave in that cabin with no mirror and no electricity?"

"Painfully," Rick said.

"I'm thinking of growing a beard," Adam added.

Rick said, "That'll be an awesome sight."

Laughing, they relaxed and talked happily about Samantha. Rick turned on the receiver. "Let's see who's wandering around before we get too far from the project." Adam held the antenna out the window. They picked up Samantha almost immediately, and then as Rick fiddled with the receiver, he suddenly slowed the truck. "Hot damn, that's Jenny!" He turned toward them, a beautiful light in his eyes. "Maybe we'll snare her tomorrow, and we can change her collar."

When they reached the laundromat, Rick said, "Would you two mind washing clothes while I go gas up and get some groceries?" He glanced at Kelly. "I guess I'm next week's cook." Kelly's spirits lifted even higher. Rick might not like the kitchen arrangement, but he was going to accept it.

She climbed out of the truck after Adam and hauled her box of clothes into the laundromat. She was slightly embarrassed to think of dumping her clothes in with the men's, but Adam was matter-of-fact. "We'll save quarters if we do all the light colors together and all the darks together. Okay by you?" Kelly nodded and sorted the clothes, amused by the fact that Rick's collection held white boxer shorts and that Adam's colored shorts were cut along the Italian line she had seen in magazine ads.

While the clothes sloshed through the cycles, she and Adam used more quarters in the pop machine and then thumbed through the available reading material. Given a chance to catch up on the news—even the news in the day-old paper that lay on the table—Kelly preferred reading to talking. It was amazing how out of touch one could become in a few days away from radio and television. Adam reached for a news magazine and was soon absorbed, too.

They were folding the last of the clothes when Rick returned. He handed Kelly a package. "I spent some of the university's money on a present for the cabin."

Kelly opened the package, which contained a wall mirror about a foot square. She held the gift toward Adam. "Look, you'll be able to chart the growth of your beard."

They loaded the clean clothes into the pickup bed where the groceries were already stashed and retied the tarp so that it covered everything. Rick drove east to a large building with a "Steak House" sign. "I'm afraid we'll have to go Dutch, here," he said. "The project funding doesn't cover eating out."

Kelly didn't care. She was happy to pay her own way. They were about to start into the second week of the bear project; she had done her share in setting snares and processing Samantha; her hair and her clothes were clean. She felt foolish and carefree. She winked at Adam when he opened the door of the restaurant for her.

The hostess seated them in a large corner booth that had room for at least six people. They spread out on the comfortable seat and ordered. They had just been served their entrees when three men stepped into the restaurant and looked around. Spotting Rick, one of the men—a burly redhead—said, "Hey, Santini."

Rick tossed his head in brief greeting, but said nothing. The three men waved the hostess aside and came to the corner booth. "So, Santini . . . you're back on the mountain."

Rick nodded. "On the other side, though."

The men looked at Adam and Kelly and then again toward Rick, who seemed slow to respond to their obvious wish to be introduced. He finally nodded his head briefly toward Adam and said, "Adam Wainwright." There was a moment of hesitation before he added, "And Kelly Jones."

"I'm Walt Johnson," the redhead said, and indicated the other two. "Harry Selnick and George Walker. Mind if we join you? You can tell us where the bears are walking."

Again Rick was slow to respond, but he finally scooted closer to Kelly on the seat, and she scooted closer to Adam. The three men slid into the booth. Walt Johnson, the redheaded one, was chunky. He looked rock solid. He wore a short-sleeved shirt and a leather vest with blue jeans. The arms that protruded from the shirtsleeves were thick ropes of muscle; his hands were broad and flat. Coarse red hairs covered the freckled arms, and Kelly could see a mat of red chest hair at the top of his shirt. When he scowled at the menu, his bushy red eyebrows met in the middle of the scowl. She glanced at the other two men. George Walker was smaller than Walt Johnson, but had the same rugged look. He was dressed in jeans and denim jacket and wore a billed cap with an elk pictured on the front.

Harry Selnick was different. His clothes were western, but they were fancier than those of the other two. He wore saddleman's pants and a western-cut shirt with pearl buttons. He had placed a light-colored Stetson on the back of the booth as he sat down.

The three men ordered and then Walt Johnson said, "So, Santini, where are the bears? My dogs are raring to go." Kelly and Adam exchanged a glance. *Houndsmen.* Kelly thought of Samantha and Jenny and willed them toward higher ground.

"I don't know the exact location of any bears on this side of the mountain," Rick said. "We've only been up here a week."

"We?" Walt repeated. "Have you already got your crew up here?"

Kelly could see Rick take a deep breath. "This is my crew," he said, nodding his head toward Adam and Kelly.

The three men turned their gaze. Then Walt grinned. "You're not so dumb, Santini. These mountain cabins need a few more of the comforts of home."

He and George looked Kelly up and down. George's eyes rested on her breasts. She had left her shirt top unbuttoned a little and now she wished she had closed it clear to her chin. As Kelly turned her eyes away from Walt Johnson and George Walker, she glanced at the other man's face. Harry Selnick had flushed a bright red. Kelly looked down at her plate and tried to pretend that she was interested in her dinner. But George Walker was not willing to leave it at that. "How'd you manage a crew assignment like this, Santini? I thought those university types were tight-assed about boys and girls together."

Rick said shortly, "Kelly is a biologist."

"No shit." All the men were looking at her. George said, "And what do you do when you and the boys are not studying biology in the cabin?" Walt Johnson laughed and George continued to smirk at her.

Kelly felt stripped bare. She was no longer a mind or a personality or even a name. As the men looked at her, she knew that every one of them, Rick and Adam included, were speculating about her as a bed partner. There was a change in the atmosphere, a subtle shifting of attitude. No matter what she said, no matter what she might tell them about the fieldwork, the three strange males were thinking only of what went on in the cabin, and for the first time, Rick and Adam seemed to be considering what might go on there. Rick's face held a deep flush. Adam looked at her with new intensity.

Kelly felt defiled . . . defeated. It took all her courage not to get up and leave, to climb out of the booth if she had to. But determined not to show any emotion, she picked up her glass, took a sip of milk, and forcing a smile, said to Harry Selnick, "Are you from this area?" *Is this what you mean by discretion, Dr. Andrews? A couple of stupid jerks insult me, and I pretend that I don't even notice and go on making inane conversation? Is this why you're so proud of me?*

Harry Selnick's face had returned to its normal color. "No," he said, in answer to her question, "I'm from Arizona. I come up in the spring to hunt."

So he was a houndsman too. Rick asked a question then, and the men's attention was diverted. Kelly nudged Adam and said, "Will you let me out?" He stood, and Kelly slipped from the booth and headed for the ladies' room. Sitting in the toilet, Kelly thought about how casually the houndsmen had demoted her from crew member to camp follower. *Despite thirty years of outward progress, women are not any closer to equality in the minds of men.* Aware that she was as angry at Rick and Adam as she was at the other three, Kelly tried to be objective about her feelings. She realized as she picked through her emotions that she had somehow expected them to defend her honor. *I'm as chauvinistic as they are. I claim that I want to be one of the team, but the moment someone treats me like a woman, I expect the men to come to my rescue.*

She washed her face and hands and redid her lipstick. She hated to return to the booth. The joy of the trip to town had been ruined, and she just wished that she could see Peggy. The houndsmen's comments brought on a kind of loneliness that couldn't be eased by learning the right words. There was no way to fit in. As long as she was on the project, men like the houndsmen would think of her as a fringe benefit for the male biologists. She couldn't look to Rick and Adam for help. The defense of her honor was up to her.

When she returned to the men, Harry Selnick said, "Why don't you let us pick up the tab here?"

Rick and Adam smiled, but Kelly said, "No, I'm afraid we can't do that. Technically, we work for the government. We can't take gifts from the public." She smiled at the man. "However, if you run across any dead animals, we will accept donations to our bait barrel." She took the ticket for her dinner and said, "Thanks, anyway," and went to the cash register. She had sounded a little abrupt, but Dr. Andrews or no, she was damned if she'd say that it had been nice to meet them.

She went to the truck ahead of Rick and Adam, opened the door and climbed up into the seat. They got into the truck too, but the mood was no longer carefree. There was tension in their silence as they left the parking lot and headed south. Finally, after they had left the lights of town behind them, Adam said, "So it's legal for those guys to set dogs on the bears, even though it's spring and the bears are in poor shape?"

"Oh yeah," Rick said. "All kinds of bear hunters show up here in the spring."

"How long do we have to put up with them?" Adam asked.

"The season runs from mid-April until mid- or late June."

"You mean from now until June, while we're snaring, someone will be killing bears?"

"Yes. So far, the department is still giving unlimited permits."

"Are those guys a fair sample of what we'll see?" Adam asked.

"Walt Johnson is a slime ball," Rick said, "and so is his buddy, George. But they're good with their dogs, so they've always got business. Selnick's not a bad guy. Too rich for his own good maybe. I think he just hunts bear because he's bored with life."

Adam started to put his arm across the back of the seat behind Kelly, and then seemed suddenly aware of the motion, and put his arm back in his lap. *Damn*, thought Kelly. *He's aware of me as a body instead of a buddy.* She sighed. She had enjoyed kidding with him and had not minded his occasional touch. The conversation lapsed, and they drove along silently for miles until suddenly, near their turnoff, Rick slammed on the brakes.

"What the hell?" Adam said as he bounced forward, at the same time throwing a restraining arm in front of Kelly.

"Roadkill of some sort," Rick said. He put the truck in reverse, and began backing up. "I think it's a calf. I hope it's not a deer."

"Why?" Adam asked.

"It's illegal to use game animals for bait."

The dead animal was a heifer, already decomposing. Kelly winced as Rick and Adam hoisted it into the truck next to the groceries and the clean laundry. She hoped that the rotting corpse wouldn't be jolted closer to her clothes as the truck turned into the rutted road toward the cabin.

Kelly helped Adam unload the heifer. "Let's cut it up tonight," Adam said.

Rick said, "We can get up early and do it."

"It will stink worse tomorrow," Adam said, "and the flies will be all over it."

Kelly laughed. "You just can't stand to smell good for a whole day, can you?" She turned to Rick. "I'll help him."

"Don't kill too much time," Rick said. "We've got to be up early tomorrow to move those lower sets." Before Kelly could answer, he was in the truck and down the road.

Kelly took the sharp-edged hunting knife and stepped to the animal. She had helped her father cut up venison. "If you'll stretch this beast out and hold it," she said, "I'll slit it up the middle." Working silently, they gutted the animal, hacked the rest of the carcass into chunks, and heaved them into the bait barrel.

It was dark by the time they started up the road. They walked quietly for a while, then Adam said, "If you get to be manager of this project next year, how are you going to deal with those houndsmen?"

"I don't know," Kelly said. "I don't even know what I'll say to them the next time I see them."

"Why didn't you stop them today?"

Kelly could not keep the bitterness from her voice as she said, "Adam, the rules of this game never allow the woman to win." She sighed. "What were my choices? If I'd called them on their comments, they would have denied any evil intent. They're just kidding, and of course, if you can't take kidding, you're a rotten sport or a hysterical female. I was damned if I'd laugh—that's like saying it's okay to insult me. All I could do was to ignore them."

"If I were you, I'd have slapped that Walker guy across the mouth."

"Sure, and prove Rick Santini right about a woman's not belonging in the field."

Adam reached out and put a hand on her shoulder. Kelly flinched and stepped aside. Adam dropped his hand. "I was only trying to be sympathetic," he said.

"My only two choices," Kelly said, "lust or pity." She shouldn't take it out on Adam. He seemed the best of the lot, but that wasn't saying much. She didn't apologize, and they walked silently back to the cabin. ❧

Chapter Sixteen

Kelly woke to the irritating smell of hot grease. She dressed and went to the kitchen where Rick was cooking breakfast in a skillet half-full of shortening. Wrinkling her nose, Kelly went outside. When she returned, she joined Rick and Adam at the table. Adam looked at the hard-fried eggs and grease-sodden potatoes and said to Kelly, "Until this moment, I never truly appreciated your cooking."

Rick said, "I suppose you're going to do better?"

Adam said, "Veritably." Rick grunted. Kelly didn't feel like joining the conversation. She poked at her eggs while Adam and Rick chatted about the chance of snaring Jenny. "I hope Samantha's leg is healing okay," Adam said. Before Rick could answer, they heard the baying of dogs somewhere northwest of the cabin. "Will Walt and George be the only houndsmen here?" Adam asked.

"No, we usually get some out-of-state houndsmen, and there's always good old Doc Morrison."

"What's so good about Doc Morrison?"

"He never shoots the bears he trees," Rick said. "He's a local veterinarian who also trains dogs, but when he gets a bear trapped, he just takes a picture, leaves a chunk of meat, and calls off his dogs."

Kelly was not impressed. She spoke her first words of the morning, "But the bastard still runs them for miles, doesn't he?"

Rick stared at her. Adam grinned and said, "Such language for a lady. You're in a foul mood today."

Kelly couldn't deny it. She was angry at the houndsmen she'd met the night before, and her resentment spread to all houndsmen, especially as the yelping of the dogs shredded the quiet morning. She gave Adam a small grin and said, "I'm getting more cheerful since I remembered it's your week to do dishes." She left her greasy half-filled plate and went to check the equipment box.

When they reached the meadow, Rick said, "We'll leave the lower snares where they are for a day or two—to see if we can get some data about the effect of the logging trucks. We'll add two more snares at the top of Warren Gulch."

Kelly said, "Let me build the new sets."

Rick and Adam turned to look at her. "Alone?" Rick said.

"You can pick the spots and leave me and the equipment there while you and Adam check Chase Creek."

"Can you handle it?" Rick's tone was abrupt.

"She won't know until she tries, will she, Santini?"

The two males glared at each other, and then Rick shrugged. "I hope it isn't a waste of our time."

Kelly yearned to be alone. Except for the moments she was in the outhouse, she was never alone at the cabin. *If I learned to drive a four-wheeler, I could check snares by myself.*

Rick chose a couple of spots high up the gulch, toward the ridge. Adam and Rick helped to clear the sites, and then placed bait and snares nearby. Rick gave Kelly one of the propane torches. "Are you sure you can do this by yourself?" She nodded, and the two men headed down Warren Gulch.

Kelly walked slowly around the area, looking at the familiar plants, thinking of her grandmother who had said, "You don't ever need to be lonely." Her grandmother had a strong faith, and she loved her husband and her animals, but considering it as an adult, Kelly thought her grandmother *had* been lonely sometimes, even during the lifetime of the silent man who had been Kelly's grandfather. And her only child hadn't been much help. *Daddy seems to resent his mother.*

Kelly suddenly felt a strong feeling of resentment toward her own mother. Mothers are supposed to be there for you to talk to—about men—about sex—to help you cover up when you've been stripped bare of what makes you real to yourself. Kelly began to drag tree branches toward the snare site. *If it feels this awful just to be considered a whore, what must it feel like to be raped?* Kelly felt a moment's fear of being alone when there were strange men in the woods. She took a deep breath and forced herself not to think of Walt Johnson and George Walker. It would be a blow to her hopes of leading the project if she started getting scared.

She created the first barricade, and slowly, as she worked in the sun and concentrated on making the barrier just right, her confidence began to return, and she thought about ways to deal with the houndsmen. *I will ignore anything they say that isn't on a professional level.* She gritted her teeth. *And I will do it in such a way that they never know when their comments upset me.* She built the second barricade and then began work on the snare, moving efficiently, pleased with the coordination between her mind and hands. She was careful to position the spring so she could hold it with her body when she set the trigger. Then she covered the cable and inspected the set before she placed the bait and seared it with the torch. She picked up the torch and walked the quarter of a mile down the trail to the next site. It was marvelous to be alone, doing interesting work. The second set seemed to build itself as her fingers flew.

Finished there, she strode down the Warren Gulch trail until she reached the area of one of their earlier sets and crossed the meadow to check it. A bear had stolen the bait from one side of the snare. She could see bear tracks around the set and heading away. When she heard the four-wheelers coming up the road, she hurried back across the meadow. Rick would want to know about the bait theft. Both four-wheelers skidded up to her in a cloud of dust. Kelly said, "Some bear has stolen a whole piece of bait."

"Without setting off the snare?" Rick asked.

"Didn't even go near it."

Rick said, "The bitch!"

Adam laughed and explained Rick's remark. "We picked up Samantha's signal over here."

Kelly could have cheered. She pictured the dark brown bear nosing around the bait and then clamping down on the meat with her huge teeth and moving away without once getting near the snare. "Oh, she's smart," she said with a grin at the others. "She's so smart."

"You're supposed to want to snare bears. That's what you're here for." Rick frowned. "I hope that sow doesn't make a habit of stealing bait."

Kelly knew she was not being the least bit scientific about this bear, but the audacious theft delighted her. She gestured toward the high ridge near timberline. "Her prints show that she took off that way." It suddenly dawned on her that Rick and Adam were supposed to be checking Chase Creek. "What are you guys doing over here anyway? Have you checked all the sets already?"

"No," Rick said. "We only got to the fourth set on Chase Creek. We came to get you."

"Why?" Kelly asked. Rick's manner was strange.

"We've got an angry black bear in the number-four set, and we need your help."

Adam said, "Hop on." Kelly stowed the torch in the equipment box and climbed on the four-wheeler, puzzled by the way the other two were acting. Was this just a ruse to get her away from Warren Gulch? Rick and Adam roared away down the trail, and Kelly hung on. Adam's gun bounced against her leg and some of the dust from Rick's machine flew into her mouth. She spit to the side and then closed her mouth firmly.

They went up Chase Creek and stopped near the site of the fourth set. As Kelly followed Rick and Adam through the grass and into the aspen, Rick said, "Move slowly and be ready to run. He's really riled up." They moved a few feet closer, and suddenly Adam touched her arm and pointed. Kelly's heart was beating fast as she looked toward the snare, and for a moment she didn't see anything. Then there was a movement near the tree.

A small black bear was in the snare. He was sitting in a nest of grass on his haunches with one foreleg around the aspen, watching them quietly with shiny little eyes. "Oh," Kelly said, "he's beautiful." She looked around. "Where's his mama?"

"We don't know. We aren't getting any collar signals," Rick said, "so she's certainly a bear we haven't met. He's a yearling, but he's probably still running with her. We'll have to be careful."

Kelly said, "I thought you said this bear was angry. He's just a scared baby."

Adam said, "Watch this." He walked slowly toward the tree. The young bear scrambled up the tree a foot or two, dragging the snare with him. He stuck his head toward Adam and made a huffing sound. "Huff, huff, huff."

Kelly laughed. He was so little, maybe fifty pounds. "He says this is his territory." Adam moved a step closer. The little bear began to clack his teeth together, creating a staccato warning. Adam just stood there. Rick and Kelly didn't move. The bear kept popping his teeth. Adam took another step or two. Suddenly, the little bear gave it up, slid down the tree, huddled in the grass, and whimpered. "Oh, the poor boy," Kelly said.

"He wants his mommy," Adam said.

"Yeah, and if we don't hurry up and get him out of there," Rick said, "we might see his mommy." The little black bear leaned against the tree, moaning, his small eyes focusing on Rick as he talked. Stalks of green grass around the bear contrasted with the white bark of the aspen tree.

"He makes a pretty picture with the tree," Kelly said.

Adam snorted. "He's made a pretty mess of that tree," he said.

"Look at the scratches in the bark." It was true. The young bear had vented his frustration in long, deep gashes.

Rick stepped toward them with the jab stick. "Keep an eye out for the mother, Adam." Kelly distracted the yearling while Rick delivered the anesthetic. When the needle went in, the bear whirled away from Kelly and lunged at Rick, who backed up quickly, laughing. "He's got spirit."

The anesthetic went to work immediately. As she watched the little furry black creature get sleepy and lick his lips, Kelly was grateful that Rick and Adam had come to get her. Forgetting for a moment all the problems of the bear project, she just enjoyed being close enough to see the young healthy animal. Maybe they could do something to make his life safer.

When the bear tumbled over, they worked swiftly to process him. They put ear tags on him and did all the measurements, but they didn't collar him. "We don't need to collar as many males as females," Rick said. "It's the movement of the females that tells most of the bear story. Besides," he added, "he's too young and he's growing fast, and we might not be able to get him back into a snare to remove the collar."

"What shall we call him?" Adam asked. Rick looked at Kelly.

"Why not call him Andy, for Dr. Andrews?" she said. Rick laughed and nodded. When they finished with Andy, they stretched him out in the shade of the aspen and re-covered his eyes. "He'll be awake in no time," Rick said. "Let's finish checking the rest of the Chase Creek sets, and then we'll go back up Warren Gulch, inspect Kelly's sets, and replace the bait that Samantha stole."

They picked up Marie's signal somewhere around the seventh set on Chase Creek. Rick said, "She had two new cubs when we processed her in the den in March. It would be great to get more data on her. She's moved a little farther than some bears do." But as they neared the set, Rick said, "Damn. We got the baby instead of the mother." ❦

Chapter Seventeen

Kelly looked toward the snare and saw a tiny cinnamon-colored cub. As they approached, the little bear began to squall. Rick looked around nervously. "We've got to shut it up quick, or we're going to be dealing with Marie, and she's a *big* bear."

Working in the same way as they had with Samantha and Andy, they put the cinnamon cub down. It was a female. Kelly covered the cub's eyes, relieved that the baby had gone to sleep quickly and stopped her sounds of distress. She already had a tiny ear tag.

"We put that on in the den just to identify her," Rick said. "We generally don't plan any long-term data collection until we know that a bear has survived a full year."

Kelly was holding the cub when the first convulsion rippled through its body. "Rick, there's something wrong with this bear."

Rick turned from the drug kit. The convulsion was over quickly. Rick knelt by the cub and checked the animal's pulse. "Her heart rate seems okay." Rick began to loosen the clamp on the cable. "But this is a lot of stress for a little bear." Before the cable came over the paw, the bear stiffened and shook. Rick picked the bear up and held it close to his body, stroking it and making low guttural sounds. When the convulsion passed, Rick pulled the cable away and checked the bear's leg. "No cable cuts," he said.

Turning to Kelly, he said, "Let's keep complete notes of this. She could have had an allergic reaction to the drug. We'll want to ask Doc Morrison about it."

"Damn it, Santini," Adam said, "why don't you take the cub to the vet right now?"

"We can't take her away from her mother. If we get out of here and leave her alone, Marie will come get her and feed her and hide her away where it's quiet. The cub will be better off that way."

"Don't you have some sort of antidote?"

"We're not carrying any. Besides, I've never seen this sort of reaction before." They spread the cub out and re-covered her eyes. Kelly and Adam loaded the four-wheelers and waited there. Rick stayed by the little bear. Kelly noticed that he occasionally glanced around the wooded area, but for the most part, he watched the cub. She felt renewed respect for Rick. He was obviously trying to make the best decision for the bear.

Finally Rick left the cub and climbed the hill. He turned the dial on the receiver until he was at Marie's frequency. The signal was clear and close. "The cub's breathing okay," Rick said. "I think she's coming up a little, and her mama's nearby. Let's leave her." As they left, Kelly looked back at the small cinnamon-colored spot in the grass. The tiny bear only weighed nine pounds.

There were no bears in the eighth snare or the conifer set. They ate a late lunch in the meadow. Kelly could hardly stomach the cold, grease-laden bacon sandwiches.

Supper was fried, too. Adam said, "Has it escaped your attention that we own other cooking utensils besides a skillet?"

"It's a rule in the field that if you gripe about the food, you have to do the dishes," Rick said.

"I *already* have to do the dishes," Adam said. "I just hope we've got enough soap and hot water to cut that grease."

Kelly went outside to put Andy's scat into the drying box. The evening air was cool, and it was pleasant outside until dogs started yelping close by. Kelly took an armload of wood and started toward the cabin. As she reached the steps, a battered pickup came down the road loaded with a pack of noisy dogs. Kelly paused. A large man got out of the vehicle and smiled at her through a full white beard. "You must be the 'bear woman' I've been hearing about."

"I'm Kelly Jones."

"I'm Doc Morrison. Here, let me help you with that." The man took the armload of wood, strode up the steps, and flung the door open. "Hey, Rick," he bellowed. "I've killed off a couple of cows for you." He roared with laughter as he dumped the wood into the wood box and turned to greet Rick with a whack on his shoulder. Kelly stood in the door watching the huge old man and listening to the racket of his dogs.

Rick said, "Hey Doc, I'm glad you're here." He introduced Adam and then turned and lit the kerosene lamp. The veterinarian sat down in a chair by the table, his belly touching the table even though the chair was not close.

"You got a cup of coffee or, better yet, a shot of bourbon?"

"Cocoa or Pepsi," Rick said.

The man scowled and his white eyebrows joined above his eyes. Then he grinned; his teeth and the beard hair nearest his mouth were stained tobacco yellow. "You at least got a place I can spit?" Rick fished a tin can out of the trash sack, and Doc shot a stream of tobacco juice into it, then grunted and said, "A guy down near the Abajos had some bad luck. Called me too late. A couple of his cows died. I dumped them up near your bait barrel."

"Thanks." Rick opened two Pepsis and sat down at the table. "I've got a problem."

The veterinarian suddenly seemed focused and professional. He listened closely to Rick's report of the cub's reaction to the drug and then said, "Well, as long as the cub was breathing okay, you probably did the right thing. I'll look into some antidotes for you." He pushed his bulk up from the table. "I got to get those dogs to bed." He grinned around the room. "They ain't as young as they used to be." He nodded at Adam and waved a hand at Kelly. "G'nite, Bear Woman." Kelly smiled at him. At least he didn't shoot the bears he treed, and he *had* brought bait.

They went directly to the seventh Chase Creek snare the next morning. The cinnamon-colored cub was gone. They stood for a moment, and Kelly could feel the relief that swept over all of them. Rick walked around the site. "Marie must have come back." He bent to retrieve some scat and began studying the area. "There're tracks heading down-slope. Let's follow them." He saw the mound first. "Oh, shit."

"What's wrong?" Kelly asked.

Rick didn't answer. He stepped forward and knelt by the dirt and leaf-covered lump. He cleared away the debris, revealing the small body of the cinnamon-colored cub. "It died."

"How did it get down here?" Adam asked.

"The mother came back, found it dead, and buried it." Rick's voice was gruff.

"Buried it?"

"Well, covered it up anyway. She probably planned to return and eat it."

Kelly could hear Adam's sharp intake of breath. Rick stood up with the bear cub in his hands. "What are you doing with it now?" Adam asked.

"Collecting it as a specimen."

"Just leave it. Cover it up again," Adam said. He looked grim. Rick glanced sharply at Adam, then shrugged and kneeling, put the cub on the ground. Kelly blinked away tears as Rick scraped leaves across the body. The three of them stood in the grass near the aspen tree staring at the mound for several minutes before turning silently and going back to their machines for the equipment and bait to reset the snare.

Samantha—or some animal—had stolen bait on Chase Creek again. But after they replaced the bait, there were no snared bears, no processing, to take their minds off Marie's cub. They ate lunch silently and then Rick said, "We might as well go cut up Doc Morrison's cows."

The cows were crawling with maggots. Kelly swallowed repeatedly while they butchered, hardly able to keep at the work until they finished. As they were covering the meat with water, they heard a vehicle bouncing along the road.

"I hope it's Doc Morrison," Adam said. "I'd like to talk to him. He sounded as if he knew what he was talking about the other day, and yet that cub died. We'd better find out what we're doing wrong." Rick flushed. Kelly knew that Adam was truly concerned, but she wished he'd keep his mouth shut. They felt bad enough.

A red pickup came into view and pulled to a stop. Before it dawned on Kelly who it was, Matt had hopped out of the truck. He strode quickly toward her and reached out, grinning, as if to grab her in a hug, but when he got close, he dropped his arms and said, "Whew! You stink!"

"Matt! What are *you* doing here?"

Matt said, "Well, I came with the idea of taking you out to dinner, but . . ." He glanced at the bloody knife in her hand, at the cowhides and the bait barrel swarming with flies, and wrinkled his nose.

Kelly wiped her face on her sleeve. She did stink. She could smell the bait on her clothes. She turned to Rick and Adam. "This is a friend of mine—Matt Cook."

As she looked at Matt, Kelly remembered their last meeting. She had told him she didn't want to date him, but here he was planning to take her out to dinner as if there were no question about it. Anger made her stomach knot.

Confused as well as angry, she stooped and ran her knife through the grass, cleaning the blade. She had to admit that she was glad to see Matt. Most of the time he treated her like a real person, not just a female body. And yet, she resented his showing up like this. *One more male to deal with.* Gritting her teeth, she put the knife in her pack and stood up. "Why don't you follow us down to the cabin where we can wash up and visit—away from the smell of bait?"

Rick and Adam climbed into the truck when she did. Adam said, "Who's he?"

Rick said, "He's the guy she meets outside the bear lab. Don't see why he minds the smell of bear bait. He didn't seem to mind the smell of scat."

And what's it to you, Rick Santini? He didn't own her either. Maybe she *would* go out to dinner with Matt.

Matt had parked his truck near her car. "How's the Buick running?"

"I don't know. I haven't started it since I got here."

Matt followed Kelly into the cabin and stopped. He looked around. "This is some dump. Where do you sleep?" Rick and Adam had come in behind him in time to hear the question. Kelly led him to the storeroom. Matt stuck his head in and looked around. "You need a door."

Kelly said, "What we need right now is a fire to heat some wash water." Rick entered the kitchen area and reached into the wood box. Kelly asked Matt, "You want some pop?"

"Aren't you going to wash?"

"Soon as there's hot water." But suddenly Kelly knew that she wasn't going to take a bath with Matt and Rick and Adam all in the cabin. She had been bathing after dark when the others were in the main room or already in bed. Rick and Adam had been considerate about not intruding or making it uncomfortable. Now she was uncomfortable.

"I'll take a rain check on the pop," Matt said.

Adam pulled out a chair. "You wanna sit?" Matt sat down and Adam said, "What do you do for a living? Are you a rancher or what?" His voice was friendly, and Kelly felt grateful to him for trying to ease the tension that had been in the room ever since Matt had asked where she slept.

"I'm a logging contractor. As a matter of fact, I've just won a bid on this mountain. I'll be working here all summer, and maybe into fall if I can get the Forest Service to agree to a clear-cut contract on one section."

Rick dropped a stove lid. It hit the stove and ricocheted into the larger area. Landing first on its edge, the lid spun, then wobbled and fell to the floor. Kelly watched it to the last wobble, afraid to look at Rick's face. Rick ignored the lid and focused on Matt. "Clear-cut?" The fury in his voice was like a blast of thunder. "You can't clear-cut this mountain." The smoke from the fire rose from the hole in the stovetop and spread in a choking cloud.

The men ignored the smoke. "Why in hell can't I clear-cut this mountain? If the Forest Service okays it, I am clear-cutting."

Kelly stood up, coughing. "Matt, let's go outside where we can talk, and I'll tell you what clear-cutting does to bears."

She took his arm and practically dragged him out the door and off the porch. When they reached his truck, Matt turned and said, "Who does that son-of-a-bitch think he is anyway, trying to tell me my business?"

Kelly sighed. "Matt, he's a bear biologist, and we lost a bear cub this morning. We're upset already." Some of the red left Matt's face.

"Well, what's that got to do with clear-cutting? I didn't kill any bears."

"Bears like deep, dense cover. Clear-cutting wrecks habitat and pushes the bears out of their home range. It causes problems, Matt."

Matt was silent for a moment. Then he ran his hand through his blonde hair. "I'm just trying to make a living, Kelly."

"Did you bid down here on purpose?"

"No," he said, but as she continued to look at him, he said, "Well, yeah. I didn't think you'd mind if I was around once in awhile."

"I thought we settled that."

Matt's face turned red again. "You settled it. I didn't have anything to say about it. You just decided I wasn't good enough."

"That's not true, Matt."

But once again he was furious and red-faced. "So those are your big deal college men. Well they stink too. I don't suppose they mind how you smell. Have you got something going with one of them? Or *both* of them?"

Kelly slapped him. She was not going to take it from Matt. Maybe she had to take it from strangers, but Matt knew her better than that. She turned and started away. Matt grabbed her arm. "Don't go, Kelly. I'm sorry. It's just that I've been crazy since we busted up. Please, Kelly. Talk for a minute—at least talk to me."

Kelly turned back. "Matt, there's not much to talk about right now. I'm tired and I stink, as you've so kindly told me, and I've got a job to do here. At the moment, I wouldn't date any man within four hundred miles. I am thoroughly sick of men."

Matt stared at her. Then he grinned. "I am glad to hear that, Kelly." He opened his truck door. "I'll be around all summer. I'll drop by when you smell better."

"Matt, I *never* smell better. Why don't you just give it up?"

He climbed into the truck and started the engine. "I'll see you, Kelly. You can count on it." He went up the road in a cloud of dust and before Kelly could go into the cabin, another pickup came through the dust toward the cabin. Kelly felt like screaming. *We might as well be on Interstate 70.* But when she saw that the pickup belonged to Jim McCarthy, she waited for him.

"Hi, Jamie," she said, going around to the driver's side. "Please don't tell me you've got another dead something."

The rancher laughed. "Nope. I just thought you might like to check my windmills and water tanks with me."

Kelly hesitated. "Jamie, there's nothing I'd like better, but I'm filthy dirty."

The old man said, "Would you like to come up to my place and take a shower?"

Kelly wanted that shower in the absolute worst way, but she said, "Your place is pretty far from here. If we go there first, you won't get your tanks checked before dark."

"Well, I've smelled dead cows before. I can stand you until we get the tanks checked."

She could have hugged him. She smiled and asked, "Have you got anything to eat at your house that hasn't been fried?"

"I've got a pot of beans on the stove. I could stir up some cornbread."

Kelly felt the saliva flow into her mouth. She ran up the stairs and hurried toward her room. "I'm going out to dinner," she said over her shoulder. The cabin was still smoky.

"With that clear-cutter?" Rick said.

"The clear-cutter took off in a cloud of dust," said Adam, who was standing by the window. "She's going out with that old rancher again."

Kelly grabbed clean clothes, her shampoo, soap, towels, and a hairbrush. "Jamie McCarthy's going to feed me after we check his tanks," she said as she reached the door.

Adam stepped over to her. "What's that you've got?" Kelly held her bundle closer, but Adam pulled out the shampoo bottle and held it up. "You don't need shampoo to eat dinner with an old cowpoke." He turned to Rick and said, "She's cheating. She's going to take a shower."

Rick was spooning shortening into the skillet. He looked up and said, "Are you really going to eat with McCarthy?"

"He's got beans, and he's going to make cornbread."

"Can I come, too?" Adam asked.

She didn't blame him, but she smiled and said, "Nope, this is my date, and I won't share him." ～

Chapter Eighteen

Jamie McCarthy's ranch house was extremely tidy. Except for a few stoneware dishes in the kitchen, nothing seemed out of place, and little seemed in use. The dining-room hutch displayed a set of fine china. A glass-fronted case in the living room held tiny glass animals.

"Betsy's things," Jamie said. "I kinda like to look at them." He moved toward the stairs and pointed. "Bathroom's the first door on the right. Take your time. I'll get going on that cornbread." Kelly could not remember a shower that had felt so good. She let the hot water run over her hair until it began to feel lukewarm, and she realized that she was putting a strain on Jamie's water heater.

Jamie and Kelly lingered over dinner, did dishes together, and talked until late. She told him about the new kitchen schedule, and he laughed about Rick's fried food. He talked about his Betsy; he talked about his kids. Kelly told him about her grandmother and the plant book. When Jamie asked, "Who was the fellow who roared away from the cabin as I was comin' in?" Kelly told him about Matt and his clear-cutting plans.

The lights were out in the cabin when the rancher dropped her off by the steps. "Thanks, Jamie, that was a feast."

"Nothin' fancy about cornbread and beans," he said.
"I was speaking of more than the food."

∾

Just as Rick and Adam and Kelly began to unload the four-wheelers
the next morning, Walt Johnson, George Walker, and Harry Selnick
came down the mountain with a truckload of dogs. They pulled into
the meadow and got out. The dogs were multicolored and rangy, if not
skinny, and they yapped and snarled in the truck bed. Walt Johnson
turned every minute or so to yell, "Shut up," and George Walker slapped
the side of the truck periodically. "Well, Santini, I see you killed a bear
yesterday," Walt said. George snickered and Walt added, "But he ain't
much of a trophy."

"What bear are you talking about?" Rick asked.

"Our dogs nosed out that cub."

"What did you do with it?" Adam asked.

"Oh, hell, I don't know. One of the dogs carried it off I guess. They
kinda mauled your bait, too." Adam looked a little sick.

Kelly stepped forward and said in a calm voice—a voice so
professional that she was proud of herself—"Mr. Johnson, you might
want to keep the dogs a little farther away from the sets. I know you've
spent time and money training them, and you'd hate to have a valuable
dog break its leg in a snare. Not to mention a bear/dog encounter when
the *dog* was trapped."

Walt Johnson looked startled. He didn't say anything, but he gave
Kelly a look that was different from the way he'd leered at her in the
cafe. For a moment, she thought she'd made some progress, but when
he spoke, it was to Rick and not to her. "Your playmate has a point,
Santini. You guys shouldn't be here during hunting season, and if one
of my dogs gets hurt in a snare, I may sue the university."

Before Rick could express the anger she could see building under
his skin, Kelly retrieved the clipboard they used in the field and said to
Rick, "Do we need to add Mr. Johnson's information to the data sheet
on the cub?"

Rick took a deep breath and focused on Kelly. "No, I don't think
it's pertinent," he said. "We knew she was dead." He turned toward one
of the four-wheelers. Adam was already on the other. Kelly climbed on
behind him, and they left the meadow before the houndsmen could say
anything else.

While Adam and Kelly were checking the Chase Creek snares,

Adam said, "You always seem so much happier when you've been with that rancher. You really handled those dog guys well."

Kelly smiled at him. "Jamie treats me like I'm just another human being. He does make me feel good." She ran a hand through her hair, which was silky. "Or it could be that all it takes to put me in a good mood is clean hair."

There were no bears in any of their snares, but there was work to do—rebaiting a set where a coyote had dragged bait away and chewed on it and lugging new bait to the set on Chase Creek. Samantha had again taken the easy way to get food. "Damn that bear," Rick said, picking up her signal very clearly, "she's had a good breakfast and gone to bed for the day." He kept fiddling with the receiver and suddenly he said, "Be quiet, be quiet." He tuned the receiver carefully, and then he turned to Adam and Kelly with a huge smile. "Now here's an important bit of information. This old boy was over on the other side of the mountain last year. He's the oldest male we've snared."

Adam and Kelly stepped closer, as if the signal brought the bear. "How old is he?" Kelly asked.

"He's six, and that's old around here. Bears can sometimes live to be twenty, but with hunters on this hill, males seldom make it past four or five." As usual when Rick was happy—and that was always when things were going well with the project—he was attractive. Kelly enjoyed the way he poured out information. "This is Roscoe. He's red and he's huge and he's healthy."

"Do you think we'll snare him?"

"You can bet on it," Rick said. "Roscoe ended up in our snares three times last summer. He's too lazy to walk around a barricade." Cheerfully they went on with the work. Rick had decided to move the set from where the cinnamon cub had died. "No self-respecting bear will come near a site that reeks of dogs." He had also decided to move the lower Warren Gulch sets. He said, "Kelly's clear-cutter is so damned noisy, we're just wasting our time with those sets."

"Matt's not my clear-cutter or my responsibility," Kelly said.

Adam laughed. "He doesn't see things that way."

"I can't help how men see things. They're a strange breed."

"Stranger than bears?" Rick asked.

"Crueler than bears anyway," Kelly said. "Bears hunt for food, not for trophy."

They didn't snare a bear on Thursday either, but they found some scat, and they used the daylight hours afforded by their early return to the cabin to bring the data sheets up to date. When he glanced at

Samantha's field sheet, some of which Adam had filled out, Rick said, "Damn, Adam, you ought to be a doctor."

"Why?"

"Your handwriting is practically illegible." Rick handed the clipboard to Kelly. "You print as well as I do. You can record this on the permanent data sheets."

After she was done with the sheets, Kelly wrote a quick note to Peggy and to her parents, and she and Adam drove to the store, where they gassed up the truck and mailed her letters. Adam bought a sack of groceries. At dinner he said, "Well, just Friday, Saturday, and Sunday to get through, and we're done with fried food. My gall bladder may hold on until Monday."

Kelly laughed. When he wasn't angry about a bear's welfare, Adam relaxed back into his joking ways and made things pleasant. "I'm glad you've taken on the job of family clown," she said cheerfully, but thoughtlessly . . . and could have bitten her tongue because Adam flushed a bright red. Damn. She had hit a painful spot. She had been teasing, and meant only the "family" in the cabin, but he had obviously taken her remark in a deeper way.

"That's how us underachievers deal with the movers and shakers," Adam said. "We make 'em laugh."

"Peggy makes *us* laugh," Kelly said, trying to take the focus from Adam and his family so that he could recover his poise.

"She's probably hurting," he said and rose from the table to begin clearing the plates. Before Kelly could respond, they heard a pickup and dogs again, and in a moment, Doc Morrison was in the room, filling it with his voice and his bulk. "I've got some antihistamine you can carry," he said to Rick. Adam turned from the sink, his eyes alive with interest.

Kelly stepped into the kitchen. "I'll finish up the dishes," she said. "You were wanting to talk to Doc Morrison." It was all she could do. It would have been awkward to apologize, but she felt awful for having invaded Adam's privacy.

"Thanks, Kelly, I appreciate it." Kelly picked up the dish towel, listening with half her mind to Doc Morrison's discussion of allergic reactions in animals, but more deeply absorbed by her thoughts about the complications of living and working full time with people who were strangers. *How can a field manager act to ease tensions? Rick doesn't do anything. He pays attention to the project, but he just lets the rest of it happen.* She took the dishwater outside and dumped it. She was beginning to appreciate how much faith Dr. Andrews had shown in letting them try to be a team.

The next morning they found a healthy three-year-old female in one of the Warren Gulch snares. Kelly asked Rick to let her give the anesthetic.

"What makes you think you can do it right?"

"I've got to learn. What if something happened and you weren't here? You need a back-up crew that knows something."

"I'll be here," he said, his skin muddy, his eyes cold. "You don't need to know how to use the jab stick."

Kelly stood her ground, set her jaw, and glared at him. "I'm part of the team," she said. "I'm supposed to learn how to do the work." Adam was silent. Kelly waited.

Finally, Rick glanced at the bear and shrugged. He filled the syringe and coached her on the jab and follow-through, repeating himself several times. "You don't have much time. That bear is going to turn and lunge toward you the moment she feels the needle. You have to think quickly."

Kelly tried to hide the slight trembling of her hands when she picked up the jab stick. Rick hovered as she approached the bear. "Adam, you go around and distract her. I'll stay here." He stood to one side so that Kelly had room, but she could tell that he was ready to step in and take over if things didn't go right.

Kelly shut her eyes and pictured the way Rick's arm arched and turned when he used the jab stick. Then she looked at Adam. "I'm ready."

Kelly lifted the stick and when Adam yelled, "Hey, bear," and the brown bear turned its head toward him, she brought the jab stick around. She could feel the momentary resistance before the needle penetrated the hide under the furry coat, and then she followed through, pushing the syringe clear down and jerking the stick away just as the bear whirled and lunged at her. She backed up quickly, out of the bear's reach, and looked toward the cable on the bear's leg. Her heart was beating fast. The cable was well placed.

"You'll be on an adrenaline high the rest of the day," Rick said. He took the jab stick from her and checked the syringe. He turned to Kelly. "You got it all into her. She'll be down in no time." It was decent of him not to say it grudgingly.

Kelly did feel high. Wired, alive, and intensely happy. She grinned at Rick, at Adam, and at the bear, who was already licking her lips. While they waited for the bear to go down, Kelly said, "When we check her, if she's definitely a female, can we name her Betsy?"

"After whom?" Adam asked.

"Jim McCarthy's wife."

Rick nodded. "Why not? That's a good public relations move, Kelly."

Rick was definitely charming when things were going well. They processed the bear smoothly. Adam said, "You do the data sheet, Kelly. Rick doesn't like my handwriting."

Kelly did not feel like she had been demoted again. She was far too high and besides, it made sense. Adam did have lousy handwriting. She recorded the data Rick gave her, helped with the measuring, and read the scale while the men held the heavy bear on the hook. Then they stretched Betsy on the ground with her eyes covered, and Adam said, "We don't have any other bears to process. Let's stay here until she comes up. We don't want those damned houndsmen setting their dogs on her."

Rick agreed, and they sat down on the slope and ate lunch. "If we'd catch Jenny and change that collar and if we could figure out how to keep Samantha away from our bait," Rick said, "this project would be going smoothly."

"Yeah," Adam said. "Doc Morrison said there wasn't anything we could have done about the cub." Betsy began to come up. They watched with satisfaction as her head cleared, and she made her way into the safety of the woods. ∾

Chapter Nineteen

Matt returned Saturday night. Afraid that his presence in the cabin would lead to a confrontation between Matt and Rick, Kelly agreed to go for a ride. "You smell better tonight," Matt said.

"That means our project's not going well," Kelly said. "We didn't snare any bears today, so we didn't need to mess with the bait."

"Do you expect to snare bears every day?"

"Heavens no. It would be a tough job if we were processing bears and redoing sets daily."

"How many hours a day do you work?"

Kelly relaxed against the padded seat back. For a change, Matt seemed more interested in her work than his. "We do an equipment check before we start out, and then we fill the bait box." Matt wrinkled his nose, and Kelly smiled at him.

"We wait to check the snares until most bears have bedded down for the day. We go to the mountain about nine to process and release the bears we have snared. We have nineteen sets now." Pleased that

Matt was listening, she went on. "Just riding and walking the trails and checking all our snares, we work from nine until about two." She paused. "Of course, it takes more time if we have a bear to process." Matt nodded, and she went on to tell about processing a bear and then, with another smile, she said, "It's fun to tell you about my work."

Matt said, "I'll be glad when you get this fieldwork out of your system, Kelly, so we can talk about more important things."

"Such as?" Kelly said, unable to conceal the edge in her voice.

"Getting married, settling down, raising a family."

"Matt, I'm not ready for marriage—to anyone." She shifted toward the door. "I've got all I can handle until I finish my thesis. I don't want to hurt you, but I'm not in love with you. Why can't we just be friends?"

"Damn it, Kelly, I've got friends." He gripped the wheel. "I don't want you for a friend. I want you for a wife."

"Matt, that's exactly what's wrong with our relationship—you don't want me for a friend."

"The only thing wrong with our relationship is that you've got the hots for those college guys." He turned, frowning. "I can see it."

"What are you talking about? *What* can you see?"

"Every time you start talking about bears and scientists, you get a kind of fired-up look in your eyes."

"Did it ever occur to you that I'm interested in my work?"

Matt laughed. "Kelly, *look* at your work. You're scraping up bear shit and propping sticks against trees. You live in a dump without even a bathroom, for cripes sake. The only reason you're out here is because Santini has you mesmerized."

"Damn it, Matt, most the time I don't even like Rick." Kelly studied him. "There's something I don't understand. You told me once that I'm uptight. You even implied that I'm frigid. Now you're talking as if I'm ready to jump into bed with the first available man. Why?"

"There's something in you, Kelly, like hot coals ready to burst into flame. I'd just like to be the guy who fans them."

It was useless, and if she let it go on, she'd be screaming at him. "Matt, if there *is* anything in me, it belongs to *me*. If it's fire or ice, it still belongs to me, and not some male." She looked out the window. "I've got to get up early in the morning, Matt, and this conversation is only going in circles. Please take me home."

"Your home is in Provo, in case you've forgotten. You haven't mentioned your family once. Don't you care what's happening to them either?"

Kelly felt a charge of anxiety. "I know something's going on. Do you see them?"

"I see Peggy once in awhile. She says it's like living on a rumbling volcano."

"I miss Peggy. I wish she'd come up here to visit."

"Why can't you go home?"

"Because if we leave here we have to take down the sets."

"Well, those two guys could take care of them for a day or two."

That was true. Kelly considered her feelings. "I don't want to go home, Matt. I think Peggy ought to move out, too. We've hung around our folks so long they don't have any life of their own."

They seemed to be on calmer ground, and Kelly wanted to leave it that way. "Let's go back, Matt." He reached over to pull her to him. Damn him. "Matt, will you stop!"

He took his hand away. "Okay, Kelly. For now." He put the pickup in gear. "But I'm not giving up."

There were no bears in the snares on Sunday either. Rick picked up Jenny, Roscoe, Marie, and Samantha on the receiver, but they weren't close by. "Too much commotion in the woods," he said. Matt came back on Sunday evening, and when Kelly refused to go out with him, he settled himself in a chair by the dining room table, creating a tension so tangible that, crossing the room, Kelly felt as if she were breaking thick spiderwebs.

After chatting about pickups and four-wheelers, Matt was silent for a few moments and then he said, "So, you two are in the university. Did you sign this Honor Code that Kelly signed?"

Rick and Adam looked at each other. Kelly didn't know where to look. Matt was only a little less crude than the bear hunters. She stood up. "Everybody signs the code, Matt. Listen, I've got to wash my hair and write to my folks. Will you excuse me?"

Matt flushed and rose from the chair. "I'm going to Provo for supplies, you want me to tell them anything?"

"Tell Ryan that I can't guarantee he'll see a bear, but he's welcome to come up anyway."

There were no bears on Monday. Rick made them rework and rebait every set. He was grim and silent, and it was a relief when he went off to Chase Creek on his own. Monday evening, Adam took over the cooking. "Do I need to hide the Crisco can?" Kelly asked him with a grin.

"I fry nothing," he said. "You are in for a treat."

"Oh, sure, you're some super chef."

"Veritably," Adam said. He put an outstretched hand on her head and twisted her toward the door. "You go gas up the four-wheelers and leave the kitchen to me." Kelly joined Rick outside and helped with the vehicles and the wood until Adam stepped to the door and yelled, "Soup's on."

The cabin smelled wonderful. "What are you cooking?"

"Just the same old pork chops."

Kelly looked over Adam's shoulder. The pork chops were in a mushroom sauce with bits of garlic and onion. A pan of rice steamed at the back of the stove. In a dish on the reservoir, cheese melted across asparagus spears. "Look, Rick. We've got a closet gourmet."

Rick sniffed the food and smiled for the first time all day. "Where'd you get all this stuff?"

"Oh, I picked up a few cans of this and that."

Supper was more fun than any meal they had eaten at the cabin. Matt didn't show up. The houndsmen seemed to have taken Kelly at her word and were avoiding the drainage areas where the snares were set. What baying they could hear was at a distance.

The sets were empty on Tuesday as well. "Damn it," Rick said when Kelly and Adam reported back to him in Warren Gulch after checking the Chase Creek sets. "We're doing something wrong. We're going to go over every set."

"Aw come on, Santini," Adam said, "we've done everything we can think of. I'm not resetting the damn sets for no reason. We'd probably have better results if we just stayed away from the sites, so the bears can come to the bait."

Rick shrugged. "Maybe you've got a point." He climbed on his four-wheeler. They returned to the cabin. Rick was irritable. He erased and rewrote map locations, grumbling aloud about the lack of bears. Adam was critical. He pointed out map lines that he felt more nearly matched the actual location of the sets. As the two men wrangled over minor points on the map, Kelly felt like screaming at both of them. Adam's supper was the only thing they enjoyed.

The next day was worse. The snares were empty. The receiver offered no welcome beeps. They found no scat. The cabin chores were minimal. Kelly washed her hair and dried it in the sun. And then there was nothing to do. She asked Rick if she could learn to drive the four-wheeler, but he said, "This damned project is not paying its way now. We can't use gas for frivolous stuff."

Frivolous? Kelly thought she had made progress in proving to Rick that she was able to do her share of the work. She *needed* to learn to run the four-wheelers, but Rick's mouth was set in a grim line. She glanced at Adam, who shrugged and said nothing. She went to her room and picked out tunes on her guitar, but she didn't feel like singing.

Late that afternoon, Walt Johnson, George Walker, and Harry Selnick dropped by and banged on the door. Their pickup bed was empty. "Where are your dogs?" Rick asked as he let the houndsmen into the cabin.

"We left them tied up at camp. No point in running dogs when there's no sign of bear." Without invitation, Walt pulled a chair away from the table and sat down.

George said, "What the hell have you been doing to the bears? We can't even pick up a scent."

"We've got the same problem," Rick said. "Maybe they've gone high to feed and aren't coming down in the drainages. I don't know." Adam joined them at the table.

George Walker smirked and asked, "So if you're not trapping bears, what do you three do with all your extra cabin time?" Walt laughed. All the men looked at Kelly. Adam had the grace to look away quickly.

Rick flushed and said, "We sit around knowing our bait is rotting and the project is going to hell. Where are those damn bears?"

Kelly was grateful to Rick for returning the focus to the work, but after the houndsmen finally got up and left, and Adam served a late dinner, there was a kind of tension in the cabin that hadn't been there before, despite their bickering and their inactivity.

Adam came into the kitchen while Kelly was doing dishes and reached for a dipper of water from the pail. When Kelly stretched to put the plates on the shelf, her arm brushed his, and he moved quickly away as if he'd been burned.

They stayed up late, each trying to read by lamplight, but their attention span was short. Their chairs creaked as they moved restlessly. Each of them made trips outside. When the lamp began to smoke, Rick said irritably, "We're wasting kerosene and wick. We might as well go to bed." He flushed as he said it and looked away from Kelly. ∽

Chapter Twenty

The week dragged by. The snares and the hours were vacant; the receiver was silent. Mornings and evenings they heard the dogs. During the day the logging trucks rumbled in the distance. The sky was empty; no clouds eased the endless blue; it was hot.

Thursday afternoon they left the stuffy cabin and sat outside. Flies droned around the screen of the drying box, lifting lazily away as Rick opened the lid and turned the pieces of grass-filled scat. Adam took a few noisy shots at a makeshift target. The smell of gunpowder rose hot and acrid. He inspected the target, then returned to the concrete porch. Rick and Kelly watched as he reloaded the gun and slowly polished it with the tail of his shirt.

"Maybe we should go see a movie."

Rick said, "There's not enough gas in the truck."

"What's for dinner?" Kelly asked.

"Meatloaf and baked potatoes," Adam said. He got up. "Do you want to make a salad?"

"You'd trust me in your kitchen?"

"It's your turn again next week." He bent and tousled her hair. "I want to give you a few pointers." She moved away from his touch.

Rick came into the cabin with them and filled the wash pan. He took one end of the counter. Kelly put together the greens that Adam washed in the dish pan. Standing between Rick and Adam, she could smell them—each had his own distinctive odor. It wasn't unpleasant; no one had been at the bait barrel for days. But their odors made her feel tense and wary, and she could feel the tension in their bodies as they stood near her.

They lingered over the meal. Adam asked questions, forcing Rick to talk. "So, Rick, what does your family do?"

"My old man is a miner. My mom runs the general store in Owl Creek . . ." He grinned slightly and said, "And she also runs my old man."

"You got any brothers and sisters?"

"More than I ever wanted. I'm the oldest of seven kids."

Adam glanced at Kelly with an I-told-you-so smirk. Kelly said, "Are any of the others in school?"

"Nope. I'm the first and only college graduate in the whole clan." Rick tossed the remark off casually, but Adam said, "That's a load to carry," and Rick flushed. There was a moment of quiet before he said, "They don't expect more than absolute perfection, instant fame, and immeasurable wealth." Kelly and Adam laughed, but Rick's smile was thin and momentary.

They lit the lamp, but didn't leave the table. Talk drifted to the bears. Kelly said, "I'm proud of my bear."

Rick looked at her. "Which one is your bear?"

"Samantha. The first bear we snared."

Adam snorted. "She's stolen bait three times that we know of. She's a real pain in the butt."

Kelly laughed. "I'm proud of Samantha because she's smarter than all of us. She's good at adapting to the annoyance of man on the mountain."

"I hope she's not giving lessons to the other bears," Rick said. He stretched and yawned. "Anyway, she'll be going into estrus in a few weeks, and then she'll have more on her mind than stealing our bait." There was silence again. Kelly did not want to think about the bear's mating or any mating. She didn't want Rick and Adam to think about it either.

She considered what Rick had said about his family. He treated the subject almost as a joke, but it explained something about him to know that he was the first one to go to college. *It must be hard to have the whole family watching—expecting great things.*

Adam broke the silence. "So what do you two think about the Honor Code? Rick, you're from outside. Does it bother you to have to sign the code anyway?"

Rick shrugged. "It's part of the deal. I knew about it from the beginning, and I wanted to go to this graduate school, so I signed it."

Adam frowned slightly and looked at Kelly. "I'm not sure if you're from outside or what. Is your family in the church?"

Kelly felt uncomfortable. "My grandmother was in the church. My father has sort of . . . strayed, I guess you'd say. My mother is a non-Mormon."

Adam persisted. "So what do you think about the code?" Kelly wished he would shut up. But Adam was waiting for a reply, and Rick was looking at her.

"It's got a good moral base. I guess the code makes it easier." She thought of Peggy and wondered if that was the truth. Adam frowned again, and she felt slightly irritated. Her assessment of the code didn't seem to suit anyone. She turned the question back to him. "What's your opinion?"

"I think it's important for the church to try to protect its kids," he said. "If I had a kid, I'd want him—or her—to have a few rules to back up his own judgment." Adam grinned a little as he added, "If he's got any."

Adam's questions and Rick's silence made Kelly uneasy. She knew almost nothing about these strangers who were sharing her summer. *I wish we had more work to do.* She made dishwashing last as long as possible, yet it was only seven-thirty when she finished. She went out into the early dusk to dump the water and lingered, reluctant to go back inside. Her flashlight batteries were fading. There would be no place to work but at the table under the kerosene lamp.

Rick and Adam were reading at the table. Taking a pen and tablet, she sat down next to Adam. She wrote the date and "Dear Peggy," and then hesitated. I can't write *what I'm feeling. Not with* them *sitting here.* She settled for facts.

"We have trapped four bears." Sixteen days, and they'd only trapped four bears. "We would have snared more than that by now, but Matt's logging trucks are noisy, and there are some houndsmen in the area with dogs." Kelly paused in her writing, thinking with distaste of Walt Johnson and George Walker and their rich friend Harry Selnick. "There's not enough to do when we don't have bears to process." Kelly glanced up. Rick was staring at her. Just staring. She had no idea what he was thinking. When she met his eyes, he flushed and looked back down at his book.

She started to write again, but Rick turned a page, and she was caught by the grace of his motion. Rick's hands were slender. The fingers were long and lean with smooth-looking nails trimmed to a slight point. As she watched, Rick reached his right hand to scratch the back of his left, which held the field manual he was reading. The fingers arched as they moved. Kelly followed his hand up and down with her eyes as he scratched himself lightly.

Adam stirred next to her. She caught his eye before he turned a page of his book. He blinked and shifted slightly so that he had somehow moved closer. He extended his arm on the table to hold his book nearer to the lamp. The light picked up the golden hairs on his arm. She traced the shadows of his muscles along his arm and toward his wrist. .

Watching Adam, she thought of riding behind him on the four-wheeler. She had grown accustomed to the gun's pressure against her leg and to the movement of their bodies together as they adjusted to the change of the slope. But now she was acutely aware of the way Adam's legs felt against hers on the four-wheeler, and she was so embarrassed that she could not sit at the table any longer.

She scooted her chair back and went out into the darkness. She walked to the woodshed and leaned against the inside wall while her face cooled and her thoughts rioted from Adam to Rick to the Honor Code to Dr. Andrews. She concentrated on her interview with the professor in his office. Her answers to his questions now seemed incredibly naive. She had begun to feel calmer when she heard footsteps through the grass and Rick's voice. "Kelly?"

"Here," she said, turning to leave the shed just as Rick stepped inside. He was a blur in the darkness, but his hand found her face. "Oh, there you are," he said. "We're just about ready to shut things down for the night." His fingers grazed her cheeks and lips before he dropped his hand, and she thought of the graceful way his hands moved. Her breath quickened as she stepped away from Rick, heading toward the cabin with a sense of being afloat in a dangerous sea.

She floundered up the steps and crossed quickly to her room, aware that Adam had been standing by the front door. She waited for the light to go out and then undressed in the dark and slipped into bed, but she could not sleep. Tense and hot and very much aware of the men in the beds on the other side of the wall, she lay listening to the sounds they made as they moved restlessly in their cots. Neither of the familiar snores started up. Their breathing was loud.

Kelly tried to shift her thoughts and was suddenly considering her mother and father. She had always felt a sort of disdain for her mother's weakness. It was stupid to throw away a whole college career because you couldn't control your own feelings.

She sat up abruptly and reached for her guitar case in the dark. Leaning against the pillow Peggy had sent, she positioned the guitar across her lap and moved her hand along the neck until she fingered the right frets. Strumming softly, Kelly began to sing. She sang all the old country and western cheatin', hurtin' tunes she could remember, stopping only when she heard snores from the other room.

The next morning, they picked up Jenny on the receiver. "Do you suppose she's okay?" Adam asked.

"I have no way of knowing," Rick said, "except that she's still moving, so I assume she's eating and growing and that collar is getting tighter." Roscoe—the big male Kelly had heard Rick describe but had never seen for herself—was in a different area. "The males and females won't be too close together until mating season later in the summer," Rick said.

"I'd like to snare Samantha again," Kelly said, "just to record how much weight she's gaining on our meat."

"I'd like to catch some bear—any bear—before Jerry shows up Friday," Rick said.

Dr. Andrews did not arrive at the cabin Friday night, but Matt did. "I wanna talk to you outside," he said to Kelly, without greeting Rick and Adam. Kelly followed him to the porch, shutting the door behind her. Outside, Matt turned and said in a fierce tone, "I've just come from a session at a trucker's bar, and guess who is the talk of the town." Kelly waited. He was going to tell her whether she wanted to hear it or not. "The houndsmen can't joke about anything but you and those guys." Matt pointed a thumb over his shoulder toward the cabin.

A warm flush rose to her face; she was glad it was dark. "Well, what do you think I can do about it?"

"I think you should leave the project before your reputation is totally shot."

Kelly's jaw tightened into a hard knot as she clenched her teeth. Fury rose in her throat with the taste of bile. She said in a low cold voice, "My reputation depends on what I *do,* not on what other people say. We have some problems here—problems that are most likely caused by you and those houndsmen—but those problems have nothing to do with our sharing the cabin. Nothing has happened in this cabin, Matt. Absolutely damned nothing."

"Something's changed."

"Are you calling me a liar?"

Matt said, "You're different." There was a hard edge to his voice.

It was time to end this. Her emotions—her sexual feelings—her sexual actions—her life—were none of Matt's business. She said, "It's time that you stopped coming around here, Matt. I am on this project to work toward a degree that really matters to me. I can't help what those jerks say about me, and I don't want you to think you have to defend me." Matt started to speak, but she said, "Let me finish. I can only prove that I am professional by being that way. Having an old boyfriend show up just adds fuel to the fire. I want you to stick to your lumbering project and stay away from this cabin. I won't go out with you, and I don't want to see you anymore."

Kelly didn't stay to hear his reply. She went into the cabin, slamming the door behind her. It was only when she heard the roar of Matt's truck that she realized that the cabin window was open. Rick and Adam had very likely heard every word. She didn't care. She had forgotten for a while that she had a serious reason for being here, but she wouldn't forget again. Tomorrow, if there were no bears, she was going to learn to run a four-wheeler whether Rick liked it or not. She stepped into the bedroom for her project notebook and spent the rest of the evening making careful notes about every bear they'd contacted, sighted, snared, or missed snaring. ∾

Chapter Twenty-One

Saturday morning, there weren't even any beeps on the receiver. They checked all the sets, found no bears, and returned to the cabin. Kelly took her purse, her car keys, and the gas cans, and said to Rick, who sat on the edge of the porch, looping a cable, "I'm going to go get some gas and then learn to drive a four-wheeler."

He glanced at her. "Damn it, Kelly, we can't afford it. Jerry is probably going to chew us out anyway for wasting gas and showing no results."

"I'm not going to use project money. I'll take my own car, and I'll spend my own money. But I *am* going to learn how to operate that machine."

"You won't get paid back."

Adam interrupted the conversation. "Give it up, Santini. If Kelly's going to get a chance to run this project, she needs to operate the equipment." Kelly could have killed him. Rick sat up straight. "Run the project?" Adam didn't respond. He *would* open a snake pit and leave her to deal with it.

"Someone has to run the project next year," Kelly said. She smiled at Rick. "Train me right, and I could do it when you've gone on to bigger and better things." She waited, wishing Adam had kept his mouth shut. Rick just looked at her, a faint scowl crimping his forehead. Then he shrugged and stood up. He fished the truck keys from his pocket.

"No point in wasting a trip." He handed her the university credit card. "Take the truck and fill it, too." Kelly started toward the pickup.

Adam said, "I think I'll ride along."

"What for?" Rick sounded suspicious.

"To pick up some pie filling."

Kelly turned back to stare at him. Rick laughed. "Damned if you don't sound just like one of my sisters." Adam flushed, but Rick had shifted his attention to Kelly. "Call the zoology department while you're at the store. Leave a message for Jerry. Just say we're okay, and we don't need bait." He didn't bother to make it a request.

Adam put the gas cans in the back of the truck, and Kelly climbed in the driver's seat. When they were out of sight of the cabin, Adam said, "Sorry about that. I thought he knew of your great ambition." Kelly looked at him, but didn't say anything. She was pissed off at both of them, and she didn't believe him. He had some ulterior motive.

Adam said, "As long as I'm apologizing, I suppose I ought to mention that I could have shut the window last night." She glanced at him again. He was grinning and there was a spark in his brown eyes.

She gave up her anger and laughed. "I could have remembered that it was open. But, since we're already the talk of the county, I guess I can't expect any privacy at home."

"It was an interesting conversation," Adam said, still grinning, "but you lied to Matt."

"I did not. I don't want to see him again."

"No, I mean when you said that nothing has happened in the cabin."

"Nothing *has* happened."

"You're kidding yourself, Kelly. We're wasting five hours of daylight every day just because we're not willing to split up and do some real fieldwork."

"I'm willing."

"Yeah, but you can't run the four-wheeler, and Rick's not about to leave me alone with you at the cabin while he does habitat work or looks for better places to put the sets."

"That's stupid, Adam, he could let *me* go."

"We're not ready to let you go roaming in the woods alone."

"Will you stop it? You're giving me claustrophobia."

"And we're all dying of boredom, too, Kelly. But we *can't* stop it. We're obsessed with one another."

"That's ridiculous." Kelly pulled the truck up to the stop sign at the highway.

"No it's not. Santini spends half his time staring at you. You flinch at the slightest touch from either of us."

He was too damned perceptive. Kelly felt invaded. "And what about you?" she demanded. "Are you just an unbiased observer, taking field notes?"

He laughed, "Nope. Me . . . I lust for you in my heart." His laugh eased the sting, but only slightly. She turned on him.

"That's what I hate. I hate being just a body to all of you."

Adam drew away from the force in her voice, but his reply was still in a joking tone. "You scare me when you yell." He ran a finger along her arm. "I don't see why you mind so much. It's a real nice body."

Kelly jammed her foot onto the accelerator, and the pickup roared down the highway. The speedometer rose to sixty-five, then seventy. Adam said, "There's a cop behind us."

Kelly flicked her eyes to the rearview mirror. The narrow highway was empty for miles. She slowed the truck and turned to Adam, who was grinning with such delight that she had to join in his laughter. When they stopped laughing, there was a companionable silence for a moment and then Adam said, "You've never spent any time away from home have you? Never been to summer camp or anything like that?"

"I used to spend summers with my grandmother."

"Must have been lonely."

"It was not lonely. My grandma taught me all sorts of things."

"Didn't you want to be with your own kind?"

Kelly was quiet for a long moment, and then she said, "I've never met anyone who was my own kind."

"Well *excuse* me. Who named you a unique species?"

Kelly was suddenly standing at the far corner of the playground again, watching a laughing, wriggling line of students bunch toward the door and disappear inside. And as she had then, she gathered herself together in her mind and ringed herself with a fortress of calm. Turning to Adam, she said, "You're good at that."

"What?"

"Turning the spotlight away from yourself and onto someone else." He flushed a bright red. Kelly pulled the truck up to the gas pumps in front of the small store.

When she had filled the truck and the gas cans, she called Provo. The zoology department didn't answer, which wasn't surprising. Rick must have forgotten that it was Saturday. She called Dr. Andrews at home. "Rick wanted me to report in."

"You guys okay? You need bait?"

"No, Dr. Morrison brought us a couple of cows." She didn't tell him that they were rotting in the barrel.

"Well, tell Rick I'll be up Monday afternoon with some people from the DWR and maybe the Forest Service." Kelly could feel her pulse lurch as her heart started to beat faster. Rick would be frantic when she told him that.

"Everything okay?" Dr. Andrews asked.

Kelly swallowed and said, "Fine. We've got a good work schedule going." No need to tell him it stopped at mid-afternoon every day.

"Okay. I'll see you guys on Monday."

Adam stowed a sack of groceries on the floor of the truck by his feet. "I'm straining the food kitty a bit," he said.

Kelly ignored the comment to say, "Dr. Andrews is coming up here on Monday with some representatives of the Wildlife Department and the Forest Service."

"Oh, damn. Santini will keep us working night and day."

"I'm not going to tell him right away."

Adam turned to stare at Kelly. "He'll strangle you when he finds out that you didn't tell him first thing."

Kelly shrugged. "Please don't tell him, Adam. I may never get another chance to learn to run that machine."

Before Rick would let her drive the four-wheeler, he insisted that she learn more about it. "The oil's on the right side; the gas tank is under the seat." Kelly swallowed. She hadn't realized that she'd been bouncing all over the mountain on top of the gas tank. When he finally let her mount the machine, Rick continued to coach her. "Start in neutral. The brake is on the left hand control. Also the button for shifting to reverse." He explained the transmission controls on the foot pedal, then he climbed on the machine behind her. Thinking of what Adam had said about her flinching at their touch, Kelly did not move a muscle when she felt Rick's body close to her own.

She put the machine in gear and started off, jerking and bucking. Rick kept up a distracting stream of instructions. She finally concentrated only on shifting and began to hear what the four-wheeler's engine was telling her as it ground its way up hill asking for a lower gear and then whining with eagerness for a higher gear as she came to a level spot. She let her body feel the machine and began to enjoy the challenge of coordinating her hands and feet to keep it running smoothly. They had gone almost to the meadow when Rick told her to head back. "Be careful to give yourself enough room. It needs a wide turn-around."

The machine steered hard. The accelerator on the hand grip was tiring to her thumb and she could feel tension in her hands and shoulders, but she turned the machine and delivered Rick back to the cabin. As he got off, he said, "You did okay for the first try."

Kelly smiled at him and said, "I'm not finished." She put the four-wheeler in gear and swung out around Rick, turning in a wide circle near her Buick and then gunning the motor as she swept past him and headed up the road alone, laughing with the joy of freedom.

She spent the rest of the day practicing. She started, stopped, sped up, slowed down, turned, climbed the hilly road near the meadow, descended and banked on a steep curve. The sun roasted her head, and the dust dried her lips, but she couldn't remember ever having had so much fun. When Rick and Adam pulled up beside her in the pickup and Adam yelled, "You're late for dinner," she was stiff and tired. She wheeled the machine away from the truck and headed for the cabin.

The bears had evaded the sets again on Sunday. Rick looked grim, but he stopped at the bait barrel on their return to unhook the trailer and let Kelly unload the four-wheeler. The houndsmen came rattling down the road with their yelping dogs just as Kelly roared up the road. She grinned at the look on Walt Johnson's face, ignored George Walker's yell, and escaped.

This time she took one of the small, rough side roads, starting slowly, but as she gained confidence, increasing her speed. She kept at it most of the afternoon. Just before she turned back toward the main trail, she took a deep breath, studied a rocky hump, and took her machine over it. The four-wheeler tilted dangerously, but she compensated with her body, and when the machine righted, she laughed aloud, swung around, and crossed the hump again. By the time she reached the cabin, the houndsmen were gone, and the cabin smelled of apple pie.

Adam's final dinner was a feast. When their plates were empty and the three of them were sitting lazily with their elbows on the table, Kelly said to Rick, "I forgot to tell you yesterday, but Dr. Andrews is bringing some DWR people up here tomorrow afternoon." ∾

Chapter Twenty-Two

"I told you he'd kill us off," Adam grumbled to Kelly as they finished redoing their fourth complete trail set at noon on Monday, after checking all the snares and finding them empty.

"Be grateful I didn't tell him Saturday, or we'd have had to rebuild every set on the mountain." Kelly placed the last piece of reeking bait and burnt it with the torch.

"I wish to hell he weren't the flag bearer for his whole damned tribe," Adam said. "He might let us stop just short of perfection once in awhile."

Even though she was aggravated at Rick, Kelly felt uncomfortable with the conversation. She was going to have to face Dr. Andrews in a little while herself. "What would you do if you had all the responsibility?" she asked Adam.

"I'd try to see the whole picture," Adam said. "I wouldn't get so caught up in the popular aspects of this project."

"That's an odd word—popular. What do you mean?"

"Snaring the bears. That's the popular, glamorous, exciting part of this project, but it isn't the only way of gathering information. You said it yourself. Even the lack of information is a data point, but we don't know that we lack information. We haven't gone looking for it."

"Why haven't you said something before?"

"This project doesn't need *three* bosses."

Kelly swallowed and climbed silently on the four-wheeler. They met Rick at the meadow and returned to the cabin. The university van was parked in front of it. Inside the cabin, three men and a woman sat at the table with cans of pop in front of them. Dr. Andrews stood near the map. As he introduced the bear biologists to the department people, Kelly was very much aware of her odor and the mess that her hair was in after riding on the four-wheeler.

"Will you excuse us while we wash?" she said. "We've been rebaiting snares."

The woman, whose name was Mary Powers, wrinkled her nose and smiled. Kelly dipped warm water from the reservoir and listened to the general conversation. Two of the men were from the Department of Wildlife Resources; the other man was from the Forest Service. She turned in surprise when Dr. Andrews said that Mary Powers was a pilot for the Forest Service. "She'll be doing some of our fall flyovers for us," he said.

Kelly felt a rise of excitement. "I hope I'll get to fly with you," she said to Mary.

Mary said, "We'll make sure you do." She had a pleasant, peaceful-looking face. Her gray eyes sparkled as she looked around the roomful of men and then back to Kelly. "I'd enjoy it."

Adam and Rick were taking their turn washing. Standing near Rick, Kelly could feel his tension. His mouth was grim, and his skin looked muddy. He glanced frequently toward Dr. Andrews. Smelling Rick's nervous perspiration, she suddenly felt great sympathy for him.

"So," said one of the department men, "how's this bear-trapping project going?"

He had looked toward Rick, but Kelly knew that Rick was not ready to answer. His flush had deepened to an angry red. He looked miserable. Mentally reviewing the notes she had been working on and including the four snarings, every beep on the receiver, both contacts with the dead cub, her sighting of Samantha, and even Samantha's stealing of the bait, she figured swiftly and spoke before Rick could reply.

"Taking into account all types of contact—including snaring, tracking collared bears with the receiver, and actual sightings—our average bear contact has been one to two each day we've been here."

"Not bad," the man said.

Rick was still silent. Damn it, why didn't he help her out? She said, "We've discovered that two females and one male that were collared in earlier stages of the project in a different area have traveled to this side of the mountain."

She was aware that her voice sounded calm and professional and that the visitors were listening with respectful attention, but she was about to run out of information, and she was certain that Dr. Andrews knew it. He was looking at her in an odd way, as if he were trying not to laugh. She glanced at Rick. His skin had cleared, and suddenly he swung into a discussion of spring feeding habits and the high content of grass in the scat and, turning their attention away from bears, spoke of the damage done by the cattle.

When Rick's information began to grow thin and his voice to grow taut, they suddenly got help from another quarter. Adam entered a momentary silence with an invitation. "How would you all like a piece of apple pie? There's enough left from the pies I baked yesterday."

Mary Powers laughed, the delight in her voice dancing through the room like sunbeams. "You baked?" She looked from Rick to Adam to Kelly. "You're a surprising crew. Sure, Adam, let's have some of your pie."

Kelly dared a full look at Dr. Andrews as she brought a piece of pie to him where he sat on the bed. He took the fork from her hand and said softly, "Average daily bear contact. . . . You'd be a damn good politician, Kelly."

After they finished the pie, the group drove to the meadow, and Rick and Dr. Andrews took the visitors in turn to the lowest trail-set in Warren Gulch. When the group had reassembled, the visitors got into the van. Dr. Andrews came to stand with the crew by the pickup.

"We'll head back to the main highway when we leave here." He studied the three of them. "They were suitably impressed with your progress. That's not bad bullshit you presented, but I think you could all work a little harder. If you don't snare a bear, take those four-wheelers and go as far as you can. Then get off and walk. You're not going to find decent scat samples if you don't get nearer the bears."

"What about the cost of gas?" Rick said. "I've already used the university credit card twice."

Dr. Andrews sighed and then said, "Don't worry about the cost. That's my department." He gestured toward the truck with his head. "I'll hit them up for more money, or I'll talk to the university or some of my friends." He shook his head. "The next project is going to be properly funded, or I'm not going to take it on." He looked back at them. "But that's not your problem. Your problem is to get out there and get some real data."

Kelly was ashamed. She had let her personal reactions get in the way of her work. She had never thought that just sharing the same cabin with two men could sidetrack her. She stared at her shoes, feeling miserable. She was startled when Dr. Andrews put a hand on her shoulder.

"Cheer up, Kelly. You're *supposed* to get a few rude shocks from fieldwork. You'll be a lot better biologist when you finish this project. Books and lab work never prepare you for the downright deadly boredom that sometimes goes along with field research."

She was surprised into saying, "How did you know?"

He laughed. "I didn't get my doctorate in the library."

She watched him turn and walk to the van. As the visitors drove out of sight, she said, "I almost forgot that *he's* the one who's really in charge of this project."

She tried to figure out what Dr. Andrews had done that had made her feel so much better. She respected him for seeing the truth of their first three weeks. It gave her mind a good clean feeling to recognize his intelligence, training, and skill. He was a better model than Rick. But Dr. Andrews had done more than see the whole picture.

He'd jarred them out of their torpor, chewed them out, and then reaffirmed his faith in them with his last understanding remarks. He had probably even brought Mary Powers along on purpose, just to keep Kelly from feeling overwhelmed.

Adam said, "I wish I'd had a chance to talk to him."

Kelly and Rick turned toward him. "What about?" Rick said with a trace of hostility.

"About whether or not I even belong on this project."

"Of course you belong on this project," Rick said. "If you weren't here, Kelly and I would have blown the whole thing by now."

It was Kelly and Adam's turn to stare. Before they could reply, Rick said, "And speaking of how valuable you are, I have a proposition for you. If Kelly and I do all the dishes, chop wood, and do house chores, will you sign on as permanent chef?" Kelly was amazed at how much he, too, had benefited from Dr. Andrews's visit to the camp. He had managed his request with real tact.

Adam laughed and said, "Sure. I'll cook full time. That's a good deal."

Kelly had hoped somehow that their renewed energy about the project would have changed the bear situation, but the sets were empty again on Tuesday. This time, though, they didn't go back to the cabin. While they ate lunch in the meadow, Rick outlined a different sort of afternoon schedule.

"We've got to take the sets to the bears since the bears won't come down to the sets." He looked around. "But we've got to find them first. I think we're too low."

He leaned forward and drew a map of the high ridge in the dirt. "Adam, take Kelly up Warren Gulch and drop her off as high as you can get. Then you go high on Chase Creek. Look for sign. Avoid the houndsmen if you hear them. Stay out of trouble and keep your bearings." He looked at Kelly. "Can you do that?"

She nodded. She had been carrying the compass for three weeks, and she was far surer of her reply than she would have been in the beginning. Adam dug out canteens and backpacks from the extra equipment in the pickup. He tossed an apple to each of them.

Rick said, "I'm going to cut over to Moreno Creek and go up from there. Be back here by five-thirty." He grinned and added, "With your backpacks full of wet bear poop."

Eager to get into the woods alone, Kelly hopped off the four-wheeler at the top of Warren Gulch, scarcely acknowledging Adam's parting words. Before the sound of the machine had faded away on the downhill trail, Kelly was striding the uphill trail, a faint game path that wound through the shadowy forest. Sunspots speckled the forest floor. The old needles that carpeted the ground were as gray as the shadows.

The air was filled with subtle scents. Kelly wrinkled her nose, wishing she had as keen a sense of smell as the bears. A grasshopper flew up in front of her, buzzing like a small chain saw. A little cloud of gnats dive-bombed her; she waved a hand around her head, dispersing them.

Bent slightly forward to ease the climb and to spot sign more quickly, Kelly slowly came into alignment with the mountain. Her breathing steadied into an efficient rhythm, her body moved smoothly, her thoughts centered on the messages left on the ground: elk had passed along the trail, deer too, and something else, perhaps a weasel.

As she entered a clearing at the edge of the forest, she almost stepped in a large plop of bear scat. Excited because it was fresh, she looked around, trying to spot the bear who had so recently relieved itself along the trail.

She saw no bears, but she was exhilarated by the knowledge that she might be close to Samantha or Jenny or one of the other bears that walked so often through their thoughts and conversation and beeped the receiver so tantalizingly. Kelly prepared labels, noting the area so that it could be plotted with the appropriate coordinates on their map. Using a piece of bark, she scooped the scat into the plastic bags, zipped them closed, labeled them, and put the bags into her backpack.

She continued up the hill and into the sunshine on a rocky hump, still below timberline, but marked by twisted trees that toed the crevices and bent away from the wind. Looking toward the ridge of rocks, she spotted a small dark opening. A den?

Determined to see into the cave, she removed her backpack and stored it at the foot of one of the crooked trees. Grasping small faults in the rock face, she inched her way up toward the black mouth. She dragged herself onto a wider ledge and lay for a moment, looking up into the blue sky where a few clouds were beginning to gather. She listened—

fairly certain that the bears had left their dens for the summer.

She heard nothing but the drone of a jet. Reassured by the silence in the cave above her, she climbed from the ledge to the mouth, knowing that Dr. Andrews would chew her hide for climbing the cliff alone. But glorying in being alone—away from the guys, free to use her body and mind in any way she chose—she scooted into the rocky opening.

Just past the narrow maw, the tunnel widened and curved to the left. Sunlight angled part way into the opening, but farther back, the shadows turned smoky blue, then steel gray, and then lost themselves in velvety black. In the near edge of the gray shadows, she could see a riff of pine needles and grass, maybe two inches deep, and she knew she was looking at part of a bear's winter bed.

She lay full length, feeling the rocks in the barren floor of the cave bite into her body, and tried to feel what it would be like to crawl in here and wait the winter through while the snow piled up and covered the cave mouth. Bears didn't really go into a true hibernation state. Maybe they got restless sometimes and yearned for spring, waking from dreams of green grass and ripe berries to find themselves in the dark, stiff and alone, and wondering if this was how it had to be.

Kelly grinned and stretched. Dr. Andrews would chew her out *more* for thoughts like that than he would for climbing rocks alone. She had heard him snort and say, "Romantic!" when students had tried to connect human feelings to animals. But thinking of Samantha, who had successfully avoided their snares when other bears did not, Kelly was tempted to think that some measure of conscious determination and planning was involved.

How do we really know them? How do we relate to them without invading their lives and controlling them, however briefly? Lying in the bear's den, she felt the intrusion as she never had when she studied books about denning habits of the bear and denning techniques of the bear biologist. Thinking of the three beer cans she had smashed and put into her pack with the bear scat, she knew it was useless to say, "We should leave them be, leave them free." It was too late. *Rick and Adam and I have to live with the knowledge that the mountain is already scarred and scratched and scraped by man. And we'll leave our own marks as we try to ensure the bears a place in it all.*

Kelly scooted backward out of the den—glad not to have met an angry, newly awakened bear—slid down to the ledge, and descended the rock face to her backpack. The clouds were bunching together now and growing higher. Swinging downhill, Kelly could smell the fresh bear scat in her pack, her own sweat and, as she went lower, the wet, rich odor of rotted leaves in the drainage along the trail. She shifted the pack and glanced at the sky. It was going to rain. Thank goodness the baggies were waterproof; she didn't relish scat soup in her backpack. A sudden movement in the drainage on her left caught her attention. She stopped dead still. Someone was at one of the sets. ❧

Chapter Twenty-Three

Kelly couldn't tell if the slender figure was male or female because the head was hidden by a huge blue backpack, but she hurried forward as the person raised a large stick and deliberately set off the snare. "What are you doing?" Kelly asked, stepping into the cleared area around the set.

The backpacker started, turned toward Kelly, and let go of the stick. It was a girl with fuzzy brown hair held in place with a beaded headband. She wore a faded maroon tank top, faded jeans, and dirty sneakers. Brown eyes narrowed, she stared at Kelly a moment before gesturing toward the snare. "I'm springing this trap. Can you believe someone is still monster enough to set traps?"

The stupid girl had no idea what she was doing. "It's dangerous for you to be releasing that strong spring," Kelly said.

"I don't care," the girl said. "We should leave the animals *completely* alone." The backpacker began kicking over the guide sticks around the snare. When she was satisfied with her destruction, she turned to Kelly and said, "What bastard do you suppose set that thing?"

Kelly took a deep breath and said, "I set the snare."

"You! How *could* you?"

Kelly waved a hand toward the mountain. "Somewhere up there are several groups of men with dogs, hunting the bears to kill them for trophy." She waved a hand in the direction of Jamie's ranch. "That way, there's a herd of cows invading the bears' habitat. Coming from north, west, east, and south are trucks, jeeps, bikes, four-wheelers, and backpackers. I am trying to do something to help the bears."

"By trapping them? That's crazy and cruel. You should just leave them alone." The girl put her hands on her hips and glared at Kelly, who suddenly felt very tired. Silently, she bent and began to rebuild her trail set. The girl watched, her entire body discharging hostility. Kelly glanced up from her work.

"We're trying to help the bears," Kelly said, "but we have to have the data before the Department of Wildlife can act. We have to show that the bears are impacted before anyone can help to save them."

"I don't care," the girl replied, repeating herself. "You should just leave them alone."

With a quick sympathetic thought for Dr. Andrews who had to deal diplomatically with the public all the time, Kelly said, "You and I could do that, maybe, but you can't tell men to leave the animals alone. They won't do it. They think that hunting is their God-given right."

Replacing the stepping sticks and smoothing the center of the snare, Kelly said, "Let me tell you about a report I read in a book by George Laycock." The girl watched with a frown, but she seemed to be listening.

"In California about seventy years ago, a man came upon a huge grizzly bear when he was hunting. He got terribly excited because not one of the huge bears had been seen in the state for some time. Knowing that he was probably looking at the *last* grizzly in California . . ." Kelly paused, took a long ragged breath, and said, "The man raised his rifle and killed the bear anyway."

The girl said, "The son-of-a-bitch."

Kelly nodded and strained to set the spring. The girl watched, saying, "I still think it's wrong to trap them." Kelly grunted with the effort, slid the tongue into place, and then stood. The backpacker looked around. "And I still might set off whatever traps I come upon."

Kelly brushed the dirt and pine needles from her jeans as a spattering of rain hit the tree leaves. She looked at the girl. "I wouldn't do that. Those snares are the property of the state of Utah and the U.S. Government." But the girl had forgotten the snares. "Oh, shit," she said. "It's raining. I've got to get out of here."

Kelly stood in the drizzle and watched as the blue pack disappeared down the trail. Then she started through the wet grass toward the nearest downhill trail-set. *What if she's sprung every one of the snares?* Kelly felt burdened by Dr. Andrews's warning to be discreet. Instead of the explanations that had sounded so awkward, she wished she could have said, "You'd be more help to the bears if you'd just stay off the mountain yourself and leave my equipment alone."

The next set was intact, but Kelly didn't dare to leave without checking each snare. The rain fell steadily, and her hair was wet and stringy by the time she reached the lowest set in Warren Gulch. As she slipped down the wet slope, she could see the long branch that had been jammed into the center of the snare. *Damn that girl.* But it wasn't until she reached the grassy area under the aspens that she saw the complete mess the girl had made.

Grabbing a chunk of bark, Kelly scraped and cleaned the area around the set, her teeth clenched in fury. The rain dripped from the aspen tree above her and soaked her shirt and underclothes. She had just finished camouflaging the cable with soggy leaves when she heard the four-wheeler. She started up toward the road as Rick passed the flag that marked the set. She waved, and he made a wide return circle, got off the machine, and called to her. "Have you got something in the snare?"

Kelly climbed the slope toward him and said, "No, some dumb girl set it off with a stick."

"Probably the one who's down at the meadow lecturing Adam."

Kelly gritted her teeth briefly and said, "Well, you'd better keep her away from me."

Rick stared at her. "What did the poor little tree hugger do to you?"

Kelly reached the road and paused to look at Rick. "Not only did she set off two snares, which I reset in the rain, at this last one, she left a sample of her own scat. I had to clean it up before I could rebuild the set."

Rick's dark eyes lit with a wicked light, and he burst out laughing. Kelly glared at him for a second and then turned and stepped onto the four-wheeler. Starting it up, she put it into gear and headed down the trail. She heard Rick's startled yell, and she considered ignoring him, but instead slowed the machine just enough so that he could catch up if he ran hard. He wasn't laughing anymore when he climbed on the four-wheeler behind her.

It rained most of the night. Kelly slept uncomfortably in the chilly cabin and woke irritably to the smell of smoke and bear scat. When she passed through the kitchen, Adam was hunched over the stove. The scat-drying box was sitting just inside the door by the table. Kelly wrinkled her nose, but she knew Rick was right to get the box out of the rain. No sense in letting data points turn to slop. As she walked through the sopping grass toward the outhouse, Kelly felt uneasy about all the things Rick remembered that never occurred to her. She sat shivering on the damp seat, out of sync with the project, her hair in lank strands around her face.

Adam's breakfast had the same out-of-sync quality: limp, underdone bacon, greasy eggs, soggy bread scorched on the outside where Adam had tried unsuccessfully to toast it on the stove lid. Kelly could easily have hated Rick, just for the cheerful way he ignored the smells in the cabin and attacked the sickly looking breakfast as if it were one of Adam's best. His skin had the golden-olive glow that usually meant he was relaxed and happy.

He grinned at Adam and said, "I thought sure you'd bring that poor little tree hugger home with you. She needed shelter from the rain."

Adam grunted. "I needed shelter from her tongue." Kelly had never heard him sound so grouchy. He scowled at Rick. "But you know, maybe she's right. Maybe we all ought to get off this mountain and let it revert to some sort of decent habitat."

Rick returned Adam's scowl. "Get real, Wainwright. You could go home, we could all go home, but that's not going to stop humans from running over the top of every mountain they can get wheels or hiking boots onto. The size of the population will doom the wilderness." He looked around, the clear tones of his skin darkened by emotion. "Hell, the entire United States considers the Rocky Mountains as a playground."

Kelly was fascinated by the strong feeling in his voice. He cared so much about some things. Rick continued. "Unless you ground every plane, outlaw every four-wheel drive vehicle, chain every tree hugger to a parking meter in the city, you're not going to keep the influence of humans out of the hills."

"No need to get on a soap box," Adam said. He stood, scraped his breakfast into the trash, and left the cabin.

Kelly did the dishes and helped Rick gather the equipment for the day's work. "Thanks for saving the samples from the rain," she said as they left the cabin. Rick flashed her a smile.

The ride behind Adam to check the snares was uncomfortable. Adam was silent, the four-wheeler was noisy, the grass along the trail was still wet, and by the time they reached the top of Chase Creek, Kelly's pant legs were soaked through. It was a relief to get off the machine. Kelly started briskly through the shrubs and tall grass toward the trail-set behind Adam. The sun was high enough now to offer some warmth when they reached the open meadow.

Adam slowed down, waiting as if he were at last ready for company, and Kelly moved forward to walk beside him. "What upset you?" she asked.

Adam grinned. "I hate that damn stove, and a lousy breakfast accompanied by a lecture from Santini is more than I can handle." He gave her a piercing look. "And what's your problem?"

"Dirty hair and the fact that I forgot the drying box and Rick remembered it."

Adam laughed, but he put a comforting hand on her shoulder, and they stood in the shining meadow for a moment enjoying the sun sparkles on a clump of wet bushes just above the trail-set. Kelly saw a movement beyond the bushes. "We have a bear!" She moved forward, her eyes on the huge cinnamon-colored bear that crashed around in the tangle of sticks and branches that had been a barricade.

"He's big," Adam said, stepping quickly toward the set, "and hey . . . he's got a collar and tags. I bet that's Roscoe."

But Kelly wasn't listening. She had seen something else as the bear strained against the cable and lifted his leg into view. Her breath caught in her throat and became shallow and quick. She grasped Adam's arm to halt his forward motion. "We've got to go get Rick . . . and in a hurry." She pointed toward the restless bear. "The snare didn't go around his leg. He's caught by just two toes." ∽

Chapter Twenty-Four

Rick parked the four-wheeler and moved down the slope until he could see the bear. When he turned to them, his face was ashy; along his forehead, beads of sweat caught the sun. Seeing his face, Kelly felt a zigzag of fear travel down her chest and settle into her stomach in a hard knot. She glanced at Adam, who was equally pale, but his eyes were opaque, showing no emotion.

Rick spoke in a low voice. "Move slowly and quietly. Adam, take your gun from the holster and sight in on his chest." Rick ran a hand across his forehead. "Damn. I hope we don't have to kill him. That's Roscoe. He's a fine old bear, and we've got good data on him."

Rick flicked a glance at Kelly and frowned slightly before turning back to Adam. "If he pulls loose and charges either of us, you'll have to shoot. Aim for his chest—for his lungs—and be prepared to keep shooting until you stop him."

Adam checked the gun and nodded his head. His arms were steady as he raised the Ruger and sighted on the bear. The animal shuffled around in the debris from the broken barricade, occasionally lifting his paw to tug against the cable, his head moving from side to side. "You won't use the dart gun?" Adam asked.

"Not if we can get near him. That barbed dart causes too much damage."

Adam nodded. Rick looked at Kelly again. She could practically read his list of objections to her presence, but he said nothing. She reached for the drug bottles and offered them to him in turn as he readied the syringe. "He weighed about three hundred pounds at the end of last summer," Rick said. "He looks that now, and maybe more."

Kelly swallowed. A three hundred-pound bear caught by two toes. Rick screwed the needle into the top of the stick and turned to Kelly. "We need to distract him. The first lunge is going to be the most dangerous." He frowned. "Do you think you could manage the jab stick?"

"That doesn't make sense," Kelly said. "We need your experience and strength on the jab stick." Rick flushed, but waited silently as she continued, "I'll distract the bear. You jab him." She turned to Adam and, managing a weak smile, said, "Try not to shoot me."

She could hear Rick's deep indrawn breath. "Okay," he said, "I guess we'll have to do it that way." She listened carefully as he issued instructions. "Give wide berth to the bear. Get on the far side of him well out of his reach, and when I'm in position, you yell. Be prepared to retreat. Keep your feet under you and move."

The bear had raised his head at the sound of Rick's voice. He watched Kelly as she made her way up the mountain. She slipped through the grove of trees and across the drainage, always keeping an eye on Roscoe. As she moved to position herself up slope from the bear, he began to make the same sort of huffing sound the little black male had made. Kelly slowed. This bear was not little and cute, and his bluff seemed truly menacing. He started the strange tooth-clicking noise.

Kelly risked a quick glance at Rick. He nodded. Her heart started to pound. She could feel it hammering in her chest. She took a deep breath. She had to yell loud enough to get Roscoe's total attention, so Rick could get a good clean shot at the bear's rump and get safely away. The bear's mouth was open. She could see the long canine teeth. Kelly closed her eyes, but the bear kept clacking his teeth. Rick was waiting. She opened her eyes, raised her arms, and with one great rush of effort yelled, "Hey bear!"

Roscoe lunged forward, and she stumbled backward. The bear continued his charge, the cable stretching, pulling taut, straining. The bear's small eyes focused on her as he surged toward her. Kelly scrambled awkwardly away, trying to keep her footing in the wet grass. She was vaguely aware of Rick's raised arm beyond the bear.

Suddenly Roscoe whirled and rushed back through the ruined set toward Rick, who was moving away. Kelly turned and ran up the mountain and along the slope to Adam, who swung the gun smoothly, keeping it positioned on the bear. Kelly was wet with perspiration. When Rick joined them on the slope, clutching the jab stick, she could smell the pungent odor of his nervous sweat. They stood tensely as Roscoe moved around the tree to which the snare was chained. Silently, they watched as the bear's head began to bob. After another minute or two, the big bear sat down abruptly. And then he lay over in the grass. Rick said, "He's down. Are you ready to process him?"

Kelly could feel herself flush. "I think I have to go to the bathroom."

Adam looked at her with a wide grin, his eyes sparkling. "You mean you didn't already?"

It took all three of them to tug the big bear into a clear spot and stretch him out after they released the cable from his toes. "I'm so weak, I feel as if you jabbed *me* with that stick," Kelly said.

"Yeah," Adam said, "I noticed your head drooping."

"It's the aftermath of the adrenaline rush," Rick said. "You want to take care of his eyes?"

Rick was abrupt. *But he's right,* Kelly thought, *there'll be time enough after the bear is processed to discuss the experience.* She squeezed the ointment into the bear's eyes and covered its face with a cloth, trembling a little as she touched the strong jaw. The big bear was rusty red in his outer coat, but the softer underneath hair was a thick creamy beige.

"He's in great shape," Rick said. "Give him a ten for pelage and a five for fat layer."

"Where did he den?" Adam asked. "Do you know?"

"Yeah, that's the marvel of it. Last time I saw this old boy, he was asleep in a cave clear over on the other side of the mountain."

"Will you recollar him?"

"No. He's full grown. This collar has plenty of space, and there's time left on the battery."

The sun came out as the three of them worked the animal. The snare site was humid and steamy. The bear's wet hair smelled like wet dog hair. He had produced a large amount of scat. While the other two measured the bear, Kelly set the clipboard aside long enough to collect and label scat samples. Rick glanced up. "Are you still carrying that come-along in your pack?" he asked. Kelly nodded. "You want to get it?"

Kelly climbed up to the four-wheeler and retrieved the small winch. She had read that bears often lose weight in the first few weeks out of the den, but Roscoe had had little to do but eat and rest—no cubs to sap his strength, no bad weather, a fair amount of food. Coming back toward the bear, Kelly had a sudden flash of the moment she'd caught the bear's attention, and he had lunged toward her. She shivered, wondering if she could ever do that again.

She joined Rick and Adam in positioning the winch cable over a tree branch. "He's amazing," Adam said. "There's not a mark on him. The cable just rubbed the hair some."

Kelly nodded. "When he wakes up, he'll scarcely be aware that he was snared, but he's added a whole batch of information to our work sheets." Adam grunted with effort as he pulled Roscoe around and bound his front and hind legs.

"I didn't finish checking the snares in Warren Gulch," Rick said. "Let's get this guy weighed and pack up." Roscoe weighed three hundred and twenty-three pounds. Kelly shivered when Rick told her. She recorded the figures, aware of the stink of fear that permeated her clothes.

Rick returned from Warren Gulch as Adam and Kelly were finishing their lunch in the shade of the pickup. He looked hot and tired. Kelly handed him a can of pop. He shook his head when she offered him a sandwich. "No time," he said. "We've got another bear."

Kelly hated to get on the four-wheeler. The machine radiated heat. Where her legs touched Adam's legs, it was hot, and when she held on to him, his shirt was damp and sticky. She reached behind her and clung instead to the metal rack.

Processing the second bear was anticlimactic. It was a docile, brown two-year-old male, who was caught firmly around the right leg. This time Adam used the jab stick and the bear went down smoothly. They named him Ryan, for Kelly's little brother.

"We've been—what?—three-and-a-half weeks out here," Adam said, "and I would have bet that being this close to a bear would never seem routine, but this one's almost too easy."

Rick looked up from where he knelt affixing the ear tags, and said, "Yeah? Well you'd better train yourself to regard every bear as your first bear, or someday you'll make a mistake, and the bear will remind you." *Damn him,* Kelly thought. *He could allow us a little time to feel good about Roscoe.* They finished the bear in silence, pulling the tooth and measuring and weighing him, but not attaching a collar.

Back in the meadow, they scanned the area, picking up Jenny and Samantha. As usual, Rick worried aloud about Jenny. "I may get the houndsmen to help me tree her if she doesn't take one of those snares before long."

"I'd hate for us to use dogs," Kelly said.

"Better than Jenny's choking to death."

Even with the windows open, the truck was hot, and with the three of them crowded onto the seat, the cab stunk. Kelly scooted close to the door and thought about the day. She was tired, but she'd done her share. She was feeling proud and happy because she'd faced Roscoe and still been able to yell, when Rick said, "Now that we're catching some bears, we need to review the project." He reached up and scratched his head at the hairline and continued in a conversational tone. "Kelly's still our weak link." ∾

Chapter Twenty-Five

Kelly took in a sharp breath, feeling as if he'd slapped her. Adam glanced at her and then said to Rick, "How so?"

"Well, she can't use the gun. She didn't trust herself with the jab stick, and it's more difficult when we have to put a girl out in front of the bear." Adam nodded and said nothing else.

A *girl!* Kelly's sense of pride in her day's efforts vanished. She had done her share as a part of the project team, and she hadn't expected praise from Rick, but this wasn't fair. He had interpreted her rational decision to put the strongest team member on the jab stick as indecision about her own skills.

She was almost nauseated with anger and disappointment, but there was nothing to be gained by disputing Rick's words, especially since Adam seemed to agree with Rick. They rode in silence until Rick stopped the truck by the bait barrel and glanced across the cab at Kelly. "You might as well fill the bait box before cleaning up."

Kelly opened the door and stepped down. When Adam joined her at the barrel, she looked up in surprise. "I thought you agreed with Rick that since I'm only fit to lug bait, I might as well be the one to do it."

"I didn't say that." Adam's face was red.

"You agreed that I'm the weak link on the project."

"I did not. I agreed that it's difficult to put a woman in danger." Adam hauled a chunk of putrid meat from the barrel.

Kelly felt a little less angry, but she said, "So you don't think a woman belongs in the field after all."

Adam met her eyes. "In theory, Kelly, I believe women have the right to be part of the project, but . . ." He grinned slightly. "It's hard to aim that Ruger at a cute little green-eyed blonde, when you're scared you might shoot her, or else the damned bear will eat her alive." She knew that Adam meant to be kind, but his words showed her how little progress she'd made. She swung the last chunk of rotten meat into the box and fastened the lid.

The cabin was hot even before Rick fired up the stove. "Let's get these data sheets filled out while the water heats," Rick said, spreading the sheets on the table. "Adam, you can put Roscoe's donation into the scat box." As Adam stepped outside, the houndsmen pulled up in front of the porch. "Damn," Rick said. "Last thing we need is them snooping around our records." But Walt and George were into the cabin before Rick could regather the data sheets.

Walt nodded at Kelly and said, "Hey, Rick, how's it going?" He picked up the field sheet for the young male bear and began to read it. Rick's face darkened, but he didn't say anything.

Exasperated, Kelly stood and collected the rest of the sheets. Reaching for the paper the bear hunter held, she said, "Would you like something to drink?" She took hold of the data sheet. Walt's forehead creased into a frown, but Kelly kept the paper in her grasp, and he released it.

"You guys got beer?"

"Not allowed," Kelly said, "but you're welcome to a can of Pepsi or 7-Up." She pushed the paperwork toward Rick who stuffed it into the file and moved to shove the file under his bed.

"We've got beer in the truck," Walt said. He and George turned toward the door. Kelly took a six-pack of 7-Up from the cooler and pulled three cans from the plastic rings. She gave one to Rick, and they stepped onto the porch where Adam took the can she offered him. Walt and George had popped the top of two beer cans. As Walt and George settled onto the cement porch, their client, Harry Selnick, got out of the pickup and joined them.

"How come you guys aren't hunting?" Rick asked.

"Too hot," George said.

"Where are your dogs?" Adam asked.

"Tied up at camp," George said. "Your whole place stinks of bear shit. Drives the dogs crazy." Kelly leaned against the cabin, too tired to join a conversation, glad that no one focused on her, but still determined to show Rick that she was a team member.

At first, the talk was of bears. The guides tried to pump Rick, but he gave evasive answers. Adam hunkered down by the scat box and spread Roscoe's samples on the screened floor. Walt said, "Where'd you get all that shit?"

"On the mountain," Adam said. He latched the cover, wiped his hands on his pants, and sat down on the edge of the porch.

Harry Selnick looked hot and tired. He drank from the beer can Walt handed him, but finished only one beer to the houndsmen's three apiece. Rick went in once and fed the fire. Adam didn't mention dinner, and Kelly knew by the look on his face that he had no intention of cooking for the whole group. *Why don't they just go back to their own camp?* But the houndsmen didn't leave, and the conversation deteriorated.

Walt and George reeled off exaggerated stories of bear kills, and then they began to tell jokes. Kelly stayed in place, trying to be just part of the group, but the jokes grew raunchier, and when George launched into a story that began, "This little gal was raped one night, and she told the cops, 'Well, I couldn't see him, but I know he was a Texan . . .'" Kelly turned and went into the cabin. She didn't care what Rick thought about her leaving. She wasn't such a weak link that she had to listen to rape jokes.

She poured hot water into the dishpan and bent over to shampoo her hair. She rinsed by pouring cupfuls of water over her head. When she reached out for her towel, she couldn't find it. She fumbled a moment before someone placed the towel into her hand. Startled, she raised her head. Harry Selnick was standing in the kitchen. Kelly dried her hair quickly. The man just stood there. Finally, nodding over his shoulder toward the porch, he said, "I'm sorry about that." His words had a soft edge. Kelly picked up her comb. The man still stood, his big Stetson in his hand, as if waiting for her to excuse him, or forgive him, or something.

"Why do you hunt with them?" she asked, bending her head to comb the tangles from her hair.

"They're good houndsmen," Harry Selnick said. "They organize a successful hunt, provide a decent camp."

He was different from the houndsmen, and Kelly was suddenly interested in learning more about him. She laid the comb aside and wrapped the towel around her head, turban style. "Would you like to sit down?"

He pulled a chair from the table and sat, knees slightly apart, turning the hat in his hands. Dusk was approaching, and the cabin was shadowy. Kelly lit the lamp and sat down, too, studying the rich man from Arizona. He was smaller than she had remembered, five feet eight inches maybe, and not over one hundred sixty pounds at the most. His hair was a dull blonde and thinning, though he probably wasn't yet forty-five. His eyebrows were nearly colorless. He kept turning the white Stetson around and around in his small hands, which were graceful and beautifully manicured. He seemed to be staring at his feet, which were also small. His expensive snakeskin cowboy boots shone, even in the fading light. He certainly hadn't done much bear hunting in *that* footwear. "How can you hike in those boots?" Kelly asked.

The man looked up at her, his eyes a surprisingly rich gray-blue. He glanced again at his feet and then back at her, his face flushing. "I haven't hiked any," he said. "I've mostly been in the truck." He laughed in a nervous way. "Walt and George are having a little trouble locating bears this year."

"Maybe there aren't as many bears as there used to be," Kelly said, understanding now why Walt had reached so greedily for their location sheets. She studied Harry Selnick, not sure what to say next.

He seemed to be having the same problem. He cleared his throat and looking back toward his boots, said, "It's not just for the bears, you know. That's not why I come."

Kelly said, "Then why?"

He met her eyes briefly, but once more directed his answer toward his boots. "For the company—for the camp as well as the hunt."

"You *like* those guys?" It wasn't a polite question, but Kelly was so startled she couldn't have held it back.

"I have liked them. Yes." His face muscles were taut; a nerve jumped in his cheek. She knew he was seeing his companions in a different light because of her presence on the mountain.

"Why?" She had to know, because to her, the big, hairy, filthy-mouthed houndsmen were boors—ignorant, crude, and cruel, totally unlike this apparently cultured man.

"They're free. They live unfettered lives, doing mostly what they choose to do. Their own skills lead directly to results." He hesitated and then added, "Their work isn't filtered through a thousand employees and middle-management and accountants and lawyers and PR men and . . ." He let the rest of it trail away.

Kelly knew he was talking about his own business, and she had never heard a man sound so tired. "Doesn't the money—your money— make up for it?"

He smiled at her, but his eyes were bleak, more gray now than blue. "My money goes to my ex-wife, to my kids, to a house I hate, except for the trophy room." He stopped abruptly.

"Do you have a lot of trophies?"

His smile was real now and reached his eyes, returning their blue. "Yes, I have some magnificent animals."

Kelly swallowed, knowing Dr. Andrews would tell her to keep her mouth shut, but she had to ask. "Then why do you need to shoot another one?"

She had overstepped her bounds. She could see him turn into the forceful executive who had made all that money. His face closed, and he answered brusquely. "That's the whole point of hiring houndsmen. I wouldn't be here otherwise." He rose from the chair and Kelly stood, too. "Thank you for your hospitality, Miss Jones." He raised the Stetson and tipped it to her before placing it on his head and stepping out the door.

Kelly took the towel from her hair and picked up the comb. Adam and Rick came into the cabin. "So what were you and Selnick having such a cozy conference about?" Rick asked. Kelly realized that she and the bear hunter had been spotlighted by the lamp as the sun had faded. Adam had halted to hear her reply, too. Kelly combed her hair with strong irritated strokes. Couldn't she even have a conversation that belonged to her? "Did he pump you about the bears we've located?" Rick demanded. "Did you tell him anything?"

Kelly laughed. All Rick ever cared about were bears. "No," she said, "we talked about his money and his snakeskin boots." Kelly went into her cubicle and began to take the last of her clean clothes from her suitcase.

Adam came to lean against the doorjamb. "Is that really all you talked about with Selnick?"

She nodded. "Mostly. I seem to make him nervous." She smiled at Adam. "I asked him why he needed another trophy."

Adam whistled. "Dr. Andrews would frown on questions like that. What did Selnick say?"

"I got the idea that he hunts to make up for all that he's not; to try to get back all that he's lost." She added her flashlight, a washcloth, towel, and soap to the pile of clothes and picked it up.

Adam stepped aside as she moved out of her room. "Where are you going?"

"To take a shower."

"You aren't going to McCarthy's place this time of night?"

"No, Mother," Kelly said, putting the pile of clothes on the counter while she dipped hot water into the bucket and took a small sauce pan from the nail. "I'm going to take a shower in the *privy*. You know where that word comes from don't you? It means *private*."

"It's dark out there," Adam said. "Do you want me to come and hold the flashlight?"

Kelly grinned at him. "Well, I would, Adam, but I'm awfully hungry, so you'd better stay here and cook my dinner." Adam saluted and held the door open for her. She was suddenly aware of Adam as a leavening factor. Like yeast in bread dough, Adam's kidding raised her heavy spirits. *He may not approve of my being on this project, but at least he treats me like a friend.*

Once in the outhouse, she stripped, lathered her entire body, and gave herself over to the pure pleasure of scrubbing with the washcloth. Then she took the saucepan and, dipping it into the bucket again and again, she dumped water over her shoulders and splashed it onto her body. As the water drained away through the floorboards and she stood on the damp wood, naked and clean, she felt enough better that she could allow herself to think about Rick's description of her as a weak link.

Maybe it was partly true. She needed to learn to shoot a pistol, but she'd used most of her spare grocery money for gassing up the four-wheeler. Without money for a gun and ammunition, she couldn't learn to shoot. Sighing, she picked up the empty bucket and her dirty clothes, and went toward the house.

"Do you think man really has the right to dominate, to make management decisions for a bear?" Adam asked as they finished dinner. Kelly took his empty plate and started the dishes.

Rick reached to the lamp, which had started smoking, and adjusted the wick. Then he said, "With the intelligence man has, it's his nature to dominate." Rick glanced at Kelly. "And that includes women, too—the human species."

"Don't bears try to dominate?"

"Yeah, in their own way, all species try to dominate."

"Do bears mark territory?"

"In some areas they mark trees and chew on signs, perhaps evidence of territoriality. But last fall in a drainage over on the other side of the mountain, there were eight bears within a quarter of a mile of each other: All ages, male and female, even cubs sharing the same area for almost a week."

Kelly was intrigued. "Isn't that unusual?"

"Yeah, perhaps. There was an abundance of acorns, which may have thrown them out of their normal behavior." Rick was into his favorite subject. "Usually mothers and cubs are together, and adult females may have overlapping home ranges. A male may overlap several females." Rick stretched and yawned. "That's why we're seeing these young males. Their mamas have kicked them out and they have to find new turf." He pushed his chair back and bent to pull the data file from under his bed. "We'd better finish our work and hit the sack." He spread the papers on the table. "I want to put two or three new sets at the top of Moreno Creek tomorrow." He turned toward Kelly. "One of these days, I'm going to outsmart *your* bear. That sow Samantha is dominating us, and I'm tired of lugging dead meat up and down hill for her." ∾

Chapter Twenty-Six

Thursday was a long, hot day with no bears, but more scat than Kelly felt like collecting and too much bouncing around on the steep trail along the Moreno Creek drainage. Adam grumbled out loud. "Damn it, Santini, these Moreno Creek sets will add three hours work to every day, just getting up here to check them."

If Rick had been gracious or diplomatic or had even bothered to ask their advice, it would have made the day easier, but all he said was, "You're on this project to work, and there's good sign up here." Kelly was silent, but she also had her doubts about putting twenty-two sets so far apart. If they ever snared more than two bears in a day, they would be well after dark finishing the processing.

On Friday morning, Andy, the little black bear, was snared in Warren Gulch. "Well, what are you doing over here?" Rick asked in the gentle tone he reserved for the animals. He turned to Kelly. "Didn't we catch him on Chase Creek the first time?" She nodded, and at the movement, the little bear swung his head toward her.

Each time their crew snared a bear, the boredom, fatigue, and irritation dropped away from them immediately, but Andy added even extra attraction to the work. He was brave and funny. Kelly was determined to get experience, but she was sorry that she had to jab the little bear. He definitely had character.

As Kelly and Adam approached him from different angles, he couldn't decide what to do. He made a rush at Adam, clacking his teeth, and then whirled to face Kelly. When they didn't go away, but just stood and laughed, Andy sat down and leaned against the tree. "If his thumb weren't so hairy, he'd be sucking it," Rick said. "Go ahead, Kelly. Put him down and let's get him out of the snare."

"Maybe you've learned your lesson," Kelly said to the little bear as Adam positioned himself to distract him. The bear looked at her, his head tipped to one side, small brown eyes mournful. Adam yelled. The black bear spun toward him, and Kelly delivered the anesthetic.

They checked him, measured him, and weighed him. He had gained five pounds, but he still seemed tiny to Kelly as she looked back to where he was sleeping off the drug. Adam had the same thought. "He has a long way to go before he's as big as Roscoe."

They split up to check the rest of the sets, and Adam and Kelly met a logging truck. Matt was riding in the passenger's seat. He jerked his head in a curt greeting, but didn't wave. Seeing Matt, Kelly was washed with regret. He hadn't even smiled. She felt a sense of loss as she watched the truck go down the road. Adam was watching *her*. He said, "He'd probably come back if you asked him."

She shook her head. "I don't want to do that. I just wish he'd valued our friendship more. We had a lot of fun together."

They had to replace stolen bait at one of the sets on Moreno Creek. Kelly was tired and dirty when they pulled around the curve to the cabin late Friday afternoon, and she was dismayed to see the university van. Dr. Andrews would be wanting detailed reports, and if he'd brought visitors, the cabin would be crowded. Adam and Rick must have felt the same way for almost in unison, they said, "Oh, shit—company."

But the next moment, Kelly's fatigue was forgotten. As Rick shut off the engine, Peggy and Ryan stepped from the cabin door. In an instant, Kelly was out of the truck, hugging first Peggy, then Ryan, and then both together. Ryan wriggled from her grasp as Rick and Adam emerged from the truck. There was a sudden bustle of introductions and fire-building and unloading the van. The table was soon covered with grocery sacks. Kelly unrolled Peggy's sleeping bag next to her own bed, filling all the floor space.

Peggy looked around. "This is the smallest room we've ever shared. Do you mind?"

"Mind? I'd sleep in the outhouse if it meant I'd have your company."

Peggy smiled at her, but she seemed subdued. There was neither time nor privacy for conversation. Dr. Andrews wanted to review the bear reports. He accepted their scat samples with a grin. "You've been working." He stepped around his and Ryan's sleeping gear to study the map. Turning to Rick, he asked, "Aren't you pushing it with this many sets so far apart?"

Rick flushed. "The bears are high yet," he said. "I thought it would be worth the chance." Kelly wished they would hurry and finish discussing business. She was dying to talk with Peggy. But Dr. Andrews had to have the whole report of the three bears they'd processed.

Rick started with Andy. Their professor was interested in knowing that the little black male had crossed over into a different drainage. When Rick spoke of the two-year-old bear they'd named Ryan, her brother's eyes took on a shine. "Really? You named a bear after me?" Then Rick told the story of Roscoe's capture and processing. Peggy perked up, Ryan said, "Oh, wow," and even Dr. Andrews seemed to be enthralled. Kelly herself felt the drama of it as Rick depicted the big cinnamon-colored bear straining against the cable, caught by just two toes.

Dr. Andrews questioned Rick at length about the processing. They discussed the pros and cons of dart guns over jab sticks, and finally,

Dr. Andrews gathered the data sheets and handed them to Rick. "You've had a busy week." He looked around the cabin, which was hot and stuffy. "Why don't we stow all this stuff, fry some hamburgers, and picnic on the porch?"

Rick said to Ryan, "You want to come help me gas up the four-wheelers?"

Ryan left without a backward glance. Peggy said, "Once again the Santini charm strikes the Jones family."

Kelly caught Adam's quick look at Peggy. His face had turned red, but he said nothing. She had no idea what he was feeling, and Adam didn't say anything but "I'll get some wood."

Before Kelly could speak, Peggy said, "I've got some stuff for you in the van," and she left the cabin, too. Kelly returned to her room to put the canned goods on the narrow shelves.

Dr. Andrews came to the door and watched her for a moment. Then he said, "It took courage to face that big bear, Kelly." She could feel herself flush as she thought of the bear and of Rick's saying, "Kelly's our weak link." She looked silently at the can of pork and beans she held in her hand. Dr. Andrews leaned his tall frame against the doorjamb. "Is there some sort of problem?"

She met his eyes. It wouldn't help the project for her to complain, and besides Rick wasn't entirely wrong. She said, "No, but you're the first person to mention that distracting Roscoe took courage."

Dr. Andrews laughed, and the tension dissolved. "That doesn't surprise me, Kelly. Those two guys were probably scared stiff, and it didn't make them feel any better to see you acting brave."

Kelly was engulfed in a rush of feeling: understanding, relief, and a kind of fierce joy. She had been so depressed by Rick and Adam's criticism, it had never occurred to her that they had been just as scared as she was. She said to Dr. Andrews, "How do you do that?"

He looked puzzled. "Do what?"

"Find just the right words to make a situation better. You also did that the last time you were here." Dr. Andrews flushed, but he looked pleased, and Kelly was surprised by another moment of insight. *He needs a little praise now and then, too.* She smiled at him. "It must be tough, scrounging for money, keeping track of equipment, and leaving home every weekend to check up on us."

Dr. Andrews nodded, still blushing. He fished in his pocket for a package of gum and unwrapped a stick as Adam came in with a load of wood, followed by Peggy, who brought a shopping bag to Kelly's room. Dr. Andrews turned away and began to get out paper plates and cups. Peggy dumped the contents of the shopping bag on Kelly's bed. "Mom sent you an entire new wardrobe—jeans, shirts, and underwear." Instead of staying to chat while Kelly finished stowing the groceries, Peggy stepped to the table to help Dr. Andrews. Kelly lost some of her holiday feeling. What was eating Peggy?

Rick dominated the dinner conversation. Ryan asked dozens of questions about the project and Rick, his face clear and handsome, answered every question patiently and fully without being condescending to the twelve-year-old. Peggy seemed remote. Dr. Andrews ate silently.

Adam had chosen a spot slightly apart from the group. If he and Peggy were the clowns who were supposed to entertain their families, neither one was doing a very good job. Kelly thought of asking Adam to show Ryan the Ruger Redhawk, but remembering Adam's sour comments about her being "activities director" when Jonathan and Kevin had visited the project, she said nothing. The meal dragged along.

Finally, when the air became chilly, they carried the remaining food into the house. Smiling, Dr. Andrews said, "I'll do the dishes." He scooped up the paper plates and napkins and stuffed them into a garbage sack that he stowed in the van, and at last Kelly had a chance to be with Peggy.

"Come to the outhouse with me," she said, and the two of them went to the privy. Sitting in the dark, Kelly waited for Peggy to speak, but her sister said only, "The stars are pretty here."

Kelly ignored that and said, "Peggy, what's the matter? Is there something wrong at home?"

Her sister sighed in the dark. "There's enough wrong at home, yes, but that's not why I came up here. I have to ask you something."

"Well, what?"

Peggy cleared her throat and then blurted out, "Would you care if I started dating Matt?" ❧

Chapter Twenty-Seven

Kelly started to laugh. "Is that all? Is that what's been keeping you so uptight?"

Peggy sounded defensive. "Well, you went with him a long time. When he asked me, he told me you were all through, but I wanted to be sure. I like him, but I wanted to be sure."

They stepped out of the privy, and Kelly turned to draw her sister into a hug. "Honey, it would be a big favor to me if you'd date Matt. Then I wouldn't have to worry about his coming to the cabin again." She looked around. "Let's go sit in my car and talk."

Once the dam was broken, their conversation poured out. Though she could not bring herself to use the term "weak link," she told Peggy about the men's comments after the processing of Roscoe. Her sister's immediate understanding was a healing balm. "And they didn't even tell you how brave you were? Oh, pooh. Men and their stupid pride. I think you're a heroine."

But when Kelly described the various encounters with the houndsmen, Peggy said, "I've been reading some women's stuff, Kelly, and kind of looking around at the men I know. Maybe in the big cities, men have changed, but I don't think they're changing very fast out here. You be careful." She was silent a moment, and then she said, "I think things are changing at home, though."

Kelly tensed. This was more what she had expected. "What's happening?"

"It seems as if we were all odd-shaped pieces held together like some Rubik's cube, and when you pulled away, the whole thing started falling apart." Kelly put a hand on Peggy's shoulder. "I'm so tired," Peggy said. "They argue at night and sometimes even during the days. They're both just miserable, and they're making us miserable."

Kelly had a flash of her father's face on the day he had encouraged her to go to the bear project. "I knew that Dad wasn't happy."

"I wish you hadn't gone away. It's too hard to keep Ryan cheered up. He kind of mopes around the house." Peggy took a deep breath. "Kelly, I'm thinking of leaving home."

"How can you do that?"

"I've got a job, and I may quit school."

"Oh, Peggy." There was a firmness in her sister's statement that made Kelly feel sad. "What do the folks think about that?"

"I haven't told them. I wanted to talk to you first. Kelly, do you think it would be fair to Ryan?" Kelly's pretty, happy sister sounded old. Her voice was flat. Kelly felt such a rush of anger toward her parents that she could not speak. They'd blundered into marriage. They'd let Grandma run their lives. When were they going to grow up? Ryan was their responsibility, not Peggy's; but she knew how Peggy was feeling, because her own heart leaded up with guilt. By coming into the field, she had left Ryan and Peggy to fend for themselves.

"I don't know, Peggy, maybe I should go home." The words were hard to say. She absolutely did not want to go home.

Peggy said, "I don't think you would fit back into the puzzle. You've changed somehow." She sighed and then asked, "Did you ever try to talk to Mother about anything serious?"

"Not often," Kelly said. "It doesn't work very well for me. She avoids serious subjects; and if you push her, she offers literary allusions that aren't much help."

"I hate the way she does that." Peggy scrunched down in the seat and tapped a curled fist on her knee. "She's always been so uptight about quitting school, I'm half afraid to quit. I wish I could talk to her about it."

Rick came out onto the porch. "Kelly? We're about to shut down for the night."

Kelly laughed. "There's my keeper. We'd better go in."

As they left the car and went toward the cabin, Peggy said, "I've got Santini figured out. He's the big cheese, but what's with that Adam? Does he just cook, or is he really part of the crew?"

Kelly considered the question seriously, picturing Adam as the three of them worked together. She said, "Well, as you know, Rick seems to be the focal point, but Adam never makes a misstep. He has learned everything I've learned." It was true. Adam talked very little about the project, but he was adept at all phases.

"You like him don't you?"

"Yes, I do. His sense of humor keeps Rick and me from each other's throats."

Of course, everybody wanted to go to the snares on Saturday morning. Ryan continued to shadow Rick, and no one had the heart to deny him a spot behind Rick on the four-wheeler for a trip to Moreno Creek. Dr. Andrews said to Kelly, "You take your sister and check Warren Gulch; then let us have the machine, and Adam and I will go to Chase Creek."

There was an old female snared about halfway up Chase Creek. Dr. Andrews sent Adam back to help ferry the group to the site. Watching Ryan's interest in everything and his eagerness to help, Kelly wished he were old enough to be on a crew. He caught on much more quickly than Kevin had. Rick studied the old bear and then said to Ryan, "Do you want to holler at her?"

Ryan nodded eagerly and listened intently to the instructions before he turned to go around the bear. When he yelled "Hey Bear!" it was loud enough to startle everyone, including the bear, but Ryan didn't seem frightened when she turned his way.

When the bear was down, Peggy followed Kelly to the snare, but she backed away from the smell of the bait, saying, "Yuck, how can you stand that day after day?"

The bear was a mousey brown, and she was in poor shape. Dr. Andrews eyed her for a moment and then said to Rick, "What do you think? Is she about eleven?"

Rick nodded. "Yeah, and she shows it." He tipped the bear's lip back to expose a broken canine tooth and general tooth wear. Then, running a hand through the fur, he said, "She's got some gray hairs, too."

Kelly knelt to look closely at the bear. Dr. Andrews said, "She's pretty emaciated. Collar her, Rick. Let's see if she makes it through the winter."

When it came time to name the bear sow, Rick turned to Peggy and said, "Shall we name her Peggy?"

Peggy wrinkled her nose. "No. I don't want you to name an old, sick bear after me." She considered and said, "Name her Marilyn." Kelly was surprised and troubled. Marilyn was their mother's name. She caught Ryan's quick glance, but neither of them said anything, and Rick nodded at Kelly, who reluctantly wrote Marilyn at the top of the data sheet. Peggy seemed so angry.

It was a relief when Dr. Andrews and her siblings went away on Sunday morning, and that knowledge made Kelly sad and quiet. *I don't want to deal with the family's problems. I don't even want to be part of the family right now.* When they got back from checking the snares, which were empty, Kelly and Adam cleaned the cabin. Visitors meant clutter, no matter who they were. She said to him, "I'm always glad to see that ugly vinyl again because it means that there aren't sleeping bags spread all over."

"Really," Adam said with a nod. He wrung out a mop and began swinging it across the garish flowers on the floor covering. "Your sister wasn't what I expected."

"She has a few problems at the moment." Kelly was cleaning the stove, which had hamburger grease on it. She stopped to smile at Adam. "But she's going to solve one of my problems."

"How so?"

"She's going to start dating Matt."

Adam leaned on the mop to look at her. "And you really don't care?"

Kelly shook her head. "I don't want to be owned."

"Is that what you think a relationship is all about? Possession?"

"Of one sort or another."

"Mature relationships don't have to be that way."

Thinking of her parents, Kelly scowled and said, "I've never seen a mature relationship." Then she grinned at Adam and said, "Mature relationship. That sounds funny coming out of your mouth—too old and too wise for a junior in college. How old are you anyway?"

"I'm twenty-three."

"Just a year younger than I am. Did you start college late?"

"Not for a member of the church. I did a two-year mission first."

"Oh, that's right." Kelly smiled at him again. "That's what aged you."

"Tell me about it." He made a sour face. "I was in Detroit."

Rick was in Kelly's room, storing the new drug bottles Dr. Andrews had brought. He looked down at Kelly as she came in to fold her new clothes and store them in her suitcase. "Your brother's a smart kid."

❧

Kelly enjoyed a visit with Jamie McCarthy Monday evening when he came by to take her with him to check his tanks. Tuesday, they snared a tan three-year-old female in Warren Gulch. Before Kelly took the jab stick, she said to Adam, "Do you mind if I do all the jabbing from now on? Rick knows how, so he doesn't need to do it, but I'll split the job with you if you want to get experience, too."

Adam shook his head. "I've done enough to know that I can do it. Have at it, Kelly."

They named the three-year-old Pamela. "That's my little sister's name," Rick said, with a friendly glance at Kelly. "It tickled your little brother so much to have a bear named after him, it might mean something to Pammy. I'll send her a postcard one of these days."

Kelly jabbed the bear and helped with the collaring. Then Rick pulled the tooth. Kelly administered a shot of penicillin carefully, but she was thinking more about the things that affected the team than she was about the bear. Each surge of visitors left its flotsam on their beach. Ryan's visit seemed to have brought out emotions in Rick besides his concern for bears.

Wednesday morning, when Adam and Kelly got to the top of Moreno Creek and walked in to check the first snare, they found Andy with the cable around his leg. "Oh, you dumb little bear," Kelly said. Andy wasn't happy. He jerked at the cable and clawed the tree and moved around and around the set site.

"It won't do you any good to huff and puff," Adam said. "We'll still have to come back and poke you."

They checked the other two sets and then went to find Rick. They could hear his four-wheeler roaring down Warren Gulch as they shut theirs off at the meadow. "We've got Andy again," Kelly said.

Rick laughed, but said, "Well, we can't do him at the moment. We've also got Roscoe."

Kelly's heart began to pound. "How is he snared?"

"Perfectly. But it looks like he's been there all night, and I want to get him processed and on his way." Adam started the four-wheeler again, and they bounced back to Roscoe. Kelly delivered the anesthetic to the big bear with a strong jab and a good follow-through. By the time Roscoe had swung away from Adam, who had yelled at him, she was back in a safe zone.

"It's fun processing him when your palms aren't sweaty," she said. There wasn't much to do. They double-checked their previous measurements. He hadn't gained more weight in the ten days since they had caught him the first time, but he was huge anyway and a magnificent creature. Kelly lifted his lips and looked at the long canines and the powerful, grinding teeth. She sat down on the ground beside him and held his forearm in her lap while she extended his claws.

"What are you doing?" Adam asked.

"Looking at this bear for the first time," Kelly said with a laugh.

Rick watched as Kelly ran her fingers through the bear's thick fur and inspected his belly and genitalia and tail. "When you're done invading that animal's privacy, we'll get on up to Moreno Creek and release Andy." Kelly helped to stretch Roscoe out, and she covered his eyes again, but even when they were finished, they lingered. "Damn, but he's beautiful," Rick said, and Adam knelt suddenly to touch the bear once more.

"I'm glad we didn't mark him in any way," Adam said. "Doc Morrison said that the snare burns don't really hurt them that much, but it's great when we can process him clean."

They stood in the drainage silently, looking down at the red-coated bear, and Kelly knew that she would put up with anything—Rick's scorn, the houndsmen, the smells, dirty hair, anything—to stay on the project. Each time they were close to a bear, they shared a feeling she couldn't describe, but she knew what Adam meant when he said, "How can city people understand their relationship to nature and to God if they never get into the wilds?"

"That's what draws them," Rick said. "And then it overwhelms them, and they have to drive fast vehicles and shoot loud guns to prove that they're still top of the heap." Kelly shivered with emotion, feeling closer to these two than she had ever felt to anyone.

Andy was a comic relief. They clowned around and observed the little bear's reactions longer than they should have. When Kelly finally put him down, and they released him, Rick said, "I'm tempted to set a snare in a fourth drainage, just to see if this little guy will cross over the ridge and catch himself again."

"He should take lessons from Samantha about avoiding snares," Kelly said.

Adam laughed. "That brown sow is a thief."

"She's a survivor!"

They decided to redo Andy's set and wait for him to wake up. When the little black bear had wobbled groggily into the trees, they returned to Warren Gulch and rebuilt Roscoe's barricades. He had trashed them thoroughly during his all-night stand.

It had been such an absolutely perfect day that they prolonged it after dinner by naming all their bears—Samantha, Andy, Betsy, Roscoe, Ryan, Marilyn, Pamela—and remembering how they looked—their condition, weight, and color. They even spoke briefly and sadly of Marie's cub. It was like spending an evening looking through family photo albums.

As they moved to put the data sheets away, Adam said, "Kelly, I need to ask you a favor." Kelly turned toward him. "Tomorrow is my folks' anniversary. I'd like to go into Moab and send flowers. May I borrow your car?"

Kelly said, "Sure."

"Is that okay with you, Santini?"

Rick nodded. "Kelly and I can check snares." He took out his wallet. "Here. Use the university credit card and fill our gas cans. And stock up on groceries. No sense wasting a trip. We need peanut butter for the bait, too."

After Adam left the next morning, Rick and Kelly gathered their equipment and checked the snares. They processed a brown female yearling on Chase Creek. Rick said, "Your sister wouldn't mind if we hooked her name onto this little one. She's in good shape and good looking, too." So they named the bear Peggy; and when she woke up, they rebuilt the set.

At the meadow, they picked up some dead aspen to be used for firewood. After they reloaded the four-wheelers and climbed into the truck, Rick reached, as usual, for the antenna to the receiver. He stuck it out the window with his left hand and fiddled with the knob on the receiver with his right.

Kelly listened idly until she heard something different. She raised a hand toward the volume knob, but Rick had heard it too, and he increased the sound before she could. He turned to her, and his face was white as chalk. "That's a mortality beep."

Kelly's throat tightened. She squeezed her eyes shut for a moment and then said, "Which one?"

Rick's voice was absolutely flat. "Roscoe." Kelly heard him swallow. "We're getting a mortality beep on Roscoe." ⌒

Chapter Twenty-Eight

"Where is he?" Kelly asked.

"I don't know, except that he's not up near the ridge, or the signal wouldn't be so clear." Rick handed the antenna to Kelly. "Hold it out your window," he said as he started the truck. "We have to find him."

"What do you suppose happened to him?" Kelly asked. "He didn't seem to have any reaction to the anesthetic." Rick just shrugged.

They followed the signal along the lower road until suddenly Rick said, "I know where he is." Kelly looked at him. His mouth was set in a straight tight line and his face was dark.

"Where?"

"He's in the houndsmen's camp."

"Oh, Rick, no." He just nodded, and there was nothing else for her to say. They drove in miserable silence toward the small grove of trees at the edge of a level meadow where the houndsmen had pitched a tent. As they followed the hunters' tire tracks to the camp, Kelly could hear the dogs snapping and snarling and the men's voices as they cursed the dogs.

She saw the form hanging in the tree just as Rick said, "They've already skinned him." Kelly's stomach heaved.

"Can that really be Roscoe?" she said, unable to take her eyes from the body. It hung upside down, the hind legs stretched apart and fastened to a heavy stick, which swung by a rope from a branch. "It looks human." Her mouth twisted as she spoke, and she had to swallow the rise of bile.

Rick's Adam's apple bobbed, and then he said in his lecturing tone, "Bears are plantigrade, which means they walk on the palms of their feet like humans do, and a lot of their bone structure is similar to humans. When a bear stands up on its hind legs, it can walk just like a human." He sounded so cold, so remote, that Kelly knew he was as upset as she.

"Are they just going to leave him there?"

"Probably," Rick said. "Ninety percent of the hunters we get up here only want the pelt." As Rick brought the truck to a stop outside the camp, she could see that Roscoe had been totally skinned, even the paws. Without fur and claws, the paws that hung down looked like human hands.

Rick said, "Some poachers kill for claws and gallbladder—Orientals consider a bear gallbladder an aphrodisiac—but it's illegal to sell them." He sounded as if he were controlling his breathing with his cold, careful words. "Experienced guys like Walker and Johnson skin the bear totally—skin out the knuckles, the hands, and then skin out the head and just take the hide with them."

"What are we going to do?"

"*You* are going to do nothing." Rick put a hand on her shoulder. "These guys will be defensive enough knowing that they've shot one of our collared bears, but if you show up in that camp, they'll be downright belligerent." He tightened his grip on her shoulder. "No matter what happens, you stay in the truck."

Kelly nodded dumbly, and Rick released her and opened the truck door. "I'm going to try to get the collar and tags back without getting into a hassle." Kelly watched as Rick went toward the campsite and spoke to the houndsmen. She scrunched down in the seat as Walt Johnson glanced toward the pickup.

Folding her arms across her stomach and trying to stop the churning of her insides, she looked away from the carcass. But it didn't help to look away. She had already registered every detail in her mind: Roscoe had kept some of his fat over the winter, and the layer of fat gave the body a yellowish tinge. The skull had been skinned, but the eyeballs were still there, bulging in the bony sockets. If she thought about that terrible carcass as belonging to Roscoe, she *would* throw up. She took a deep breath as she recalled the magnificent bear, caught by two toes and rushing toward her. She remembered the lush feel of his thick coat when she had held him in her lap the second time they had snared him. He was in his prime. He would have been a good mate for Samantha. She looked back toward Roscoe.

Rick was now standing by the bear's carcass. If she knew him, he was getting as much data from the remains as he could before leaving the camp. In a moment, he came to the truck. Climbing in, he handed Kelly the collar and tags. "He wasn't in bad shape. He had more fat than you'd think. He wintered well." She glanced at him. The muscle in his jaw was a solid knot.

When they reached the cabin, Adam was carrying groceries up the steps. He turned from the table where he set them and looked at Kelly, who still held Roscoe's tags. "What's wrong?" Adam said, and then he saw the broken collar and took a deep breath. "Who?"

"Roscoe," Rick said shortly. He dug in his pocket and brought out several bills. "Selnick gave me two hundred dollars to have the collar redone."

"You mean the houndsmen killed him?" Adam said. Rick nodded and dumped the money on the table. Adam erupted with such anger that Kelly stepped back. Adam seldom even used slang, but now he poured out a cascade of furious words. Kelly, and Rick too, just stood while Adam called the houndsmen names. It helped to listen to him, as if he voiced their own anger. Finally, Adam turned to Rick. "Can they do that? Can they shoot a collared bear?"

Rick looked spent. He nodded and said tersely, "It's legal." He took the collar and tags from Kelly. Then he pulled the data file from under the bed. Kelly knew it had to be done, but she could not watch Rick record Roscoe's death on the data sheet. She went to the wood shed.

She chopped wood while tears ran down her face. She didn't stop working until Adam came to the shed. "Supper's ready," he said. She leaned the axe against the shed wall and turned. Adam stepped forward and put his arms around her. For a brief moment, she leaned her head against his shoulder. Then he said, "Rick's waiting."

They ate little and went to bed early. Kelly couldn't sleep. Her grief over the big bear had turned into hot steady anger: *This is just one more thing that Dr. Andrews expects us to be discreet about. Well, it's stupid to try to study a bear that is fair game for every holdover from the Old West who feels that shooting a bear will make him a man.*

But Kelly knew that she would have to swallow this, too, and keep her mouth shut. She wasn't here to change the system. Rick was already concerned about her aggravating the houndsmen, and Dr. Andrews would remind her that hunting impacts were part of the study.

Friday there were two bears, one on Chase Creek, one in Warren Gulch, both females. But the fun had gone out of it. Rick worked efficiently and silently. Adam was morose, and Kelly felt despairing. "Does collaring make it easier for the houndsmen to find our bears?" she asked.

Rick looked up from where he was pulling the tooth from the young female. "They're not supposed to track them that way."

"Yeah," Adam said, "but you can bet that Johnson-Walker crew would do anything to get their client a bear."

They named the three-year-old female Kendall after one of Adam's sisters, recorded her tan color and her weight, and left her while they processed the other bear, a nine-year-old female they named Eleanor.

"This old gal is in estrus," Rick said, pointing out the swollen vulva. "And," he said, "she's in real good shape." He ran his hand through the thick light-brown fur. "She'll probably conceive."

"What makes them conceive or not?" Adam asked.

"Well, actually a bear sow *conceives* right after mating," Rick said, "but bears use a unique reproduction system that allows for delayed implantation. They breed now—in June and July." Rick had switched into his teaching voice, and Kelly listened as intently as Adam, although she had studied the system herself.

"Fertilization takes place, and a few divisions of the egg occur. Those few cells are called a *blastocyst*. That little ball of cells just floats around in the uterus. It doesn't attach and start growing. It remains that size until November or December, and then if the female bear has gotten enough fat on her to be able to nourish the young, the egg implants in the uterine wall and starts to develop."

Rick stood up and looked around at the general area. "But if it's been a poor year, say the acorn crop has failed, or the berry crop got frozen out or something, and the sow wasn't able to put on enough fat to bring the cubs through, the blastocyst is diverted. It's not even implanted." Rick stared down at Eleanor. "But this old sow is in good shape," he said. "We'll be seeing cubs from her in the den in January."

"How do we keep track of their dens?" Kelly asked. "We can't possibly find all of them by walking these hills in the snow."

"The Forest Service has a plane. We fly the bears. Track them from the air by collar signals. You met Mary Powers. She's one of the pilots."

It helped to talk about procedure, but each time they stretched a bear out on the ground, Kelly saw again the hanging naked carcass that had been Roscoe. Maybe that's why Rick was talking so much—to keep from thinking of the big red bear. Rick was now speaking of Jenny. He said, "Before the houndsmen are gone for the spring season, I may get one of them to bring his dogs and track Jenny."

"You said that before," Adam said. "Is it really necessary?"

Kelly said, "You won't use Walt Johnson's group will you?"

"No, more likely Doc Morrison's dogs. He has some pretty well-trained hounds." Rick pulled Eleanor's quiet body out to full length on its stomach, and Adam covered the eyes. By the time they gathered scat and reset snares and checked all the others, it was late. Rick replaced the equipment box and headed down the mountain on his machine.

Adam was silent. When Kelly climbed on the four-wheeler behind him, he took off abruptly with a roaring of the engine and tore down the mountain. Kelly tried to hang on to the rack behind her, but she bounced around dangerously. Finally, she grabbed Adam around the middle and held on to him tightly.

Adam skidded the machine around curves and bounced it over humps in the trail. He was about halfway down the mountain when the machine tilted dangerously to the right. Kelly could feel the wheels lift. Adam leaned toward the left, and Kelly threw her body weight in the same direction. The four-wheeler settled back down on all wheels, and Adam brought the machine to a stop. Kelly climbed off and turned toward him. "What is the matter with you? Do you want to kill us both?" ⌒

Chapter Twenty-Nine

"I'm sorry," Adam said.

"You crazy idiot! You scared me half to death." Adam took a step away, and Kelly softened her tone. "Are you still upset about Roscoe?"

Adam moved to the dirt bank and sat down. He picked up a stick and drew aimless circles in the dirt. "I don't belong out here." He frowned. "I didn't expect us to cause these animals so much trouble."

"We didn't kill Roscoe, Adam."

"We collared him." Adam's anger at the houndsmen and his concern for the bears had firmed the line of his jaw. In fact everything about him seemed firm. The muscles in his arms were tight as cables. Kelly thought of the feel of his body as she had clutched him on the wild ride down the mountain. He had recently switched to plaid cotton shirts. Under the light material, his body was lean and muscled.

"I'm not the same kind of scientist you are," Adam said. "I know that over the long run, our data will contribute to balance in management." He crisscrossed the circles he'd drawn. "But I want to do something that helps the animals right away." He looked up at her. "I'm thinking of quitting the project."

Kelly felt as if she'd been kicked in the stomach. The project without Adam? She said, "You can't do that."

"Why not?"

Briefly, she was at a loss for words. Then she said, "You committed yourself to Dr. Andrews for one year, didn't you?" Adam nodded. "Well, then, you have to stay." Kelly got up and moved around on the trail. Then she turned to Adam. "My gosh, Adam, don't you know what it would be like for me up here if I was alone with Rick?" She looked at him for a long moment and said, "You keep the seesaw steady. You can't desert me."

Adam tossed the stick aside and stood up. He grinned at her. "The real reason you want me to stay is that you don't want to be put back into the kitchen."

Relieved by his smile, Kelly said, "True, true. And I would have to cook or drown in Rick's grease." They got onto the machine. Adam reached back and pulled Kelly's arms around his body. Startled, she asked, "You're not going to bounce me all over the mountain again, are you?"

Adam flung a wide grin her way. "Nope. I just like the way it feels when you hold on tight." She pinched him on his firm belly, but she didn't take her arms away until they were almost in sight of Rick at the truck.

When they returned to the cabin, Dr. Andrews was there with a summer-session zoology class. Rick grumbled, but Kelly was relieved. The three of them still suffered over Roscoe's death. They needed the distraction of company. And was there company! The class had ten males and four females. Dr. Andrews said, "The men can sleep on the porch."

The commotion of spreading sleeping bags and preparing dinner diluted the pain of telling Dr. Andrews about Roscoe. After dinner, the professor reviewed the use of the anesthetic and the proper procedure at the sets. Two of the women asked intelligent, perceptive questions. One student in particular—Elizabeth—was poised and calm, and she seemed totally focused on the lecture while some of the others started side conversations or moved restlessly on the floor where they sat.

As the evening went along, and Dr. Andrews and Rick lectured in turn about the project, Kelly noticed something that first annoyed her and then became of concern. The male students in the group surged forward to look at the snares, drugs, and scat samples. As they grouped around the table, they left no space for the female students, who seemed unsure about moving forward. Elizabeth made a tentative effort to wedge through the group to see the equipment, but a new wave of motion among the men eased her back.

It was not deliberate. Kelly could see that. The men were unaware that they had blocked the women's access, but Kelly could see Elizabeth's increasing frustration. As the lectures were concluded, Kelly moved to Elizabeth's side and said, "We can probably get close to the table now." Elizabeth gave her a quick bright glance and moved to the equipment display immediately. Before Rick could reach to repack the snares and the jab stick, Kelly was showing them to Elizabeth and explaining as quickly as she could. The other women moved closer and listened.

On Saturday morning, Rick, Adam, and Kelly happened to meet at the pickup at the same time to stow gear. Rick said, "These damn classes make it doubly hard on the bears. I almost hope the snares are empty." Adam and Kelly nodded in agreement. But there were two bears: the two-year-old male they had snared before and named after Ryan and an untagged cinnamon-colored female.

Even with students sitting on the bait box and the rack, it took three trips with the four-wheelers to get the class to Warren Gulch. Without a glance at Kelly, Rick chose five of the men, distributed equipment, and gave instructions. Then he turned to the rest of them. "It is essential that you be absolutely quiet. Your presence alone is causing stress to the bear."

It took extra time to process a bear with the students helping, especially since Rick decided to collar Ryan. Because of Roscoe's death, they needed another collared male. It was late by the time they went on to Moreno Creek and the female. Rick chose the other five male students, who blundered about and trampled the scat before it could be collected. At Dr. Andrews's request, they named the new sow Christine. In the pickup on the way back to the cabin, Rick said, "Some of those damn kids don't even think. I'm tempted to make them all take turns filling the bait box."

"Don't do that," Adam said. "No way am I hauling in enough water to bathe that whole crew."

"And I don't want to sleep near them if they lug bait and don't get a bath," Kelly said. "Drop me off at the bait barrel, and I'll fill the box."

After supper, Kelly invited Elizabeth to join her while she transcribed field sheets. She enjoyed their quiet, intelligent conversation as they worked. It was like being in the peaceful eye of a hurricane. The rest of the students were in constant motion. Some of them complained. They didn't like the hard floor of the porch. The food hadn't been to their taste. When she heard that, Kelly glanced up to meet Adam's eyes. He winked at her. She thought he'd done a masterful job of preparing meatloaf for the whole group.

The next morning they delivered the crowd to the road above the first set on Chase Creek. When they trekked down to the site, they found a bear in trouble.

A medium-sized brown bear had been snared, but he had not just trashed the site. He had also clawed his way twenty feet up the tree, dragging the snare and the chain after him. He had climbed over a branch and then around it, pulling the chain with him. When he had started up again, he had snubbed his right front leg tight to the tree. He couldn't get down, and he couldn't go any higher. When the group came near, the bear began to thrash about.

Dr. Andrews took over. "Go back up the slope and sit down," he said to his class. "Don't talk. Don't even whisper." The awed students did as they were told, and Dr. Andrews turned to Rick. "He's safe as long as he's hanging on to the tree, but if we tranquilize him, and he slips off that branch before we release him from the snare, his weight is liable to pull his foot right off." The brown bear stared down, his small dark eyes focused on the scientists, his ears alert. Dr. Andrews said, "Use the dart gun, Rick, and when he's about half under, someone will have to go up that tree and get a rope around his waist."

Adam stepped forward. "I'll go up the tree."

Kelly prepared the anesthetic and handed the syringe to Rick who had loaded the gas cartridge on the dart gun. Adam took off his shoes and socks, stuck the ratchet wrench in his pocket, and coiled the rope over one arm. Rick steadied the gun on Kelly's shoulder and darted the bear. They waited tensely for about three minutes. Dr. Andrews said to Adam, "We can't wait until that bear is totally out, so you be careful."

Adam nodded, his eyes on the bear. When Rick said, "Go," Adam wrapped himself around the tree and shinnied up it. The bear stirred groggily. "You've got about two minutes before he drops," Rick said.

Adam swung one leg over a branch and reached to slide the rope around the bear's middle. He knotted the rope close to the belly and dropped the loose end over the branch to the ground. Then he began to unscrew the clamp. Rick and Dr. Andrews grasped the hanging end of the rope. Clutching part of the rope, Kelly joined her weight to theirs just as Adam shouted, "He's free," and the bear—totally unconscious— fell away from the tree, dropping two feet before the rope caught his full weight. Even with the two men holding the rope ahead of her, Kelly could feel the jolt and the pull of the bear's weight as they slowly lowered him to the ground.

The group on the hillside broke into a raucous cheer as Adam slid down the tree. Dr. Andrews turned to quell them, but Rick, Adam, and Kelly paid no attention to the students. They stretched the bear out on the ground, covered his eyes, and checked him for damage. Except for a bloody cable cut on his wrist, the bear was unhurt. Adam let out a long breath as they moved quickly to begin the processing. Rick said to Kelly, who had picked up the data board, "We'll call this one Adam." Adam looked up from where he knelt pulling the tooth, his face bright red. Kelly smiled at him and wrote Adam at the top of the sheet.

After they finished processing the bear, they loaded equipment and people and moved along the trail. When they reached the snare in the conifers at the top of Chase Creek, there was a dark brown bear in the trap, and Kelly knew the moment she saw her that it was Samantha. Before Rick or Dr. Andrews could speak, Kelly turned to the students and said, "Let's make this an all-woman crew." Rick started to say something, but she continued, "The men have all had a chance to process a bear."

Dr. Andrews looked at her with a grin and stepped back from the equipment. "You guys go up the slope and be quiet," he said. He started uphill, but turned briefly to Rick and Adam. "You, too."

Kelly shared facts about Samantha as she prepared the jab stick. Then, turning to Elizabeth, she said, "Go around the slope and catch the bear's attention. I'll slip down behind her. When I nod, you yell 'Hey Bear!'" The processing of Samantha went very smoothly. The women were eager to help, and when Kelly explained the value of the scat samples, they weren't squeamish about collecting them. Elizabeth was deft and professional. They used a minimum of time to weigh and measure Samantha and record the data. Kelly took a moment to stroke the quiet bear. Then she checked the eye cover and climbed the hill. "She's gained twenty pounds," she said to Rick.

He scowled. "Peanut butter will do that to you."

Dr. Andrews was looking at his watch. "I need to start getting these guys down the hill, so we can load the van and head for Provo."

Before the group left, Rick asked Dr. Andrews about hiring dogs to tree Jenny. The professor agreed, but said, "Doc Morrison doesn't have much time, but if you can get him, he'll do it for free. I'm scrounging for money again. I want to keep your crew trapping through July and it's still only mid-June." He glanced at Kelly with a grin and said, "We need free bait, too. Can't you get your rancher buddy to kill off a couple of cows?"

They worked all week resetting snares. Rick had decided that each of the chains should be nailed to the tree at the set to prevent bears from pulling the snares and chains up the tree. "We were lucky to get him down safely," Rick said. Adam frowned, but Kelly just nodded. She was working on a barricade and the sun was hot, the air under the trees, humid. Each night, she tried to scrub away the smells of heat and sweat and bear, but she never entirely succeeded.

One evening, completely frustrated with the effort to keep her hair clean, Kelly had asked Adam to cut it. She held the scissors out toward him. "Just cut it short all around so I can wash it more easily."

Adam had backed away from her, holding one hand palm forward in protest. "I will not cut your hair. I like the way the light comes down through the aspen trees and picks out strands of gold."

Kelly turned to Rick, but he shook his head, and said, "That's not the solution. We have to rig up some sort of shower. We all need it, and it's going to get worse in July when the temperatures rise above ninety."

"Here," Adam said. "I'll wash it for you." He ducked her head into the dishpan and scrubbed with such firm fingers that Kelly wriggled away from him.

"It's not dirty on the inside of my scalp," she said. Adam laughed and grabbing her shoulders pushed her back to the pan to rinse her hair. Then he toweled it thoroughly before he released her.

They snared a two-year-old female on Moreno Creek, and at Kelly's request, they named her Elizabeth. Each day Rick picked up Jenny's signal. Each day, she refused to be snared. Rick continued to worry out loud. Fear that Jenny was being injured by her collar affected Adam as well, and he was morose. Kelly yearned for time alone. On the third Sunday in June, she said, "Let me work Moreno Creek by myself. One of you can drop me off up there, and I'll walk to the snares and rebait where it's necessary."

It was a relief when Adam wheeled away. Kelly worked her way slowly down the mountain, lugging the bait in a plastic garbage bag and carrying the propane torch, tools, and a jar of peanut butter in her backpack. Most of the snares were in good shape. She stopped often to enjoy the wild columbine and the Indian paintbrush in the lush grass in the aspen meadows. She had just started to burn the bait on the last and lowest set in Moreno Creek when she heard the sound of the four-wheelers coming back. They stopped at the road behind her, and she bent over to hurry her job.

"Well, well. What do we have here?"

The strange male voice startled Kelly, and she whirled around, torch in hand, to stare at the four young men who formed a half-circle in front of her. ∾

Chapter Thirty

The four were clad in faded jeans and black T-shirts with a lightning-bolt insignia in red and orange on the fronts. Their hair straggled down their necks from underneath brimmed caps. "Seems like the lady is all alone," one of them said, taking a step forward and raking his black eyes up and down Kelly's body. Kelly could feel the short hairs on her neck move.

"What are you doing out here?" another asked her, looking at the scorched bait and wrinkling his nose.

Kelly swallowed and said, "I'm setting a bear trap."

The four glanced over their shoulders and around. "I don't see no bears," the black-eyed man said. "All I see is a sweet little blonde that looks lonesome." The four focused their eyes on the vee of Kelly's shirt. Hot and sweaty from the work, Kelly had unbuttoned the shirt at the neck and opened it for cool air. The damp shirt clung to her body. As the men looked at her, one of them licked his lips.

The sight of the animal-like tongue and the sudden shuffling motion that advanced the four males closer to her filled Kelly with a clear, empowering anger. Once again she had been reduced to nothing more than a body—a target. But that was now to her advantage. If these four creeps didn't know she had a brain, they wouldn't expect much from her.

The four moved forward again, blocking Kelly from the front. The barricade was behind her. Kelly took a side step that she knew looked only like an attempt to escape, but which placed her between the bait and the hidden snare. If they kept advancing, she might lure one of them into it. As she moved, she turned the knob on the propane torch, and the jet of flame lengthened. When one of the men reached a hand to grab her arm, Kelly swung the propane torch forward. The man jumped back, but the four of them stayed close, their feet just at the edge of the bait. "Whew," one of them said, "that damned stuff sure stinks." The half-circle of men moved slowly from side to side in a stalking maneuver, but avoiding the huge pile of rotten meat in front of them. Kelly held her ground behind the bait, clutching the torch. She could smell the acrid odors of the men—stronger, more offensive to her than the odor of the bait.

She darted her eyes from man to man. The black-eyed man made a quick motion toward the torch, and Kelly met his hand with the flame. Cursing, he backed away. Kelly kept her eyes moving. When another of the four reached toward her, she swung the torch toward the lightning-bolt insignia and held the long blue flame steady on the fluorescent paint. An odor like that of burning rubber joined the other smells, and the second man cursed as he beat at his chest.

"Oh, hell," the black-eyed man said, half turning. "What do we want with a female that stinks of dead meat and shit?"

Just at that moment, the loud report of a gun crashed through the grove, and a bullet tore into a stump next to the black-eyed man. The four men whirled to look toward the road. Adam stood there, pistol in hand. "You crazy bastard," the black-eyed man said. "You could have shot me."

"If I'd meant to shoot you," Adam said, "I would have shot you. Now get on your machines and get out of here." The four scrambled toward their four-wheelers, making a wide detour around Adam, who turned with them, holding the Ruger. Kelly closed the gas jet and began to pack her gear into her backpack. Moving slowly up the hill, she buttoned her shirt to the neck before she arrived to stand near Adam and watch the four-wheelers go down the trail in a cloud of dust.

Adam turned. "You okay?" Kelly nodded, and Adam said, "You shouldn't be out here alone."

Kelly was suddenly angrier at Adam than she had been at the other men, and she turned and walked away, fighting an urge to hit him. Adam followed and put a hand on her shoulder. She whirled, striking the hand away. Adam said, "What's wrong?"

"I can't believe that *you*," Kelly said, "you, of all people, could say something like that."

Adam looked truly puzzled. "What did I say?"

"Like every other male in the whole damned world, when it comes to predators that go after women, you blamed the victim instead of the criminal."

"I didn't!"

"You did. You said that *I* shouldn't be out here." She glared at Adam. "Well, I have every right in the world to be out here doing my job, or to be any other damned place I want to be. Don't blame me for what those bastards tried to do."

"Oh, Kelly," Adam said. "I wasn't blaming you. I was blaming Rick and me for leaving you here."

But Kelly would not accept that either. "Then you're saying that you and Rick should post a guard on me when I'm not behind my veil or locked in the harem." She took a deep breath. "I know you're trying to be decent, Adam, but locking up the women is not the ultimate solution."

She turned and climbed on the four-wheeler. Adam joined her, but before he turned the ignition key, he said, "What did you mean when you said, 'you, of all people'?"

Kelly considered his question. She hadn't thought before she said it. What did she mean? "Well," she said, speaking slowly, "you seem to be different from the others to a certain degree. You seem to have some grasp of the idea that there's more to sex than lust, some grasp of the honor in the Honor Code."

She could feel Adam's body tighten, but he didn't say anything for a moment, and then he said, "What are we going to tell Rick about this?"

"Do we have to tell him anything?"

"Kelly, he's responsible for the crew. Don't you think he's entitled to know when something endangers one of the crew members?"

"Yes, I would, if he really thought of me as a crew member. But, Adam, he'll just use this against me. Didn't you see him when that class was here? Not once did he ask a question of a woman. Not once did he give even Elizabeth a chance to try out the equipment. Please, Adam. I'm not hurt. Can't we just keep this to ourselves?"

Adam turned around so that he could meet her eyes. "Okay, Kelly, but only on one condition."

"What's that?"

"That today you start letting me teach you to use this gun, and as soon as you can manage it, you get a gun to carry."

Kelly nodded. "I need to know how to use a gun anyway. That's a good idea, Adam."

When they reached the meadow, Rick said, "I saw some of those fat-tire faggots roaring out of Moreno Creek just ahead of you. I hate Sundays and mid-summer. It's going to get worse toward the Fourth of July when that jeep thing is held."

After dinner that evening, Adam said, "Kelly wants to learn to use my gun, Santini. That okay with you?"

Rick glanced up. "I don't care. As long as you've got the scat all labeled and spread, and if you two pay for the ammunition." He went back to his data work as Adam took the gun and cartridges and walked with Kelly to the small meadow a few hundred feet past the bait barrel.

He took two sets of earplugs from the ammunition case, and giving her one set, inserted the other two plugs in his own ears. Kelly followed his example. Then, rigging a pile of logs about twenty-five yards away, Adam wedged a small piece of aspen bark into them near the center. "That's your target, Kelly." He took the Ruger from its holster. "This is a versatile pistol. It's possible to have both single and double action, but double action is not as accurate, and if you're not used to the recoil, you might shoot wildly. I want you to start with single action."

"Will it kick a lot?" Kelly asked.

"It's going to buck a little," he said, "but it's not like a shotgun or a rifle. The rifle or shotgun recoil, you take in the shoulder. You'll learn to take the pistol's recoil in your arms." He handed her the pistol. When she lifted it, he said, "Use both hands." He showed her how to grip the pistol with her right hand and then support her right hand with her left hand. "The palm of your hand will absorb most of the kick, but having both hands there will help because your arms will take some of the pressure."

As she extended her right arm and bent her left arm to support the right, Adam reached to straighten her left arm. "The arms have to be straight, or you've got a chance of the pistol coming back and hitting you in the face." Kelly shivered as she looked at the heavy stainless steel barrel. It could break her nose. Standing behind her, Adam extended his arm in support as her arms trembled. Kelly cocked the hammer and squinted to see through the sight, which wavered up and down.

Adam explained the way he had the sight adjusted. "Put the top of the orange square on the bottom of the front sight. That's where this one is set to shoot because that gives me the biggest view of the target when I'm sighting in." Kelly squinted through the sight again. When she thought she had the orange square in alignment and the white piece of bark firmly in view, she pulled the trigger.

The force of the explosion bucked her arms upward, and she stepped backward into Adam, who caught her body and held it briefly next to him before he said, "After a while, you'll adjust for the motion." He grinned at her as he added, "You missed the target, but you did hit the logs."

"Let me try it by myself," Kelly said. She extended her arms, careful to hold them straight, sighted, and shot. Once again her arms flew upward. The recoil slammed into the heel of her hand, and she winced. Adam fished in his case and handed her a leather glove.

"This will protect your hand some." She slipped her hand into the glove and tried over and over, stopping only to watch as Adam reloaded. Finally, she nicked the edge of the aspen bark, and Adam said, "Yeah. Now you're getting it."

But when she lifted her arm to try again, her arm trembled worse than it had in the beginning. "I'm losing my grip."

"You're getting tired," Adam said. He stepped behind her again and reached to steady her. Kelly could feel his body trembling, too, and suddenly he moved away from her.

She turned and said, "What's wrong?"

There was a strange expression on Adam's face. He smiled, but the smile didn't reach his eyes. "I think I'm losing my grip, too."

"On what?" Kelly knew they were no longer speaking of the Ruger. She removed the ear plugs from her ears.

"On the Honor Code," Adam said. He reached out and took the

Ruger from her hands. Stepping further away, he cleaned the gun and replaced it in the holster on his hip. He gathered the spent shell casings and picked up the ammunition box.

"I'm sorry," Kelly said. "I am so self-centered, and I was so intent on learning to shoot that thing, that I wasn't even thinking about you."

"I know that," Adam said. "You have the best array of submersion techniques I've ever seen. Matt was right about you in some ways. I don't think you're even aware."

Kelly met Adam's level look. "You're wrong, Adam. I'd never have gotten this far if I weren't aware. I learned a long time ago that it's all part of the same creative energy. I use it. I learn things, I do things, I move, I work, I keep my mind focused on other ideas and . . ." Kelly grinned slightly as she told him something she'd never told anyone before, "When I'm really desperate, I make music. That old guitar is a lifesaver." She moved her feet in the grass of the meadow as Adam continued to meet her gaze, but didn't smile. "It's all creative energy," she said again.

"Do you know just how insignificant that makes a man feel?" Adam asked.

The sun was almost down, and a cool breeze whirled through the meadow. Kelly shivered. She took a long deep breath and said, "Adam, you are not an insignificant friend. I am sorry if I made things difficult." Adam did not reply. Not knowing what else to say, Kelly waited a moment and then turned and walked toward the cabin. ❧

Chapter Thirty-One

Rick seemed unaware of the tension between his crew members. He was checking every spot on the map where he had marked Jenny's signal. Kelly looked over his shoulder, surprised to see how many times they had contacted bears on the mountain simply through the beep from the receiver. Rick turned to her. "I went up to the store and called Doc Morrison. He's bringing his dogs on Wednesday."

Monday and Tuesday as they rode to check snares, Kelly was careful not to touch Adam more than absolutely necessary. She clung to the rack behind her and held her body rigidly away from him. They worked in silence, the strain leaving her exhausted.

"Oh, shit," Rick said on Wednesday morning when Doc Morrison pulled into the yard with his pickup loaded with dogs. "There's somebody coming in behind him." As Doc Morrison entered the cabin, Rick said abruptly, "We don't need more than one crew."

The veterinarian shrugged. "You know how it is. Houndsmen hear of a bear hunt, and they want to be in on the chase."

"Maybe they can help," Adam said. "The sooner we tree her, the better."

Doc Morrison said, "Before I forget, I've got a dead cow located for you across the line in Colorado." He handed Rick a piece of paper. "I wrote the directions. I told the guy one of you bear people would be down."

"Thanks," Rick said, taking the paper and sticking it into his pocket. Looking around the cabin, he returned to the plans for the hunt. "We'll split into two groups. Adam can take one receiver and go with you and your dogs." He stared at Kelly for a moment before saying, "Kelly can come with me and the others." She heard the reluctance in his voice. But he really had no choice. It was difficult to process a bear alone, and she knew he didn't trust strangers. Kelly was glad to discover that all the houndsmen were unfamiliar to her. They scarcely acknowledged her presence, and she was glad of that too.

The biologists led the houndsmen in their pickups as close as they could get to Jenny's signal. Then the men got out and gathered their dogs from the trucks. Doc Morrison and Adam went one way with eight dogs. There were fourteen dogs in the group that stayed. Rick frowned and said to her in an undertone, "That's too damn many dogs." But he and Kelly dropped in behind the houndsmen, who gave the straining dogs the lead.

The dogs were quiet at first, looking for the trail. Hunting dogs had always seemed to her such a raucous bunch of brawling mongrels that Kelly was surprised to see how well disciplined they were when they went to work. They trotted along on their leashes, businesslike noses to the ground. Kelly was surprised by the men, too. They were totally in tune with their dogs. And despite a general tendency toward beer gut, these men were not as out of shape as she had supposed them to be. They moved swiftly and strongly, holding the dogs' leads and keeping pace with the dogs.

Suddenly the dog at the point began to whine and tug at the leash. The other dogs quickly joined in. One of the other men turned to Rick and said, "I think we've got her scented, but we're not close enough yet." Everyone picked up speed, the men breaking into a kind of jog trot, the dogs pulling the leads taut, whining and straining forward. In spite of herself, Kelly's heart began to beat faster, and she could understand the excitement that the men were showing.

The lead dog suddenly began to bark insistently. The houndsman who controlled him bent and released the dog from the leash. When the lead hound seemed to be firmly on the trail, the other men released their dogs. The animals raced into the woods, barking and baying. The men followed the sound, and Kelly and Rick followed the houndsmen. The dogs kept up their noise, and though the hounds increased their distance from the men and were soon out of sight, the persistent sounds of pursuit cut through the woods.

Rick said, "That poor damned bear only has three legs." Kelly shot a glance at him. His skin was flushed, his mouth, a tight line. "I wish to hell we'd been able to snare her."

They followed the sounds of the dogs for a long exhausting time before the baying changed suddenly to a higher, more excited pitch, and one of the houndsmen said, "They've treed her." The frantic barking continued and grew louder as the houndsmen and Rick and Kelly went down the slope.

The hounds had treed Jenny in a huge aspen at the edge of the meadows in the Moreno Creek drainage. The cinnamon-colored bear had climbed fifty feet and now sat panting with her broad rump on a relatively small branch, the claws of her good front leg dug into the tree. Her tiny eyes never left the howling dogs at the base of the tree.

"Call them off," Rick said, "and back away." The houndsmen moved to restrain their reluctant dogs. Rick turned to Kelly. "That's going to be tough to climb, and we won't want to try it twice. So we'll dart her with the gun."

Kelly said, "I can climb a tree, Rick. It would give us some time if I started up with the rope as soon as you darted her."

"Can you tie a decent knot?"

"I can tie knots. I've hung venison in a tree with my knots. I never tried anything heavier."

Rick considered this briefly and then said, "Can't chance it. I'll dart her from the bottom of the tree. You have the rope ready for me." Rick was heavier than Kelly. It would take him longer to climb the tree, and he'd have less time to tie the rope on Jenny. But he had made his decision and was already preparing the dart. Kelly readied the rope.

The houndsmen had released their dogs and backed away. Kelly said quietly, "I'll need a couple of you to help me hold the rope once Rick gets it tied onto the bear." Two of them stepped forward.

Rick's hand trembled on the dart gun. He leaned against a smaller tree and steadied his arm before he shot. The dart hit the bear and quivered briefly, but it stayed in the tawny rump. Giving the gun to Kelly and taking the rope, Rick began to climb, pausing as the bear moved on the branch, then saying, "Clock the anesthetic, Kelly. Don't let me wait too long." He pulled himself from one shattered branch to the next, and by the time he secured himself on the stub of a branch that Jenny had broken during her own frantic climb, the bear had begun to lick her lips.

"You'd better tie her, Rick." Jenny was too far under to object to his pulling the rope around her middle. Rick dropped one end toward Kelly and quickly began to tie a knot with the other end. "She's letting go," Kelly said, grabbing the dangling rope as Rick gave a final tug to the knot. The houndsmen grasped the rope behind her as the bear's claws came away from the tree, and Jenny toppled from the branch. Since there were no branches left to break her fall, her whole weight hit the rope.

Even wearing gloves, Kelly could feel the rope burn as it slid through her palms. She tightened her grip and braced her legs. The rope strained, but held. The bear was forty feet in the air, totally unconscious, a dead weight. Kelly and the houndsmen began slowly to let out the rope, lowering Jenny gradually, inch by inch.

And then suddenly, without warning, the knot that held the loop around the bear's middle gave way, and the bear fell to the earth with a solid, sickening thud. Kelly lurched backward into the houndsmen, who stumbled backward too, but stayed on their feet and kept her from falling. Rick shinnied down the tree, jumping from the last five feet. In a moment, he had reached the bear and turned her over. The bear's crippled front leg was bent under. One of the bear's rear legs was broken: a sharp bone end protruded at an angle. Rick looked up at Kelly, and she had never seen so much pain in a human face. "Kelly, can you find Doc Morrison?"

She knew it was useless, and Rick must have known too, but she scrambled up the slope, not having the slightest idea of which way to go to find the other group. She had moved only a few hundred feet along the trail, however, when she heard the baying of dogs. In moments, the other group of dogs came into view. She stepped aside as the dogs tore past her, then she moved up the trail until she sighted the veterinarian, puffing along after the sound of his dogs. When he saw Kelly, he slowed and paused near her, panting. "They're hot on the trail," he said. His face was beet red above his white beard. Adam was close behind him.

"Rick needs you. The bear's hurt." Kelly turned immediately toward the return trail, but Adam stepped forward and put a hand on her arm. "Hurt?" Kelly nodded, swallowing. "How bad?" She met Adam's eyes and said nothing.

Doc Morrison had trotted around them, and when Adam and Kelly reached the area, he and Rick were kneeling by the bear. Kelly noticed that the collar was almost buried in the fur around the bear's neck. Rick had been right to worry about the collar. The veterinarian looked up at Rick and shook his head. Rick rose and, unsnapping the holster on his hip, said to the houndsmen, "You want to back off? I'm going to put her out of her misery."

The houndsmen were subdued, but their dogs still whined and jerked toward the bear on the ground. The men tugged the dogs away and started up the hill. Rick turned to Adam. "Take Kelly out of here." It was more a matter of Kelly's taking Adam, however. Adam seemed to be in shock, and Kelly had to pull hard on his arm before he moved slowly away with her. He flinched as the shot rang out.

In a few moments, Rick appeared, carrying the equipment. Kelly and Adam relieved him of part of it. Rick clutched the collar and tags. The three of them walked silently down the trail. The silence continued in the truck, but when they reached the turnoff to the meadow where they had unhooked the trailer and unloaded the four-wheelers, Rick said, "Doc Morrison is going to make sure that bear carcass gets back to the lab for study. You two go ahead and check the snares." He gripped the steering wheel with both hands; his knuckles were white; there was a white line around his mouth, but the rest of his face was mottled.

"What are you going to do?" Kelly asked.

"I'm going to Colorado to get that cow." ❧

Chapter Thirty-Two

Adam and Kelly worked the gulches separately. Andy was snared again in Chase Creek, but they didn't play with him. They put the black bear down, processed him, and released him. The rest of the snares were undisturbed. "I'm not surprised," Kelly said. "With men and dogs all over the mountain, the bears are probably in the darkest forest."

Since Rick had taken the pickup and was not in the meadow when they got there, they had to ride the four-wheelers back to the cabin. It was already early evening by the time they arrived, but Rick was not at the cabin either. They recorded the data and took care of the equipment. Kelly did her daily target practice alone while Adam fixed supper.

They ate in near silence. Neither of them spoke of Jenny, but Kelly knew that each thought of little else. It didn't help to know that they were steadily gathering data that would make the mountain safer for bears. It didn't help that they'd already made many safe contacts with bears. "I feel sorry for Rick," Adam said. "He's not going to forgive himself for this."

"I know it. At least with Roscoe, it was beyond our control."

Rick had not returned by dark. They did the dishes together, changed the scat in the drying box, and filled the wood box. The work would have been a comfort if they had been companionable, as they were before Adam had started teaching her to shoot. But they were stiff with each other now in conversation, and they avoided physical contact of any sort.

When they had done all the work they could think of, they sat down at the table. Each had a book, but neither read. They started at the slightest sound. Once, Adam got up and went outside to listen. Kelly joined him on the porch. The engine noise was a jet. They watched its lights until they disappeared in the east. The nighthawks were hunting; an owl hooted. There was no sign of Rick. "Where is that blasted Santini?" Adam said.

"He should have been back. We're not twenty miles from the Colorado line."

When they went inside, Adam said, "Play your guitar, Kelly. I can't concentrate on anything else." He stretched out on his cot. Kelly took the guitar to Rick's cot, and leaning against the back wall of the cabin, extended her legs and settled the guitar on her lap.

She played and sang for a while and then said, "Sing with me, Adam." They sang all the songs they knew, and finally, Kelly said, "My fingertips can't take any more tonight."

Adam sat up. "You're right about that guitar, Kelly. It does help." He yawned. "I guess there's no point worrying about Rick. There's probably a logical explanation."

"I hope so. Anyway, we need to get to bed because we'll have to ride the four-wheelers all the way from the cabin tomorrow if he doesn't show up." She put the guitar away and used the outhouse.

When she came back in, Adam was standing by the table. "Shall I leave the lamp on for him?"

Kelly nodded. "A light might be a comfort."

Adam fiddled with the lamp until he had a low but steady light. Then he turned and met Kelly's eyes. Sad about Jenny and worried about Rick, Kelly would have welcomed a hug, but she couldn't make the first move because she didn't know what Adam was feeling. Without their sparkle, his brown eyes made her unsure. She held the look until Adam shifted slightly and said, "Thanks for the music, Kelly."

In bed, Kelly lay awake thinking of Jenny, worrying about Rick.

Where was he? *If I had to tell Dr. Andrews about today, I'd be miserable. Why hadn't she insisted on climbing that tree?* If there had been just a couple more minutes, the knot might have been tied better. *It was careless work on our part. We shouldn't have let the frenzy of the chase affect our thinking.* As she turned over one more time in her cot, she heard Adam begin to snore. She focused her mind on the bubbling sound and finally began to drift toward sleep.

The roar of the pickup woke her, but she was more immediately aware of Adam's cot jolting against the wall. She jumped from the bed and stepped into the kitchen just as Rick slammed the door open. "Santini, what in the . . ."

Adam had only begun when Rick roared, "Jones, Wainwright. Let's get up and get going. We've got to move all the sets and rebait them." His voice was loud and thick. In the dim light of the kerosene lamp, his face was shadowed, and before Kelly could say or do anything, even that light was gone. Rick lurched against the table, swung out his arm and swept the lamp to the floor. The flame went out, but the lamp exploded, throwing shards of glass. Kelly could feel the prick as a splinter of glass hit her bare foot. The strong odor of kerosene pervaded the cabin. Kelly moved backward, feeling for the storeroom door with her hands, reaching for her flashlight.

Shining the light on Rick, she was appalled by his looks. His face was puffy, his eyes red and wild, his hair uncombed. He muttered angrily as he stumbled toward the light, swinging his arms, narrowly missing her. He had the truck keys clutched in one fist, and as he swung his arm again, his fist connected with the water bucket, which had been half full. It crashed to the floor, splashing cold water on her feet and legs.

"He's drunk," Adam said. "Let's get him out of here before he knocks the place down."

Rick began yelling their names again. "Kelly. Adam. Get up, damn it. We've got to get to work before this whole sorry project goes down the drain." He reeked of alcohol and cigarette smoke and sweat and dirt and dead meat.

Adam took hold of Rick, and using Rick's angry shift of body to turn him, he aimed him toward the door. Kelly set the flashlight on the counter and, grabbing the arm Rick swung at Adam, she forced Rick's fist open and grasped the keys. She ducked the next erratic swing of Rick's arms and helped Adam shove him out onto the porch. He stumbled down the stairs and staggered away toward the pickup.

"Oh damn," Adam said, "He's heading toward the truck. We can't let him drive."

"He won't," Kelly said. "I took the keys away from him."

She heard Adam let out a huge sigh. "Good. So let's just let him sleep it off."

They went inside and locked the door. They heard Rick's continued grumbling, a banging sound as if he had hit the tailgate, and a grunt as he fell. Then there was silence. "He's passed out," Adam said. "Go back to bed, Kelly. We'll deal with this in the morning."

Kelly peered at her watch. "It's almost morning now." She went back to bed, but as she reviewed Rick's last sounds, she realized that they had heard Rick climb the tailgate and fall into the truck bed. She shivered. Rick was lying with that dead cow. She sat up and reached around under the cot for her shoes. By the time she opened the front door, Adam was with her. They made their way to the truck and looked in the bed. Rick had fallen slantwise on the bloated belly of the dead Hereford; his head lay across the cow's neck. The flashlight sparked on the greasy-looking eyeball of the cow. The stench was horrible, worse than the bait barrel.

"The poor guy," Adam said. "We can't let him sleep there." He looked around. "We could put him in the wood shed." Kelly went for the keys and a blanket and then backed the truck to the shed. Lowering the tailgate, Adam climbed into the bed and tugged Rick's body off the cow. Rick snored in a loud loose way and never opened an eye as they dragged him out of the truck and settled him under the shelter. They stood for a moment to catch their breath.

"He weighs more than most bears," Kelly said. Adam tucked the blanket around Rick and turned to Kelly.

"That's all we can do for him right now." He wrinkled his nose. "Let's take that truck up and park it by the bait barrel."

They walked back in the darkness to the cabin where they dipped tepid water from the reservoir and washed. Adam poured them each a glass of juice. They stood in the kitchen, sipping it. "He's blown the Honor Code all to hell," Adam said, "but I don't blame him."

"Nor I," Kelly said. "Every time I shut my eyes tonight, I heard Jenny hitting the ground." She ached with fatigue. "Let's go to bed, Adam. Tomorrow is going to be difficult."

Adam took the glass from her hand and put it in the dishpan with his own. And then he just stood there beside her, and she could feel the heat of his body and a slight trembling. The flashlight did not spread light the way the lamp had. She couldn't see Adam's face, but she remembered how he had looked when he stepped away from her at the meadow. Tears came to her eyes, and she was so startled by them that she moved backward.

"Poor guy," Adam said again as they headed toward their cots.

Kelly lay awake a long time, listening to Adam's restless turning, thinking about sex. Everything she had learned about sex when she was growing up had been from her own observation. Despite the wild sounds she made in the nights of Kelly's childhood, Kelly's mother had never spoken directly to her about sex. Only rarely had she spoken of her marriage, but when she did it was in bitter tones as if she had been trapped, as if she herself had nothing to do with it; and Kelly hated the lie, even before she fully understood that it was a lie.

Her grandmother had never discussed sex with her either, but she was matter-of-fact when it came time to breed an animal, and Kelly had known that mating was meant to produce young. Her grandmother was candid about the facts. It was the feelings Kelly was left to discover on her own. The first time her own body responded to the touch of a boy, she could only think of her mother's cries in the dark. *It will never happen to me. I will never be as miserable as my mother.*

She had hated the dishonesty of sex from the beginning, and nothing she found out in dating changed the feeling. Boys were not honest. They wanted to touch her body, and they said words that were meant to lull her mind, while their hands crept up her leg, and their mouths crept toward her breasts. And she was dishonest, too. She enjoyed some of the touching, but she never said anything but "no," "don't," and "I have to get home."

Moving from town to town, she had found all young men equally dishonest. What a relief it would have been if one guy had said, "I don't want to go steady; I don't want any responsibilities; I'd just like to feel your body and get some relief for my own." Kelly sighed in the dark. Peggy said she hid from sex behind the Honor Code. And in ways that was true, but Kelly wanted more than had ever been offered to her. She heard Adam turn over again. At least Adam was honest. He had told her that she caused him trouble.

She understood her tears now. Because of the damned hormones, she was going to lose something more valuable than sex. Adam's warmth and the affection in his touch had kept the summer from being just hard work and sorrow over the bears. Kelly sighed again, and pulling the blankets close around her, forced herself to plan the next day's work.

Rick was still passed out in the woodshed when Kelly went to the outhouse in the light of dawn. Adam brought in a fresh bucket of water, but when Kelly knelt to begin picking up the shards of lamp glass, he said, "Don't do that, Kelly. It's Rick's problem, not yours."

Kelly held the glass for a moment, considering, and then put it back on the floor. "Yeah," she said rising, "our problem is to get that stinking cow out of the truck so we can load the four-wheeler." The bloated, reeking cow weighed nearly half a ton, and they had to use the winch to drag her from the truck, dumping her off to the side of the barrel before returning to the cabin.

After loading the equipment boxes and the four-wheeler in the truck, they hooked up the trailer. Then Adam stepped over to the woodshed and looked in. "He's still snoring. We might as well leave him here and get going." When they passed the cow's carcass, Adam said, "You know we'll have to cut that thing up when we get back." Kelly wrinkled her nose, but said nothing. They checked Chase Creek and Warren Gulch separately and then Adam said, "Why don't we do Moreno Creek together and eat lunch on the mountain somewhere when we finish? Santini is not going to be overjoyed to see us anyway."

Kelly was glad not to go up Moreno Creek alone. The death of Jenny was strong on her mind. "I'm glad Doc dealt with Jenny's body for us," she said. "I didn't want to see her yesterday, even though a good biologist collects every specimen he can."

"I shouldn't have objected when Rick tried to collect Marie's cub," Adam said. "If it had gone to the lab, its death would have served some purpose." Adam clipped the words as if he were biting them off. Kelly dropped into silence.

It was a sweet, hot June day. The odors of the grassy meadows were crisp and clean. It was nice not to be driving the machine, and she rode along without thinking. Her body ached from lack of sleep and from the strain of dragging Rick's weight and that of the cow. There were no bears, and the sets had not been disturbed. Adam chose a sunny slope well away from the site of Jenny's tree. They settled into the grass and ate quietly.

Adam repacked the food, and, stretching out on the ground, said, "This project owes me a couple hours of sleep." He shut his eyes, and to Kelly's amazement, was snoring almost immediately. Kelly leaned back in the grass, listening to the birds chittering in the bushes.

The sun warmed her body, and she let herself relax until Adam woke, stretched, and gave her a sleepy grin. When they got back to the bait barrel, the cow had been butchered and the barrel filled to the top with chunks of meat. Kelly looked at Adam. "What are we going to say to him?" ∾

Chapter Thirty-Three

"Oh no," Kelly said when the cabin came in view. "He's taken my car. You don't suppose he's gone to get drunk again?"

"I doubt it. If he had that in mind, he wouldn't have cut up the cow."

"What are we going to do?"

Adam glanced at her as he turned off the engine. "Nothing we can do unless you want to chase Santini all over Utah." Stepping down from the truck, Adam unbuckled his gun belt. "There's a little ammunition left. Why don't you go practice? I'll unload the truck and start a fire."

Kelly's aim was erratic at first. She tried not to think of her good old car upside down in some ditch, but forced herself to concentrate, not stopping until she was hitting the center of the target consistently. She was loading the rest of Adam's bullets when she saw her car moving slowly over the rutted road. She shot the last round before walking back to the cabin.

The table was covered with an assortment of groceries, bags, and boxes, and Rick was fiddling with a Coleman lantern, trying to tie the small net mantel around the gas jet. He looked up when she came in. His face was gaunt, but he had cleaned up. His hair was combed; his clothes were crisp and spotless. He said, "How'd your shooting go?"

Kelly said, "Pretty good. But I'm out of ammunition."

Rick nodded a head toward the table. "I picked up some more while I was in town." He bent his head over the lantern again. Kelly stepped to the table. A large pizza box and a six pack of colas stood near several boxes of ammunition. She glanced at Adam, who raised both hands palm up, but said nothing. "Look in the plastic sack," Rick said.

Kelly pulled out a lumpy roll of black plastic and a rubber hose with a shower head. "What's this?"

"Unroll it. It's a camp shower."

The black plastic was actually a large bag with a screw-capped mouth. The bag had a hook at the top and a spigot at the bottom. "How do you use it?"

"It's made for solar heating. Fill it in the morning and hang it where the sun hits it. Before long the water's hot." Rick tried a brief smile on her, but he seemed so nervous that the smile didn't hold. "I thought we could use the outhouse for a shower stall like you did before."

Adam said, "There's hot water in the reservoir. You want to try washing your hair?"

Rick set the lantern aside and stood. "I'll go screw a hook into the ceiling for you."

He left the cabin and Kelly said, "Did he say anything?"

"He asked about the sets."

"Did you say anything?"

"I told him about Andy, and then he started hauling in all that stuff."

"What should we do?"

Adam grinned. "Enjoy a hot shower and eat Rick's pizza."

Kelly dipped water from the reservoir with a cup until she had filled the black bag. The shower was wonderful. She stood under the soft warm spray until the last bit of the water had drained into the pit. While Adam showered, Kelly sat on the front porch and dried and combed her hair. When Adam came around the corner looking freshly scrubbed, she stood to enter the cabin with him.

Rick had put the groceries away, cleared the table, and set it for dinner. Hanging from a hook above the table, the gas lantern hissed softly, spreading a light that far surpassed the kerosene lamp in brilliance. Rick divided up the pizza and poured cola in the glasses. For a while, the silence was broken only by the sound of chewing and the gentle whisper of the lantern. Then Rick said, "I think it's time to bring down the high sets. Now that the berries are coming on, the bears will be in the thickets and not on the ridges." His face reddened slightly. "Spring hunting will be over this weekend."

It took most of Friday to move and rebuild the sets. Saturday morning, Dr. Andrews drove into the yard just as they were ready to leave. Rick said, "You guys want to go ahead and start checking sets?"

Adam was already out of the truck. He looked over his shoulder. "In a few minutes, Rick. I need to talk to Dr. Andrews."

Rick's skin darkened, and his eyes narrowed. All three of them went into the cabin with Dr. Andrews. Adam said, "We're about to head out, but I have to ask you something."

Dr. Andrews said, "So ask."

"My family is having a reunion the week of July eighth. We're celebrating my grandparents' fiftieth, and my mom and my aunts have got all sorts of things planned that week. My folks wanted me to ask you if I can get off for five days." Kelly glanced at Rick. His face had cleared.

Dr. Andrews looked at Rick. "What do you think? Can you and Kelly handle it by yourselves for a few days?"

Rick didn't even look at Kelly. "Sure," he said, and the three men settled the matter immediately.

"You can ride out with me, Sunday the seventh," Dr. Andrews said.

"Thanks. And the Friday after that, I think some of my relatives can drop me off at the store on their way home."

"Okay. Do as much as you can on the mountain until then." He glanced at Rick. "You feeling okay? You look a little peaked."

Rick flushed again. "Yeah, I'm all right." He took a deep breath. "But we lost a bear this week." He turned to the others. "Go on ahead. We'll come up when we're done here."

As they drove toward the meadows, Adam said, "I don't blame him for getting rid of us. It's going to be hard enough to tell Dr. Andrews about Jenny without having an audience."

Kelly nodded, but she wasn't thinking about Rick's problem at the moment. She was thinking about her own. "Do you have to stay away for a whole week?" she asked. "Most anniversary celebrations are just for an afternoon."

Adam grinned at her. "When my family decides to celebrate, they do it up right."

"What am I going to talk about with Rick while you're gone?"

"Bears, snares, habitat, and scat. Same old stuff he always talks about."

They split up to check Chase Creek and Warren Gulch, agreeing to do Moreno Creek together. As Adam started up Chase Creek, he took out the receiver and Kelly waited to see what he would pick up. "Marie and Marilyn are both up there somewhere," he said. "I'll come get you if either one is snared."

The sets in Warren Gulch were empty and undisturbed. Kelly burned the bait again and returned to the meadow to meet Adam. As they went along the Moreno Creek trail, Adam stopped occasionally to check the receiver. Kendall was roaming the area, moving about quite a bit. "Damn," Adam said suddenly. "I was hoping we wouldn't have to open that bait box, but we might as well, because Samantha has just been somewhere in the vicinity of the second set."

"Hurrah for Samantha," Kelly said, grinning at Adam. "I hope she was smart enough to avoid the snare."

"Stop that. We're supposed to be snaring bears, and one way to get Santini past his current humiliation is to give him some bears to think about."

Samantha had stolen one piece of bait and chewed on the other. They had not caught a glimpse of her, but her signal was loud in the area. "You carry the bait," Adam said, "since you think that bear is so smart."

They rebaited and cleared their tracks. As they reached the four-wheeler again, Kelly said, "Adam, are you coming back?"

"Back from where?"

"Back from your family reunion, if there really is one."

Adam's eyes showed his shock. "Do you really think I'd make up something just to leave the project?"

"No, I guess not, but you haven't answered my question. Are you coming back?"

"Of course I'm coming back." He grinned at her. "You and Rick can stand each other's cooking for five days, can't you?"

"I hope we have lots of bears. Rick is bound to be touchy, and if we don't have plenty of work, I don't know how I'll handle it."

"Kelly, you don't always have to be in control." Adam put the torch in the equipment box. "Just take the days as they come and stop thinking your whole future depends on what Santini thinks of you."

"Dr. Andrews really respects his judgment."

"Yeah," Adam said, "do you think he would if we told him about dumping Rick into the woodshed at two o'clock in the morning?"

"But we aren't going to tell him, are we?"

"No, and I doubt if Rick does either."

When they started down to the first Moreno Creek set, Kelly spotted the bear in the set and stopped for a moment, her heart beating so fast she could hardly breathe. The big cinnamon-colored bear who tugged at the cable looked just like Roscoe. "Do you suppose he's a twin?" Adam asked as they moved closer and eyed the cable loop.

Kelly took a moment to clear her memory of Roscoe's carcass hanging in the hunters' camp. Then she began to prepare the ketamine and Rompun. When the bear was down, Kelly said, "It's a male. I think we should collar him to take the place of Roscoe in our data sheets. He's closer to Roscoe's age than Ryan is."

They tugged the big red bear over on his stomach, covered his eyes, and put on the collar and tags. She handed the flesh plugs from the ear tagging to Adam, who put them in the solution and labeled them. Kelly measured his long claws and the height of his massive shoulders. "What do you think? Is he about four years old?" Adam asked.

"I'd say so, and if he is, he can't be Roscoe's twin. Let's pull the tooth and get a lab report." Adam pulled the tooth. Kelly gave the penicillin shot. As she took the clipboard to record the data, she asked, "What shall we name him? What's your grandfather's name?"

"Adam, just like mine, but we've already got an Adam. Let's name this bear Santini." Kelly laughed and wrote the name at the top of the data sheet.

The bear weighed 275 pounds. His coat was not as fine as Roscoe's.

He'd been rubbing it against something and it looked patchy. They left him sleeping in the shade and started back toward the four-wheelers, just as Rick and Dr. Andrews walked down the slope. Dr. Andrews looked toward the bear. "A male, isn't he? Have you got a name?"

"Veritably," Adam said, exchanging a glance with Kelly.

"We named him Santini," Kelly said. Rick blinked and gave a short nervous laugh, but he looked pleased.

Dr. Andrews laughed, too, and said, "Okay, that's an apt name. But if you snare another male, will you name him Harry? That Selnick guy gave me enough money for three more collars before he left for Arizona." The professor dug in his pocket and took out a stick of gum, unwrapped it, and stuck it in his mouth. "Know what he said, Kelly?"

"No."

"He said, 'I like your bear woman.'" Kelly scowled. Harry Selnick hadn't even listened to her when she was talking to him. He had gone out and shot Roscoe anyway.

Back at the cabin that evening, Dr. Andrews noticed the lantern. It would have been surprising if he hadn't. It gave much better light than the lamp. "I see you replaced the lamp."

Rick said, "I broke the lamp."

"Well, the lantern's an improvement. We can probably reimburse you."

"Forget about it. I broke the damn lamp, and I replaced it. That's all."

Adam and Kelly looked at each other. Rick had not told Dr. Andrews about getting drunk. She glanced away. Rick was looking at them, and he looked so guilty and miserable that she had to do something before Dr. Andrews started probing. "Rick brought us a whole cow, a new light, and look what else." She brought the camp shower bag to Dr. Andrews for inspection. "It's like being in heaven to stand in the outhouse and let hot water pour over my hair."

After Dr. Andrews left the next morning, Rick lingered in the cabin, moving restlessly, fingering the equipment, but not working with it. Adam took the ashes out and brought wood and water in. Kelly did the dishes. The silence was heavy. Finally, as Kelly wiped out the dishpan and turned it upside down on the counter and Adam buckled the gun belt around his waist, Rick took a deep breath and said, "I owe you guys an apology."

Adam said, "It wasn't so bad, Santini."

Rick looked at him with a scowl. "I know just how bad it was. My old man's a drinker, and when he's drunk, he yells and busts stuff." He turned to Kelly. "Let's bring the data sheets up to date." His face was dark. "And then let's get to work on the mountain."

Kelly brought out the data sheets, and Rick dictated the facts of Jenny's death including the knot that had given way, the broken leg, and the shooting. Kelly's hand trembled as she wrote. "Do Santini, too," Adam said, and Kelly recorded the data about the new red male.

They tried to put Jenny's death behind them, but the ten days that followed were the most frustrating the bear crew had spent on the mountain. The human race swarmed over it, and the bears withdrew. "Blast these tourists," Rick said on July second when their snares were once again empty. "Why don't they stay in town and celebrate the Fourth with beer and firecrackers?"

Though they saw no bears, they saw humans every day. A jeep safari came into the mountains, and the constant roar and the dust was irritating to ears and eyes. The tires dug deep ruts in the creek bottoms, and when the jeeps didn't stay to the trails, they damaged the ground cover. Plastic sandwich bags and other bits of plastic blew into the bushes. Checking snares, Kelly and Adam picked up beer and soda cans and caught what paper debris they could. Hikers were just as bad. They seldom covered their toilet paper or their piles. Kelly began to carry a small shovel and did the distasteful job herself just to keep the mountain clean.

"If it weren't so much work to put them back," Rick said at dinner one night, "I'd be tempted to pull all the sets until after the holiday."

"I'm glad we haven't snared a bear," Adam said. "This confusion would cause them double stress."

"It will calm down some after the holiday," Rick said, "but all of August will be a pain, as the plains heat up and more people start taking their vacations."

"One good thing resulted from two weeks with no bears," Adam said one evening as he and Kelly scrounged the scrub oak behind the cabin for more firewood.

"Yeah, what?"

"We haven't used up our bait, so it will probably last until we're done snaring for the summer."

Kelly gathered some broken limbs for kindling and stacked them on top of the load, which Adam carried on his outstretched arms. "I just hope we snare some bears while you're off playing." Adam grinned around the pile of wood and headed for the woodshed.

On the following Saturday night, while Dr. Andrews and Rick discussed the human depredation of bear habitat, Adam came into

Kelly's room with the Ruger, the cartridge belt and holster, and the boxes of ammunition. "You'd better wear these while I'm gone. You'll be working alone most of the time."

"Do you trust me?"

"You're not a bad shot, Kelly. Keep practicing the way you've been with good concentration and mind/eye coordination. Some day you'll be nearly as great as I am." Adam's smile was warm, and his brown eyes sparkled.

Kelly returned the grin. "If you don't come back as soon as that dumb reunion is over, I'm going to track you down and shoot you." Adam reached out and, gripping her shoulder, pulled her close to him. He cupped his other hand around her head, bent, and kissed her on the mouth. Startled, Kelly wriggled from his grasp. Adam was red-faced, but still smiling as he turned to leave her room.

Early Sunday morning, Adam and Dr. Andrews got in the van and went up the road and out of sight around the curve, leaving Rick and Kelly alone. ❧

Chapter Thirty-Four

They stood near the porch and, before they could turn to go in, the van came into view once more, backing up. When the vehicle was near enough, Dr. Andrews leaned out the window and handed Kelly two letters. "I forgot to give you your mail." The van took off again. The letters were from Peggy and Ryan.

"Go ahead," Rick said. "Read them. And then I want to show you what I've got in mind for the next week."

Kelly nodded and sat down on the porch. To her annoyance, Rick sat down beside her. Feeling pushed, she glanced through the letters quickly. When she looked up, Rick was watching her. Kelly said, "Ryan wants a picture of his bear."

"You got a camera?"

"In my suitcase."

"Well, if you want to lug it around and if we catch that bear again, we can snap a picture for the kid. Now, let's get going." His tone was bossy. Rick stood and headed for the door. Kelly went to the outhouse. Rick didn't need to expect her to hop to his commands. She knew how Adam would see her attitude about this, but she didn't care. She always worked as hard as Rick did, and there was no point in his rude ways. She frowned, thinking of Adam. Why had he kissed her? Wasn't that just making the situation worse? What had he expected from her, with

Dr. Andrews sitting not ten feet away? Maybe that was the point. It was safe. Remembering the grin on Adam's face, she stopped frowning. Adam was fun and funny. She was going to miss him.

She reread her sister's letter. Peggy had moved into an apartment with two other girls. She had written, "I've been so jealous of you, getting to leave home and do exciting things, and now I'm away from home, too. You don't know how good it feels." *Yes, I do. It's like putting down a heavy package that you've carried for a long time.* Ryan's terse letter made her worry about him. He wasn't escaping from home.

Kelly went inside and put the letters away. Rick had unfolded some finely detailed maps. "The Fourth-of-July commotion has scattered the bears." She looked where he pointed. "We're going to make a big sweep through here with the receivers and find out where our collared bears went." Rick continued, "When we get some sort of overview, we can replace the sets accordingly." Kelly nodded. The plan made sense. Rick folded the maps and put them into his backpack. "But first, we have to check the snares."

The heat from the four-wheeler's engine made Kelly's legs and crotch sweat, and despite a brimmed cap she'd borrowed from Adam, the sun got to her face. The weight of the Ruger caused the gun belt to chafe her skin through her damp shirt. Her hands were sweaty on the handlebars of the machine. Driving the lower Chase Creek trail, she looked around, noting the thickets where the service berries and chokecherries ripened in the hot sun, but her thoughts were on Ryan. She wondered if anyone were giving him good information about sex. *Could I?* She and Ryan were good enough friends that she might talk openly to him. *But I don't understand the way men feel about sex.*

Who could anyone talk to? Who had ever managed to keep sex from being a game for power and possession? She thought again of Adam's kiss. His lips had been strong against her mouth as he held her head in the vise of his hand. It would be fun to play with Adam, to lie on that warm slope on Moreno Creek and kiss and touch. If they could be honest. Kelly shook her head. Thoughts about Adam's mouth and his firm belly were not cooling the day down any.

Back at the meadow, Rick's businesslike manner turned her thoughts quickly to the project. *If there were a bunch of us, all hot and bored and horny, it would be tough to keep the crew on track. Work is probably the only antidote.*

After they'd checked all the snares, Rick allowed them a few moments for lunch during which he discussed range and habitat. Whatever else he was, Rick was informed about the subject of bears, and his previous fieldwork gave him experience that Kelly wanted to hear about. "What's the difference between home range and territory?"

"A home range can encompass several different types of habitat."

"Is your thesis on home range?"

"Well, yeah, that and population age structure and sex ratios. For example, we have a lot of young bears on this mountain. There are not very many old ones."

"Is there a reason for that?"

"Nothing but pressure. The average age of our females is four years and the average age of our males is three."

"And what's their natural lifespan?"

"Bears in other studies—where there are no people—have lived to be twenty years old. The oldest bear we've caught here has been eleven. That's probably because of hunting pressure."

Kelly nodded. "Harry Selnick brags of his magnificent trophies."

"At least he donates a few collars," Rick said. He took a huge bite of his lunchmeat sandwich and looked at her. "You could do some habitat studies," he said, "if you're up to the work." He stuffed the last of the sandwich into his mouth and gathered his sandwich bags and the pop can. "We better get going if we're going to cover enough ground." He handed her the trash, and she stored it in her backpack. "Are you cooking dinner tonight?" he asked.

Startled, Kelly looked at him. He had actually *asked*. She said, "I'll flip you for it."

Rick fished in his pocket. "Heads you fill the bait box, tails you cook dinner."

"That's no choice. I hope it stands on its edge."

Rick flipped the coin and said, "It's tails." He turned toward the four-wheelers in the meadow. "We'll reload one of these and hook up the trailer so we'll be ready to head out when we get back." Kelly drove her four-wheeler up the ramp onto the pickup and then helped Rick position the trailer tongue over the hitch. "We'll take the portable receiver and antenna and the maps. Better take the canteens. We're going to do some walking."

"Do you think we'll see any of the bears?"

"Maybe if we walk far enough." Rick grinned at her. "It's not easy hiking. Bears like the thickest, nastiest cover they can find." His face was the golden olive color that meant he was at ease.

"Have you seen bears in the wild—away from the sets?"

"Yeah, I've been able to get within about fifty yards of them before they detect me. But then they'll smell me or hear me and take off."

"Then what do you do?"

"I go to the spot where I saw them and look for evidence. I usually find a day bed or scat. And then I look to see what they were eating."

Rick swung a leg across the saddle of the four-wheeler, settled the receiver in his lap, and held the antenna until Kelly climbed on behind him and took it. As they started up the smooth road toward the first turnoff, Kelly asked, "If there are cattle and sheep and elk and deer and bear all in the same area, how can you tell who was eating what?"

"It's mainly by other signs in the area, but they do eat in different ways. If you find a log that's torn apart, it's probably a bear; they do that to dig out the ants. A deer won't do that. And if you see an area where just the flowers have been eaten off, that's what bears do. Or look at berries and acorns. The bears pick 'em off."

"It's a lot to learn."

"It's just experience. After you've been out there a while, you become familiar with what it looks like." Their conversation was far easier than Kelly had expected. Without the strain between Adam and Rick and her own constant awareness of Adam's blasted seesaw, Kelly could concentrate totally on the mountain and the project, and as she did, Rick seemed to relax more too.

When they picked up the first signal, which was Marie's, they parked the four-wheeler and walked quietly along a game trail. Rick was ahead of Kelly when he stopped abruptly and put out a hand to slow her down. He nodded his head slightly forward. Across the gully, near a tangle of chokecherry bushes, Marie and a cub were moving through a patch of sunlit grass. Kelly froze. This is what she had always wanted to see—a bear in her own world, unaware of the human race. She held her breath as the big blonde mother bear lumbered toward the chokecherries, and the small red cub scrambled after her.

Rick leaned close to Kelly's ear and whispered. "This is no place for us. If she smells us, we might have trouble. Most likely, she'll just run away, but she'll be defending both cub and food, so we won't take the chance. Back slowly away." Kelly obeyed his instructions and moved quietly up the trail and away through the scrub oak. Rick followed silently until they had reached the crest of a small hill. "I think we're okay now. I'm glad we were across the gully."

"I'm glad she had two cubs, so that she has one left."

"Looks like a twin to the one that died."

Kelly liked the companionable mood they had established, and she discovered that as long as she asked questions, Rick was responsive and pleasant. They moved on and picked up signals from Elizabeth and

Christine. Rick showed her how to mark the map. "How do you write up the habitat data?" Kelly asked.

"To begin with, you record elevation, slope, aspect, soil type, distances to creeks and ponds and to roads and other disturbances." He folded the map. "When we get back tonight, I'll show you some of the habitat sheets."

They were late getting in, and Kelly just scrambled some eggs with bits of Spam. Rick looked at the plate she set in front of him and said, "For the first time all day, I miss Wainwright." After they ate, Rick brought out the habitat sheets, and Kelly studied them while he lectured. "What you do is set up a ten-meter-by-ten-meter plot—a hundred square meters—at the center of some bear activity. Identify all the plants within that area and write them down. Estimate the percent of cover of each plant species, their mean height, how much of it is living material. Record the plant phenological stage—is it in the flower stage? Is it in the seed stage? Is it dying off?" Rick stretched and yawned. "You done looking at those?" Kelly nodded, and he gathered the habitat sheets and refiled them. Kelly went to the outhouse feeling grateful that one of the five days alone with Rick had passed so smoothly.

By Monday evening, after hours of exhausting hikes through the scrub oak and up one hill after another, they had located most of their collared bears. Although they hadn't pinpointed the exact spot where each bear lingered, they had a good enough general idea. "We'll pick up the highest snares out of all three drainages tomorrow and rebuild closer to the oak shrublands." Rick had the grace to smile at Kelly as he planned three days' work in one. After his apology, Rick had never mentioned the day of Jenny's death again, but he seemed determined to add more bears to their data sheets before the July trapping was done.

Tuesday morning, Rick decided that they should split up so they'd have some chance of getting all nine sets redone. "Once you've moved the equipment, go ahead and start rebuilding." He started his engine. "I'll check your sets when I've finished building mine." Exasperated, biting her tongue not to say "and then I'll check *your* work," Kelly got on her machine. She'd been building barricades and placing foot snares for two-and-a-half months. If Rick told Dr. Andrews that he still had to follow behind her, what were her hopes of advancing on the project?

Kelly went up the logging road toward Moreno Creek, moving to one side to let one of the big trucks pass. The driver was a stranger. She wondered if Peggy and Matt were dating. Peggy had not mentioned him in her letter. It would be lonely at home this fall with Peggy not there to talk to. *I wish I had more of Grandma's money left. I'd move out too*. She parked the four-wheeler, still thinking of her arrangements for fall. *If I can get a lab teaching job, I can pay the rest of my tuition, but I don't see how I can work for Dad on weekends if I plan to do any of the fall trapping and the early den work.*

Kelly decided to go high and work her way down. Just retrieving the sets was difficult. The gun and holster were constantly in the way. When she carried a snare and chain, she had to hold her hands away from her side or the gun rubbed her arm. When she swung the holster to the back, her pack bounced off it. If she moved it to the front, the gun banged her leg and made her stride awkward. She worked around it the best she could and finally moved downhill to start the new sets. The scrub oak and the thickets were not as pleasant to work in as the sun-spangled aspen meadows. She splashed her face with water from the trickle in the deep vee of Moreno Creek. The water smelled of moss and earth. Refreshed, she began erecting barricades.

It took all day to move and rebuild the sets. It was after dark before they ate and did the cabin work, but it didn't take them long. Kelly was learning a lot from Rick about running a businesslike project. Keep your thoughts, your feelings, your comments to yourself and—as Adam had said—talk only about bears, habitat, and scat.

They started early Wednesday to check the new sets and all the others. Walking toward the first of the new Chase Creek sets, Kelly caught a motion. She squinted to see through the thick cover, and her pulse quickened as it always did when she saw a bear. She went closer. Firmly snared, the cable a little too high on his leg, a red bear with white ear tags prowled around the tree. It had to be Santini. He had pulverized the barricades, mauled the bait, and left huge piles of scat.

She wanted to tell Rick immediately, but she had to check the rest of the snares. She gunned the four-wheeler and covered the distance between sets faster than she ever had before. The third new set also held a bear—a young blonde bear without ear tags. Two bears. They were going to have a busy day. Kelly checked the rest of the snares and then headed for Moreno Creek. Her new sets were undisturbed, but Ryan was snared in the very top set of the drainage. The brown bear tugged at the chain and huffed as Kelly came near.

The skin on Kelly's arms was covered with gooseflesh. Three bears! They'd never snared so many in one day. Rick had been right to move the sets. A filling joy made Kelly raise her arms. Ryan whirled toward her at the movement, and she decided that she could celebrate later. Right now, she needed to catch up with Rick and tell him that they had three bears.

"Make it four," he said, his dark eyes gleaming with a matching excitement. "We've got Samantha in the berry thicket up Warren Gulch." ❧

Chapter Thirty-Five

"We'll need the winch," Kelly said. "Santini is in one of your new sets, and he weighed two hundred and seventy-five pounds two weeks ago." She leaned to her pack. "And I want the camera, too. That's Ryan up top in Moreno Creek."

"Still high, huh. Wonder what he's eating up there."

"Our bait. He's stolen several pieces this summer. He just got careless this time."

With few words, they swung into the bear processing. Rick handed Kelly the jab stick, and with swift strides, crossed in front of Santini to distract him. Kelly set the needle into the bear's rump and delivered the anesthetic fully with her follow-through and then moved away as the big bear whirled to lunge at her.

When the bear went down, they approached him. "So this is the bear you guys hooked my name onto," Rick said as they stretched him out. "He's kinda ratty-looking."

"He had an itch to scratch."

"Or a tree to mark."

They worked quietly and quickly. When Santini was bound for weighing, Kelly attached the winch and, using a tree branch, they lifted the bear just high enough so that the field scale could register his weight. "Two hundred and eighty-seven pounds! This fellow has really been scarfing down those berries."

Kelly nodded and let the bear sag to the ground. They untied his legs and stretched him out again. Kelly picked up one paw and extended the claws. The bear's paw hid most of her hand. She eased the leg into a position that looked more comfortable for the bear.

"We'll be able to do a Lincoln-Peterson estimate with these recaptures," Rick said. Kelly nodded. The Lincoln-Peterson index was a statistical method of estimating the bear population using the ratio between captures and recaptures. Their data was getting stronger each time they snared a bear.

It was nearly two o'clock by the time Kelly took her share of the equipment back to her four-wheeler, but she bet herself that Rick would want to do one more bear before they stopped for lunch. She slipped an apple from her pack and ate it on the way to the blonde bear.

They moved into a smooth routine, processing the blonde bear as if they were one person. Before Rick reached for something, Kelly had extended it. At the moment she was ready to do a measurement, Rick took up the other end of the rule. Collar, tags, tooth, flesh plug, shots—each was applied or removed efficiently. The bear was female, two years old, ninety-five pounds with a fair coat, but not much fat. "Let's name her Mary, after Mary Powers, that woman pilot that came up with the department people," Kelly said. "I liked her."

"Suits me, and it might impress them," Rick said, printing Mary at the top of the data sheet and recording the information Kelly dictated.

Before and after they put Ryan down, Kelly snapped pictures for her brother. Ryan was frisky. He whirled from Rick toward Kelly three times before she could get close enough to place the jab stick. She was sweating and tired by the time he went down, but they worked him with the same efficiency, and she felt less tired as the harmony between them made the work easy.

There was no need for conversation. Total focus on work with someone else who had the same focus put Kelly into a kind of timeless sense of well-being. Her mind felt sharp and her eyes keen as she surveyed the set area, collected scat, and recorded data.

By the time they got to Samantha, it was late, and the barricade, thicket, and set were tromped, clawed, and pulverized. "This bear is a rotten sport," Rick said.

"How so?" Kelly could hear the defensive tone to her voice. She admired this bear.

"She steals our bait all the time, but she gets mad when she loses a round."

Samantha was slow to go down, as she had been the first time they snared her. It seemed a lifetime ago, but it had only been early May. Rick sighed as if he were getting tired. "Damn it, Kelly," he said, "give her another half-round. She resists that anesthetic worse than any bear I've ever put down." They ate salami sandwiches while they waited for Samantha to give in and go to sleep.

Samantha had gained another ten pounds, and she was in estrus. "We'll be seeing her in her den with cubs this winter," Rick said. "She's in such good shape from eating our dead cows that she's bound to implant." Kelly ran her fingers through the beautiful chocolate-colored hair. This was an animal to remember all her life. It would be fun to follow her in a habitat study, to see her mate, and meet her cubs. She was strong and determined, and she seemed to have a sense of self.

It was early evening by the time they had processed all four bears, but Rick wasn't ready to go back to the cabin when they reached the meadow. "We won't reset the snares tonight, but I want to make damn sure that every bear we processed today got up and walked away." He nodded toward a four-wheeler. "Hop on behind me, and we'll make a quick run up each drainage."

He really meant *quick*. Kelly hung onto the rack and to Rick, too, as he gunned the machine and took off. The rush of cool evening air past her face felt good, and she relaxed into the motion of the machine, swaying with Rick's body when he leaned sideways, leaning forward with him when they climbed a hill, feeling the swift sure motions of his legs as he shifted. The sun was already behind the higher peaks, and the deeper parts of the conifer forest were shadowy, the tall tree trunks just dark emphatic lines. Each of the four bears had recovered and left the sites by the time they checked them. Satisfied, Rick headed at last toward the truck.

The cabin was dark and musty after being shut up all day. It was a relief to get rid of the Ruger. "Let's take care of the equipment and get that scat drying before we clean up and eat," Rick said. Kelly was tired, and her muscles ached, but she was happy. The processing had been perfect. The bears were safe and not damaged. Two quiet people caused the least stress for the bears. She and Rick had worked like a well-matched team—like partners. She took her backpack and tools into the storeroom and with the aid of the flashlight put them on the shelf. Rick followed with the ice chest.

"You want to shine that light up here?" he said. Kelly complied, and Rick unlocked the cabinet doors above her head and placed the chest of drugs and DNA samples on the shelf. When he had relocked the cabinet, he turned slightly and looked down at Kelly.

In the gleam of the flashlight, his eyes took on a strange glow, and as he continued to stare into Kelly's eyes, her pulse quickened. She could feel his body tense, and then, as smoothly and efficiently as he had moved all day long, Rick closed the distance between them and with one strong arm pulled her body tightly against his. With his other hand, he grasped her chin and turned her mouth upward.

His mouth on hers was powerful and demanding. Kelly had been so tuned to him all day that her response was automatic. Her body formed itself to him, and her mouth met his with a natural, easy response. She was totally alive and aware of everything. She could feel the long hard shape of him against her body. She smelled sweat and bear and the scent of pine needles and the salami on his breath and the odor of male excitement and a hint of gasoline.

His mouth was so determined she could feel the bruising to her lips, but she did not want him to stop because as Rick kissed her, Kelly felt some inner barrier drop away, and she slid into a satisfying, deep, hot place inside herself. She moved forward when Rick's hand moved to her buttocks and pressed her closer to him. His belt buckle cut into her, and the zipper of his jeans bit her stomach where his hard erection pushed against her body.

Holding Kelly in the continued vise of his arm, Rick moved their combined bodies toward the cot and onto it. His mouth never left hers. The weight of his body was immense, but it simply made the fire inside of Kelly leap higher and burn brighter. She could see the flames behind her eyelids, blue and hot and orange and red. The joining of their bodies after the day-long joining of their minds seemed inevitable.

Rick's mouth had moved to the vee of her blouse and his hands to the top of her jeans. As he struggled on top of her, her arms were trapped, and there was no way for her to help, despite her need to be free of clothes and restraints and be even closer to him. His weight and intensity immobilized her. Then he said, "Damn it, give me a hand."

And at the imperative tone, so like the usual Rick, Kelly remembered with a rush of panic the project and the Honor Code, and she began to struggle. This was not how she wanted it the first time, not against her honor, not something she would have to regret afterward. "What in the hell?" Rick continued to try to remove her clothes, and now Kelly was fighting with real determination.

"Don't, Rick," she said, writhing beneath him and freeing one leg. "We signed the code," she said. But Rick paid no attention, and now she began to be afraid. *This is not what I want.* Rick had pulled her blouse open, and she could feel the roughness of his day's growth of whiskers against her breast. The fire in her was still alive, but she knew—her mind knew, anyway—that she would be sorry if she let that fantastic fire burn up thoughts of the other things that mattered to her. She craved his mouth and his hands and his hard body on her, and she had to fight her own body and her own emotions as she fought Rick's wonderful, muscled, determined body. *This is what the Honor Code is all about. But this is also the way this day should end, partners in every way.*

She continued to struggle because she knew without a doubt that if she let this go to the conclusion her body wanted, she would have to leave the project. There would be no way to keep the truth from Dr. Andrews if she dishonored the code. He had trusted her enough to let her come to the field. She could not do this.

With these thoughts, some of the fire died away in Kelly, and the cold truth gave her the strength to free a hand and push against Rick. Swinging her head away from the lips that had sought her mouth again, she began to talk. "Rick, we can't break the code. Rick, we're not here to do this. This will ruin the project."

When Kelly said that, she felt Rick's mind take it in, and he slackened the thrust of his body enough that Kelly could slip off the cot and onto the floor. She lay there for a moment making no movement because the movement her body wanted warred with her mind, and she fought herself—wanting to reach up and draw Rick to the floor with her.

She couldn't see his face. The flashlight had fallen and lay on its side aiming its beam toward the kitchen. She could hear him panting. And then suddenly he gave a great shove that banged the cot against the wall. She winced, but Rick's motion was not toward her. He pushed himself up—his dark shape was huge above her—and then he turned and went out of the storeroom, careening against the doorframe and stumbling over the flashlight. She heard the front door slam and the outhouse door slam, too.

She stayed on the floor trying to grasp some rational thought that would get her through the next few hours. All she really wanted to do, if she couldn't follow Rick and make hot love in the grass, was to think about the depth of the fire that had roared through her. *I always knew that if my mind and body and emotions were all in alignment, it could be this way.* There was something so beautiful about the sense of being whole that she could hardly let it go.

Casting around in her mind, she thought of the Honor Code, but it seemed shallow and faceless. Then she found Dr. Andrews's face in her mind. He trusted her discretion. He trusted her to keep the project going smoothly. She felt more strongly about keeping her honor clear with Dr. Andrews, really, than she did about the Honor Code itself. Holding to her thoughts of the professor who had given her the chance to come on this project, surely knowing the hazards, she got up from the floor and picked up the battered flashlight.

She washed her face in cold water and combed her hair and straightened her clothes. Then she lit the lantern and began to build up a fire. They needed food and regular routine. She didn't know if Rick would come back in, but she didn't think he would leave because there were four sets to rebuild tomorrow and all the other sets to check, and he wouldn't trust her to do them alone and do them right.

Just as she was slicing potatoes into the skillet to fry along with the pork chops she had browned, Rick came into the cabin. He stopped to pump up the lantern and then silently took plates and silverware and set the table. She threw a quick glance his way. He looked sullen. His mouth was set in a straight line; his eyes seemed hooded. When she served the meal, he sat down, and jerking the meat plate close to his, forked two pork chops onto his plate. He piled potatoes beside the chops and ignored the dish of mixed vegetables. The silence was so heavy, she felt it like smog. She took deep breaths and tried to think what she could do. This had to get worked out some way before Dr. Andrews came again, even before Adam returned on Friday.

When Rick pushed his empty plate away, she took one more deep breath and said, "Rick, I think we should talk." He raised his eyes to hers for the first time since he had looked into them in the storeroom. She added, "For the sake of the work."

He nodded slightly and said, "Yeah. Maybe."

Her own need to know what kind of joining they might have had helped her to phrase her question. "Why did you . . . ?" She didn't know how to finish the question, but a little spark of light leaped in Rick's eyes, and she knew that he wasn't over the feeling any more than she. Would he tell her?

The spark died and the sullen look returned. "Do you want an honest answer?"

She swallowed, but said steadily, "I don't think we can clear the air without honest answers."

Rick gave a half shrug and then straightened his shoulders. "It just kind of built up. My project was going well; you were pretty good help; I'd taken four bears. It seemed natural to take the bear woman, too." He could have hit her in the face, and it would have hurt less.

What a *fool* she had been to assume that their feelings were the same. Rick had never wanted her, and he still didn't want her as a person. But she was damned if she'd let him know how much pain his words had inflicted. She forced a smile and said lightly, "Just another trophy, huh? Like Harry Selnick takes for his trophy room?"

Rick looked down, but he nodded and said, "Something like that." She was silent. Maybe this was all he was going to say, and maybe this was all she wanted to hear. But Rick surprised her by asking, "And why do *you* think it happened?"

She was tempted to evade the question, but she bit her lip and then said, "I felt that we had worked so smoothly as partners that it was almost a natural outcome of these three days' work."

He jerked his head as if he were offended. "I didn't . . . I don't . . . think of us as partners. I don't *want* a woman for a partner."

There wasn't anything Rick could say that could wound her more than he had already, so she pushed him further because she wanted to know how a man felt about this. "Not even an intelligent woman? One who could think and work on an even basis with you?"

"No, damn it. I don't want to spend my life competing with a woman. Competing at work is hard enough. I want a woman who is ready to take care of me at the end of the day—to listen to my ideas, cook a decent meal, and be willing in bed."

This was more than she had ever heard Rick say before about his personal feelings. Despite his reasons for making a move on her, he seemed to have been as shaken by the fire between them as she was. She said, "So what is an intelligent woman supposed to do with her life?"

"Give birth to intelligent sons and get out of their way." The words infuriated her. The rush of anger smothered the fire inside her. She was swept with a tide of relief that she had not had sex with Rick. His contempt would have left her feeling dirty all her life. She remained silent, drained by emotion. But Rick spoke again. "This is just another reason why you shouldn't be on this project. This would not have happened if you hadn't been here."

And now her fury was boiling over. "Are you trying to tell me that this is all my fault?"

"I tried to tell Jerry in the first place, and I'm going to tell him again." Rick's face was totally mud-colored. "This wouldn't have happened if you hadn't been here."

"And *you* had nothing to do with it?"

Rick only repeated a third time, "It wouldn't have happened if you hadn't been here." ∽

Chapter Thirty-Six

It will never happen again. Kelly grabbed the dirty dishes and washed them with quick, angry movements. Finished, she flung the dishwater from the porch, carried more water from the spring, banked the fire, and filled the wood box. It wasn't until she dug the data file from under the bed and began to record the day's bear information that Rick stirred. "I'll do that."

"Just dictate the information as you always do," Kelly said, her voice as cold and as businesslike as she could make it.

By the time they had recorded the data, Kelly's anger had faded into fatigue and the sour flat feeling of receding sexual frustration. Rick said, "We need to get an early start tomorrow. Checking snares will use the morning. Four sets will take up most of the afternoon. The bait box is half empty, and we might have other bears."

Kelly looked at him as if he were a stranger. "I've been ready to go to work every morning since I've been here. I'll be ready tomorrow morning."

She undressed in the dark and crawled under the covers. The light in the big room went out, and she heard Rick's cot creak as he lay heavily upon it. She could not go to sleep. The evening began to replay itself backward in her mind, starting with his words, "It wouldn't have happened if you hadn't been here." Adam had said that too when she had faced the men who had accosted her in the woods. So many times. So many times. She had read it in newspapers, heard people say it. "She shouldn't have been there."

Kelly sighed. Adam was basically a very decent person. If he believed what he had said, what hope was there for women who wanted to work safely in the field? Rick turned over in his cot, and she shivered. She had to admit that he was basically decent too, or she would have been raped this evening. Or maybe he was just basically selfish. He cared nothing for *her*, but he cared enough about *his* project to put it ahead of his sexual need.

Rick coughed and turned again. She could not keep herself from thinking of the way his body had moved on hers. But remembering how she had felt when he had held her so tightly against him, she also remembered his words, "I thought I'd take the bear woman, too," and her anger returned with a rush of acid to her stomach. She'd never go to sleep feeling this upset. She tried to regain some of her objectivity.

Even if they made her raw with humiliation, she had gathered several valuable data points tonight—the most important being: there is no true union with a man who only wants to count coup on your body. Sex with Rick would never really be satisfying, no matter how hot and eager her body felt. *I learned something else about myself, though. And it's not so bad.* An inside blockage—like a false floor—had burned away, and she felt a kind of awe at the beauty of something when it felt right. Even if it wouldn't have been right with Rick, it was right with her. When she was total, and all parts of herself connected, she felt real power. Thinking of what Matt had said about a fire inside of her, she had to acknowledge the truth of his words. But she still felt as she had before. *Whatever it is, it belongs to me.* If that kind of fire was what her mother had stumbled into as an undergraduate, it's no wonder that she had escaped into marriage. At the moment when Rick's mouth had joined with hers, nothing had been more important then his hand on her buttocks, his hard penis pressing into her body, his weight on top of her. She gritted her teeth as she felt the flames rise through her again. Gripping the cot she fought thoughts of his body. He was lying awake, too. All she had to do was make one move, and they would finish what they had started. *You're a fool, Kelly. That's the way to total destruction of everything you value about yourself.*

It didn't make any difference. It would be a long time before she could look at Rick without remembering. And there was no way to go back to the placid, controlled feeling that had protected her before. Why hadn't her mother warned her that one's body could turn on with such force? *Because if she thought about it at all, she didn't want me to know it was in me.*

As she tossed and turned, the covers bunched up around her. Rick's cot moved again against the outside wall. Go to sleep, Santini. She hated him. She had worked as a partner with him, but he was still going to tell Dr. Andrews that she shouldn't be here. Kelly turned on her side and stared at the window. The sky was lightening. It was nearly dawn. In an hour or two, she would have to face Rick. *I will never touch him again, nor let him touch me.*

Rick took bait with him toward Chase Creek the next morning, assigning Kelly to rebuild the Moreno Creek set after checking the others. They were businesslike and coolly civil, and Kelly was aware that Rick avoided being near her as much as she avoided him.

Hefting the fifteen-pound chunk of stinking meat from the bait box to replace stolen bait on Moreno Creek, Kelly felt as if she'd faint. She had not slept at all, and she was fairly certain that Rick hadn't either. He looked like a shack in a ghost town—faded color, no lights, frame sagging. A wreck. She burnt the bait and then went up creek to rebuild the top set. Her fatigue made her slow, and it took her an hour and a half. The spring fought her like something alive. She forced her tired body to push against it, until the catch slipped into place.

When she got back to the meadow, Rick wasn't there, and he should have been there. They had agreed to do Warren Gulch together. *Maybe he has a bear in trouble.* She took her four-wheeler up Chase Creek, where she saw that Rick had rebuilt the first set. Driving higher, she could tell by the tracks that he had checked others. When she rounded the next curve, she saw his four-wheeler parked beside the trail, but Rick was nowhere in sight. Kelly stopped her machine behind Rick's and started down through the scrub toward the set. She saw a movement, low in the brush, and her heart leaped and started beating in her throat. Moving slowly and carefully, she crept toward the spot until she could see clearly. Rick was crawling up the hill, half dragging his left leg. Kelly hurried toward him. "Rick! What happened?"

He looked up at her. His forehead was beaded with sweat. "The spring got away from me." Kelly moved closer and looked at the leg. Just above his shoetop, there was a deep gash that had bled down into his sock and over the white canvas shoe. His ankle was badly swollen.

"I'll be right back." She sprinted up the hill where she lifted the small ice chest from Rick's four-wheeler, along with the strip of cloth from which they tore eye coverings for the bears. Why weren't they carrying a first aid kit? She took the spray that they used on cable cuts and the vet wrap. Rick had moved a few more feet up the hill. Kneeling by him, Kelly poured melted ice water from the bottom of the chest into the gash and, using a scrap of cloth, cleaned the dirt and leaves and finally the blood from the wound. "This isn't sterile. Have you had a tetanus booster recently?"

"Yeah." Rick's face was pale. The ankle was swelling more. Kelly sprayed the cut liberally with the antiseptic, then took most of the ice from the chest, leaving the drugs buried under one layer. She spread the cloth and laid the ice on it, folded the cloth to trap the ice, then pulled it around Rick's ankle. She secured the bulky ice pack with the vet wrap. Rick watched her silently, his mouth tight.

She stood. "Can you get up?"

"Yeah, I think so." She extended her hand to him and Rick pulled himself up onto his good right leg, wincing as he stood.

Kelly moved close to him and said, "Put your arm across my shoulder and use me as a crutch." For one brief moment, one brief flare of heat, Kelly was aware that they both were thinking of the last time his arm had gone around her. Kelly shook her head slightly. *This is the damndest job I ever had. No matter what happens, you keep on doing the next necessary thing.* Rick put his arm across her shoulders, and they made slow awkward progress up the hill. At the top, Kelly helped Rick onto his four-wheeler. "Do you think you can drive?"

"Just help me get it into low. I can go back to the truck without shifting." Once at the meadow, Rick said, "There are two more sets to build. If we fashion some sort of crutch, I can do the Warren Gulch one. The slope's not bad."

Kelly stared at him. She knew he hadn't slept all night. He was pale with pain. "Don't be a fool, Rick. For all you know, that ankle might be broken."

"But the sets have to be rebuilt."

Tired to the point of desperation, Kelly had nothing left of tact or discretion. "Get in the back of the truck and lie down before you fall down. I can rebuild those sets, and it will take me a damn sight less time alone than it would if I have to drag you up and down the hill." Rick's eyes opened wide, and then he blinked and turning to the tailgate, crawled up on it.

Please, don't let there be a bear in the Warren Gulch sets. Kelly went there first and breathed a tired sigh when she found the sets empty. She rebuilt the trail set where they'd snared Samantha the day before and made the long trek to Chase Creek and took care of the second set. Back at the meadow, she used one four-wheeler to tug the trailer close to the truck, helped Rick climb into the passenger seat of the cab, and finished loading.

Rick didn't want any supper. He took some Tylenol from his Dopp kit and then hopped to his cot, collapsed, and fell into a deep, snoring sleep. Kelly ate and went to bed, too tired to work on data sheets.

Friday, she left Rick on his bed after a verbal battle that was irritating and stupid. The leg was still swollen, and Rick could hardly walk. She had to help him outside to the outhouse and back in. How did he think he could climb mountains? She rewrapped the wound. "Just work on data sheets or something."

"What if there's a bear?"

"Then I'll have to go and find some help." Male pride was exasperating, and it got in the way of the work. Maybe *he* didn't belong here.

It took most of the day to check the sets. Her luck held and there were no bears. She returned home and began the rest of the work. It was dusk when Jamie McCarthy's truck pulled up in front of the cabin and Adam got out with an armload of packages. The truck drove away, and Adam came up the steps, smiling when Kelly opened the door. But his smile faded as soon as he stepped into the light and looked at her. "What in hell happened to you?"

Kelly was suddenly grateful for Rick's accident. She pointed toward the bed where Rick was once again sleeping with the bandaged leg elevated on pillows. "Rick got hurt. I've been doing most of the work."

Adam put his packages down with a whistle. "I'm sorry, Kelly. Why didn't you call me?"

"It just happened yesterday." She moved to a chair and sank into it. "I'd have had to call you if there had been any bears. We snared four of them on Wednesday."

"Four! I should never have left."

"I'm just glad you came back."

"I'm glad to be back. I'd forgotten how complicated a family reunion can get." Kelly smiled ruefully. He'd never know how complicated a *bear project* could get.

⚬

Saturday morning, Rick agreed to stay home one more day, but he said, "Can I borrow your car, Kelly? I need to call Jerry and report." She looked at him in amazement. She should loan him her car so he could sabotage her graduate work and the next two years of her life?

"No, I don't think I want to loan you my car," she said. "You can wait until we get back, and one of us will drive you. Your leg's not ready to operate a clutch."

Rick scowled. Kelly put her car keys in her backpack. Adam stared from one to the other. When they got into the pickup, he said, "What was that all about?"

She said, "You don't want to know." She was grateful that they had to split up to do the work because Adam was too perceptive, and she didn't have any barriers in place against the probing questions she knew he would get around to sooner or later.

They had caught a nice little brown yearling on Chase Creek. He snuffled around the set trying to reach the bait, gave it up to sit down on his haunches and scratch himself, then yawned and rolled over in the leaves, kicking his free feet in the air for a moment before struggling upright once more when Adam and Kelly approached. He huffed in a tentative way, as if he'd never tried it before. The bear worked the same old magic in Kelly. Laughing, she turned to Adam. "Aren't you glad you're back—just to see him?"

Adam nodded, and they went to work processing the little bear. When he was down, and she had released the cable, Kelly knelt and pulled him into her lap. She hugged his fat little body to her and laid her face on his warm fur a moment before stretching him out and covering his eyes. "I hope he gets a chance to grow up and grow old," she said as she applied the ear tags, took the flesh plug, and then pulled the tooth.

Adam said, "Let's call him Kelly."

"Kelly is a girl's name."

"Could be a boy, too. We don't have a bear named after you, and we may not catch another female this summer."

"You are *not* going to put my name on a male bear!"

"Okay. Not Kelly. I'll just call him Cubby Jones."

For the first time since Rick had dumped his honest answers on her, Kelly began to feel that the pain might go away someday. She smiled at Adam and petted the little bear once more. "Cubby Jones. I like that. I'd like to keep him on the foot of my bed."

"That's the first time your eyes have smiled since I got back," Adam said. He hesitated and then said, "Kelly . . ."

She interrupted. "Don't, Adam. Let it go. Don't spoil a nice day." His face closed for a moment, and then he nodded and picked up the bear's paw to measure it.

When they returned to the cabin, Rick was sleeping. Adam said, "Let him sleep. I'll go check in with Dr. Andrews." Kelly glanced at him. His report to Dr. Andrews would be a lot different from Rick's. With a sense of reprieve, she nodded, and watched the pickup until it disappeared around the curve.

Rick insisted that he accompany them on Sunday, and Kelly insisted that Adam drive Rick's four-wheeler for him. Rick's leg was still obviously painful, and besides, she didn't want to be alone with Adam. But Rick foiled her attempt to avoid Adam. After they'd checked Chase Creek and Warren Gulch, Rick said, "Why don't you two do the Moreno Creek run? I'll hang around the truck and mark bear locations." He limped slowly around the truck and reached inside for the antenna.

Some human had tossed the bait from both sides of the first set into a pile of brush. They could see boot tracks all around. The other sets were undisturbed. As they turned away from the last set at the top of the drainage, Adam walked toward the sunny slope where they had rested once before. "We need to get back, Adam."

"Santini will be okay. He can prop his leg up in the truck."

"I'm tired."

"You're avoiding me, Kelly." He turned toward her with a serious expression. His eyes bored into hers. "I'm part of this crew, too, and when something happens that so blatantly affects the crew, I'm entitled to know."

"Maybe not."

"Damn it, Kelly. I had serious doubts about coming back here. I talked it over with my parents, and they encouraged me not to quit. I've seen bears hurt and bears die, and now I see Santini hurt physically and you hurt in some other way." He stomped around in a circle and then turned once more to her. "You and Rick have from the very first moment acted as if this was your project and the only question to be answered was who got to be boss. Well, I've worked as hard as you, and

I've learned as much as you, and I'm not some dumb flunky you can put off by saying I don't have any rights." Kelly was astonished. She just stood still and looked at him. "Well?"

She sighed and then said, "Rick is going to tell Dr. Andrews in strong terms that I don't belong on this project."

"How in hell can he do that? It looks to me like you did your share of the work through Wednesday and all of the work Thursday and Friday. He should be telling Dr. Andrews you're totally capable."

"It's not what I do, Adam, it's what I am."

"And what are you?"

"A woman."

"Is he still harping on that?"

"He's adamant about it."

Adam reached out to Kelly, put his hands on her arms, and turning her toward him, forced her to meet his eyes. "What happened, Kelly? Did Santini make a pass at you?" ❧

Chapter Thirty-Seven

It would be so easy to let Adam believe that, but she couldn't lie to him. "Not exactly."

"Not exactly? You mean you can't tell when a guy makes a pass at you?"

"I mean that it wasn't entirely his fault." Adam still held her, staring into her eyes. She shifted uncomfortably. "Nothing happened, Adam."

Adam shook his head slightly and let go of her arms. "You're quick to say that. You told Matt the same thing, and it was a lie then too."

"The Honor Code is intact," Kelly protested. "My honor is intact."

"Your honor . . ." He sounded hurt somehow, but he left the sentence unfinished and dropped into silence, his look probing like a long knife. Kelly glanced away. "You're different," Adam said. "Even totally exhausted as you were the other night, you seemed more alive. What in hell did Santini do to you?"

"Adam, can't you let it be?"

"No."

Kelly bent and picked a long blade of grass. Smoothing it through her fingers, she tried to explain to Adam. "It was a misunderstanding. We worked those four bears efficiently. I was feeling close to him because of it. He was feeling triumphant because of it. Somehow, we came together for a few confusing moments."

"And?"

"When we sorted it out, he blamed me, blamed my presence here. He's going to talk to Dr. Andrews."

"That's not what's making you so alive."

"I learned a few things about myself, Adam. It doesn't really have anything to do with Rick."

"Doesn't it? Then why do you two crackle with electricity every time you look at each other or rather avoid looking at each other?"

"Adam, why are you going on about this? Nothing happened."

"I hate to see you making a god out of him. Just because Santini has a steel trap for a brain, you practically worship him."

"I do not."

"Yes, you do. You've been obsessed with him from the first moment we started working the bears." Adam took the blade of grass from her fingers. "Kelly, Rick Santini is a perfectionist and a workaholic, and besides that, he's scared of women. He's got you buffaloed because he's smart. He doesn't own you." Adam put a peculiar emphasis on the last statement. Why was he so upset? *He* didn't own her either. "And he doesn't own your future unless you let him."

"Why are you so angry at me?" Adam tossed the blade of grass to the ground and turned toward the four-wheeler. "Adam?"

He swung around and shouted, "Because for someone as smart as you, you're damned unperceptive, and it's a stupid waste."

Kelly was startled by the loud response. "You don't need to yell at me."

Adam gave her a brief grin. "Yes, I do." He nodded at the machine and said in a much milder tone, "Get on this thing, and let's head back to the truck before Santini has a heart attack worrying about his project."

Kelly was glad to be quiet and let the men make small talk as they drove. When she saw the strange car in front of the cabin, she was pleased. If they had to deal with company, Rick and Adam wouldn't have so much time to concentrate on her. Rick wasn't pleased. "What are *they* doing here?"

"They who?" Adam asked.

"My folks."

Kelly felt a thrill of curiosity. They'd had only a few hints about Rick's family. She smiled to herself with anticipation and then felt herself flush when she caught Adam's eyes on her. She stuck her tongue out at him. She knew that he was every bit as curious as she. When Adam stopped the truck, Rick was slow to get down. Kelly slid out after Adam and went toward the car. The woman in the driver's seat opened the door and swung her legs around. She stood and held out a hand to Kelly. "Hello, I'm Joan Santini." She nodded to the man, the boy, and the girl who stepped out of the car from different doors. "My husband Ricardo, our son Anthony, and our daughter Pamela."

Kelly smiled at the girl. "We named a bear after you."

"Really?" The girl's eyes, dark like Rick's, warmed to a sparkle.

Kelly nodded to everyone and said, "I'm Kelly Jones, and this is Adam Wainwright."

Rick had moved slowly to the group. While he greeted his family with an obvious lack of enthusiasm, Kelly studied them. Rick's mother was almost as tall as he. Her hair was raven-wing black with a few streaks of gray that emphasized the beauty of the dark color. She had intelligent gray-blue eyes. She was looking at Rick as he spoke, and her focus on him was intense. Kelly realized that Rick was no less intense. He had scarcely greeted his father and siblings. Rick's father seemed anxious. He stood stiffly by the car, watching his wife and son. His eyes and skin were like Rick's, but he lacked the golden vitality that made Rick seem so attractive at times. Rick's mother was explaining their visit. "We went to your great-uncle James's funeral yesterday. You said that you couldn't get away all summer, so we decided to swing by on our way home."

Adam had acknowledged their greetings and then stepped back beside Kelly. Now he said, "You're just in time for dinner."

Rick's mother turned toward him with a warm smile. "We wouldn't think of your providing dinner for us. We brought dinner. Pam, Tony, get the hamper out of the trunk."

Kelly had not expected Rick's mother to be either warm or beautiful. Rick had said, "My mother runs the general store, and she runs my old man, too." Kelly had pictured an older, tougher-looking woman. Joan Santini was vibrant. In a whirlwind of organization, she had the hamper and several other bundles into the cabin and onto the table—with plastic tablecloth, paper plates, plastic utensils and glasses in place before Kelly could offer to help.

Once dinner was underway, Rick's mother turned her attention in turn to each of the bear crew. She asked pertinent questions. She was charming in the way she focused on the speaker's face and listened intently. When she turned to Kelly, Kelly felt as if Rick's mother really cared about the project and Kelly's part in it. Her understanding was immediate, and her intelligent eyes, registering every word, became the loveliest part of her face. Kelly warmed to the woman, even as she noticed Rick's continuing coolness.

Rick's father wasn't quiet exactly; it was more that he was

acquiescent. He passed food, refilled drink glasses from the cola bottles on the counter, and was generally pleasant. When his wife was speaking, he looked at her without expression. But Rick was not acquiescent. He answered his mother's questions with paragraphs of complicated information, and there was some sort of tension between them as they finished one sortie into the scientific aspects of the project and launched into another.

Kelly felt confused. This woman truly cared about her son and what he was doing. It was obvious she had gone to some trouble to learn about his work. It was equally obvious that Rick resented her, that he had not wanted his family to come here, and that he was impatient for them to leave. "You're not staying the night, are you?" he asked in a tone that was so blunt it verged on rude.

Adam said, "Of course they are. It's too far from town for them to return in the dark, and besides, your brother and sister would probably like to see our bear sets." Rick frowned. Kelly was amused. Adam had said he was a full part of this crew, and he was certainly acting on his belief. He said, "Tony, you and Rick and I can sleep on the porch. Your folks can have the main room, and Pamela can share with Kelly." And between Adam Wainwright and Joan Santini, the arrangements were soon made.

They didn't catch a bear on Monday, but Rick's family seemed to enjoy the outing on the four-wheelers, and Rick's mother continued to ask questions, listen attentively, and respond intelligently. When she asked Kelly about being the only woman on the crew, Kelly answered as honestly as she could without discussing Rick. "The bear hunters don't like having a woman on the project, but we work well as a crew and we share the cabin work equally."

"Still, it must be tough for a woman." If Joan Santini had not been Rick's mother, Kelly would have been tempted to confide in her just how tough it was. She was puzzled by Rick's resentment of intelligent women. His mother was so very nice along with being bright. Rick's father continued to be a puzzle too. He was not really interested in the bear project as the others were. He seemed to be turned inward in a nervous, wary manner. Rick had said, "When my old man drinks, he breaks things." This man? She couldn't imagine it.

After a picnic in the meadow, Rick's family repacked their car and prepared to leave. Kelly and Adam held back, to allow Rick a moment of privacy. "I like Rick's mother," Kelly said.

Adam turned and gave her a sardonic look. "You would."

"What is that supposed to mean?"

"You're a lot like her."

"I take it that is not a compliment."

"It's more an explanation."

"Of what?"

"Of why Santini doesn't want you on this project."

"Adam, what are you talking about? Mrs. Santini is a lovely, intelligent woman."

"From whom Rick has probably been trying to escape for most of his life. He said she runs his dad; maybe she doesn't leave Rick anything of his own, either."

"No one needs to leave him anything. He takes everything as his own."

"He's just building walls for his fortress."

Kelly wasn't sure she liked this new side to Adam. He was talkative, but he was no longer close to her. "Do you know that you've started speaking to me as if I were some stranger?"

Adam gave a short, cold laugh. "We three have known each other for only two-and-a-half months. We *are* strangers."

"That's not true, Adam. You can't live through the death of three bears together and still be strangers." Adam's eyes were as cold as his laugh. He had created a fortress of his own. It made her feel lonely, and she would have said that to the old Adam, but this new person was unapproachable. She said, "I wish we'd trap another bear. Dealing with the bears is a lot simpler than dealing with people."

"That's because you can put the bears down and control them."

Kelly winced. Adam turned and went into the cabin as Rick's family drove away, and Rick came up the steps, still limping slightly. Kelly lingered outside—not feeling welcome inside—and she was standing there when Dr. Andrews's van drove in, followed by her family's car. Her mother was driving, and she was alone. Immediately forgetting the Santinis, Kelly ran down the steps. "I didn't expect you!"

Her mother got out, looking terrible, thinner than she had ever been. Her eyes met Kelly's briefly, but slipped downward. "I came because I need to talk to you."

Kelly was alarmed by the greeting. She wasn't prepared for another crisis. She had to postpone it. "Come inside and meet the others first. You just missed Rick's family."

Dr. Andrews had called a hello to Kelly and gone into the cabin. Kelly's mother straightened her shoulders and moved them around briefly. "It's a long drive down here," she said. "I can see why you haven't come home."

Kelly stopped on the porch. "We have sets out on the mountain seven days a week, Mother. We can't leave them. We have to check the snares every day."

Dr. Andrews stuck his head out the door and said, "I thought I'd take the lot of you out to dinner. How do you feel about that?"

Kelly smiled with relief. "I'd love to go out to dinner, as soon as I take a shower." Kelly's stomach had tightened with her mother's first words and nothing helped her to relax, not the warm shower, nor the leisurely dinner filled with general bear talk. Dr. Andrews was very much interested in the story of the four-bear day and wanted to know every detail, but Kelly's mother never asked a question. Kelly could not help contrasting her mother's strained features with Joan Santini's active, excited face. Sitting in the group, with Adam polite and distant, Rick getting chummy with Dr. Andrews, and her mother looking like she was trapped behind her own eyes, Kelly felt totally alone. Her mind buzzed with worried questions. What did her mother want to talk about? What was Rick going to say to Dr. Andrews? What was Dr. Andrews going to say to her?

When Dr. Andrews parked the van in front of the cabin on their return, the three men went inside, but Kelly's mother made no move to join them. "Is there some place we could talk?"

There was no way to postpone it further. Kelly said, "Let's go sit in one of the cars." ❧

Chapter Thirty-Eight

Outside, Kelly walked toward her Buick, needing her own space while she heard the important words that had made her mother drive halfway across the state. When they were seated in the car, which was warm and stuffy from being parked in the sun, Kelly opened the driver's window. She listened for a moment to the familiar sounds of the night before asking, "What do we need to talk about?"

She heard her mother's indrawn breath and the sigh that followed, and then her mother said, "Your father and I are making some changes, and some of them will directly affect you." She took another breath and said, "We have sold the house, we plan to sell the store as soon as we can, and your father is going back on the road."

It was more than Kelly could absorb all at once. "What are *you* going to do?"

"I'll run the hardware store until it sells, and then," her mother paused before finishing, "I'm going to go back and get my degree."

"Does this mean that you and Dad are separating?"

"Not exactly." Her mother moved in the seat. "I'll see him when he is in town. We don't want to separate." A breeze stirred the leaves of the scrubby trees around the yard. Off toward the ridge, a pair of coyotes conversed in shrill yips. Her mother continued slowly, "There won't be any place for you to stay, Kelly, and there won't be a job at the store." Again the huge sigh. "And I don't think there'll be any money. The store is paid for, but it is barely paying expenses. The house was not paid for, and there wasn't much left after the sale."

She sighed again. She seemed so full of sighs. "Ryan and I will need the money from the sale of the store to see us through the next few years while I study and your father gets a start on the road." There was an odd, almost petulant tone to her voice as she added, "You'll have to make do with what's left of your grandmother's money."

What was it about that legacy that caused so much emotion in her family? Each one of them in some way carried her grandmother's will like a cocklebur. Kelly shrugged in the darkness. Her mother's news was all she could deal with right now. Dr. Andrews had said they would pull the traps in just ten days. She had no idea what she could do or where she could go after the trapping ended.

She felt a sudden rush of anger. Her parents had rearranged her whole life without even consulting her. "What about Peggy?"

"Peggy is working full time, and she lives in an apartment."

"Is she happier?"

"I don't know, Kelly. Peggy doesn't come home."

Kelly was silent. Her mother seemed so desperate. There was no point in making the situation worse with anger. She said, "Maybe that's not so bad, Mother. Maybe we've hung around home longer than we should have anyway. It's your turn to do what you want."

Kelly's mother put a hand on her shoulder. "It's generous of you to say that."

Kelly hesitated. She wasn't feeling generous. She was just following Dr. Andrews's orders one more time. Be discreet, be diplomatic. For a brief moment, she was washed with a bitter sense that she was a hypocrite, that her discretion increasingly became dishonesty. But what else could she do? She tried for more honesty. "Mother, I've never known you when you weren't interested in learning, and you were always a good teacher. Why did you give up college in the first place?"

Her mother's hand dropped, and she felt her mother shift away from her on the seat. Kelly waited. If her mother were ever going to open up and talk to her about the strong feelings inside her, she might do it now, and then Kelly might be able to talk about her own strong feelings. The silence grew. Finally, Kelly's mother said, "There were reasons." And that was all she said, though Kelly stayed still in the quiet car, hoping that she would continue.

When it became apparent that her mother was not going to say anything else, Kelly opened the car door. Turning toward her mother, she peered at her in the dimness of the dome light. "It was nice of you to come and tell me yourself. Didn't Dad want to come along?"

"Your father has been gone for two weeks, Kelly. He got a chance to start selling, and he took it almost overnight."

And left you with the details as usual. Kelly did not say the words out loud because, looking at her mother's face, she could see the additional strain that the conversation had caused. "You are exhausted, Mother. It's a long drive down here, and it will be a long drive home. We'd better get to bed."

When they reached the cabin, Rick and Dr. Andrews were sitting on the far edge of the porch in deep conversation, the light from the window just grazing their faces. Kelly swallowed and went on up the stairs.

Kelly gave her mother her own bed and made a makeshift bed on the floor. She was awake long after the others fell asleep. *What am I going to do?* She didn't want to go back to Provo, but if she left the project, there was no place else to go. She turned on the miserable pile of blankets that were supposed to be padding the floorboards. She wondered if Rick had had the nerve to tell Dr. Andrews about the moments they had spent on the cot. *How could I ever have believed we were partners?* Just remembering her starry-eyed assumptions made her cringe. Her anger at Rick turned into shame. *And how could I be so turned on by someone like him? He's disloyal to his crew, arrogant, and afraid of his mother.*

But I don't have to assume that Dr. Andrews will be so unfair as to take Rick's word for everything. Dr. Andrews. That was the man she should be thinking about. Could she come up with a plan that would convince him that she was competent to continue the work? Grateful for the privacy afforded by the darkness, Kelly considered for a moment how nice it would be to live in the cabin alone and think of nothing but research. Suddenly those thoughts gave her a glimmer of a plan. She began to put together a presentation for Dr. Andrews.

Before her mother's car was out of sight the next morning, Kelly had turned to Dr. Andrews. "Could I speak with you? Somewhere private?"

Dr. Andrews nodded. "We need to talk." He stepped over to Rick and Adam, who were loading the pickup. "You two go ahead and check snares by yourself." He grinned at them. "Kelly and I will go wash your dirty socks."

When Rick and Adam were gone, Kelly and Dr. Andrews went into the cabin and sat down at the table. Dr. Andrews studied Kelly silently, which made her stomach tighten. Then he said in a friendly voice, "Rough week, huh?"

For one brief moment, Kelly was tempted to blurt out her mother's bad news, to voice her sexual confusion, to confess her anger at Rick and the rest of the men she'd met during the summer, and to complain of her frustration at never being able to do her work without being watched and judged as a woman. But she knew suddenly, and with certainty, that this was not the time to confess and confide, and especially not to Dr. Andrews. This was a time for strength and discretion beyond any the professor had ever asked for.

She acknowledged his kind question briefly. "Not so bad. It was interesting to process four bears in one day." And then she changed the subject. "I have a plan for the rest of the summer, and I'd like to discuss it with you." She was proud of the confident tone of her voice. It certainly wasn't her hastily conceived plan that inspired it.

Dr. Andrews's shrewd gaze focused sharply on her. "Oh?"

Kelly didn't give him a chance to say anything else. "After we pull the traps, I want to spend the month of August and the first two weeks of September doing habitat studies. I plan to stay on at the cabin." *Because I have nowhere else to go*, she thought, but continued aloud, "I'll use the receiver to track each of the bears we've collared. I'd like to collect more movement data and also spot bears feeding and do habitat sheets on as many as I can in six weeks."

Dr. Andrews seemed a little taken aback. "Alone? You want to stay up here alone? Kelly, are you sure that's wise—that you'd be safe?"

"I've been driving the four-wheeler for weeks now. Adam has trained me in the use of his gun. I know the mountain, and besides, I always carry the compass." Taking a breath, she plunged on. "I do not intend to go near enough to the bears for them to be threatened by me, or me by them. In fact, I hope to be undetected most of the time." Dr. Andrews made a gesture with his hand, but Kelly went on. "I am particularly interested in seeing the bears away from human influence. We get good information from snaring, but it's still a man-controlled situation."

Dr. Andrews laughed and said, "Slow down, Kelly. When I said it wasn't safe, I was thinking primarily of the cabin." He tipped his head on its long neck and peered at her. "Rick seems to think that the men in the area are somewhat threatening to you."

Count on Rick to pick something like that. He couldn't point to her work. "Which men?"

"He mentioned several incidents with the bear hunters."

"Mr. Selnick wasn't rude. He even apologized for Walt Johnson and George Walker, and," Kelly said, meeting Dr. Andrews's gaze, "those two are the foul-mouthed type a woman learns to ignore from the time she's about twelve." Another hypocrisy. Saying that was like saying you could be splashed with sewer slime and ignore it. But at least Dr. Andrews could see that she wasn't torn up by it. He seemed to accept that statement, but immediately voiced another concern.

"But you'd be vulnerable here, alone at the cabin, and the bathroom and shower situation would make it more so."

Kelly could feel the bitter humor well up inside her. Rick had done a real job on Dr. Andrews, making it look like the men *outside* of the cabin were the real threat. She hadn't thought about the cabin, but she smiled, and planning quickly how to meet this objection, said, "I have a few changes in mind for this cabin."

Dr. Andrews said, "I don't think the department will underwrite modern plumbing." She laughed with him and said, "My father owns a hardware store." *At least for a while yet.* "I plan to take a few days in Provo and get the equipment I need. I'll bring back a propane camp stove with some fuel canisters and a porta-pot from his sporting goods section. I'll also bring a tub for my shower to drain into." She was beginning to enjoy this as she remembered last night's wish to have the whole cabin to herself. "I'll move my bed out here and turn the storeroom into a bathroom and dressing room, so that I can lock the cabin door and bathe in privacy and safety." Dr. Andrews was listening intently. "Using propane, I won't need to chop wood. I'll lock myself in at night, too, and keep a gun handy." *I'll have to see if Dad will let me take a gun and holster.* "The cabin chores can be done in broad daylight."

"You've been planning this for quite a while, I see," Dr. Andrews said.

All of five minutes, Kelly thought, but she said, "Probably from the first moment I looked at my grandmother's stove there. That's a ridiculous old dinosaur. With propane, I wouldn't have to worry about wood and ashes. Cabin work would be cut to an absolute minimum, and I could focus on the bear studies."

"Well, the houndsmen won't be around again until fall," Dr. Andrews said. *Damn. I'd forgotten that there's a fall season, too.* "But," her professor was still voicing doubts, "what about your logger boyfriend? Rick said he was hanging around, too, and giving you a hard time."

Matt was giving her a hard time? Rick was really rotten to name Matt when he should have named himself. Though Kelly felt a surge of anger, she laughed lightly and said, "Dr. Andrews, I told Matt to stop coming here sometime around mid-May and since then he's been happily dating my sister Peggy . . ." She added firmly, "In Provo."

Who else had Rick named as a menace? Jamie McCarthy? Doc Morrison? She decided to turn the discussion back to her work and the habitat studies. "I'd like particularly to study the bear we named Samantha. She's an intelligent creature. She steals bait without setting off the snares, and she has always fought the ketamine and Rompun. She's in good health and probably in estrus. I'd like to get as much information about her as possible in the next six weeks."

"That might be an interesting project, Kelly, but I wouldn't want you to get romantic about this bear. Rick mentioned that you're pretty fond of her. Don't humanize her."

What a picture Rick must have painted. Totally exasperated, Kelly gritted her teeth. Then she said, "Dr. Andrews, I am not a nineteenth-century poet; I'm a scientist. If it didn't help with identifying these bears, I wouldn't even give them human names. I'm not all *that* impressed with the human race."

Dr. Andrews laughed out loud. "Well, Kelly, this is not exactly what I had in mind when I said we needed to talk." He reached in his pocket for his chewing gum. "Rick still seems to be set pretty strongly against a woman on the project." He unwrapped the gum. "What do you think of your crew?"

Kelly was tempted to say, Rick has a few problems of his own, but she was still certain that fighting Rick's accusations in a defensive way would only sway Dr. Andrews toward believing them. She said, "Adam says that Rick and I are too competitive and it's probably true. Adam has been a good leavening factor. But Rick certainly knows what he's doing with the bears, and Adam and I have both learned a lot." She shook her head when Dr. Andrews held the pack of gum toward her, hoping he hadn't noticed the slight emphasis she had put on the word bears. "For three people who were virtual strangers in May, I think we've turned into a competent crew. Despite our personality differences, when we have a bear to work, we operate smoothly."

Dr. Andrews studied her face for what seemed a long time, but was probably only a few seconds, and then he glanced at his watch. "We'd better go do that laundry."

Dr. Andrews actually helped with the washing. On their way home from town, he said, "I think Rick has probably done the fieldwork he wants to do for the time being. He needs to get back to a computer and start pulling his thesis together."

It was only fair that Dr. Andrews consider the needs of each of his graduate students, but feeling as she did about Rick's attempt to abort her fieldwork, she resented the idea that Rick's wants must be considered first.

Dr. Andrews continued, "Adam only agreed to work through July and then to come back for denning." He was briefly silent and then said, "This proposal of yours comes as a surprise. I'm not sure I could get it past the department. It might stick in the craw of some of the more conservative members—the idea of a woman up here alone." He glanced at Kelly. "I'm sorry to say that I still feel a bit that way myself." He shook his head. "We read too much about women who disappear, women who are assaulted. I'm not sure but that I agree with Rick to a certain extent. You shouldn't be here."

There it was again—the statement she would be up against for the rest of her professional life. You shouldn't be here. Because we can't control the men in this world, we must imprison the women. If men and women work together, sex will become a factor. Thinking of the four bikers who had found it fun to harass her—thinking of the fire that had built up between Rick and herself after the four-bear day—Kelly admitted to herself for the first time that there really were problems with a woman in the field. She had to convince Dr. Andrews that she could handle them.

"I am aware that there is a measure of risk, but I will be both alert and well-armed. The fieldwork with these bears matters more to me than anything else in my life at this point, and I would not do anything to jeopardize it."

Dr. Andrews said, "I can't give you an answer now, Kelly. I really do have to be accountable to the university." He glanced at her with a twinkle in his eyes. "I suppose you'd expect your salary to continue?"

Kelly smiled. "Of course." She hesitated, but deciding that she might as well go for the whole thing added, "And speaking of money, do you think there would be a spot for me in the department this fall? My mother has decided to go back to school, and money is going to be tight."

"Well, good for your mother!" He nodded. "I'll see what I can do, Kelly." As they unloaded the clean laundry, he said, "I'll be back up here next Tuesday, a week from today, to help pull the snares. I'll try to give you an answer then about this summer plan of yours." ∾

Chapter Thirty-Nine

The first time that Rick touched her on Wednesday, Kelly thought it was accidental and simply moved away from him. There wasn't much room at the kitchen counter. It could have been inadvertent. But when they were loading the truck, and Rick reached his arm around her—though it would have been easier to place equipment from the other side—she had to believe that he was doing it on purpose. *As if he's found a vulnerable spot and intends to take advantage of it.* The thought filled her with anger. He'd done enough damage with his little speech to Dr. Andrews. She moved away again.

The July day was hot. Storm clouds began building early, and the air was humid and sticky in the truck. Sitting in the middle, Kelly tried to tighten her body so she didn't have to touch either of the two sweaty men. She flinched when Rick reached to the gearshift and grazed his hand across her leg. She felt Adam tighten, too, and when she glanced his way, he frowned. *What does he think I can do about this?* At the meadow, Rick said, "Kelly, why don't you drive for me? My leg's still not back to normal."

Drive for him? With his body behind her, jolting against hers? No, Rick, I don't think so. She said, "It's too hot to double up, Rick. Why don't you just stay here and rest your leg and let Adam and me go check the snares?"

"Oh, hell, if you're going to make a problem out of it, I'll do Chase Creek myself." Rick climbed onto the four-wheeler, and shifting a little awkwardly with the stiff leg, roared out of the meadow.

Adam said, "It's a good thing we're pulling the snares in a week. This crew is disintegrating."

His critical tone was stinging. "Adam, please don't be upset."

"He doesn't honor the Honor Code, and despite what you say, you're not much better."

"That's unfair, Adam. What do you think I can do?"

"Well you must have given him some encouragement."

"What? By working well together? Adam, the stupid incident just happened, and we didn't violate the code."

"Not on the surface maybe, but, Kelly, the code isn't just a rule. It's deeper than that; it implies that we have a responsibility to our community as well as ourselves." He took a breath and added, "It's based in spiritual principles." He glanced away from her. When he spoke again, he had the same hurt tone she'd heard before. "The code is supposed to be an inner part of you."

The gulf between them was immense and deep. Surprised at how much his words had hurt, she was silent a moment; then she tried to phrase her response very carefully. "Adam, I know that you have a deep, clear faith. My grandmother had that same faith. And I envy you your upbringing and your certainty. You don't know how lucky you are to be able to discuss your problems with your parents. I wasn't raised the way you were, and I have to work things out on my own. *I do* honor the code, although I think it could cause problems of conscience for some people . . ." She thought of Peggy, hoping it wasn't true. "Because they might end up signing a lie, just to be able to go to school at Provo." She looked at Adam squarely. "But the problem between Rick and me doesn't have anything to do with the code."

Adam looked away again. She waited, and when he still didn't speak, she moved toward the four-wheeler. Then he said, almost sullenly, "Do you want me to come with you?"

"Of course I want you to come with me."

"It's not too hot to be near me, just Rick."

She felt like screaming. "Can we forget Rick Santini for a few moments and go see if there are any bears in the snares? It's hot for them too, and they'll be stressed and miserable." The crew *was* disintegrating. When she and Adam found a broken barricade, they were awkward in repairing it. Underneath the trees, the shade was not cool. It was oppressive. As the temperature rose, the mugginess increased. It was hard to breathe. Their physical misery was intensified by the muggy silence between them. She missed their small jokes and the sparkle of fun in his eyes.

An old mouse-colored bear was caught in a snare in Warren Gulch. The cable had thrown high on her arm. "We need to get Rick here in a hurry," Kelly said. Adam nodded and drove away. Kelly waited on the hillside watching the bear, which walked awkwardly about pulling against the cable.

Kelly was startled to discover that she and Rick still worked as a smooth unit. During the four-bear day, they had broken into a new rhythm, and it quickly reestablished itself when they had a bear to process. For a moment, she felt miserable. They could work this way, and yet he had tried to dynamite her progress.

"She isn't in bad shape for her age," Rick said. "She's at least eleven, but she already has a layer of fat under the skin, and she'll winter well if she can get herself into a good den." Rick and Kelly decided to name her Grandma. Adam worked as silently as he had earlier, distancing himself. The storm broke just after they had finished the bear. "Damn," Rick said. "I was hoping we'd get her up and away before it rained." He looked up into the pouring rain. "We ought to stay and see that she's okay."

"I'll stay," Kelly said.

But Rick would not allow her to do that. "The trail will be muddy when you come down, and the machine will be hard to handle."

"Well, I could stay," Adam said, but Kelly wasn't about to get on the other machine with Rick, and she shook her head.

Rick looked tired, but she knew that if they stayed, he would, too. Their reactions were so stupid that she couldn't believe they had let things deteriorate to this point. They huddled beneath bushes on the hillside in the rain, each one of them more miserable than Grandma, who finally stirred and moved her head about, then rose and shook herself vigorously before climbing the opposite hill at a fast pace. "It's a relief to know she's okay," Adam said, actually sounding cheerful.

"Yeah," Rick said. "If she's our last bear, I'm glad she came through the processing safely."

Grandma *was* the last bear. Though they picked up most of their collared bears on the receiver each morning, and though they spotted Ryan leaving a set where the bait had been disturbed, the snares stayed empty, and the last of the bait rotted in the bait barrel. "I hope we don't catch another bear," Adam said as they passed the barrel on Sunday. "I wouldn't touch that bait without a full suit of armor."

In the cabin, it was even more obvious that the trapping was coming to an end. The excitement and sense of anticipation they had shared each day during the earlier snaring were missing now. She did not mention her plan for habitat studies. Adam continued to be aloof. Rick spoke of putting his thesis on the computer, but also mentioned fieldwork as if he assumed that whatever he planned on doing, he could do. Kelly had to immerse herself in work to keep her mind off Dr. Andrews. She cleaned the cabin from one end to the other, dusting, mopping, and even taking down the roller shades and brushing them clean. She polished the stove. She washed her car and took it into Moab for an oil change and lube job.

Adam told her to continue practicing with the Ruger. She was grateful that Rick's guilt trip had resulted in extra bullets. It cost fifty cents to shoot one time. She knew she needed to keep practicing, but her own money was running very short. She added *lots of ammunition* to the list of things she planned to get from the hardware store.

The three of them had everything in order by the time Dr. Andrews returned on Monday evening. Kelly was nervous, but she was proud of the data sheets and samples and location information. When

Dr. Andrews asked them to sit down at the table for an evaluation session, Kelly's heart began to pound. Dr. Andrews seemed relaxed. He stretched his long legs under the table, unwrapped a stick of gum, and grinned around the circle. "Well, you guys have done a good job this summer. You've got a lot of data; the department is impressed; and the neighbors like you." He stuck the gum in his mouth. "The undergraduates in the lab aren't thrilled with you, though." He smiled even more broadly. "I came into the lab the other day just in time to hear one of them say, 'Don't those damn bear people do anything but pick up shit? I never saw so much of the stuff.'"

The four of them laughed and there was a general easing of tension. Once again, Kelly was impressed by Dr. Andrews's skills with people. She knew that he was about to tell them something that was going to make either Rick or her unhappy, but he was easing the stress first.

Dr. Andrews looked at Kelly. "Your friend Harry Selnick gave the project another shot in the arm. He sent a check for a thousand dollars."

"Guilt money," Kelly said.

"Don't care what you call it," Dr. Andrews said, "that's one-fifteenth of next year's budget." Dr. Andrews picked up the gum wrapper he had dropped on the table and began to roll it into a tiny ball. He cleared his throat. "About the rest of the summer . . ." Kelly's pulse leaped as he looked at her. "As you may know, before I left last week, Kelly presented me with a plan." He looked at the men, who shrugged and said nothing. "I've discussed this plan with my colleagues, and they have reluctantly agreed to let Kelly give it a try." Kelly couldn't hold back her big grin. She was going to get her chance to study the bears in their own territory without the cable holding them tight to human control.

"Kelly will stay up here for six weeks beginning August first and do habitat work." The professor looked at her. "Their one stipulation, Kelly, is that you have to check in twice a week instead of just once—Wednesday and Saturday, faithfully." Kelly nodded. She would agree to any stipulation. She glanced at the others, who had been totally silent since Dr. Andrews had started talking about her plans. Rick's face was the color of dried scat. Adam's mouth was tight. She could guess Rick's emotions, but she hadn't a clue to Adam's.

Dr. Andrews said, "We'll pull those snares tomorrow, and I'll take some of the equipment back in the van. We'll leave Kelly one four-wheeler. She can drive her car home and bring the pickup back."

"What if I need to come up to check something out?" Rick asked, his tone aggressive.

"You can use the van," Dr. Andrews said. He looked at Kelly. "Take the antenna and receiver and that fine lantern home with you so that nobody loots them while you're gone."

Adam said, "Is Kelly going to be safe up here alone?"

Dr. Andrews sobered, but he said, "She has some plans for being safe in the cabin, and I'm trusting her good sense and her new skills to keep her safe in the woods."

Kelly was torn. She was glad that Adam still cared enough to worry about her safety, but his comments were no help to her work. "I'm grateful to the university for giving me the chance to do this," she said.

"Well," Dr. Andrews said, "we agreed that if we're going to let women into graduate studies, they have a right to do the fieldwork, too."

Kelly was sure that it had been Dr. Andrews who had brought them to that conclusion. She sat still for a moment, remembering her thoughts about half-truths during her first interview with him last April. All of them were still operating through half-truths, evasions, and lies of omission: Dr. Andrews would not discourage her by telling her how some of the older professors had reacted to her plan. Rick would not tell the truth about his objections to her presence in the field—her presence in his life—if he even knew the truth. She and Adam had somehow lost their ability to be honest with each other. She and Adam and Rick had never revealed the real reason for the broken lamp. And as far as she knew, the episode on the cot was still a distasteful secret between Rick and herself. What was the truth about this project? For a moment she felt covered with a grimy layer of deceit, and she was tempted to tell Dr. Andrews the whole story of their summer.

But of course, she did not. She rode with Dr. Andrews the next day and listened closely to his lectures about how to do habitat work and how to measure horizontal obscurity. When they joined the others for lunch, she ignored Rick's rigid jaw and Adam's silence. When the equipment was loaded in the van and the pickup, she packed her own car.

Adam was returning from the outhouse when she called his name. He came around to the driver's side of the Buick. "I have a favor to ask. Would you be willing to meet me at my father's hardware store and look at the guns he has? I don't know how to choose the right one for use up here if he doesn't have a Redhawk."

Adam said abruptly, "I'm not going to be using that Ruger for the rest of the summer. You ought to carry the gun you're familiar with." He turned and went to the van, returning with the holster, gun belt, pistol, and cartridge box. When he handed them to her, Kelly remembered the last time he had given her the gun. He had kissed her then and grinned.

But now, without smiling, without saying a word, he stepped away toward the van, the cold look in his eyes denying every warm moment they had shared as friends. Kelly blinked back the sudden stupid tears that made a haze in her eyelashes, and then she was angry. He didn't have to be so rude. She felt like dumping the gun and all the paraphernalia out the window. But she turned and placed them on the back seat of the Buick, put the car in gear, and started the long drive to Provo. ❧

Chapter Forty

Kelly had to change a flat tire near Wellington and by the time she got in to Provo, it was late. Without thinking, she drove to her home. It wasn't until she saw the wide red banner announcing "SOLD!" across the real estate sign in the yard that she realized that her mother had not given her a new address. She sat in the Buick, disoriented and close to tears. *Where are my things? My clothes?* Turning, she fished in the clutter on the back seat for Peggy's letter.

She drove to the address on the letter, which was an apartment building in the downtown area. Matt's truck was parked outside, and she was reluctant to go in, but where else could she go? She climbed the stairs and knocked on number two-twenty. A tall blonde opened the door. "Is Peggy here?"

"Yeah." The blonde backed up, and called over her shoulder, "Peg, you've got company."

Peggy appeared in a doorway across the room. "Kelly! I didn't know you were coming home."

"You can hardly call it that, Peggy. I went by the house and then remembered that I didn't have a home."

"Why didn't you go to Mom's apartment?"

"I don't know where it is."

"Oh, Kelly. I'm sorry." Peggy moved forward. "Well, you can stay here tonight. Did you bring your sleeping bag?" Kelly nodded, and Peggy, seeming very grown up, began to take control. She went to the kitchen door. "Matt? Can you help us out?"

Matt came from the kitchen with a pop can in his hand. "Hey. The bear woman came out of the woods." He turned to Peggy, "What do you need, hon?"

"Kelly's an orphan for the night. We need her suitcase and sleeping bag out of her car."

"Okey-dokey," Matt said, setting the can on the coffee table. Things were moving faster than Kelly could react to them. She glanced around at the apartment, which held a motley collection of used furniture. "You comin'?" Matt asked.

"Oh, excuse me. I'm sort of spacey. It was a long drive and I had to change a tire."

"Was your spare up?"

Kelly smiled at Matt. This was something familiar. "You taught me to keep it full of air."

Peggy walked downstairs with them. "Is your project over, Kelly?" she asked as she looked at the car loaded with Kelly's belongings. There was an odd tone to her voice.

"No. I'm going to spend another six weeks in the woods." Peggy seemed to relax a little. Kelly added, "I just brought my stuff to keep it safe."

Matt said, "Yeah, there are a lot of strangers roaming around your hills. They harass my loggers sometimes."

"Are you still planning to clear-cut?"

"No." Matt shook his head. "We didn't get the permit. The Forest Service is waiting on your data."

The relief she felt gave Kelly a burst of energy, and she reached into the trunk and hauled out her sleeping bag. "Are you sure I won't be a bother?"

Peggy and Matt exchanged a look. Peggy said, "Of course you're no bother. If you don't mind sleeping on the floor, you can stay as long as you need to."

Matt's face was red, but he said in a cheerful tone, "Hey, I'd better get going. I've got some people to call." He picked up Kelly's suitcase and backpack and, moving ahead, he went up the stairs and into the apartment. Peggy took the sleeping bag from Kelly and followed him.

She said, "Did you have supper? We were just finishing, but I can put together a meal."

"I ate a hamburger." Kelly felt as if she had entered a play in the second act and was two lines behind the action. Though Peggy seemed welcoming and totally in control as hostess, she scarcely met Kelly's eyes.

Matt kissed Peggy on the cheek. "I'll call you."

After he went out the door, Kelly followed Peggy to a small room off the hall near the living room and watched as she spread Kelly's sleeping bag out on the floor beside the three-quarter-size bed.

"There. At least you'll be warm, and it doesn't smell like your bear camp." Peggy swung her head toward the kitchen. "Come and meet my roomies." The kitchen was large and brightly lit. A pretty brunette lounged in a chair at the table, nibbling on a chocolate-chip cookie. Peggy said, "That's Susie." Turning to the blonde who had opened the door, she said, "And this is Beth."

The women nodded, and Susie scooted around to a chair behind the table. "Sit down."

Peggy moved to the stove, piled a plate with spaghetti, and smothered it with a pungent red sauce. She set it in front of Kelly. "Do you want a salad?"

Kelly was suddenly ravenous. "I'd love a salad. I haven't had many salads this summer. Without refrigeration, it's hard to keep fresh vegetables."

"Peggy says your living quarters are absolutely primitive," Beth said. "Can't they do better than that for you?"

"Not out in the middle of the woods where we need to stay to be near the bears."

The women began to ask about the bears, and Kelly remembered Adam's comment about the glamour of their project. Everyone was interested in bears. But the questions were ill-informed.

"Do they roar and growl at you?"

"Are the little babies soft to hold?"

"Aren't you scared to stay in the woods? What if the bears came into your cabin?"

Kelly smiled and said, "If you could see us, just trying to find a bear, you'd know how shy they are." She could tell by the women's faces that her information was not what they wanted. She stopped talking and returned to the meal.

Susie rose and slid out from behind the table. "Nice to meet you, Kelly. I've got to grab a shower."

Beth rose too and began to clear the table. She said, "It's my turn to do the dishes."

Kelly nodded and tried to look pleasant, but she was suddenly pierced by a wild stab of homesick longing for the woods. She shut her eyes briefly and saw the cabin in lamplight in the good days before Rick had broken the lamp, before Adam's eyes had turned cold.

Peggy said, "Let's go to my room. You can get a shower after Susie and Beth finish. Susie has to go to work, and Beth has a date."

"What about you?"

Peggy flushed. "Oh, Matt and I usually poke around. He'll call later."

Kelly settled on the sleeping bag and leaned against the wall of the little room. "How do you like being on your own?"

Peggy didn't answer directly. She said, "It's a good thing I made some plans before the folks tore things apart. There isn't extra room in Mother's apartment for a mouse."

"What about Ryan?"

"Mother gave him the bedroom. The whole apartment is just two small rooms. She strung a curtain across one end of the other room and put a cot back there for herself." The phone rang in the hall, and Peggy went to answer. Kelly could tell that she was talking to Matt. She wished Peggy had shut the door because what she overheard was disturbing. Trying to move her focus, she glanced around the room. Items on the dresser and a pair of shoes under the bed hinted at Matt's more than casual presence.

"Well, I can't help it," Peggy said. "I don't know. I'll ask her." Peggy came into the room. "Matt wants to know if you want to go bowling or something."

"Heavens no!" Kelly was amazed that Matt could be so stupid. She watched as Peggy's fair skin turned red from brow to neckline, but Peggy smiled and met Kelly's glance straight on for the first time. "But you go ahead," Kelly said.

"No. I'll stay home, too." Peggy closed the door as she went back to the phone. She was gone for a long time, and when she returned, she carried a large bowl of buttered popcorn and two colas. She plopped down on Kelly's sleeping bag and put the bowl between them. They ate and caught up on the family news.

"Dad's in and out. He and Mom talk on the phone a lot. I get reports from Ryan. Mom is just frantic to get the store sold so she can register at the university."

"How's Ryan holding up?"

"Who knows, really? He seems fine. Mom lets him drive that old van around the parking lot, and he unloads for her."

"Have you quit school for good?"

Peggy looked uncomfortable. "I don't know. I guess so."

"Peggy, is there something bothering you? Something I can help with?"

Peggy dug a hand fiercely into the bowl, and popcorn spilled onto the sleeping bag. "You're the last person I need to talk to."

Stung, Kelly reached under the bed and pulled out one of Matt's shoes. "Does it have something to do with this?"

Peggy looked down and picked up the popcorn, piece by piece. When she looked at Kelly again, she seemed like a lost child. "I have gone off the Honor Code. I didn't think it would matter if I quit school first." Tears rolled slowly down her face. "Only it does matter. I feel like I've cheated some part of me by breaking my promise."

Hearing Peggy say "I've gone off the code," the way one might say "I've gone off the pill," made Kelly think of Adam's comments about deeper meanings and inner principles. She shook her head, uncomfortable with the memory.

"Why don't you go back on the code?" The phrasing troubled her, but she didn't know how else to ask the question.

"Because I'd lose Matt."

The look on Peggy's face made Kelly's throat tighten with worry. She tried to comfort her. "You don't know that for sure."

Peggy swallowed the rest of her cola and squeezed the aluminum can fiercely between two hands. "I'm only a substitute for you anyhow."

Kelly said, "I don't think that's true, Peggy. It's quite obvious that Matt likes you and wants to please you."

"He treats me like a little sister!"

Kelly glanced at the bed and said, "Well, hardly."

Peggy caught the glance. "That's not such a big deal, either. He's nice to me, but I don't know what I'm supposed to be doing, so I just let him do what he has to. It's awkward because we have to be sort of quiet. They know he's here, but really . . . I don't want my bed banging." She rolled the can around again and then said, "It's not the way I thought it would be."

"Have you two considered getting married?"

"Matt hasn't mentioned it, and I'm scared to bring it up, because I know he'll leave me." Peggy's blue eyes were bleak. "Kelly, I love him. I've loved him forever—all the time you were dating him." Peggy sighed. "Matt used to talk to me about his troubles with you. But Matt and I can't talk, not really talk, about this." Kelly felt a surge of sympathy. She knew what a conversation with Matt was like, but hadn't managed to solve the problem herself, and she couldn't think of advice for her sister.

Peggy continued twisting the can silently for a moment, and when she spoke, she changed the subject. "How are your bear scat buddies?"

"Mad at me."

"No kidding. I suppose Santini's uptight because you're continuing with the project."

Kelly wished that she and Peggy could go back to the relaxed days when they had done a data sheet on Rick, but Peggy didn't laugh that way now, and it would be uncomfortable to discuss the Honor Code, so Kelly didn't tell Peggy about the four-bear day. She said lightly, "He never changes."

"And what's Adam's problem?"

"He doesn't like much of anything about the project, and I guess that includes me."

"Well," Peggy said, "he'll be back in school and off your case this fall anyway."

The comment made Kelly feel lonelier. Ignoring it, she said, "Peg, I don't know much about this, but are you using some sort of protection?"

"I kinda mentioned it to Matt. He said not to worry." Peggy gathered up the cans and popcorn dish and stood up. "Could we just not talk about this anymore?"

Kelly rose and slowly began to get ready for bed, feeling as helpless as she had when she watched Jenny fall. ☙

Chapter Forty-One

Her mother was stocking shelves when Kelly entered the store. "Kelly! I didn't expect you."

"You didn't give me an address or phone number, so I spent the night with Peggy." The sting of not knowing where her belongings were had welted into resentment, and Kelly did not smile. "I need some of my stuff, and I need some things from here."

Her mother flushed. "I'll give you the key to the storage locker, and you can take whatever you want from here. I'm going to put most of it on sale anyway."

"Really? I can just take stuff?"

"If it will be a help to you."

"It will be a lifesaver. I hope Dr. Andrews will give me a check before I go back, but he didn't say, and I hate to push since the project is always hurting for money."

"Isn't everybody's project?" her mother said.

After Kelly had put the camp stove and several propane bottles and a large plastic tub into the trunk, and crowded a small porta-pot onto the front seat, she came back in to look at the guns. There was no Ruger in the case, but she saw a pair of binoculars and a spotting telescope. Feeling greedy, but wanting them both, she said, "Will it break the store if I take these?"

"We owe you something." Her mother reached into the case and handed both of the expensive items to Kelly. "When you go to the storage locker, take whatever curtains and bed linens you want. That cabin of yours is dreadful."

The cabin, dreadful and bare as it was, seemed more and more attractive, but Kelly just said, "Thanks, I'll dig around."

"Come by for dinner tonight," her mother said. "Ryan loved the pictures of his bear."

Though the storage locker was crowded and messy, at least her mother had boxed and labeled Kelly's things. She spent the day unpacking and repacking boxes and piling the car even higher. The storage-locker attendant wandered by and said, "You're going to need a moving van."

She smiled and said, "Or a dumpster." He laughed and went on his way. It was the first human exchange since her return that held no undercurrents.

Ryan's dinner conversation was refreshing. *He* was interested in the truth about bears. He had been reading some terrible Alaskan grizzly stories, but Kelly could tell that he was not sympathetic with the storytellers. "They shouldn't have been in the bear's territory, messing around with the bear's food," he said. "Rick told me that bears are shy, and they only attack when they feel threatened."

"Well, that's not always true," Kelly said. "Once in a while, an innocent human—a hiker or such—may come upon a bear who is feeling grouchy because of an encounter with another animal or another human, and he might take it out upon the hiker."

"Are you scared to go into the woods?" Ryan asked.

"No, but I plan to be careful."

It was Kelly herself who ruined the openness of her conversation with Ryan. The real estate agent had called, and when Kelly's mother went out, Kelly tried to express her concern about Ryan's life and to offer him a chance to talk about the changes. "Are things okay with you and Mother?"

"Sure," he said.

"Don't you need to see more of Dad? To talk to him?"

"About what?"

"Well, the kind of things men talk about."

Ryan snorted. "Nobody talks to anybody in this family." His sweet, intelligent face was cold and closing. Kelly wanted to stop the movement, hold the moment open.

"Ryan, we could talk. I know that there are things about growing up that are confusing."

"Don't poke around, Kelly. I'm not some bear for you to study."

Kelly let it go, appreciating his quickness. He knew what she was talking about, and he didn't want to join in. She smiled. "Why don't you come up and visit me in my woods?"

Ryan's face clouded. "I probably can't. I think I'd better look for a job here."

Kelly stood, feeling useless to him. "Well, I'd better get over to Peggy's before she rents out my bed." She forced a laugh.

Ryan just looked at her. "She goes out with Matt. Did you know that?"

"Yes, I know that."

"Don't you care?"

Grateful that he could ask open questions even if he couldn't answer hers, she said, "Matt and I were only friends, Ryan. I'm glad that he and Peggy are dating if they're having fun."

"You should be poking around in *her* life," Ryan said, "instead of mine."

Kelly said, "I already tried that." She and her brother exchanged a level, grown-up look. Their mother came in again just then, and Kelly left for Peggy's apartment.

She didn't sleep well. The apartment building was poorly soundproofed and other people's lives seeped into her ears. Quarrels, music, loud laughter, and loud plumbing invaded the bedroom. The next morning Kelly waited for the other three to take showers, and when she entered, the cluttered bathroom was humid. The plastic shower curtain clung to her skin when she brushed against it. She thought of her airy "shower stall" on the mountain, the sun shining through the cracks in the door, blue jays squawking in the scrub outside. Then she laughed at herself. *I'm nostalgic for an outhouse.*

At breakfast, she managed to bring a light to Peggy's eyes. "They're letting me take the pickup back to the cabin. Would you like to use my car for the rest of the summer?"

Peggy's smile turned her into her old self. "Oh, may I?"

Peggy's hug was spontaneous and comforting, but Provo continued to feel alien to Kelly. The morning drivers were rude, their vehicles smelly—the acrid oily odor as bad in its way as bear bait. She used up most of her cash on ammunition for the Ruger and some cotton camouflage clothing from the army surplus store. When she parked by the Widstoe Building, it was with a sense of relief.

Rick was in the bear lab, reading. He looked up when she entered, and his eyes actually warmed. "Hi, Kelly." He held up the journal he was reading and said, "This guy from Colorado is making a real case against cementum annuli. He questions the reliability of telling age by the teeth."

"Do you agree with him?"

"Our lab's estimates and our known-age bear information have always been pretty close, but I've wondered sometimes if enough data has been collected."

"Do you think we could devise some way of checking our system more closely?"

"Maybe, if we started with cubs in the dens and pulled teeth over a period of years."

Oh, it was wonderful. Kelly was at home again. She pulled a chair away from her old desk and sat down to talk about bears and aging and statistics. Finally, Rick said, "Well, I'm supposed to be using the computer next door. I guess I'd better get going. When are you heading back to the cabin, Kelly?" There was a wistful sound to his voice, and having just dragged herself out of the city's excesses, she knew that it hadn't been any easier for him to come back to town.

She smiled fully at him. "As soon as I can get Dr. Andrews to release me."

Rick's softened manner was very dangerous. For a moment a sort of hazy electricity flickered between them, but it didn't last past Rick's next words. "So," he said, "you think you can really handle being alone in the woods for six weeks?"

Irritated, she said, "I can handle it."

Rick's face hardened slightly and he asked, "Have you ever spent that much time alone?"

"No."

"Well, I doubt you'll last two weeks."

Kelly gritted her teeth and changed the subject. "Have you seen Adam?"

Rick flushed. "Not since he and Jerry and I rehashed the project. He was pretty mouthy about the snare burns."

Kelly wondered why she hadn't been included in that evaluation session, but she said only, "I know that Adam feels that we do too much harm to the animals. Maybe we should try some culvert traps."

"Well, hell. I've thought of that, but everything takes extra money. What good does it do to complain when the project already limps along without adequate funds?"

"Speaking of which, are July's paychecks on the horizon?"

Rick put the journal he'd been holding back onto the desk and stood. "Yeah. Jerry's down in his office with the loot."

Rick left her at the next office, and she went down the hall and poked her head into Dr. Andrews's door. "Hi."

"Well, hello, Kelly, come on in. I tried to call you, but your family seems to have vanished." That was why she hadn't been included. No one could find her.

Kelly took the chair across from the desk. "I practically had to hire a private detective myself."

"What can I do for you?" Dr. Andrews said, picking up a pack of gum from the desk, "aside from giving up your money?" He offered the pack to Kelly, and she took a stick.

Unwrapping it, she said, "I would like to go back to the cabin a few days early." She smiled. "Right after I'm paid, as a matter of fact." She stuck the gum into her mouth.

"Any particular reason?"

She tried to speak lightly. "My 'habitat' got sort of rearranged in my absence. My current home seems to be a storage locker on the other side of town. My mother and brother live in a shoe box. My father is rambling around the West on a new job. My sister is dating my old boyfriend, and . . ." She smiled at him. "Three is definitely a crowd."

Dr. Andrews didn't say anything. The silence was uncomfortable. She said, "Besides, I want to spend some time fixing the cabin to suit me." She moved in her chair. "And then I want to get back to work. I'm wasting time here."

Dr. Andrews stopped looking at her as if she were under his microscope. He opened his desk drawer and took out a check. Handing it to her, he said, "I robbed Peter and Paul both. I'm paying your back pay and advancing your next six weeks' pay too. If you get lonesome up there, go into town once in a while for dinner." Had Rick voiced his latest stupid opinion to Dr. Andrews? She *wasn't* going to get lonesome. She could hardly wait to be alone. The professor frowned slightly. "Be sure to get a chain lock for that cabin door." She nodded and he said, "Be careful, Kelly. Please be careful."

"I will."

"You'll be wanting the pickup." He took the keys from his desk. "There's a fantastic count of ant heads in one of the scat studies. You might want to see them." He handed the keys to her. "You could work in the lab the rest of today, and plan to head out tomorrow."

Bless him, he was offering her a place to spend the day. Kelly was tempted to give the professor a big hug, but she settled for a big smile. One more night in town and she could go back and check out Samantha and the rest of their bears. ∾

Chapter Forty-Two

Someone had broken a window in the cabin and damaged the door lock. Feeling nervous and invaded, Kelly made a trip to town for glass, putty, and a new lock set. When she had replaced the window glass, she worked on the lock. The old screws were rusty, and she wore a blister into the palm of her hand with the screwdriver, but by dark, she had installed the dead-bolt lock and the chain lock that Dr. Andrews had wanted. She was too nervous to unload in the dark. She took her sleeping bag, the lantern, and the porta-pot inside and went to bed on the cot in her old room.

She woke the next morning still feeling apprehensive. When she went to the outhouse to empty the pot, she found that someone had dumped garbage down the toilet hole, and the roll of toilet paper was soggy and yellow-stained. *Sometimes I hate the human race.* Gritting her teeth, she picked the roll up with a stick and tossed it in on top of the garbage. Then she took strong cleanser from the kitchen and scrubbed the whole outhouse. Only when the seat and boards were scrubbed nearly white was she satisfied.

"Vandals are so stupid." She said it aloud because she had discovered something else that troubled her. Despite the fact that she was glad to be away from Provo, the silence was hard to adjust to. She had not expected solitude to feel so heavy.

After she cleaned the outhouse she was hungry and dirty, but the cabin seemed empty without Rick and Adam, and an odd lethargy made her sit down on the front step. Her emotions about her family roiled her mind. *Ryan needs more security. Peggy needs some method of birth control and disease control! I hope Matt knows what he's doing.* She forced herself to get up and begin pulling her belongings from the back of the truck, trying to recapture the sense of relief that she had felt all summer, just being away from her family. But as she set up the camp stove on top of the cold iron range and screwed on the propane bottle, her anger at her parents was as compressed and dangerous as the propane. It wasn't necessary to do things in such an abrupt and stupid way.

Sure, Dad, take off down the road and never look back, or you might see that poor little worried boy who thinks he has to get a job to support his mother. Kelly lugged in the equipment boxes and then headed back to the pickup, thinking of her mother. *You're self-centered and adolescent. If you wanted an education, why didn't you stay in school and get an education? If you wanted children, why didn't you forget your damned education and be a mother?*

Her anger gave her energy and helped her finally to finish unloading. But the clutter inside the cabin was disheartening and reminded Kelly of the disorder in the storage locker her mother had rented. *Where am I going to live this fall?* At least, all the other times they'd packed up and moved, there'd been a house to go to. *How am I going to write a thesis in the middle of chaos?*

Kelly heated soup and ate it from the can, as depressed as she could ever remember having been. She wasn't sleepy, but her feeling of being insulated from her own self by a cloudbank of emotions gave her a dull sense of purposelessness and, despite the mess in the cabin, she pushed a few boxes off a cot and went to bed early.

She woke with a headache. It irritated her to have to dig around in the pile of boxes to find a bottle of aspirin. She brought in a bucket of water, but since the counter was cluttered, she just set it on the floor. She broke open a box of cereal and ate several handfuls from the box. She took it with her and went onto the porch. Sitting in the sun, she ate half the box of sugar-coated flakes before she began to feel cloyed, her tongue thick. She said out loud, "Why did I buy these? They're just junk." She slapped at a fly that buzzed around her mouth.

When she went inside for a drink of water, she stood for a moment aghast. In the morning light, it looked like a drunk had hauled in her belongings. Things were dumped in random piles, dishes in the living room, bedding on the stove. What if Dr. Andrews drove up right now? Worse yet, what if Rick arrived? He had predicted that being alone would get her down. She drank several glasses of water and brushed her teeth. Then she spent the rest of Sunday hauling the whole mess out on the porch and starting over.

She dusted everything before she hung the rose-colored curtains she had retrieved from the storage locker. The soft color helped to tone down the garish linoleum. She put all three cots in the living room, setting them in a U-shape around the back walls. She spread sheets and blankets on all the cots. There would be company eventually. She might as well be prepared. Then, using some more of her mother's belongings, she created a daybed effect with dark rose bedspreads and contrasting pillows. She placed a rose-colored rug in front of her "sofa." She hung the big map again, this time on the wall that separated the living room from the storage room.

After dividing the storage room in the middle by putting a spring-loaded shower rod across near the ceiling and attaching a green shower curtain to it, she hung the plastic shower bag on a ceiling hook and positioned the large tub under the spray head. She set the porta-pot just inside the curtain. As she started on the kitchen, she turned for a moment to look at the storage room. It was totally different from the bedroom where Rick had backed her up and laid her down on the cot. It gave her renewed energy to set the place up in a way that totally eradicated Rick's presence.

After she had cleaned and organized the entire cabin, swept out the truck, and parked it in the shade near the woodshed, she took a shower and put on clean clothes. But the pall that had settled around her would not dissipate. Nothing broke the silence but small birds chittering in the scrub, and they only emphasized the heavy, empty air around her. She took her hairbrush and went to the porch. *What am I going to do?*

As clearly as if she were there in front of her, Kelly heard her grandmother say, "You must work, child."

A flood of memories brightened Kelly's mind. After her grandfather's death, Kelly had asked her grandmother, "What do you do now that Grandpa's gone?"

Her grandmother had put her arm around Kelly and said, "Honey, I do as I always did. I work. I have animals and a house and a life God gave me. Work is the blessing he added to my life."

"Do you still prepare your year's supply?"

"Of course." Her grandmother took her to see the shining jars on the shelves of the cellar, and then they walked in the garden looking at the growing things that would join the jars of fruit, jams, vegetables, chicken, and venison.

"That is a *lot* of hard work."

Kelly's grandmother laughed, her laugh as golden as the jarred peaches they had just admired. "It's never too hard to do the work you love." She took Kelly's hand, and they wandered on to the flower gardens, but her grandmother was still talking about the year's supply. "People in cities are just one big storm or one long trucker's strike away from having no food to buy. It's such a good smug feeling to think of my root cellar and its treasures."

Peggy should have had a chance to see how Grandma did things. Why wasn't Peggy ever sent to visit Grandma? Why was I sent? Kelly brushed her hair until it was dry and went in to comb it in front of the mirror. Seeing a sudden glint of gold in her hair as sunshine sparked through a window, she thought of Adam saying, "I like the way the sun looks on your hair." She wrapped her arms around herself in misery. She hated losing Adam's friendship.

Fighting the lethargy that made her consider skipping dinner altogether and thinking of the way her grandmother had served a meal, Kelly set the table with a place mat and cloth napkin. After dinner, she went outside. The four-wheeler, which had been stored in the woodshed, didn't want to start at first, but Kelly coaxed it, being careful not to flood the engine. Finally the stubborn machine came alive, the sound bringing a rush of memories of Rick and Adam and snares and bears. Where was Samantha right now? For the first time since her return, Kelly began to think about the bears. By bedtime, she had made sure all of the equipment was ready for fieldwork on Monday morning.

The equipment was ready, but not the biologist. As she drove away from the cabin Monday, past the bait barrel which had been turned upside down, she still felt heavy, her mind distant. Maybe Rick knew more about this business than she. Maybe his days alone up here last year had been difficult. She missed the teamwork and Adam's jokes, and though she hated to admit it, she missed the feeling that if something went wrong Rick would know what to do.

Driving toward the first area she had decided to scan, she felt nervous. She glanced at the Ruger in its belt on the seat beside her. The damage to the cabin had left her feeling vulnerable and not so sure of her skills. She parked the truck in the meadow, buckled the gun belt around her waist, and unloaded the four-wheeler. High up Warren Gulch, she stopped the machine and activated the scanner. Grandma's signal came through. The bear wasn't near, but the coincidence made Kelly smile. *Okay, Grandma, I'll get to work.*

Annoyed with the lingering fog in her mind and the scattering of her focus, she loaded her backpack and stepped away from the four-wheeler reluctantly, aware that she was a long way from the truck. The pack was heavy, the gun chafed her thigh, the trail was steep, and despite Grandma's gimpy leg, the bear was moving quickly. The signal kept receding.

"Why aren't you sleeping in some day bed where I can find you?" Kelly grumbled aloud. She didn't pick up any other signals, so she felt she had to follow the one she was locked onto. She needed to start habitat work today. Shifting the gun belt, she started through a clump of ponderosa pines, walking slowly, looking at the receiver as if she could spot Grandma's location by viewing the sound, which was still moving away. Glancing up, she caught a glimpse of an open meadow ahead. The trees were just beginning to thin out. She took a step forward toward a large pine tree, and at that moment, a bear rose up from behind the tree. ॐ

Chapter Forty-Three

The huge black bear charged toward her, and without thinking, Kelly raised her hands high, still clutching the receiver and the antenna and yelling, "No! Go! Hey!" and then a series of garbled noises.

Like some slow-motion sequence on television, the next few seconds seemed an eternity. The black bear hesitated, his eyes looking sleepy and confused. He shook his head slightly. And then with an awkward motion, he veered off to the right—passing within five feet of her—and crashed through a clump of bushes on the edge of the meadow. She stood with her arms still raised, watching him move swiftly through the grass and into the woods on the other side.

When he was gone, she lowered her trembling arms and stumbled forward to lean against the tree. The antenna and receiver slipped from her hands and landed in the pine needles. She gasped, drawing deep shuddering breaths over and over. Then she sank to the ground, shivering violently as if she were freezing. She huddled there shaking for at least half an hour. Finally, she got up and picked up her equipment. Grandma had moved even farther away. Her signal was almost out of range.

Kelly stepped around in front of the tree. The bear's day bed was on the other side—pine needles and leaves pawed into a pile. The big black animal was not one of their collared bears, and there was no way she could have known he was sleeping there. *But I should have had my mind on the work.* She realized suddenly that her mind was clear; the weighted foggy feeling was gone. With a thrill of pleasure, she began to search the area for evidence that the bear had been eating. This could be her first habitat study.

The bear had not been feeding in the open meadow. She continued her search, moving in a measured, careful way so that she would miss no signs. She gritted her teeth with aggravation when she saw evidence of Jamie's cattle. Surely there was a way for ranchers to survive without destroying wildlife habitat. She finally found raspberry bushes where the berries had been picked off. Then she found large plops of bear scat around a rotting log that had been torn apart. A few remaining ants crawled in the rust-colored pith inside the log. She collected and labeled the bear scat, smiling as she remembered what the lab volunteers had said.

Humming to herself, Kelly chose a spot equidistant from the berries and the stump and named it the center of the habitat. Taking the tape measure from her pack, she marked off five meters each direction and flagged the boundaries of her study.

She spent the rest of the day crouched or crawling—the Ruger scooted around to rest on her back and buttocks—recording everything inside her area of study. She identified and listed the plants, then estimated the percent of coverage of each plant species. She wrote their mean height and recorded the phenological stage. She wrote of the cattle encroachment, noted signs of elk, and described the bear that she had seen in the area. When she had printed each bit of information carefully onto the field sheet for transfer to permanent habitat sheets, she put the clipboard into the backpack and stood up, a little wobbly. It was late afternoon, and she had not eaten. She carried her sandwich around with her as she slowly walked the stiffness from her back and knees. She still had to get the horizontal obscurity data before she could go down the mountain.

She unfolded the horizontal obscurity grid—a square meter piece of canvas—and rigged it at the center of the plot. She moved ten meters away and counted the number of squares obscured by vegetation; then she moved twenty meters away. From that distance, the bear's chosen eating spot was eighty-five percent hidden. She wasn't surprised by that figure. She'd had to scramble through dense cover as she moved out from the center. If she hadn't startled the bear from a deep nap, she would never have seen him at all.

She stood still in the midst of the bramble bushes, rubbing a sore spot where a thorn had poked her, and thought about the bear. Now that she wasn't shaking, she could appreciate what a marvelous moment she had experienced. She stretched her arms up toward the treetops in a quick movement of exultation. A few birds rushed chattering away from her. She laughed aloud and repacked the grid and her data sheets and took the flags from her boundaries.

The cabin was a nice place to return to, but as Kelly worked through the evening, recording the day's haul of information, she realized that she had not exorcised her ghosts. Adam and Rick were present in everything she did. Rick would be interested in the fact that there was so big a bear in the area—one they had not seen, snared, or collared. Adam would study the map and remember each marked spot, but he wouldn't make a show of his good memory, his quick perception. He'd laugh and fix a gourmet supper. She missed them more than she had ever missed her family.

In bed, she was even lonelier. She listened for the sounds of their snoring. The house was too clean. She wanted to smell them. She remembered the feel of Adam's arm across her shoulder and her arms around his belly. She tried not to think of Rick and the four-bear day, but relived it anyway. *What is the matter with you, Kelly? You could* hardly *wait to have this cabin to yourself.* Getting up, she took her guitar and, unbolting and unchaining her locks, she sat on the steps and sang to the moon.

Tuesday and Wednesday were frustrating. She tramped and drove and scanned and listened, but she didn't pick up any signals. Tired and discouraged, she stayed out on the mountain late on Wednesday and only remembered as she drove toward the cabin that she was supposed to report in. She turned around and drove out to the highway, preparing a concise, cheerful, professional report for Dr. Andrews, which she ended up delivering to his wife.

Thursday, trying for any collared female on the theory that the females might have stayed closer to their last location, she finally picked up Pamela. Samantha's signal had flickered once and then gone out of range. *Darn you, Samantha, how can I study you if I can't find you?* She got only close enough to see Pamela's tan rear moving rapidly away, and she had to use the long-range scope to do that. *I'm probably never going to see a whole bear again.* But at least Pamela had been feeding. Kelly marked the spot and began her day's work on her hands and knees. Friday, she picked up Kendall's signal in the same area. She didn't spot Kendall, but found fresh scat and started the study from there.

Each day she recorded every scrap of information she found, including the continued encroachment by cattle and the coyote skins stretched over a fence. The skins made her feel slightly sick. Several of the skins were female. How many small coyotes were now orphans?

Saturday morning, she thought she had Samantha's location pinpointed. She took the four-wheeler as high as she could go and then wasted the whole morning following the signal of the elusive brown bear before losing her on the ridge. Following a creek bed back down, Kelly caught a movement in the drainage and, glad that she was wearing camouflage clothing and that there was no wind, she stood absolutely still as a young black bear emerged from the bushes. She thought she could see a white ear tag, but she wasn't sure and she didn't want to reach for the scope for fear she'd scare him.

Kelly held her breath as the young bear began to play with a flower stalk, batting it with one curved black paw and worrying it with his teeth, until yellow petals flew off in all directions. Then the bear rolled over on its back and waved its paws in the air, squirming in the dirt as if scratching itself. When that didn't do the trick, the little bear righted itself and padded over to a tree, where it scratched its back vigorously on the rough bark.

It had to be Andy. He had never had much sense about getting caught, and he wasn't paying attention now or he would have picked up her presence. Andy eased his itch and turned his attention to the red berries on a currant bush. He ate for a while, and then, like some little sleepy kid, he ambled to a clump of bushes, scrabbled for a moment or two at the base, and lay down. Kelly hated to keep him from his nap, but she needed the data, and it was getting late. When she came near, the black bear sat up, made the brave huffing sounds that had always amused the biologists, and took off across the creek and up the other side of the drainage. Kelly laughed aloud, loving the dumb little bear, and then began to record the data from his patchy, scratchy habitat. It was nearly dark when she reloaded the four-wheeler and headed for the cabin. She was supposed to report in again, but she wanted food and a bath first. When she pulled up in front of the cabin, Rick was sitting on the steps. ∾

Chapter Forty-Four

"I can't get in," Rick said as she got out of the truck. "And it's hot." He sounded like a sulky child.

Kelly looked around. "Did you hitchhike or something? Where's the van?"

"Jerry got all bent out of shape when he couldn't find you." Rick's face cleared as he grinned. "He's gone up to the store to see if they know your whereabouts."

"Why didn't he go to the meadow?" Kelly was annoyed, and to hide the fact, she stepped past Rick and unlocked the door.

"He didn't think you'd be up at the meadow this late." Rick stepped in and looked around. "Looks like my grandma's house."

"I didn't know you had a grandma." Kelly's mood was not improving. She didn't need these males checking up on her.

She went back outside to get her gear. So much for her bath. She'd probably have to cook supper for Rick and Dr. Andrews. Damn. She had just begun to enjoy the rhythm of her own solitude. She had scarcely stepped inside the door when Dr. Andrews arrived. "You had me worried," he said, without further greeting. "What happened? Why did you change the locks?" She knew his abrupt tone was caused by concern, but she still felt invaded and spied upon.

"As I told your wife when I reported in last Wednesday, someone had broken a window while we were gone from here."

Dr. Andrews looked embarrassed. "She told me you called." He coughed. "I just asked if you were okay. I didn't have time for the complete report." He smiled at her. "I knew I'd be up here today."

Kelly nodded, but she still didn't feel like smiling at him. "The lock had been tampered with, so I replaced it when I fixed the window."

"*You* fixed the window?" Rick asked.

"*I* fixed the window." Kelly wondered why she had ever been lonesome for Rick. In a few moments, he and Dr. Andrews had reestablished male dominance of the cabin and the project. Rick picked up her field sheets and began riffling through them.

Dr. Andrews looked around. "You've followed through on your plan to fix the place up. It looks good." He smiled at her again and asked, "Have you got enough groceries to share some for our supper?"

Kelly was still aggravated because he had gone to the store asking questions. "Yours, maybe, but not enough for the posse you alerted to hunt for me." Dr. Andrews raised his eyebrows. She didn't care if she wasn't tactful and hospitable. She wanted a bath; she wanted to take care of her own data sheets; and she wanted to be alone. What if their visit ruined her adjustment to being alone? Damn it. Why were they here anyway? And where were they going to sleep?

Dr. Andrews had reached for the habitat sheets. He studied the three she had done earlier and then checked the field sheet she had finished just before returning from the mountain. "Andy? You really think this little guy is Andy?"

"He had white tags, and he sure acted like Andy."

"Well, great. It's a thorough study of the site. But it seems like you've had a long day. Why don't you go ahead with your shower, and Rick and I will fix something to eat."

There was a twinkle in his eye. *The blasted man can read my mind.* For a moment she was envious of Dr. Andrews's wife. It would be fun to be married to a man with a sense of humor and a sense of humility. Rick didn't look too pleased about the cooking plans, but Dr. Andrews was whistling between his teeth as he stepped to the food shelves and began studying the cans there. Ignoring Rick, Kelly went outside for the plastic bag that had been warming the water all day. She gathered her things, and going into the back room, closed the curtain, and took a shower.

At dinner, Dr. Andrews said, "Kelly, I'm going to be gone for about four weeks. I've got a black-bear convention to attend, and then I have to pacify my wife and family. They claim that I like bears better than I like them." He wrinkled his forehead slightly. "I hate to leave you, but this is the only time we'll have for a vacation before school starts again."

"That's okay," Kelly said, "I'm not going to do anything but what I've already been doing."

"Did you get extra keys?" Rick asked.

"Yes, but I'd rather not pass them out indiscriminately," Kelly said.

Dr. Andrews nodded. "Good idea." He glanced from Rick to Kelly and then added, "But Rick is going to need one. I may want him to come up here every now and then."

So, Rick had been appointed substitute keeper. Kelly could feel her face muscles tighten. She finished her dinner silently, and then, pushing her plate back out of her way, copied Andy's habitat information on the permanent sheet. After that, still without speaking, she went to the map and noted location information. She didn't turn around when Dr. Andrews suggested that they do the dishes, but when the two men brought in sleeping bags and started to spread them on the floor, she felt ashamed of her fit of pique. "Here," she said, reaching to remove the covers from the other two cots. "Put your bags on the cots."

When they were ready to leave the next day, Kelly said, "If you're going to be gone anyway, do I still have to check in so often? It's a pain to drive down to the store."

Dr. Andrews hesitated and then said, "I guess you could skip the Wednesday call, Kelly." He nodded at Rick. "Get his home phone and check in with him on Saturdays. Okay?" It was galling, but there was nothing she could do about it. Nodding, she dug in her pocket for her key ring and handed each of them one of the spare keys. She was glad to see them go.

She had decided that it would be easier to find Samantha when the bear was feeding in the early morning hours and again in the evening, so she rose before dawn the next morning and packed enough food to last her for lunch and supper. *I'll find Samantha first every day, and do data work on her, including a habitat study. Then I'll find another bear and learn what I can about its area. In the evening, I'll go back to tracking Samantha.* Using her copy of the complete file of all bears ever collared on the mountain, she wrote down the signal numbers, even of bears that had been on the other side of the mountain the year before. It was fascinating to note how far the bears were roaming and where they fed. This was what her work was all about. She was grateful for the scanner.

She separated her field notes on Samantha from the rest of the notes. If Rick showed up, he'd be into the files as soon as he was into the cabin. Since he had already told Dr. Andrews that she was obsessed with Samantha, she didn't want him to know how much time she spent on the bear.

Hunting for Samantha, she worked on her scanner skills. The more she understood about the direction and volume of the signal, the faster she could focus on a bear's location. Samantha liked the high country. The bear usually traveled the ridge near timberline, dropping down into the lower forest only to feed in an area of berry bushes. Kelly made up a spotting sheet, a bit like a child's follow-the-dots puzzle, and connecting the dots with lines, she could "see" Samantha's trails, but she still felt frustrated. *I want to see that bear with my eyes and not just my mind.* Samantha was wily and smart. For days, Kelly knew that she was there only because of the signal from the collar. Kelly rose earlier, determined to glimpse Samantha, at least to tell where she was feeding. She was on the mountain near the ridge as soon as the dawning light allowed her to see the trail, shivering in the chill high-altitude air, but alive and alert. Other creatures were out at the same time.

One morning, she spotted a herd of elk in a meadow below the ridge and watched them for a time through the binoculars. She admired the cow elk that seemed to stand guard as the others grazed, her head moving to allow her to scan the area and sniff the air. Even from a distance, Kelly could hear the sharp little calls the elk cows and calves exchanged, keeping in touch as they moved about, feeding. There were no adult bulls. She knew they kept apart until rutting season in late September.

When Kelly sat still, the other creatures seemed to forget about her. Birds chattered and fluttered about the trees and bushes. Chipmunks flicked their tails as they stood on stumps or rocks surveying their world. A coyote hunted on a grassy plateau with a magpie trailing it across the field, waiting for a share of mouse or ground squirrel. When Kelly moved, the animals moved to cover.

When the sun was high and the air hot, the animals took to their beds. Kelly finished her habitat work, set aside her tools, and sat in the soft grass eating her sandwich and fruit, scarcely thinking as she kept her senses tuned to the sounds and motions of the mountain. Often, she cleared away twigs and stones and scratched together pine needles for a day bed of her own. She napped in the way an animal might, occasionally slapping away the flies that nibbled at her, aware of the buzz of a grasshopper and the whine of a high fast airliner—more sharply aware of noise and movement close by. When she heard humans on the mountain, she froze, knowing that her green-and-brown splotched camouflage clothes kept her hidden in the grass and bushes.

Sometimes she woke up hot and horny. Her own body was as interesting as the rest of the wildlife, and she let her feelings rise, the keen sexual urges highlighting the sharp clear edges of her mind, joining parts of her that had been long divided. Once or twice, she lay back and fantasized a male. It was never a male she knew, just a perfect mate, matching her fire, matching her mind. In the warm grass bed on the mountain, she felt no social burden. Her grandmother's rigidity, her mother's urgency were from some other world. Seeking animals, being animal, she felt the earth under her as part of her bones; the grass and the sun were not separate from her skin. When the cool of evening made its way into her nostrils, she rose and went back to work in search of Samantha.

One evening, scanning the area, she picked up Santini and then a moment later, Samantha. Male and female together. It was almost too late for breeding season, but maybe Samantha was still in estrus. Moving slowly and stopping frequently, Kelly inched toward the spot where the signals seemed to collide. *Oh, if I could see them, even for a moment.* When she judged that she was a hundred and fifty yards from the bears, Kelly stopped and eased the spotting scope from her backpack. Holding it as steady as she could, she adjusted the focus and began to scan the mountain slope and the meadow ahead of her. The signals weren't far from timberline. When the lens caught a cinnamon-colored motion, Kelly's heart began to beat rapidly. Holding her breath, she centered the lens on Santini, and then suddenly she was seeing Samantha, too. The two big bears were playing with each other like cubs, pawing and nuzzling.

Samantha was gorgeous. Her coat gleamed golden brown in the shafts of the late afternoon sun, shading almost to black on the round fat side of her that was away from the sun. Santini was not so shiny, but he was big and determined to court Samantha. He approached her where she seemed to wait demurely and followed when she changed her mind and ambled away from him. She was definitely in estrus, or Santini wouldn't be interested. The brown bear was a tease. She nuzzled and bit the big red male and then rolled away from him. Once she allowed him to grasp her and roll too, before scrambling up and away, to wait as Santini vented his feelings on a nearby sapling, which he uprooted with one swipe of his huge paw.

Kelly watched until the bears decided they were hungrier for berries than for each other and wandered down hill into the brambles. It was dark before Kelly took the four-wheeler to the pickup, but she wasn't tired. She knew that she had seen something few people, even few biologists, ever get to see. *Nothing monogamous about bears,* she thought, *but what a fun courtship.*

She was awake late that night, recording every tiny detail of what she had seen on the mountain, and she was awake again early the next morning, with a sense of rested well-being, and eager to be back in the woods.

As she had predicted to herself, she seldom saw a complete bear. She heard signals from many yards away. The bears were too keen of ear and nose to allow her to approach any closer. She didn't take time to use the spotting scope for habitat work. If she could glimpse enough of a bear to determine that it had been in the area, she went ahead with the study. She was getting faster with her habitat surveys. The same plants grew in most places on the mountain, varying somewhat from one altitude, one aspect, one slope to the next, but increasingly familiar—she had to spend less and less time refreshing her knowledge in identification books—and as Rick had said, she soon recognized who was eating what, including always the blasted cattle.

Even with the scope, she could not spot Santini and Samantha again, although they stayed together for nearly a week, their signals almost on top of each other every day. And then it was over. The signals separated. She assumed that the two had mated. She hoped so. If Samantha had cubs and they found her in the den, it would add wonderful information since Kelly could almost certainly name the boar with whom she had mated.

After that, Kelly managed to get the scope on Samantha twice more, usually from a distance, and after Kelly had sat still for a long time. Samantha was always eating when Kelly saw her. Kelly began to know the rhythm and pattern of the signal movement as Samantha ate, early and late, and rested midday. The big brown bear stayed in Kelly's mind, even when she couldn't see her. Having held and touched the bear twice, Kelly could picture the powerful paw shredding a log, the tongue swiping through a swarm of ants, the teeth clipping berries.

The bear stayed high and stayed hidden. Kelly kept her files hidden, too, recording her data in minute detail each day, but squirreling the information away in her own suitcase instead of in the general equipment storage, because, after Dr. Andrews left for the convention, she suddenly began to have more company than she wanted. ❧

Chapter Forty-Five

Jamie McCarthy was her first Wednesday-evening visitor. He pulled into the yard and said, "I heard that the bear woman was living up here alone. I thought I'd see if she was cooking anything tasty."

Kelly laughed and invited him in for dinner. She could be mad at his cows and disapprove of the whole practice of putting cattle into wildlife habitat, but she could not be mad at Jamie. "You neglected us during early summer," she said, setting the table for two.

Jamie placed his Stetson on the end of the bookcase. "Your buddies didn't have much use for me. I hated to rattle their cage."

Kelly remembered the rude way Rick had questioned the rancher. "Tell me something, Jamie. I hear so much rumor, I'm never sure what to believe. If you didn't have public range, would it put you out of the cattle business?"

Jamie pulled a chair away from the table and sat down. "Our profit margin is very slim, Kelly. The people of this country holler if we get a little subsidy, but they would scream to high heaven if they had to pay the true cost of food—if we passed along every penny of interest and every hour of work we put in." He unfolded his napkin before continuing. "The federal deficit is our biggest problem. It makes operating money so high, we can hardly keep going. Any increased expense puts us in jeopardy."

Kelly served a simple meal and joined him at the table. "But what about the public range? Do ranchers need public range?"

Jamie said, "Not all ranchers have access to public range, but almost none who do could make it without the extra pasture." He ate silently for a while and then said, "But I don't know what I'm hanging in there for. None of my kids want the place."

"Why not? I'd think they'd love to come back here."

"I educated them too well." He grinned at her. "I've got me a bunch of yuppies. My oldest son's a lawyer, my daughter's a banker, my youngest son's an engineer. Their mama was determined that they'd be educated—get to do what they wanted to do." His grin slipped a little. "And what they *don't* want to do is the twenty-four-hour-a-day work on a ranch."

"Do you want to leave?"

Jamie looked up at her, and all the loneliness he had felt in the three years since his wife's death was showing in his eyes. "No, I want to die there and be buried near Betsy on that sunny slope behind the house. I hope she still wants me beside her like we planned."

"Jamie," Kelly said, thinking of the way her mother's unhappiness had invaded the family, "stop punishing yourself over Betsy's journal. You know, she had choices, too. Since she had time to write in that journal, *she* had time to write something else. You didn't fail her." Rising to clear their plates, Kelly rested her hand briefly on his shoulder. He didn't look at her, but he raised his hand to pat hers.

After they had eaten fruit and cookies, the rancher stood up and reached for his hat. "Well, I see that you're okay out here alone, and I've got stock tanks to check."

Kelly picked up on his words right away. "Of course I'm okay." She stepped in front of Jamie who had headed for the door. "Did Dr. Andrews send you down here?"

The rancher looked sheepish. Nodding his head, he said, "Yeah. I ran into him up at the store, and he asked me to check on you from time to time."

Her visitor on the next Wednesday was Doc Morrison. He didn't stay for dinner, but accepted a bottle of pop and sat on the porch. Amused, Kelly said, "Did Dr. Andrews delegate you to see that I was safe and sound?"

Doc Morrison nodded, his white beard flopping up and down. "Said if I was in the area to drop by some Wednesday and see how you were doing." He smiled at her. "Looks to me like you're doing real well."

Kelly decided to pick his brains a bit since Dr. Andrews had so kindly sent him her way. "I'm interested in seeing more bears in the wild, and I understand that you like to take pictures of bears. How do you get them to stand still and face you?"

Doc Morrison erupted in a big booming laugh. "Seen a lot of tails and rumps, have you?" He drained the bottle and set it down. "Well, you have to trick those bears. They're smart and private. You could use a blind or a stand."

"What's the difference?"

"Well, a blind hides you, but it doesn't necessarily draw the bear. You could sit in a blind all day, even along a known trail, and never see a bear." He smiled at her. "With a stand, you cheat. You put your platform up in a tree and your bait around the bottom. Then you climb that tree and wait until the bears come."

"Do they come?"

"If they're in the area, they come. Trouble is, sometimes they don't go when you want them to. That stand is a pretty cramped spot for waiting on a bear's whims." The veterinarian hoisted his bulk up onto his feet. He said, "Tell you what. My youngest daughter hunts with bow and arrow from a stand. She knows all about it. I'll get her to help you out."

Kelly hated to think of baiting the bears—it wasn't really a natural situation—but she felt a thrill of excitement. *I'd like to see Samantha up close again.*

Rick was the Wednesday visitor that Kelly didn't welcome. He poked through the files, he complained because she served rice and fish, and he crowded her. Mentally and physically, he crossed boundaries and made her feel invaded and edgy. When she stood at the map marking bear locations, he stood right beside her, critical of the markings, questioning her about the spots she flagged. When she worked at the table, he hovered, reading over her shoulder. He would lean forward suddenly to point at a figure he doubted or a plant identification he thought was wrong. His body was too hot, his breath too moist, his hands too close.

Exasperated, she said, "Rick why did you come down here? You're not doing any fieldwork, and you should be home compiling your own data instead of nitpicking mine."

"I hate that damned computer, and you're having all the fun."

If that excuse had sounded like the truth, she could have felt sympathetic. She *was* having fun on the mountain, and she knew Rick loved the work the way she did. But he didn't even look at her when he said it, and every criticism, every gesture he had made seemed aimed at making her feel uncertain about her work. When he announced that he was spending the night, she was so annoyed that she didn't even answer. She folded back the bedspread on the cot farthest from her own and went silently to bed, determined to get up and start at her usual early time.

The next morning Rick was slow to leave. She went ahead with her work and made a lunch. He said, "That's enough for four people."

"I work hard. I get hungry." She hoped he wasn't thinking of going with her.

He diddled around after packing up her latest scat samples, scanning the map one more time, going through the files again. There was no point in what he was doing. She picked up her gear and headed for the door, turning only to say, "Rick, from now on, why don't you just let me report by phone? There are plenty of people here who look out for me." When she reached the truck, Rick delayed her again by deciding suddenly to check the oil. *As if I hadn't brains enough to see to my own equipment.* After he slammed the hood down, he followed her to the driver's side. As she grasped the steering wheel and started to step up into the cab, Rick put his hand on her bottom, squeezed her buttock briefly, and boosted her into the truck. Startled, she jerked away and settled awkwardly behind the wheel.

It took her half the morning to restore her confidence in herself. *I have to do something about this.* The strong, invasive hand had taken her back to the beginning of the project when he had smacked her on the bottom and called her an earth muffin. *But how can I handle it without making so big a deal of it that Dr. Andrews gets involved?* Catching the signal from Elizabeth's collar and tracking her until she saw the bear briefly near a creek, Kelly thought about the student named Elizabeth. *I owe her some help and advice, but I've got to solve the problem before I can talk about it.*

There was comfort in Samantha. Kelly got close enough that evening to watch her through the spotting scope. Strong and confident, with no natural enemies but man, the bear moved through the woods taking what she needed. Now out of estrus, she no longer needed a male, and she wouldn't tolerate a male's presence. *The damned males wouldn't get kicked out if they weren't so dangerous to the young.* Kelly was feeling very sour about all males as she packed away her study of Elizabeth and marked Samantha's location for a habitat study the next day. It took all of her good sense to overcome the feeling that Rick had polluted her studies and debased her somehow. Dr. Andrews had approved her data sheets. She belonged here, doing her work.

Early Saturday morning, she got gas and groceries, and then called her keeper, getting a wicked feeling of pleasure when she discovered that she had awakened him. Then gradually, as she focused on her work, she regained the sense of flow, of belonging to the rhythm of the land she walked. She increased her search for bears, determined to complete two habitat studies each day, one of them always being Samantha. Sometimes it was hard to find another bear after spending so much time on the chocolate brown bear, and she extended her working hours. On Wednesday night of her fifth week on the mountain, she was so late she almost missed Mary Powers. ∾

Chapter Forty-Six

The pilot greeted her with the same lovely smile that had lighted their cabin on her first visit. Kelly took her offered hand and said, "I suppose Dr. Andrews suggested that you drop by?"

Mary Powers laughed. "He's quite the mother hen, isn't he?"

Dinner was fun. Mary Powers seemed to be a self-contained and happy person. She asked intelligent questions and listened with respect to Kelly's answers. After dinner, they sat on the porch, sipping cocoa and enjoying the stars. Kelly said, "Are you married?"

"I was. My husband died of cancer when I was thirty-three."

"I'm sorry."

"Thank you. I still miss him. He was unusual in his way of letting me be myself and do my work."

"Has it been hard, being a woman in a field that men have claimed for themselves?"

"I made a lot of mistakes before I learned how to survive."

"Were you ever sexually harassed?"

Mary Powers heaved a big sigh and set her empty cup on the porch. "It never really stops, Kelly. I'm afraid you'll find that out. But there are ways to deal with it."

Suddenly feeling safe and comfortable in the dark, Kelly decided to tell the woman about Rick, though it was probably not discreet to air project problems to someone from the sponsoring department. The pilot listened quietly as Kelly told of Rick's resistance to her presence on the project and his unwelcome touches. Kelly even told her about the four-bear day and the attraction between them.

When Kelly stopped talking, the woman's first words surprised her. "Poor Rick."

"Poor Rick?"

Mary Powers laughed. "There he was, top of the heap, brilliant in his field, with a clear run ahead of him for the choicer jobs. And then you came up behind him, bright, hard-working, sensible. There aren't that many jobs in Utah—in the entire West even—demanding the skills of bear biologists. Once you get experience in the field, he knows you'll be applying for the same jobs he's after."

"It doesn't have to be so competitive. We work well together. We could cooperate."

"Men don't cooperate, they compete. Anyway he's sexually attracted to you, and that confuses him. He can't treat you like a man because of the attraction, and he can't treat you like a woman because you're in his territory. The rules are screwed up for men these days."

"Well, what am I supposed to do? I have a right to work, don't I? A right not to have him always grabbing hold of my butt."

Mary Powers reached a hand to Kelly's shoulder. "Honey, of course you do. But if you're in this for the long run, and I'm convinced that you are, you need to stop sexual harassment privately if you can. Because, if you go public, the men in power will brand you a trouble maker."

Kelly felt a sickening sense of despair. "I don't know how to stop it."

Mary Powers said, "There's a little formula called, Say, Say, Say: Say what he's done. Say you don't like it. Say that you won't stand for it to happen again." She stretched back and looked at the starry sky and was quiet as if remembering. "It's hard the first time you do it, but it will be easier for you than it was for me. Men are not so certain now that they can get away with it. Company policies are changing."

"I hate all the rules and restrictions on my life. I've got chains and locks and guns . . ." She let the comments trail away. She sounded whiny.

"What is, *is*," Mary Powers said. "No point in using your fine energy on hating. Use it to try and change things."

Kelly was grateful that Dr. Andrews had sent this particular Wednesday nursemaid. Wanting to know more about her, she said, "Do you think you'll ever marry again?"

"No." The answer was so brief that Kelly felt rebuffed, but before she could apologize, Mary Powers began to talk. "I enjoyed my first husband a great deal. He was from a loving, faith-filled family, and he had a grand sense of humor. I wanted to die, too, after he was gone." She stirred on the porch as if the pain were still with her. "And then my education began. Men began to show up at my front door for no reason—the husbands of my friends, our insurance man, the plumber, you name it. I was so innocent at first, innocent about why they came—thinking maybe they truly felt protective and concerned about my grief—appalled when I discovered that they were there to provide the sex they were certain I was craving." She moved again and made an angry gesture with her hand. "As if any one of them could make up for the loss of Johnny."

After a moment's silence she said, "When I got angry enough, I asked the insurance man just why he thought he had the right to invade my home. 'Oh come on, Mary,' he said, 'you know that divorcees and widows are fair game.'"

Kelly said, "The bastard."

"Wasn't he. He's also the one who told me that an intelligent, spirited, career woman like me would be fun to have an affair with, but that when he went home, he wanted a woman who was ready to take care of him, ready to listen to him."

"Rick said the same thing. It makes me feel that what they want is to come home from school and find Mama."

"It's incredible how grown-up and vital and exciting a man can be at work, and what a spoiled child he is at the end of the day. There's the crux of our problem as career women, Kelly. When they are high on their work, men are exciting—fascinating—and they simply ooze sexual magnetism. If you are also high on your work, you probably have the same effect."

Kelly nodded in the dark. It was true. Rick was the most attractive when they were working the bears well, and the electricity was highest between them when they focused on an interesting problem.

"I made one horrible mistake, Kelly, and I lost a good job because of it. I made the mistake of getting involved with a man at my first job, a year or so after Johnny's death. The man was a pilot and he loved to fly. We had that in common, but it wasn't enough." By the light from the door, Kelly could see Mary Powers shake her head. "Boy, was it not enough! He wasn't married. He had been a couple of times, but he wasn't when I knew him. He decided that our affair gave him total rights to everything about me, including my home, my money, and every minute of my time."

Kelly was fascinated by Mary's honesty.

"When I resisted his need to own me, he became abusive. Of course, I ended the affair, but there was no way we could work together. When people were around, he was the most charming, capable, intelligent pilot in the company. When we were alone, he was sadistic. There was no one to complain to. I didn't think anyone would believe me. So I quit." She sighed. "I wish someone had given me a set of rules. When I went to work for the Forest Service, I was determined not to get involved socially with anyone there. That was a good rule for me, but it still didn't help me to deal with pats and pinches and comments about my breast size and questions about how I passed the long nights."

"But you did finally get some sort of system—this 'say, say, say' system?"

"Yes, though it wasn't my own idea. I went to a professional women's group where we discussed the problem of sexual harassment."

"Does this system really work?"

"I think you have to judge your harasser pretty closely. I always found it best to speak to him in private with a strong, certain voice, showing absolutely no fear or uncertainty about my rights."

"And that was it?"

Mary Powers laughed. "Well, I must admit, sometimes I had to give a little boost to my warning. I would add that I had written a detailed description of the harassment and had dated the information so that if I had to go to our superiors I would have the appropriate back-up material."

"Did any of them try again?"

"Once. Then I got a male friend in the department to stand by, and I said in front of him, 'Just so you won't think that by silence I am welcoming your advances, I want you to hear me say, in front of a witness, that I don't like for you to touch me or to speak of sexual matters.'"

"What did he say?"

"He was very embarrassed, but he didn't bother me again."

Kelly felt that Dr. Andrews had given her a gift in sending Mary

Powers to the cabin. *She is generous to share her own secrets, so that I don't feel indiscreet and disloyal to the project by telling her mine.*

The pilot stood and stretched. "I suppose I'd better go down the road."

"Why don't you stay? I get up early. You could leave when I do."

"Okay." Mary Powers was so direct and decisive that she was a joy. They got ready for bed, talking about bears and a flying trip to pinpoint bear dens in the fall.

When the lantern was out and they were in their cots, Kelly said, "I appreciate your talking to me."

"You're a lot like I was when I was young, Kelly. We have to help each other."

"I know a girl named Elizabeth who wants to work in the field. I've been trying to think of a way to guide her. You've given me that."

At breakfast the next morning, Kelly said, "You were so emphatic when I asked if you'd marry again. Why wouldn't you?"

Mary Powers laughed. "Because I'm fifty, self-centered, and selfish. I don't want to marry at this late age and take care of some guy who over-indulged his body and under-indulged his mind."

Kelly smiled, and Mary added, "I have a couple of nice kids, and I'll have a grandchild by Christmas." She looked at Kelly. "I'm also lucky enough to know a sweet guy who travels around the country, living his own life. He's good company when he's here, and I don't worry about him when he's gone."

When Mary was ready to leave, Kelly walked to the car with her. "Kelly," Mary said, "as long as I'm giving you advice, let me add one more thing." She studied Kelly. "Do you mind?"

Kelly shook her head. "Your advice seems to be just what I've needed."

"I've flown Rick several times to spot bears. He's very intelligent, very attractive. But don't let yourself be blinded by him. At your age, with your verve, you need a mate that brings his own strength to your union—not your strengths. When you're ready to marry, don't look for a duplicate of yourself." The words seemed harsh, but Kelly felt their integrity in the pit of her stomach. When Mary had gone, Kelly went into the cabin and, finding the bear capture sheet that had Mary at the top, she changed the name to *Mary Powers*. ∾

Chapter Forty-Seven

Doc Morrison dropped by again early on Sunday with his daughter.

"This is Leslie," he said, as a tiny girl stepped forward.

"You're the one who hunts with bow and arrow?" Kelly's surprise made her almost rude. She laughed. "I'm sorry. I didn't mean to sound so incredulous."

"Aw, she gets that all the time," the veterinarian said. "I swear she took up hunting to prove that she's as good as her brothers despite being the runt of the bunch."

Leslie was not fazed by the conversation. "Dad says you want to build a bear stand. Any particular place?"

"Near the ridge. I'd like to attract a brown bear named Samantha if we can."

"Well, let's go do it." The young woman sounded very capable.

"You young'uns have at it," Doc Morrison said. "I'm too fat to go up to the high altitude." He took a bucket of bait from his truck and set it into Kelly's truck. Leslie and Kelly unloaded the plywood, the two-by-fours, the carpet, and the nails and tools that were also in Doc's truck. When they reached the meadow where they parked the pickup, they transferred the materials to the rack on the four-wheeler and laughed their way up the mountain, Leslie balancing the load while Kelly tried to keep the machine level.

They carried the equipment through a meadow to a thick stand of trees below Samantha's ridge. Leslie chose four tall spruces that stood close together. She nailed short sections of fallen aspen log to the back of one tree to serves as footholds, climbing up the tree a little farther as she finished each step. When she was about twelve feet up in the tree, she nailed longer pieces of two-by-four to the four trees to serve as supports for the platform.

They cut the plywood to fit the space between the trees, and tugging it up the tree with the help of Kelly's come-along, they nailed the platform to the two-by-fours. The needles on the branches below them were thick enough to conceal the platform fairly well. Leslie nailed the carpet to the plywood. "It's easier to sit on, and it keeps us quieter," she said when Kelly joked about the luxury of carpet.

"You're good at this," Kelly said, admiring the little treehouse.

"I've done it lots of times," Leslie said. "My family's been hunting and eating bears for as long as I can remember."

"We had venison," Kelly said, "but I've never tasted bear." And she didn't want to, but she didn't say that aloud. She respected hunters who used their kill. "What do you do with the skins? You don't have them stuffed?"

"No, we're not trophy hunters. We use them for blankets and rugs.

We keep the fat for greasing our boots and saddles."

They put the bait fifteen yards from the base of the tree, partially concealing it in a pile of brush to give it a natural look. Then, late in the afternoon as the sun was slanting toward the west, and the hot summer day was chilling down, they obliterated their own tracks, and made the steep climb to the platform. "I hope we didn't brush against the bushes coming in," Leslie said. "Sometimes I wear rubber knee boots, just to keep my smell off the foliage. Bears are cautious."

They made themselves as comfortable as they could on the tiny square of wood amongst the scratchy needles. Leslie simply sat cross-legged. Kelly had to deal with her longer legs by folding them and sitting sideways. Then they waited silently. Leslie was good at silence. She relaxed into her lotus position and was still. Her breathing was close-mouthed. She allowed the little gnats to circle her head without moving a muscle. It was harder for Kelly to be that still. Her thigh muscles cramped, and her lower back pulled too tight. But she forgot her discomfort when Leslie suddenly touched her and pointed toward the meadow that stretched away from their tree. Andy scrambled through the grass, heading straight for the bait pile.

The moment he reached the bait, the little male began to sniff and chew at the rank meat. He was in good shape, his black coat was shiny and full, and he looked like he'd gained at least twenty pounds. He was so busy with the treasure he'd found that he paid attention to little else, and Kelly was so engrossed in watching him that she was startled when she heard a half snuffle, half growl, and Samantha showed up below her. Andy backed away from the bigger bear. Samantha watched the little male for a moment before beginning to nose the bait. Andy took a tentative step closer. Swirling her head around, the female raised one huge paw and swatted the yearling. He scrambled away into the grass and then sat and watched Samantha, making the moaning sound that had made the bear biologists laugh.

Kelly turned her attention to Samantha. The brown bear lifted her head often, swinging it from side to side, sniffing the air and listening. Kelly held her breath as the bear moved close in and began tearing a piece of the bait with her huge teeth. From her vantage point, Kelly could see the bear's right paw, the paw that had sustained a cable cut in the first snaring. Now it seemed fully healed, and no scarring showed through the heavy brown fur. Suddenly, Samantha picked up the chunk of meat she had been eating and moved rapidly away toward the ridge. At the same time, Andy turned tail and scrambled into the trees.

Leslie touched Kelly again and lifted a finger to the north. A huge red bear lumbered toward the bait pile. Looking down at him, Kelly saw the ear tags. Santini. The male was bigger every time she saw him. Snuffling and grunting like some large furry pig, Santini made a full dinner on the rest of the bait while Kelly studied his body and muscles and his use of jaws and paws.

It was late by the time Santini finished the bait in the brush pile and grunted his way up the slope. The summer light lingered just long enough to aid Leslie and Kelly as they climbed cautiously down from the stand. They used Kelly's flashlight to return to the four-wheeler. "We were lucky," Kelly said.

"Bears will often come the first night," Leslie said, "and then they get wary about returning."

Not certain that Dr. Andrews would approve of this method of bear study, Kelly kept the stand sheets with her Samantha file. Leslie returned twice more during the first weeks of September. Each time a bear showed up under the tree, Kelly's pulse rate jumped and she could feel the adrenaline rush. These were the unfettered bears she had wanted to observe, but it was a bit nerve-wracking to see just how big and powerful they were. They saw Samantha once more and a strange young male and a female she thought was Eleanor, though she didn't dare make noise by trying to pick up the signal from her collar. The male noticed them in the tree and stood up on his hind legs to reach toward the platform, but he didn't make any attempt to climb the tree. The vigils at the tree stand were exhilarating, and Kelly was tempted to go to the stand alone, but she didn't want to push her luck. She had had a safe, productive summer, and by the time Dr. Andrews showed up again at the cabin, Kelly was ready to share her considerable information on Samantha.

"How much of your information came from the stand?" Dr. Andrews asked after looking at the Samantha file.

Chagrined, but trying to make light of the situation, Kelly said, "Doc Morrison has a big mouth."

Dr. Andrews did not smile. "Kelly, is there some reason why you think you have to hide your data from me?"

"Rick told you that I was too involved with Samantha." Her throat tightened as her professor nodded, but she went on. "I couldn't take the chance that you'd tell me to stay away from her, because I knew I could get some good information if I just worked hard enough."

"Well, you've worked hard enough." Dr. Andrews didn't seem entirely satisfied, but he continued. "I hope you're ready to work even harder—at something you're going to hate if you're anything like Rick. And from what I can tell, half the trouble around here is that you and Rick are too much alike." His criticism made her feel tired and defeated. She didn't want to be like Rick. She waited silently, dreading whatever Dr. Andrews had planned for her next.

"Rick needs to do some more bear-range studies," Dr. Andrews said. "He wants to come back to the cabin." Kelly remained silent. She certainly wasn't going to make any extra trouble. "So, if you'll leave the cabin set up just as it is," Dr. Andrews continued, "Rick can spend week-days down here this fall, and you can come down on weekends to help with denning locations and maybe a little fall trapping if we have the money, and if you can get away from your work."

"What work will I be getting away from?"

Dr. Andrews smiled. "I was coming to that. I've arranged for you to be a lab instructor for freshman science classes. There's a salary with it. You could probably manage a room in a dormitory."

Kelly took a huge breath in and let it out. The job would solve her problems. "Thank you so much. This is what I needed."

Dr. Andrews laughed. "I wouldn't be too hasty about declaring overwhelming gratitude. You've never taught a group of captive freshmen."

∾

She had never taught freshmen, and by midterms in October, Kelly never wanted to teach freshmen again. They were as noisy and wriggly as kindergartners; most of them hated the required science labs; they didn't study for tests, and yet they complained when she gave them low grades. One day, dropping by to see Dr. Andrews, she said, "If I promise never to be any trouble again, and if I do everything Rick tells me, can I go back to the cabin?"

The professor laughed. "Tired of paying your dues already, Kelly?"

"How do you stand being a teacher?"

"Oh, every now and then I get a couple of complicated, dedicated, aggravating students such as you and Rick, and I remember why it was I wanted to teach."

Kelly didn't have time for more conversation—she *never* had time for more of anything except grading more papers and planning more lab exercises—but she left his office feeling better about their summer project.

She spent one wonderful weekend flying the bears with Mary Powers. The pilot was always relaxed and open. After they were done concentrating on the scanner, Kelly told her about her family situation.

"Sounds like they're all growing," Mary Powers said calmly, and then, with a keen look at Kelly, she added, "Change is a constant, but as long as everyone is alive, there is hope that change is for the better. Don't judge people too harshly. If you do, you'll feel guilty when they die." Some old pain surfaced briefly in her face.

I love you, Kelly thought. *You are the way I'd like to be.* She said, "Thank you, Mary. You're always good for me."

The next weekend she and Rick and Elizabeth took her flight data and, using the scanner, managed to mark some of the dens they would visit during the winter. "You'll be glad we set up these long poles when you see how deep the snow lies in here," Rick said.

She didn't have a chance to visit with Elizabeth because Rick was hovering, interrupting, correcting. Watching him, she felt a moment of sadness. *Isn't there some way that we could all cooperate, instead of competing? We women have so much to give.*

Kelly could hardly wait for snow and Christmas vacation and denning, even though she knew she would have to grade the finals from her lab classes during part of her vacation.

Just before the holiday break, Kelly was in her room with planning sheets spread over her desk when someone knocked tentatively at the door. When she opened it, Peggy stood there clutching a shoe box.

"Peggy, what's the matter?" Her sister's face was bleak, the skin drawn tight to the bones, her eyes shuttered by half-closed, swollen lids. Pulling her sister into the room, Kelly shut the door and led her to the desk chair. Seating herself on the bed, she said, "Tell me."

Peggy looked at her, still hanging on to the shoe box. "I'm pregnant."

"Oh, honey," Kelly said and then asked, "does Matt know?"

"Nobody knows." Peggy began to cry. "What am I going to do?"

"Well, first of all, you're going to stop crying. I can see you've done enough of that already." Kelly went to the small sink and, warming a washcloth under the tap, she stepped back to her sister and gently washed her face. Then she said, "Peggy, Matt wants a wife and family. He'll make a good daddy." Kelly hoped she was telling the truth. What if Matt turned and ran? "You've got to tell him. He has a right to know, and you need his help." She put her arm around Peggy, who leaned against her. "And then, you've got to see a doctor and get a good medical plan going."

"What about the folks?"

"You'll have to tell them, of course, but why not wait until you've told Matt?"

"I'm so scared."

"Of course you're scared, who wouldn't be?" *Damn that Matt. Where is his head?*

"Will you tell him for me?"

Kelly was too astonished to speak for a moment. "No, Peggy. This is strictly between the two of you. If you think you want to be married to that man, you have to learn how to talk to him." *And good luck.*

"What if he doesn't want me?"

"Well, you need to know that. There's no point in kidding yourself about anything at this stage of the game. If Matt doesn't want you, we'll have to figure out how to help you be a single mother, unless you want to give the baby up for adoption."

"Give up Matt's baby? Never!"

"Then go tell Matt about it. I think he'll be pleased that you love him so much."

"Are you sure you don't care? Are you sure you don't love him?" Peggy shifted the box on her lap and looked at Kelly, who was sitting on the bed again.

"Peg, all I love at this moment are you and Ryan and a bunch of bears."

"Do you love the folks?"

"I suppose I do. I'm trying to understand them."

Peggy handed the shoe box to Kelly. "This might help you understand them. I don't know if I should give it to you, but you have a right to see it."

"What's in it?"

"Some papers. I knocked the dumb box off a shelf when I was digging around in that impossible storage place. I couldn't help reading this stuff as I was picking it up." Peggy stood up and said, "I think you need to be alone when you look at this, but if you want to talk, call me and I'll come over again." Kelly swallowed. Peggy was suddenly acting as if she were the older sister. Peggy hugged her. "You're such a comfort. I'm lucky to have you for a sister." There was some kind of extra meaning in her words.

Peggy left and Kelly sat still, clutching the box, her heart beating wildly. She couldn't bring herself to open the box. She set it on the bed and gathered the papers from her desk and put them in her briefcase. She uncapped a bottle of pop and drank it slowly. But the box seemed to get bigger and bigger.

She reached to the lid and took it away. The box was full of papers and letters. She looked at the top document. It was her parents' wedding certificate. But the date was wrong. It said January 15, 1967.

That couldn't be right. Her parents had been married in January of 1966. And she had been born in March of 1967. Suddenly, grabbing the rest of the papers, Kelly read everything in the box. The wedding certificate, her birth certificate, Peggy's and Ryan's birth certificates, and in the very bottom of the box, the letters postmarked in 1966 and 1967 from a woman named Jane Lister. Kelly skimmed the letters.

"You can always go back to school after the baby is born. It's not the end of the world," and "I know you love Keith." Keith was Kelly's father's name. She was reading her own history. In the next letter, Jane said, "He'll want the baby when it's born, Marilyn, and you will, too. You wouldn't really consider abortion?" And in the next, "His mother is a blessing even if you feel like she's taken control over everything. I know you don't want to tell your own folks." And another letter. "You will want this baby. Don't keep telling me that you hate it. It's part of Keith. You love Keith."

Kelly couldn't read any more. She folded the letter and returned it to the envelope. She knew that Jane Lister was her mother's college roommate. She had died in a car accident six months after she had graduated from college—the college from which Kelly's mother had never graduated because she had a baby she hated. ❧

Chapter Forty-Eight

Numbly, Kelly restored the papers to the shoe box, closed it, and put a rubber band around the lid. She couldn't think about this right now. She had lab plans to make. It was hard enough to teach freshmen when she was prepared. If she wasn't prepared, especially this week as the students strained toward Christmas break and the ski slopes, it would be easier to round up wild turkeys than to capture their attention. Half of them were sniffling and coughing because of the flu outbreak on campus; the other half might as well have brought their skis to class. The next evening, she set the box on her closet shelf. Eventually she would have to do something about it, but she had paperwork to finish if she, too, were going to escape to the mountains after her last class.

Before she could leave Provo, she needed to check in with her family about Christmas. The thought of talking to her mother made her stomach tighten. She went to see Peggy instead. "Are we having a family Christmas?"

"Sure. Mom and Ryan have already got a tree. Dad's coming home." Peggy eyed her. "Did you look in that box?"

"Yes."

"I should have just stuck it back together and left it there."

"No, Peggy," Kelly said. "This family needs to dig out the truth." Her eyes filled with tears, embarrassing her. She turned away.

"Oh, honey," Peggy said, following to draw her close. "Oh, Kelly." Then she said fiercely, "My baby is never going to feel this way. Not ever. I'm always going to say how much I loved it from the very first moment." Her voice faltered. "Even if Matt doesn't want us."

"Have you told him?"

"After Christmas. I'll tell him after Christmas."

It was Kelly's turn to offer comfort with a hug. "I know Matt wants you. You've got to tell him. The sooner the better. Don't wait until after Christmas. Tell him now."

"I'll try." She drew back to look at Kelly. "You're going to be here for Christmas, aren't you?"

"I'm going denning. We want to reach the females with yearlings and all the males during school break." She sighed. "I suppose I have to come home for Christmas."

When Peggy dropped Kelly off at the Widstoe Building, they saw Rick and Adam waiting by the pickup. "Well," Peggy said, "your buddies are here."

Kelly didn't answer, for she was suddenly filled with apprehension. She had not talked to Adam all semester. Once or twice, she'd caught a glimpse of him near the zoology building, but too rushed to try to catch him and too uneasy about their parting, she had let it go. She was relieved to see Adam's smile and the sparkling brown eyes. He was dressed in a heavy wool-plaid logger's jacket in rich shades of tan and brown that went with his complexion. "Hey, Teach," he said, "I hear you're real mean."

"Yeah," Rick said, "they're calling you Sticks-and-Stones Jones."

"You guys are just jealous that I get all the fun." Kelly climbed into the pickup, feeling happier than she had in three months and able to release a little of the ache that had settled inside her as she read the letters in the shoe box.

Rick was grumbling. "I hope to hell it doesn't snow. I wanted to take the snowmobiles back to the project, but somebody else was using the snowmobile trailer—probably some prof's son who went off to play."

Adam stretched his legs forward. "I'm so glad to get away from classes, it even feels good to hear you griping, Santini." He sneezed, shielding his face with his hand.

"You sound like most of the kids in my lab," Kelly said. "I should have carried a hanky and wiped noses the last three days."

There was no new snow in the high country, but it was cold. They decided to move the propane stove to the counter and build a fire in the range to warm the cabin. Adam looked around. "Who fussied up the place?"

"Folks at the store tell me the bear woman lived here all summer," Rick said.

"You'd think she'd decorate with bear skin rugs and coyote tails instead of pink curtains. Adam shook his head. "Pink!" Rick had taken the center cot. Kelly folded back cot covers for Adam to place his sleeping bag and then did the same for herself. "So," Adam said, "you're going to be sleeping with us?"

Rick laughed. "Go take a peek in her old bedroom."

Adam snooped around in the shower stall, saying, "All the comforts of home." He sneezed again and blew his nose.

"Wash your hands before you cook dinner," Kelly said.

"Me? Who says I'm the cook?"

"If you don't cook, you're a sadist and a masochist both," Rick said.

Adam came out of the bathroom. "Listen to the big words. You must think you've got your MS already."

"It's just BS," Kelly said and they all laughed—the laughter warming the cabin faster than the stove, which was beginning to make a satisfying roar as the kindling caught fire. *No matter what happened between and among us as individuals, we actually did turn into a team. No other three people could walk into this cabin and feel so much together.*

The fact that they worked well together was a help during the days before Christmas because denning was difficult work. As they slogged their way through old snowdrifts and up a steep slope, Adam groaned aloud and said, "Leave it to a namesake of yours, Santini, to den on a perpendicular face. What did he do—use rope and crampons?"

"At least when we get there," Kelly said, "we won't have to dig through six feet of snow. Nothing could settle on a rock so steep." Santini's signal was very clear. He was denned in a cave or crevice above them.

"I just hope he's sleepy enough to let us put him down easily," Rick said. "They don't really hibernate, and they're not always under. I don't want him to take a swipe at me."

"He's one strong brute," Kelly said. "I saw him uproot an aspen this summer." The men were interested in the story, and Kelly told it between moments of panting for breath as they climbed.

Santini's signal drew them to a small opening on a ledge about midway up the rock face. Rick studied the opening and then crouched on the ledge and directed a flashlight beam inside. "I can't see clear to the back, but it looks like it widens out," he said. "I think I can get in there to jab him; then we'll drag him out here for processing."

"Is this ledge wide enough?" Adam asked. He looked a little pale, and he didn't inspect the den entrance as Kelly and Rick had.

"I think so. We'll move slowly." Rick was preparing the jab stick. "I'm going to crawl in and check on this old boy. When I get through the opening, tie the rope around my feet, and if I say 'pull,' you guys get me out of there fast."

Kelly swallowed. "The rocks would tear you up," she said.

Rick had put a miner's light on an elastic band around his head and clipped the battery pack to his belt. "Better the rocks than Santini." He pushed the jab stick inside the opening, and then, crouching on all fours on the ledge, he slowly flattened himself until he could fit his head and shoulders through the hole in the rock, tipping his head to get the light safely through. When he was stretched out, they tied the rope to his legs. Like a wide worm, he inched his way into the hole and disappeared. They reeled out the rope as he scraped across the rock floor of the passageway, pulling steadily. Then there was silence, and the rope no longer tugged in their hands.

Kelly looked at Adam and was startled to see that there were beads of sweat on his forehead. "Are you okay?"

He shook his head slightly. "I don't know. There's something about that hole that gives me the creeps. I hope we don't have to go in there after him."

"After who?" Rick's head popped out of the hole, his grin as bright as the light on his head. "Me or that old bear? He was sawing logs when I jabbed him. We can process him in a few minutes. Which of you guys wants to help?"

"What's the den like?" Kelly asked.

"Wide and comfortable, with a couple of inches of bedding."

Kelly felt Adam's body stiffen beside her. He coughed, then took a deep breath. "I'll help."

"Okay," Rick said. "What you need to do, Adam, is to get a rope on him so we can pull him out. Then while Kelly and I work on him, you can measure the den, describe it, measure the bedding, and name the contents—leaves, pine needles, whatever. When you're out, you can help weigh him before we stuff him back."

"How are we going to get a bear that size out of a hole that small?" Kelly asked.

"Well, he musta squashed himself to get in there," Rick said. "Luckily, the passageway's not bad. It's just the opening that's small. We'll only have to squash him a little to get him out."

"Is the stress the same for a hibernating bear as for the ones we snare?" Adam asked, frowning.

Rick nodded soberly. "Every contact with humans causes stress for the bear. We need to work quickly, quietly, and gently."

It was cold on the ledge, and Kelly's fingers and toes were stinging by the time Adam extended the rope to her from the cave mouth. The huge sleeping bear was extremely heavy. It was difficult to brace themselves in the small space on the ledge, and it took their combined efforts to extract him from the hole. As they positioned him on the rocks, Rick said, "Go ahead, Adam, check out the den while Kelly and I check out my namesake."

Santini's fur was thicker and less patchy than when they had last seen him. Kelly warmed up with the effort of processing the bear. After a short time, Adam crawled out of the den to help weigh him. Putting the bear back in the den was even more difficult than pulling him out because there was no way to get behind him on the narrow ledge to push, and sideways motions to move him were awkward. Kelly followed Rick through the tight opening to help pull the red bear inside. Rick kept his eye on Santini, and once they had the bear spread out on his stomach in the passageway, Rick said, "He's coming up. Let's get out of here."

Outside, Adam coughed and said, "Thanks for going in, Kelly. I wasn't ready to crawl through that hole again." The growly cough seemed to be getting worse.

"We need to get you home and rub Vicks on your chest," Kelly said after they picked their way down the rock. Adam gave her a flashing look, and she remembered the moment on the firing range when he had stepped away from her. She raised her gloved hands, palm up, and said, "Sorry, I know you don't need a mama." Just saying the word mama brought a jolt of pain to Kelly—the box and its papers swimming into her mind with Jane Lister's words loud as if they'd been spoken. *You don't hate this baby, no matter what you say.*

Adam had taken her arm. "Kelly? Are you okay?" She shook her head to dispel the floating words, and gave Adam a glance, but she couldn't focus. Moving away from his arm, she stumbled through a tangle of scrub and crusted snow.

They were exhausted by the time they got into the cabin. Wet, dirty, cold, hungry, and silent, they recorded their data, ate, and went to bed.

The next day was even harder. Rick had targeted a gulch where

Ryan had denned. "The gullies on the way to the top are probably deep with drifts. We'll take the snowshoes."

Disliking the look of the clumsy snowshoes, Kelly tried at first to walk without them, but after she plunged through the surface of a deep drift, trapping her legs clear to her hips, she accepted Rick's hand to help her free herself and Adam's offer to strap the snowshoes on for her.

The snowshoes kept her on the surface of the snow, but maneuvering around thickets and trees and downed logs, always climbing uphill, took concentration and effort. She was already tired by the time they reached the area where Ryan was sleeping under about seven feet of crusted snow.

Each team member extracted a small fold-up shovel from its loop on the backpack and, snapping it into full length, began to dig through the snow. The cold air, the high altitude, and the effort left them no breath for conversation. Kelly didn't feel like talking anyway. Exhausted and cold, she was having trouble controlling her emotions.

She could not make the box stay on the closet shelf; she could not stop the misery of its contents from seeping like sewer water through her mind, contaminating the joy of gaining knowledge about the bear-denning process. *I always wanted to unearth the reasons for Mother's unhappiness*, she thought, tossing a heaped shovelful away from the den. Somewhere in the area of her breastbone, she felt a tight burning sensation, and tears pricked the corners of her eyes. *But that was before I knew that the reason for her unhappiness was me.*

Their shoveling must have disturbed Ryan because when they finally uncovered the opening, the bear was awake and feisty. They settled on using the gun instead of the jab stick. "At least," Adam said, "this opening doesn't make you feel like the middle of a rock sandwich." He went through the wide maw of the cave and measured the den after tugging Ryan close enough for Kelly to reach him.

On Christmas Eve day, they planned to process Kendall, but after following her signal high on the ridge, they somehow took the wrong turn up a canyon and lost the signal completely. They backtracked and zigzagged, but they were too close to the huge snowy mountain. They lost perspective, and they couldn't tell one gulch from another. Tired and discouraged, they descended late in the day and left for Provo without warming the cabin or eating a hot meal.

"Are you going to Colorado for Christmas?" Adam asked Rick.

"Yeah. My mom sent an airplane ticket." Kelly couldn't tell if Rick was pleased or displeased or neutral. She pictured his bright attractive mother. *What would I do if I had a son like Rick?* Kelly thought of the withdrawn man who was Rick's father, and she felt sorry for Rick and his mother both. *If Rick were my son, and I were stuck in a small town, lonely for intelligent company, I'd probably hang on to him—at least to his mind—in any way I could.* Kelly remembered that Rick had said, "Have intelligent sons and get out of their way." It would not be a relaxed Christmas at the Santini household.

"What are the Joneses doing for Christmas?" Adam asked.

"Throwing out all the old traditions," Kelly said. Her voice sounded odd, even to herself, and Adam turned to look at her with a piercing glance that made her think of all the times they had shared honest discussions. He cleared his throat. She did not want Adam to start probing with Rick around. She said, "You ought to go home and go to bed until the day after Christmas if you're coming back up here to work with us."

Rick said, "Speaking of that, Wainwright, have you decided to stick with the bear program or not?" *Oh, great,* Kelly thought. *Adam's already miserable, Rick. Let's add to his problems.*

"I don't know," Adam said. "I'm not sure how I feel. I still think we do too much damage, and we don't know enough about caring for animals in the wild." He coughed and then said, "I've got enough credits to graduate at the end of this semester, but I don't know what I'm going to do." He looked down at Kelly. "I'm not sure how I feel." She felt that this time, he was not talking about bears.

She met his glance briefly, but there was no privacy, no time to explore their feelings. It would take skill to get them back on some steady basis of friendship, and emotionally exhausted, she was scarcely holding on to the casual conversation in the truck. ✆

Chapter Forty-Nine

Since the dorm was closed for the Christmas holiday, Kelly went to her sister's apartment. Beth said that Peggy was out with Matt, but she invited Kelly in, gave her clean towels and a smile, and left her alone to recuperate under a hot shower before she called her mother's place. Her father answered, and Kelly was surprised almost into tears at the pleasure of hearing his voice. "Well, hi," she said. "I've missed you. How's the road?"

"Challenging, exciting." He paused and added with a lower voice, "And lonesome."

Startled by the confession, Kelly tried to find the right response. "I know how that can be. My work offers little social life."

He asked, "When are you coming over?"

"Are we having the big to-do in the morning?"

"Same as always."

"Well, I haven't bought a thing. Why don't you ask Ryan if he wants to help me go Christmas shopping?"

"Just a minute." She heard the rumble of conversation. "Kelly? He says he'd like to go to the mall. That suit you?"

"Sure."

He said, "Thanks, Kelly. I just got here an hour or so ago. I haven't had a chance to be with your mother."

Ryan seemed just as grateful. "I didn't want to be around to get in their way," he said.

"Let's go play Santa Claus," Kelly said. "Or I'll shop, and you can hang out with your friends if you want."

Ryan stayed with her, though, and they laughed as they picked through the department-store leftovers, trying to find something for each family member. They fell into a fit of giggles when Ryan held up a pair of red silk shorts and said, "How about these for Dad?"

It was fun to shop with Ryan, fun just to be with him. His quick mind was a pleasure, and there were no complications. She was suddenly aware of what a blessing a brother could be. He was male, intelligent, and no problem. She invited him to share hot chocolate, and while they sat at a table in the mall, she told him about finding Ryan Bear in his den.

When they finished, Ryan said, "Why don't you come back with me? You can wrap your stuff in my room and sleep on my floor." Grateful for the niche in the family that he offered her, she began to feel that she might get through Christmas okay.

"Wake up! Wake up! Wake up!" Peggy's voice rang like a clarion through the apartment. There was a lilt to it that Kelly, even sleepy and disoriented, recognized as relief and happiness. She stretched in her sleeping bag, smelling the piney scent of the large tree that crowded the corner just outside Ryan's door. Suddenly that door burst open, and Peggy plopped herself down on Kelly's sleeping bag with her hand extended under Kelly's nose. "Look what Matt gave me for Christmas!"

Kelly squinted down her nose, and the sight of the diamond ring made her sit up. "Oh, Peg! That's super." She hugged her sister tightly. Then she asked softly, "Did you tell him?"

"No," Peggy looked away. "I didn't want to spoil his gift."

"You have to tell him."

"Not if we get married right away."

"Are you going to tell the folks?"

"After reading the stuff in that box? Never!" Peggy tossed her head. "Nobody is going to manage our lives but us."

Matt stuck his head in the door. Peggy hopped up to go to him, and he put his arm around her shoulder, his large hand curved protectively toward her. "So what do you think of our news?"

"Fantastic!" Kelly said. "Congratulations."

Matt met her look without a smile, studying her briefly before saying, "Thanks, Kelly." He turned to Peggy. "Your folks are up. Let's go tell them."

Kelly lay back in the sleeping bag, a riot of feelings inside her. But Ryan wouldn't let her have the moment for reflection. He rolled off the bed and sat on top of her. He was grinning, and he seemed like an innocent, happy kid again. "Will you get off!" Kelly said, pushing her little brother and laughing as she struggled to get out of her sleeping bag.

There was no time for thinking. The day became a rich stew of noise and motion, stirred occasionally by emotion. Uneasy about talking with her mother, she was relieved when the day was filled in other ways, and she never had to make a decision about the box.

But as the day wore away—the rich food making them drowsy and less noisy, the apartment feeling smaller with the clutter of too many things and too many people—Kelly began to wish she were back in the cabin. In late afternoon, Peggy and Matt left for her apartment, and Kelly's parents slipped even deeper into their own emotional whirlpool. When Ryan went to be with his friends, she felt irrationally deserted. She didn't know where to go to get out of her parents' way. She finally went into Ryan's room and tried to read about denning techniques, but she could not concentrate. She thought suddenly of Mary Powers. What did she do on holidays? Was her nice friend with her—or off walking his own path? *I don't want a life like that.*

She tried to picture the life she did want, and her grandmother's place came into her mind. It always seemed to be sunny there, the hillside filled with flowers—birds, animals, sky, trees, and land all a part of the warmth, the richness. She closed her book, attempting to remember the relationship between her grandparents. Her grandfather had been quiet, seeming stern, but she had a residual memory of respect. They were too reserved to speak of love, but they remained . . . she sought a word . . . solid.

Mary Powers had spoken of each person's strengths. That was what her grandparents had—strengths that made them seem whole together. And somehow, that strength had stayed with her grandmother. Even when her grandfather had died, he had left the wholeness.

Kelly was suddenly wiping away tears. But she didn't know if she was grieving for the two dear dead people, or for her own loneliness. *I wish I were like Samantha, needing a mate only for breeding and the rest of the time content to be in my own world.* She imagined Samantha curled up asleep in a rock den, but it was not a comforting picture.

∞

They hauled the snowmobiles back on the day after Christmas. Kelly could tell that the break for Christmas had interrupted their sense of being a unit. Rick was silent, remote, and almost curt when he gave orders, and he was the most abrupt when giving orders to Kelly. Adam still coughed.

"Why didn't you stay home?" she asked, turning toward him in the pickup.

"There's nobody to take my place," he said. "I didn't want to leave you two to do the work alone." He changed the subject. "So what did you get for Christmas?"

"A brother-in-law."

Adam's eyes focused sharply on her. "Matt?" Kelly nodded. "How do you feel about that?"

"Relieved." That was true, but it wasn't the whole truth. Kelly also felt jealous. She had realized it when she saw Matt and Peggy whispering something to each other at dinner and Peggy giving her fiancé a sparkling private smile. Peggy would never confide in her again in the same way. It was stupid to think that she had lost her sister, but it was a definite splitting of their paths.

Adam was still looking at her. "You mean you aren't one little bit sorry that he's chosen someone else?"

Kelly laughed. "Adam, I don't want Matt. I told you that last summer. I want him to make my sister happy. If I miss anyone, it will be her. She's been my best friend."

"It's pretty easy for you to toss away an old boyfriend," Adam said.

"Bears come first with the bear woman," Rick said suddenly.

What was the matter with these two? It was as if they had joined forces in some odd male way to feel resentful because she didn't want Matt. They had been equally resentful when they had thought she wanted him.

"Bears are a lot easier to understand," Kelly said, but she didn't want to talk about her feelings—for bears *or* boyfriends. She asked, "What did you guys get for Christmas?"

"Money enough to keep on until I finish my damned thesis," Rick said. He seemed to resent the money. "My mom dug it up somewhere." Or maybe it was just his mother that he resented.

Adam said sourly, "I got a lot of advice."

It was like sitting between two porcupines. She changed the subject again. "Is it supposed to snow?"

"It's snowing now," Rick said, lifting a hand toward the windshield. ∽

Chapter Fifty

By the time they reached the turnoff to the cabin, there was a steady wet curtain of snow, and new drifts had crossed their road. "We'll never make it to the cabin with that trailer hooked on to us," Rick said. He and Adam got out and, unhitching the trailer, jockeyed it to a wide spot, and then climbed back in, wet and muddy. Rick put the truck into four-wheel drive and bucked his way through the drifts for several minutes. But somewhere near the bait barrel, the truck slid into an old rut, and they were stuck.

Adam and Kelly climbed down to push and to help rock the truck. It was cold. The snow coated their faces. Footing was slippery. When the truck gave a sudden leap forward, jerking away from their grip, Kelly slipped and fell. She sat still for a minute recovering from the jolt. Rick and the truck roared out of sight around the curve.

Adam slogged over to her and offered her a hand. Helping her up, he pulled her close to him and held her there briefly in the middle of the blizzard. She caught her breath and clung to him silently. Then he began to cough, and he let her go, but held on to her hand, and they tugged each other through the drifts to the cabin.

It was interesting again to Kelly how any outside threat, even from nature, renewed them as a team. Safe in the cabin, with the fire warming it, they settled in, their holiday prickles subsiding. Adam cooked a huge pot of spaghetti followed by apple pie he'd brought from home. The stove roared inside; the storm roared outside. They sat around the table drinking hot chocolate, discussing the difficulties of the next day's denning trip.

"Let's try for some bear that's low," Adam said.

"Well, Peggy's low, Marilyn's low, Eleanor's low, but we shouldn't do her because she's probably pregnant."

They decided to try for Marilyn on Friday and Peggy on Saturday, and then Rick said, "Jerry told me that you've got a lot of good data on

Samantha. Can we see your work sheets?" He seemed truly interested, and Kelly was happy to share the information now that Dr. Andrews had more or less approved her summer work.

"You've got a good start with her," Rick said, "especially your luck in catching her with Santini. If we can follow her over the other three years of the project, we'll have a good picture. The female is actually the most important to study."

"She denned awfully high," Kelly said. "I hope we can find her after she has cubs."

Rick studied the map. "She seems to have a love affair with that ridge. She's probably in some impossible hole in the rocks."

"Do they always den in the rocks?" Adam asked.

"No, sometimes they'll choose an opening at the base of a tree, but that's fairly rare here. I don't think our trees are big enough."

They finally put the data sheets away after discussing every angle of their denning trip on the following day. "I'll take Kelly on the big snowmobile," Rick said. "You can take the small one and haul gear." Adam nodded. They lingered at the table. Provo seemed far away. It *was* far away because the blizzard was surely making the roads impossible, Soldier Summit impassable. Rick said, "You guys want to play a game? Pammy gave me this dumb board game."

It was fun. They squabbled and laughed over every move, every point. Around midnight, they decided to heat up the rest of the pie, and then Adam said, "Hey, I'll make some snow ice cream to go with it." They scooped up a big panful of new snow, and Adam added canned milk and sugar and vanilla. The concoction was grainy and then watery when it melted on the pie, but it made them laugh again, and Kelly relaxed into sleepy contentment.

The snow had stopped by morning, but it was still cloudy and cold. Kelly hid her face behind Rick as they roared through the new snow and along a trail that led them up Moreno Creek. The gassy smell of the snowmobile was unpleasant, and the sound of the engine racketed against the peaceful mountain. The huge white snowdrifts resembled clouds or pillows, so white they made the aspen bark look gray.

The drifts didn't feel like pillows, though. Rounding one curve a little too swiftly, Rick lost control of the machine, and it tipped over into deep wet snow at the side of the road, dumping them both. Adam roared up behind them laughing, until he started coughing. After they set the heavy machine back on its runners, Rick picked up the scanner. He fiddled with it for a moment and then turned. "Let's get going," he said. "Marilyn's restless."

When they reached the point of the strongest signal, they dug through the drifts until they found the mouth of the den. The old bear they had named after Kelly's mother was denned in a shallow cave, and she hadn't made much of a bed. They pulled her out to the light where they recorded every piece of information, despite the intermittent snow and the freezing temperatures. She was thin and mangy, and her fat layer was not nearly as thick as that on the other denned bears they had checked. Her teeth were badly worn; the broken canine they had noted before was infected.

Adam said, "Could we have done something about that tooth when we snared her in June?"

"We gave her a shot of penicillin," Rick said. "That should have killed any infection." The bear's tail was bony, almost hairless from the mange. There were white circles of mange around her eyes, making the eyes themselves seem even smaller than usual. They measured her, took hair samples, and scraped a little of the mangy skin into a plastic sack.

Kelly had hoped for some time alone to talk to Adam, but the denning process was exhausting, and at the end of the day, all they wanted was to finish their work, to eat something, and to sleep. Rick insisted that all equipment be checked each evening. "Our denning days are limited. We don't want to miss a bear because of equipment failure."

Friday morning Adam woke with a worse cough, but he insisted on driving the snowmobile anyway. By the time they reached the upper reaches of Warren Gulch, snow was falling thickly, and an icy wind funneled through the gulch, blowing the snow in their faces. Glad for the broad shield of Rick's shoulders, Kelly bent her head behind him. She did not see what happened. One moment the machine was roaring along what seemed like a trail, and the next moment it was on its side, tunneling through the snow to end up against a tree. She heard Rick cry out. He crawled off the machine, holding his right hand. She was stuck with one leg buried in the snow beneath the snowmobile.

Adam came first to her, tugging at the snowmobile, but unable to move it by himself and finally digging under it to give her room to maneuver. When she was standing, they turned to Rick, who was obviously in pain. "Are you okay?"

"I hit my hand on the tree." He removed his glove to look at the injured hand. It was swelling already. He pushed it awkwardly into the glove.

"Shall we go back?" Kelly asked.

"No! We're almost there. We don't want to do this again tomorrow."

Adam and Kelly did most of the work of righting the snowmobile, with Rick putting his body weight against it to keep it from sliding down the gulch. "We can't go much farther on these, anyway," Rick said. "The trail peters out."

"I hope Peggy is in a spot we can get to easily," Kelly said after they parked the snowmobiles and strapped on their snowshoes.

"We'll just get the bear data," Rick said. "We can mark the den and come back and do den measurements in the summer." *We?* That was the second time he'd used the word with reference to the future of the project. She wondered how long Rick thought he'd be hanging around after he finished his thesis.

When they finally dug down to Peggy's den and checked the opening, they looked at each other in dismay. The passageway was cramped—long and narrow, and the rock ceiling hung low all the way back. And then they discovered that Rick could not hold the jab stick with his swollen hand. "Okay, Wainwright, I guess it's up to you."

Adam took the jab stick and got down on his belly in front of the opening. As Kelly knelt to tie the safety rope to his feet, he turned to speak to her, and she noticed that he was pale. She put a hand on his forehead. He was hot with fever.

"Rick, Adam's sick. We ought to abort this."

But Adam said, "No, he's right. We don't want to come back again." He looked at the hole in the rock face. "I just wish that damned passageway were bigger." He began to slide into the hole on his belly, and Kelly let the rope out slowly.

Suddenly Adam cried, "Pull me out." Kelly gripped the rope with two hands, Rick with one, and they pulled Adam backward as fast as they could. When his head and shoulders were near the opening, they could see him scrabbling frantically with his hands. They grabbed hold of his legs and helped him out. Rick reached in and retrieved the jab stick.

"Is she awake?" Rick said.

Adam's eyes looked wild. He shook his head. "I didn't hear anything."

"What's the matter, then?" Kelly asked. Adam's eyes were now glassy as if he were about to go into shock. "Here, sit down."

Adam sat down in the snow, breathing hard. After a moment or two, he looked up at them. "I think I have claustrophobia. I got a little panicky the other day, going into the first den, but I thought I'd get used to it." He was still breathing oddly. He seemed terrified.

"Maybe it's just because you've got a fever," Kelly said.

Rick looked at Kelly. "You want to give it a try?"

"We probably ought to get Adam out of the cold."

"No," Adam said abruptly. "I've already screwed things up." He picked up the rope and said, "Let's get it over with."

Kelly said, "Let's think this through a little. What should we be doing here?"

Rick held his hand close to his chest. He nodded and said, "Okay. First of all, Adam, are you sure that bear's quiet?"

"Yeah. All I could hear in there was my heart beating." He looked at Kelly. "Do you think you can go in?"

"Do you think you guys can pull me out?"

Adam said, "We can do that. Can you put her down?"

Kelly had no idea what she could do inside the den, but she was the only one left who could keep them from wasting this day of denning. She reached for the jab stick. "I'll give it a try."

She knelt, inserted the jab stick into the hole, and pushed it as far ahead as she could. Adam leaned over her and fastened the head lamp band around her forehead; she clamped the battery pack to her waist. She lay down and inserted her head and shoulders into the opening. After the rope was tied firmly about her ankles, she began to inch her way along the rocky passage, her headlight lighting the roof more than it lighted the space in front of her.

As soon as her whole body was inside the opening, she knew what had happened to Adam. On all sides of her, the rock was solid. Underneath her, jagged corners of stone pressed into her legs; above her the ceiling of the tunnel brushed her head, then her back, some projections catching at her clothing. On both sides, the rock pressed close, cramping her shoulders. Thank goodness her arms were in front of her. There was no other space for them. She could only hope that the battery pack at her waist would not get knocked off.

The darkness made it worse. It was so close, so black, except in the small area the flashlight beam touched, that even the air seemed to imprison her. She rested a moment, listening for sounds from the bear.

But resting was the wrong thing to do, for suddenly she was aware of the weight of the mountain above her and the snow on that mountain. Even if the rocks didn't move, an avalanche could sweep Rick and Adam away and bury her in the den. She listened again, this time for sounds of the mountain, but heard nothing except her own rough breathing.

She had to keep moving. Surely the passageway widened out. She shivered as she thought about the bear. *If Peggy wakes and comes to investigate the scraping sounds, there's no way Rick and Adam can pull me out without injury. This is just plain dumb.* But she dragged herself forward through the dark narrow tube of rock until she saw a glimpse of brown fur. ∾

Chapter Fifty-One

Peggy was breathing, but not moving. She seemed to be deeply asleep. Kelly drew the jab stick up to the point of a wider space in the rock and delivered the drug, scraping her elbow as she forced the follow-through. Since the bear was quiet, she decided to wait for the drug to take effect. No point in traversing that passageway more often than she had to. She studied the den—if anything so small could really be called a den.

The wide crevice was big enough for the young bear and nothing else. Peggy had managed a fair bed. It had taken patience to scrape bedding materials through the narrow opening. Kelly shivered and pushed away the thought of her own return trip.

When she was certain that Peggy was down, she uncurled the little brown creature and positioned her so that she could pull on the bear while Rick and Adam pulled on the rope. She pushed the jab stick as far back down the passageway as she could, then stretched out and gave a tug on the rope, holding her breath until she felt the answering tug.

The pull on the rope was like the touch of someone's hand, comforting and reassuring. She grasped the small bear's ankles and as Rick and Adam moved her slowly backward, she pulled the bear along. She had to keep her mind away from the idea of being trapped. When the battery pack caught briefly on a rock projection, her pulse rate surged. She could feel the rush all over her body. She took a hand from the bear and shoved on the rock floor in front of her. The motion freed the pack, and she exhaled the breath she hadn't realized she was holding. The two outside continued the steady reassuring motion. She pushed the jab stick along when she came to it.

When Rick and Adam pulled her through the opening, Kelly drew the bear out and then released it to Rick who said, "It's a good thing she's a little bear." She could tell by the way he held his hand and by the strain in his voice that he was hurting. But she had done all that she could do for the moment. Her hands were trembling and she could not get enough air. Adam took the rope from her ankles.

She gasped and shivered. "That passageway is a nightmare." Adam was silent. He stood apart, rolling up the rope, but huddled in obvious misery. *We should have aborted this one*. Rick muttered something, and she realized that he was having trouble holding the measure. She moved to help him because *Adam's coughing shook his whole body. Adam's in no shape to drive back. The next thing I'm going to learn is how to drive a snowmobile.*

It turned out that it was the next thing, but she didn't drive for Adam. Rick's hand was too swollen for him to use the controls. He tried, wincing each time he exerted pressure. Finally, he put Kelly in front of him and coached her. It was not as difficult as learning to drive the four-wheeler, and she soon had the hang of controlling the machine, although going around curves frightened her. Rick didn't need to be dumped into another snow bank. She settled for driving much more slowly than Rick had as she carefully retraced their trail.

Finally back in the cabin, Kelly built a fire and put the dishpan on the stove to heat water. Adam stumbled to the cot and collapsed as soon as they got inside. Kelly felt his forehead, which was extremely hot and dry. "You better get that wet jacket off," she said. She put her arm behind him and lifted him up as she might have done Ryan, tugging his sleeves until he pulled each arm out. She unlaced and removed his boots. Adam turned on his side and jerked the bedspread around him, coughing.

"You ought to give him something for his fever," Rick said.

"Should we give him a penicillin shot?"

"If it's a virus flu, penicillin's not going to help. Better you get him to breathe some steam for the congestion and give him aspirin to bring down the fever." Rick had buried his hand in a washpan of snow.

Kelly took a bottle of aspirin and counted out four tablets. "Here," she said, offering two of them to Rick. "These should ease the pain a little." He opened his mouth for the pills and took the dipper of water with his good hand. Adam bent his face into the pan of steaming water until the steam no longer rose. Kelly returned the pan to the stove and gave him the aspirin.

She made soup and sandwiches, but Adam shook his head. Rick ate only a little before retiring to his cot. Adam coughed all night; Rick groaned and thrashed about. Kelly got up several times to stoke the fire. She felt Adam's head each time, and it was always burning. Once Adam reached up and clutched her hand. She stood in the darkness, holding his hand, feeling comforted herself, until the rasping coughs started once more.

She had never been happier to see anyone than when Dr. Andrews pulled up in front of the cabin on Sunday morning, despite the fact that he chewed them out royally for not aborting the denning after Rick's hand was hurt. The hand was somewhat better, but Rick's skin took on the mottled look it always did when things went wrong for him. Adam's cough was still rough.

"So," Dr. Andrews said. "Kelly did the den work because Rick was hurt and Adam was sick." He smiled at her. "Do you still think this bear project is more fun than anything?"

Kelly laughed. "You should have asked me when I was on my belly in that tunnel."

Adam spoke up suddenly. "There's something you should know." Dr. Andrews turned toward him. "Even if I hadn't been sick, I would have screwed up. I started into that tunnel and panicked." He shook his head. "I didn't know I had claustrophobia . . ." He coughed. "But I don't think I'm reliable denning help."

Dr. Andrews looked at him soberly. "I appreciate that, Adam. It's hard to keep track of the project without honest reports when things go wrong." He glanced around the cabin.

"This place is too drafty for a sick bay. What do you say I take Rick and Adam back with me, Kelly, and send you some other help?"

"Do you think you can get anybody to come up here before New Year's Day?" Rick asked. "Everyone will have New Year's Eve plans."

"If nothing else," Dr. Andrews said, "I'll come myself and bring my wife."

"Don't cancel your holiday plans on my account," Kelly said. "I don't mind being alone for a couple of days. I can write up data and do a little planning."

"I can stay," Rick said.

"You can return, maybe," Dr. Andrews said, "but first you're going to have that hand X-rayed."

The night alone was weirdly mobile. Fire shadows from around the edges of the stove lids jiggled the ceiling; the wind harried the screen door; burning wood murmured and moved; and Kelly's thoughts skimmed along her mind like dried leaves blown in the wind. She slept restlessly, reliving the denning days in complicated, frightening dreams. She lay in the dark tunnel held by sharp corners of her life, facing an angry bear who raised a wounded paw and turned into Rick, who fumbled her body with heavy groping claws. Adam blew around them like smoke, his face and eyes shaping and dissolving into sorrow and blame. She awoke once, cold, to get up and renew the fire, and when she went back to bed, she dreamed that she sat on the ground at the far edge of a schoolyard, tearing papers into little pieces while her mother watched from the bushes. When the school bell rang in her dream,

Kelly woke and decided to get up though it was only five o'clock. She drank hot chocolate and reread the denning locations. She wouldn't dare to go denning alone, but she wasn't ready to stay in the cabin all day. She decided to practice maneuvering the snowmobile.

She walked out to the trailer, enjoying the crisp air and the high cold blue of the sky. The snowmobile was reluctant to start, but she finally got it going and began to learn the quirks of driving the thing. She drove up the snow-covered road toward the highway and returned. On the second trip, she met the university van. She turned around and drove back to the turn-off, parked the machine, and hopped in the van when it pulled up beside her.

"Hi," Rick said. "I'm glad you've got that machine warmed up. We came early so we could get to the mountain today, at least to another low den."

Kelly greeted Jonathan, who was the other part of "we," and then said, "How's your hand?"

"Usable," Rick said. "Not broken. We can manage."

"What about Adam?"

"I don't know. We dropped him off at his folks' place."

During the rest of the Christmas break, they managed to reach a den a day. It was hard, cold, physically exhausting, and yet, as they added more and more information to their files, they were renewed and ready to go each morning. They worked intensely. Jonathan was a good, focused crew member. All Kelly's wavery feelings disappeared under the discipline and joy of the project. She slept without dreaming. They went back together in the van. Rick took Jonathan home first and then delivered Kelly to the dorm. "Can you get away for denning work in January?"

"I don't know. We'll just be getting into the new semester."

Rick nodded. "And I've got to get a preliminary draft of my thesis put together for my advisor." He touched the denning file. "We've done the males and the young females. We can let up a little until March."

❧

Starting into the second semester, Kelly was too busy to even visit the bear lab, but she agreed to join her family the weekend of January twenty-fifth to be Peggy's attendant at the simple wedding she and Matt had arranged.

It was a dishonest, uncomfortable day. Kelly knew too much. Peggy's pregnancy did not show in her body, but there seemed to be a change in her face. It was disconcerting to think of the child who would be Kelly's niece or nephew, arriving too early, facing questions all her life or being shielded by lies. Her family seemed to be without anchor. Her father was only home for the day of the wedding; Ryan was adjusting to a new school; her mother was focused on her college problems. Kelly left the wedding reception uneasy and lonely, missing her grandmother, and with a rawer feeling of loss, missing Adam.

Rick was usually in the computer room, but she didn't see Adam nor hear from him. She wished she had the courage to call him, but she was uncertain about his response. She would find herself remembering the warm hillside or a ride on the four-wheeler when she was close to him—laughing into his brown eyes as he looked over his shoulder to make a joke—and she was certain, briefly, that something real had happened between them. He had felt something for her before the four-bear day. But then she remembered the way he had withdrawn and turned so cold, and she felt a surge of anger and confusion. *I didn't do anything to you, Adam.*

As she endured university politics, adjusted to her crowded schedule, and tried to offer something worthwhile to her new classes, she looked forward to March denning. Trying not to think of Adam, she thought of Samantha and the golden moments when she had seen the bear with Santini. Samantha might be giving birth at this moment in the dark of her den. But Adam would not stay out of her thoughts, and time and time again her mind returned to the moment when Adam—feverish, sick, and miserable—had told Dr. Andrews a truth he hadn't needed to tell. She and Rick would never have mentioned Adam's claustrophobia to Dr. Andrews. They would have added it to the little shoe box of omissions that held Rick's drunken spree and the four-bear day. She respected Adam's sense of honor.

I have to talk to Adam. I can't just let it end this way. But how could she call and say the right things to him if she didn't know what was wrong? *If he cared at all, he would call me.* But he didn't call her, and she didn't call him, deciding that it would be better to talk during the next denning trips.

The miserable winter continued with a blizzard of paper: ungraded projects piled on her desk, books and notebooks for preparing the next projects spread all over her bed, research material for her thesis set aside in piles on the floor.

Dr. Andrews dropped by her classroom one day in late February. "I think I've got a replacement for your crew, Kelly."

Puzzled, she said, "Who needs replaced? Has Rick finished his thesis?"

"No, Rick will be around through denning and maybe longer."

Kelly sighed. She had hoped to hear that Rick would be gone and that Dr. Andrews actually meant her crew. But if it wasn't Rick who was leaving . . . She looked at Dr. Andrews. "Adam?"

Dr. Andrews hesitated and then said, "I thought you knew. Adam graduated at the end of the semester. He withdrew from the project and left the university." ᏬᎳ

Chapter Fifty-Two

Kelly could not stop the tears that came into her eyes. She bent to pick up her briefcase, hiding her face from Dr. Andrews. *Adam had gone? Without even saying goodbye?* Her hands trembled as she stuffed papers into the case. She swallowed and then swallowed again. Finally, she said as calmly as she could manage, "Who is the replacement?"

"Jonathan wants to be permanent, so does Elizabeth, but they've both got heavy class schedules. They'll work with us when they can."

"They're good help. Both of them." Her emotions now under tight rein, she asked, "Did Adam get a job somewhere?"

"No, I don't think so. He mentioned grad school, but he didn't say where." Dr. Andrews stepped to the door and then turned. "Try to get caught up as much as you can. You'll want to be free to spend every weekend in March at the project."

Kelly tried to heed his advice, but in the days that followed his announcement about Adam, she would sit at her desk attempting to work, only to discover time and again that she had drifted into a daze of misery and depression, doing nothing, thinking nothing. She would force herself to look at the papers in front of her and see them through a blur of tears. *If only we had resolved something before he left.* And then she would be angry, wiping away the tears with strong gestures and saying out loud, "He's a stupid, judgmental nerd." But it wasn't true. She had known religiously opinionated people in some of the places they had lived, and she had heard her mother's opinion of people who imposed their beliefs. Adam wasn't like that. He lived what he believed, just as her grandmother had. She put her head down on her desk and sobbed into the stack of papers.

She wasn't accomplishing anything. She couldn't talk to her parents or Peggy. One Sunday morning, after a sleepless night, she dressed and went to church, just to feel closer to her grandmother. The next week's work went better, and Kelly returned to church the following Sunday, where the hymns and the words she heard made her think of Adam's family with an aching, lonesome envy.

Night after night, she worked alone in her room, desperate to catch up with schoolwork as March denning grew nearer, but she couldn't concentrate. She kept thinking of Adam's family and the strength Adam seemed to find in his family and his faith. And suddenly, one evening, as she red-penciled a correction on the edge of a paper, she realized what she had done to Adam.

She could hear him say so clearly, "The Honor Code is supposed to be a part of you."

And she had said, "I honor the code, Adam. We didn't violate the code, Adam." But just signing the code wasn't what Adam was talking about. In the same way that men had always looked at her body and overlooked her mind, she had looked at Adam's body and mind and discounted his spiritual strength.

A year ago, she had been angry because Matt had joked about not needing to learn from her, ignoring the chance to share more deeply with her. But when Adam had tried to share the spiritual side of himself, she had done the same thing to him, rejecting something he valued, as if they were having a casual conversation. She hadn't even asked him a question. She had said—she flinched as she remembered how cold she had sounded—"I have to figure this out in my own way."

Thinking of the night when Matt had responded with a joke instead of sharing real thoughts with her and remembering her certainty then that her relationship with Matt was hopeless, Kelly knew that Adam would not be back. The knowledge was too painful for tears.

For the first time, Kelly recognized another barrier inside herself. She might know her own mind and body, but she knew nothing of her spirit and its connection to something larger. She stared into space for a long anguished time, wishing she could talk to Adam, wishing she could talk to her grandmother, wishing she could pray. But all she could do, at last, was to go numbly back to work.

The first weekend of March, both Jonathan and Elizabeth joined the crew, and they found Marie and her yearling in a cave with a complicated—but not tight—entry. Rick went in and put them down. Marie still had a fair fat layer. Her yearling was a furry red bundle. Their work was accomplished quickly, and they snowmobiled home under a blue sky with sunshine sparkling on the drifts.

Grandma had two cubs. The old bear had denned in a narrow crevice on a steep slope, and they spent so much time on Sunday getting to the den that they had to hurry the processing. It was difficult to drag the bear out. While Elizabeth held the cubs, the other three of them pulled the sleeping mother from the den, processed her, and pushed her back inside before placing the squawking cubs on her belly.

The next Saturday, Rick and Kelly had only Dr. Andrews to help. He said, "Elizabeth has a couple of heavy term papers; Jonathan has a cold."

Rick was in an odd mood. He didn't initiate any conversation, but when Kelly and Dr. Andrews began to discuss the bears, Rick interrupted Kelly to make a point. When they started to gather equipment, he said to her, "Why don't you fix the lunches?"

She decided not to make a big deal of it. It was going to be a long, cold day, and there was no point in starting it out in a squabble with Santini. But when Rick came in from helping Dr. Andrews check the snowmobiles and, moving past her to go to the storage room, patted her bottom and said, "That's a good little girl," she almost lost it. If Dr. Andrews had not stepped back into the cabin just then, she was sure she would have slapped Rick. He strode past with an arrogant grin and went out the door.

"What's the matter?" Dr. Andrews asked, eyeing her.

"Rick's acting strangely." That was as honest a response as she could manage without telling him about Rick's roving hands.

"He's got a few problems at the moment," Dr. Andrews said, and hesitated before adding, "The committee is being real picky about his thesis."

Oh swell. I hope I'm not going to be stuck with him all summer while he redoes his data. If Rick hadn't called her a "good little girl," she might have felt sympathy for him.

They drove through a snowstorm, following Eleanor's signal on the scanner, up Chase Creek and into a fairly heavy forest. When their snowmobiles could no longer manage the drifts, the biologists strapped on the snowshoes and kept going. Rick was sure that he could pinpoint the den exactly, and he moved rapidly ahead of them. Dr. Andrews was puffing a little. "I'm getting too old for this sort of thing." He pointed, with sudden excitement. "Look at that. She's denned in a tree."

Eleanor had chosen a huge white fir. Rick dug away the small drift in front of the opening. "She's awake," he said. They could hear the cubs grunting as they suckled, and squalling when they lost the nipple. Working quickly in the falling snow, Kelly prepared the jab stick and handed it to Rick, who knelt in front of the almond-shaped hole at the bottom of the tree and delivered the anesthetic. The bear moved in the opening, and Rick rolled away from it.

Dr. Andrews had taken a small tape recorder from his pack. "I'd like to get those cubs on tape," he said. They waited until Eleanor seemed quiet, and then the professor bent and set the tape recorder inside the opening. Just as he took his hand away, the bear raised up and swatted the tape recorder with a huge paw. It tumbled inside the darkness of the tree den. Dr. Andrews jerked his hand away. A little pale, but laughing, he said, "I hope she didn't hit the off button."

Kelly and Dr. Andrews each sheltered a cub until Rick had finished work in the den, then Rick and Dr. Andrews took the cubs to weigh them. The little brown babies were wriggly. Rick used his knit cap as a cradle, hooked the scale to it, and started to read the figures, but the little bear wouldn't stay still. It tipped the cap and tried to escape. Rick righted the baby and finally got a weight. "Five pounds."

"Can you believe that?" Dr. Andrews said. "Only five pounds, and he'll probably grow up to weigh three hundred."

Rick handed the cub to Kelly again. She held it close to her face. It smelled like a wet puppy. The cub squawked constantly until she tucked it back inside her jacket and put her arm around it to warm it. Then it stopped squawking and made little grunting noises as it poked her with its nose. She could feel the sharp claws dig in as it moved around looking for something that smelled like mama. Rick handed the second cub to Dr. Andrews. "Four pounds," he said and took a moment to note the cub weights on the field sheet. They had already tagged the ears.

"I want to see inside the den," Kelly said. Dr. Andrews took her cub, and Kelly went to her hands and knees to look into the tree where Eleanor was still down. The inside of the tree was hollow up to about nine feet. The floor of the den, which Kelly judged to be twenty square feet, sloped slightly toward the back. It was a roomy, cozy place to hole up. Kelly pulled her head out. "I like this much better than those cold rock dens."

"Here." Dr. Andrews handed her a cub. "Put this baby on his mama's belly." He laughed ruefully. "He just wet on my shirt."

Kelly took the cub, suddenly overcome with amazement. *I'm holding a new bear cub; I'm going to place it on the belly of its mother who weighs two hundred pounds.* Filled with renewed joy in being where she was, she wished Adam had stayed to see this part of the project. The cubs were so intensely alive. She reached back for the other cub and settled it in the warm belly hair of the mother. The cubs immediately started grunting around to find the nipples, and then there were only the squeaky sounds of suckling. Kelly leaned past Eleanor's huge shoulder and retrieved the tape recorder. "It's still running," Dr. Andrews said as he inspected it, "but she broke the rewind button."

It snowed all night, and Dr. Andrews decided that since he and Kelly both had classes to teach on Monday, they should cancel the Sunday denning and return to Provo. He took the van while Rick and Kelly followed in the pickup. "Damn waste of time," Rick said, "to make a four hundred-mile round trip and only do one bear." Kelly leaned against the doorframe silently, remembering Adam's arm around her shoulder and the smile in his brown eyes.

Working with an untried volunteer on the next weekend, Kelly missed Adam more fiercely than ever. The young man complained about the cold and was loath to carry equipment. They managed to reach Christine only after a long cold hike up a gully that was too deep for the sun's winter rays to reach.

"No way," the volunteer said when he looked at the den opening. "No way am I going in there." Not that they really needed him. Kelly and Rick worked the bear smoothly together, ear-tagging the female cubs and insisting only that the young man keep them warm until they were done with Christine. "They're ugly little things, aren't they?" The volunteer wrinkled his nose. "And they stink."

There was no way to feel that this insensitive young man was part of a team. *Why did he volunteer anyway?* Kelly paused to feel concern about the summer project. If Rick was upset because of his thesis, and they couldn't get a permanent crew with someone like Jonathan, the project would just limp along. She tried to say the right thing to the volunteer. "Tagging these little bears in the den gives us a great chance to track them all their lives, to really learn what they need for survival."

The young man turned to Rick. "Do we really have to do this all over again tomorrow?"

"That's what we're here for," Rick said.

They had an easy trip on Sunday to a southern-facing slope where the sun had melted most of the snow away from the opening of Elizabeth's den. But the bear was restless. She resisted the anesthetic, and even after she went down, she didn't seem to go deeply under. "Keep those cubs quiet," Rick said. "If she hears them, she's liable to wake herself up."

Kelly put a tan cub under her jacket, admiring the mother's powerful concern for her babies. Taking the other cub, the volunteer said, "Yuck. This dumb little thing pissed on me."

Despite the success of both days' denning, the return trip to Provo was tense and uncomfortable. They smelled of bear, and the volunteer complained steadily. Rick looked across the cab at Kelly. "Do you ever hear from Wainwright?" She shook her head. Rick turned on the radio and put the volume high. The volunteer subsided morosely. Kelly tried to rest. They'd be late getting back. She had papers to grade. Rubbing her face, she wished that she could just go into some den and sleep. When Rick dropped her off at the dorm, he said, "Well, next weekend, we'll go visit your pet, Samantha, and see if Santini really did get to her." ✺

Chapter Fifty-Three

The spring sunlight was lemony yellow. Rick and Kelly made good time into the high country on the four-wheelers and then used snowshoes only part of the time. The kinnikinnick's shiny green leaves poked from under the dwindling snow banks; there were open places for walking. "I'm glad that other guy backed out," Rick said. "He was a pain in the butt."

"Veritably," Kelly said, and immediately wished she had not because Rick picked up on Adam's word and said with a scowl, "Wainwright backed out, too. I didn't think he would."

Kelly just shrugged and moved along the trail. Samantha's signal was strong. Along the top of the ridge below timberline and the stark rise of the higher peaks, a cluster of gray rocks shouldered their way out of the earth. Where the huge boulders leaned together, dozens of dark shadows indicated openings, crevices, and caves. Rick's attention was focused on the scanner. Kelly's heart beat faster. She could hardly wait to see Samantha and the cubs. Would they be brown, black, red? Twins, triplets?

"There," Rick said suddenly, pointing to a place on the slope above them where two large rocks met at right angles. "She's back in that hole." He put the scanner in his pack. "I hope she's asleep. It would be a lot easier."

"When did Samantha ever make things easy?"

They stopped talking as they approached the hole in the rock. Fair-sized at the mouth, the entryway narrowed and curved to the left. Rick slipped into the hole and inched partway toward the curve. Then he moved rapidly backward. "Damn it. She's awake. I can hear her and the cubs." He thought for a moment. "I hate to do it, but I think we'll have to put her down with the dart gun."

"Can it be done safely?"

"There's a rock that partly blocks the den itself. I can work from behind it. There's quite a bit of space in there." He began to assemble the gun, saying to Kelly, "Fix the syringe and put enough in it to put her down the first time."

They said nothing else. It was essential not to upset the bear. In a few moments, the equipment was ready. Kelly indicated the rope, but Rick shook his head. He adjusted the light and reentered the cave. Practically holding her breath, Kelly waited. She trusted Rick's knowledge; he would do nothing stupid. But Samantha had always been independent and aggressive. Protecting cubs, she would be even more so.

Above Samantha's ridge, the highest peak of the mountain reared a snowy head against the blue sky. She and Adam had been almost this high on some of their best working days. She remembered daydreaming in the sunny grass while he slept.

"Time the drug," Rick said, poking his head out of the entry hole. Kelly checked her watch. "We could go ahead and eat lunch," Rick said, sliding free of the rock. "She's got Santini's cubs all right," he said with a grin as he opened a sandwich bag. "They're both red."

By the time they ate, the drug had taken effect, and Samantha was asleep. Kelly followed Rick into the entryway and waited behind the boulder that narrowed the access to the den. "You'll have to baby sit both of these little guys," Rick said, handing her one squawking red cub and then another. Kelly opened her jacket and tucked a baby bear in on each side of the zipper. The cubs were shivering slightly, and she put her arms around them, snuggling them close to her belly. When Rick had pushed the mother partway out of the den, they tagged the cubs and put them back into the bedding and then tugged Samantha down the passageway and into the open. After processing her, they used a tree branch and the come-along to weigh her. Samantha was in good shape despite a small flesh tear where Rick had removed the dart. Her fat layer was not totally gone. She would come out of the den weighing more than she had the previous spring.

"She's a beauty," Rick said. He had released the rope from Samantha's feet, and he ran a caressing hand from the bear's head to her tail.

Kelly knelt beside Rick. She slid her fingers through the thick dark hair, matched her hand to the huge paw, and then rested it on Samantha's head. "She's the first bear I ever saw on the project, and she's been the most interesting."

Rick said, "We'd better put her back. She's just strong enough to wake herself up if the cubs holler very loud."

Kelly helped him to tug the bear back to the boulder inside the stone tunnel, then she slipped into the den and, moving the cubs aside, pulled on the huge bear while Rick pushed. They settled her in the bedding, and then shone the light on the little red cubs one more time. Their noses were pink, and their eyes seemed larger than they would later when their heads were bigger. They scrambled awkwardly back to the warmth of their mother, their cinnamon color showing light against Samantha's dark fur.

When the cubs were suckling peacefully, Rick shut off the light. They stood for a moment in the dark, resting from the physical exertion, feeling the den the way a bear might, listening for outside sounds. After Rick turned the light back on, they made their way silently out of the tunnel, crouching and creeping along until they could stand.

Outside, Rick said, "Well, we did a good job with her. She could have given us a lot of trouble." He nodded toward the north. "Let's hike toward the area where we lost Kendall. Maybe we can pinpoint her location and process her tomorrow." Happy with the thought of Samantha and her healthy cubs, Kelly strode along behind Rick. Everything was clean from the harsh scrubbing of winter storms. Little trickles of water seeped from under crusted snow; the earth smelled rich and ready for new growth. They had crossed one small gully and moved out onto a plateau when Rick stopped suddenly and said, "Don't touch anything."

Kelly moved around him to see what he was talking about. The carcass of a sheep—belly bloated, putrid flesh torn—lay in the dry grass. A few feet to the other side of the sheep was a coyote, also dead, and beyond it a dead bird. "What happened?"

"Somebody has baited the sheep with poison." Rick shook his head. "He doesn't care what he kills. We'll have to report this to the DWR."

Angry, their joy about Samantha soured with worry, Rick and Kelly moved past the dead animals and across the meadow until they picked up a faint signal from Kendall's collar and pinpointed it close enough to be sure they could locate her the next day. In the pickup on the way to the phone at the store, Rick said, "Ranchers. I wouldn't give you ten cents for their ethics."

Kelly waited in the truck, but when she saw Jim McCarthy pull up to the store, she got out and went to his window. He greeted her, and she told him about the baited sheep. He frowned and said, "I guess your buddy is in there frothing at the mouth already. He doesn't need to see me today."

Kelly said, "He knows you wouldn't use poison."

"He's going to be teed off at *all* ranchers." Jim started his truck again. "I'll see you later, Kelly." Kelly sighed and went back to the university pickup. There was no way to meet the needs of everybody on the mountain.

Rick came from the store and, climbing into the pickup, handed her an ice cream bar. "They'll try to get someone up here today."

"I just hope they move that sheep before the bears come out of their dens."

"The bastard who put it there is probably after bears, too." They sat in the truck, united against all human predators, licking their ice cream bars. They discussed Samantha and the cubs, more for the pleasure it gave them than for any forgotten data points.

They were late getting to the cabin, and it was chilly inside. Rick built a fire, and after they both washed, Kelly started supper. She was reaching to take the plates from the shelf above the counter when Rick came up behind her. Putting his arms around her, he cupped her breasts in his hands and pulled her toward him. She could feel his body hard against her and his breath on her cheek when he put his face close to hers.

As he moved his fingers to squeeze her nipples, Kelly felt nothing but fury. It roared through her like wildfire, containing none of the confusion she had felt the first time Rick had embraced her. Her body belonged to her, and no matter what Adam thought about her spiritual ethics, her own moral code mattered to her, and she did not have to put up with this. She began to struggle in Rick's arms.

He shoved her forward, pinning her against the counter. She reached up and grabbed his hands and jerked them away from her breasts. Then she arched her body abruptly, slamming against him to gain space, and forced her way past him. Breathing hard, thinking of Mary Powers's advice, she straightened her clothes. Then she turned and said, "Ever since the beginning of this project, you have put your hands on me in inappropriate places. I do not like to have you touch me. I don't want you to touch me again."

"Oh, come off it, Kelly. You know you'd like a little of what Santini gave Samantha." Rick stepped forward as if to take hold of her again. She moved to the table and put a chair between them.

"Rick, I am serious. I am no man's trophy. I do not want sex with you." Rick's eyes narrowed, and he shifted his body slightly. He was as arrogant and predatory as the houndsmen and the ranchers, and it would be dangerous to make him any angrier. She tried to sort out something to say that would convince him that she was serious, but would still calm his temper.

"Rick, there is something between us when we work, but that doesn't mean it should carry over into our personal lives. Even if we weren't bound by the Honor Code, I wouldn't go to bed with you."

Rick's face was still angry. What right did he have to be angry? She hadn't grabbed him. She swallowed and continued. "I am telling you as plainly as I know how, so you won't misunderstand. I admire the way you deal with bears. You're smart and focused and perceptive. I look forward to working with you on other bear projects, but when I'm excited about my work, I don't want you to misread my emotion."

He frowned. He wasn't going to make it any easier. She followed more of Mary Powers's advice. "I'd like to get things clear, here and now, and keep this private between us, but I'm prepared to write down each incident from this summer and to talk to Dr. Andrews if I have to."

Rick's nostrils flared. She could smell her own scared sweat. If Rick didn't back off, would she be safe spending the night in the cabin? He suddenly tossed his head and said, "Oh, hell, I was only teasing you."

Her own anger rose again. "No, Rick, I won't accept that. Touching me or any woman on the bottom, on the breast, anywhere she doesn't want you to, is not teasing. It's sexual harassment and it's not funny. I've earned more respect than that, and I won't accept anything less." *Adam was right. I should have stopped this the moment it started. I should also have told the houndsmen to shut up.*

Rick stood by the counter, looking at her. She met his glance and held it without wavering, though her legs were trembling. Rick turned and took a dipper of water from the bucket. He drank deeply, replaced the dipper, wiped his mouth, and then turned back to her and said, "Well, are you going to cook dinner or what? ∾

Chapter Fifty-Four

Kelly blinked. And then she laughed. She simply could not help it. It was too funny. *If you can't get them into bed, put them back into the kitchen.* "Shall I take my shoes off?" she asked, thinking of a stupid old joke about keeping women barefoot and pregnant.

"What in the hell are you talking about?"

Kelly shook her head. "Never mind." Adam would have understood, but Rick took himself too seriously to have a decent sense of humor. She dreaded spending the evening alone in the cabin with him. "I have a suggestion," she said. "If you'll drive us to Moab, I'll *buy* dinner."

They got back into the truck where Kelly sat as far away from Rick as she could get. On the long drive, they spoke only of bears and of the danger of the baited sheep, and Kelly remembered Adam's telling her what to talk about with Rick. She wished that she had followed more of Adam's advice.

Rick seemed to pick up on her thoughts of Adam. "I'm sorry

Wainwright felt that he had to pull out. He was actually a lot better help than most."

"Did you talk to him before he left?"

"Nope, he avoided the whole department. Just finished up and split."

"I don't think he likes either of us very much," Kelly said.

Rick glanced her way. "Did he say so?"

"He thinks we're both too bossy, and he said that we have no respect for the deeper meaning of the Honor Code." Rick flushed, but did not respond, and there was an uncomfortable silence until they reached the restaurant where they had a stilted conversation about the denning procedures and the upcoming summer of snaring.

A sudden spring storm whirled around them on their way back from dinner. It continued all night, and by morning they knew they'd have to use the snowmobiles again. "We'll take them both," Rick said. "It would be damned dumb to go on one machine and get stuck up there." Kelly was glad. She had no wish to ride behind Rick.

The trip toward the ridge, which had been gentle and pleasant the day before, was so difficult in the storm that it took their total concentration. There were no visible trails and though the snow had stopped falling, a biting wind kept the new snow swirling in front of them. When they reached the area of the strongest signal, they had to dig through a deep drift. Kendall's den was an elongated hole that angled into the ground under a section of gnarled tree roots and led back to a cave under a large rock outcropping.

The altitude and the cold robbed them of energy. They worked without talking, each taking an equal share of the shoveling, digging, crawling, and dragging. They got every bit of data they went after, but by the time they stowed their gear and climbed back onto the snowmobiles, Kelly's hand trembled on the controls. She yearned to turn the driving over to Rick or Adam or any other willing man. Ashamed of her desire to have it both ways—equality when it was easy, chivalry when it was not—she offered to share the drive to Provo, and Rick agreed, falling immediately asleep in the truck and snoring through her half of the drive.

The next weekend Kelly had a miserable cold. She knew that Dr. Andrews and Rick were planning to try for some of the bears Rick had collared the year before on the other side of the mountain. She stopped by Dr. Andrews's office. "Could I beg off this weekend?" Her voice croaked, and she coughed roughly.

He offered her a stick of mint gum and said, "Sure. We can manage."

She was almost grateful for her cold. It gave her a reason to avoid spending the last denning weekend with Rick. She said, "Thanks," and turned to leave the office.

Dr. Andrews said, "Oh, by the way, Kelly," and she looked back at him. "I forgot to tell you. After reading some of our data, the DWR is going to limit bear permits next year."

"Hurrah!" It was raspy, but loaded with feeling. "Are they still going to allow spring hunting?"

"There's tremendous hunter resistance to a ban on spring hunting. A change like that will take more data than we can offer right now."

Kelly rested Saturday and on Sunday she went to church where she paid attention to the music and the spoken words, and afterward was welcomed by friendly faces. A woman who had known her grandmother greeted her warmly, and she went back to her room feeling less alone.

March and den work were over. The bears would be waking, the mothers bringing their young cubs out into the sunlight for the first time. The focus of the project returned once more to completing the scat analyses of the past year, compiling data, and preparing equipment for a new year of snaring.

No one heard from Adam. Dr. Andrews did not name a crew. Rick was morose as he struggled with his thesis. Kelly was trying to outline her own thesis plans and keep up with teaching. She helped in the bear lab when she could, and the month of April swirled by in a fog of pressure and fatigue. Sometimes at night she rested in thoughts of Samantha and the red cubs, but as often as not, the scene with Rick spoiled the memories. Would she have to follow through on her threat to tell Dr. Andrews?

Peggy dropped by one evening in early May. "Matt's gone bowling, so I thought I'd come to see you."

"You look like you swallowed a bowling ball yourself." Peggy grinned and patted her stomach. "What does Matt think?" Kelly asked.

"He is going to buy us a house."

"Does he know that the baby is going to arrive early?"

"Yes, and he doesn't care. He says he always wanted to be a family man and have a wife and kid at home."

Thinking of her mother's lifelong misery, Kelly asked, "And what about you? Will you be sorry that you didn't finish school?"

Peggy shook her head. "I have no grand ambitions. Anyway, Matt wants me to learn to keep books for his company." She smiled almost shyly and amended the words: "For our company." She eyed Kelly. "Have you talked to Mother about that box I found?"

Kelly rose from her chair and removed the box from the closet shelf. Taking a roll of cellophane tape from her desk, she taped the lid securely to the box. "No. And I'm not going to."

"Why not? Don't you want it all out in the open? No more secrets?"

"Those are Mother's secrets, Peg, not mine." Kelly paced around the room finding answers for herself as she formed them for Peggy. "I have no right to wrest anything from her."

"But she did you such wrong, hating you, giving you over to Grandma."

"She did herself wrong. She's filled with wonderful creative energy. I know what it's like. I've felt it too, and I've made some mistakes." Kelly paused, thinking of the things she'd never told Peggy about the bear crew. "Before Mother was old enough to figure out that it wasn't just sexual energy, she was caught in a trap."

"Well, it sounded like sexual energy." Peggy frowned. "All those nights . . ."

"Those nights were the only way she found to express that energy."

"I still don't understand why you don't feel cheated. I'd hate the lies."

Kelly looked closely at her sister. Maybe Peggy was beginning to wonder how she was going to explain things to her own child. She answered the surface comments. There was no way to answer Peggy's unspoken fears. "Mother tried to *protect* me with the lies. And, as you said, I had Grandma."

"All you did with Grandma was work. I hated that dumb old farm."

Kelly did not protest Peggy's statement. She was suddenly aware that her sister—and Ryan, too—had each grown up in a totally different family environment from her own. "You didn't need Grandma as much as I did," she said. "I can remember how happy everyone was when you were born. You were a wanted baby, and Ryan was the son. Each of you had a place of your own. Grandma gave me my place . . . and my work."

"I want my baby to have a grandma," Peggy said, "but I'd never let her steal my baby the way Grandma took you." Kelly was silent. *Where would I be now if my grandmother hadn't loved me until my mother stopped hating me?*

Peggy said, "I still think you should tell Mother that you know."

"If we hadn't read the letters I wouldn't know. It's not our secret."

Kelly sat down as she repeated the words and looked into her sister's face. "Peggy, I can't hold Mother accountable for something a scared nineteen-year-old did. It's obvious that she couldn't be honest with her own parents. I wasn't real to her. She was in love with Daddy and afraid of losing him."

Peggy, of all people, should understand that. She had felt the very same way about Matt just six months ago. Her sister said nothing and Kelly was suddenly tired of talking about it. "Our mother is forty-three years old and is only now discovering her own needs. I don't think it's fair to go crying to her to fill mine."

She could tell by the look in Peggy's eyes that her comment had hit home. Peggy wanted to talk to their mother for her own reasons. She said gently, "Peggy, we can't return to the past and fix things. All we can do is to try to be honest, to be loving, in our own lives." She shoved the box into Peggy's hands. "Put this thing back where you got it."

Peggy took the box, but she didn't turn to go. She studied Kelly's face and then suddenly reached out and touched her sister's cheek. "Are you really okay? You look tired and sad."

"I *am* tired, Peg. I'm trying to do three different things at once all the time."

"But there's something else the matter. I think Mother's box upset you more than you're admitting."

"Well, no one likes to find out they were unwanted, but I think I always knew that something wasn't right."

"So if it's not the box, what is it? Is Santini still giving you trouble?"

"Santini is the same as he always was, but I'm learning how to handle him." She met Peggy's eyes and hesitated. Then she said, "Adam left the project."

"Why?"

"I don't know. He didn't tell me goodbye." Tears started in Kelly's eyes. She turned her head, but Peggy grasped her chin and turned her face back around.

"And it hurt you. Kelly, are you in love with Adam?"

"No. I don't know. I don't think so. We were so close sometimes." She jerked her chin from Peggy's fingers. "What difference does it make? He doesn't want me either."

"Did he say that?"

"He didn't say *anything*. He just left. Isn't that enough?" Peggy was suddenly hugging her tight, and Kelly was crying. "I don't know what to do."

"It will work out somehow. Look at Matt and me. I used to think I'd die if he didn't want me someday, and now he's buying us a house." Peggy stepped to the dresser for a tissue. She wiped Kelly's eyes and then held the tissue to her sister's nose. "Blow."

Kelly laughed and took the tissue. "You're just practicing on me. Take that dumb box and go home. I'm not a baby, and I've got more work to do."

"Are you okay now?"

Kelly nodded. "It helped to tell somebody. Thanks, Peg." After her sister left, she returned to her desk, but she couldn't concentrate. *If this is love, it hurts too much. I'd rather be like Samantha and Santini.* She steadied herself, thinking of the bears, and resolutely not thinking of Adam.

The next day, she dropped by to see Dr. Andrews. She took it for granted that she would be part of the crew, whether Rick's thesis was finished or not, and she entered the office with none of the fear she had felt during her first interview the year before. "What's our summer plan?" she asked, shaking her head as he offered a stick of gum.

"Well, I haven't got all my volunteers lined out yet, but we'll piece something together." He leaned back in his chair, stretching his long legs under the desk. "I can't get up there until Sunday. Do you want to take a load of equipment up on Friday and start looking for good snare sights? I'll get Rick to cover your classes."

Once she was back on the mountain, the scanner was a glorious temptation. Kelly unloaded the pickup and put the cabin in order as soon as she arrived, but she could hardly wait to finish and go high, listening for the signals that brought pictures to her mind. Marie with a cinnamon-colored yearling, old Grandma and her cubs, Samantha and her two red furballs.

She put the spotting scope in the equipment box. Dr. Andrews had asked her to talk to Doc Morrison about bear bait, but after that, she could head toward the ridge. The equipment box still held Adam's Ruger. She would have to return it to him someday.

Doc Morrison knew of a dead goat. He went with Kelly to load it into the pickup. It was small, and she was able to drag it out of the truck by herself when she got back to the bait barrel. She cut up the carcass and, turning the bait barrel over, stored the chunks of meat. Then, after a shower, and with a sense of joy in the new beginnings in her work, she took the four-wheeler toward Samantha's ridge. ~

Chapter Fifty-Five

The woods were sweet with life. In the gullies, silvery creeks whispered across the rocks and through the willows. Birds picked up the melody and scattered it across the meadows where it became a visual song in the green and silver of new ground cover. Kelly leaned against the four-wheeler and watched two tufted-ear squirrels chasing each other up a tree to the end of a branch and in a flying leap into the bushes below, only to begin again in the wild exuberance of youth and spring. She hated to intrude into the scene, even with the tiny beep of the scanner, but she set it to Samantha's frequency, and in a moment, she could hear the signal.

She's not going to let me get close to those cubs. Kelly adjusted the holster holding Adam's Ruger to a more comfortable position and then took the spotting scope from her pack and stepped quietly through the woods until the signal was fairly strong, but she was still far enough away to keep Samantha from sensing her presence. She set up the scope, using a low branch for a support, and focused on a cleared area below the ridge. The signal came from that area. Kelly settled behind the scope to wait. The bears would be foraging in the early evening.

She stilled her body. The birds, which had gone silent when she moved, renewed their bubbles of song. Through the eyepiece, she could see the rocks on the ridge and a shallow gully. For a long time, nothing moved except the wind in the trees. Her legs were cramping, and her hands were cold on the scope by the time Samantha ambled into the clearing and into the magnified circle of the eyepiece. Kelly caught her breath. The two little red cubs gamboled after their mother, pausing to wrestle with each other, then scrambling to catch up.

When one of the cubs ventured to go ahead of Samantha, she smacked it with her paw, and it retreated. But then Samantha rested and allowed them to crawl onto her belly where she draped one huge paw across them, licking a baby ear when it came in range. The cubs wallowed in the soft fur, until suddenly, Samantha lifted her head and turned it from side to side. Then she rose, spilling the cubs into the grass, and moved swiftly out of Kelly's range, the cubs galloping after her.

Kelly sighed and watched the empty circle for a moment more, feeling suddenly deprived. When the cool air caused her to shiver, she put the scope in her pack and made her way down the hill in the dusk, resolved to see Samantha and the cubs again the next day if she could.

During the night, she could hear the houndsmen's dogs. She got up and checked the double locks on the cabin doors. She hated to start another season of dealing with Walt Johnson and George Walker and their innuendos. *I won't listen to any insults. This year, I won't put up with their filthy mouths.*

In the early morning when she returned to the ridge, Samantha's signal was farther away, as if the bear were higher up or behind the rocks. Kelly waited for a while with the scope, but the bear did not come into range, and she decided that she'd better start checking out snare sites. She searched for evidence of bears, found some fresh grass-filled scat and other signs, and made notes. In a couple of promising areas, she gathered barricade material and chopped and cleared in preparation for snare building.

She did not need to adjust to being alone this time. She didn't even feel alone with the small creatures skittering through the woods and Grandma's signal on the scanner along with Samantha's. *Maybe Grandma is Samantha's mother. Bear mothers and daughters sometimes share the same home range.*

Samantha and the cubs were puttering around in the woods during the early evening on Saturday. Kelly could pinpoint Samantha with the scanner, but her scope could not penetrate the deep cover. She went home tired and dirty, glad that she didn't have to eat grass and ants for supper as Samantha was probably doing.

Early Sunday morning when she turned the scanner on, she was not prepared for anything but the joy of seeing the cubs again. The mortality beep did not register at first. She moved the dial and retuned it to Samantha's frequency. And then the distinctive sound reached her brain. Her jaw went rigid, and her heart began to pound. *Please God, let me be mistaken.* She fiddled frantically with the dial, but the horrifying signal was always the same, distant but steady. Sick with its message, Kelly began to climb. The bear was nowhere near the den, and there was neither sight nor sound of the cubs. Tears ran down Kelly's face as she followed the signal higher on the mountain, into the tundra above timberline, and toward the sparse trees on the peak above. Dread iced her stomach and her throat. *Oh, please, let the collar be malfunctioning, let Samantha have scraped it off, let it have broken, anything, anything.*

She could not move fast enough. The mountain above her was steep and rocky. She slipped and slid as she scrabbled for hand holds. She couldn't climb and carry the scanner at the same time, but she stopped frequently to check the signal. It was always sickeningly the same. If Samantha had not scraped the collar off, then Samantha was lying dead somewhere. Kelly's heart pounded as much with dread as with the effort of scaling the steep slope.

She was breathless, and her lungs ached from the exertion of the climb when she reached the barren area around the highest tree on the windy peak. She followed the signal to a bush where she found the collar. She picked it up and inspected it. It had been removed, not broken. It was definitely Samantha's collar. The number was right, the signal was loud. There was little to hope for as she looked around the bush, a leaden feeling slowing her steps.

She searched the area. The ground showed the marks of dogs' paws scrabbling at the base of the tree; the tree was clawed, the scratches emphasizing the bear's frantic climb to the branches twenty feet up. But there was no bear in the tree. Kelly moved under the branches. She swallowed a sudden rise of bile when she saw the blood near the spot where the bear had fallen. Following drag marks in the dirt, she rounded a large rock and found the carcass.

It had been skinned by an amateur, or someone in a terrible hurry. The head and paws had been chopped off, the body stripped without being hung, the belly mangled in the process. Beheaded, the bloodied naked carcass was a horror that Kelly could not take in.

This could not be Samantha. But the collar signal was steady. She shut the scanner off. She could not endure the sound. Anger and grief rose in a searing wave. She leaned against the rock and vomited until her stomach was empty, and then she continued to heave in dry, gagging convulsions.

When her body finally stopped reacting, Kelly wept, her head buried in her arms on the rock, memories of Samantha surging through her mind from the moment she had first seen the lovely chocolate-colored bear until her last view, through the scope, of Samantha and the tiny cubs. *The cubs*. She had forgotten about them. If she didn't find them, they would probably die. Kelly blew her nose and put the scanner away, adding Samantha's collar to the pack with a hand that trembled.

Then she began a careful, systematic search, following the track of the dogs backward, hoping to come upon the spot where they had first picked up Samantha. Samantha would have sent the cubs up a tree before leading the dogs on a long chase away from her young.

Hour after hour, through the long miserable morning, she searched for the red babies she had warmed inside her jacket. There was no way to ease her grief over Samantha's death. She could not even think of the bear without trembling, without crying again. But all she could do now for Samantha was to try to save the cubs.

She managed to find some trail sign of bear and dog and man, but Kelly could not find the cubs. Thinking that they had perhaps been near the den, she returned to the rocky ridge. Though she was not carrying a light, she crept into the dark rock passageway, listening carefully. There was only silence. To be absolutely sure that the cubs were not there, she felt her way into the den and ran her hands through the bedding. Nothing. Crawling back out into the light, she sat for a moment on the ground, holding her arms close to her chest, rocking in misery. *I have to keep looking.*

She took the four-wheeler back to the truck long enough to leave a note on the windshield. Surely Dr. Andrews and his volunteers would come to the meadow. She needed more help. There was no way of knowing where Samantha had been when the dogs started running her.

She returned to the mountain and combed the gullies and slopes, stopping often to use her binoculars to study the trees and grass. But there were a million places for two little cubs to hide. Exhausted, she started once more at the den on the ridge and moved down the mountain.

Late in the day, having seen no sign of the cubs, and finding the note still undisturbed on the pickup windshield, she decided to go to the houndsmen's camp. It was the only place where there might be humans to help in the search. Remembering the professional way that Roscoe had been skinned, she did not think that George Walker and Walt Johnson had killed Samantha. Maybe for once, their dogs could do some good.

Leaving the note where it was, she drove the four-wheeler toward the clearing where the houndsmen had camped the year before. When she was near enough to see the tent and two pickups, she decided to park and walk in so that she wouldn't disturb the dogs so much.

She recognized Walt Johnson's truck, but the other one was strange—fire red and brand new with shiny chrome. She could see the gun rack and high-powered rifles through the windshield. The dogs set up a cacophony as she approached, and three men emerged from behind the tent. She started to move closer to make herself heard above the hounds. Walt Johnson stepped toward her with a scowl on his red face. "If it isn't the bear woman. What are you doing here?"

"I need help to search for some cubs," she said, stepping alongside the new pickup. But before Walt could speak again, she saw something from the corner of her eye, and turning away from him, she moved close to the strange truck and looked over the side. In the bed of the red pickup, rolled and tied, was a brown bear hide with the head stretched out on top. The eyes were glassy in death, and on each ear there was a yellow tag. 〜

Chapter Fifty-Six

Stunned at the sight of Samantha's head, Kelly could not say anything else. She leaned forward and lifted one of the brown ears, which was stiff and cold to the touch. The number on the ear tag left no doubt. These were the houndsmen who had killed Samantha. Suddenly, her fury rose like a geyser, hot and powerful, and there was no way she could have kept it from erupting. "You killed a collared bear!" Her voice was so harsh she hardly recognized it.

Walt Johnson frowned and shifted slightly. "There's no law against killing a collared bear."

"But there *is* a law against killing a female with cubs."

"We didn't see no cubs." His tone was belligerent.

"That's because you set your dogs on Samantha before you ever saw her." She glared at the houndsman. "But as soon as you saw that she'd been nursing, you knew." Kelly was sure that the butchering had been done in a way that hid all signs of the swollen teats. "You didn't *care* if she had cubs."

"God damn it, we didn't see no cubs." The man's profanity made Kelly more certain that she was right about the houndsmen's actions. "Besides," Walt Johnson said, "there ain't much harm done. I read that no more than one percent of spring kill is female with cub."

"I've seen that statistic," Kelly said coldly, trying to control her voice, "but it doesn't mean anything to this bear's cubs. They've lost one hundred percent of their mother." She stepped forward. "With the killing of this bear, you've left those cubs unprotected—prey to mountain lions, male bears, hunger, cold." Despite her attempt at control, her fury made her voice rise, and Walt Johnson moved backward a step, as if he feared her attack might turn physical.

When he moved, Kelly suddenly saw the two men behind him more clearly. One was George Walker, the other was Harry Selnick. Selnick started forward, and Kelly directed her words to him. "How could you? I didn't expect them . . ." she said, flinging a hand toward the guides, " . . . to have a sense of honor. But somehow I expected you to be different." The tone of her voice held all of her pain, her grief, her contempt. She could hear it—see it when Selnick flinched—but she didn't care. She only cared about Samantha. "The Old West is gone.

You're not killing bears to protect your home and family."

Selnick turned fiery red, but Kelly could not stop. This man had paid people to chase Samantha with dogs. "The houndsmen trained the dogs. The dogs found the bear. What did *you* do? You shot a tired, frightened bear out of a tree. That took a *lot* of skill." She was crying now. "Bear hunting for trophy is an example of everything that is wrong with this world."

She sniffed back her tears and gestured toward his truck. "What you paid for this truck and those rifles would have kept our bear project going for a whole year. We're trying to keep bears alive." Harry Selnick started to speak, but Kelly continued. "If we don't find those cubs you've probably killed *three* bears today. Have you finally done enough killing to prove that you're a man?" Kelly stared straight into the man's eyes. "Why don't you go home and do something constructive with your money? Stay out of these woods and leave the bears alone." Harry Selnick looked down toward his boots. Suddenly exhausted, Kelly turned from the Arizona man and said to Walt Johnson, "I want the ear tags."

"No," he said. "I'm not giving you the ear tags. And you can't prove nothin', even if you did take them to the DWR. We didn't know that damn sow had cubs." His mouth tightened. "And we don't need some bleeding-heart bitch in here telling us what to do."

Kelly moved the cartridge belt around on her hip and laid her hand on the butt of the Ruger. Walt Johnson's eyes narrowed. Harry Selnick said in a flat voice, "Give her the tags."

The houndsman still hesitated. George Walker spoke up for the first time. "Give her the damn tags and let's get out of here."

Walt Johnson took out his knife and moved to the truck. Kelly could not look again at Samantha. She stood with her hand on the gun and waited. When the houndsman turned to hand her the yellow tags, his eyes suddenly shifted to something behind her. He muttered a curse.

Kelly took the tags and turned. Rick and Adam were standing at the edge of the clearing. She was too filled with grief to think of what Adam's presence meant. She stumbled toward them, holding the tags. "They killed Samantha. I can't find the cubs."

"We know," Rick said. "We read your note."

"Will you help me look some more? Maybe we can find them before dark." Rick and Adam did not need explanations. They were part of the team, and they understood about the danger to the cubs.

Rick stepped over to Walt Johnson. "Where did your dogs pick up the bear?"

The houndsman said sullenly, "I'm not sure. Somewhere off that ridge below Craigs Peak."

They consulted a map, and the three of them went back up the mountain, separating to cover more ground and hunting in vain for the cubs until total darkness made it useless to continue. It had probably been useless from the start. They had just come together again back at the cabin when Dr. Andrews pulled up and parked. As they let themselves in and lit the lantern, Dr. Andrews said, "The damnedest thing just happened to me." He laughed. "I had stopped at the store for some chewing gum and was just coming out, when that hunter from Arizona, that Selnick guy, pulled in, driving a bright red truck. The houndsmen were behind him in Walt Johnson's truck."

Dr. Andrews seemed to be unaware that Kelly and the other two were disheveled and tired and totally silent. He was having such fun telling his story. "That little dude in his ten-gallon hat hopped out of his truck and came over to hand me something. I thought it was another check until I looked at it." Dr. Andrews shook his head. "But it was the title to that Chevrolet pickup, signed over to the university. He just put it and the keys in my hand and got in Walt Johnson's truck and drove off, leaving the rifles on the gun rack." Dr. Andrews laughed again. "Damned strange. Selnick never said one word, but as they drove away, Walt Johnson leaned out of the truck and gave me the finger."

Kelly exchanged glances with Rick and Adam. Kelly said, "Was there anything in the bed of the truck?"

"Some camping gear. That's all."

Kelly stepped to the counter for a drink of water. Catching a glimpse of herself in the mirror above the counter, she tried to smooth her hair. Her tears had long since dried up, but her face was dirty, and she looked old. She felt old.

Her hair was hopeless. She let it be and turned back toward Dr. Andrews, who seemed to realize that nobody was exclaiming over his strange story. He eyed her face. "I can see you've been working hard. Well, I think I've got Elizabeth and Jonathan committed to being your summer crew, as soon as their finals are over."

Kelly glanced at Rick and Adam, who had flopped down on the rose-colored bedspreads. They didn't look much better than she did. She was puzzled. "You mean this isn't our summer crew?" *If that's true, then what is Adam doing here?*

"No," Dr. Andrews said. "Those two are just a couple of tourists who came along to gawk." He grinned. "What do you think, Kelly? Do you think you can head up a new team?" He smiled at her as if he were giving her a gift. And it would have been a gift. Yesterday, it would have been a wonderful gift. Yesterday, all she had wanted from Dr. Andrews was to have him ask that question. ∽

Chapter Fifty-Seven

She glanced again at Rick and Adam, but they said nothing; they simply waited as if it were her move. "I thought the committee wanted you to get more data," she said to Rick.

"They weren't quibbling about data. It was the wording that held up their approval." Rick tried to smile, but Kelly knew by the color of his face that he, too, was hurting about Samantha and the cubs. The anemic smile didn't last. He made a sound of disgust. "They wanted me to write like an English major."

Dr. Andrews said, "But he made it. They approved his thesis. He's going job hunting." The professor pulled out a chair and sat down, stretching his legs under the table. "So what do you say, Kelly?"

Kelly moved her glance to Adam. She still didn't know what he was doing here, or elsewhere. He just looked at her without smiling. She thought of how he had put his arms around her on the day that Roscoe was killed by houndsmen, and her feelings whirled in confusion.

She couldn't deal with emotions about Adam right now. She had to answer Dr. Andrews. She fished in her pocket for the yellow tags and, clutching them as if they might give her courage, she moved toward the table and sat down facing him. She took a deep breath and said, "There's something you have to know."

"Oh?" Dr. Andrews's eyes focused sharply on her face.

She laid the tags on the table. "Walt Johnson and George Walker set their hounds on Samantha; the hounds treed her above the ridge; Harry Selnick shot her out of the tree." Kelly could see the shock register in Dr. Andrews's face, and then a gathering of sympathy, which she could not allow him to express or she would never manage to say what she had to say.

"They skinned Samantha on the ridge and threw the collar in the bushes. They cut off her head and her paws." Kelly swallowed. "It was such a bloody mess, I didn't think professional houndsmen had done it, and I couldn't find the cubs, so I went to the houndsmen for help, but Samantha . . ." She faltered. "Samantha's hide and head were in that red truck." She could not stop there and look at the picture in her mind again. She couldn't endure it. She rushed on. "I have to tell you . . . you have to know this. I chewed them out. First, Walt Johnson, and then Harry Selnick. I was not quiet, nor tactful, nor diplomatic, nor discreet." She paused, took a breath, and put her future on the line.

"I *want* to head up a new crew, but I want you to understand first that I'm not sorry about yelling at the houndsmen and Selnick. At some point, I have to stand up for what I believe is right, and I have to try to change what I think is wrong, and if you don't want me on the mountain, I will understand." She stopped abruptly. It was out, and if she lost her place in the project, that was how it would have to be.

Dr. Andrews was totally quiet. He looked into her eyes for a long time before he said, "I want you on the mountain." And then, as if he could not stand the emotion of the moment, he turned away from her and said to Rick, "Don't you think I should hang onto a woman who slings bear bait the way *she* does?" It was an awkward joke, but Kelly was grateful for it.

Rick said, "Yeah, keep her up here until I get a job." Startled at the tone in his voice, Kelly met his eyes. The respect there was reassuring. Maybe she had won something in this day of harrowing loss.

She took another deep breath and said to Rick, "You were right, you know. Considering the data we already had on hunter impact, I should not have let myself get emotionally involved with Samantha."

"I can hardly blame you," he said. "She was a neat bear. I hope you find another one like her to study." He was turning the project over to her.

With the matter of his crew chief settled, Dr. Andrews was back to thinking of the problem at hand. "Those cubs still have a chance if they make it through the night," he said. "I'll arrange for somebody to take your classes and somebody for mine, and we'll all four head for the mountain as soon as it's light. We know the area; Kelly especially is familiar with it. If anybody can find those cubs, we can." He sounded so certain the cubs might yet be found that for the first time since she had tuned in the mortality beep, Kelly's heart lifted a little.

He stood up. "Come on, Rick, let's go get the university's new truck before Selnick recovers from the bear woman's tongue-lashing and changes his mind." The warmth in his smile was a balm, and Kelly didn't mind the title when he used it. The professor continued. "We might even go for a pizza." He looked from Kelly to Adam, who had not moved from the cot. "You two want to come?"

Kelly shook her head and said, "I'm too tired and dirty, and I don't want to be in town with those hunters." She was so drained that she couldn't even react to the fact that she would be continuing on the mountain the way she had dreamed from the beginning.

Adam, who had been silent for a long time, only shook his head. The others left, and Adam still didn't say anything. Nervous and too exhausted to think of dealing with Adam alone, Kelly went to the files that she had unloaded onto the table on Friday, and took out the information sheets on Samantha. Flipping through her data, she once more remembered every time that she had seen the bear.

Hating the job, but needing to get it over with, she picked up her pen and filled in the permanent data sheet. "Bear #63, Samantha, killed on Craigs Peak by houndsmen during spring hunting. Fate of cubs, unknown." She put the sheets back in the file with a sense of futility. "I should quit," she said. "It's not worth it."

She was speaking mostly to herself, and she was surprised when Adam responded. "That's not the answer, Kelly."

She turned toward him. "What *is* the answer?"

"Begin again. There are nearly a hundred bears in that file. You can't give up your work because you lost one bear. We didn't give up after Roscoe. Rick hung in after Jenny, even though his error caused her death. You can't quit. You have to begin again."

This was not the way she had expected to start a conversation with Adam. She looked at him, not knowing what to say, and he continued, "You're good at what you do. You're here to get data, not yell at houndsmen." A wisp of grin went across his face as he added, "Although you're pretty good at that, too."

She felt awkward attempting to respond. She didn't know why he had left the project, and now he was telling her that she *couldn't* leave. She said abruptly, "Why are you here?"

Adam got up from the bed and came toward the table. "I'm moving to Colorado and . . ."

She interrupted him to finish the sentence. "You want your Ruger Redhawk." She went to her bed, where she had dumped the gun, holster, and cartridge belt, turning her back to hide her emotion, too tired to deal with one more disappointment. Only now did she realize how much she had hoped that Adam had come to see her. His presence in the cabin had helped her to tell Dr. Andrews the truth. Just having him near had eased some of her grief about Samantha. But she was stupid. He hadn't come to see her. He just wanted to reclaim everything that was his and clear out for good. When she thought she was calm enough to face him, she took the gun and the accessories to the table.

"Here," she said, "there are a few cartridges left in the box."

Adam took what she offered and, setting it immediately aside said, "I don't want the damned gun. I came up here to talk to you, Kelly, but you're too tired right now and in too much pain, and I know you haven't had anything to eat. Why don't you take a shower while I fix you some supper?" He practically shoved her into the storeroom. He filled the black bag with hot water, handed it to her, and slid the curtain across the bar.

The hot water revived her, and while she was combing her hair, the smell of meat cooking made her realize that Adam was right. She hadn't eaten lunch, and it was way past dinnertime. She was hollow with hunger.

When she emerged from the storeroom, Adam sat her down in front of a plate of corned beef hash with two fried eggs on top of it. A cup of hot chocolate steamed next to the plate. She started to speak, but he said, "Eat," and joined her at the meal. She was still nervous about talking with Adam, but she was grateful that he had insisted that she eat. She might gain strength enough to deal with his leaving one more time.

Adam took the empty plates and set them on the counter, and then he just leaned against the counter and looked at her. This was getting them nowhere. "For Pete's sake, Adam, talk. Dr. Andrews and Rick will be back here, and I still won't know why you're moving to Colorado."

"I didn't like the snaring," Adam said, "and I hated the denning, even without the claustrophobia. And you know I was unhappy when we caused pain and stress to the bears." Kelly nodded, and Adam continued. "I left to see if I could find something I liked, something I wanted to do for the rest of my life."

"And did you?"

"I floundered for a while, and then I went and talked to Doc Morrison, who put me in touch with a wild-animal vet in Colorado. I've been working there for two months now." Adam moved over to the table. "My folks can't afford any more school, but if I get resident status in Colorado, I can keep working and pay my way to vet school at CSU." His brown eyes were unusually sober. "I'm going to specialize in treating wild animals."

"So you can undo the damage I do?" She couldn't help saying it. Everything he had said so far seemed like more criticism of her and her work, and it hurt to have him disapprove of her. His next words were no better.

He didn't respond to her comment, but said instead, "I always thought my mom offered the perfect example of how a woman ought to run her life: do her own thing for a little while and then settle in and take care of her family. And then I met you, and you lived for your work." He shook his head. "I didn't even know how I wanted to make a living, and here you were putting up with hard work and grief and the stink of bear bait and Santini's passes just so you could stick with the project." Kelly had no idea where his monologue was going. What difference did all this make?

"I felt like such a failure after you had to take over for me in that tunnel that I couldn't face you, even to say goodbye. I just quit the crew and left." Kelly had thought she was drained of all emotion and would never feel anything again, but the misery in Adam's face moved her. She made a sound of sympathy.

He ran the back of his hand across his mouth. "I faced a few facts about myself while I was looking around for work, and I finally found something I wanted to do. But even that didn't make me feel any better. So I decided to go home and let my mother comfort me." He tried to grin. "Instead she gave me a jolt."

"Adam, do you realize that you've been saying stuff for five minutes, and you haven't yet made sense? What are you talking about?"

Adam wiped his mouth again. "My mother told me that women aren't necessarily thrilled to devote their entire lives to someone else's projects. And she said that it was no wonder you wanted nothing to do with me if I was preaching to you about Rick, when I should have been telling him to knock it off and leave you alone. And she said, furthermore, that sexual harassment is not just a woman's problem; it's a human problem, and that you had every right to do your work in peace and with dignity, and that I was stupid to be jealous about something I should have helped you to handle in the first place."

Kelly was laughing by now. "I like your mother," she said and then spoke to the important part of his rambling speech, "but who told you I wanted nothing to do with you?"

Adam flushed. "You didn't want anything Matt offered you, even though he owns a whole company, and you didn't want Rick, who is a lot more high-powered than I am. Why would you want me?"

Kelly was beginning to feel as if she could get over Samantha's death someday—as if she could be happy. "Maybe because you're a good cook," she said, but he didn't smile. "Maybe because you know how to laugh." Adam wasn't laughing now. His brown eyes had never been so serious.

Kelly continued softly. "Maybe I might want you because you cared enough to feed me before you unloaded your troubles. Maybe because you stepped away from me at the firing range and never once made a pass at me." She took a deep breath, knowing how deeply he too would mourn Samantha. "Maybe because you hurt for every injured bear." She smiled at him. "Adam, there might be a thousand reasons why I would want you."

Adam's face had cleared, and he said with the beginning of a grin, "Well, my mom said that too. She said that if you were as smart as I said you were, you might find a reason to want me."

Kelly reached out and put a hand on his. "Veritably," she said.

After having been in Adam's church—after hearing what sort of commitment was required for a serious relationship—Kelly knew how much trust Adam's mother had placed in her son. *She encouraged him to come back and talk to me, not knowing if I would honor his beliefs, not knowing if she could also trust me.* Kelly breathed a prayer of gratitude and promise.

Adam took her hand and stood up, pulling her with him. He took her other hand and, holding them both, looked into her face. "Kelly, I know that you have to begin your work again. Can *we* begin again too?"

"No," she said, as her pulse quickened, and she felt the fire build between them. Adam's brown eyes sobered once more, and she hurried to add, "I don't want to begin again. Don't you think it would be better if we went right on from here?"

Adam's eyes began to sparkle, and the dimple in his cheek deepened with his grin. "Veritably," he said and took her in his arms. ✷

Crooked Adam

Books by D. E. Stevenson

Crooked Adam

by
D. E. STEVENSON

HOLT, RINEHART AND WINSTON

NEW YORK   CHICAGO   SAN FRANCISCO

Part One

Chapter One

The great clock in the tower of Rockingham School chimed the hour of twelve—it was midnight. Adam Southey laid down his pen with a sigh of relief for he had been correcting examination papers and that was the last one finished . . . He collected them into a bundle, clipped them together, and laid them aside. It was the end of the summer term and Adam was not sorry, for he found it extremely galling to spend his time teaching modern languages while his friends and contemporaries were taking active part in the war. The newspapers were full of accounts of battles on land and sea and in the air, the wireless announcers described heroic deeds . . . and Adam Southey was spending his days cooped up in a classroom with a score of fourteen-year-old boys.

Adam lifted his eyes from the papers and looked across the little room. His face was reflected in the mirror of his dressing-table: a firm, somewhat rugged-featured face with a clear golden-brown skin which told of good healthy blood and clean living; the eyes beneath the dark eyebrows were a curiously light grey—the colour of dry pebbles—and a lock of dark hair had fallen across the broad, open brow.

He threw back the lock impatiently. "Damn," he muttered. "I mustn't think about it. I mustn't get all worked up again or I shan't sleep a wink . . ." But the resolution came too late for he was "worked up" already.

Adam put out his light and drew back the thick curtains and he saw that it was a bright moonlight night, perfectly still and windless. In the distance he could hear a dog barking; there was no other sound. He leaned his elbows on the sill and looked at the sky; there was wind up there for a few solid-looking clouds were moving across the dark blue vault. Adam watched them and wondered what it would be like to fly above those clouds, to fly over Germany and drop bombs, to meet an enemy and fight him thousands of feet above the sleeping countryside.

Rockingham had been a ducal palace before it became a school and the great house was surrounded by parkland and fine old trees. Here and there, scattered about the estate, there were new buildings such as art studios, science laboratories and workshops, swimming baths and gymnasiums, and houses for the masters. Adam Southey was accommodated in one of these "outhouses" and from his bedroom window he could see the avenue stretching in both directions —up to the main school building and down towards the gates; it was like a white curving ribbon in the bright moonlight.

The scene was so quiet and peaceful that it had a soothing effect upon Adam's nerves, and he began to recover from his distress. He reminded himself that six weeks' holiday lay in front of him; he intended to spend it at a forestry camp in Wales—six weeks of hard manual labour was exactly what he needed after his term at Rockingham School.

"All the same I'm lucky to be here," said Adam. He said it aloud in the hope of convincing himself that it was true. He *was* lucky in one way, for, although he had spent several years abroad and could speak French and German fluently, he had no degrees in languages and no experience in teaching. He had been offered the appointment because he was an "old boy" and knew Dr. Cooke, the Headmaster of the school. Dr. Cooke had met Adam in London, soon after the war started, and had said: "Would you like to come back to Rockingham?"

It was curious—thought Adam—how small things influenced one's life. If he had not decided that he needed a new pipe, and strolled into the tobacco department of the Army and Navy Stores to buy one, he would not have met Dr. Cooke and he would not be here now. Adam remembered the meeting well; he remembered how he had hesitated when he saw the tall gaunt figure . . .

Shall I speak to him . . . or shan't I? Adam had thought.

Dr. Cooke had been Adam's housemaster and now he was the Head, but he was just the same—his figure had not changed and neither had his thin eager face with the high cheekbones and the pale blue eyes which were usually rather dreamy, but which sometimes looked at you so piercingly that they seemed to see your soul. Adam had not been able to resist the urge to speak to Dr. Cooke; he

8

had accosted him . . . and Dr. Cooke had known him at once and greeted him cordially and, after a few minutes' conversation, had invited him to come back to Rockingham and teach French and German to the lower forms.

"I know you, Adam," Dr. Cooke had explained. "You haven't a degree, of course, but it is extremely difficult to get qualified masters at the moment and I feel sure you would be able to manage the work. I want someone who will not be snatched away by the Military Authorities when he has begun to get into the way of things."

Adam had very nearly said: "So that's why you've chosen a cripple!" but he had managed to bite back the bitter words.

A cripple—thought Adam, who was now "all worked up" again—a man with one leg shorter than the other . . . a man who was useless to defend his country . . . "Crooked Adam"—that was his nickname in the school.

Adam was just about to turn away from the window when he heard the sound of quick footsteps coming down the avenue from the big house and he knew, even before he saw the tall gaunt figure striding along in the moonlight, that it was the Headmaster on his way to the science buildings. It was by no means the first time that Adam had heard the familiar footsteps going past in the night, and he wondered—not for the first time either—how on earth Dr. Cooke managed to carry on without sleep, how he managed to run the school by day, to attend to all the perplexing business which his position entailed and work in the science buildings most of the night.

Dr. Cooke passed at a good pace and then (while Adam still watched and wondered) a shadowy form darted out from amongst the bushes bordering the avenue and ran along the grass and disappeared.

Adam hesitated. The figure had been so shadowy that he almost disbelieved his eyes—almost but not quite. It *was* somebody, and it was somebody who was up to no good. There had been a suggestion of stealth in the appearance and disappearance of the figure which had made a very unpleasant impression upon Adam . . . furtive and stealthy were the words that sprang to his mind. It might be a

9

boy, of course, but even if it were—and somehow it had not seemed like a boy . . .

Adam seized his stick and, without waiting to put on his coat, he hurried downstairs and out of the house.

It would have been obvious now—if anyone had been there to see —why Adam's nickname had been bestowed upon him, for his gait was curiously lopsided—long, short, long, short; it was like the loping canter of a prairie horse and incidentally it took him over the ground with incredible rapidity. (Few of his colleagues cared to walk with Adam for he could cover miles without tiring or slackening speed and it was a little galling—so his colleagues found—to be outwalked by a lame man even though he was a good deal younger than oneself.)

To-night Adam's gait was even more peculiar than usual for he was in a hurry. He loped along the grass, keeping in the deep black shadow of the trees . . . He stopped and listened . . . and then went on again. There was nothing to be heard, nothing except the firm footsteps of Dr. Cooke on the hard-baked avenue. There was nothing to be seen either; the shadowy form, which had startled Adam so much, seemed to have vanished into thin air.

The Headmaster had reached the door of the science buildings and was searching in his pocket for the key . . . and now, once more, Adam caught a glimpse of a shadowy form which melted into the bushes as he approached . . .

"Sir!" called Adam breathlessly. "Dr. Cooke, wait for me—it's Adam Southey . . ."

"Adam!" exclaimed Dr. Cooke, swinging round and staring at Adam in amazement.

"Open the door," gasped Adam. "Open the door."

Dr. Cooke opened the door and switched on the light and Adam followed him into the building and shut the door firmly. But now that he was here, standing face to face with Dr. Cooke in the brilliantly lighted workshop, Adam's feelings underwent a reaction and he could find nothing to say. What possible excuse could he offer for forcing himself upon Dr. Cooke in such an unceremonious fashion?

"Were you following me, Adam?" inquired Dr. Cooke, looking at Adam with his piercing stare.

"Yes . . . no," said Adam uncomfortably.

"What are you doing here at this unholy hour?"

"Nothing," said Adam. "I mean—the fact is I saw you pass my window and I thought—I thought someone else was following you, sir."

"Ah, that was it!" said Dr. Cooke. "I knew—I had a feeling that someone was following me." He sat down on a convenient bench as he spoke and drew his fingers across his brow as if he were very weary.

"It's absurd of course——" began Adam, somewhat incoherently. "I mean why should anyone—It was just that the figure seemed—well—a bit furtive . . ."

"Furtive!"

"Yes—a bit furtive—so I just thought—no, I didn't think at all, really—I just *came*."

"Without stopping to put on your shoes," said Dr. Cooke, pointing to Adam's carpet slippers which were stained with the wet grass.

Adam looked down at his feet a trifle ruefully and admitted that he had not remembered about his shoes. "It was silly of me," he added. "I mean who could it have been? Why should anyone—what could anyone——"

"I believe I know the answers to some of your questions," said Dr. Cooke quietly.

"You mean——"

"I mean it might have been someone with—shall we say *ulterior motives*, and by coming after me without stopping to change your shoes it is possible that you may have saved my life."

"Saved your life!" echoed Adam incredulously.

"Possibly," said Dr. Cooke. He hesitated and then added: "It sounds somewhat fantastic, doesn't it? Perhaps you think I am mad."

"I never knew anyone saner," replied Adam quickly.

"Thank you. I'm glad you said that. I believe it might be a good plan to tell you about it; things are getting a little too much for me."

"You can trust me, sir," said Adam. "You know I would do anything for you."

"I believe you would," replied Dr. Cooke, smiling very kindly. "I have always known you were trustworthy and to-night you have proved yourself a man of action. I think the best thing I can do is to tell you about it from the very beginning."

Chapter Two

"Have a cigarette, Adam," said Dr. Cooke, opening his case and offering it to Adam. "This is going to be a long story because, if you are going to help me, you must understand everything. I do not want you to undertake anything without understanding what you are in for."

They lighted cigarettes and disposed themselves as comfortably as they could. Dr. Cooke crossed his long legs and leaned back against the wall and Adam perched himself upon a solid wooden table. There was a short silence while Dr. Cooke arranged his thoughts and Adam had time to look round and to wonder at the strange machinery which he saw on every side. He was aware that Dr. Cooke had provided a good deal of the machinery out of his own pocket. (The place was known throughout the school as "Cookie's Chamber of Horrors.") He was aware that Dr. Cooke was a brilliant scientist and possessed degrees in electrical engineering and radiology. Some people were of the opinion that Dr. Cooke was more interested in science than in schoolmastering . . . but the school had grown and prospered exceedingly under his aegis.

"What do you think of it all?" asked Dr. Cooke suddenly, and Adam realised that Dr. Cooke had been reading his thoughts.

"I don't know anything about science, or engineering——" began Adam.

"If you had taken my advice and devoted your energies to the pursuit of science—instead of frittering away your time on languages—you would be able to appreciate what you see."

Adam smiled, for this was a very old bone of contention between them.

"You may smile," said Dr. Cooke, "but how am I going to explain my invention to a man who does not know the A B C of science and engineering?"

"You have invented something, sir?"

"Haven't I just said so?" inquired Dr. Cooke. "I *could* explain it to you of course, but you would not understand, so you will just have to take my word for it."

"I'm quite willing to do that."

"Very well then. To begin at the beginning, I must tell you that the idea at the base of my discovery is by no means new to me, but it was not until two years ago that I began to work upon it seriously and to construct a small working model in my leisure hours."

"I've often wondered how you found time," Adam said.

"It has not been easy," admitted Dr. Cooke. "But the fact is there was no other course open to me. I have money of my own, but not sufficient, for radiology is a costly hobby. I do not think the school has suffered."

"No, indeed it hasn't."

"The school authorities were good enough to grant me a private workshop and I fitted it up myself. I shall show it to you in a few minutes, Adam, but first I must——"

"There's just one thing," said Adam, interrupting him a trifle diffidently. "I mean before you begin. Hadn't we better do something about that fellow who was following you?"

"What should we do about him?"

Adam's idea was to go out and find him and, if necessary, hit him pretty hard on the jaw. He explained this to Dr. Cooke, but his suggestion was turned down.

"There is no need for any such drastic measure," said Dr. Cooke. "The man cannot get in here for I have had wooden shutters fixed upon all the windows. The place could withstand a siege if necessary, but I do not anticipate a siege."

Adam looked at him in amazement. He said: "And I was just thinking how dull it was here . . . and that nothing ever happened."

"That's where you were wrong, Adam. It is not only in the dust and heat of bursting bombs that the battle is fought and won. The battle is not to the swift and strong—not nowadays."

"You are speaking metaphorically, sir."

"I am speaking the literal truth," replied Dr. Cooke earnestly.

As far as Adam could see he was speaking in riddles, for Adam was completely in the dark. Dr. Cooke was excited and enthusiastic

14

but Adam could not work up much enthusiasm over this unknown invention . . . It must be something important, thought Adam, looking at Dr. Cooke's eager face and flashing blue eyes, or at least it must be something that *he* considers important . . .

Dr. Cooke caught Adam's gaze and smiled. "No wonder you are puzzled," he said. "I am telling you the whole thing back to front. Let me get back to the beginning. I started out with the intention of improving upon the searchlight which is being used by the Military Authorities for spotting aeroplanes."

"A searchlight!" exclaimed Adam. Somehow or other he had not expected to hear that the invention was a weapon of war.

"That was the beginning," nodded Dr. Cooke. "My idea was to find a ray which would pierce clouds, and I was working on this super searchlight when, quite by accident, I discovered something more important still. At first I scarcely realised the terrific potentialities of my discovery and when I did realise them I became quite alarmed. I could not sleep for thinking of the frightful responsibility which lay upon my shoulders . . Sometimes I felt that I ought to smash up my model and burn the blueprints . . ." Dr. Cooke paused and pulled himself together. "Of course I could not do that," he continued in a more sober tone. "One cannot go backwards; one dare not shut one's eyes to knowledge. I had made this discovery so the responsibility was mine. It is still my responsibility and will be until the invention has been handed over to the proper authorities."

"What is it?" asked Adam eagerly. There was no need for him to feign enthusiasm now.

Dr. Cooke rolled up his sleeve and showed Adam his arm. It was very badly scarred from the wrist to the shoulder.

"Good heavens, that must have been a severe burn!" Adam exclaimed.

"It was," admitted Dr. Cooke. "But I was so excited at the time that I scarcely felt it. I had been working at the small-scale model of my searchlight which is operated by a dynamo and I happened to require a tool from the other end of the workshop. When I crossed the path of the ray it set fire to my clothes . . ." He stopped suddenly and looked at Adam.

"It set fire to your clothes?" repeated Adam.

"Yes. Do you realise what that means?"

Adam was beginning to realise what it meant. He looked at Dr. Cooke with startled eyes. "Then, of course," he began, fumbling for words, "of course if your small model . . . the ray . . . but how far would it work?"

"This is a question I cannot answer," replied Dr. Cooke. "I have no means of computing the distance at which the ray could operate, but it would depend very largely upon the power at one's disposal . . ."

His voice died away and Adam saw that he was thinking deeply and did not disturb him. Adam was thinking, too. He was no scientist, but he had imagination. He seemed to see a plane soaring in the sky; he seemed to see it caught in the beam of a searchlight . . . bursting into flames . . . falling to earth. Adam shuddered—no wonder Dr. Cooke had felt a heavy responsibility for his invention. Hitherto radiology had been used for curative purposes, to diagnose and heal, but Dr. Cooke's invention was destructive . . . But Adam's second thoughts went further and he realised that radiology healed because it destroyed disease. Was it too much to hope that this invention might be the means of destroying the terrible disease of war? If it were powerful enough, if it were placed in the proper hands and used in the right way it seemed to Adam that it might. He was aware of his own ignorance on the subject; he knew nothing about radiology nor engineering; he was groping in the dark. There were so many questions that he wanted to ask that he scarcely knew where to begin. He had no proper words for his questions.

"Is it a sort of tongue of flame?" he asked at last.

"No, it is not a flame-thrower," replied Dr. Cooke, laughing. "The Romans used flame-throwers, didn't they? It is quite impossible to go into details without becoming technical but, quite simply, my invention is a ray of light which possesses the power of igniting any inflammable material with which it comes in contact."

"Is it a sort of X-ray?"

"Yes," said Dr. Cooke. "I dislike the nomenclature exceedingly, and I dislike your slipshod method of speaking but I suppose that cannot be helped. We will descend to the level of your intelligence and call it 'a sort of X-ray'."

16

"Thank you, sir," said Adam, smiling.

Dr. Cooke sighed. He said: "You always were quite irrepressible, Adam."

"So you always said, sir," agreed Adam respectfully.

Dr. Cooke left it at that. He said: "Is there anything else you want to ask me before I show you the model?"

"What are you going to *do*?" asked Adam. "I mean what's the next step?"

"I have put things in train," replied Dr. Cooke. "I wrote to John Brownlee who is the senior partner of Mitchell & Freis, the big iron and steel people. John is a friend of mine—we were at the Edinburgh Academy together—and I knew he would do what he could. It took a little persuasion to get him interested, but I sent him the specifications and he is now building a full-scale model of the machine in his Edinburgh works. This morning I received a letter from him," continued Dr. Cooke, taking a typescript letter from his pocket and opening it out. "The letter is full of technical details which, unfortunately, you would not understand, but this is how it goes on . . ."

Dr. Cooke put on his spectacles with two swift movements— to right and to left—and cleared his throat. (It was a familiar gesture and had been aped, more or less successfully, by every boy in the school. Adam, himself, had been rather good at it in the far-off days when he was a grubby little fag and Dr. Cooke was his house-master. The putting on of the spectacles and the clearing of the throat were usually the prelude to some important—or unpleasant— announcement: "Er-chm, will the boys who know anything about the cricket ball which shattered the window in number five dor-mitory come up to my study to-night after prayers." . . . But this was no time to hark back down the years, and Adam pulled himself together and prepared to listen.)

"Er-chm," said Dr. Cooke. "This is what he says:

" 'Apart from these difficulties in the construction of the full-scale model, which may be due to some slight error in your calculations or in our workmanship, the machine appears to have possibilities more important than I had anticipated. The difficulties must be overcome.'"

"You ought to go there at once," said Adam thoughtfully.

"I must," agreed Dr. Cooke. "John Brownlee is a queer mixture. He's a great talker but when he puts his hand to paper he is chary of words. When he says that the difficulties must be overcome it means a great deal."

"Of course it does. It means that he's prepared to go all out in helping you to overcome them," exclaimed Adam, excitedly. Adam had not disbelieved Dr. Cooke's story, of course, but this letter from the cautious head of a big business firm seemed to give the whole matter a more solid foundation.

"It means just that," agreed Dr. Cooke.

"What else does he say?" asked Adam.

"He goes on to tell me about some trouble in the workshops. Ah, here it is:

"'You may have expected to hear from me before but the work has been delayed. We were obliged to dismiss several of our best hands at short notice. It appeared that they were taking undue interest in the model. We had taken the precaution of having the parts turned in different workshops so no leakage is possible but in view of the nature of your invention I cannot urge too strongly the necessity for caution at your end.'"

"There must have been leakage!" Adam exclaimed. "Those men must have realised the importance of the invention, and, when they were sacked from the works, they found out where you lived——"

"It looks like it, I admit."

"I've been wondering all the time," cried Adam, getting up and beginning to walk about in his excitement. "I've been wondering how anyone could have found out; now we know."

Dr. Cooke nodded. He said: "To tell you the truth I shall be glad when the whole thing is out of my hands. Several rather disquieting occurrences have taken place. For instance, the other night when I was out to dinner a man called to see me and when Jenkins asked him his business he said it was in connection with Oxford and Cambridge examinations. He was an elderly man 'like a professor' Jenkins said. Jenkins left him in my study to await my return but by the time I got home he had gone. I am almost certain—no, I am positively assured that he had been through the papers in my desk, but there was nothing of importance there so it did not matter."

"And then that fellow to-night," put in Adam.

"Yes, and several other odd occurrences. I am not alarmed for my own safety—or perhaps it would be more exact to say that I am less alarmed for my own safety than for the safety of the invention . . . better that it should perish than fall into the wrong hands."

"Good heavens, yes!" exclaimed Adam. He hesitated and then added in a lower tone:"Those men must be German agents."

"It looks like it," agreed Dr. Cooke. "It looks uncommonly like it, Adam." He rose as he spoke and led the way across the big workshop to a solid oak door in the wall, and taking a Yale key from his pocket he unlocked the door and showed Adam a smaller workshop, full of the most awe-inspiring machinery. The room was so full of machinery that there was scarcely space to move and Dr. Cooke was obliged to bend his head and squirm his long body between the masses of iron and steel and glass . . . In the middle of the room there was a solid table, screwed to the floor, and on the table was the model which Dr. Cooke had made.

Adam looked at the model curiously. It was not nearly as large as he had expected; in fact it was more like a toy than an engine of destruction. There were wheels and cogs and levers all made of shining steel and a long-shaped funnel (like the horn of an old-fashioned phonograph) which pointed towards the door. A thick cable ran from the base of the model to a large dynamo in the corner of the room.

Dr. Cooke fingered the machine lovingly. "You would like to see it working, wouldn't you, Adam?"

"Yes, I should, sir."

"I want to see it myself," said Dr. Cooke. He sighed and added: "It will be the last time—yes, I have made up my mind to dismantle it to-night. I cannot go north and leave the model in working order. It would be most unsafe . . ." He touched a switch and the room was filled with the hum of the dynamo and a ray of violet light flowed from the steel funnel through the door, into the large workshop and was focused upon a huge iron plate which hung on the opposite wall.

"There," said Dr. Cooke, raising his voice above the humming sound. "That is the ray, Adam. There is no flame, you see. It is a ray of light. Perhaps you would like to make an experiment with it?"

This was exactly what Adam wanted to do. He accepted a pair of tongs and a piece of newspaper from Dr. Cooke and went back to the end of the big workshop. The ray of light was not very strong; it was a pale violet colour, and Adam found it difficult to believe it would set fire to the paper. He rolled the paper into a tight ball, gripped it with the tongs and held it out in the path of the ray . . . There was a flash of fire and the paper fluttered to the floor in charred fragments.

Chapter Three

The sun was rising behind the tower of Rockingham when the door of the science laboratory opened and Dr. Cooke and Adam Southey came out. Adam blinked in the morning sunshine like a sleepy cat and Dr. Cooke stretched his arms above his head and filled his lungs with the fresh sweet air. It was no wonder they were tired for they had been working all night; the small model which had taken years to build was now dismantled and the parts scattered . . . the specifications were in Adam's pocket.

"Well, are you ready?" asked Dr. Cooke.

Adam was ready. He locked the door and put the key on his chain and they walked up the avenue together. There were no lurking shadows this morning—the day seemed innocent as Eden before the Fall.

"But you will be careful, sir," Adam urged.

"There is no danger by day," replied Dr. Cooke in confident tones. "To-day, especially, there will be so many people about the place——"

"It might be the opportunity they've been waiting for," interrupted Adam.

Rockingham School was breaking up to-day and the boys were going back home for their summer holidays. It was always a muddled sort of day and Adam could not help wishing it were over. Dr. Cooke usually stayed on at Rockingham for a few days after the end of term, but this year he had decided to vary his procedure and go north the first night. Adam had offered to accompany him and his offer had been accepted.

"To-night, then," said Adam as they parted at Dr. Cooke's door. "I shall be waiting for you at eleven o'clock and we will drive straight up to London."

"I shall be ready," replied Dr. Cooke.

"You won't tell anyone you are going?"

Dr. Cooke laughed. "Don't worry," he said, "I shall tell everyone that I am staying on as usual . . . good-bye, Adam. I shall not forget what you have done for me."

"Eleven o'clock," repeated Adam.

"Yes, eleven. Go and have a few hours' sleep, now."

Adam did not reply for he had no intention of going to bed—he was too excited to sleep; he had made a plan of his own and, once he had seen Dr. Cooke safely into the house, he proceeded to carry it out. He went straight back to the science workshop, opened the door with the key and went in. He left the door slightly ajar, crossed the workshop to the changing-room, found a green baize apron and put it on. It was part of the plan that he should look rather dirty and dishevelled and Adam was prepared to anoint his face with smears of oil . . . but on looking into the mirror in the changing-room he saw that his face was quite dirty enough already. His collar was smeary too and his tie had worked round under one ear. Adam smiled (he had a curious smile for one corner of his large mobile mouth went up much higher than the other) and decided that he would do.

Having provided himself with a dustpan and brush, which he found in the janitor's cupboard, Adam sat down upon one of the benches and lit a cigarette. The trap was laid; it remained to be seen whether the rat would walk into the trap or not.

The workshop was very quiet; Adam could hear the birds singing in the bushes outside the door; he had opened a skylight in the roof and a beam of golden sunlight fell on to the strange machinery with which the place was filled . . . motes of dust were floating in the beam and Adam, as he looked at them, wondered why they remained suspended in the air. He thought vaguely: if I were a scientist I should know the answer to that, too.

What a strange night it had been! He had spent it with a screwdriver in his hand. Screws and screws and screws, each smaller and more fiddling than the last, but gradually he had attained a certain proficiency which had earned a grudging approval from his companion. It must have been very trying for Dr. Cooke to demolish the model—Adam realised that—but he had not complained. He had gone ahead manfully and his long thin fingers had not faltered.

Adam finished one cigarette and lighted another. He was begin-

22

ning to think, very longingly, of breakfast. Why hadn't he brought something to eat? A bar of chocolate would have been better than nothing . . .

Suddenly there was a slight sound and the door which Adam had left ajar began to open a little wider . . . Adam seized the dustpan and brush and fell on his knees on the floor. The temptation to look at the door was almost irresistible, but he managed to control it. He brushed industriously and kept his eyes down so the first thing he saw was a pair of brown shoes, somewhat worn and shabby.

"Hallo!" exclaimed Adam, sitting back on his heels and looking up in simulated surprise.

The man who had entered looked down at the figure kneeling on the floor; there was nothing very alarming about it—he saw a blank sleepy face with a smudge of oil across one cheek. "Hallo, are you the—er—janitor?" asked the man.

Adam sniffed and drew his finger across his nose. "Looks like it, don't it!" he said.

"Sweeping up the place?" said the man in a friendly voice.

Adam did not answer that. He said suspiciously: "Look 'ere, what are you doin' 'ere? I got orders no one's to come in 'ere—not without they 'ave a permit."

"I've got a permit, all right," replied the man.

By this time Adam had taken a good look at the man for he wanted to be certain of recognising him if he happened to see him again. He had a big nose and deeply sunken eyes, his hair was brown and lifeless. His voice was a trifle nasal, but not unpleasantly so. He was dressed in a neat navy-blue suit and a blue tie with white spots and he was carrying a Burberry over his arm. If Adam had seen him in ordinary circumstances he would have put the man down as a clerk in the city—perhaps the head clerk of a small business; that was the impression he gave.

"You'll know me again, won't you?" said the man jokingly.

"That's part of my job," replied Adam. "I got to know people that comes round 'ere. I got to know their business, what's more."

"I see—well—er—the fact is we've had orders from the school authorities to examine one of the models and put it in order."

"Oh, 'ave you?" said Adam incredulously.

The door opened a little wider and another man appeared. Quite a different sort of individual. He was tall and gaunt with broad shoulders and long arms. His face was dark; it had the blue tinge of a man who ought to shave frequently; it was a long-shaped face with the long upper lip which is so often seen in people of Irish extraction. He was dressed in the same fashion as the first man, but the garments did not suit him and Adam had a feeling that he would have looked more at home in oil-stained overalls.

The first man was still talking, explaining that they had come down from London by the early train and that they must get to work at once.

"Well, I dunno," said Adam, interrupting him. "I ain't got no orders about anyone comin' in 'ere. Strikes me you'd better see the 'Eadmaster about it."

"He works here at night, doesn't he?"

"That's roight," agreed Adam. "Works 'ere the 'ole bloomin' noight. Doesn't like bein' disturbed, neither."

"If we came down here to-night we could see him."

"You'd better not."

"Why?"

"Because 'e doesn't like bein' disturbed—not unless it's important business."

"It's very important business," said the man solemnly.

The second man had begun to prowl round the workshop, and to examine the machinery with interest. Adam felt more than ever convinced that he was an engineer.

"'Ere, you!" cried Adam. "I never said you could snoop round the plaice. I'd lose my job if the 'Eadmaster saw you."

"He won't do any harm," said the first man in a soothing tone. "He's very interested in machines, aren't you, Pat?"

The second man agreed that he was. He spoke in a husky voice and his accent was as Irish as his name. He pointed to the door in the wall and asked what was in there.

"That's Dr. Cooke's private room," said Adam. "Nobody can't go in there."

"I suppose you go in to tidy up, don't you?"

"Sometimes I does," agreed Adam. "And a nice mess it is, I can tell you."

"Have you got the key?" asked the first man, and, as he spoke, a pound note fluttered down on to the floor in front of Adam's nose.

Adam looked at it in dismay. He felt slightly sick for it was proof —if proof were needed—that the men meant business. He knew that he must accept the bribe and act—act as he had never acted before. "Oo!" he exclaimed, simulating amazement. "Gor' lummy, a quid! . . . But I ain't got the key, mister," he added in regretful tones. "I couldn't get it neither. There's nobody 'as the key but the 'Eadmaster."

"That's a pity," said the man. "But perhaps you could arrange for us to see the Headmaster. Put the note in your pocket—there will be another for you if you can help us."

Adam took the note and put it in the pocket of the green baize apron. He could not help wondering who would find it there and what he would do with it.

"Well, I dunno," he said dubiously. "I don't want to get into 'ot water and lose my job . . ."

"You won't get into trouble," said the man confidently.

"What d'you want me to do? You ain't givin' away quids for nothin'."

The man hesitated and then he said: "I'll tell you what. We'll come back to-night and see the Headmaster; it's very important that we should see him. All you need to do is to leave the big door open—like it was just now. You could do that, couldn't you?"

"I moight . . ." said Adam in a considering tone.

"I suppose the Headmaster is sure to be here?"

"Certainsure," replied Adam. "If you was to come down round about eleven-thirty 'e'd be 'ere. But why d'you want the dooropen? If 'e's expectin' you——"

"That's my affair," replied the man. "You leave the door open and there will be another pound for you—and keep your mouth shut, see?"

"Two quid," said Adam. "Two quid more. It's worth that to you—I moight lose my job over it and then where should I be?"

"Very well. If the door's open you'll get your two pounds. It's easy money."

They went away after that, and Adam was not sorry to see them go. His heart was thumping uncomfortably as he followed them to the big door and watched them walk down the avenue towards the gates. He realised that he had underestimated the danger to which he had exposed himself . . . he had been in considerable danger . . . and not only that but half-way through the interview he had remembered that Dr. Cooke's specifications were in the inside pocket of his coat. What a fool he had been!

The day passed slowly; it seemed to Adam even more muddled and noisy than usual. Boys rushed up and down the passages looking for stray garments and cricket bats; their voices echoed in the vaulted roofs. The big hall was cluttered with luggage, with tuck-boxes and cricket bags. Buses drove up and were filled with boys and luggage and rattled away down the avenue to the station. Parents arrived in cars and hung about the precincts, waiting for their offspring, or searched feverishly up and down the corridors; and through it all moved Dr. Cooke, placid and urbane. Adam spent most of the day shadowing Dr. Cooke from afar. He was unhappy when the tall thin figure was not in sight; it seemed to him that the hurly-burly and the coming and going of cars provided good cover for anyone who had designs upon the Headmaster's person. His only comfort lay in the fact that he had misled those two men—or hoped he had misled them. They would return to-night at eleven-thirty expecting to find the door open and Dr. Cooke at work, and by that time Adam and Dr. Cooke would be on their way to London.

The day dragged on. Adam was so tired that everything seemed vague and dreamlike. He said good-bye to hundreds of boys and shook hundreds of hands.

"Good-bye, Mr. Southey!"

"Oh, good-bye, Brown. Have a good holiday."

"Thank you, sir. Hope you will, too."

"Good-bye, Mr. Southey!"

"Oh, good-bye, Falconer. Mind you have a good holiday."

"Good-bye, Mr. Southey!"

"Oh, good-bye, Yates. We shall miss you badly."

"Thank you, sir. I shall miss Rockingham and everyone . . . It seems funny to think I shan't be coming back."

"Good-bye, Mr. Southey!"

"Oh, Turner—I was looking for you! Let us know how you get on at Cambridge."

"I'm not going to Cambridge, sir. I'm going straight into the RAF."

"Oh, good work. Let us know how you get on, won't you?"

"Yes, sir."

"Good luck, Turner."

"Thank you, sir. I hope you—I mean good luck to you, too."

Yates and Turner had been inseparable for four years. They walked out together talking earnestly and Adam wondered what they were feeling; he wondered what they were talking about. They were good boys, both of them, and somehow Adam felt that Rockingham would not be the same without them—but he had felt that before when other boys left and it was always just the same. Boys grew and developed and stepped into the vacant places . . . Rockingham went on. Turner and Yates would not be here next term; they would be fighting for their country . . .

"He's a frightfully decent sort," Turner was saying as he and Yates walked away. "It must be pretty foul for him to have to stick on here and see everyone leaving."

"Crooked Adam," said Yates thoughtfully. "Why do we call him that, Turns?"

"Why do we?" exclaimed Turner in surprise. "Well, because of his funny walk, of course . . . and he's got a crooked smile too. You know the way his mouth goes up at one corner when there's a joke on."

"Yes, I know," agreed Yates. "But I can't help thinking that one of the reasons we call him Crooked Adam is because he's as straight as a die—if you know what I mean."

This was a bit beyond Turner, and he said so.

"I mean," explained Yates, "I mean it would be difficult to be absolutely straight if you were a bit lopsided. Some people would

27

be pretty sour—they'd feel they'd had a rotten deal—but Crooked Adam makes the best of it. He's as fit as you are," added Yates, feeling his friend's iron muscles beneath the cloth of his grey flannel jacket.

"He's fitter if anything," agreed Turner.

They walked on for a few moments in silence.

"Come on, Yates," said Turner. "Let's have a prowl around Long Acre. It seems funny we shan't be here next term. It seems damn funny to think everything will be going on here just the same."

"Nice," declared Yates, swinging into step. "I mean that's what we're going to fight for, isn't it? . . . Rockingham and all that . . ."

"Sentimental ass," said Turner affectionately.

Chapter Four

The narrow platform at King's Cross Station was a scene of bustle and confusion. Porters ran hither and thither carrying suitcases; passengers struggled through the press with anxious expressions on their faces.

"Have you found your seat?"

"Do you want a paper?"

"Where's Edward . . . he'll lose the train."

Gradually order arose out of chaos and people sorted themselves out, found their seats, found their friends and made their last-minute farewells.

Adam Southey had been standing on the platform near the entrance to a first-class carriage; he had been smoking a cigarette, and now, as the whistle blew and the long heavy train began slowly to move out of the station, he swung himself on board and made his way along the corridor to the compartment in which he had taken his seat. The compartment was empty except for Dr. Cooke who was comfortably ensconced in a corner.

Dr. Cooke put down his paper and smiled: "Have you seen anyone?" he asked.

"No," replied Adam.

"Who or what did you expect to see?"

Adam could not answer. He did not know—that was just the difficulty; he did not know whether he was being too careful or too careless; he did not know whether there was any danger or not.

"What kind of danger do you anticipate?" asked Dr. Cooke in a conversational tone.

"I know it seems absurd," said Adam doubtfully. It seemed absurd . . . and yet . . . the blueprints of Dr. Cooke's devilish machine were in Adam's inside pocket. He could feel the bulge and they crackled when he moved. He sat down opposite to Dr. Cooke and leant forward. "I think we should be careful, sir," he said. "Those two fellows meant business."

"I agree with you there," replied Dr. Cooke. "But you have put them off the scent. They cannot know that we are on our way north —therefore we are safe."

"Yes," said Adam doubtfully.

"What could they do, Adam?"

"They might try to kidnap you."

"Good lord, Adam!" exclaimed Dr. Cooke, laughing. "You have been reading too many detective novels."

"I don't read them at all," replied Adam with a grin. "I'm not clever enough or something—at any rate they don't appeal to me."

"I suppose that was why you haunted me all day yesterday like Banquo's ghost?"

"I'm afraid it was," admitted Adam. "I may be making heavy weather of it, but the fact is those two fellows frightened me . . ."

"You were very foolish to expose yourself unnecessarily."

"I know," agreed Adam. "I underrated our adversaries. I don't want to make the same mistake again."

"If they meant me harm, they could have shot me half a dozen times——" began Dr. Cooke.

"But they don't want to shoot you . . ."

"I see," said Dr. Cooke, looking at Adam with a grave expression and twinkling eyes. "I see what you mean. They want to kidnap me and hold lighted matches to the soles of my feet—then I shall be obliged to give away the secrets of my invention."

"But, sir——"

"Never mind, Adam," added Dr. Cooke with his kind smile. "I was only teasing you, my dear boy. I agree that we should take reasonable precautions."

The door of the compartment slid back: "Will you be taking the first lunch, sir?" inquired the attendant politely.

If Adam had not been so anxious he would have enjoyed the journey to Edinburgh (he had never been on that line before and there was much to see), but he was too uneasy in his mind to enjoy anything; he felt his responsibility keenly. Dr. Cooke slept most of the way and Adam would have liked to sleep too for he had slept very little last night and not at all the night before, but he was determined not to sleep. He sat in his corner hour after hour and watched the fields slip past. How green they were, how fresh and bright and tidy. Miles and miles of cornland, pastures with cows grazing placidly, woods and villages, roads and towns.

The train was delayed a little for it was the beginning of the holidays and it was late when at last they approached Edinburgh and ran through the tunnels into Waverley Station.

Dr. Cooke was refreshed by his sleep; he became quite excited. "Here we are!" he exclaimed. "By Jove, it's good to see old Edinburgh again. The air feels quite different."

They had decided to leave their luggage in the station and go straight to Mr. Brownlee's house. Adam wanted to take a taxi but Dr. Cooke refused. He led Adam up a long flight of steps and introduced him to Princes Street.

"There!" he exclaimed, gripping Adam's arm. "You won't see a finer street than that . . . and there's the Castle, Adam! Isn't the air marvellous? By Jove, it's good to be back!"

Adam was amazed at the change in Dr. Cooke; he seemed years younger and full of boyish enthusiasm. He seemed quite a different being from the staid and dignified Headmaster of Rockingham School.

"We'll take a tram," continued Dr. Cooke. "We'll get one opposite Scott's monument. Come on, Adam, there's no time to lose . . ."

They caught a tram which took them along Princes Street and down Shandwick Place. Dr. Cooke talked all the time pointing out the various buildings and giving Adam a good deal of interesting information, and at Coates Crescent they descended from the tram and plunged down a side street. It was beginning to get dark now, dark and cold and cloudy, but Dr. Cooke led the way with confidence. He turned up one street and down another and Adam cantered along beside him in his usual peculiar manner.

"I was born there," said Dr. Cooke, pointing to a bleak-looking house in a row of bleak-looking houses.

"Were you, sir?" said Adam. "Perhaps some day there will be a plate on the wall."

31

"A plate on the wall!" echoed Dr. Cooke in amazement.

"Saying you were born there," explained Adam.

Dr. Cooke laughed. "A plate on the wall—eh? Not much chance of that . . . a waste of money anyway."

The streets all looked the same to Adam but his companion knew them well and after they had been walking for about ten minutes they came to a terrace of houses with gardens in front of them and beyond the gardens a fine open view.

"You could see the Forth from here if it were not so dark and misty," said Dr. Cooke. "You could see the hills of Fife. It's a grand view on a clear day . . . This is John Brownlee's house; let's hope the man's at home and not gadding out to a concert or something . . ."

Mr. Brownlee was at home. His visitors were shown into a comfortable well-stocked library and after a short delay the door opened and Mr. Brownlee appeared. For some reason Adam had expected him to be like Dr. Cooke, tall and thin and a trifle gaunt, but instead of that he was tall and broad-shouldered with a round red face and bushy grey eyebrows.

"Sam!" he exclaimed, hastening forward and seizing Dr. Cooke's hand. "Sam, by all that's blue! I've been thinking of you all day and wishing you were here—and here you are! When did you arrive?"

"Half an hour ago," said Dr. Cooke, laughing.

"Good—you came straight here. Where are your bags?"

"We left them at the Waverley—this is Adam Southey . . ."

"How are you?" said Mr. Brownlee, turning to Adam.

"Very well, thank you, sir."

"Good—we'll send for your bags. You'll stay here, of course, both of you."

"But, John——"

"You'll stay here," repeated Mr. Brownlee. "I'll take no denial so you can spare your breath."

He was so fierce about it that Adam could not help laughing inwardly. It was the oddest invitation he had ever received.

"Sit down," said Mr. Brownlee. "I've got half a hundred questions to ask you, Sam, but first I must tell you that we haven't much time . . ." He paused and looked at Adam doubtfully.

"Adam knows," said Dr. Cooke. "Adam is in it up to the hilt— you can say what you like."

"Fine," said Mr. Brownlee, smiling at Adam. "Fine. Maybe he's been helping you with that searchlight of yours—we'll just call it a searchlight if you've no objection . . ."

"I'm not an engineer," said Adam.

"He would have been if he had listened to me," put in Dr. Cooke. They all laughed.

"Now look here, Sam," said Mr. Brownlee, "we've made the full-scale model—as I told you in my letter—but the fact is it isn't right. I'm not saying whose fault it is—it may be our fault—but you'll need to get down to it and see where the fault lies."

"That's what I've come for," said Dr. Cooke simply.

"Was the small working model satisfactory?"

"Perfectly satisfactory."

"Have you the blueprints of the model?"

"Adam has them in his pocket."

Mr. Brownlee nodded. "That's all I want to know," he said. "If the small model worked, we're not far off it. It's a matter of adjustment, but the adjustment must go ahead quickly and I'll tell you why. I was in London on Saturday and I was speaking to Handicote. I gave him a hint that we were experimenting with a searchlight and he wants to see it as soon as possible."

"But it's not finished!" cried Dr. Cooke in dismay.

"You'll get on to it," replied his friend in soothing tones. "I'll give you a couple of my best men. It'll not take you long. Handicote is coming north next week to have a look at an improvement in a retractable undercarriage—it's a small thing to my way of thinking and not worth the trouble, but they're making a fine hullabaloo about it . . ."

"Next week!" exclaimed Dr. Cooke in horrified tones.

"Now, Sam, there's no need to get all het up about it," declared Mr. Brownlee. "You can leave it to me. If the searchlight is not ready Handicote won't see it—but we'll have a good try."

"Is it to be demonstrated here?"

"No, there's not enough room. The parts will have to be taken north and reassembled at my place in Ross-shire. We want plenty of space to demonstrate the machine properly—you see that, don't you?"

"But, John——"

"You'll manage it fine, Sam. It's always better to do things with a rush; they get done, then. We'll go down to the works to-morrow morning and look through the specifications together and see what's what. Then the parts will be packed into a van and sent north. There's no difficulty about it."

"Have you a workshop at your place in Ross-shire?" inquired Dr. Cooke faintly.

"Have I a workshop!" exclaimed Mr. Brownlee. "Wait till you see my workshops; they're the pride of my heart."

"I didn't know——"

"Nobody knows. It's a dead secret, Sam. The whole thing started in a casual sort of way. I had bought Lurg House some years ago—it's an out-of-the-way place—and then when we began to do a lot of secret work for the Government it struck me that I might make use of Lurg to experiment on aircraft . . . different types of wings and suchlike. That was the way it started and now it's one of the most secret places in the Kingdom. I have a staff there, of course, and my nephew Dick flies the aircraft . . . Wait till you see it, Sam."

"I'll need to, I suppose," said Dr. Cooke, smiling.

Chapter Five

Dr. Cooke had said a great deal about his old friend John Brownlee, but had never mentioned that Mr. Brownlee was a widower and had a daughter, so Adam was very much surprised, on following the two older men into the drawing-room, to see an attractive young woman sitting there reading a book. She jumped up as they went in and greeted Dr. Cooke cordially and smiled at Adam in a friendly way.

"You're grown up now!" exclaimed Dr. Cooke in surprise.

"Of course I am," replied Miss Brownlee. "I'm nineteen—quite a hag."

"They're staying here, Evelyn," said her father. "You can fix that up, can't you?"

"Of course—quite easily."

"And they'll be coming to Lurg with us."

"Good!" said Evelyn, nodding.

Adam had said nothing. He had been rather taken aback at Miss Brownlee's appearance; she was the prettiest girl he had ever seen. She was of medium height and very slim with fair fluffy hair and blue eyes and a complexion of milk and roses and her small regular features were full of character and expression.

"John" and "Sam" had so much to say to each other that the younger members of the party were obliged to entertain each other as best they could, and at first Adam was somewhat shy. He always felt shy with girls for he had met so few and knew nothing whatever about them. He felt clumsy and awkward and his lame leg gave him an inferiority complex. What girl could take any interest in an impecunious schoolmaster with a lame leg? Fortunately Evelyn was not shy; she was gay and friendly and after a little Adam found himself talking quite naturally.

They went to bed early and Adam was very glad for by this time his head was buzzing with fatigue. His suitcase had been brought from the station and unpacked for him and there was a hot water bottle waiting for him in the comfortable bed. Adam's last thought —as he laid his head on the pillow—was one of gratitude for the small comforts of civilised life.

The next day was fine and sunny. Dr. Cooke and Mr. Brownlee went off early to the works and Adam was left to amuse himself as best he could. He decided to go out and have a look at the city and was on the point of departure when he was intercepted by his hostess.

"Are you going out?" asked Evelyn Brownlee. "If you wait a minute I'll get my hat and come with you . . ."

She ran upstairs as she spoke and Adam was obliged to wait. He would rather have gone alone for he was sensitive about his lameness . . . Miss Brownlee wouldn't like it when she found she had saddled herself with a lame companion . . . but there was no help for it.

Presently Miss Brownlee returned and they set off together for a country walk. They went by Ravelston and over the hill which is called "Rest and be thankful" and as they went Evelyn Brownlee chattered away in a friendly manner until at last Adam lost his shyness and found his tongue. It was easier after that; they talked about books and music and discovered that their tastes were curiously alike.

"What on earth is that?" Adam exclaimed suddenly, stopping and looking all round him with an expression of blank amazement.

"The lions roaring," replied Evelyn laughing heartily. "The lions in the zoo. We might go to the zoo to-morrow if you would like to see it."

Adam said he would. He was beginning to feel that he would go anywhere with Evelyn Brownlee.

The two older men returned from the works about seven o'clock. Dr. Cooke looked gaunt and weary, but Mr. Brownlee seemed as full of vitality as ever.

"Have you had a good day?" asked Adam as he took his seat at the dinner table.

"It's been a worrying day," replied Dr. Cooke.

"We've been through the specifications," added Mr. Brownlee.

"We've spent the whole day on them and we're going back to the works after dinner to have a look at the model. Perhaps you'd like to come with us, Southey. You might be interested."

"I should be very interested indeed," replied Adam eagerly.

They finished dinner quickly and Mr. Brownlee—who was always in a hurry—bustled them out of the house and into a large car with a long shining bonnet which was waiting at the kerb. Dr. Cooke leant back in his corner; he seemed lost in thought, and Adam took the opportunity to inform Mr. Brownlee of the strange events which had taken place at Rockingham, of the man who followed Dr. Cooke to the science laboratory and of his own interview with the two odd-looking individuals on the following day. Mr. Brownlee listened with interest and amazement.

"But this is serious!" he exclaimed. "We'll need to keep an eye on Sam until the searchlight is out of his hands."

"I wondered how the men knew about it," said Adam in a significant tone.

"You're not suggesting there's a leakage here?"

"I just wondered," repeated Adam uncomfortably.

"There's no leakage here," said Mr. Brownlee firmly. "I'll stake my oath on that—but we'll need to look after Sam, that's one thing certain. Sam needs looking after. He's too much in the clouds—you've realised that, of course."

It was extremely odd—so Adam found—to hear his revered Headmaster referred to in this familiar way, and criticised in this slightly condescending manner; it was all of a piece with the strange unexpected experience in which he had become involved

"Sam has no head for business," continued Mr. Brownlee. "Anybody could swindle the boots off him—he was always like that—but I'll see to it that he doesn't get swindled out of his rightful dues."

"As you always did," put in "Sam" with a chuckle.

"Oh, you're listening are you?" said Mr. Brownlee. "I thought you were in the clouds. Yes, I always saw that you didn't get swindled when we went to the Academy together . . . and you did my science papers for me. It was a very satisfactory sort of partnership you'll agree."

By this time they had reached the works and although it was now after nine o'clock, the place was still humming like a hive of bees.

"We're working night shifts, of course," explained Mr. Brownlee as he led them past the doorkeeper and along a stone passage which sloped down steeply into the bowels of the earth. "I've got to get hold of Ford," he added. "That's the first thing to do. Hi, there, Williams! D'you know where Mr. Ford is?"

The man thus addressed replied that Mr. Ford was in number seventeen—or had been there a short time ago.

"Seventeen, eh?" said Mr. Brownlee, adding in a lower tone: "That's where your searchlight is, Sam."

They walked on and after turning down another passage and passing through an enormous workshop where men in overalls were working busily amongst masses of buzzing machines, they came at last to a big iron door let into the solid stone wall. Mr. Brownlee rang a bell and a moment or two later the door was opened by a short stocky man with large features and iron-grey hair.

"Ha!" cried Mr. Brownlee. "The very man I want. Sam, this is Mr. Ford—he knows all about your searchlight. Ford, this is Dr. Cooke."

A slow smile lighted up the somewhat dour face. "I'm real pleased to see you, Dr. Cooke. We've been needing you here."

"So I heard," said Dr. Cooke gravely.

"Aye, we've been needing you badly. We're dismantling the sairchlight now. She'll be away north in the morning."

Dr. Cooke looked rather taken aback but Mr. Brownlee was delighted.

"That's fine," he said. "Ford doesn't let the grass grow under his feet . . . Come in and see how they're getting on."

It was a huge workshop and at first it seemed to Adam that the whole place was in the most frightful confusion, but after he had watched for a few minutes he saw that his first impression was wrong. Two men were busily engaged in taking the machine to pieces, two others were wrapping the pieces in rags and packing them into straw-lined crates. Two other men were bringing straw, bringing empty crates and moving the full ones.

"You might have got more men on to it, Ford," said Mr. Brownlee looking round at the scene with a practised eye.

"I might," agreed Ford, "but I'm not just very keen on it. I'm a wee bit nairvous about the machine and I like to keep my eye on what's happening. There's some hanky-panky going on and I haven't got to the bottom of it yet."

"Hanky-panky!" echoed Mr. Brownlee in surprise.

"Queer things have happened. You're aware I had to dismiss O'Connor; I'm thinking I'll need to get rid of Crole as well."

"Crole's been here for years."

"I know that as well as you do, Mr. Brownlee."

"What's the meaning of it?"

Ford shook his head. "There's big money at the back of it—whatever it is. I'd like you to hear what Dow was telling me this forenoon." He called to a tall thin man with a round back and the man put down a piece of metal and waded over to them through the straw. Adam had a feeling that he came reluctantly.

"Dow," said Ford. "I'd like you to tell Mr. Brownlee what you told me this forenoon. There's no need to be nairvous, just you tell him the truth."

The man shifted uneasily from one foot to the other. "He wus waitin' for me," said Dow. "A big feller, he wus, nicely spoken, too. I'm no' one to get talkin' wi' strangers—Maister Ford kens I'm no' a gasbag—but this feller wus friendly like. We'd been crackin' away for a wee while and then I found the feller wus pumping me . . . and that's the truth."

"But not the whole truth, Dow," said Mr. Brownlee, shaking his head.

Dow looked up with startled eyes.

"Come on, my man," said Mr. Brownlee. "You'd better come clean, you know. What else happened? What did the man want?"

"A wax mould of the key," replied Dow in a low voice. "The key of the side door—it was big money he was offering . . ."

"And what did you say to that?"

"It was as much as I could do to keep ma hands off him," declared

Dow, raising his eyes and looking Mr. Brownlee in the face. "I wus mad with masel', too. I just said he'd come to the wrong shop . . ."

"Mr. Brownlee!" exclaimed Adam. "This man is in danger."

"Och, I can look after masel'," said Dow.

There was a short silence.

"Dow had better go to Lurg with the van," said Mr. Brownlee at last. "See to it, Ford. You'll need to send a few hefty fellows with the van."

"I was thinking I'd go myself," said Ford.

"And I!" cried Adam. "Let me go too!"

Ford looked at him critically from under his bushy eyebrows. "Aye," he said slowly. "You can come if you like. It'll not be a picnic, mind you."

"What's this about Crole?" asked Mr. Brownlee, going back to the subject. "What's Crole been doing, eh?"

"Betting," replied Ford. "It's betting that's the trouble with most of them . . . and trouble's the word. O'Connor was one of my best hands till he got bitten with the craze . . . and now it's Crole. They get dipped and then along comes a fellow offering big money for some wee scrap of information—you haird what Dow said. Betting's worse than drink by a long chalk."

"It's not new——" Mr. Brownlee began.

"It's wurrse," declared Ford, rolling his R's more fiercely than ever. "There's been nothing but trouble since we started on Dr. Cooke's sairchlight. I'll be glad when it's out of this place and that's the truth."

"You're making heavy weather of it, Ford."

"I hope so," said Ford doubtfully. "It's a good deal safer at Lurg, anyway."

Adam could see that Mr. Brownlee was annoyed. He said: "Very well. Get the van away as soon as you can."

"We'll be away at the back of six, and if the young gentleman is coming he'll need to be ready."

"I'll be ready," said Adam eagerly. "My name is Southey."

"It's a good name, too," said Ford. "Would the man who wrote the *Life of Nelson* be an ancestor of yours?"

Adam smiled. "I'm afraid not," he replied. "I suppose you aren't related to Henry by any chance?"

Ford looked at him for a moment, somewhat blankly, and then his face broke into a wide grin. "That's good," he said. "Aye, it's a good one that is. I'm thinking we'll get on pretty well, you and me."

Chapter Six

It was exactly five-thirty when Adam presented himself at the big door of the works and asked for Mr. Ford. He was wearing his Burberry and a soft green hat and had a small suitcase in his hand. The doorkeeper was expecting him and he was hurried through the stone passages and ushered into number seventeen workshop without a moment's delay. At the other end of the workshop two large doors stood open and in the yard outside was an enormous brown van. Ford was standing on the step of the van directing the packing, but when he saw Adam he jumped down and came towards him, picking his way across the floor which was strewn with tools and shavings and paper and straw and rags.

"You're airly," said Ford. "I was hoping you'd be airly for we'll get away before our time. There's you and me and Dow going and the driver—four of us. Berwick is the driver's name. You can sit in front, Mr. Southey. We'll change about later." He took Adam's suitcase and handed it into the back of the van. Adam climbed up in front and as he did so a burly man with a small black moustache began to crank the engine . . . it stuttered and started . . . the man straightened himself, came round to the cab and climbed in. They moved off slowly up the steep slope.

The morning was grey and misty and a fine rain was falling so there was little to be seen except black dripping houses on either side, but Adam scarcely noticed the rain for he was thinking over the events of the last few hours and especially his conversation with Mr. Brownlee. There was nothing very new in what Mr. Brownlee had said, but he had the knack of putting things into clear forceful words.

"We all know this thing's important," Mr. Brownlee had said. "I could ask for military protection for the van, but I scarcely think that's necessary. Our vans go to and from Lurg at least twice a week and there's never been any trouble . . . However you can take this revolver just in case. You know the way to use it? That's right. Put

42

it in your pocket . . . you'll use it if necessary. Now about Sam—
I'll look after Sam so you needn't worry. We'll be going north in
the car and maybe we'll be there before you. Ford is a good fellow
—a wee bit dour but staunch and sensible . . . He's cottoned to you
and that's a feather in your cap if you want one. I wouldn't let you
go if Ford hadn't cottoned to you; he takes some understanding.
I'm sending Dow and Berwick. Dow is—hum—doubtful. Berwick
has been with us six years—you ought to be all right."

Adam had exclaimed: "But, sir, Dow must be all right——" and
Mr. Brownlee, who had the strange faculty of knowing what you
meant to say before you had formed the words, interrupted and
said: "He may be all right, but I'm not so sure. He didn't tell us *all*
the truth . . . yes, I'll tell you how I know. Supposing you were
anxious to obtain the mould of a key would you hit on the first man
you saw coming out the works and stand him a drink and offer him
'big money' for it? You would be a fool if you did."

"No," said Adam thoughtfully. "You mean——"

"I mean Dow's been in tow with that fellow. He's been selling
little bits of information—little things that Dow thought were of
no consequence at all. Then all of a sudden Dow found he had gone
too far, he was getting into deeper water . . . that's my reading of
it."

"I see," said Adam more thoughtfully still. He hesitated and
then added, "But even then, sir, even if that's what happened it
may be all to the good. He had the guts to refuse—and he'll be
more careful in the future."

"Let's hope so," said Mr. Brownlee.

Adam had been lost in thought, but now he rose to the surface
and noticed that they had left the town behind them and were on a
country road. There were trees on either side of the road and fields
and hedges and here and there a farm with a cluster of cottages.
Adam had not yet spoken to Berwick. He opened the conversation
by offering the man a cigarette.

"I suppose you've been to Lurg pretty often," said Adam when
they had lighted up.

"Twice a week for three years," replied Berwick in a deep rumbling voice. "It's a good road as far as Inverness and then not so

43

good. Surface isn't bad but it's narrow and winding—stiff gradients too. Gets worse and worse. I usually take two days . . ."

They chatted for a little and then Adam closed his eyes. He dozed uneasily and awoke to find that they were passing through a big town.

"It's Stirling," said Berwick. "Mr. Ford said we was to come this way. I wouldn't mind a glass of beer to tell the truth."

Adam was thirsty too, but he decided not to think about it.

They passed through the town and climbed a very steep hill which had a bad hairpin bend about half-way up. It seemed odd to have such a bad turning on a main road and Adam said so.

"Aye, it's bad," agreed Berwick. "The rest of the road is pretty good, though."

They were on a good bit of road now and were rumbling along smoothly when a bell rang beside Adam's right ear . . . Berwick pulled in to the side and stopped.

"That's Mr. Ford," said Berwick with a grin. "He's had the same idea as me, most likely."

He had guessed right. Ford came round to the front with a bottle of beer in each hand.

"Good man!" cried Adam, jumping down to stretch his legs.

They each had a bottle of beer and a large cheese sandwich. Adam and Ford stood in the road and talked.

"That's Sheriffmuir," said Ford, waving his hand. "My mother was a MacDonald and she was never done talking about Sheriffmuir. You'll no doubt remember that the MacDonalds did uncommonly well in the Battle of Sheriffmuir—you being a schoolmaster."

"Yes," said Adam. He knew very little history and Scottish history was a closed book to him, but he had not the moral courage to admit his ignorance.

"Aye," said Ford nodding. "You'll remember that Argyll's Dragoons drove back our left wing; it was one of those battles that both sides claim as a victory."

"Yes," said Adam meekly.

At this moment a small car passed, going north. It passed the van and drew up and a lady got out. Adam went forward to meet her, taking off his hat as he went—she was that kind of lady, quite young and extremely pretty and clad in a brown tweed coat and a scarlet beret. She had dark curls and brown eyes and a pale, rather delicate complexion.

"Can you tell me if this is the way to Perth?" she inquired, smiling at Adam in a friendly way.

"Yes," said Adam. "I'm a stranger here, but we're making for Perth so I know it's all right. Difficult without signposts, isn't it?"

"Very difficult," she replied. "I've been this way before, several times, so it's rather silly of me to be uncertain. It's pretty country, isn't it?"

"That's Sheriffmuir," said Adam.

She seemed interested so he told her what he knew about the battle and explained that he had just been informed of the facts by a descendant of one of the combatants. The girl laughed—she had a merry laugh—and Adam laughed too.

By this time the men had finished their beer and were ready to start so Adam was forced to cut short his conversation. He returned to the van and climbed in.

"We'll go right through Perth," said Ford. "We'll have our dinners north of Pitlochry."

"Could we not stop at Pairth for our dinners?" asked Berwick in dismay.

"No, we've got our dinners with us—it will save time," replied Ford. "And push on a bit faster, Berwick, you're not making the most of your speed."

"It's better to go steady——" Berwick began.

"You're dawdling," interrupted Ford. "You're having to change down on every gradient—get a move on, man."

Berwick was annoyed. He let in his clutch with a jerk and they moved off. He said: "We always stop at Pairth. It would be a sight more comfortable to have our dinners at the Inn. There's a good Inn. It's run by a cousin of mine."

"Is it?" said Adam.

"Aye—could you not suggest it to Mr. Ford?"

"No, I couldn't," replied Adam, smiling. "I'm only a passenger on this trip."

45

The mist had disappeared and the sun was shining, but the wind was extremely cold and Adam was glad of the leather waistcoat which he was wearing. He was surprised to see that the country was not mountainous and rugged; it was rolling country with enormous fields and good solid farmhouses in sheltered nooks.

"Where are we now?" asked Adam after some time.

"Getting near Pairth," replied Berwick. "Strikes me we'll have to stop here after all. The engine's not pulling too well."

Adam had noticed that the van seemed to be labouring on the hills. He said: "Well, if we have to stop we'll have to—that's all." He had hardly spoken when the engine gave a stutter and a gasp and stopped . . . Berwick said nothing. He put on the brakes, got out and raised the bonnet.

"What's happened?" inquired Ford, coming round to the front.

"Seems to be engine trouble," replied Adam.

Ford turned and spoke to Berwick. His remarks were blistering— most of them were new to Adam.

"We're not far off Pairth," said Berwick sullenly. "It's as well this didn't happen at Dalwhinnie or some such place."

"It shouldn't have happened at all," declared Ford, poking his head under the tilted bonnet.

There was silence for a few moments and then Ford applied himself to the cranking handle and the engine started humming very pleasantly . . . but Ford did not seem pleased. He and Berwick stood in the road talking in undertones; they were both frowning.

"Well, I can't help it," said Berwick in sullen tones. "I overhauled it yesterday and it was O.K. We'll just need to stop in Pairth and have it seen to."

After some consultation Ford decided to stop. He explained to Adam that they might get through to Lurg without any further trouble, but he thought it wiser to be on the safe side.

"I'd rather stop here at a garage I know than maybe have to stop farther north at a garage I don't know," said Ford anxiously.

Adam agreed with him.

Perth was reached without any difficulty, the van turned into a side street and drew up at a garage and by this time Ford seemed to have recovered his equilibrium.

"Away you go, Mr. Southey," he said. "Take a look around—it's a nice place, Pairth, awful clean and neat. If you're back in an hour we'll be ready to take the road."

Dow had already wandered away—the repairs were not in his line—and Adam took off his Burberry and put it in the van (the revolver that Mr. Brownlee had given him was in the pocket, but he would not need it here). Then he followed Dow down the street. He had decided to have a look round first and then find somewhere to have a meal . . . it was pleasant to stretch one's legs after the long run.

The shops were very attractive, Adam found. He was especially interested in a "Man's Shop" which had a fine display of tartan rugs in one window and cardigans and pullovers in another. There was a very nice brown pullover—dark brown with a polo collar—which looked comfortable and cosy but as he had not got his ration card in his pocket he could not buy it. There ought to be gloves here, thought Adam, remembering the Fair Maid of Perth, but so far he had not seen any unusual display of gloves.

Adam was turning away from the window when he caught sight of Dow coming back down the street at a tremendous pace, and Dow looked so strange, so wild-eyed and disordered, that for a moment he wondered if the man had been drinking . . . but there hasn't been *time*, thought Adam in bewilderment. He pursued Dow and caught his arm and at this Dow gave a yelp of dismay.

"Dow, what on earth is the matter?" asked Adam.

"Maister Southey, what a fright ye gave me!" exclaimed Dow. "I thocht it wus *him*."

"Who——"

"I've seen him. He's here in Pairth—I'm thinking he's after me——"

"Who?" repeated Adam, shaking Dow's arm.

"Maister Black," said Dow, looking back over his shoulder as if it were the devil he expected to see.

"Black? Who's Black?"

"Yon feller—the feller that wantit the key off me. There was a wee feller with him, too."

"Where?" demanded Adam. "Where did you see him?"

47

Dow was in such a state of fright that it took some moments to persuade him to retrace his steps to the place where he had seen the man. They walked back along the street and round the corner and were just in time to see two men disappearing into a small commercial hotel.

"That's him," said Dow. "That's Black—the big feller in the grey suit; I'd ken him anywhere on airth. What are you going to do, Maister Southey?"

His last words fell on empty air for already Adam was hastening after the two men.

Chapter Seven

When Adam reached the entrance of the hotel the two men had vanished; he hesitated in the small dark hall and wondered where they had gone . . . and then he heard voices coming from the direction of the staircase so he went up the stairs. There was a landing on the first floor and a long dark passage with doors on either side so he went along the passage very quietly, listening at each door. When he came to the third door he paused, for he heard the sound of movement inside . . . it was the sound of a drawer being opened and a window being shut.

Adam knelt down on the mat and put his ear to the keyhole; he could not help smiling as he did so for he had often read of people listening at keyholes and sometimes he had wondered whether a keyhole was any use or whether it was just a "wheeze" invented by the authors of thrillers to enable their characters to be overheard. He soon discovered that a keyhole was an excellent listening post. . . . He could hear every word that was said.

". . . is this the map you were telling me about?"

"Yes, I have the place marked," said a second voice with a curious guttural accent. "Killicrankie it is called. De road is narrow dere—trees on both sides."

"That ought to be easy to block."

"Dere are only tree men and four with de van."

"Your three men are armed, and they'll have the advantage of surprise."

"I do not like it—no."

"What's the use of saying that now when the whole thing is arranged?"

"I said it all de time. I said it would be better farder north, but I was told no, it is to be here."

"Yes, because if it fails we can have another try farther north—that's the reason."

"If it fails we haf warned dem. It will not be so easy again."

"Well, it mustn't fail, that's all; it shouldn't fail if you've done your job properly."

There was an exclamation of disgust and the second voice broke into a torrent of German . . . and this did not surprise Adam unduly for he had been certain of the man's nationality from the beginning. It did not trouble Adam either . . . he could understand every word.

"*Ach, ich kann es nicht tragen* . . . I cannot stand it. It is not fair to me. If the ambush is not successful I shall be blamed, yet how can I ensure that the road shall be empty of traffic at the right moment. If there is a car or a lorry passing at the same time as the van, the whole plan falls through. I have watched the road for hours, counting the vehicles, and have come to the conclusion that the ambush has an even chance of succeeding and no more. I do not like these chances. I like to see the way clear and to prepare thoroughly for every eventuality. My plan was better yet nobody would listen."

"I'm listening—or trying to," said the first man in English. "If you wouldn't jabber so fast I could follow it easier. What was your plan, Stein?"

"I think we should hire a car and follow the van. Then we could choose our own time to attack—when there was no other vehicle in sight; then we should have our own men all together and not spread out in different places. We have too few men."

"Why shouldn't we combine the two plans? Leave the first plan as it is and hire the car as well. If the first plan succeeds, well and good; if not we can pick up your three fellows and go on."

"That sounds a good idea——"

"It will have to be a large car."

"I have the right vehicle in mind. It is a baker's van. The baker would lend it to me, but we should have to pay a good deal of money for it."

"Pay him what he asks. It will be worth it. A baker's van will do splendidly."

"We shall have to be quick about it."

"I know that as well as you do."

Adam only just had time to rise from his knees and turn away when the door swung open and the two men came out.

"Here, you!" cried the big man, seizing Adam by the arm. "What are you doing here, eh?"

"What the devil has that got to do with you!" exclaimed Adam, throwing off the man's grip and turning away. He looked over his shoulder as he walked towards the stairs and added: "Have you bought the hotel, or what?"

For a moment Adam thought that his ruse had succeeded. (He wanted to run for it but realised that this might be a fatal mistake.) But the next moment the men were after him and had seized him firmly by his arms.

"Look here!" cried Adam. "What's this all about? I suppose it's your idea of a joke; it isn't mine."

The big man hesitated, but the smaller man gripped Adam more tightly. "It is one of dem," he said in a low voice. "I am sure of dat. He was listening outside de door."

"One of who?" asked Adam crossly. "It strikes me you're rather a suspicious character yourself——"

"I am Norwegian," said the German quickly.

"Well, I don't know what you're getting at," Adam said. "I've been up to my room to fetch my hat and now I'm going out. I have an appointment at one o'clock, if that's of any interest to you."

"It is a lie!" cried the German. "He is not a guest in dis hotel. I haf been staying here tree days and I haf not seen him."

"You see?" said the other man. "My friend says you aren't staying here, so you've no right to be prowling about the passage."

Adam was getting desperate now for the time was passing and Ford would be wondering why he did not return. He *must* get back and warn Ford; they would have to get police protection for the van before proceeding farther. All this passed through Adam's mind in a flash and he decided to take a chance. He bent forwards suddenly and then threw himself back and, shaking off the grip on his arms, made a dash for the stairs. Black was taken by surprise but the German was on his guard, he put out his foot and tripped Adam . . . and Adam, trying to recover his balance, stepped on a mat which slid across the polished floor . . . He staggered and fell with a sickening thud, bumping his head against the rail of the banisters.

The blow dazed Adam though it did not actually stun him. He

felt the two men lift him and carry him back to the bedroom and hoist him on to the bed. His head was aching horribly and buzzing like a beehive and he felt sick and faint with the pain. Far in the distance—or so it seemed—he could hear the two men discussing the situation.

"He's heavier than he looks! He's not dead, is he?"

"*Nein, er ist betaubt*——"

"Speak English for heaven's sake—someone might hear you."

"He is stunned—dat's all. He has a big lump on de back of de head."

"He hasn't a gun. He's probably a perfectly innocent commercial traveller. It would have been better to let him go."

"He is one of dem, I tell you. He was listening at de door."

"What the blazes are we to do with him?"

"Could we not take him wid us?"

"How could we?"

"I could get the baker's van and bring it to the door——"

"Wouldn't it be better to leave him here on the bed?"

"He would be found and dere would be trouble. Questions would be asked. Dis is my room; it would mean trouble for me."

"Put him into someone else's room."

"*Nein—nein*. The devil was listening. He knows too much. We must take him wid us and leave him in some lonely spot where he will not be found . . . We must make sure dat he cannot interfere wid our plans."

Adam's head was aching so badly that he could scarcely understand what he heard. He lay quite still with his eyes shut. All he wanted was to be left to lie there in peace, but after he had lain there for some time he was dragged out of bed and taken downstairs, his two jailers supporting him, one on either side. He had recovered a little by now and had begun to think of escape. Surely there would be somebody about, either in the hall or in the street, who would help him.

There was a man in the hall, a fat man with an apron round his middle, and as Adam was dragged past he made an effort to enlist the man's aid.

"Help!" cried Adam. "They're taking me away——" His words sounded strangely blurred to his own ears.

"Aye, he's properly sozzled," said the man with a laugh. "He'll have a sair heid the morn, I'm thinking."

The baker's van was large and new and well sprung so it was not uncomfortable. Adam had been shoved in at the back and lay on the floor with a folded sack under his head. The pain in his head had lessened and his thoughts were clearing . . . he felt quite desperate. Would Dow tell Ford what had happened? If so Ford would probably push on quickly . . . he was sure Ford would push on . . they would run straight into the ambush . . . three armed men and the road blocked! Hell, why hadn't he been quicker. Why hadn't he got away before the men came out?

It was no use thinking of that. He must think what to do; he was in a serious mess. The conversation that he had overheard sounded pretty ominous; they intended to dump him in some quiet spot where he would not be found and Adam was certain that the man "Stein" intended to make sure that he would not be found alive . . . They were desperate men.

Adam sat up and looked around. His head swam, but he was beginning to feel more like himself. He found a lump on the back of his head—it was the size of a large marble—but his skull was hard and he was as tough as leather . . . Lucky that he had good bone, thought Adam, feeling the lump somewhat ruefully. It was lucky, too, that his jailers had not thought it necessary to tie him up; they were in a hurry and had shoved him into the back of the van and shut the doors—but Adam discovered that there was a handle inside the doors, so he could open them quite easily.

The van was buzzing along pretty fast, but when it slowed down he could open the doors and jump out. They would choose an empty solitary stretch of road to stop and get rid of him and Adam realised that he would have to be pretty nippy if he were to make good his escape. He did not feel particularly nippy at the moment. Perhaps he should jump for it while the van was still in motion; he might hurt himself but he would have to take the risk.

Adam was still considering the matter when the van slowed down and stopped . . . He opened the door and leapt out into the road and was just about to make a dash for the woods when he realised that the road was not an empty, solitary stretch of road—as he had expected—but on the contrary was crowded with people and cars. There were three private cars drawn up in a line and a grocer's van and a large army lorry, and the people to whom these vehicles belonged were standing about in groups and talking excitedly. Adam walked across and attached himself to an elderly major who looked large and solid and exceedingly safe, and as he did so he saw his two jailers leap down off the front of the van into the road. They stood and stared at Adam in amazement, but they were powerless to take any action to prevent his escape.

"Can you tell me what's happened, sir?" said Adam to his quite unconscious protector.

"There, you can see for yourself," replied the major. He pointed ahead and Adam saw that a tree had fallen across the road blocking it completely.

"Good heavens!" exclaimed Adam, looking at the tree in dismay.

"Most extraordinary thing," said the major. "Nobody seems to know anything about it. I was just in time to see the crash. There was a van in front of me—a big brown van; it had a devilish narrow squeak."

"Really?"

"Never saw a nearer thing," said the major, nodding. "The van was going like hell and I suppose it couldn't draw up in time. Some of these heavy vans are badly underbraked."

"Are they cutting down trees here?"

"I suppose they must be—though as a matter of fact I use this road a lot and I've never seen any lumber work going on. In any case it's sheer damned carelessness to let a tree fall across the road. I've sent my driver to find out how it happened; he ought to be back any minute."

Adam had been thinking. He said: "Is this place called Killi—something?"

"Killiecrankie—yes," replied the major. "It's a pretty place, isn't it? Have you been here before?"

"No, never, sir."

"There was a battle here—the Battle of Killicrankie."

"Scotland seems full of battlegrounds!" exclaimed Adam in surprise.

The major smiled. "Yes, I suppose there has been a good deal of fighting in Scotland, but Killicrankie is especially interesting for it was here in this Pass that a small force of Highlanders under Claverhouse beat an army of twice their numbers. The redcoats were taken by surprise and the Highlanders rolled rocks down the hills on to them; it was a great victory but Claverhouse was killed . . ."

"I thought Claverhouse was a sort of devil incarnate," declared a young woman who had been listening with interest to the tale.

"So his enemies said," replied the major. "His enemies called him 'Bloody Clavers' and his friends called him 'Bonnie Dundee'."

"And which do you call him?" the girl asked with a mischievous smile.

The major smiled back and replied: "I'm a loyal subject of His Majesty King George the Sixth."

It was obvious that this was no answer, and Adam was about to inquire further into the matter, but at this moment the major's driver returned and, saluting, tendered the information that he had searched industriously, but could find nobody in the woods.

"What d'you mean—nobody?" asked the major. "D'you mean the tree fell of its own accord?"

"No, sir, it's been sawed."

"Who sawed it, then?"

"I dunno, sir. There's nobody there now."

"What an astounding thing!"

"Per'aps the chaps who sawed it got a fright when they saw it fall across the road and made off, sir," suggested the driver.

"It looks uncommonly like it," the major said. "You had better turn the car if you can. We shall have to go back to Pitlochry and send some fellows to clear up the mess."

By this time a bus had appeared and about fifteen more people were standing about in the narrow road. Some of the cars had started to back—it was a scene of chaos and confusion. Adam looked round for his erstwhile jailers and found that they had disappeared into thin air. He was not surprised. For a moment he hesitated, wondering whether it was his duty to tell the major what had happened, but he decided that it would take too long. His story was so fantastic that it might not be believed and the major might insist on taking him back to Pitlochry to explain things to the proper authorities. Adam's first duty was to catch up with the van; the van had got through all right—that was one comfort.

Chapter Eight

The van had got through and was on its way north and Adam had made up his mind to follow it as quickly as possible. He walked up the road and climbed over the fallen tree and found, as he had expected, that there were several cars held up on the other side of the block—southbound cars. One of these, a small post-office telephone van, was already manoeuvring backwards and forwards across the narrow road trying to turn. Adam asked the driver if he would give him a lift and the driver agreed.

"I'm away back to Kingussie," he said, "but I'll need to stop at Blair Atholl on the way and tell them to clear the road. Hop in."

Adam hopped in.

"There'll be trouble about this," declared the man. "It's a miracle there wasn't a bad accident. A big van passed me on the hill; it must have just got through before the crash." He was signalling to another car as he spoke, signalling to it to slow down. "Look at that," he added. "That car was going sixty at least—there may be a bad smash yet unless somebody has the sense to stand at the corner and warn people . . ." He was silent for a moment and then added in a thoughtful voice: "It's the sort of thing the Gairmans might do —blocking the only road to the north."

"It was done by German agents," said Adam.

"How d'you know that?"

"I heard someone say it," replied Adam cautiously.

"Is that so?" exclaimed the man. "I'll tell the police at Blair Atholl; they ought to search the woods."

Adam agreed. It could do no harm for the police to search the woods—though he was extremely doubtful if it could do much good. By this time Black and Stein and their three armed men might be many miles away.

"This is Blair!" said Adam's companion in a proud and satisfied sort of tone. "It's a nice wee place, isn't it?"

It certainly was a very pretty place, sheltered and peaceful, with hills all round and a crystal clear stream running through the meadows.

"It's my home," said the man. "That's my cottage with the sweet peas in the garden. I'll just stop a moment and tell the wife—maybe you would like a cup of tea."

Adam was anxious to get on, but he was extremely hungry and a trifle lightheaded as well. He reflected that a cup of tea might make all the difference to his feelings—it was poor policy to go on until he dropped—so after a moment's hesitation he accepted the offer and followed his new friend up the path.

The door opened before they reached it and a nice-looking young woman looked out.

"This is Mistress Fraser," said her husband proudly. "Jean, I've brought this gentleman in for a cup of tea."

"My name is Southey," said Adam, smiling and holding out his hand.

It was taken in a firm clasp. "Pleased, I'm sure," said the woman. "Come away in and take a seat. The kettle's on the hob and it'll not be long—you're back sooner than I expected, Donald."

"There's a tree down in the Pass," said Donald Fraser. "I'll need to go round to the Police Station about it but there's no need to wait on me—you and Mr. Southey can begin."

Adam was glad to go in and sit down in the beautifully clean little kitchen; the grate was shining and the tall dresser was decked with a fine array of snow-white china. There were chintz curtains in the windows and chintz covers on the chairs; it was obvious that Mrs. Fraser was an admirable housewife.

"Are you feeling well enough?" asked Mrs. Fraser, looking at her guest somewhat anxiously.

"Not awfully well," replied Adam, trying to smile. "The fact is I had a fall and bumped my head, but I shall feel better when I've had some tea—it's nothing to worry about."

"You sit still, then," said Mrs. Fraser, placing a cushion behind his head. "I'll have a cup of tea ready in a minute."

She bustled about and soon she had set the table and made the tea; it was a good substantial meal with scones and butter and jam and the tea was hot and brown and stronger than any tea that Adam had tasted. Adam—as he had predicted—began to feel quite different and was able to take an intelligent interest in the conversation.

"Some folks might find it dull," said Mrs. Fraser in answer to Adam's question. "But there's always plenty to do in the house and sometimes we have a dance or a whist drive or maybe a bazaar. There's been a circus here the last two days; it's a great treat for the bairns."

"A circus!" echoed Adam in surprise.

"Not a very big one," said Mrs. Fraser, smiling. "It comes here every year—it tours about from one place to another; it's away north to Kingussie or Newtonmore to-day. Maybe you wouldn't think much of it," she added apologetically.

"I like a circus," Adam said.

"I liked it fine, myself," said Mrs. Fraser, nodding. "Donald and me took the bairns yesterday afternoon—it was a real good show, we thought. There's an elephant and two lions and a conjuror and a lady with performing dogs . . . and there's side-shows as well. Coconut shies and such like. Donald got two coconuts and he was real pleased about it."

She talked on in a friendly manner while they had tea and Adam had a feeling that, in spite of her assertion that she did not find the country dull, she was quite pleased to have someone new to speak to.

Donald Fraser came in a few minutes later; he winked at Adam and said he had arranged matters and Adam took this to mean that he had passed on the information which Adam had given him and that the police were taking action.

"We'll need to hurry," added Fraser. "I've got to get to Kingussie—so if you've finished your tea . . ."

Adam rose at once for he was quite as anxious as Fraser to waste no time, and soon they were back in the post office telephone van and on their way north.

"You didn't mention the Gairman agents to the wife, I take it?" inquired Fraser. "Aye, I'm glad of that for she gets ideas into her head . . . and even the best of women are apt to talk a wee bit wildly. Are you wanting to come all the way to Kingussie or what?"

"I'm trying to catch up with a van," replied Adam. "It's a big brown van—I think it's probably the van you saw at Killiecrankie Pass. The driver is a pal of mine and promised to give me a lift, but I was delayed at Perth and he started without me."

"Is that so? We'll catch it easy, for it's a heavy van and the hill's pretty steep. It's uphill all the way to Dalnaspidal—more or less."

Fraser was a good driver and he was pushing along pretty fast when suddenly they rounded a bend and came upon a small cart drawn by a white pony.

"Gosh, if I hadn't forgotten the circus!" Fraser exclaimed. "That's the beginning of it and I wish it was the end."

Adam echoed the wish. He looked ahead and saw the circus straggling up the hill. There was a man leading an elephant and a bunch of very pretty piebald ponies and, beyond that, several gaily-coloured vans. It took a little while to pass the circus, but the post office van was small and nippy and Fraser seized every opportunity he could find. Some of the vans were quite small and were drawn by horses, others were larger, petrol-driven vehicles, and there were two very large vans which were being towed by a steam tractor. Adam waved to some of the people who were looking out of the windows of the vans and they all waved back and smiled at him cheerfully.

"That's the last of them," said Fraser. "We got through pretty quick really. It's lucky for you, in a way, because I don't mind betting that the van you're after took double the time."

They were still climbing and it was getting a good deal colder. The scenery was becoming wilder and more rugged . . . there were mountains and moors and small silver burns which swept down the hillside and dived beneath the road. This was the sort of scenery that Adam had expected to see in Scotland and he was suitably impressed.

"It's a wild place!"

"Dalnaspidal," said Fraser. "Aye, it's a wild spot. You should see it in winter when there's snow on the ground—I've seen drifts thirty foot deep and more . . . Hallo, would that be the van you're looking for?"

"Yes," cried Adam. "Yes, by Jove—there it is, safe and sound!"

It was drawn up at the side of the road on a flat piece of ground and beside it stood Ford with a cup in one hand and a slice of bread in the other. His short stocky figure was the most welcome sight on earth to Adam's eyes. An angel form could not have been more delightful.

Fraser swept past the van and drew up and Adam got out.

"Thank you very much indeed for all your kindness," said Adam, offering him a ten shilling note.

Fraser looked at it and drew back. "No, no, I don't want money for giving a man a lift," he declared, and so saying he let in the clutch and drove off.

That was a mistake, thought Adam, looking after the little car regretfully. The man had been so friendly and pleasant and now he was hurt. It was a bad mistake and he had made it from lack of understanding . . . These Scots, thought Adam with a rueful smile. I must be more careful in future. He was still standing there when he heard a shout and saw Ford coming towards him.

"In the name of fortune!" exclaimed Ford. "Where have you dropped from, Mr. Southey? My, but I'm glad to see you."

"And I'm glad to see *you*," replied Adam fervently. "I got held up pretty badly—in more ways than one—and I was very worried about you . . ."

"It's a wonder we're here!"

"I know that. The tree was intended for you, but apparently you just scraped through."

"Scraped is the word," declared Ford. "It's a funny thing, Mr. Southey, but I had a feeling that events were conspiring to delay the van. Berwick was driving too slow and there was that breakdown at Pairth; I never got to the bottom of it properly. Then you disappeared and Berwick was all for waiting . . . I waited a wee while for you, but by that time I was beginning to get very suspicious of Berwick and the more he said wait, the more I felt we should push on. You may think it was just that I was thrawn but it was a sort of feeling I had."

"A presentiment," Adam suggested.

"Maybe," agreed Ford doubtfully. "I'd think it was more a kind of mind reading. Anyway there it was and that was the reason I left you in the lurch and pushed on as fast as I could."

There was a lot more to be explained, but this was not the time for explanations. "We ought to get on," said Adam. "There's no time to be lost. There are five men on our tracks. They've had one try to stop the van and they'll have another."

"We'll be all right, now," replied Ford confidently. "We know what we're up against and there's two of us. I don't trust either of the men a yard . . ."

Berwick and Dow were sitting in the back of the van having their meal; they were very much surprised to see Adam, and Adam had a strong feeling that they were not much pleased.

"Come on now," said Ford. "You've been long enough over your meal. If we don't get a move on we'll be overtaken by the circus and I'm not wanting the trouble of passing it all over again. You might sit at the back with Berwick, Mr. Southey, and I'll take Dow in front."

Adam climbed in. He found his Burberry (with the revolver safely in the pocket) and put it on.

It was quite comfortable at the back of the van for there was a pile of sacking to sit on. The big doors of the van were clipped back and there was a three-foot board across the opening. Adam hooked his elbow over the board and leaned against the side of the van with his legs stretched out in front of him . . . yes, it was very comfortable indeed. Looking back he saw the road coming out from beneath the van like the ribbon in a tape machine and streaming away in the distance . . . it was rather fascinating to watch but he found if he looked at it too long it made him dizzy.

Berwick was in a sulky mood. He sat there glowering and biting the stem of his pipe and when he was spoken to he answered in monosyllables. Adam left him severely alone and after some little time he suddenly burst out into a spate of words.

"Am I the driver of this van or not?" growled Berwick in a deep voice which seemed to emanate from his boots. "Is this my van that I've driven for three years or isn't it? What right has Ford got to oust me and drive himsel'—that's what I'd like to know. He's been driving since we left Pairth . . . you could have knocked me down with a feather . . . 'I'll drive,' says Mr. Ford. 'I'm wanting to reach

62

Lurg before Christmas. You can get in at the back with Dow.' I was that taken aback and affronted that I could scarcely speak."

He stopped and looked at Adam, and Adam gave a sort of grunt for it was difficult to know what to say.

"Ford may be an engineer," continued Berwick, "but he's no driver—my hairt's been in my mouth half a dozen times and that's the sober truth. He's been pushing the van as if she was a racing motor—and then he complains that she's not pulling well. Who'll be to blame if he rattles the engine to bits? Tell me that. It'll be me that's to blame, *me* . . . and it'll be me that has to overhaul the engine when we get to Lurg."

"A tree fell in the Pass, didn't it?" asked Adam, trying to change the subject.

"It missed us by an inch," declared Berwick. "It isn't Ford's fault that we're alive. He misjudged the distance badly. There was ample time to stop, but he wasn't going to stop—not him. He was in a rage, that's the whole explanation of it . . . so instead of stopping, what does Ford do but tread on the gas . . . I thought we were done for. The branches scraped the top of the van and that's the truth— you can ask Dow if you want."

Adam was silent and presently Berwick added: "I'll not stand for it. I'll speak to Maister Brownlee himsel'."

"Yes, I should," said Adam. He was so pleased to think that he was back in the van and that they were on their way north—with all their troubles behind them—that even Berwick's grumblings and mumblings could not disturb his content. They were on their way to Lurg and Evelyn would be there. He was thinking of Evelyn and there was a gentle smile on his lips when suddenly he heard a curious scraping bumping noise and the van came to a halt.

"That's the big end gone," declared Berwick triumphantly. "I knew that would happen sooner or later."

Chapter Nine

It was nine o'clock and very dark, for a thick black cloud had obscured the rising moon. Adam came out of the little inn—where he had been fortunate enough to obtain a room for the night—and looked up and down the village street. It was very quiet and peaceful and the air smelt sweet with the scent of flowers—night-scented stock which was growing in the cottage gardens. So much had happened that Adam could hardly believe it was only sixteen hours since he had left Mr. Brownlee's comfortable house in Edinburgh and started off for the works; sixteen hours—it seemed more like sixteen days. Adam was tired and his head was still aching—though not very badly—and he intended to turn in early for a good night's sleep, but first he would walk along to the garage where the van was housed and have a talk with Ford.

Ford was in the garage, sitting on the step of the van smoking his pipe. He looked somewhat dejected, but he smiled at Adam in a friendly manner as Adam came in.

"Did you get on to Mr. Brownlee?" he asked.

"No, there's a block on the line. I couldn't get through."

"We'll need to wait till the morning, then," said Ford. "It's the big end, so there's nothing to be done but wait here till they send another van." He sighed and added: "It's the delay that matters and I'm feeling it's maybe my own fault for pushing her along too fast. I'm feeling pretty sick about it, and that's the truth."

Adam sympathised with Ford. He was feeling none too happy himself. It was ignominious—to say the least of it—to have to sit down and wait to be fetched. He felt that he had failed in the task which Mr. Brownlee had entrusted to him. He said this to Ford.

"You couldn't help it," said Ford reasonably. "It was me that was driving the van."

"It was because I was a fool and got held up by those men that you had to hurry."

"Partly," agreed Ford. "But it's no use crying over spilt milk."

"What about hiring a van here?" Adam inquired.

"Aye, I thought of that. Wylie has a van—that's the chap that owns the garage—but it's a lightly built vehicle, so it would be no use. We'll not get a van that'll take this stuff, Mr. Southey."

"Bad luck!" said Adam.

"Aye, the luck's been against us," agreed Ford. He sighed again and added: "You go off to your bed. You're looking like deith and it'll do us no good if you crack up. I'm sleeping in the van for I'll feel safer; I'm taking no chances."

Adam left him and went out into the street. It had been quiet before, but now it was full of movement for the circus was arriving in the village and half the population seemed to have turned out to welcome it. The street was thronged with people and a host of small boys had appeared; they were running along beside the vans waving and shouting. Adam was bitten with the general excitement and he, too, followed the vans and saw them lurching in at a gate and taking up their allotted positions in the field where they were camping. He watched the scene with interest and as he watched he began to have the glimmerings of an idea. At first this idea seemed fantastic, but it grew upon him and took shape.

There was a man standing near the entrance to the field directing operations—a short fat man with a very red face and a voice of stentorian proportions—and it was obvious from his manner and from the manner in which his directions were obeyed that this was the boss.

In about twenty minutes the last van had rolled in through the gate and the man was about to walk away when Adam accosted him.

"Are you the—er—manager?" asked Adam.

"We've got permission," said the man quickly.

"Yes, of course," agreed Adam. "I just wondered if you were on for a deal—if you would be interested in—er—ten pounds, for instance."

"Ten quid! What for?" asked the man suspiciously.

"It's rather a long story."

"Oh, it is—is it?"

"I could explain it better if you could come along to the hotel and have a drink."

"Now you're talking," declared the man in a more friendly tone. "You'll have to wait for me, though. I've got one or two things to see to—five minutes you must give me."

"That's all right. I'll wait."

"Patch is the name. Not Hengler nor Barnum but just plain Patch."

"Mine is Adam," Adam said.

The five minutes which Mr. Patch had demanded were more like twenty and Adam got tired of hanging about in the cold and went to look for him . . . It was nearly an hour before he managed to recapture Mr. Patch and conduct him to the small inn where he had taken a room for the night.

"We shan't get drink here," said Mr. Patch in disgust.

"I've got a flask," replied Adam. "If you don't mind coming up to my room . . ."

Mr. Patch did not mind at all, and presently they were sitting in Adam's bedroom drinking whisky and discussing the proposed deal.

"It's a rum go, that's all I've got to say," declared Mr. Patch. He had had several whiskies by this time and his big round face was red and glossy. "It's a rum go, but if you'll swear it ain't a police matter——"

"I do swear it," declared Adam.

"I don't want to get into trouble with the police . . . a man in my position 'as got to be careful."

"You won't get into trouble, Mr. Patch. It's perfectly fair and square."

"Is it for a bet?"

"Not exactly. There's valuable furniture in the van and I happen to know that several people would like to get their hands on it. We've got to get it safely to Inverness."

"I'm going to Nairn," said Patch.

"Nairn will do," replied Adam.

Patch laughed. "It's a funny ideer. Strikes me you're a bit of a card, Mr. Adams."

"You'll do it?" asked Adam, pouring the last of the whisky into Mr. Patch's glass.

"I don't mind . . . fifteen quid is fifteen quid these days."

"I thought I said ten!"

"Come now, you said yourself it was valooble stuff. Fifteen quid won't break you."

"I don't see what you're doing for it——" began Adam, trying to hide a smile.

"I'm doing a lot," retorted Patch. "I'm giving you a tow, I'm giving you a stand in my field . . . and I'll give you the paint into the bargain. There now, what d'you say?"

"Done," said Adam.

"Good," said Patch. He held out his hand and Adam shook it solemnly.

"I'll tell you what I'll do," added Patch as he rose to go. "I'll send a man with the paint to-morrow morning. I'll send Lovell . . . he'll give you a hand . . . Funny thing, you can't beat a gipsy when it comes to painting vans."

In spite of his excitement over his brilliant plan, Adam slept soundly and awoke at seven o'clock the next morning feeling like the proverbial giant. He dressed quickly and hastened along to the garage before breakfast to see Ford and tell him of the new arrangements, for there were various details which must be settled, and he could brook no delay. He was so in love with his plan and so delighted with himself for thinking of it that it was irritating to find Ford in a carping mood.

"I'm not saying it isn't an *idea*," declared Ford, who looked somewhat tousled and unkempt after his night in the van. "I'm not saying it mightn't be a good plan to get a tow to Nairn, but where's the sense of painting the van to look like a—like a raree-show?"

"But that *is* the whole idea," replied Adam impatiently. "The van must be disguised to look like part of the circus."

"What's Mr. Brownlee going to say if we arrive at Lurg looking like Barnum's menagerie?"

"What will he say if we don't arrive at all?" demanded Adam.

"The men'll not stand for it, Mr. Southey."

"We must get rid of the men. We'll send them on by train. . . . No, by Jove, hold on a minute. We'll hire that light van and send them on by road."

"And why will we do that?" asked Ford wearily.

"Listen to me," said Adam. "You're the boss of this outfit—I own that. Very well, then, let's hear your plans and I'll fall in with them."

Ford scratched his head and then his dour face broke into an unwilling smile. "You've got me there," he said. "I've been thinking most of the night and I can see no other way but to stay here until they send and fetch us."

"That's what you want to do?"

"No," said Ford quickly. "It's not what I'm wanting at all. It means we're beat."

"Of course it does," said Adam. "Well, which is it to be? You can't have it both ways, you know. Are you on for my plan or not?"

Ford shuddered. He said persuasively: "Could you not think of some other way?"

"No, I couldn't. It must be all or nothing. It would be far too great a risk to go with Patch unless we paint the van. Those men will stick at nothing to get hold of the stuff."

"We'll just need to do it, then," said Ford in a grudging tone. "But what Mr. Brownlee will say when he sees his van . . ."

Adam smiled. "I'll fix it," he said. "I'll make all the arrangements and take all the responsibility—but you'll have to play up like anything. It will be your job to hire the other van and fill it with scrap and send it north with Dow and Berwick while I get on with the painting."

"So that's the idea!" exclaimed Ford, looking at his new boss with dawning respect.

"That's it," agreed Adam, rubbing his hands. "Hire the van and fill it with scrap—there's a heap of scrap metal behind the garage— tell the men you're sending them on with the most important parts of the machinery and that you and I are remaining here with the rest of the stuff——"

"I doubt they'd believe me," objected Ford.

"They've got to believe you—and why shouldn't they? You think they won't believe you because you know you don't trust them, but *they* aren't to know that."

"It's true enough," agreed Ford when he had thought out this somewhat complicated statement.

Berwick and Dow did not put in an appearance until nearly ten o'clock and by this time the hired van was standing ready loaded in the yard outside the garage.

"This is a nice time to come in!" exclaimed Ford, trying to make his voice sound suitably annoyed but not succeeding very well.

Fortunately Berwick was too full of his own grievances to notice the tone of Mr. Ford's voice. "What was the use of coming in airly?" inquired Berwick with an insolent air. "There's nothing to be done till we get a new big end from the works. I'm not responsible for the breakdown—that's one thing certain. It's a wonder to me there's anything left of the engine at all."

"I'll trouble you to hold your tongue," replied Ford, who no longer needed to feign a wrath he did not feel. "That's quite enough from you. If I choose to drive the van, I'll take the responsibility. I'll be responsible to Mr. Brownlee and nobody else . . . and since you're so anxious to drive you'd better get a move on," added Ford, waving his hand in the direction of the hired van.

"That van——" began Berwick in surprised tones.

"Aye, that van," repeated Ford. "We've hired it and moved the most important parts of the machine. You're aware that Mr. Brownlee wanted the stuff rushed through in a hurry."

"You've moved the stuff!"

"Some of it," replied Ford. "We've been up all night, Mr. Southey and me, while you've been snoring in your beds. Away with you and don't dawdle on the road. You should be at Lurg before nightfall."

"But, Maister Ford, are you not coming?" inquired Dow in a bleating tone.

"I'm away to my bed," replied Ford, yawning. "It's about time you did some of the work. Warm up your engine, Berwick, and see that your radiator's full. Hurry up, man."

Berwick obeyed quite meekly and a few minutes later the van

moved out of the yard. It had no sooner gone than a tall dark gipsy appeared with a handbarrow full of paint pots and a pair of steps balanced on the top.

Adam had always liked paint; he had dabbled in it from his earliest youth, and now at last he was about to have an absolute orgy of paint. He went forward to greet the gipsy rapturously.

Chapter Ten

When the circus had been in the village for two days it packed up and continued on its way north and the village turned out *en masse* to see it go. Some of the villagers noticed that there was an extra van in the procession—the steam tractor was pulling three vans now—and this extra van was very large and gaily painted in red and blue with the intriguing inscription

THE DISAPPEARING LADY

in large letters on its sides.

The girls and boys felt very much annoyed to think that they had missed seeing what was obviously the best show in the circus and one boy—more daring than the rest—ran along beside the van and called out in his shrill treble:

"Whaur's the lady? I never saw the lady at the circus."

"She had disappeared, of course," replied a man, with a very brown face and a red handkerchief tied round his neck, who was sitting on the front seat of the van.

"Smart, aren't you, Mr. Southey!" exclaimed his companion in a grumpy tone.

"Adams to you," said the first man, smiling and showing a set of very white teeth which looked all the whiter in contrast with his unusually tanned skin. "Just plain Adams without any frills. I think I shall call you 'Jim,' it seems to suit you, somehow."

"You can call me what you like. If I've to sit here all the way to Nairn, you'll not find me a very good companion. Yon lions smell —stink would be nearer the truth; I'm wishing we'd taken a place in front of them."

"We needn't sit here," Adam (or Adams) replied. "We can sit in the back of the van or get out and walk if we feel like it."

"We could walk a deal faster," declared Ford (or Jim).

This was not true, of course, for once clear of the village the

71

tractor gathered speed and rolled along at quite a respectable pace, and the country through which they were passing was so beautiful and the scenery so variegated that Adam did not feel their progress was too slow.

So far none of the circus people had spoken to Adam; they looked at him askance as if he were a new boy at school, and they seemed to take no interest at all in the van. (Adam felt that they were inimical and did not like it.) He pointed this out to Ford, and Ford snorted and replied that he wanted no truck with circus trash.

While they were rolling along Adam took out a sheet of paper and began to compose a letter to Dr. Cooke. He had been too busy painting the van to think of doing this before, but now that he thought of it he realised that it was a necessary task.

Dear Dr. Cooke,

We have had some unpleasant adventures but no harm has been done and the stuff is perfectly safe. Ford and I are bringing it north slowly. We were obliged to arrange for the van to be towed. We are both very sorry there has been this delay but it was unavoidable. Perhaps Mr. Brownlee will be good enough to meet us at Nairn and arrange for the van to be towed to Lurg.

When he had got thus far Adam showed the letter to Ford, who put on his spectacles and read it carefully.

"Uhha," said Ford. "It can do no harm, that's one thing."

"I thought it would relieve their minds. I thought they might get a shock when the men arrived with the light van and they started to unpack it."

"Will the men arrive?" said Ford.

"You've been thinking that, too!" exclaimed Adam. "I've been worrying about them a good deal. I never thought of the danger until they had gone and then it was too late."

"They'll be O.K.," said Ford unsympathetically.

Adam took up his unfinished letter and continued:

We sent Berwick and Dow ahead with a light van full of scrap. It occurred to us that this might divert attention from ourselves. If the men have not arrived it might be as well to make inquiries and call in the police.

"Uhha," said Ford. "That's neatly put. It's clear and all in a few words. That's what comes of being a schoolmaster, Mr. Southey."

"I'm a gipsy," replied Adam. "My name is Adams—and don't you forget it."

"There's no need for all this play-acting when we're by ourselves," objected Ford.

"You will call me Adams all the time," said Adam firmly. "I like being Adams, the gipsy, and it's good practice for you, Ford."

"I thought my name was Jim," said Ford with perfect gravity.

Adam laughed. "That's one up to you," he admitted. "Come on, Jim, I must get this letter finished. Is there anything else I ought to say?"

"You better say where to meet Mr. Brownlee at Nairn—there's nothing else as far as I can see. Tell him you'll meet him at the County Hotel," added Ford. "That's where he always stays."

"I can't go to the County Hotel looking like this!" exclaimed Adam in horror-stricken tones.

Ford was obliged to smile. He said dryly: "There's nothing to prevent you calling at the back door and asking to speak to Mr. Brownlee."

Soon after Adam had finished his letter he began to feel hungry but nothing could be done about it for they had brought no food in the van. Adam had thought that they would proceed at a walking pace and that he would be able to buy what they needed on the way, but now he saw his mistake. There were very few villages on the road and the tractor was pulling them along about ten to twelve miles an hour . . . if he left the van to buy food he might have difficulty in catching up with it.

At midday they stopped on the road, but it was an open road with nothing in sight but moors and trees and far-off mountains so there was no chance of getting a meal. Adam and Ford sat at the back of the van and smoked to still the pangs of hunger. There was coming and going between the other vans and a great deal of talk and laughter, but The Disappearing Lady was left severely alone.

"Rabbit stew," said Ford, sniffing the air. "Greedy pigs, that's what they are."

"I thought you didn't want any truck with circus trash," retorted Adam crossly. "Anyhow it isn't their fault—it's mine for being such an idiot. We ought to have brought food with us."

Ford said nothing.

Presently Mr. Patch came along and asked if everything was all right and Adam replied in the affirmative for he did not intend to betray his lack of foresight to Mr. Patch.

"You look a proper gipsy," declared Mr. Patch, with a glance at Adam's brown face and red handkerchief. "I suppose you got Lovell to paint you as well as the van."

Adam laughed somewhat feebly and replied that he liked to dress the part.

"We'll be at Grantown to-night," added Patch. "Come and 'ave a bite of supper with me, Adams. I'll expect you after the show."

He walked on without waiting for an answer and Adam realised that it was less an invitation than a royal command.

"I suppose we'll get a meal in Grantown," said Ford with a sigh.

The circus arrived at Grantown about four o'clock and by this time Adam and Ford were starving. They had tossed a coin to decide who should feed first and the lot fell to Adam so he dropped off the van as they rolled through the town and found a teashop where they gave him a very good meal. He hurried over it, for he did not want to keep Ford waiting. As he walked across the field where the circus was camping he noticed that The Disappearing Lady had been placed quite near the entrance—why on earth had Patch put them there? The answer to this question was obvious of course. Patch was a good showman and The Disappearing Lady was the most attractive-looking van in the show; it was large and newly painted and the inscription was intriguing, so Patch had put it in his window. Adam felt annoyed. If he had been on the spot when the circus arrived he would have seen to it that they got a less conspicuous position; it was too late to do anything now. He released Ford to go and have a meal and sat on the steps of the van smoking and watching all that was going on. Everyone was busy. The show people were unpacking and talking, running hither and thither and hammering industriously. Adam was a sociable person and would have liked to speak to them; he would have been glad to lend a hand in setting up the stalls, but not a creature came near him—or even looked his way. There was something odd about it.

Presently Ford returned looking a good deal more cheerful and the two of them sat and smoked and talked in a desultory fashion. They had not much to say to each other, Adam found, for although Ford was quite friendly and pleasant his interests were different from Adam's and despite Adam's efforts to make contact he would not come out of his shell. The gates had opened by this time and people were streaming in. Most of them made a beeline for The Disappearing Lady and were disappointed on being informed that they could not see the show . . . Adam got so tired of repeating the same thing over and over again that he and Ford got inside the van and shut the doors. It was dark inside the van and cold and stuffy and it smelt of oil . . . Adam reflected that they would have to sleep in the van and did not view the prospect with enthusiasm. At last it was time for Adam to go to supper with Mr. Patch; he tidied himself as best he could and sallied forth. He was walking across the field, winding his way between the stalls, when a curious incident occurred. Adam was stepping over a rope which lay on the ground when the rope was suddenly pulled taut, and Adam, who was not expecting it, took a header over the rope and fell full length on the field.

The grass was soft and he did not hurt himself, but he was exceedingly angry and he rose and dusted himself and looked round to see who had accomplished his downfall. Two women with babies in their arms were standing outside the door of a van; they were laughing heartily, and the coconut-shy man, whose stall was adjacent, was smiling in a nasty way.

"Who did that?" asked Adam, scowling and doubling his fist. "Who tripped me up with that rope? I suppose it's someone who hasn't the guts to show himself and take what's coming to him."

Round from the back of the van strolled a man with the end of the rope in his hand. He stood and looked at Adam without speaking and Adam looked at him. He was well over six feet tall and broad in proportion, his arms were long and his hands enormous.

The women were laughing more heartily than ever now and the coconut-shy man was leaning against his stall and shaking like a jelly.

"Oh," said Adam uncertainly. "It was you, was it?"

"Ar," replied the man in a gentle voice. "Hast any complaints, laad?"

"Er—no," said Adam. "I mean of course it was an accident, tripping me up."

"Naa," said the man, shaking his head slowly. "Naa, thaat wasn't no accident. Did tha waant a fight, laad?"

For a moment Adam hesitated and then he smiled and shook his head—the whole thing was so ridiculous. "I shouldn't think many people want to fight you," he said.

"Naa, laad," said the big man turning away.

He looked enormous as he turned away. He looked like a giant and suddenly Adam changed his mind. "Here, I'll fight you," he cried. "Come on if you want a fight—take off your coat." But the man was walking away and did not turn round, and when Adam shouted at him he paid no attention.

"You can spare yer breath," said the coconut-shy man. "'E won't fight. 'E's allus arskin' fellers ter fight, but 'e ain't keen on it, not really. Soft, that's wot 'e is, just a bit soft. I'll fight yer if yer loike. I was 'oldin' the other end of the blinkin' rope."

"I don't want to fight anyone," replied Adam. "There's no sense in it. I suppose it was your idea of a joke, tripping me up."

The man did not answer, but one of the women called out: "You ain't wanted 'ere, mister, that's what."

"Why?" asked Adam. "Why aren't we wanted? We haven't done anyone any harm."

"We don't want the likes of you," said the other woman in a sulky voice. "Comin' 'ere and gettin' round Patch—takin' the best pitch. We got an illusionist 'ere already and Patch 'asn't any right to fix up with someone else . . . Disappearing Lady, indeed!" added the woman scornfully.

"We aren't showing," said Adam when he could get a word in edgeways.

"Not showing!" exclaimed the woman in surprise.

"No," said Adam. "We aren't going to join the circus; we're travelling with you as far as Nairn, that's all."

He walked on and left them, but he could hear the buzz of talk which followed his statement and he realised suddenly why The Disappearing Lady had been sent to Coventry—he might have thought of it before. These people led a precarious existence, their vans were shabby and their shows were second-rate, and The Disappearing Lady with her new coat of paint was a positive menace to the community. Adam was glad to find a solid reason for the scowls and slights which had been his portion. He hoped that the news he had given the woman would go round the camp and that things would be more comfortable in future.

Chapter Eleven

Mr. Patch's caravan was at the other end of the field next to the roundabouts. It was a large green van decorated with yellow scrolls. As Adam approached, he saw his host waiting for him so he hastened his steps.

"There you are, Adams!" exclaimed Patch. "Come in and shut the door and I'll put on the light. This black-out gets my goat."

"It must be very inconvenient for you," said Adam.

Patch laughed mirthlessly. "Inconvenient!" he said. "I'm losing 'undreds over it—'specially on the side shows. Who wants to walk 'round side shows in the daytime? There's no glamour about it, no romance. It's when the darkness falls and the stalls are lighted that you get romance and glamour, and it's then," added Patch nodding seriously, "it's then that the boodle begins to roll in."

He seemed depressed, but his nature was volatile and once they had shut the door and put on the light he began to cheer up. He was very proud of his caravan and pleased to display its conveniences and luxuries to his guest, and his guest responded suitably and admired everything he saw.

The caravan was divided in half by a thick curtain; the inner half was Mr. Patch's bedroom and the outer half his living-room. Everything moveable was clipped into position so that there was no rattling when the van was in motion. There were cupboards on the walls and pictures of high-stepping horses and of performing dogs. The seats were of the "tip-up" variety and were upholstered in red plush.

"It's cosy," declared Mr. Patch. "It's nice and bright too, isn't it? I run the electric light off the roundabout engine and the cooking and 'eating is all electric—no messing about with paraffin for me."

"Delightful," declared Adam who had almost exhausted his vocabulary and could find no more terms of approval and admiration. "Most attractive. It must be tremendous fun living in a caravan."

78

"I wouldn't call it fun, exactly," replied Mr. Patch. "It's my 'ome, you see. It's the only 'ome I've got—and the only 'ome I want for that matter. I wouldn't exchange it for a palace," said Mr. Patch, nodding his head at his guest. "No, I wouldn't, really. Some people might find it a bit cramped, but I was brought up to this sort of life —born and bred to it."

"Were you, really?"

"Born and bred in a caravan," nodded Patch, "and of course in those days it wasn't as comfortable as this. My mother was a fortune-teller—an artist at the job, she was—and my father 'ad a troupe of performing dogs. I've gone a bit farther down the same road. Yes, I wish they could see me to-day."

Adam agreed that Mr. Patch's parents would be very proud if they knew to what heights their son had risen. He had begun to like Patch a good deal better for there was something pleasantly ingenuous in the man. His frank delight in his position and possessions was rather an engaging trait.

"Do you live here by yourself?" Adam inquired,

"I'm not married," replied Patch, twisting the question to suit his own convenience. "I *was* married once, but it wasn't much of a success. She was a poor thing. If you ever feel like getting married choose a woman of spirit—that's my advice. You may 'ave trouble with 'er sometimes, but you'll 'ave more fun."

Adam laughed and promised to remember the advice.

"But it's better to be free," continued Patch thoughtfully. "And there's plenty of women that'll come in and do a bit of cooking and cleaning up. I like to 'ave everything just so. I like to know just where to lay my 'and on everything."

Sitting at his dining-room table, which was about three feet by two, Mr. Patch demonstrated to his guest the convenience of his arrangements. Without moving from his seat he could reach the electric stove where the food was keeping hot, he could reach the cupboard where his china and glass were stored—each plate and cup and glass held in place by a little clip to prevent it from rattling —and by stooping and stretching to one side he could reach the zinc-lined "cellar" where he kept his drink.

"Admirable," declared Adam, who had suddenly remembered this useful adjective.

"We'll 'ave supper now," said Mr. Patch. "I 'ope you're 'ungry because I am. I do myself pretty well, reely."

Adam was not surprised to hear it for Mr. Patch looked like a man who enjoyed his food. He assured his host that he was very hungry indeed and proceeded to demonstrate the truth of this assertion. They had duck in a casserole and green peas and fried potatoes and for a pudding course there was a suet dumpling with golden syrup, and for drink there was beer. Rather an odd mixture, thought Adam, but he was far too hungry to cavil at that.

"You've got enemies, Adams," said Mr. Patch suddenly.

"I know. I told you that, didn't I?"

"A tallish chap in a grey suit and a little fellow that talks bad English—is that them?"

"Yes."

"Yes," repeated Patch, nodding his head. "Yes, they come up and spoke to me in Grantown this afternoon . . . wanted to know if I'd 'appened to see a big brown van on the road."

Adam looked at him.

"Oh, I didn't tell them nothing," said Patch. "I said I 'adn't seen a big brown van on the road—and neither I 'ad. I said I'd arsk some of my people if they'd 'appened to see the van and I'd let them know about it if they came 'ere to-night."

"That was good of you, Mr. Patch."

"It was only fair," replied Patch. "I wanted to see what you'd say before I told them anything."

Adam had not expected Black and Stein would turn up again so soon, for he had hoped they would follow the other van as far as Inverness—if not farther. It was difficult to know what to say to Patch.

"It's like this," declared Patch. "It's a bit of a problem. You say one thing and they say another, so 'ow am I to know which of you to believe?"

"What did they say?"

"They said the brown van 'ad been stolen, that's what they said."

"And you believed them?"

"Not altogether," replied Patch, "but then I didn't believe you either if you want the truth. Your story was a bit thin, Mr. Adams."

Adam had been aware of this from the beginning. His only excuse was that he had not had time to think of a better one.

"I don't want any more lies," declared Patch quite amiably. "You needn't set your brains to work on another story. I didn't believe all that about the valooble furniture. I took it on as a business deal—fifteen quid is fifteen quid—but I'm beginning to wish I 'adn't taken it on. I'm a peaceable man and I don't want no trouble."

"You aren't going to let me down, Mr. Patch?"

"I like you, Adams," Patch replied, "but there it is—I've got to think of myself."

"What do you propose to do?" asked Adam after a moment's thought.

"Why not 'ave a showdown—you and them?"

"What sort of a showdown?"

"Meet them 'ere," said Patch. "'Ave it out with them. There's two of them and two of you—what say?"

Adam hesitated. His inclination was to say yes, but there was the safety of the van to be considered.

"You don't like the ideer," said Patch in disappointed tones.

"I do," replied Adam quickly. "But I'm not my own master. I've got to get the van safely to Nairn. Nothing else matters."

"What's your ideer, then?"

"I believe we ought to get the police."

"No," cried Patch, bringing down his hand on the table with a thump. "No, I'll not 'ave the police brought into it. I know what the police are when they start nosing round. You swore it wasn't a police matter or I wouldn't never 'ave agreed to the bargain."

There was a short silence. Patch's round red face wore an anxious expression and there was a frown between his eyes.

"All right," said Adam at last.

"'Tisn't all right. I'm a peaceable man and 'ere I am up to the neck in trouble. 'Ow am I to know it isn't true that you made off with the van?"

"I wouldn't want the police brought into it if I had."

"Well, that's true," said Patch grudgingly. "That's true enough, but what am I to say to those men? 'Ow am I to get rid of them? Why can't you see them yourself and keep me out of it altogether? They're coming 'ere to-night . . . They'll be 'ere in a few minutes. Why not see them yourself and 'ave a showdown and put all the cards on the table."

Adam was smiling now for Patch's words had given him an idea. He leant forward and said: "I'll tell you how to get rid of them, Mr. Patch. Just you listen to me."

Adam was lying on Mr. Patch's bed. He noticed that the mattress was buoyant and extremely comfortable. He noticed also that there was a tiny hole in the curtain in a most convenient place so that anyone lying on Mr. Patch's bed could see into the outer portion of the caravan without lifting his head from the pillow. In this, as in other matters, Mr. Patch's aim had been to spare himself unnecessary trouble. Through this peephole Adam could see Mr. Patch sitting at his table. The white cloth had been removed and a green baize cover had been substituted, and Mr. Patch was busy dealing out a pack of somewhat dirty cards.

"Do you mind my using your peephole?" asked Adam in a low voice.

"Oh, you've found it, 'ave you?" said Mr. Patch, without looking up. "Don't put your eye too close and don't move the curtain."

"And don't cough and don't sneeze," added Adam. "And if you go to sleep don't snore."

"You seem in good form."

"Yes, I'm going to enjoy this," declared Adam.

"Don't laugh either," replied Patch, gathering up the cards with one sweep of his hand and beginning to lay them out in a different formation.

"That's nice," Adam declared. "I like to see you doing it."

"I'm out of practice," complained Patch. "I wish my old mother was 'ere. I've forgotten most of the patter——" He stopped suddenly, raised his head and listened, and a moment later there was a knock on the door.

The two men came into the caravan and sat down. Black was full of self-confidence, but Stein seemed a trifle uncomfortable and was careful to choose a seat next to the door.

"Now then, you'll 'ave a glass of beer," said Patch in a friendly tone. "'Ere's three glasses and 'ere's the beer. Now we're all set for a nice chat and you can tell me all about it."

"I thought you were going to tell us," said Black. "I've told you already about the van. It's a big brown van and it was stolen out of a garage in Perth. There's a lame fellow, a fellow with dark hair and light grey eyes—goes along like a crab—that's the man who stole it. We want to lay our hands on him."

"I see," said Patch.

"He's the one we want," continued Black. "He's a bad lot, that fellow . . . and of course we want to get the van back too. We've reason to believe the van came north and we thought you might have seen it on the road."

"I told you I 'adn't seen it," replied Patch.

"Yes, but you said you'd make inquiries . . ." Black began and then he paused for Patch had begun to lay out the cards on the table.

"Yes," said Patch. "We talked about it this afternoon. I've made a few inquiries, but I 'aven't much to tell you and I don't know why I *should* tell you for that matter. It's a good plan to keep your mouth shut sometimes, then you don't get into trouble . . . Of course I could 'ave a look at your cards," added Patch in a casual tone. "That wouldn't be telling you anything . . ."

Adam moved slightly so that he could see Black's face. He saw its expression change from blank amazement to comprehension. He saw Black wink at his companion.

"Good idea," said Black. "I'll have my fortune told. There's sure to be something in it about a big brown van."

Patch swept up the cards. "You shuffle the pack," he said. "You think of what you want to know while you're shuffling . . . give them a good shuffle, that's right. Now then, we'll see what the cards 'ave to say about it." He took the cards and began to lay them out, talking all the time. He was perfectly serious about it and if Adam had not happened to know that the whole thing was a fake he would have sworn that Patch believed every word he was saying.

"First we look into the past," said Patch, gravely. "'Ere's the square, you see . . . and we get the two black jacks together with the two o' clubs between them. That's a funny thing, that is. That means there's some funny business going on. They're 'atching a plot, I shouldn't wonder . . . and 'ere's the jack o' diamonds. Now what's 'e doing? Well I never, 'e's listening in . . . listening in through the key'ole!"

"Look here, I don't know what you're playing at——" began Black, but Patch silenced him with a wave of the hand.

"'Ush," said Patch. "No talking if *you* please . . . We lays out another square inside the first one . . . there. Now 'ere we 'ave a journey. The five o' diamonds means a journey by road . . . all three jacks go off together in a van. It's a baker's van, though; that ain't the van you're after——"

"Now, look here," said Black. "Look here, what are you up to——"

"Let's see what 'appens next," said Patch, laying out another deck of cards. "This is getting int'resting, this is. Oh, 'ere's an odd thing! 'Ere we 'ave three more men and the six o' spades beside them. That's a saw, so they're woodmen and they're cutting down a tree . . . funny business this is! Looks like a road block to me. You don't 'appen to know anything about a road block, I s'pose?"

"I'm afraid we ought to be going," said Black. His face had gone a curious mottled colour beneath the bright light.

"But we 'aven't come to the van!" cried Patch. "I'm only just starting. Look 'ere, I'm putting out your future now. 'Ere's the jack o' spades, that's you, Mr. Black. We put you in the middle of the circle. 'Eaven's, 'ere's trouble!" exclaimed Patch. "'Eavens, I wouldn't be in your shoes for a good deal!"

"We must go," declared Black, rising.

"Sit down," said Patch. "Sit down and finish your beer—and you too, Mr. Stein."

"Feiborg is my name. I am Norwegian," said Stein quickly.

"Norwegian!" cried Patch, laying down the cards. "Now isn't that lucky! We've got a Norwegian lady 'ere—she's the wife of the lion tamer. I'll send for 'im to come along and bring 'er with 'im. She's a peach . . ."

"Please do not trouble. We must go . . ."

84

"No trouble at all. I'll send for them both to come. 'E's a moody sort of chap—a bit violent sometimes, a bit of a temper if you know what I mean—but you'd get on with Ingeborg like a 'ouse on fire."

"Do not trouble her——" began Stein, laying his hand on the door.

"Nonsense, she'd like it. She gets a bit down'earted sometimes. It would do 'er a power of good to 'ave a chat with one of 'er own people."

"I do not have time," declared Stein, opening the door.

"Yes, we mustn't stay," agreed Black. "The hotel shuts at half past eleven so unless we get back pretty quick we may find ourselves locked out."

"Did you say 'locked up'?" asked Patch significantly.

The departure of Mr. Patch's guests was more in the nature of a rout than of an orderly retreat, and when Adam emerged from the inner compartment he found Mr. Patch sitting on the steps of the caravan laughing uproariously.

"You got rid of them all right," Adam said.

"Yes," said Patch, mopping his eyes with a large yellow handkerchief covered with blue horseshoes. "Yes, I got rid of them. It was a mighty poor show, but I was out of practice. 'Aven't done anything of that nature for donkey's years."

"It was good enough for them."

"I don't know what it was all about," said Patch, blowing his nose like a trumpet. "I just said what you told me to say."

"If you want to know——"

"Better not," interrupted Patch. "I'm a peaceable man and I don't want to get mixed up in trouble. I'd just as soon not know what all that nonsense meant—'atching plots and bakers' vans and woodmen cutting down trees and what not; it sounded double Dutch to me."

"They understood."

"Gave them the jimjams," agreed Patch. "Oh well, I'm glad you're satisfied."

"I'm not satisfied," replied Adam seriously. "I should have liked to lay them both by the heels—especially Black. I shan't be satisfied till I've got Black where I want him."

"Black's got 'is knife into you, all right."

"Yes, but that isn't the reason," replied Adam. "They're both dangerous, they're both vile, but Black is an Englishman which makes it——"

"Stop," cried Patch. "You'll be telling me the 'ole story in a minute and I don't want to 'ear it."

Chapter Twelve

Mr. Brownlee was sitting in the lounge of the County Hotel drinking a glass of sherry. He was restless and out of humour for his plans had all gone wrong. Mr. Handicote had come to Lurg and had seen the demonstration of the new gadget—the improvement on the retractable undercarriage—and he had not thought much of it. Then he had asked about the searchlight and had been annoyed on being told that it was not ready. He had seen the blueprints, of course, and had spoken to Dr. Cooke, but it was obvious that he was not impressed. "I shall have to come north again—that's all," he said. "I shall bring Professor Fullerton. He knows all about radioactivity." Dr. Cooke had remarked in his mild voice: "He must be a wonderful man." That was one up to Sam, anyway.

Mr. Brownlee thought of this incident as he drank his sherry. He took Adam Southey's letter out of his pocket and read it again. The letter had been read and reread a good many times but neither he nor Sam Cooke had been able to make much of it. They had tried to read between the lines . . . What on earth had happened? What had delayed the van? What were Ford and Southey playing at? If Mr. Brownlee had not trusted Ford as he trusted himself, he would have put the police in possession of the facts and told them to trace the van, but Ford was absolutely reliable and, according to Sam, Southey was absolutely reliable . . . two reliable men . . . The other two men, Dow and Berwick, were anything but reliable. Dow had arrived at Lurg himself—full of the most hair-raising stories—but of Berwick and the light van, which Southey had mentioned in his letter, there was no trace at all.

Mr. Brownlee grunted and looked at his watch. The whole thing was intensely irritating and now, to crown all, that young Southey was late for his appointment. Mr. Brownlee was frowning so savagely that the good-looking waitress paused uncertainly before she dared to speak to him.

"What is it?" asked Mr. Brownlee who had become aware of the hovering figure. "What do you want, eh?"

"It's someone wanting to speak to you, sir."

"Bring him in—bring him in."

"It's a man," said the girl doubtfully.

"It'll be Mr. Southey—I'm expecting him."

"No, sir. It's just a man. He's waiting at the back door. He asked me to give you this." She held out a dirty piece of paper—a leaf torn from a notebook and folded several times.

Mr. Brownlee took it and unfolded it. There was only one word written on it: *Southey*.

"I'd better see the fellow," said Mr. Brownlee, rising from his chair and finishing his sherry at a gulp. "Lead on, Macduff. Where do you keep your back door, eh?"

They went down a flight of stone stairs and along a stone-flagged passage and presently arrived at the back door which opened into a yard. A man was waiting there, leaning against the lintel, a well-built man with a brown face and a red cotton handkerchief tied in a knot under his chin.

"Well, my man——" began Mr. Brownlee . . . and then he stopped and gazed at the man in surprise.

The man laughed. He said: "I wondered if you would recognise me, sir. Ford and I had a bet on it. The van is here quite safely."

"Where?"

"In a field at the other end of the town. Perhaps you'd like to come and see it yourself."

"There's nothing I'd like better," Mr. Brownlee declared.

Adam suggested that Mr. Brownlee should follow him to the field, walking some paces behind, but Mr. Brownlee had no qualms about being seen in strange company. He did what he liked and if anyone objected to his actions it mattered nothing to him—besides he was extremely anxious to hear what had been happening and Adam had his work cut out explaining everything and answering a fire of questions. By the time they reached the field, Mr. Brownlee was in possession of the salient points of the story and was chuckling delightedly over the idea of "Sam's Searchlight" parading over Scotland disguised as a circus van.

They turned in at the gate, wended their way between the Fortune-teller and the Shooting Gallery, and presently came to The Disappearing Lady, and when Mr. Brownlee's eyes lighted upon it he stood back stock-still and rocked with laughter.

"Oh, Adam," he cried. "What a prodigy! You'll be the death of me before you've done. Man, it's a work of art; we'll need to put it in a museum. 'The Disappearing Lady'—what in the name of fortune made you think of that?"

"It just came to me," said Adam modestly.

"It was an inspiration," declared Mr. Brownlee.

Ford was much relieved to find that Mr. Brownlee approved of what they had done for he had been wondering somewhat anxiously how the boss would take it. He came out of the van where he had been having a cup of tea and they all three sat on the step and talked.

"Your letter saved my life," said Mr. Brownlee. "It saved my life and Sam Cooke's reason, but you might have given us a little more information while you were about it. The light van never arrived at Lurg——"

"Never arrived!" cried Adam in alarm.

"Never arrived," repeated Mr. Brownlee. "Dow arrived by himself in the bus. He had a mighty queer tale to tell. You know the first part of it, of course, so I needn't repeat that, but I can tell you that when I heard about the tree and about the transfer of the machinery to another van I felt like tearing my hair out by the roots. Dow's tale was that he and Berwick got to Inverness without any untoward adventures; they left the van in a garage and went off to have a drink. Somehow or other Dow lost sight of Berwick—missed him in the crowd—and instead of going straight back to the garage what does the fool do but wander about the street looking for Berwick."

"He's a mutt!" exclaimed Ford.

"Just about it," agreed Mr. Brownlee. "No gumption, that's what's the matter with Dow. Eventually, when he did think of going back to the garage he found that the van had gone, and the mechanic said that Berwick had come back and driven it away. Dow was a bit annoyed at that, he caught the next bus and came on to Lurg expecting to find that Berwick had arrived before him."

"Dirty work," said Ford.

"I don't think there's any harm in Dow," said Adam thoughtfully. "He isn't very bright, of course."

"Berwick and the van have disappeared," continued Mr. Brownlee. "The police have been searching everywhere for the last two days."

"Where can he have gone?" exclaimed Adam.

Mr. Brownlee nodded. "That's the question," he said. "I'm wondering what's become of the wretched man."

"He's in the racket," said Ford confidently.

"But even so," Mr. Brownlee pointed out. "Even supposing he *is* in the racket, his pals won't be too pleased when he turns up with a vanload of scrap." He hesitated and then added: "Those men— Black and Stein and the others—we'll need to put the police on their tracks. I must see about that at once. You'll need to give a description of them to the police, Adam. You said they were at Grantown two days ago; I wonder where they've got to now."

Adam was wondering the same thing. He said: "If only Patch hadn't been so afraid of trouble we might have bagged them easily. . . . You won't get Patch into trouble, will you, sir?"

It was a few minutes short of eight o'clock when Adam walked into the County Hotel—by the front entrance. He had been invited to dinner by Mr. Brownlee and although he had explained that he had not any decent clothes and that he felt exactly like a tinker—having lived the life of a tinker for the last four days—Mr. Brownlee would take no refusal. "Evelyn's with me," Mr. Brownlee had said. "She'll want to hear the whole thing and I'll never be able to satisfy her. You can wash your face and put on a collar and we'll expect you at eight o'clock."

Adam had tidied himself as best he could. He had scrubbed his face and hands with a nail-brush and had brushed his hair assiduously, but in spite of all his efforts his skin was still uncommonly tanned and his hair would not lie down and the clean collar, which he had in his suitcase, felt much too tight for his neck.

How very odd it seemed to be sitting at a table with a snow-white cloth upon it, and shining silver and glass! What a strange contrast to his last meal which had been fish and chips in a paper bag! He looked at Evelyn across the table and smiled at her—and Evelyn smiled back.

"Go on," said Evelyn. "Tell me more. What happened after you had painted the van. It must have been fun painting the van, wasn't it?"

"Tremendous fun," replied Adam in fervent tones.

"I wish I'd been there to help."

"I wish you had. Poor Ford watched us until he could bear it no longer and then he groaned and went away."

"Go on," said Evelyn delightedly.

How pretty she is! thought Adam as he went on with his story. He felt large and clumsy and awkward beside her daintiness. His clothes were shabby—their texture and fit had not been improved by his recent activities—his shirt was dirty and one of his cuffs was frayed.

"Mr. Southey is coming to Lurg with us, isn't he, Daddy?" inquired Evelyn.

"That was my idea," replied Mr. Brownlee. "I've brought half a dozen stout fellows and a tractor to take the van to Lurg so there's no need for Adam to worry about that. Adam has done his bit."

"I'm so glad," said Evelyn. "I want to show you Lurg, and it's such a lovely drive. The view as you come over the hill and look down the valley towards the sea is simply marvellous."

"That's Evelyn's special view," declared her father laughing. "I'm just warning you, my boy. If you don't admire it properly, you'll go down with a thud in Evelyn's estimation."

"We drive right across Scotland from east to west," said Evelyn. "It's a perfect drive . . . I do hope we'll have a fine day for it."

"You'll stay on with us for a bit," Mr. Brownlee said. It was his usual method of tendering an invitation—more like a royal command than the invitation of an ordinary person. "You'll stay on and have a holiday. You certainly deserve one."

"I'd like to stay and see the demonstration of the ray," Adam replied. He realised as the words left his lips that they sounded awkward and ungracious, and was annoyed with himself for his stupidity.

Evelyn's eyes were twinkling. "Of course," she said. "The ray is a very potent attraction . . . you'll have to try and bear Lurg for the sake of the ray . . ."

She continued to tease him, but she teased him kindly and Adam found that he did not mind. Like many serious-minded people, he enjoyed being with people who were naturally merry.

Soon Adam discovered to his surprise that Evelyn had followed her father's lead and was calling him "Adam," so he summoned up all his courage and began to call her "Evelyn"—and Mr. Brownlee seemed quite pleased and was exceedingly friendly and kind. When the evening was over—and it was over far too quickly—he came to the door of the hotel with Adam and handed him a wad of notes.

"Pay Patch," said Mr. Brownlee. "It's better that the money should come from you."

"But this is far too much," declared Adam in amazement. "I told you, sir. It was fifteen pounds——"

"The rest is for you," replied Mr. Brownlee, smiling. "Nonsense, Adam, of course you must take it—fair wear and tear in the service of the firm."

The road went forward over the moors—up hill and down dale. The sun was shining brightly in a cloudless blue sky and there was a crisp dry feeling in the air. It was the sort of day that should have sent Adam's spirits soaring with the larks, but his spirits were clouded by a deep depression. He had been mad last night but to-day he was sane, and he saw quite clearly that there could never be anything except ordinary friendship between himself and Evelyn. Last night he had let himself go; he had been excited at the success of his mission and by the kindness shown him by his host . . . last night he had dared to dream that Evelyn's gay friendliness was the beginning of something more . . .

Adam had never wanted marriage. He had always been scornful of young men who rushed into matrimony without counting the cost (how much better it was to be free, Adam had thought) but

Evelyn had made him change his mind and he had begun to think that marriage might be very pleasant indeed. He was not in love with Evelyn of course, but it would be easy to allow himself to fall in love with her. What madness to think of it! He was lame and awkward, with no money and no prospects. Mr. Brownlee's smiles would change very soon into frowns if he suspected that the lame schoolmaster had designs upon his daughter.

The car swept on. It was a five-year-old Rolls, exceedingly comfortable and powerful. Adam had never been in such a comfortable car before. The low hum of the engine and the rush of the wind gave one the feeling of flight . . . Adam sat in his corner and listened to Evelyn's gay chatter and his heart was like lead.

"Isn't it lovely?" Evelyn was saying. "Look at that line of hills against the blue, blue sky!"

"Marvellous," Adam agreed, feigning an enthusiasm he did not feel . . . There are occasions when the most magnificent scenery fails to produce the correct reaction in the human breast.

They lunched at a large hotel which stood back from the road, surrounded by trees, and, if anything was needed to depress Adam's spirits further, the reception of his companions by the landlord would have accomplished it. Mr. Brownlee often stopped here on his way to and from Lurg and he was well known for his genial personality and for the generosity of his tips. Only the best table in the dining-room was considered good enough for his party . . . the cook would produce a special pudding . . . the head waiter some special brandy. All this Mr. Brownlee accepted in a perfectly friendly, natural manner. He accepted it as his due; and it *was* his due—for he was an important man, bighearted and full of drive, bursting with vitality.

Lunch was over and the waiter was bringing in the coffee when Adam heard a noise in the road, and glancing out of the window he saw a gaily painted van lumber into sight. It was towed by a tractor and was accompanied by two men riding motor bicycles. He smiled when he saw it—and this was his first real smile to-day though his face felt quite stiff with false ones.

Mr. Brownlee saw it too. He waved his table napkin and laughed heartily.

93

"The Disappearing Lady!" said the waiter, gazing out of the window as if he could not believe his eyes. "That's a funny thing. It's the first time I've seen a circus come this way."

"Perhaps you'll go and see it," suggested Mr. Brownlee with a wink at Adam.

"I wouldn't mind," replied the waiter. "Disappearing Lady sounds pretty good. I wouldn't mind having a sixpence-worth if she camps anywhere near."

"She'll have disappeared before you get there," declared Mr. Brownlee, and he laughed louder than before.

The waiter looked puzzled but, as he was hoping for a fat tip, he joined in the laughter as heartily as he could.

"Adam is pleased to see his old friend," said Mr. Brownlee when the waiter had gone.

"I'm very jealous of her," Evelyn declared.

"You haven't a hope," Mr. Brownlee said. "You haven't a dog's chance. Adam has been thinking of The Disappearing Lady the whole morning. That's true, Adam, isn't it?"

"Only partly," Adam replied in a somewhat embarrassed manner. "You see—you see she's been on my mind for so long, night and day; it's very nice to know she's on the last lap of her journey."

"We'll follow her," said Mr. Brownlee, rising. "We'll keep behind her and see her safely in. Adam shall have the felicity of escorting The Disappearing Lady to Lurg."

Part Two

Chapter One

The car drew up at the top of the hill and Evelyn jumped out. Adam followed her to a big rock and they stood and looked down the valley.

"There's Lurg," said Evelyn, clasping her hands together. "I do love it so! It is a lovely view, isn't it?"

"Perfectly beautiful," said Adam.

The valley was narrow here and a small burn ran along the bottom of it between giant boulders, but soon the valley widened, the mountains drew back farther and farther, and the burn became a small river which wound its way in silvery curves to the far-off sea. There was heather, not yet purple, on the slopes of the mountains, and in some places there was pale green bracken or patches of dark green conifers. Here and there was a farm, or croft, surrounded by small fields. In the middle of the valley lay Lurg House, a square grey-stone building with trees and gardens round it. The road wound down the valley, taking the easiest way, and about a half a mile ahead Adam caught a glimpse of scarlet and blue and yellow—The Disappearing Lady was nearing her journey's end.

"That's Lurg," repeated Evelyn. "The works are beyond those trees; you can't see them from here. They're camouflaged of course, but you can see the smoke rising above the woods. I was frightfully upset when Daddy decided to make workshops here. I thought it would spoil the place, but it hasn't, really."

"Is that an airfield?" asked Adam, pointing to a green patch of meadow near the house.

"No, the airfield is beyond the hill. It's a saucer-shaped depression in the moors. That's where all the experiments are carried out."

It seemed that Miss Evelyn Brownlee knew a good deal about the secret activities of Lurg.

"I suppose there's fishing," said Adam thoughtfully. "That river looks as if it might be pretty good."

"It's very good indeed," nodded Evelyn. "That's the Tinal River.

Daddy used to fish all day when we came here for his holidays; he never has time to fish now."

"We must make time," declared Mr. Brownlee, who had followed them to the rock. "If you're a fisherman, Adam, you'll find plenty to amuse you at Lurg. I tell you what we'll do, we'll ask Mr. Taylor's permission to fish his stretch of the Tinal—it's the best stretch of river in the strath."

"There's Mr. Taylor's place," said Evelyn. "Right away down the valley on the edge of the sea. Two squat grey towers—can you see them, Adam?"

They were looking due west and the sun was setting so it was not easy to see, but Adam shaded his eyes with his hand and far away in the distance he saw the squat grey towers of Tinal Castle.

"We'll ask Taylor," repeated Mr. Brownlee. "He'll give us permission I'm certain . . . and maybe we'll have a couple of days on the loch into the bargain."

All this sounded very pleasant and peaceful. Adam had always wanted "a real fishing holiday" and it seemed that his wish was to be fulfilled. He began to ask Mr. Brownlee all sorts of questions about the size of the trout in the Tinal and the best flies to use and Mr. Brownlee was only too pleased to give him the information he desired. They were still talking about fishing when they drove up to Lurg House.

There was nothing pretentious about Lurg House. It looked solid and comfortable and it lived up to its appearance; it suited Mr. Brownlee down to the ground. Adam was given a room on the second floor with a fine view across the valley; he was told to amuse himself, to make himself at home and do as he liked. The river was very low and the sun was too bright for fishing so he walked over the hills and explored the countryside and returned at night comfortably tired and hungry. It was very pleasant indeed, but after three days of it Adam decided that it could not go on and he tackled Mr. Brownlee.

"Look here, sir," Adam said. "I can't go on like this. I'm not pulling my weight; haven't you got anything for me to do?"

"What about Evelyn?" asked Mr. Brownlee. "Won't Evelyn play with you?"

Adam laughed. He said: "Evelyn's busy—everyone is busy except me. Besides it isn't that I'm bored with pottering about by myself. I'm enjoying it in a way, but—I can't explain it properly—I feel I ought to be doing something."

"You want a job?"

Adam nodded.

"But this is your holiday, Adam."

"I know. I intended to spend it cutting down trees. Holidays aren't much fun in wartime when everyone else is working full steam ahead . . . the best holiday is a change of work."

"We're shorthanded," said Mr. Brownlee, looking at Adam keenly.

"Well then, there you are! I'm not an engineer, but surely, there's something I could do. I don't mind what it is."

"You can try it," said Mr. Brownlee. "I dare say Ford might be quite glad of an extra hand."

They walked down to the works together and, as they went, Mr. Brownlee chatted to Adam in a confidential way.

"I wish Sam would take things a bit easier," he declared. "He works on that searchlight all day and half the night. I'm afraid of his cracking up before the machine is ready. Could you not have a word with him, Adam?"

"Good heavens!" exclaimed Adam, laughing at the idea. "You don't suppose Dr. Cooke would listen to me!"

"Why not?"

"Because I'm still a grubby little schoolboy to Dr. Cooke."

Mr. Brownlee laughed.

"I don't think you need worry," continued Adam in more serious tones. "Dr. Cooke won't break down under the strain—not until he's finished his work, anyhow."

Mr. Brownlee looked at Adam sideways. "H'm, I believe you're right," he said. "You don't say much but you see a good deal—h'm."

Ford was quite pleased to see Adam and agreed to give him some unskilled work, so Adam donned a suit of overalls and took his place at the bench. He was happier now for he felt that he was doing something really useful, something definite to help on the war. He worked under Ford's direction, rubbing down pieces of metal to conform to measurements, polishing this and painting that and running messages. The "searchlight" was being assembled under Dr. Cooke's supervision and various small adjustments were being made—adjustments which required endless patience and perseverance before they were passed as correct. There was other work going on in the workshops, but the "searchlight" was the most important and occasioned the most interest among the hands. Adam, as he went about his business, heard them discussing it and arguing about it and weighing up the chances of its success. Dr. Cooke was discussed, too. Some of the men declared he was "barmy," for he had a vague way of wandering about the workshops when he was not actually at work, but others, who had worked under his directions, held a very different opinion. One and all were looking forward eagerly to the day when the machine would be ready for demonstration.

"You'd make a good apprentice," said Ford one day when Adam had completed rather a troublesome piece of work.

"Nonsense," replied Adam, laughing. "I'm slow and I know it. Look at the time it takes me to get a thing right."

"But you get it right," said Ford. "If I give you a job to do, I know it will conform to the measurements. It's true you've a lot to lairn but you're capable of lairning. You're reliable and you're neat-fingered, forbye. Come on, now, Adams—Mr. Adam, I mean," continued Ford earnestly. "You don't like schoolmastering, do you? Let me speak to the boss about it."

In one way the idea attracted Adam for this was real war work, and much more to his taste than teaching boys, but there were several reasons why Adam hesitated to accept the job. (He knew that if Ford spoke to Mr. Brownlee the job was his for the taking.)

"I can't decide now," said Adam. "I couldn't leave Dr. Cooke in the lurch."

That was only one reason of course; for another there was Evelyn Brownlee. It seemed to Adam that the sooner he departed from Evelyn's vicinity the better it would be. If he stayed on to help Ford, he was bound to see a good deal of Evelyn and he would not be a guest in the house but merely a junior apprentice at the works. He would see her in the distance, as high above him as the stars, and Adam did not think he could bear it.

"Think about it, Adams," urged Ford more earnestly still. "Talk to Dr. Cooke and the boss. I'm needing a man I can rely on and I'll train you myself—we've always got on well, the two of us."

"I'll think about it," Adam said, but already he had made up his mind. His adventures were over now and it was better to make a clean break. He would stay on at Lurg until the demonstration and then say good-bye to his new friends . . . And perhaps there would be time for him to have a fishing holiday before he returned to Rockingham for the Christmas term.

Adam's work brought him into close touch with Mr. Brownlee and they began to understand each other even better than before. Mr. Brownlee made no secret of the fact that he liked Adam (indeed this preference caused a little jealousy) and sometimes he would call Adam into his office to talk to him or to introduce him to contractors who called on business.

"I'd take you on as my secretary if you could manage a typewriter," said Mr. Brownlee one day as they walked back to the house together.

"I can do typewriting," Adam replied.

"You can? Why the devil didn't you say so? We'll talk to Sam about it——"

"No, sir," said Adam. "It's awfully kind of you but——"

"I can depend on you," declared Mr. Brownlee. "I want a reliable fellow with his head screwed on the right way. You'd be useful to me, Adam."

"It's very good of you, but——"

"Leave it open," said Mr. Brownlee. "If you get tired of schoolmastering, let me know. Sam can easily find somebody else to teach his boys French."

"Thank you, sir. I think I'd better stick to schoolmastering in the meantime."

"You're dependable," repeated Mr. Brownlee. "It's the first thing I ask of a man . . . it's the one thing that matters . . ." He hesitated and then he said: "You get on well with Evelyn, don't you?"

"Who wouldn't!" exclaimed Adam in surprise.

Mr. Brownlee was silent for a few moments, then said: "Dick has been a disappointment to me. I can't depend on Dick."

Adam thought it was a great pity that Mr. Brownlee and his nephew did not get on well. There was so much good in both of them, but they did not appreciate each other and were always rubbing each other the wrong way. Dick did not live at Lurg House; it would have been impossible under the circumstances. He had a room at an inn called the Highland Bull about three miles farther down the valley and he roared over to Lurg daily on a supercharged motor-bike. He explained to Adam that he preferred to be free and the Highland Bull was a comfortable howff and did you well. Adam not only liked Dick Brownlee, but admired him tremendously for he was everything that Adam would have liked to be. He was tall and fair and extremely good looking and he treated life as a joke. At Cambridge Dick had played a brilliant part in athletics, but had shown to less advantage in the examination room. He explained to Adam, quite seriously, that he had not had time to do much work, there were so many other things to do at Cambridge. "Of course Uncle John was a bit fed up," said Dick confidentially. "He expected me to take a First in engineering . . . well, I ask you! I mean I haven't got that kind of brain. Even if I had worked like the devil I couldn't have done it, so what was the use of trying?"

"You might have taken a Second——" began Adam doubtfully but Dick shook his head. "No use," he said. "No use at all. I got my rowing blue and I learnt to fly; Uncle John shouldn't complain."

There was a good deal of truth in this—more perhaps than appeared on the surface—for Dick was a brilliant and intrepid pilot and was extremely useful to "Uncle John" on that account. His job at Lurg was to try out new gadgets for aircraft and he had been given exemption on the grounds that he was indispensable to the firm. His work was difficult and dangerous and it would have been practically impossible for Mr. Brownlee to find anyone to fill Dick's shoes.

Chapter Two

One evening Mr. Brownlee announced that he had been over to Weston and had met Mr. Taylor and arranged for Adam to have a day's fishing on the Tinal. "You can borrow a motor-bike from Ford," said Mr. Brownlee. "You can take my rod and tackle; we'll look it out for you to-night after dinner."

"But I promised Ford——" began Adam.

"Nonsense," said Mr. Brownlee, who was a benevolent autocrat and liked his own way. "Perfect nonsense. This is your holiday and you're working like a slave. I'll not have it, Adam. Besides I've arranged the whole thing with Taylor so you can't back out of it now."

Adam had no real desire to back out of it and when he saw Mr. Brownlee's twelve-foot trout rod and began to look through his fly-book he felt a surge of pleasurable excitement.

"I wish I were coming," Mr. Brownlee said. "Look, Adam, you might try this butcher on the tail . . . but to-morrow is a hopeless proposition for me. I've a man coming from Inverness to see me."

"Perhaps you could have a few days' fishing after the demonstration," suggested Adam.

"Perhaps," said Mr. Brownlee in a doubtful tone. "But there's always something. I'll certainly be easier in my mind when Sam's searchlight is off the bill. Handicote is to be here the day after to-morrow," added Mr. Brownlee with a sigh. "Handicote and Professor Fullerton and Colonel Winch and goodness knows who else besides. It's to be hoped that Sam will play up."

Adam smiled. He knew what Mr. Brownlee meant. Dr. Cooke was getting more and more irritable as the great day approached—even at the best of times he was apt to be a trifle difficult over his beloved invention. If Dr. Cooke thought that his invention was not being properly appreciated, he might retire into his shell and remain there like a sulky snail.

Adam thought of all this as he rode over to Tinal on the borrowed bike; but as he neared his objective he forgot about Dr. Cooke's little peculiarities and began to think about his day's sport. The river had risen considerably—it looked just right—and although the sun was very strong there were plenty of clouds about. Evelyn had given him directions and he followed them faithfully, turning right at the Highland Bull and left at the cross-roads. He stopped at the top of the hill and looked down at Tinal Castle—what a fine old place it was! It stood on the cliffs overlooking the sea and the little river swept past its door. The castle consisted of two squat towers, massively built and so weathered by the storms of centuries that they seemed part of the solid rock. It was not a very large castle but there was something awe-inspiring about it—or so Adam felt.

Evelyn had told him a little about Mr. Taylor who was the present owner of the Castle. He was an Englishman with business in London and had bought Tinal some years before the war. He was a bachelor, but had a niece who kept house for him. They lived here most of the summer and returned to London for the winter months. "Everyone likes Mr. Taylor," Evelyn had said. "He's a great acquisition to the neighbourhood. He's a J.P. and something pretty big in the Home Guard, and he's awfully generous and always heads the list when money is wanted for local charities."

"A good fellow and a fine shot," Mr. Brownlee had added.

Adam was still looking at Tinal Castle and wondering about its history when he saw a man, clad in a Harris suit, coming towards him up the hill.

The man waved in a friendly manner and shouted: "Hallo, are you Mr. Southey? I'm Taylor."

"It's most awfully good of you——" Adam began.

"Not at all, I'm delighted," declared Mr. Taylor.

He was quite different from Adam's mental picture, much younger and more approachable. His Harris tweeds were well worn and comfortable-looking, his shoes were obviously old friends. For some unknown reason Adam had expected Mr. Taylor to be "quite old," he had expected to see a smart London businessman. Mr. Taylor looked like a retired soldier—perhaps he had soldiered in the last war, Adam thought.

He was talking now in an easy friendly manner, explaining that the best pools were about a quarter of a mile up the river beyond the bridge. "You can fish there as much as you like," he was saying. "I'm no fisherman—I haven't the patience for it; I'll potter about all day with a gun, but fishing doesn't appeal to me—so come whenever you like. You're on leave, I suppose?"

"No," said Adam. "As a matter of fact they won't have me. I'm lame, you see."

"Bad luck!"

"I'm a schoolmaster."

"You don't look it."

"Thank heaven for that!"

"Why?" inquired Mr. Taylor, laughing. "Schoolmasters are usually admirable people. We couldn't do without them, could we?"

"Perhaps not, but all my friends are in the Services—all my contemporaries. Sometimes it's almost more than I can bear. I'm very strong and fit—you'd think there was something I could do . . . I say, it's awful of me to bore you like this!"

It was not only "awful" but it was most surprising that Adam should have let himself go like this to a complete stranger . . . what on earth had possessed him!

"You aren't boring me," said Mr. Taylor gravely. "You felt I was interested or you wouldn't have told me. I know exactly what you're feeling for the same thing happened to me in the last war. They wouldn't have me because there was something wrong with my heart; I felt as fit as a fiddle, too."

"I thought you looked like a soldier, sir."

"No, they wouldn't have me." He hesitated and then said: "Come and have lunch, Southey, I might be able to suggest something that you could do. You won't catch any fish as long as it's so bright—you see I know something about the sport though I don't indulge in it myself."

"It's awfully kind of you——" began Adam in a doubtful tone.

Mr. Taylor laughed. "Come along and we'll have a chat—and a good grouse. You won't mind taking potluck, will you?"

Adam could not refuse for there was something about this man that drew him like a magnet and soon they were walking down the hill towards the Castle and Mr. Taylor was telling Adam the history of the place—or as much of it as he knew. It had been built in the twelfth century and had belonged to a robber chief, who had ruled the countryside with a rod of iron. The place was in reality a miniature fortress for it was protected on one side by the sea and on the others by the river and a moat. There was a drawbridge over the moat and Mr. Taylor admitted with a smile that he had had the drawbridge put in order and that he drew it himself every night.

"Just for fun," said Mr. Taylor with a slightly apologetic air. "Just because it amuses me to feel that I'm living in a real castle."

"It's a fascinating place," declared Adam.

"I was fascinated by it," nodded its owner. "The moment I saw it I fell for it and I felt I had to have it at all costs. It was almost a ruin when I bought it—the inside I mean, for of course the outside walls will stand as long as the rocks on which they are built. I had the whole place done up and put in electric light and bathrooms and what not, so it's very comfortable now. Unfortunately my niece doesn't care for the place. She finds it lonely and isolated."

"It is very isolated."

"The petrol restrictions make it worse," continued Mr. Taylor. "People can't drop in and see us as they used to do, and Brenda finds it very dull."

"What a pity!"

"Yes. We had rather a bad time in London before we came north. The bombing upset Brenda's nerves. I thought the peace and quiet of Tinal would do her good, but it hasn't been a success."

Mr. Taylor sounded so worried that Adam felt sorry for him. "Perhaps Miss Taylor would be happier if she had something to do——" began Adam.

"She isn't strong," replied her uncle, shaking his head. "Her nerves are easily upset . . . she couldn't take a job like other girls. The fact is her mother was—well, a trifle unbalanced mentally, and I'm afraid Brenda . . . but I'm boring you, Southey."

"No, of course not," declared Adam. "I just wish——"

"You'll realise what I mean when you see her," said Mr. Taylor with a sigh.

"It must be worrying for you!"

"Yes. I don't know what to do for the best—whether to leave Brenda here or take her back to London."

"Are you going back to London, yourself?" asked Adam.

"Yes, of course," replied Mr. Taylor, smiling. "I suppose you are thinking the same as other people and wondering what sort of business I could do. I don't look like a businessman—or so I'm told. The fact is I'm on the social side—if you know what that means; my job is to go about and meet people and make social contacts. It's a very pleasant job, but my partners seem to think I earn my salt."

The Castle was furnished in a very comfortable style, with thick carpets and curtains to keep out the draught. They lunched at a small round table in the dining-room window and were waited on by a middle-aged butler and a very young tablemaid. Miss Taylor had slipped into her chair as silently as a ghost—Adam had not heard her approach and was quite surprised when he saw her. She acknowledged Adam's introduction with a quiet inclination of her head and took no further interest in him. In spite of this there was something about her that attracted Adam—he felt as if he had seen her before. She had a fair delicate skin and dark curls. He could not see her eyes, for they were fixed upon her plate and her dark lashes lay upon her cheeks like two little fans. He tried to talk to her and to draw her into the conversation, but he could make no headway and he was forced to give up the attempt.

The window of the dining-room looked west, there was nothing to be seen from it except brilliant blue sea. Adam commented on this to Mr. Taylor.

"Yes," replied Mr. Taylor. "That's one of the attractions of Tinal Castle. I love the sea. Sometimes Brenda and I go over to Balfinny . . . it's a fishing village about four miles down the coast. We take a boat and go out and catch mackerel—don't we, Brenda?"

She did not reply.

"We can't do that now, of course," continued Mr. Taylor with a sigh. "The war has put a stop to that—as it has to so many innocent pleasures."

"Do you keep a boat here, sir?" asked Adam.

Mr. Taylor laughed. "No, we don't," he replied. "It wouldn't be any use. If you look down on to the shore you'll see the reason why."

Adam leaned forward and looked down. He saw that the cliff on which the castle stood dropped steeply, almost perpendicularly, to the shore below. Just below the castle there was a tiny bay enclosed by rocks. Inside the rocks the water was calm, but outside the sea fretted against the reefs so that they were edged with white foam. Some of the rocks were low and flat and covered with glistening seaweed; others were tall and black with jagged teeth. The rocks and reefs stretched for some little way in both directions and farther out to sea the waves seemed to be breaking on covered shoals.

"It wouldn't be any use keeping a boat here," repeated Mr. Taylor.

"No, it wouldn't," Adam agreed.

"Some of the villagers say there used to be a channel through the reefs," said Miss Taylor suddenly.

Adam was startled to hear her speak. He looked at her in surprise and could find nothing to say in return.

"It's an old wives' tale," said Mr. Taylor in a soothing voice.

"Brenda is nervous," explained Mr. Taylor as he ushered Adam into the library and shut the door. "She won't believe me when I tell her that the Germans couldn't land here. She thinks this place is too isolated to be safe. As a matter of fact I've had the reefs examined most carefully—just to relieve her mind—and there isn't any channel and never could have been . . . but she still worries about it."

"She seems very—er—depressed," said Adam uncomfortably.

"I believe I ought to take her to a specialist," declared Mr. Taylor. "I'd have done it before but I was afraid of upsetting the poor child. It's this horrible war," he added with a sigh. "It seems to have got her down completely . . . and she was such a bright little thing."

The library was one of the most comfortable rooms Adam had ever seen. It was just the sort of room he would have liked to have as his very own; there were several comfortable chairs grouped about the fire and the walls were lined with books; there was a large desk in one corner, a solid sensible desk, and a round table which stood in the middle of the floor was covered with periodicals such as *The Sphere*, *The Spectator*, *Country Life* and *Punch* and half a dozen others all up to date and clean and glossy. They looked tempting—quite unlike the tattered dog-eared copies of illustrated papers which were handed round the masters' common-room at Rockingham—and Adam would have liked to linger and turn them over at his leisure. How nice to be rich, thought Adam ingenuously, how pleasant it would be to order all these interesting papers for oneself, to read them when they were straight from the press all new and shining . . .

". . . very draughty, of course," Mr. Taylor was saying.

"Draughty!" echoed Adam in surprise.

"These old houses always are. I put in central heating, of course, but the wind still whistles under the doors. What do you think of that screen?"

Adam was sitting with his back to the door, so he turned and looked at the screen. It was of carved oak with five leaves and each leaf was carved in a different pattern. It was a beautiful piece of work and Adam said so.

"Yes, it is," agreed its owner with a satisfied air. "It's beautifully carved and so solid. I like solid furniture. I picked it up in a sale-room. Got it for a fiver; I don't know when I've been so pleased with a bargain."

"It was dirt cheap," Adam agreed.

"And what's more it achieved its purpose," continued Mr. Taylor. "This room was always cold no matter how big the fire. The draught swept in under the door and the flames roared up the chimney."

"It's very comfortable now," said Adam. He rose as he spoke for he felt it was time to go.

"Must you go?" said Mr. Taylor. "We haven't had our grouse, have we? Oh well, you must come another day, that's all."

"Thank you, sir."

"I'm afraid you won't get much fishing—it's still far too bright—but come again, come whenever you like."

"Thank you very much," said Adam.

They walked across the big hall, which was paved with grey flagstones and carpeted with thick blue rugs, and as they reached the front door a man came up the steps and stood aside to let them pass. Adam glanced at the man . . . and then he looked again . . . Yes, he knew that man . . . Yes, he had seen the man before, not so very long ago but in very different surroundings. There was no mistaking those strongly marked features, the long straight nose and deeply sunken eyes. Adam had memorised those features so carefully that he was not likely to forget them. This was the man with the brown shoes (and oddly enough he was actually wearing them now), the man who had walked into the science building at Rockingham and bribed the janitor with a crisp pound note. "Rat Number One" was the label that Adam had attached to this unpleasant creature . . . what, in heaven's name, was Rat Number One doing at Tinal Castle?

Adam's heart almost stood still with amazement and dismay (for if he had recognised the man it was only reasonable to suppose that the man would recognise him) and then he remembered the circumstances of their previous encounter and decided that it was unlikely, for the guest at Tinal Castle was a very different sort of person from the janitor with a green apron and a dirty face.

The man's glance swept over Adam unwaveringly and Adam met the glance with a disinterested stare . . . Adam passed on down the steps.

"Oh, Cheller," said Mr. Taylor. "I'll be back in a few minutes. Wait for me in the library, will you?"

"Who is that, sir?" asked Adam, as they walked across the strip of garden to the river bank.

"You mean Cheller?"

"Yes, I just wondered . . ."

"Cheller is my secretary," said Mr. Taylor. He smiled a trifle ruefully and added: "At least that's what he's supposed to be. To tell you the truth he doesn't fill the bill very satisfactorily."

Adam hesitated. It was on the tip of his tongue to tell Mr. Taylor what he knew of the man, but something held him back.

"He was recommended to me by a friend," continued Mr. Taylor. "I was sorry for the fellow for he seemed in pretty low water and I thought I'd try him out. It's difficult to get a competent secretary just now."

"Yes, but as a matter of fact——" began Adam and then he paused.

"Yes?" said Mr. Taylor inquiringly. "What were you going to say?"

"Nothing important," replied Adam uncomfortably. He had suddenly realised that he could not tell Mr. Taylor about Cheller without telling him about the ray—and that was not his secret.

"I thought perhaps you knew him, or knew something about him," Mr. Taylor said.

"No, I don't know him."

"Poor Cheller," said Mr. Taylor, shaking his head. "I'm afraid he drinks a bit and he has a taste for queer company. He's down at the Highland Bull far too much. Perhaps you've seen him there?"

"No," said Adam. He did not add that, as he had never been to the Highland Bull, it was quite impossible for him to have seen Mr. Taylor's secretary there.

"I'm afraid I shall have to get rid of Cheller," said Mr. Taylor in a thoughtful tone of voice. It was such a very thoughtful tone of voice that the words stuck in Adam's memory and he remembered them later.

Chapter Three

Adam had never been to the Highland Bull, but he had promised Dick Brownlee to look in at the first opportunity. It seemed to Adam, as he rode back to Lurg, that this was as good a time as any to pay his promised visit to Dick, so he stopped at the Inn and left the motor-bicycle in the yard. Dick was just finishing a much-belated lunch and he hailed Adam in a friendly way.

"Have you fed?" asked Dick. "Quite sure you don't want another guzzle at the trough? Right oh, we'll sit on the terrace."

Dick was as friendly as ever, but in spite of that Adam was sure that there was something wrong. Dick wasn't quite so talkative as usual, his sparkle was a trifle dimmed.

"Life's absolutely foul," said Dick in answer to Adam's inquiries. "Everything seems to have gone wrong at once if you know what I mean."

"Yes, I know," said Adam in sympathetic tones. "I thought you seemed a bit under the weather."

"Yes," said Dick. "Everything has suddenly gone askew . . . at least that's what I feel about it. Take my bomb release, for instance," said Dick in a grumbling tone. "Of course you don't know about it, but the fact is I hit on quite a neat little gadget, an improvement, you know. It was quite a small thing but I was rather bucked about it—old Handicote took it up at once."

"Good work!"

"Yes," agreed Dick. "Yes, it was quite good really—and now the Hun's got it."

"No," cried Adam in dismay.

"Yes, isn't it foul? The official explanation is that one of our bombers came down in Germany and the Hun cribbed it . . . but I can't help wondering."

"What does Mr. Brownlee think?" asked Adam.

"He swallowed the official explanation whole," declared Dick in disgust. "As a matter of fact we had words about it this morning."

"I wish you wouldn't have words with him!" exclaimed Adam.

"Who could help it?" said Dick. "I'm sick of kowtowing to his majesty. I'm sick of hanging about here. I want to be a fighter pilot, but Uncle John won't release me."

"You're doing very valuable work here."

"Yes, of course," agreed Dick who had no false modesty in his make-up. "But I want to see a bit of fun. Uncle John can't have it both ways; it isn't fair."

"Both ways?" asked Adam.

"It's a bit complicated," said Dick. "It goes round and round if you know what I mean. Evelyn says we must be patient. She says it will all come right if I wait patiently. She says I don't understand Uncle John——"

"She's right there."

"Why should I be patient?" urged Dick. "I've got my life to live and time's passing and here I am tied down. He won't let me go and he won't let us be engaged—he's got it both ways."

"Engaged!" exclaimed Adam.

"Evelyn and I," nodded Dick. "You knew about it, didn't you? I've always wanted to marry Evelyn, of course."

"Yes, of course," said Adam rather faintly. It seemed easier to pretend he had known about it all the time . . . and, now that Dick had told him, he realised that he ought to have guessed it long ago if he had not been stone blind. Evelyn and Dick—they were the same sort of people, good-looking and merry-hearted, with the same background and the same interests. It was because they were alike and because their manner to each other was so intimate and friendly that he had overlooked the possibility that their feelings towards each other went deeper than cousinly affection.

"It's rather funny," Dick continued, blushing a little under his tanned skin. "The fact is I've never *looked* at another girl. It's always been Evelyn—and Evelyn feels the same about me—so there you are."

"Yes, of course," said Adam again.

"Uncle John has never been keen on it because he thinks I'm not good enough for Evelyn . . . well, I dare say he's right but that's for Evelyn to say."

Adam felt dazed, and it was exceedingly difficult to be sympathetic, but he did his best. "I should wait a bit," he said. "Evelyn knows how to manage him."

"I can't stick it," said Dick moodily. "Why should the old buffer have what he wants all the time?"

"You might be a little more tactful——"

"No," interrupted Dick. "No, it's a matter of principle. I want to talk it over with him *reasonably*. I want to go to him and say: 'Which is it to be? Let us be engaged or else let me go,' but Evelyn won't let me."

Adam listened to all this and a good deal more but at last he reached the limit of his endurance. "I must go," he said, rising from his chair. "I don't want to be late for tea."

It was a feeble excuse, but Dick accepted it. He followed Adam into the yard and watched him wheel out the motor-bike.

"Uncle John's rod and bag and tackle!" exclaimed Dick somewhat bitterly. "He'd see me far enough before he'd lend me his walking stick!"

"Oh rot!" replied Adam uncomfortably. "It's just that you don't take him the right way."

"I don't suck up to him," said Dick.

Adam hesitated with his foot on the starting pedal. He said: "Do you mean I suck up to him, Dick?"

"I'm sorry," said Dick quickly. "I didn't mean anything nasty. I just meant that you—you get on so well with him; he's always shoving you down my throat."

"Is he?" asked Adam in dismay.

"You're his white-haired boy."

"No——"

"Yes, honestly. He'd be as pleased as Punch if it was you that wanted to marry Evelyn——"

"Me!" cried Adam in amazement.

"Oh well," said Dick, laughing a trifle ruefully. "I mean—I mean he wouldn't mind you; it's me he can't stand. Lucky for me that you and Evelyn don't like each other, isn't it?"

"We're friends——" began Adam.

"I know. That's what I meant."

"Evelyn would never think of me."

"I know," agreed Dick.

Adam hesitated and then he said: "Well, so long, Dick!"

"So long!" echoed Dick, waving.

Adam had a good deal to think about as he rode back to Lurg. Now that he knew about Dick and Evelyn, a good many things which had puzzled him became clear, and above all Mr. Brownlee's attitude to his nephew. "Dick is irresponsible," Mr. Brownlee had said. He was always saying the same thing in different words and Adam had wondered why Mr. Brownlee was so annoyed with Dick for not being staid and sober-minded and reliable. Dick did his work well, in fact he did it brilliantly; he was always ready to try out weird-looking experimental planes, and Adam had tried to point out to Mr. Brownlee that if Dick had been staid and sober-minded he might not have been so eager to risk these flights. Now, of course, the whole matter was clear as crystal for Mr. Brownlee had not been thinking of Dick as a pilot of experimental planes but as a possible husband for his beloved daughter. Naturally he wanted a reliable man for this important post . . . A reliable man, yes, but not Adam. The idea was quite absurd . . . and even if Mr. Brownlee happened to entertain this absurd idea, it could make no difference. Nothing could make any difference as long as Dick and Evelyn loved each other . . . Evelyn could always manage her father, she always got her own way in the end . . .

"I shan't think about it any more," said Adam to himself as he sped down the hill towards Lurg.

There were plenty of other things for Adam to think of, and the most important of these was Mr. Taylor's secretary. The man's presence at Tinal was disquieting and Mr. Brownlee must be told about it at once. With this end in view Adam went straight to the works, but found that Mr. Brownlee had been called to Edinburgh on business and would not be back until time for the demonstration.

Adam debated whether or not to tell Dr. Cooke about Cheller, but he realised that Dr. Cooke was already upset about the "search-light" and the demonstration and he hated to add to his anxiety.

"I'll just keep my eyes open till Mr. Brownlee gets back," said Adam to himself. "Then I'll tell him about Cheller at once and he can report it to the police."

Chapter Four

It was a fine dry night, still and warm and cloudless; the moon was setting beyond the hills when the party from Lurg House started out to see the demonstration. There was Mr. Handicote, Professor Fullerton, Colonel Winch and Major Hamilton Walker, and several other less important personages. They went ahead with Mr. Brownlee and his secretary . . . Dr. Cooke followed slowly. Adam had hoped to walk up to the moors with Evelyn, but at the last minute she had decided not to come, so he attached himself to Dr. Cooke and endeavoured to bring him to a more cheerful frame of mind. The strain and excitement were playing havoc with Dr. Cooke's nerves and for the last few days he had been quite unlike himself, cross and irritable and contrary. His face, always fine drawn, had become quite emaciated and his eyes burnt in his head as if with fever. Adam felt thankful that now, in a few hours, the ordeal would be over and the invention would be out of Dr. Cooke's hands. He said something of this to Dr. Cooke as they followed the rest of the party up the path.

"Something will go wrong," declared Dr. Cooke.

"Nothing will go wrong," said Adam confidently. "You know the machine was working perfectly this morning."

"They don't understand it."

"You don't need to *understand* it," Adam pointed out. "All you require is a pair of eyes. I didn't understand it when you showed me your model in the science lab at Rockingham, but I saw its potentialities——"

"I can't stand that fellow Handicote," said Dr. Cooke in a querulous tone.

"I know, but it doesn't matter. He's capable—anyone can see that. He wouldn't be where he is if he weren't capable——"

"And Fullerton is an ass."

"It doesn't matter," repeated Adam in soothing tones. He put his arm through that of his companion (for the path was steep here) and was horrified to find that Dr. Cooke was so thin it was like linking arms with a skeleton. "Good heavens, you *are* thin, sir!" Adam exclaimed.

Dr. Cooke took no notice. He was a man with one single thought. He was obsessed. "They're not in the proper mood," he complained. "Laughing and talking like that . . . you'd think they were going to a fireworks display."

"They'll change their tune."

"And it's far too light. I told John it would be too light. How could anyone judge the potentialities of the ray. Look at the moon."

"The moon is setting," replied Adam.

By this time they had reached the crest of the rise and were descending into the big shallow saucer of moorland which had been the scene of so many secret experiments . . . but none (thought Adam) more secret or more thrilling than the experiment they were to witness to-night. The moon had begun to sink behind the hilltop, and a few ragged wind-blown firs stood out upon the skyline silhouetted against the bright silver disc. In a few minutes it would be dark but at present it was bright, the shadows of rocks and trees black and eerie.

Adam saw the huge truck, covered with a dark tarpaulin, and round it a group of figures, talking earnestly. He saw that Ford was there, and several other men who had been working on the machine. . . . He hurried Dr. Cooke forward.

"Come along, Sam," said Mr. Brownlee. "We're all waiting for you. Professor Fullerton wants to ask you a few questions before we start."

Adam left Dr. Cooke and retired a few paces for he had suddenly realised that he was the only person present who had nothing to do with the demonstration. He sat down on a boulder and waited patiently. It was very quiet and peaceful on the moor. There was no sound save the occasional bleating of a sheep and the murmur of voices. Ford had removed the tarpaulin now and the machine was exposed to view, a huge unwieldy mass of mechanism, a sort of Loch Ness Monster in the world of machines. It had been painted grey. Adam had helped to paint it; perhaps that gave him the right to be here. He remembered suddenly that if it had not been for him the machine might not have been here at all . . . He remembered The Disappearing Lady and smiled involuntarily.

Dr. Cooke seemed to have recovered his temper and was "playing up" quite well; he was explaining the principles of his invention to Professor Fullerton.

Mr. Brownlee was talking to Colonel Winch: ". . . quite impossible to demonstrate without actual experiment," Mr. Brownlee was saying.

"How are you going to do that?" Colonel Winch inquired.

"With an aeroplane," replied Mr. Brownlee. "I happened to have an old Moth."

The moon disappeared. It had sunk very suddenly behind the hill . . . the stars were mere pinpoints of light in the dark bowl of the sky . . .

"But look here," began Colonel Winch. "Look here, sir. If this ray is going to set fire to the plane . . . I mean it will be damned unpleasant for the pilot."

"He's got a complete suit of asbestos clothing," said Mr. Brownlee. "It will be all right, I assure you. He's used to carrying out experiments . . . Ah, there he is!"

Adam heard a low hum. He looked up and saw a small green light moving across the sky amongst the stars. His heart stood still . . . and then raced on. It was crazy. It was the maddest, craziest experiment that had ever taken place. These men did not understand. They had not seen the paper burst into flames and fall in burnt charred fragments on the floor. Oddly enough Adam had never thought of asking how the ray was to be demonstrated . . . he had never thought of this . . . it was ghastly. Dick was in that plane. That small green speck of light was Dick . . .

There was another hum now, much nearer and louder than the drumming of the far-off plane. It was the dynamo, of course. A thin stream of pale violet light streamed from the oddly shaped funnel of the machine and cut a swathe through the darkness. The swathe of light swept the sky like the blade of a sword.

"Wait!" cried Colonel Winch. "Stop, for heaven's sake! Are you sure there's no danger for the pilot? We don't want to do anything foolish."

"He's used to flying," said Mr. Brownlee. "He has a parachute, of course."

"Couldn't it be done with a kite?"

"I think we should accept Mr. Brownlee's assurances," said Professor Fullerton firmly. "I, for one, am extremely anxious to see the ray in action."

"We've come here to see the demonstration," added Mr. Handicote a trifle unpleasantly.

"I don't like it at all," declared Colonel Winch.

"I was under the impression that you were an airman yourself, Colonel Winch, and used to taking risks in the execution of your duty."

"I consider this an unnecessary risk."

"Are we to carry on or not?" asked Mr. Brownlee impatiently.

"Carry on, please," replied Mr. Handicote.

Adam felt his scalp prickle. He clenched his hands and found that the palms were wet. He did not want to look, but his eyes were fixed upon the small green light and he could not turn them away. The sword of light was stationary now, and the small green light was circling near it . . . approaching nearer and nearer at every turn . . .

Suddenly there was a flash of light, a burst of flames so dazzling that it seemed to illuminate the sky, and the next moment a mass of blazing wreckage was falling towards the hills.

Adam's eyes were fixed upon it as it fell. He gazed at it in horror, for the thing had happened so quickly that it seemed impossible that Dick should have escaped . . . and then he saw a parachute and a small white figure swinging from the ropes. . . . Dick had managed to fall clear. He had fallen quicker than the plane, but now he was held by the parachute and was coming down more slowly and the blazing plane passed him in mid air, lighting up his parachute and white clothing with a ruddy glow . . .

Ford had turned off the current and there was a sudden silence broken by the distant sound of the wreckage crashing upon the hill.

"By Jove, that was a plucky thing to do!" cried Colonel Winch, who was the first amongst the little group of spectators to find his tongue.

This exclamation seemed to break the spell and the others began to talk eagerly and excitedly to each other and to Dr. Cooke. The potentialities of the ray had been demonstrated in a manner which could leave no doubt as to the value of the machine . . . perhaps the risk had been justified after all.

"This must be put into production at once," Mr. Handicote was saying. "There must be no delay. I shall fly back to London at once and see the Prime Minister. The point is how many factories can be turned over to its production . . ."

"What effect would it produce on a tank?" inquired Major Hamilton Walker. "You could use it against infantry . . ."

"The First Sea Lord should have been here himself!"

"The effect on morale would be staggering!"

"How many thousand feet do you think——"

"How heavy? It's a question of mobility——"

"You could clear the sky in ten minutes . . ."

"Supposing the infantry were approaching in open order . . ."

". . . if we can produce enough of them, and quickly . . ."

"Oh, absolutely secret, of course. Every precaution must be taken."

"In naval warfare, for instance . . ."

It was a gabble—or sounded like a gabble in Adam's ears—for they were all talking at once and nobody was listening. Each one was thinking of how the ray would affect his own particular bit of war.

"I want to speak to the pilot," said Colonel Winch's voice at Adam's shoulder. "Could you manage it for me, do you think?"

Adam was about to make inquiries as to Dick's whereabouts when a car appeared, bumping along over the uneven ground. It drew up some yards away, the door opened and a bulky white figure squeezed out.

"Here he is, sir!" cried Adam.

Dick stood and looked around as if he were slightly dazed, and Adam took his arm and led him to Colonel Winch.

"Well done!" said the Colonel, holding out his hand.

Dick shook hands with him. He said: "Was it a good show? Were the old buffers pleased?"

"The old buffers are delighted," replied Colonel Winch, laughing.

"Oh, good," said Dick vaguely. "They're going to take it, I suppose."

"There's no doubt about that."

"No, I don't suppose there is."

"They're discussing how many can be turned out—and how soon."

"Oh, good," said Dick again, still in that queer vague voice. He added confidentially: "You know I can't help feeling a bit sorry for Jerry . . . I mean it was pretty hellish."

"I can well believe it," replied Colonel Winch.

"Yes, it was—well—well pretty hellish," repeated Dick. "I still feel a bit queer. You see, I meant to bale out just before it happened, but it happened before I expected it . . . The plane didn't just go on fire—if you know what I mean—instead of that it burst into flames all round me. The heat was frightful. The plane fell apart and every part of it was blazing . . ."

They were walking towards the house now. Dawn was breaking and the world was taking shape before their eyes. Dick had thrown back the thick white hood of his asbestos flying suit and his face emerged from its folds like the face of a young monk, clean-shaven and ascetic. His fair hair was ruffled by the morning breeze.

"Was Uncle John pleased?" he inquired.

"Very pleased indeed," replied Adam confidently.

Dick was silent for a few moments, and then he said: "It's a devilish thing, you know. I didn't believe in it, to tell you the truth. I mean I didn't see how it could work. Even now I can scarcely believe it. The man who invented that ray must be in league with the devil."

Adam laughed. It was so ridiculous to think of Dr. Cooke in league with the devil—Dr. Cooke of all people!

"Oh, I know he seems harmless," agreed Dick. "He seems mild and kind and slightly barmy . . ."

"Look here," said Colonel Winch. "How would you like a commission in the RAF?"

"A commission!" echoed Dick in amazement.

"We want people like you," explained Colonel Winch. "I dare say Mr. Brownlee would be annoyed if he knew I was trying to get you, but I just thought I'd mention it. The fact is it occurred to me that you might like a safe cushy job—such as bombing the docks at Hamburg."

Dick roared with laughter. He said: "My work here isn't all quite so spectacular . . ."

"I'm glad of that."

". . . but if you can get round Uncle John I'm on."

"We'll have a try."

"It's good of you, sir. I must say I should like to have a crack at the Hun, and there isn't much time, is there?"

"Much time?"

"That ray will finish them," said Dick seriously.

Chapter Five

The morning after the demonstration Adam awoke feeling somewhat flat. He had been living under a strain and the strain had lifted.
There was nothing more for him to do. He realised that it was silly
to feel flat for the ray was a success and that was all that mattered.
The Government was taking it up and large numbers would be
produced . . . Adam was free now, and this being so he must leave
Lurg immediately. He might stand himself a fishing holiday before
returning to Rockingham. The thought of the Christmas term at
Rockingham gave Adam no pleasure; the thought of the dingy
classrooms, the masters' common-room, the dining-hall with its
clatter of plates and cutlery; the thought of spending hours and
hours trying to din a few words of foreign languages into the heads
of reluctant boys made Adam groan.

At that moment there was a furtive knock on Adam's door and,
on permission being given to enter, Ford put his head round the
edge of it and inquired whether Adam was awake.

"Of course I'm awake. Come in," said Adam in surprise.

"It's airly," Ford pointed out. "It's just gone six, but I wanted a
wee crack with you. I'm away back to Edinburgh to-day."

"It was a good show, wasn't it?"

"Uhha, it impressed them," replied Ford, coming in and closing
the door carefully. "It's an awful machine and that's the truth. I'm
not just easy in my mind about things. I'm a wee bit worried. It's a
kind of feeling I've got."

"What kind of feeling?" Adam inquired. He was not sure
whether it was physical feeling, such as a pain in Ford's inside, or a
mental discomfort.

Ford's brow was corrugated with the effort to explain. "There's
things going on that I don't just understand," said Ford slowly.
"There's money about the place. There's money spent at the canteen that the men don't get in their wages . . . and there was a funny
thing happened in the office. Some blueprints were moved."

"Stolen?" asked Adam in horror-stricken tones.

"No, just moved," replied Ford. "Moved from one place to another. Maybe you'll not think there's much in that, but the key of the office was in my pocket and nobody had any right in the room . . . and then there's yon bomb release."

"I thought the official explanation——"

"Uhha—it was said that the Gairmans copied it from a wrecked plane, but if that was the way of it they must have been pretty quick on the job. You can't make alterations in existing mechanism in a week—nor yet in a fortnight—and turn out the stuff in mass production."

Adam considered the matter. He knew so little about conditions at the works that it was difficult for him to judge whether these apparently unrelated facts could be linked together, and, if so, what could be deduced from them.

"If you really think there's something wrong, you should speak to Mr. Brownlee," said Adam thoughtfully.

"I did," replied Ford. "Mr. Brownlee said I needed a holiday. Maybe he's right. Maybe I moved the papers myself and forgot I'd done it, maybe the men have been lucky backing winners. If there was anything definite Mr. Brownlee would listen. He's a great one for facts. You can't frighten him with shadows."

Adam knew that this was true.

"But I've got facts for Mr. Brownlee," he said, and he told Ford about his meeting with Cheller.

"There you are," said Ford. "There's something wrong."

"I shall speak to Mr. Brownlee the first thing. I didn't get a chance last night because he came home just before the demonstration and afterwards there was no use in talking to anyone about anything."

"But," Ford answered, "Mr. Brownlee's gone away again. He's gone off to Edinburgh this morning . . . I thought I'd just warn you to keep your eyes skinned—you might see something. The men in the workshops are used to you now, so you could——"

"But I'm going away," said Adam. "There's nothing more for me to do. I can't stay on and trespass on Mr. Brownlee's hospitality."

"You can't go," said Ford earnestly. "You must find out about yon man at Tinal. Could you not take a room at the Highland Bull so as to keep an eye on him?"

"I might," said Adam thoughtfully. It was not a bad idea. He had promised himself a fishing holiday, and there was no reason why he should not take it here. Mr. Taylor had given him permission to fish the river at Tinal . . .

"You must," said Ford, more earnestly still. "You must find out what yon fellow is doing in these pairts."

"I don't know what to look for, or how to look for it."

"If I could tell you what to look for I could tell the boss and there'd be no difficulty." He hesitated and then added: "I wouldn't care if it wasn't for the ray. It's kind of got on my mind. There's been trouble and nothing but trouble since we started on the machine. It's made me feel I can't trust anybody. Take Berwick, for instance, I've known Berwick for years."

"Yes," agreed Adam. He had thought that he had finished with the ray—that it was out of his hands now—but apparently he had been wrong. "You think it's the ray they're after?" he inquired.

"What else?" replied Ford. "Now see here, if you're in any difficulty and wanting help there's one man you can depend on. He's a shepherd, that's all, but he's got quite a good head on him— in some ways. You can see his wee white cottage on the hill over towards Tinal."

"What's his name?" asked Adam.

"It's Ford," replied Ford with one of his rare smiles. "Uhha, he's my brother. I'm not saying we always see eye to eye but you can trust him. Ebby's his first name."

"Short for Ebenezer," suggested Adam.

"Just that," agreed Ford gravely.

"And what's your name?" inquired Adam, finding to his surprise that he had no idea of it.

"It's the same as your own, Mr. Adam," replied Ford with a chuckle.

"I'm sorry you're going away," said Evelyn. "I wish you would stay on. I was hoping you would stay on with us until the beginning of term. It's nice having you here."

"I've enjoyed it tremendously," Adam replied.

"You're so good with Daddy," continued Evelyn with a sigh. "You understand him and he likes you. I do wish . . ."

Adam knew what she wished. He said: "Yes, it's a pity Dick isn't a little more tactful."

It was after dinner and they were sitting together in the drawing-room window. The light was going fast and the moon was rising behind the trees.

"Tactful!" echoed Evelyn with a soft laugh. "Dick doesn't know the meaning of the word. His latest idea is to join the RAF—it's a sort of blackmail. He won't listen when I tell him that Daddy is the last person to be blackmailed."

"It isn't really blackmail," said Adam thoughtfully. "He *wants* to join the RAF . . . It's difficult for Dick, you know."

"Keep an eye on him, won't you?" she urged. "Cheer him up a bit. It will be nice for Dick to have you at the Highland Bull . . . and you can come over and see us sometimes. It isn't very far."

"Of course I will," said Adam. "I'm not going to say good-bye."

"Since you're going for the fishing, take Daddy's rod and fly-book. He lent them to you before and I know if he were here he'd tell you to take them. You can send us over a basket of trout if you have any luck."

"I will," said Adam. "And thank you very much indeed for all your kindness."

Adam went up to Dr. Cooke's bedroom. He had been in bed all day, resting after the demonstration. Adam had been in to see him several times and had always found him asleep, but he was awake now and greeted Adam in a friendly manner.

"Come in, Adam," he said. "I'm feeling better, but I've got a lot of sleep to make up. What did you think of the demonstration?"

"It couldn't have been better."

Dr. Cooke smiled. "No, I don't think it could. The ray is out of my hands now. It has caused me a great deal of work and anxiety . . . yes, and a great deal of pleasure, too."

"They may need you to help——" began Adam, who felt that it was just as well to stress this point.

"They will need me," agreed Dr. Cooke. "But it will not be the same thing. I have given it to the Government."

"Given it?"

"Yes. It isn't an invention for which I could accept payment, Adam. It is too deadly. John doesn't understand my feeling—he thinks I'm mad—he's very angry with me."

"I think I understand," said Adam.

Dr. Cooke sighed. He said: "It sounds a bit highfalutin to say that I have given the ray to Britain and I wouldn't say it to anybody else . . . but that is what I have done. That is what I have always intended to do from the very beginning."

"I am sure you are right, sir."

"So am I," agreed Dr. Cooke. "You see, Adam, I couldn't take money for a lethal weapon, for an invention that will bring death to thousands of young men."

"No," said Adam. "No—but if it's properly used it will end the war."

"You think so?"

"I've always thought so. That's why it's so vitally important."

"I have thought so, too," said Dr. Cooke with another sigh.

"You're tired," said Adam. "You must rest. I just came to say good-bye. I'm going away to-morrow morning early."

"So soon?"

"Yes, it's better, really."

Dr. Cooke did not ask why it was better; perhaps he suspected the reason. He thanked Adam for all he had done and added that he would look forward to seeing him at Rockingham on the twenty-second of September. "You are coming back, I suppose," he said, looking at Adam keenly.

"Yes, of course, sir," said Adam.

"There's no 'of course' about it," said Dr. Cooke. "John wants you—he told me so—and if you think it would be more congenial work I shall not stand in your way. I should be ungrateful if I tried to bind you down after all that you have done for me."

"It's very good of you——"

"No, I know it has been hard for you—very hard indeed. You do not feel that teaching boys is war work. I disagree with you, of course, but I can see your point of view."

"I should give you a term's notice in any case," said Adam firmly.

They left it like that, and Adam felt happier. He did not intend to leave Dr. Cooke in the lurch, but it was pleasant to feel more free. It was also very pleasant to feel that Dr. Cooke understood and appreciated his difficulties. He was very fond of Dr. Cooke.

"Are you staying on here?" asked Adam.

"Only for a few days," replied Dr. Cooke. "I'm going to my sister in Wales to have a real rest before the term begins. I feel I require a rest."

"You've earned it, sir," declared Adam with feeling.

Chapter Six

It was a lovely morning when Adam set forth. He took the bus as far as the Highland Bull and left his suitcase there, and then he walked on to Tinal. It was warm by this time and Adam was tired and footsore when he reached the bridge—an old hog-backed bridge, it was, with moss growing in the crevices. He saw at once that what Mr. Taylor had said was true, and that by far the best pools lay above the bridge.

A path ran along at the edge of the river, following its windings amongst thickets of hazel bushes. The river itself looked perfect—neither too high nor too low, there was a nice steady breeze in the right direction and a cloud had covered the sun. Adam's eyes kindled . . . he was in such a hurry to get the rod assembled that his fingers seemed all thumbs.

He started at the pool just above the bridge, casting across the current towards a big blue-grey rock . . . He was sure there was a big trout lying there . . . but no trout rose. Adam tried for a bit and then he went up to the next pool. It was a delightful river to fish for there were stretches of calm water and there were pools and rapids and boulders. Here and there the trees overhung the stream, but in other places they drew back and left it open and moory. It was delightful to fish, but unfortunately the fish seemed to have no use for Adam's flies this morning. Why hadn't they? wondered Adam. The conditions seemed perfect—could that cloud on the hill mean thunder? He was very fond of fishing, but he was not one of those madly keen fishermen who can go on casting all day long without getting a rise, so presently he wound in his line, leant the rod against a hazel tree and sat down.

How pretty it was! How peaceful! The river gurgled and splashed amongst the rocks and the breeze whispered in the leaves of the hazel trees. In front of him, across the river, rose a hill clothed with heather and behind was a broad-browed mountain boldly outlined against the sky. The sun had come out from behind its cloud and was shining warmly and glinting upon the ripples in the river. Adam watched the ripples for a while and then he closed his eyes . . .

It was late when Adam awoke, the sun was declining and the wind was quite chilly. He sat up and rubbed his eyes. He was annoyed with himself for sleeping . . . but it didn't matter, really. He could have a few casts now before returning to the Highland Bull for his evening meal. He looked round for his rod and saw that it was gone . . .

Adam sprang to his feet with an exclamation of dismay—it had been stolen while he was asleep—Mr. Brownlee's rod—and then he saw a man fishing about a hundred yards up the river. The man was wading, he was casting with an easy practised swing which betokened an expert in the art, but Adam had no time to admire the man's skill for he was sure that the man was using his rod. He shouted and waved and immediately the man wound up his reel and came towards Adam along the path. The man was hatless, he was wearing a suit of shabby brown tweeds—he was a small wiry individual. As he drew nearer Adam saw that he had sandy hair and a skin of reddish fairness flecked with freckles and his eyes beneath his scraggy sandy eyebrows were very light blue.

"What the devil are you doing with my rod!" shouted Adam.

"Fishing," replied the man. "They began to rise when the thunder clouds dispersed."

"You're a pretty cool customer," Adam said.

"The truth is I couldn't resist it," explained the man. "They were boiling all over the place and *there* was your rod and you asleep." He smiled as he spoke and his eyes twinkled . . . he reminded Adam of a cairn terrier, and perhaps this was the reason why Adam's heart was melted.

"It must have been very tempting," Adam admitted, with an involuntary smile.

"Very tempting. I just couldn't resist it . . . I've a nice basket of trout for you, Mr. Southey."

"How do you know my name?"

"I know you," he said. "I've been keeping an eye on you; I thought you'd have been to see me before now. Adam said you'd be coming."

"Adam?"

"My brother."

"Then you're Ebby, of course!" exclaimed Adam in surprise. The fact was obvious now that Adam knew the relationship for there was a definite resemblance between the two men. Ebby Ford had the same large features as his brother, the same big nose and jutting brows. They were much the same height, too, though Adam Ford was stockily built and this man was thin and wiry. Adam held out his hand and they shook hands gravely.

"Pleased to meet you, Mr. Southey," Ebby said.

"You don't talk like your brother."

"I dare say not. I've travelled all over the place and picked up different kinds of talk . . . but I can talk good Scots when I want. I'm the rolling stone of the family and Adam's the good boy, the industrious apprentice."

"He's certainly very industrious," agreed Adam, smiling at this description of his namesake.

"I've been in America," continued Ebby, "and then I was in Canada for a bit . . . I did some trapping there. It's a great country. Then I was in South Africa and I went on to Tanganyika. I was lucky there for I managed to get taken on by a man who was going on safari. That was grand."

"You've seen a bit of the world."

"That's what I wanted," Ebby explained. "It's fine going about and seeing places. I was in a store at Natal for a bit, and then I had a stroke of luck and made some money, but I lost it all and came home with nothing but the clothes I stood up in. I wouldn't have come home, mind you, but my mother was getting on and I wanted to see her before she died."

Ebby had sat down on a stone while he was talking and was busy filling his pipe. His hands were large and horny but he used them neatly. Adam liked the way he used his hands.

"Did your brother tell you——" Adam began.

"He told me a good deal," said Ebby. "He told me about the funny things that were happening at the works, and about the fellow you saw at Tinal. Adam doesn't approve of me, he thinks I might have made more of my chances, but when the test comes he

132

knows who he can trust. It's a queer thing how you come back to folks of your own blood."

"What do you think of it?"

"Well, Adam isn't the man to see trouble when there's no cause. He only sees what's there and even then he only sees three-quarters. Mind you he's good at his job, Adam is, but he hasn't much imagination. You don't need imagination working with machines."

"You don't like machines?"

"I like beasts," replied Ebby. "I like an active outdoor life . . . and I like time to think. I wouldn't change with Adam for all his fine position and the money he gets. He wouldn't change with me, of course. He thinks it's a poor job to be a shepherd, but you've time to think when you walk the hills after sheep. You see the sun come up over the hills, and you feel the breeze. It smells better than oil, Mr. Southey."

"Yes," said Adam thoughtfully.

"But to get back to this business—I've been worrying about you a bit. It seems to me if you've found out anything you may be in danger yourself. That's why I was keeping an eye on you."

"How were you keeping an eye on me?" Adam inquired.

"How?" repeated Ebby. "I was just watching you."

"I never saw you."

"No, I dare say not. When you know the hills as well as I do, it's not difficult to keep an eye on a man without being seen. You see, Mr. Southey, we were brought up here. My father was the shepherd and that's how I got the job. We were brought up in the wee cottage that I'm living in now."

"Funny to come back to it after all your wanderings."

"Yes, that's true. It was a queer sort of feeling—as if the rest of the world had been a kind of dream. There were three of us—three boys, Adam, Japhet and me—my mother knew her Bible."

"Obviously," Adam agreed.

"Japhet was killed in the last war," continued Ebby. "He was the best of us, Mr. Southey. It was always Japhet that thought of things to do—although Adam was a year older; some of the things we did were pretty wicked if the truth were told."

"Poaching, I suppose?"

"Poaching," agreed Ebby, and his eyes twinkled.

Adam had a feeling that Ebby was telling him all this to win his trust, but there was no need, for he had trusted the man at first sight. He said: "You know about the ray, of course."

"I was there," Ebby said. "I was on the hill. I saw what happened."

Adam was silent. He knew by the tone of Ebby's voice that he had been deeply impressed by the demonstration. Perhaps the thing haunted Ebby as it haunted him . . . the burst of flame, the strange white figure floating earthwards lit up by the blazing fragments which were falling round it . . .

"They mustn't get that machine——" said Ebby slowly. "We'll need to do something about it, you and me."

Adam sat down beside Ebby and lighted his pipe.

"I'll tell you this," said Ebby at last. "We'll need to get on to it through the man Cheller. You'll see him at the Highland Bull. Does he know you?"

"He's seen me at Tinal, of course, but I don't think he'll connect me with the janitor at Rockingham."

"But it's risky," Ebby said. "They'll not stick at murder. There's another way of course. I'm thinking of a farmhouse that's down near the sea. The land belonging to it was taken over by another farm so the house stood empty for years, but there's people in it now for I saw smoke from the chimneys."

"You mean we could have a look at it?"

"That was my idea," nodded Ebby. He was silent for a few moments, smoking hard, and then he said: "And then there's Mr. Taylor, himself, what about him?"

"Mr. Taylor!" exclaimed Adam.

"You don't think he's in it?"

"Good heavens, no. He's all right—if Cheller is up to mischief, it's without Mr. Taylor's knowledge."

"Cheller's using Mr. Taylor as a blind," said Ebby thoughtfully.

"Yes—and I think Mr. Taylor is beginning to suspect something; he told me that he was going to get rid of Cheller."

"That wouldn't suit Cheller."

"No, it wouldn't."

"And that's where the danger lies, for Cheller may suspect that you've had something to do with it—I mean if Mr. Taylor gives him the sack."

They discussed the matter for some time but without getting much further and while they were talking Ebby took down the rod and put everything neatly away. Adam knew that he must go for if he did not get back to the Highland Bull by eight o'clock he would miss his supper, but he was loath to part from his new friend. It was pleasant to feel that he had an ally—and such a trusty one.

"Where can I get hold of you?" Adam asked as he slung the fishing bag over his shoulder and prepared to go.

"I'll not be far away," replied Ebby. "I'll be looking in to see you at the Highland Bull to-morrow morning."

Chapter Seven

As Adam walked back to the bridge along the winding path he thought of all that had happened, and especially about Ebby Ford. It was odd how two brothers, so alike in feature, should be so different in nature and character . . .

He came to the bridge and scrambled up through a tangle of nettles and brambles into the road, and as he did so he noticed that there was a man on the bridge . . . He had propped his bicycle against the parapet and was pumping up the tyre, but as Adam passed he looked round over his shoulder and Adam saw that it was Cheller. Adam walked on. It was getting dark now for the sun had set and the sky was full of heavy clouds; on the moor there was a queer eerie half-light which made the few stunted trees look bigger than they really were and gave each rock and bush a special significance. Adam's shadow was faint but long and distorted as it went beside him along the road.

Where was Cheller going? Perhaps he was on his way to the Highland Bull, perhaps not. Adam wondered about it and then he took a sudden decision, turned off the road, crouched down behind a bush of gorse and waited patiently. After a little while he heard the crunch of footsteps on the road and Cheller went past up the hill wheeling his bicycle.

Adam left his fishing gear behind the bush and followed Cheller, keeping well behind and making use of what cover there was. He did not find it easy for he had never followed a man before and it was difficult to know the exact distance at which a man should be followed. He expected Cheller to mount his bicycle when the top of the hill was reached—and then he would be able to follow him no longer—but, instead of that, Cheller left the road and took a narrow path, a cart-track, which went off at right angles across the moor. It was even more difficult to follow him now for there was no cover at all and it was becoming so dark that Adam could hardly see his quarry unless he kept pretty close behind him, but fortunately

Cheller had his work cut out pushing his bicycle along the rutty track and did not look round.

At first the track was fairly level and then it began to slope gently downhill and after about a mile Adam felt a cooler breeze with a dampness in it as if they were getting down towards the sea . . . There were several gates on the track, but these were either standing open or fallen to pieces and rotting on the ground. Suddenly the path dived steeply into a wood, a dark dank wood with swathes of mist caught amongst the trees, and here Adam had to go more carefully than ever for the roots of the trees straggled across the path like snakes and between them the ground was wet and slimy. Cheller had disappeared in the gloom, but Adam could hear his footsteps and the rattle of the bicycle as it bumped over the uneven ground. In another few minutes a mass of dark buildings loomed into view . . . and a high wall. Adam heard the sound of a door being pushed open, and then shut with a bang. Cheller had gone in.

Adam hesitated. He wondered if this was the farmhouse of which Ebby had spoken. He and Ebby had decided to have a look at it sometime, but there was no need to wait for Ebby—he could go in now himself. What better opportunity could there be? He felt along the wall till he came to the door. He turned the handle very cautiously and found that it was locked. That was a nuisance, but the obstacle was by no means insuperable; in fact it was an added incentive as a locked door so often is. He peered about in the darkness and saw an old beech tree with gnarled branches which seemed to have been made for the purpose he had in mind. Adam climbed on to a branch and looked over the wall; he saw a yard, and, beyond the yard, the dark bulk of the house against the sky. It was very quiet; there was no movement, no sound of man nor beast; if he had not seen Cheller go in he would have said that the place was deserted and had been deserted for years; there was a feeling of dereliction about the place, a smell of decay . . .

Very carefully Adam let himself down into the yard. He found that it was paved with cobblestones and there were weeds growing in the crevices between them. He moved round the yard, keeping close to the wall and feeling his way along in the darkness; first he came to a broken horse trough and then to a wooden shed and then to the wall of the house. Here was a window with broken panes mended with cardboard and—yes—here was another window, boarded up. Adam felt his way along the wall; it was made of rough stone, damp and slimy. Ah, here was the door! He pushed it gently and it yielded to his touch. He pushed it wider and slipped in through the opening. It was even darker here in the narrow passage than it was outside and there was a musty smell, the smell of dirt and dry rot. At the other end of the passage there was a faint glow of light and as Adam tiptoed down the passage towards it he saw that it came from a door which was slightly ajar.

So far Adam had been carried along by his purpose—his aim had been to follow Cheller and he had followed Cheller without thinking of what he was going to do when he found him—but now that he had tracked Cheller to his lair he began to wonder what he was going to do next. Cheller was probably armed and Adam was not . . . Once again he had left the revolver behind just at the moment when he needed it . . . and then he heard the murmur of voices and realised that Cheller was not alone.

"It's all very well," Cheller was saying (Adam had heard that slightly nasal intonation before so he recognised it easily). "It's all very well for him; he doesn't need to worry. I wouldn't worry either if he left me alone to do my work in my own way. I don't like people sent to spy on me."

"It isn't that. He asked me to come and give you the letter, that's all."

Adam was amazed at the sound of the second voice for it was a woman's voice, quiet and cultured. Somehow he had a feeling that he had heard the voice before . . .

"I'm not blaming *you*," replied Cheller. "Why did he send you —that's what I want to know?"

"He was busy and I happened to be going out."

"He shouldn't have sent you here. You had better go back. I'm expecting someone——"

"Is there any answer?"

"No. Just say you gave me the note and it will be O.K."

There was the sound of a chair scraping on the stone floor and of footsteps; they were coming towards the door and Adam was in danger of discovery. He found another door behind him in the passage and opened it. He slipped into the room and pushed the door to, but did not shut it for he wanted to see the woman if he could and, as the passage was dark, he did not think that the slit of open door would be noticed. They would not come in here, he felt certain, for the room had a damp rotten smell as if it had not been used for centuries. Peeping through the slit, Adam saw Cheller come out of the lighted room into the passage; the woman followed him; she was wrapped in a dark red cloak with the hood of it drawn over her head. The light was behind her and she was outlined against the yellow glow.

"He shouldn't have sent you," Cheller was complaining. "He interferes too much; it might spoil everything . . ."

They turned down the passage towards the door which led out into the yard and, as they passed, Adam had a glimpse of the woman's face. It was a delicate face, with a clear white skin, very pale in contrast with the rough red cloth of the hood . . . The woman was Mr. Taylor's niece.

Adam was so amazed to see the girl here, and gazed at her so intently that she seemed to feel his eyes upon her . . . she looked back over her shoulder and hesitated.

"What are you dawdling for?" asked Cheller roughly. "I've no time to waste. What are you looking at?"

"It's so dirty," said the girl. "There are cobwebs everywhere. It ought to be cleaned if you're going to live here. I'll send Jean down here to-morrow——"

"I don't mind the dirt," he replied. "The place is all right as it is; it suits my purpose. Don't you send Jean or anyone else nosing about here. Come on, I'll see you through the wood, but you'll have to go the rest of the way alone."

"I'm not afraid of the dark."

"I'll see you through the wood," repeated Cheller impatiently.

They went down the passage and out of the back door . . . and Adam gasped with relief. He had thought for a moment that the girl had seen him—it had been a bad moment. What an amazing thing to see Miss Taylor here! What was she up to? What did it mean? But Adam had no time to think about it now for he wanted to have a prowl round before Cheller returned. Adam crept across the passage and looked into the lighted room; it was the kitchen, for it had a big old-fashioned range. A fire was burning cheerfully in the barred grate and this gave the room quite a different feeling from the rest of the house; it felt warm and dry and comfortable. There was an oil lamp with an amber shade standing on the table, and the table was laid for a meal. There was bread and butter and a pot of jam and a tin of sardines and a piece of cooked ham, and there were two bottles of beer and two glasses . . . Cheller was expecting a guest, and he was going to give his guest a good supper. Who was the guest? Not the girl, of course, for his one idea had been to get rid of her as quickly as possible.

Adam looked round and saw a piece of paper lying on the table, and a torn envelope with "Cheller" written on it. He picked them up and put them in his pocket. What else was there? He pulled out a drawer in the dresser and found it full of old cookery books. . . . The drawer had knives and forks in it. He was still looking round and wondering whether there was anything to be found when he heard a knock on the door. It was a gentle, furtive knock but in spite of that Adam was considerably startled . . . He dropped a fork and it fell on the stone floor with a tremendous clatter. Who was it? Who could it be? Not Cheller, of course, because Cheller wouldn't knock—besides the knock had been on the front door and Cheller had gone out through the yard.

The knock was repeated—this time a little louder—and Adam crossed the passage and opened the door; he peered out into the darkness and saw a figure, large and bulky, standing on the step.

"I've come," said the man in a husky whisper. "I've come, but I couldn't get it for to-night. Will you tell him . . . I'll try again . . ."

"He'll be angry," Adam whispered back.

"Tell him I couldn't manage it," whispered the man. "I'll have it Friday . . . I won't come in . . . you tell him . . . Friday . . ."

"Wait——" began Adam, for he was very anxious to get a look at Cheller's visitor. "Wait a moment——" But the man had faded into the shadows and was gone.

Adam hesitated for a moment and then followed, closing the door behind him, for he was anxious to be out of the house before

Cheller returned. It was completely dark now and there was mist as well, a raw mist which tasted salty on his lips. Adam stumbled down the broken steps and began to grope his way along the path, but he could see nothing and the next moment he found himself amongst bushes and brambles. He groped about, cursing softly as the brambles tore at his clothes and the nettles stung his hands, and at last he found a thickset hedge of hawthorn and squeezed through it—for he was quite desperate by now—floundered into a ditch full of muddy water and from thence on to a road.

By this time Adam was beginning to see a little better—either because the sky had lightened or because his eyes had become used to the gloom. He peered about and saw that the road ran in two directions between dark hedges. Which way should he go—north or south? He had no idea what road this was nor where it led. Adam turned to his right and began to walk along the road pretty smartly; he was glad to be out in the clean cool night, glad to breathe the pure fresh air with the tang of salt in it; he wanted to put as much distance as he could between himself and that horrible house . . . there was something positively foul about that house. It was dirty, of course, it was in a terrible state of decay, but there was a spiritual squalor about it as well, a feeling of evil which Adam had hated more than the dirt . . . Beastly hole, thought Adam, something pretty nasty is going on there.

The road wound between the hedges and there were dark patches shadowed by trees, and every now and then Adam caught a glimmer of the sea on his left, and heard the murmur of the waves in the distance. There was no other sound at all save the occasional shriek of an owl. He walked on, and gradually his pace slackened for he was very tired by now and extremely hungry. He remembered that he had had nothing to eat since the sandwiches which Evelyn had given him for his lunch . . . He had no idea when or where he would get another meal and that made him feel even more empty and lost. He wished he had his fishing bag with him for there were one or two sandwiches left . . . He wished he had taken a piece of bread from Cheller's supper table—no, he hadn't really got to that stage yet. He wished he could find an inn of some sort. Surely there must be an inn somewhere on this blinking road. There was no inn. There were no cottages. The road went on and on between the dark hedges, up hill and down dale, and at last Adam began to wonder whether it was any use walking on and on. He stopped and looked round and saw a dark solid-looking mass on his right. Perhaps it was a cottage where he could ask the way—perhaps it was a barn. He turned in through the gate and groped his way towards it and found that it was nothing more nor less than a very large haystack. Adam lay down beside the haystack and covered himself with hay.

Chapter Eight

A thick ground mist lay on the moor; it lay in hollows like water but softly opalescent, and here and there a tree or a mass of boulders rose above it . . . the rock masses looked like islands in a pearly sea. The sky was pale grey with cloud, but there was a faint brightness in one quarter of the heavens which showed where the sun was trying to shine through the clouds.

Adam had wakened early, hungry and cold, and now he was wandering over the moor trying to find his way back to the Highland Bull. He was warmer now, but not less hungry and he had begun to think that he was irretrievably lost. It would have been better to stick to the road—for all roads are bound to lead some-where—but he had been tempted to take to the moor by a path which he had assured himself was a short cut over to the valley where the Inn was situated. He was lost now. The hills seemed quite a different shape from the hills round Lurg and Adam could not make up his mind whether they were the same hills seen from a different angle or whether they were different hills. The path had led him high up on to the moor and there was nothing to be seen but hills—no cottages, no farms, no signs of man. The only living things that Adam had seen were a few small black-faced sheep and a covey of grouse. Adam toiled up a steep slope expecting to see the valley on the other side, but all he saw was a steeper slope in front of him. This had happened at least three times already—he had been climbing for hours . . .

He came at last to a place where the path forked and because he was tired he took the downhill path. It curled round the shoulder of a hill and joined a cart-track which was deeply rutted. This looked a little more hopeful and Adam mended his pace and walked on. The cart-track was descending now, it was zig-zagging down the hill and, looking ahead, Adam saw that the valley was full of mist. He looked across the valley to the trees on the other side; it was like looking across a lake. At the bottom of the valley there was a river for he could hear the sound of it splashing amongst the rocks; if it was the Tinal River—and what else could it be—he could follow it down to the bridge. Adam went down the slope and in a few moments the mist had risen to his waist . . . another few steps and it closed over his head. It was a curious feeling for it was not dark like a fog, but perfectly light and he could see all round him for about four yards perfectly clearly. It was as if he were walking in an opaque bubble. He went on a few steps farther and then he stopped: this was foolish; it was foolish to go forward without knowing where he was going. He turned and went back, climbing out of the mist, and sat down on a rocky mound.

It was very beautiful, very quiet and peaceful, and if Adam had not been so hungry he would have been happy to sit there for a long time. The sun was gaining strength and the clouds were breaking; a slight breeze had sprung up and was soughing down the glen, blowing the mist before it like smoke. The mist eddied and rose and billowed, it assumed strange shapes which faded gradually in the sun-warmed air.

Adam was sitting there watching the curious sight when he heard a shout and saw a man coming towards him up the hill and somehow or other he was not surprised to see that it was Ebby Ford.

"Mr. Southey," cried Ebby as he came nearer. "I've been looking for you—I was over at the Highland Bull and they said you hadn't been back. Where have you been?"

Adam replied that he had got lost and had slept under a haystack. He spoke rather shortly for he was not in the best of humours.

"You got lost!" exclaimed Ebby in surprise. "How did you manage that?"

"I saw Cheller and followed him."

"You did! I wondered what had happened, but you can tell me about it when you've had your breakfast."

"Breakfast?" inquired Adam, looking round the deserted moor. "Are we anywhere near your cottage?"

"No, we're not. My cottage is away the other side of the ben."

"The Highland Bull——"

"Is three miles away or more," declared Ebby, smiling. "Besides I'm not too sure of the Highland Bull. The landlord was asking questions about you . . . but let that be till we've had our breakfasts," added Ebby.

Adam was only too ready to postpone the discussion in favour of a meal, and although he did not see how Ebby was going to conjure up breakfast in the middle of a barren moor, he rose and followed obediently. They went down the hill through the tattered remnants of mist and came to a burn which ran at the bottom between high rocks—it was not the Tinal River after all—and after walking along the bank for a few minutes they came to a place where they could cross. There were two rocks here, flat and shiny with moisture, and the burn streaming between them like brown frothy ale. Ebby took the gap in his stride and Adam followed more carefully for leaping was not his strong point and his leg was stiff and tired . . . Ebby was waiting for him and caught his elbow and steadied him as he landed, but did not say a word. They were on a path now (a sheep path perhaps, for there were little tufts of wool caught on the thick heather at either side); it snaked up the hill between giant boulders and clumps of gorse. At the top of the rise the path turned, and followed the ridge of the hill. The heather was deeper here, as high as Adam's waist, purple as a king's robe and humming with bees . . . and now the path turned again and twisted down into a marshy place and disappeared.

"The sheep come here to drink," said Ebby, pointing to a spring which bubbled out of the ground and was surrounded by thousands of little hoofmarks in the mud . . . "We're nearly there," he added in an encouraging tone.

"Nearly where?" asked Adam, looking round at the hills and the marsh and seeing no signs of human habitation.

Ebby did not reply. He was leading the way across the marsh, leaping from tuft to tuft and pausing every now and then to see if Adam was following. They came to a ridge of rock, sheer as a wall, masked by a thicket of hazel bushes and brambles. Ebby pushed aside the bushes and held them apart for Adam and so they came to a little burn and beyond the burn a grassy slope and a cave hollowed out of the rock.

Adam stood still for a moment and looked round. It was a charming spot, the burn, the grassy slope and the cave, and all round was the screen of hazel bushes thick and pathless. He went forward and saw that, at the entrance to the cave, the rock was blackened with smoke and below this natural chimney was a neat fireplace built of stones and cemented together firmly. Ebby was already on his knees, scraping away the ashes and re-laying a fire with dry heather and sticks. Beside him on the ground there was a fishing bag—which looked familiar—and a couple of good-sized trout had rolled out of it . . .

"Where did you get the trout?" asked Adam in surprise.

"They're yours," said Ebby. "They're the ones I caught with your rod. I'll tell you the whole story when we've had our meal. Sit down, Mr. Southey. There's a pile of dry heather behind you."

Adam sat down. There were all sorts of questions he wanted to ask—so many questions that he did not know where to begin—and this being so it was easier to postpone them until Ebby was ready to pay attention. He was feeling a good deal better now that breakfast was within sight and it was a pleasure to watch Ebby making the preparations. Ebby was neat-handed, he was quick and sure in all his movements, he knew exactly what he wanted to do and did it without any fuss. The fire sprang up cheerfully—as if it were glad to serve him—and when he saw that it was burning well he disappeared into the cave and returned with a saucepan and several tins. Soon there was a delicious smell of coffee in the air and the trout, slit up the middle, were being dusted with oatmeal and laid upon a home-made grill.

"Who does this cave belong to?" asked Adam suddenly.

"I guess it belongs to me if it belongs to anybody," replied Ebby with a grin. "We found it when we were boys—and what a find it was! Many a game of robbers and smugglers we used to have here."

"Doesn't anybody else know about it?"

"I don't believe anybody ever knew about it except Japhet and Adam and me . . . and Japhet is dead and Adam has forgotten it long ago . . . but before our time people must have known about it for we found an old claymore buried in the floor and Japhet said it belonged to a soldier who had fought at Culloden."

"This would be a splendid place for a fugitive," said Adam thoughtfully. "I wouldn't mind living here myself."

146

"That's just exactly what I was thinking," replied Ebby, looking over his shoulder and nodding significantly. "You'd be as free as air if you lived here."

Adam was startled at this for he had spoken at random and it had never occurred to him for a moment that he might actually take up his residence in the cave. He was about to reply and to point out the obvious disadvantages of cave-dwelling for civilised man when he was suddenly presented with a large slice of bread, a trout on a tin plate and a mug of steaming coffee.

"You're a wizard, Ebby!" he exclaimed, falling upon the viands with ravenous haste.

After that there was silence for some time, and it was not until Adam had finished one trout and was half-way through a second that his curiosity began to stir.

"You found my fishing bag," he said.

Ebby nodded. "It was this way, you see. I went down to the Bull early this morning and found you hadn't been there. It gave me a fright, I can tell you, especially when old Farl began to ask questions. It was then I thought of this place, Mr. Southey, so I took your suitcase and said you'd not be coming back. I said you'd been called away on business."

"You did, did you?"

"Maybe you think it was taking too much on myself," said Ebby gravely, "but I was a bit worried. So then I came back up the hill and I saw where you'd left the road and taken to the moor, and I found your fishing bag and the rod hidden behind a bush. I brought all the things up here. All the time I was thinking where you could be and then I thought maybe you might have taken it into your head to go down to that farmhouse, and maybe got into trouble there, so I was on my way down to the place to look for you."

"I was there," said Adam. "I saw Cheller and followed him. I'll tell you the whole story."

"Have another cup of coffee first," Ebby suggested.

Adam held out his mug and then got down to the tale of his night's adventures, and Ebby listened with his eyes fixed on Adam's face.

". . . so there *is* something pretty queer going on there," said

147

Adam. "It's a pity I didn't see that man's face—the man who came to the door; I wouldn't know him again. He was just a big burly shadow with a husky voice. I wonder how long Cheller waited for him."

"He'd be angry—Cheller would," said Ebby slowly. "He'll seek out the man, most likely, and the man will say he came and left a message——"

"And Cheller won't believe him," added Adam in confident tones.

"Maybe not," agreed Ebby. "But we can't be sure of it. Did you leave any trace of your presence in the house?"

Adam was sure he had left no trace.

"There'll be footmarks in the dust," Ebby reminded him. "Maybe Cheller won't notice them—but then again he might— and he might be wondering where the letter had gone to. Have you looked at the letter, Mr. Southey?"

"I'd forgotten all about it," said Adam, producing the crumpled piece of paper from his pocket.

Ebby rose and looked at it over Adam's shoulder. It was a half sheet of note-paper, and the message was written upon it in pencil and had no beginning nor end.

> Put the screw on.
> I must have it before Friday. E. is on his way.

"That tells us a lot," said Adam in disappointed tones.

"It tells us a little," said Ebby. "It tells us that Cheller is no more than a tool. Cheller was to have got something from the man who called at the door, and Cheller's master must have it before Friday because E. is coming."

"The plans of the ray!" exclaimed Adam.

"I think you're right," agreed Ebby soberly.

"But who is E.?"

"Ah, if we knew that!"

"And the girl—where does she come in?"

Ebby did not reply and they were silent for a few minutes.

"We don't know much," said Adam at last with a sigh.

148

Ebby agreed. He said: "There's just two roads from here, Mr. Southey. You can wait and tell Mr. Brownlee the whole story or we can set to in earnest and do the job ourselves."

"What have we got to tell?" Adam inquired. "We haven't anything definite, have we?"

"I'm all for the second road, myself," said Ebby, smiling.

Adam returned the smile. He was feeling much better now that he was warm and comfortable and well fed. He lay back on his bed of heather and smoked his pipe while Ebby washed the breakfast dishes and put them away.

"Why don't you let me help?" Adam asked him.

"Because I'm quicker working alone. I'm used to it and I know just where to lay my hands on things . . ." He vanished into the cave as he spoke and returned with Adam's shaving tackle and arranged it all very neatly on a rock; he set up a small mirror and lifted a pan of hot water off the fire.

"Ebby!" exclaimed Adam, laughing. "Ebby, you really are a wizard—there's no doubt of that."

Ebby smiled. "There's nothing very wonderful in a pan of hot water, Mr. Southey. The fact is it's a great mistake to be uncomfortable if you can help it and you can usually help it by taking a little thought. You can make yourself comfortable almost anywhere and in almost any circumstances: in a tent with the thermometer below zero, or in a dugout, or in a grass hut in the tropics. I've tried all of them so I know what can be done. I'm willing to bear discomfort if necessary, but I like to be comfortable and snug."

Adam was shaving now. He laughed suddenly—it was a kind of snort—and said: "I wish we'd had you with us in the van. I was never so cold and hungry and dirty in my life."

"Adam was telling me about it," said Ebby, and his eyes twinkled.

"He told you, did he?"

"Yes, but he didn't get much sympathy from me . . . You'll not be cold or hungry or dirty here, Mr. Southey. I'll see to that."

By this time Adam was quite reconciled to the idea of taking up his abode in the cave and this was just as well for Ebby had been set on it from the beginning, and liked having his own way.

"Do you come here much?" inquired Adam.

149

"Quite often. Sometimes I get tired of the cottage, for it's lonely living in a cottage by yourself, and I come up here for a bit of a change. I can keep an eye on the sheep—it's a grand place to stay when the lambing starts—and I bring a few books with me to keep me company. *Robinson Crusoe*'s one of my favourites; did you ever read it?"

"Long ago," said Adam.

"And *Kidnapped*," added Ebby. "*There's* a grand book for you ... Sometimes I wish I'd been there myself with David, walking over the hills."

"He wouldn't have got into so many scrapes if you'd been there," declared Adam with a sideways smile.

They chatted on while Ebby busied himself putting the cave to rights and once again Adam marvelled at the differences in the brothers. Adam Ford was taciturn; he was a good sort and excellent at his job, but not interested in anything outside his somewhat narrow orbit; Ebby was interested in everything, he was a better companion in every way, more humorous, more intelligent and more knowledgeable ... It was curious that Adam should have got to know these brothers so well—first the one and then the other.

Ebby paused in his work and seized Adam's arm. "Look!" he whispered. "There's a wee friend of mine—he always comes to visit me when I'm at the cave ... Look, Mr. Southey!"

It was a small red squirrel with a bushy tail. Ebby threw a crust on the ground and the squirrel ran down a tree and sat within a few yards of the cave, holding the crust between its paws and nibbling it daintily ... and watching the two men with its bright beady eyes.

"He's an awful wee rogue," declared Ebby, whose rugged face had broken into a delighted smile. "I've known him come right into the cave and sit there looking at me, waiting for me to give him his breakfast."

Chapter Nine

Adam lay on a bed of dry heather and gazed at his fire. He was exceedingly proud of it for he had lighted it himself and, although it had taken some time to kindle properly and had occasioned its author a good deal of anxiety, it was burning brightly now and giving forth heat and comfort. It was very quiet in the cave. Adam had never "heard" such quiet before. In a house there is always some sound to break the stillness—a door opening, footsteps, voices, the rattle of a window or the creak of furniture—but here in the cave there was no sound at all.

The cave itself was getting dark now for the sun had moved round the hill, but it was still shining on the hazel bushes and Adam could see the bright golden picture of hazel bushes and mountains framed in the dark rock of the cave's entrance. He was very much pleased with his new abode; it was dry and comfortable and there was something about it that moved his imagination. There was a good deal of the boy in Adam, and what boy would not enjoy living in a cave? Adam thought of the soldier from Culloden who had sheltered here, who had lain here where Adam was lying and lighted and tended his fire . . . and before that it must have afforded shelter to other desperate men, to robbers and cattle thieves, perhaps. There was a strange freedom in this existence—or at least it was strange to Adam who was used to being bound down by the clock; he could come and go as he liked with nobody to hinder him; he could sleep when he felt inclined and eat when he was hungry. As a matter of fact he had slept most of the day, for Ebby had left soon after breakfast and it was now well on in the afternoon . . . and he was hungry now so why shouldn't he make himself a cup of tea and eat a slice of bread and jam with it? He rose and put the kettle on the fire and found the teapot and a tin of milk and an enamel mug . . . Soon he was sitting there having his tea and no tea had ever tasted so good.

Why do we live in houses? asked Adam of himself. Why do we hamper ourselves with so much unnecessary furniture? Why do we tie ourselves down to feed and sleep at fixed hours and make ourselves slaves to the clock?

The sun was declining by the time that Adam had finished and washed up and put everything neatly away and this was the right moment to go out and shoot a rabbit for supper. Ebby was coming later and he would cook the supper and then, when it was dark, they would go down to the farmhouse together and have a good look round. Cheller might be there again to-night and, if so, he would have two unexpected visitors. Adam thought of all these plans as he picked up Ebby's gun, which was leaning against a rock, and went out to shoot his rabbit.

When he came out of the hazel thicket on to the hillside, he paused for a moment and looked around, memorising the geographical features of the place so that he would be able to find it again. There was the marsh in front, held in a pocket of hills, and from it the burn streamed down to join the Tinal River. There were hills all round, some of them rocky, some covered with heather or greenish yellow grass. The cave was in a good strategic position for it lay in the middle of a triangle made by the Highland Bull, Tinal Castle and the old farmhouse. Adam could see the Inn on the road beneath him, but he did not go down. He took a path along the edge of the marsh and round the shoulder of a hill. There was an old sheep-fank here and Ebby had said that there was a warren farther on, beyond the sheep-fank; he would get his rabbit there when the sun went down. Adam saw the sea as he came round the shoulder of the hill, and he saw the sun, an orange-red ball, almost touching the water. Far below him was Tinal Castle, its squat towers outlined against the glowing path of the sun.

The sheep-fank with its crumbling walls was behind him now and Adam was going down towards another burn which ran in a deep cleft between the hills and was masked by rowan trees, their berries pink in the evening light. He was going carefully with his gun at half cock for he might see a rabbit at any moment . . . and then his eye caught a glimpse of something which moved against the rocks at the edge of the burn. At first he thought it might be a

152

sheep, for there were plenty of sheep on the hills, but as he ap-proached nearer he saw that it was a woman.

The woman was sitting on a rock with her back towards him, she was leaning over the stream and bathing her foot in the water. The babble of the burn masked the sound of Adam's approach and he stood and looked at her for a few moments before she became aware of his presence. It seemed very strange to find a woman here on this lonely hillside with darkness falling . . . Perhaps it was a woman from Tinal village, or perhaps a visitor who had lost her way and had an accident amongst the rocks. Adam did not want to show himself, he had enough on his hands already without taking on any fresh responsibilities, but he realised that he could not leave the woman here without finding out what was the matter.

He was still hesitating and wondering what to do when she turned her head, holding it on one side and listening.

"Is anyone there?" she asked, and her voice quivered a little.

"Have you hurt your foot?" said Adam, going forward as he spoke.

She looked up at him with a white face and startled eyes and he saw to his amazement that it was Miss Taylor.

"Oh!" she exclaimed. "Oh, I thought you were—someone else!"

Adam did not know what to say. He wondered whom she had expected to see in that wild place.

"I'm afraid you've hurt your foot," he said at last.

"It's nothing. I just twisted it a little," she replied.

Adam bent down and took the foot in his hands. He knew a little first aid (enough to know whether any serious damage had been done). The foot was small and white and very cold. He moved it gently this way and that.

"You haven't broken anything," he said. "It's just sprained a little, I think."

"It's nothing at all," she replied, turning away her head, but not before Adam had seen tears quivering on her long lashes.

"I say, I *am* sorry!" he exclaimed. "I'm afraid I hurt you."

"I told you it's nothing," she replied in quivering tones. "You don't suppose I'm crying because I hurt my foot, do you?"

153

As this was exactly what Adam had supposed, he could find no suitable answer.

She took out her handkerchief and dried her eyes. "No," she said firmly, "I don't mind the pain. It isn't really bad."

She raised her chin as she spoke and looked at him fairly and squarely; he noticed that her eyes were very dark brown. He noticed also that although she was muddy and untidy, with her dark curls in disorder and her face as pale as death, she seemed to have acquired a certain dignity, she seemed to have come alive. When Adam had seen this girl at Tinal Castle her face had worn a strange blank expression; she looked quite different to-day.

"I'm glad the pain isn't bad," said Adam after a moment's pause.

"I was trying to run away," explained the girl. "I jumped off a rock and twisted my foot, that's all."

"Trying to run away!"

"Yes, from Tinal Castle. Now I shall have to go back, I suppose——"

"But why?" asked Adam in bewilderment. "Why were you running away?"

"That's a long story," replied Miss Taylor firmly.

There was silence for a few moments. Adam was trying to decide what he ought to do. The girl was "queer" of course—Mr. Taylor had said so—and the fact that she was trying to run away from the Castle proved that she was "queer." She must be taken back to Tinal, and Adam would have to take her. He would have to carry her down the hill. Meanwhile Ebby would be waiting for him and wondering where he was.

"You needn't bother about me," she said suddenly, and he realised that she had read some of his thoughts.

"It isn't a bother," he declared. "I was just wondering what to do. I think I had better take you home, you know."

"I can go home myself."

"But your foot," said Adam. "No, really, I had better see you safely home."

"I suppose you think I'm not fit to be at large," remarked Miss Taylor in bitter tones. "You think I ought to be locked up, don't you?"

154

"Mr. Taylor will be anxious about you," said Adam uncomfortably.

"He thinks I'm in bed," she replied. "I had made all my arrangements to run away and, if I hadn't hurt my foot, they would have worked out splendidly."

"I'm afraid you will have to go home," repeated Adam.

She did not answer that, but after a moment she said: "Who are you?"

"Adam Southey," said Adam in amazement. "Don't you remember me? I lunched at the Castle——"

"Yes, of course I remember you," she replied. "I didn't mean what was your name. I meant *who* are you? Why are you here?"

"I'm a schoolmaster and I'm here for the holidays."

"You spend your holidays in a funny way. What were you doing at Yowe Farm last night?"

Adam might have returned the question but he was too nonplussed. "What was I doing——" he began.

"Yes, you were there. I saw you behind the door."

That staggered him. She had seen him and had said nothing about it to Cheller. What did it mean?

"You seem—surprised," she said and there was a trace of amusement in her voice.

"I am surprised," he admitted. "I mean—I mean why didn't you tell Cheller I was there?"

"Why should I tell Cheller?"

Her voice was so scornful that Adam exclaimed: "You don't like Cheller!"

"Do you like him?" she asked. She hesitated and then added in a different tone: "I thought just now, when I heard someone behind me, that it was Cheller following me. That's why I was so startled. I thought—but it doesn't matter what I thought."

"Have you told your uncle that Cheller—annoys you?" Adam asked her.

She looked at him gravely. "You don't understand," she said. "It's true that Cheller annoys me, but I can look after myself. I'm not frightened of Cheller—not really. I'm frightened of—other things."

155

"What are you frightened of?" he asked.

"Things that I can't understand. There are queer things happening—secret things . . ."

"And that's why you were trying to run away?"

She hesitated again and then replied: "There was another reason as well. I mean it was not just because I was frightened, not just for my own sake . . ."

Again there was silence. Adam had the feeling that he was fencing with this girl. He was beginning to realise that he had been mistaken in his estimate of her. She was as sane as he was; her brain was as clear as his and a good deal quicker. Why had Mr. Taylor told him —or hinted to him—that she was not quite normal? It was most extraordinary. Was the girl playing a deep game? Somehow or other he could not believe it.

"You don't look like a person who runs away from things," said Adam at last.

"But I couldn't do any good," she replied gravely. "It's dreadful to feel helpless, to know that something is wrong and not be able to put it right. I wouldn't have run away if I could have done any good by staying. Besides I told you there was another reason, didn't I?"

"You didn't tell me what it was."

She said in a low voice: "I wanted to find someone."

"Who did you want to find?"

"Anyone," she replied with a gesture of her hands. "Anyone who would listen to me and help me."

"Wouldn't I do?" he asked.

"You!" she said. "But you think I'm crazy. You think I'm a poor mad girl who has escaped from her keepers and must be taken home."

"I think you are as sane as I am," replied Adam quickly.

She looked at him. "If only I knew who you were . . ." she said, in a doubtful tone.

The sun had vanished now and it was getting darker every moment. A band of deep amethyst cloud was stretched across the sky, shutting away the saffron light of the sunset. Ebby would be waiting at the cave, but Adam could not help that for he knew that he must hear this girl's story. He sat down on a rock and began to fill his pipe.

"What do you want to know about me?" he inquired.

"I want to know if I can trust you."

"Why shouldn't you trust me?"

"Because," she said slowly, "because I've learnt that there are very few people you can trust."

He left that and tried another way. He said: "You were looking for someone who would listen to you and you've found me."

"But how can I tell you!" she cried. "You might be the wrong person."

"We both dislike Cheller," said Adam with a smile. "We have common ground there, haven't we?"

She laughed somewhat mirthlessly and replied: "A good many people dislike Cheller."

"Why not tell me," urged Adam.

"You wouldn't believe me."

"Why?"

"Because it's incredible. You wouldn't believe that anyone could get mixed up in horrible things without knowing it . . . you couldn't believe that, could you?"

Adam was beginning to think that he could believe it. He said cautiously: "What sort of things?"

There was a word on her lips but she hesitated. She said: "I must trust you. I haven't any choice. I'm absolutely helpless and it's so important—so terribly important. But first of all tell me what you were doing at Yowe Farm. Did Cheller know you were there?"

"Not unless you told him."

"You know I didn't tell him," she said quickly. "You *know* that, because he would have gone straight back and found you."

"Why did you ask if Cheller knew I was there?"

"I didn't think of it at the time," she replied. "It was afterwards . . . I began to wonder whether you were hiding from *me*."

"I was hiding from Cheller."

"He was expecting someone——"

"Not me," said Adam quickly.

"Who then?" she asked.

"I wish I knew," declared Adam. "I would give a good deal to know who it was that called on Cheller last night."

"Why didn't you wait and see?"

"I did see the man," said Adam. "I saw him for a moment in the dark, but he made off before I could recognise him. If you have any idea——"

"But I haven't!" she cried. "I'm groping in the dark . . ."

They looked at each other gravely. There was still enough light in the sky to enable them to see each other's faces . . . and once again Adam marvelled at the change in this girl. There was no sign of "nerves" in the determined little face and proudly tilted head. Her eyes were dewy with unshed tears but her mouth was firm; she was bearing her troubles with courage and dignity. Adam was aware that she was looking at him intently, scrutinising his features, trying to read his heart and to make up her mind about him.

After a few moments Brenda Taylor gave a little sigh. "Yes," she said in a low tone. "Yes, I can trust you. I shall tell you everything from the very beginning because that's the only way to make you understand."

Chapter Ten

The sun had set some time ago and the twilight was deepening. It was very quiet, so quiet that even the sound of the burn seemed muted. In the queer half-light it seemed as though the mountains had drawn back from the valley leaving it wider and shallower. The sky was amber towards the west and here and there a faint star was beginning to twinkle. All of a sudden it seemed much colder, the wind whispering down the little glen had a nip in it and Adam realised that if they were going to talk much longer they would have to move into a more sheltered place. He rose and looked about.

"You aren't going!" exclaimed Brenda in dismay.

"No, of course not, but we shall have to move. Wait a moment till I find a sheltered place."

He went up the hill and found a pile of boulders and then he returned and helped the girl to rise. When he had got her into the cranny of rock and settled her there, she looked up at him and smiled. The smile lighted her face and made her seem more human —it was the first smile he had seen on that delicate flowerlike face.

"Warmer?" asked Adam, smiling back at her.

"Much warmer," she replied.

"Now we can talk comfortably," he said, sitting down beside her. "I want to hear everything."

"I want to tell you everything, but it's so incredible. I wonder if you will believe what I have to tell." She clasped her hands as she spoke and raised her head. The smile had vanished now and her face looked pinched and drawn as she started her story.

"My father died when I was very young," said Brenda Taylor. "My mother and I lived together in a country village. My life was narrow and rather dull—or at least I thought so at the time. I looked after my mother and ran the house with one little maid. When my mother died I had nowhere to go and I didn't know what to do— and then my uncle suddenly appeared on the scene. He was very kind to me, he managed everything; it seemed as if all my troubles were over when Uncle Roland came. I had thought of getting a job, but Uncle Roland wouldn't hear of it; he said I must go and live with him and run his house. He was rich and very generous and he gave me a big allowance to spend on clothes for he liked to see me look nice when his friends came to the house. He had a great many friends—different kinds of friends—and he entertained a great deal. It was a very different life for me—London in the winter and Tinal Castle in the summer and all the time people coming and going. Some of the people were rather queer, some of them were foreigners; Uncle Roland liked all kinds of people; he can speak several languages fluently. I took it all for granted and enjoyed it . . . I never thought there was anything wrong. No child of seventeen fresh from school could have been more gullible than I was."

There was such bitterness in her voice that Adam stirred uncomfortably. "But you don't mean that your uncle——" he began.

"You must wait," she said. "I must tell you in my own way. He was very generous, very kind, not only to me but to everyone. After the Austrian Anschluss there was a constant stream of refugees coming to the house and Uncle Roland helped them all; they were fed and housed for weeks at a time."

"Refugees?"

"That's what they were supposed to be."

"And weren't they refugees?"

"They were spies," she replied in a low voice. "They were enemy agents."

"They couldn't have been!" Adam exclaimed.

She laughed mirthlessly. "I told you it was incredible, I don't blame you for not believing what I say . . . They were enemy agents," she continued. "Oh, of course I didn't know it *then*. I was easily deceived, all the more easily because I was so fond of Uncle Roland. He was always good to me, kind and thoughtful and amusing; he took endless trouble to give me a good time. I thought he was the most wonderful person that ever lived. I thought he was perfect . . ."

Her voice broke here, but she pulled herself together and continued firmly. "It was only after the war started that I began to have faint doubts—vague formless suspicions that something was wrong

—and even then I shut my eyes. When I was with him the doubts fled and I was sure that everything was all right; it was only when he was not there that I became worried and anxious. I began to wonder what his business really was and how he made his money—so much money for so little work. It seemed queer. Then, this year, when we came north to Tinal things were different, Uncle Roland was different, and I began to realise that he was using me . . . using me in all sorts of strange ways. He was not so kind and thoughtful, not quite so—so careful. Perhaps he was tired of keeping up appearances before me or perhaps he thought I was completely under his influence and it didn't matter."

"Do you really mean that Mr. Taylor is . . . "began Adam and then he stopped for it was too frightful to put into words.

"I don't know what he is," Brenda replied. "I only know that something is terribly wrong . . . and I know, now, where all the money comes from."

"Not from Germany!" exclaimed Adam. "Not Mr. Taylor!"

"You liked him, didn't you?" she said. "I saw that you had fallen beneath his spell. I've seen it happen so often—over and over again. He's so wonderfully clever, and he knows how to talk to people—he has a different way of talking to everyone. It used to amuse me to see him exert his charm and people go down like ninepins . . . but it doesn't amuse me now. You can't believe what I'm telling you, can you? You can't believe that his charming friendly manner is nothing but a mask."

Adam did not know what to believe. He had liked and admired Mr. Taylor so much, but there was such sincerity in this girl that it was difficult to discredit her story.

"Oh, what can I say to make you believe me?" cried Brenda in despair. "What can I do? Things are working up to a climax—something is going to happen soon—something important—more important than anything that has happened before. I don't know what it is. I only know that Cheller is trying to find out something for Uncle Roland, to get some important information for him, something important and urgent, something that he wants at once. I can't tell you how I know all this for it would take too long . . . I know it in a dozen different ways . . . by putting things together . . .

a few words here and a few words there. Oh, you *must* believe me!"

"I do believe you," Adam said and now it was true for she was in such dire distress that he could doubt her no longer.

"Oh, thank heaven!" she cried. "Thank heaven—you will help me, won't you?"

"Yes, of course. What do you want me to do? Shall we go to the police and tell them what you've told me?"

She hesitated. "They wouldn't believe it, would they?" she said in a low voice.

"Why shouldn't they believe it?"

"Because of him," she replied. "Because he's so well known and respected. He has dozens of influential friends. I haven't any proof—not a shadow of proof against him and who would take my word against his? Even if they did believe me or took the trouble to go and see him and investigate he would be able to convince them that he was innocent; he can make people believe anything; he can convince them that black is white. I've thought about it so often that I can imagine the scene quite easily. He would explain that my 'nerves' were upset by the raids; he would laugh and give them drinks all round and shake hands with them in his bluff hearty manner when they went away . . . and as they went down the drive they would say to each other that it was a pity about the girl—she ought to be locked up."

Adam was silent for he had felt Mr. Taylor's charm and he saw the little scene might easily take place.

"He tells everyone that I'm mentally unbalanced," she continued in a hopeless voice. "Sometimes I begin to wonder if he's right . . ."

"Oh, no!"

"Oh, yes," she said. "You don't know how dreadful it is to be surrounded by people who speak to you cheerfully and watch you with suspicion—you begin to doubt yourself. That day when you came to lunch I could see you were sorry for me. You thought I was mad, didn't you?"

"He said—he hinted——" began Adam uncomfortably.

"I know," she nodded. "I know exactly what he would say and how he would say it. Just a few words and then a pause . . . and then in a more cheerful voice: 'but I mustn't bore you with my troubles, Southey' . . . Oh, yes, I know."

"But you," said Adam, "you never spoke——"

"I thought you were one of them—another tool. I thought I would live up to my reputation. Then when I saw you at Yowe Farm, hiding behind the door, I began to wonder about you."

Little by little the pieces were falling into place. Adam's knowledge fitted in with all that she had told him and the picture was taking shape.

Brenda sighed. "If only I could tell you more!" she said. "If only I knew what he does or how he sends his information to the enemy. If only I knew what it is that Cheller is trying to find out for him."

"I know that," Adam said. "It isn't information. He's trying to get hold of some plans——"

"Plans!" she cried, looking at Adam aghast. "I knew it was vitally important! Plans of fortifications, I suppose, so that they'll know where our guns are hidden when they try to invade us!"

Adam did not enlighten her for he saw no need, and it was safer for her not to know too much. He thought for a moment and then he said: "Your uncle is expecting someone to arrive shortly. Someone called 'E.' Do you know anything about him?"

"It must be the Baron," she replied. "Yes, Baron Ehrling von Brum. Uncle Roland said he was coming."

"Can you tell me anything about him?"

Brenda nodded. "He's a Dutch refugee . . . At least that's what he's supposed to be, but there's something rather mysterious about him. He's tall and fair—rather good-looking in his own way—and he's very polite and friendly but somehow one feels that he's an important person. I mean he has an air of authority, and even Uncle Roland is just a little in awe of him."

"Where does he live?"

"He's supposed to live in London, but we've never seen him there—only at Tinal. He's been to stay with us several times and each time he has appeared quite suddenly."

"Unexpectedly?" asked Adam.

"No, not exactly," she replied. "Uncle Roland tells me that he's coming and to have his room prepared . . . and then, one morning when I go down to breakfast, he is there. He said he had come by the night train from London, but surely if that were so Uncle Roland would have sent the car to meet him."

"How do you know that he didn't?"

"I asked the chauffeur," replied Brenda simply.

Adam was silent for a few moments and then he said: "You've told me a great deal, but we've got to find out more before we can do anything."

She nodded: "Yes, I see that. I'd do anything to help."

"Do you mean that?"

"Yes," she said. "Yes, I mean it. I'll do anything you say. I'll go back to Tinal if that's what you want me to do."

"Would you really?"

"Yes," she repeated. "I can go back. I can get back to my room without anyone knowing. Tell me what you want me to do." Adam looked at her. There was something in her small determined face that moved his heart; he felt it turn over in his breast. There was fear in her eyes, but her mouth was firm and steadfast. How could he send her back? . . . And then he saw that he must, for the affair was so desperately important that he must use every weapon in his power.

"Yes," said Adam slowly. "I know it's terribly difficult, but I think you must go back. I wouldn't ask you to do it if I could see any other way."

"It won't be so bad," she said. "I mean I shall know that you believe in me."

Adam took her hand and her fingers clung to his. He was surprised—almost dismayed—by the smallness and the softness of her hand . . . It seemed a dreadful thing to send her back to that house, all the more dreadful because so much depended upon her.

"You can bear a lot if you have a friend," Brenda continued in a low voice. "I shall know that you're—somewhere——"

"I shan't be far away."

"You want me to find out more, don't you?"

"That's only part of it," said Adam. "I want a friend in the enemy's camp."

"You shall have one," she said, gravely.

164

By this time it was quite dark and the sky was full of stars. It was time to get Brenda back to the Castle before her absence was discovered. Adam inquired anxiously how the foot was feeling.

"Much better," she replied. "I told you it was nothing."

"I could carry you," Adam said. It would not have been difficult, but Brenda would not hear of this.

They went down the slope together, slowly and carefully, Brenda leaning on his arm. He was sure by her hurried breathing that the foot was giving her pain, but she would not give in, and presently when they reached the path which wound along beside the river it was easier going and they were able to mend their pace. They did not talk much for they had done all their talking and the night was very quiet—the river flowed softly and there were stars in every pool.

"How lovely!" Brenda whispered. "How peaceful! It makes war and treachery and wickedness seem worse."

Adam squeezed her arm to show that he understood.

"There will be peace," she continued. "There will be real peace in the world, but not until men are able to understand this—this peace of mountains and rivers . . ."

"Yes," said Adam softly. He wanted her to go on talking for her voice was part of the beauty of the night.

"Yes," said Brenda. "So many people see these things with their eyes—Uncle Roland, for instance—but they don't see it with their hearts . . ."

"Blind hearts."

"Blind hearts," repeated Brenda.

They had reached the little hog-backed bridge and here Brenda stopped. "You had better not come any farther," she said. "I can manage now. How shall I send you a message? I can't trust anyone in the house."

Adam took out his cigarette case and slipped it into a crevice between two stones. "That's our pillar-box," he said, trying to speak lightly. Now that the moment had come to part, he felt miserable for he was risking this girl's life and if anything happened to her he would never forgive himself.

Once more her hand lay in his, soft and confiding. "Be careful, won't you?" he said. "I can't tell you how much I admire your courage. I shall be thinking of you all the time."

He stood there for a few minutes after she had gone and then he turned and walked back the way they had come. As he went he tried to sort out all that Brenda had told him, and to make some sort of plan, but it was difficult to think of plans. Brenda's face rose before his eyes, her voice rang in his ears, he felt the touch of her soft fingers on his hand. He had never met anyone like this girl before, never anyone who had moved his heart as she had. She was so small and yet so determined; she was frightened and yet she was brave. Oddly enough Adam had not felt shy and awkward with her, he had not thought of his lameness—no, not once. Perhaps he had been too busy thinking about her to think of himself.

Chapter Eleven

There was a greyness in the sky and the stars were growing pale when Adam reached the cave, for, although he had memorised the contours of the hills, the cave was so well hidden that it had been difficult to find. He had shot a rabbit on the way and was carrying it in one hand with Ebby's gun over his shoulder. Adam parted the hazel bushes and stepped over the burn. It was very dark in the little clearing, but a dim glimmer showed from the fire and beside the fire sat Ebby with his back against the rock and his head drooping sideways on his shoulder. He started up as Adam approached; he awoke all of a sudden just as animals do.

"Mr. Southey!" he exclaimed in reproachful tones. "I've been here for hours. You said you would wait for me!"

"I couldn't help it, Ebby."

"I've been wondering if something had happened to you!"

"I know," said Adam. "I meant to be back." He sat down as he spoke and put the rabbit on the ground.

"Have you had your supper?" Ebby inquired, looking at the rabbit in surprise.

"That's our supper," replied Adam with a smile. "It's more like breakfast time but it isn't my fault. I've lots to tell you, Ebby."

He began to tell Ebby all that he had heard and Ebby, while he listened, skinned and cleaned the rabbit and began to prepare a meal. It seemed to Adam that Ebby's hands worked of their own accord for his attention never wavered from the story.

". . . so you see I couldn't let you know," said Adam at last. "I had to find out all that I could, and I had to get Miss Taylor back to the Castle."

Ebby did not answer that, for he was not one to waste words upon what was self-evident. Instead he said slowly: "It's dangerous work for a woman."

"D'you think I don't know that?" cried Adam. "D'you think I didn't see the danger? I may have sent her to her death . . ."

"It's pretty grim."

"It's frightful, but I had no choice, had I?"

"Not much," agreed Ebby. "We've got to do what we can. I'm not as surprised as you to hear about Taylor for, to tell the truth, I thought it might be him at the bottom of it. I thought so all along but you wouldn't have it."

"I liked him so much," said Adam regretfully. "Even now I can scarcely believe it . . ."

"It all fits in," declared Ebby.

Adam agreed. He said: "Well, what now? Are we to go to Mr. Brownlee or not?"

There was a little silence. Ebby straightened his back and gazed out over the trees. "Have we any proof?" he said. "Have we anything at all that couldn't be explained away? We've nothing but our own suspicions and the story of a girl that's supposed to be half-crazy . . . and Taylor is a J.P. and the head of the Home Guard. Who would listen to us, Mr. Southey?"

"I hoped you would be able to think of something," said Adam in disappointed tones. He was tired and dispirited and his brain felt like cotton wool; there was no shadow of a plan in him.

"See here," said Ebby. "Let's get things straight. Let's see how Taylor's plans are going to work and then we can decide where we're to butt in. We know that the fellow you saw is to get hold of the plans and pass them on to Cheller, and then Cheller takes them to his master. Now supposing we butt in at the farm when the plans are changing hands—how would that do?"

"Friday night," said Adam thoughtfully. "That's what the fellow said, but Cheller might get after him and hurry him up. Mr. Taylor has got to have the plans before Ehrling arrives on the scene."

"You think Ehrling——"

"Well, don't you think so?" asked Adam. "I mean here's a mysterious man arriving in a mysterious manner just at the critical moment . . . I wouldn't mind betting that Ehrling is to get the plans and take them back to Germany."

"How does he come—and go?"

"I've thought about that, but I can't see it, somehow."

"By air," suggested Ebby.

"No, not by air—at least I don't think so. You can't land just anywhere in a plane, besides it's far too risky. Someone might see the plane and shoot it down."

"By parachute, like Hess?"

"How could he get away again?"

Ebby shook his head hopelessly. "I'd like to lay my hands on that man Ehrling," he said. "Him and Taylor, that would be a good bag."

"Well, why not?" inquired Adam in eager tones. "That's an idea, Ebby. Why not wait till Ehrling comes and bag the lot? Miss Taylor could let us into the castle, she could leave a window open or something . . . There's Cheller, of course; we should need one or two hefty fellows to help us."

Ebby nodded. His eyes were shining. "You've said it," he declared. "That's just what we'll do. I can lay my hands on a couple of trusty lads—they're fishermen from Balfinny; maybe I'd better go over and see them to-day before I'm any older."

"Fishermen!" Adam exclaimed.

"Aye, fishermen. We could depend on them if there's to be any trouble, for they're made of the right stuff."

Part Three

Chapter One

Adam was dreaming. He was standing at the end of the avenue at Rockingham and the boys were running past. It was a cross-country race and Adam was counting them in . . . Turner was leading as usual . . . "Turner, Yates, Bingham," said Adam to himself and he was marking the time in his notebook. Curiously enough Turner was dressed in the blue uniform of the RAF and looked somewhat out of place amongst the others, who were all in running shorts. Turner waved to Adam as he passed and shouted that he had been to Cologne . . . and with that Adam awoke. He found himself in the cave lying on his bed of heather. There was a heavy feeling in the air and the sky was overcast. Between the dark thunder clouds which were gathering over the hills there was a gap of tawny-coloured sky. Rain was falling in slanting rods, copper-coloured with the eerie light; the heavy drops, pattering upon the ivy leaves at the mouth of the cave sounded like running feet. Adam yawned and turned over and, stretching out his hand, he threw some dry wood on the fire . . . and as the flames sprang up he saw Ebby sitting at the other side of the fire smiling at him.

"So you're back!" exclaimed Adam, sitting up and rubbing his eyes. "Why didn't you wake me?"

"You needed sleep," replied Ebby.

"Did you see the men?"

"I saw them. They're on for anything. There's old Ben and his three sons. I said two would be enough, but they all want to come —what do you think about it?"

Adam laughed. "Four of them!" he exclaimed. "Never mind— the more the merrier."

"I think so, too," agreed Ebby. He took a piece of paper out of his pocket and handed it across. "There's a letter for you," he added.

"A letter!"

"From your private box," explained Ebby with a grin. "I went

173

down to the bridge on the way back from Balfinny just to see if there was any message for us."

"Did you read it?" Adam inquired.

"Yes, I did. It might have been something urgent."

Adam unfolded the paper. There was one short sentence written on it in a firm decisive hand:

He has gone away for two nights so we have a little time.

"She doesn't waste words," said Adam, looking at the paper thoughtfully.

"I was thinking the same," said Ebby. "Two nights brings us to Friday; it gives us a little breathing space."

"I think I had better go down to the Castle and see her," said Adam slowly.

"To the Castle!"

"Why not? I ought to see her and tell her what we mean to do." It was curious how his heart rose within him at the thought of seeing her.

"Now then," said Ebby. "Now then, Mr. Southey, you just stay quietly where you are. You're safe here and you want to stay safe until the time for action arrives."

"I must see Miss Taylor, Ebby. There are all sorts of things to arrange."

"But, Mr. Southey——"

"I want to find out where we can get in," explained Adam. "I must, really. We can't go groping about in the dark."

"And what'll I do if you don't come back?" asked Ebby, looking at him gravely.

"Carry on, of course. You could carry on perfectly well without me. I'm a passenger, Ebby."

"No," said Ebby, shaking his head. "You're not a passenger. Maybe I know a bit more about the hills, but then you think of other things; we're a good team, Mr. Southey."

"You do most of the collar-work—but never mind, Ebby, I'll come back, all right."

It was five o'clock when Adam set out from the cave; the rain

174

had stopped, but the sky was grey and watery and the clouds were low on the hills. Everything was very wet, the heather, the grass, the very mountains were so soaking with moisture that it seemed as if you could squeeze them like a sponge; and the burns, which had been mere trickles, had swollen to powerful torrents racing down the sides of the hills. Strange how a few hours of heavy rain had altered the whole character of the land. It had seemed a holiday-land, a sort of modern Eden as it lay dreaming beneath the sun, but now it was wilder, louder, lonelier. Adam found it more bracing.

He walked across the bridge and up the avenue to the Castle and across Mr. Taylor's drawbridge (in which he took so much pride) and as Adam's feet echoed upon the solid oaken planks he remembered Mr. Taylor saying that he drew it himself every night "just for fun," and wondered whether it was quite such a joke as Mr. Taylor had pretended . . . But there must be some way in, some way for resolute men to enter the castle, thought Adam as he went up the steps and rang the bell.

Adam had decided upon this extremely simple method of obtaining an interview with Miss Taylor for there was no reason on earth why a guest who had lunched at the castle last week should not return this week and call upon his host. Indeed there was every reason why he should call—it was only polite.

The door was opened by the fat butler.

"Is Mr. Taylor at home?" asked Adam in casual tones.

"Mr. Taylor is away from 'ome, sir——"

"Oh, what a pity!"

". . . but Miss Taylor is at 'ome."

A few moments later Adam was being ushered into the drawing-room . . . It was almost too easy.

Miss Taylor rose from the sofa with an exclamation of surprise at the sight of her unexpected guest; it was very nearly an exclamation of dismay.

"I called to see Mr. Taylor," said Adam, for the benefit of the butler. "I wanted to thank him so much for allowing me to fish."

Brenda had recovered a little and took her cue very well. "Uncle Roland will be sorry to have missed you," she declared.

The butler withdrew, closing the door behind him, and now

that they were alone, Brenda changed her tune. "Oh, do you think this is wise?" she asked, looking at Adam anxiously. "I never thought you would come like this."

"Perhaps you expected me to come down the chimney," replied Adam, laughing. "I had to speak to you and I saw no reason why I shouldn't call in a civilised manner."

She laughed softly and motioned to him to sit down. She was looking much better, Adam thought. There was a faint colour in her cheeks and her eyes were very bright. He remembered, now, where it was that he had seen this girl before . . .

"How is the foot?" asked Adam.

"Much better," she smiled. "It still hurts a little when I walk on it, but it will soon be all right."

He sat down beside her. There was so much to say and so little time to say it for he must not prolong his visit unduly. He must tell her their plan—such as it was—and find out how they could get into the Castle. He must ask her more about Ehrling. What he wanted to do was to talk to her simply and naturally about all sorts of things and especially to ask her if she remembered their first meeting.

"I've met you before," said Brenda suddenly.

"Sheriffmuir," replied Adam, nodding. "You were wearing a red beret."

"So you do remember! I knew you at once—that day that you came to lunch. Did you recognise me?"

"No," replied Adam. He knew it was the wrong answer, but somehow he did not want to lie to this girl. "No, I didn't know you at first. You looked so different; there was a shadow on your face."

"It was the shadow of despair," said Brenda in a low voice. "I felt alone and hopeless. I was without a friend in the world."

Adam was silent, but his heart warmed to her. He liked the frank sincerity of her manner. There was no nonsense about this girl, no sham, no affectation. Nonsense was all very well in its way, but it would have been out of place when they were engaged upon such a desperate business. Steel-true and blade straight, thought Adam as he met her grave glance and returned it with the same gravity.

At this moment the door opened and the butler appeared with a large tray of bottles, decanters and glasses which he deposited upon a side table. "Would you care for me to mix you a cocktail, sir," he inquired, "or will you take a glass of sherry?"

Adam's one wish was to get rid of the man as quickly as possible and resume his conversation with his hostess so he replied that he would rather have sherry and waited impatiently until it was poured out and presented to him with ceremony upon a silver salver.

"Won't you have something?" asked Adam, looking at Brenda.

She shook her head. "Sykes knows that I never do," she replied.

"That is so," agreed Sykes. "Miss Taylor has not developed a palate for wine. Occasionally she takes a glass of champagne——"

"Only on birthdays, Sykes," said Brenda, smiling. "And you know quite well it's wasted on me."

Adam waited until the man had gone and then he said: "I bet Sykes has a well-developed palate."

"Yes, I think so, too," agreed Brenda.

"Is he——"

"No," said Brenda, shaking her head. "No, he's honest. He has no idea what is going on—I'm sure of that."

"Would it be any use——"

"Well, would it?" she asked. "You've seen Sykes. He isn't the stuff that heroes are made of—nor conspirators. Uncle Roland couldn't have chosen a more ideal butler than Sykes. He's thoroughly respectable and exceedingly stupid."

There was so much bitterness in her voice that Adam said quietly: "It's all coming right."

"But how?" she asked. "Uncle Roland has so much personality, he can influence people. If he were to walk in now and begin talking to you and charming you——"

"What would happen?" asked Adam, smiling at her, his mouth tilting a little to one side as it did when he was amused. "What would happen, I wonder. Would I go down like a ninepin, d'you think?"

"Perhaps not."

"You know I wouldn't," said Adam, suddenly quite grave. "We mustn't underestimate his power but we mustn't overestimate it either, because, if we do, we shall never get the better of him—you see that, don't you?"

"The plans are terribly important, I suppose?"

"More important than my life—or yours," said Adam earnestly. "Do you think I'd let you stay here another hour if it were not absolutely vital?"

She met his eyes gravely and he saw that she understood. It had been necessary to make her understand the importance of the business, but it was no part of Adam's plan to depress her. He wanted to encourage her and keep her cheerful.

"I wish I could take you home with me," he told her. "You would be safe and sound and warm and dry."

This sounded such a curious description of Adam's home that she looked at him in surprise. "Where is your home?" she asked.

He pointed out of the window. "It's about half-way up that mountain—a perfectly splendid cave with all the amenities provided by nature. I don't know why people live in houses when caves are so much more comfortable."

"Perhaps there aren't enough caves to go round," said Brenda, smiling. "But do you really live in a cave?"

"Yes, really."

"And cook your own food?"

"Dear me, no. I have a butler . . . I mean a chef, of course."

Brenda laughed quite heartily and, as she was somewhat strung up, her eyes were suddenly full of tears. She brushed them away. "But we must talk sensibly," she said. "You haven't told me what you want me to do. Have you any plans?"

Adam nodded. "We want to get into the Castle while Ehrling is here, and that's where you come in. Could you leave a window open?"

"I couldn't," she replied. "It just isn't possible. You can't get into the castle at night. First of all there's the drawbridge—Uncle Roland draws it himself, *always*—and secondly Sykes shuts all the windows and fixes the burglar alarms. Uncle Roland says I'm frightened of burglars, but the truth is *he's* frightened."

"What of?" asked Adam.

"He has—enemies," said Brenda slowly.

Adam had known that it might be difficult to approach the castle, but he had not imagined it was so impregnable as this. "We must get in somehow," he said.

"There's only one possible way," said Brenda thoughtfully. "It wouldn't be easy, but you might manage it. There's a curious old stair which goes down from the cellars with a door at the bottom leading on to the shore. I could leave that door open—nobody would be likely to notice it."

"That sounds splendid——"

"It wouldn't be easy," she repeated. "You would have to climb down the cliffs on to the shore . . . I'll show you," she added, glancing at the clock. "The servants will be having their supper so this is a good time to explore."

Adam followed her into the hall and through a heavy door covered with green baize and down a flight of stone stairs. They were in the kitchen quarters now, in a stone-flagged passage with doors on both sides and they could hear the hum of voices and the clatter of knives and forks.

"It sounds like a regiment of soldiers," Adam whispered.

"There are eight altogether," replied Brenda. "Four women and four men. The gardeners and the chauffeur come in to meals . . ."

The door from whence the noise was proceeding was half-way down the passage. They passed it safely and reached the other end of the passage and went down a few steps into a cellar full of wine bins. At the other side of the cellar was another door. Brenda opened it and showed Adam a flight of very steep stone stairs which seemed to descend into the solid rock.

Chapter Two

"What an extraordinary place!" exclaimed Adam. "These stairs seem to have been hewn out of the rock."

"It's interesting, isn't it?" Brenda said. "It makes one wonder who made them—and why. They're very old, of course. I don't think Uncle Roland knows about these stairs—he has never mentioned them and neither have I. It was one day when I was trying to tidy up the cellar that I saw the door and opened it and found them."

"Rather exciting!"

"Very exciting," she agreed.

Adam had switched on his torch and was examining the walls of the stairway closely. He noticed that they were very uneven and came to the conclusion that the stair had been made in a natural fissure in the rock—the passage had been widened and the steps roughly carved.

"By Jove, what a work!" he exclaimed. "What a long time it must have taken—and I don't suppose they used dynamite or anything. There's a place in Wales with a staircase like this . . . I don't remember the name of it."

They began to go down slowly and carefully for the steps were very rough. Here and there the stairway widened into niches or small caves while in other places it was so narrow that Adam's shoulders brushed the walls. The stair twisted and turned this way and that, following the natural fissure in which it had been made. There was no light at all and the air was damp and smelt like a vault.

Brenda said in a low voice: "I could leave the door open. Nobody would know."

"You would have to come down here alone."

"Of course," she replied. "Did you think I would ask Uncle Roland to come with me and hold my hand?"

"You might ask Sykes," suggested Adam, playing up to her.

"I should have to hold his hand," said Brenda with a soft laugh.

She could laugh about it, but Adam was not deceived. It would not be easy to come down here in the darkness all by herself. He wished, with all his heart, that he need not ask her to do it.

They had come down about twenty steps when suddenly there was a rush of wind in their faces, a rush of cold pure air, and they heard a loud bang which echoed and re-echoed a score of times in the narrow tunnel before it died away.

"It's the door!" whispered Brenda, clinging to Adam's arm. "It's the door—someone's coming up!"

Adam put out his torch and seizing Brenda round the waist he dragged her into a niche in the wall where the staircase turned. He flattened her against the wall and put his arm across her shoulders; he could do no more. They stood there pressed together, and pressed against the damp rock, listening to the approaching foot-steps on the stair . . . it was a man with tackets in his shoes, for Adam could hear the scrape of the tackets on the rough steps. Even at that moment, with the footsteps of the unknown man approaching, Adam had time to savour the sweetness of Brenda's hair against his cheek. It was not scent, but the clean delicate perfume of perfectly kept hair, the perfume of Brenda, herself. Thank goodness she doesn't use scent, thought Adam, for scent would have betrayed their presence in that narrow place.

The man came on up the stairs. He was whistling softly under his breath. He had an electric torch, but the battery was not very strong and he was using it to light the irregular surface of the steps. Adam knew that if the man lifted his head he was bound to see them; he knew that the slightest movement would disclose their presence . . . the slightest movement, the slightest sound. . . . If the man hesitated for a moment Adam was ready to spring upon him . . . Adam was so strung up that his muscles were like cords. The man had reached them now . . . he was passing . . . turning the corner of the stair, and as he passed his shoulder brushed against Adam's hand.

He passed. He went on up the stairs—scrape, scrape, scrape—and a faint smell of hair oil lingered in the dank air.

Brenda was trembling now, trembling all over, and Adam was not surprised for his own knees did not feel particularly strong. He held her tightly, pressed against him, and patted her back as if she were a child.

"Cheller," said Brenda. "That's who it was."

"Are you sure it was Cheller?" he asked.

"I know by his smell," replied Brenda and there was a quiver in her voice but whether of laughter or tears he could not determine.

"Buck up," he said. "We're all right now. You behaved like a brick. You were simply grand. Buck up, we're all right now."

"I thought he was going to stop."

"Not here," declared Adam. "He was far too busy watching his step."

"If he had stopped——"

"That would have been unfortunate—for him."

"I wish I were brave," said Brenda with a little gasp.

He took her hand and squeezed it gently and felt the soft fingers cling to his. "You are brave," he said. "You played up like anything."

They went on hand in hand—Adam had been counting the steps, but he had lost count now—and at last they came to a solid wooden door with iron hinges and an enormous lock and key. The key turned quite easily and Adam saw that it had been oiled too and the door swung back without a sound. They came out on to a ledge or shelf of rock and just below was the little bay which Adam had seen from the dining-room window. The tide was out and there was a beach of white shingle, then the calm waters of the bay and the jagged reefs beyond. It was delightful to breathe the fresh air and to see the bright light of day after having been immured in the dark dank rock, and Brenda and Adam stood there for a moment or two smelling the sea scent and enjoying the gentle breeze.

All round the little bay the cliffs rose up sheer and black and dripping with moisture from the recent rain. In some places the cliffs overhung the bay, in others they were perpendicular.

"There's no path," said Brenda after a short silence.

"But there must be," said Adam. "Cheller came in this way and Cheller hasn't got wings."

"Perhaps he came down and went back again."

"To admire the view?"

"To oil the door."

This was possible, of course, but it did not seem likely, for why should Cheller take the trouble to oil the lock of a door that led nowhere except to a deserted beach? "There must be a path," said Adam confidently. "I'll find it."

"Are you sure?"

"Perfectly certain. You had better go back," he added.

"Perhaps I should," she replied doubtfully. "Cheller might wonder where I had gone . . . When shall I see you again?"

"To-morrow morning at the bridge. I'll be there about eleven. . . . I left my hat in the hall."

"I'll hide it and bring it to-morrow," said Brenda, smiling at him.

She went in and Adam closed the door. He felt a trifle anxious when he heard the key turn in the lock for he had burnt his boats . . . but there must be a way up the cliffs, he felt sure of it. He stood back from the cliffs and looked up. Yes, he could climb on to that ledge, and from there . . . no, that was no use, for there was a scree of loose stones which only a chamois could negotiate. What about trying a little farther along? Adam looked all round the bay but he could see no path, no possible place to make his attempt. He walked across the bay to see if he could wade round the corner, but although the tide was far out and the rocks were glistening with seaweed he could find no way of exit from the bay; the cliffs were sheer and the water at the bottom was deep and full of snaky seaweed. Adam considered the matter with growing anxiety. He wanted to get out of the bay but also, and what was equally important, he wanted to find a way in—a way in for himself and Ebby and the fishermen. This bay was the key to the castle . . . there must be a way out of it. Cheller used this entrance—whether he used it with or without Mr. Taylor's knowledge Adam did not know. Which way had Cheller come?

Suddenly Adam laughed. What a fool he was! He had only to go back to the door and follow Cheller's tracks. His tackets would have left a trail which could be followed easily. Adam went back to the door and stooped down. He was not used to tracking and it was not as easy as he had imagined . . . Ah, there was a footprint in that patch of mud . . . no, it was Adam's own footprint. He went down on his hands and knees and examined the ground. Here was an unmistakable scrape of tackets on the rock . . . and here was another . . . and there, in that patch of sand, was a complete print of Cheller's shoe. Adam was getting the hang of it now, he was quite proud when he discovered a piece of bruised grass and a stone which had been turned over as Cheller trod on it. The tracks led Adam to the base of a perpendicular rock-chimney, and looking up he could see that this exit from the bay had been made by man. There were steps, or rather small footholds, chipped out of the rock; and staples, with iron rings attached to them, had been driven into the rock to serve as handholds. The rings were yellow with rust, but they looked firm enough—and this was the way Cheller had come down. Adam did not like the look of Cheller's staircase for he was not good at climbing, his lame leg was stiff and less trustworthy than other people's legs; however he had no choice but to remain where he was indefinitely or make the attempt, and this was no choice at all.

Adam seized hold of an iron ring and began the ascent. At first it was not too bad for the footholds were fairly regular, and Adam's arms were exceedingly strong so he could take the weight off his bad leg, but, about half-way up the cliff, the footholds became farther apart and instead of being in line, one above the other, they were placed to right and left. It was easy enough to reach the right foothold with his right foot, but he could not raise his left foot high enough for the next step. He had to change his feet on the tiny ledge and twist his body so that he could step up with his right foot . . . then he was all lopsided and had to change his feet again. Adam began to feel the strain. His arms were tired and his legs were shaking. He paused for a moment, clinging to a ring with both hands and his body flattened against the cliff. His heart was thumping and his brow was wet with perspiration and something within him was saying: "You can't go on. You're at the end of your tether."

"But I've got to go on," said Adam aloud. He had to go on because he could not go back. He had to go on, not only because of his own danger, but because there was something more important than life at stake. As he rested there, clinging to the rock, he saw that everything depended upon him, for he alone held all the clues and he alone could save the ray from falling into the enemy's hands . . . and he reached up to the next ring and gripped it firmly and climbed on, twisting and turning and changing feet at each step.

He was almost at the top now. He could see the grass and heather which grew on the edge of the cliff—it was just above his head. He seized the last ring and put his foot in the last foothold and heaved himself up . . . and then he felt the foothold crumbling and a piece of rock, loosened by the rain, dislodged itself and fell to the bottom with a shower of earth and stones . . . and Adam was left suspended by one hand with the toes of his boots scrabbling against the face of the cliff.

It seemed hours—and Adam had time to think of a dozen different things, of the ray, of Brenda, of Ebby waiting for him at the cave—and then his toe found a tiny crevice in the rock and the immediate danger was past. He steadied himself, stretched out his other hand, caught a tuft of wiry heather and somehow or other managed to drag himself to safety. He rolled over on to the grass and lay there panting with the blood drumming and singing in his ears.

For some minutes Adam was so thankful to be safe that he thought of nothing else. He felt a passion of gratitude for his deliverance. He was alive and the world seemed beautiful . . . more beautiful than it had ever seemed before. The blue sky, the hills, the trees, every tiny flower on the woody stems of heather took on an added significance in Adam's eyes.

Gradually he recovered, gradually he began to gather up the threads of life and, as he did so, his spirits fell for he realised that his plan for entering Tinal Castle could not be carried out. He had come up the cliff, but it had taken every ounce of his strength to accomplish it. . . . He could not go down, that was certain . . . so, if this was the only way into the castle, Ebby must do the job without him (Ebby and his fishermen could go down quite easily of course). Adam crawled to the top of the cliff and looked over, in the faint hope that it might seem less formidable when you looked at it from above, but instead of looking less formidable it looked positively terrifying . . . the bare black rock, glistening with moisture, the fragile footholds, and, far below, the heaps of boulders and shingle and the jagged rocks. His head swam as he looked down and he tightened his grip on the tough stems of the heather and dug his fingers into the firm texture of the grass. It would be madness to make the attempt to go down, utter madness; he would fall and dash his brains out on the rocks below.

Adam could have wept. He had suffered all his life from his inability to do things that other people accomplished quite easily, but he had never felt so bitter about it as now.

Chapter Three

The morning was fine and bright with a stiff breeze which rustled in the leaves of the hazels and sent a few small white clouds scurrying across the blue sky. The sun wakened Adam and he rose at once and went down to have his bath . . . he had found a perfect place to bathe. The burn, cascading into a pool, had deepened and widened it and by piling up a bank of gravel at the lower end had engineered a dam. At one side of Adam's bath there were rocks and over-hanging trees, at the other side open moor. The pool was deep enough for swimming; three bold strokes took Adam across from one side to the other but it took five or six strokes to swim against the current from the bottom of the pool to the little cascade. He swam up until he felt the spray on his head and shoulders and the sting of the falling water . . then he turned on his back and was carried down to the tiny gravel beach. To-day, however, Adam decided to vary his usual procedure so he climbed down the rocks of the cascade. The swirl of pale brown peaty water was more powerful than he had expected, it pushed him and plucked at him and the sunlit spray was all round him, cold and bracing on his bare skin. He slithered down with the water and was sucked under and swept round the pool and stranded on the gravel like a piece of drift-wood . . . it all happened in a moment.

"Ugh!" gasped Adam, picking himself up and shaking the water out of his hair. It was cold. There was a tingle like ice in the water and it tasted faintly musty with the peat. His body tingled, too, a delicious fire coursed through his veins . . . He did a few exercises and plunged in again, swimming round, treading water and diving to explore the rocky bottom.

Presently Adam was walking back to the cave, clad in his dressing-gown with his towel over his arm. He felt like a king—what king had a more gorgeous palace, what emperor a more magnificent bath? He felt as if the hills belonged to him and there was no human being, nor any sign of man, to dispute his sovereignty.

Breakfast now, thought Adam, scrambled eggs and coffee. . . . He was becoming quite a cook.

Adam had not seen Ebby last night, but had cooked his own supper and gone to bed early—tired out with his adventure on the cliff. Ebby would not be here this morning, either, for he had gone over to the other side of the valley to have a look at his sheep. Adam was quite glad that Ebby would not be coming, for he could walk down to the bridge and meet Brenda without having to think of an excuse. No *excuse* was necessary, thought Adam, as he drank his coffee and shaved with unusual care; it was essential that he should keep in touch with Brenda and perfect the plan of action before Mr. Taylor returned, but in spite of this conviction he had an uncomfortable feeling that Ebby would have frowned upon the project. Ebby had not liked the idea of his going to Tinal Castle yesterday and he would have objected even more strongly to a second visit. Adam tried to examine his own motives and to weigh the pros and cons. He wanted to go, he must see Brenda, he had promised to be there and if he did not turn up she would think that something had happened to him and she would be worried . . . well, of course she would . . . Ebby might think that he was taking an unnecessary risk, but Ebby would be wrong. Besides he was not going to the castle, he was only going as far as the bridge.

As he set the cave to rights, putting everything in its place, Adam began to think of Lurg House and to wonder what they were all doing. He thought of Evelyn. He knew, now, that he had never been in love with Evelyn—not for a moment; he had admired her and liked her immensely and he still admired and liked her as much as ever, but that was not love. Love was quite a different thing—it was different not in degree but in kind; he knew now what love was. Love squeezed your heart and turned your bones to water. It made you a hero and a coward. Adam was in the first stage of love which wants to give all and demands nothing in return. He wanted to serve Brenda, he wanted to make life a bed of roses for her, he wanted to protect her and shield her from harm and instead of that he had placed her in the gravest danger and bound a heavy burden on her back. He had been obliged to do it—there was no choice open to him—for the ray was more important than one woman's life.

But if anything happens to her, thought Adam, pausing with the tin of coffee in his hand, if anything happens to Brenda, I shall do something desperate; I shall avenge her and die in the attempt. There are things a desperate man could do . . . and especially a desperate man who can speak German like a native . . . desperate things . . .

His mood of gloom and misery lasted until he had finished his chores and was walking over the hills to the trysting place, and then because the sun was shining and because he was young and was on his way to meet the girl he loved, his spirits rose and his step lightened.

Brenda was waiting for him on the bridge. She was leaning over the parapet watching the water flow past and Adam looked at her as he went down the hill and marked the graceful poise of her slight figure, and noticed how the sun shone on her uncovered head with its trim and glistening curls. He saw that she had brought his hat with her . . . she had put it beside her on the low stone wall. She turned suddenly when she heard his footsteps on the road and held out her hand and smiled at him, and Adam took her hand and smiled back.

"Am I late?" he asked.

"No, I'm early. I've been worrying about you, wondering if you managed to climb the cliff. You found a path, did you?"

"I found a way," he replied. "It isn't a very easy way for a lame man." He was watching her face as he spoke for a good deal depended upon her reaction to his words.

"I never think of you as lame," said Brenda frankly. "You seem so strong and active."

"It was a fall," he told her. "I fell downstairs when I was two years old; of course I can't remember it, but I was in plaster of Paris for six months."

"Poor little boy!" said Brenda softly. "It must have been a weary time, mustn't it?"

Adam agreed. He was wondering why he did not mind her sympathy, for, as a rule, sympathy infuriated him, and then he realised that he, too, felt sorry for that little boy who had suffered so much pain and discomfort . . . sorry for him objectively. Adam was sorry for himself, too, but he did not intend to let Brenda see that, so he proceeded to give a humorous account of his struggle to climb the cliff and added that nothing on earth would induce him to make use of Cheller's staircase again.

Brenda listened but she did not smile. "Can they manage it without you?" she asked anxiously.

"We'll think of a way," said Adam. He spoke with cheerful confidence for he was not going to worry Brenda more than he could help, and there was always a hope that Ebby might think of something.

"We must be careful," said Brenda. "We mustn't stay here long. I shouldn't have come, but I was anxious about you and I wanted to give you your hat. You had better put it on."

"Why shouldn't you have come? Surely nobody can object to your going for a walk along the river?"

"Cheller was asking questions. He came into the drawing-room last night and wanted to know why you had come and what you had said. I didn't like it."

"Cheller doesn't know me."

"He knows all about you. Uncle Roland must have told him."

"Told him what?"

"That you were staying at Lurg and working in the factory. He said you had left there now, but you weren't living at the Highland Bull although you had taken a room there."

"Cheller seems to have a fairly efficient intelligence department," said Adam in surprise.

"He's horrible!" Brenda cried. "He's slimy and plausible, he hints all sorts of things. . . . I think Uncle Roland is beginning to be afraid of him."

Adam could well believe it for Cheller must know a great deal about his master's affairs.

"He asked where you were living now, and I said I knew nothing at all about you—and cared less," added Brenda with the ghost of a smile.

"In that case he had better not see us together," replied Adam with an answering grin.

They climbed down on to the path which wound along the river bank and began to walk up the stream, talking as they went. There were hazel bushes here, but after a little the bushes stopped and the river ran through open moorland. Hills, deep in heather, rose at each side of the river-bed and here and there a patch of trees, of pines and mountain fir, had been planted to break the force of the wind as it swept down the glen in winter.

"I wish I needn't go back!" exclaimed Brenda suddenly.

"If you feel like that——"

"No, I didn't mean to say it. I must go back."

"I wish we could think of some other way——"

"No, I want to help. It was only," said Brenda a trifle unsteadily, "it was only just that it's so peaceful and lovely here. Somehow or other I hate Tinal Castle. I used to love it and look forward to coming here, but now—now there is something about it—something horrible."

Adam struggled with himself. He wanted to pick her up in his arms and take her back to the cave—she would be safe at the cave, perfectly safe and comfortable; she could stay there until it was over and the whole plot exposed and Taylor and his gang laid by the heels. Why couldn't he think of some way to manage without Brenda's help?

"It's all right," said Brenda.

"It's all wrong," replied Adam. "If Taylor suspected for a moment——"

"He won't suspect. I'll be very careful indeed. Don't worry too much about me, Adam."

"Brenda!" he exclaimed. They stood quite still and looked at each other without saying any more and he saw her dark eyes shining at him with a strange softness in their depths. He had never called her by her name before, but he had thought of her as Brenda (the name suited her for she was like a flame). And it seemed natural and right to call her Brenda. There was so much that he wanted to say; he was full of all the things that he wanted to say to her, but this was no time for personal things. The personal things would come afterwards when they had won through—if they won through alive.

Brenda seemed to understand what he was feeling for she said quietly: "We're friends, Adam. We're working together. That's all that matters."

"Afterwards——" he began.

"Yes, afterwards," said Brenda quietly.

Adam said no more for he knew that she understood.

Chapter Four

Adam and Brenda walked slowly along the path. The sun shone and the river prattled and gurgled and, far away on the tops, the sheep called to their lambs and were answered in a higher key. As they walked Adam began to tell Brenda his plan in greater detail and to tell her about Ebby Ford and his fishermen.

"Is that clear?" he said at last. "Is there anything you want to ask? We may not be able to meet again so easily when your uncle comes back."

She hesitated and looked at him. "There's one thing," she said. "What will they do to Uncle Roland?"

This was a question which Adam had dreaded. He knew, by the way she spoke of her uncle, that her feelings towards him were mixed. She had been very fond of him; she had stressed the fact that he had been kind and generous and thoughtful. It was only natural that she should feel anxious about his fate. Adam was silent for some moments, trying to frame his reply and at last he said: "Mr. Taylor will be tried. He'll get what he deserves—no more and no less; I'm afraid that isn't much comfort to you."

"No," said Brenda.

"We haven't got to that fence yet," added Adam.

"No," said Brenda again.

They walked on in silence for a little and then suddenly Brenda stopped and laid her hand on Adam's arm. "Cheller!" she exclaimed.

The man was standing on the path about two hundred yards ahead of them. He was using a pair of field-glasses, sweeping the hillside very carefully as if he were looking for something or somebody that he knew to be there. His attention was riveted to the task so he did not see Adam and Brenda coming along the path and they were able to dive behind a gorse bush and hide themselves before he turned.

"Perhaps he'll go the other way," said Brenda in a low voice.

"He's coming this way," replied Adam. "Stay where you are—I'll deal with him."

"But, Adam——"

He put his hand on her shoulder and pressed her down and then he rose and began to stroll towards Cheller with his hands in his pockets and his hat tilted to the back of his head. He had decided to brazen it out, to speak to Cheller and ask when Mr. Taylor would be home and whether he could get permission for another day's fishing. Cheller might be suspicious but he could not know anything for there was nothing to know—not yet—and then Adam heard footsteps behind him, and he saw a man running towards him along the path. There was something familiar about this man, but Adam had no time to think of that for he was between the two men—and so was Brenda. At all costs she must not be discovered and linked with him.

Adam gave a shout and leaving the path he made off up the hill as fast as he could go. He looked back and saw that his ruse had succeeded: both men had left the path and were following him, trying to cut him off.

Adam pounded on up the steep tussocky slope of the hill. He was not at his best when negotiating rough ground, and the men were gaining on him. They were shouting to him to stop and for a moment he wondered whether it would be better to stop now, and have it out with them . . . now, before they were hot and tired and angry . . . Then he decided that he must go on farther because of Brenda; he must lead them away from the place where she was hiding. He had almost reached the top of the rise when there was a sudden report and a few pellets whistled past his ears.

Just for a moment Adam felt paralysed. It was a most unpleasant sensation to be shot at, to feel that one was being hunted by one's fellow man. A queer kind of fear seemed to choke his heart and his limbs felt weak and powerless . . . and then he managed to pull himself together and to swallow his fear. He had reached the top of the rise by this time and there was a path through the heather, and the moment his feet found the path Adam felt a different man. He began to run quickly and easily with his queer lopsided gait. The path wound along the top of the rise and skirted a sheep-fank and dived into a little valley full of bog myrtle. Adam followed it faithfully for the path was his salvation . . . if he could keep to the path he was confident that they would not catch him. He looked back once or twice and saw that they were not gaining on him now; they were keeping him in sight and waiting for him to tire. Fortunately Adam was hard and fit and the last few days had toughened his muscles . . . but of course his pursuers did not know that; they were chasing a lame man and thought he would be caught very easily.

The path mounted steeply and curled across the shoulder of a hill. Here and there a fall of rock had swept it away and left a scree of loose stones and this caused Adam some delay. The men gained on him, they shouted again, threatening him and telling him to stop and he heard another report and a spatter of shot on the rocks behind him. It was a shotgun—that was all—and it was the other man who had the gun, not Cheller. Adam felt glad of that. He ran on, for, although he had led them far enough to save Brenda from discovery, he realised that it was too late now to stop and argue with them. If they had not had the gun, he might have risked it but the gun gave them too great an advantage. He lost his first path—it vanished suddenly and mysteriously in the waist-high heather—but he found another, better path and put on a little spurt of speed. He hoped that might discourage his pursuers and that they would abandon the chase, but when he looked back he saw that they were still following him. Cheller was in front, running steadily, and the other man was about twenty-five yards behind.

Adam was beginning to tire by this time, and, what was worse, he was beginning to feel a little uneasy about the outcome of the chase. It was obvious that he had underrated his pursuers or overrated his own powers of endurance. He looked back again and saw that Cheller had gained upon him. If he wanted to keep ahead of Cheller, he must increase his speed. Adam put on another spurt, but he knew that he could not last long at this pace and he was definitely frightened now—frightened not so much for himself but more for the load of responsibility which lay on his shoulders. He had been a fool to risk another meeting with Brenda; he should have waited patiently in the cave until the moment for action arrived. He should have taken Ebby's advice.

Adam was furious with himself and his fury lent him temporary strength; he cantered on. A dyke loomed up just ahead of him; he threw himself over it, picked himself up and plunged downhill through a sea of bracken. There was a peat hag at the bottom of the hill, a boggy place where peat had been cut and piled into stacks to dry, and as Adam approached he saw another man running from one peat stack to another which was directly in his path.

He was done—he was completely cut off—that was his first thought, for it seemed obvious that this third man was in league with his pursuers . . . And then something familiar about this third man made Adam look again. It couldn't be Ebby, of course . . . or could it be Ebby? Ebby had a strange faculty of turning up in unexpected places. The figure had disappeared behind the peat stack and still Adam was not certain whether it was Ebby or not but he ran on—for there was nothing else to do. He was almost at the end of his strength, his breath was coming in deep sobs and his leg felt like a dead weight. He scrambled through a deep ditch full of muddy water where the peat had been cut and he stumbled to his feet and staggered to the peat stack.

"Ebby!" he gasped.

Ebby was there, waiting for him. He seized Adam's hat, crammed it on to his head and ran on. There was no time for explanations, but none were needed for it was quite obvious what Ebby was trying to do. Adam crept farther into the shelter of the peat stack and lay there, panting heavily, and as he lay there he saw Ebby stumbling up the hill reeling to and fro with a queer sideways gait. At first he thought that Ebby must have twisted his foot and his heart sank within him for if Ebby were caught it would be the end of everything, and then quite suddenly he realised what Ebby was doing: he was imitating the gait of a lame man; he was pretending to be exhausted, to be at his last gasp.

Good heavens, do I really run like that? thought Adam, watching Ebby's antics with fascinated eyes.

The next moment Cheller passed. His eyes were fixed on the figure ahead of him, the swaying stumbling figure on the hill, and he passed a few feet from his quarry without a sideways glance. Adam was surprised at Cheller's appearance for he showed little sign of fatigue and was running strongly and steadily, and this was all the more strange because Cheller did not look like a man in good training. It was obvious that Cheller had been playing with Adam, letting him run himself out; perhaps he thought that Adam would be easier to deal with in an exhausted condition or perhaps Cheller had moderated his pace for the sake of his companion, the man with the gun, who had now dropped a long way behind.

Adam watched Ebby. He had reached the top of the rise and was disappearing from view with Cheller in full cry. In another moment they had both vanished . . . and now the other man, Cheller's companion, was approaching for Adam could hear him floundering through the ditch. He was in very different case; his breath was laboured and he moved heavily as though he were drunk with fatigue. Adam let him pass and then sprang out from behind the stack and caught him by the knees . . . They went down together, rolling over and over in the soggy ground.

Chapter Five

Adam rose and possessed himself of the gun, but this was merely a precaution for there was no fight left in the man. He lay upon the ground just as he had fallen, breathing in long-drawn sobs. His limbs twitched convulsively, his eyes were glazed.

"Black!" said Adam, looking at his captive with a good deal of satisfaction. "You're Black, of course. I was sure I had seen you before."

The man groaned.

"Of course your real name may be something quite different, but Black is short for blackguard, and that's good enough. You remember our first meeting I'm sure," continued Adam cheerfully. "It was in Perth, and you were good enough to give me a lift as far as Killicrankie. Then we parted without saying good-bye. You seemed in a hurry for some reason. It *is* nice to see you again," declared Adam with real sincerity. "I only wish that your little German friend were here too; Stein was a delightful fellow, I thought."

"I don't know—what—you're—talking—about," gasped the man.

"Don't say you've forgotten me!" exclaimed Adam in mock dismay.

"I've never—seen you—before."

"But nobody ever forgets *me*," Adam assured him. "I'm so different from other people."

"You're crazy——"

"Not crazy—crooked," declared Adam. "You've got the wrong adjective, Mr. Black. . . . No, don't get up," he added, fingering the gun in a significant manner. "You ought to lie quite still for a bit longer after that cross-country run. I'm afraid you aren't in quite such good training as your friend Mr. Cheller. Besides we've so much to talk about, you and I."

The man lay back and groaned again.

"Where's Stein now?" asked Adam in a conversational tone.

There was no reply.

"What is he doing?" asked Adam. "Come on, Mr. Black, why won't you talk? Where's your friend Stein?"

"You've got it wrong," declared the man who had recovered his breath a little by this time. "You've made a mistake. You're thinking I'm somebody else. I don't know anyone called Stein."

"Have you been having your fortune told lately, Mr. Black?"

"My name's Wilson," declared the man. "I'm Mr. Taylor's keeper; there'll be trouble when he hears about this."

"Was it Mr. Taylor's orders that you were to hunt me over his hills like a wild beast?"

"I've got to keep the place clear of poachers. I was chasing you because I thought you were a poacher, that's all."

"You told Cheller about me," said Adam slowly. "I'm beginning to see it now. You and Cheller thought you would hunt me down and present my head to your master on a salver. Quite a good idea from your point of view, though not so from mine."

"I thought you were a poacher—Cheller said you were."

"That's funny because the last time Cheller saw me I was your master's guest."

While they were talking Adam had been looking about and now he found what he wanted—a stout piece of hempen rope which had been used to tie round the peat stack. He picked it up and began to undo the knots.

"What are you going to do?" asked his captive, looking at the rope with apprehension.

"I'm going to tie you up securely, that's all," replied Adam. "I know you deserve to be hanged, but that's a job for an expert. I might bungle it—which would be a pity."

The man laughed feebly. "You're joking," he said. "I can take a joke, but it's gone far enough . . ."

"Tell me," continued Adam, working away at the knots, but keeping a wary eye upon his prisoner. "Tell me what they pay you for this sort of thing. It's pretty lucrative, isn't it?"

"This has gone far enough," repeated the man, making a movement as if to rise.

"Keep still," said Adam. "It will be safer for you because I've got your gun. You see that, don't you?"

"I see you getting into pretty hot water over this."

"I'm sorry to keep you waiting," continued Adam. "These knots are the very devil, but we shan't be long now, Mr. Black."

"Listen," said the man earnestly. "You're making a mistake; my name's Wilson and I'm Mr. Taylor's keeper. I've been with him for years."

"We'll see what Dow says."

"Dow?"

"You know Dow, don't you? You met him in Edinburgh."

"I haven't been near Edinburgh for years—nor Perth either. I don't know anybody called Dow."

"Don't you? What about Berwick? Where's Berwick?"

"I don't know him either—never heard of him. Look here, you're making a mistake and there'll be trouble."

"There's been a good deal of trouble already. I mean it isn't pleasant to be hunted over the hills and shot at. I didn't like it much."

"I'm sorry——"

"I bet you are!"

"Yes, really," declared the man. "It was all a mistake. I was mistaken about you and you're mistaken about me. I dare say I shouldn't have shot at you, but I didn't hit you, did I? I just wanted to make you stop . . . and then you rolled me in the mud. We're quits, aren't we? Let's wash it all out and forget about it; I'm not one to bear a grudge."

"Aren't you?"

"No," said the man earnestly. "We'll wash it out. We'll go down to the Bull and have a drink. We'll call it quits."

"Quits?" asked Adam with his tilted smile. "Really, Black, you must have a poor opinion of my intelligence."

"Wilson's my name."

"I prefer to call you Black. It always confuses me when people change their name. Put your hands behind your back, please."

"You aren't going to tie me up!"

"That's where you're mistaken. You'd rather be tied up than hanged, wouldn't you, Black?"

"But look here——"

"Put your hands behind your back," repeated Adam, approaching with the rope.

The man kicked out suddenly, but Adam had seen the intention in his eyes and sprang sideways. Black rolled over and was about to rise, but Adam was too quick for him and dealt him a pretty hefty blow on the ear.

"Too bad," said Adam, regretfully, as his captive sank back with a groan. "Frightfully unsporting of me to hit a man when he's down, but you asked for it, you know."

It was easier, now that Black was in a half-dazed condition, to tie him up securely, and Adam made a pretty good job of it. He tied his hands behind his back and he tied his ankles together and then he found a long pole—it was the broken shaft of a cart—and tied it on to the man's back from his neck to his heels. If Black could escape from these bonds he was a contortionist. Adam then dragged his prisoner into the shelter of a stack and covered him with some sacks to keep him warm and dry.

"You aren't going to leave me here!" Black moaned.

"Just for a little," replied Adam kindly. "You'll soon be safely in jail," and so saying he picked up Black's gun and walked away. He could hear Black shouting and yelling as he went up the hill, but it was not likely that anyone else would hear him in that remote spot.

When Adam reached the top of the hill, he looked round to take his bearings and was pleased to see that he was not as far from his mountain home as he had expected. The chase over the hills had taken the form of a semi-circle and there below him was the main road from Lurg to Tinal and about a mile down the road he saw the chimneys of the Highland Bull. Adam had intended to get into touch with the police and tell them about his prisoner, but the sight of the Highland Bull gave him another idea. He settled the gun on his shoulder and walked down to the Inn.

Dick Brownlee was just wheeling his motor-bicycle out of the garage when Adam appeared. He stood still and gaped at Adam in amazement.

"Adam Southey, by all that's blue!" exclaimed Dick when he had recovered the use of his tongue.

"Yes," said Adam, smiling. "You haven't forgotten me, I see."

"Where have you sprung from? What have you been doing? Why haven't you been back to Lurg?"

"I've been rather busy," Adam replied. "Let's have a drink, shall we?"

Dick was always ready to accept an invitation of this nature. He led the way into the bar—which happened to be empty—and they sat down at a table in the corner.

"What the devil have you been doing?" repeated Dick. "I thought you were coming *here*, and then you sent a fellow to fetch your things. Mrs. Farl said you'd gone to London. Why didn't you write or something? Your stock has slumped pretty badly at Lurg House."

"I never thought of writing," replied Adam—nor had he, for somehow the mere fact of living in a cave had divorced him from the conventions of civilisation. He saw now that he should have written to Mr. Brownlee or Evelyn; he owed them a bread-and-butter letter. (Adam could not help smiling at the thought of himself sitting on his bed of heather inditing a bread-and-butter letter to Evelyn Brownlee.)

"You may smile," declared Dick, "but I can tell you it's no joke. Evelyn is mad with you and Uncle John is madder. They can't make up their minds whether to tell the police to search for your murdered corpse or to strike you off their visiting list."

Adam laughed. "Has your stock gone up?" he inquired.

"It has—a bit," admitted Dick in a different tone. "What with your defection and the machinations of Colonel Winch—he's a tremendously good fellow, you know—it looks as if Uncle John is coming round. I was invited to dinner last night and Uncle John was quite polite to me."

"You must have been sucking up to him," said Adam gravely.

Dick had the grace to blush. "Oh well . . . " he said uncomfortably.

" 'Paris is worth a mass,' " quoted Adam, sotto voce.

"What?"

"Evelyn is worth a little boot-licking," explained **Adam**.

"But I didn't——"

"Of course not. I mean I don't blame you in the least. I've always thought you were far too high-handed. But that wasn't what I wanted to see you about."

"What have you been doing?" asked Dick, who was glad to change the subject.

"Well, as a matter of fact——"

"You've been shooting," said Dick with his eyes on the gun which Adam had lent up against the wall. "Lucky beggar, I wish I could get a day's shooting."

"I haven't been shooting—someone has been shooting at me——" began Adam and then he stopped for this was not the way to start. "Look here, Dick," he said, "I want you to do something for me. It's rather a strange story, but you'll have to take my word for it. I'm on the track of something important." He had lowered his voice and now he glanced round the room to make sure there was nobody within hearing.

"Then you haven't been just amusing yourself, shooting and fishing?"

"You remember I told you about those fellows at Perth who laid me out and tried to wreck the van? Well, I've managed to catch one of them."

"Is that what you've been up to!" exclaimed Dick, looking at him, wild-eyed.

"That's what I've been up to," nodded Adam. "The fellow's name is Black; he's the chap that tried to bribe Dow, so Dow will be able to identify him."

"Pretty good work! Where is he? How do I come into the picture?"

"He's lying beside a peat stack, trussed up like a fowl and I want you to go and fetch him and hand him over to the police."

Dick gazed at Adam in dumb astonishment.

"You can do that, can't you?" said Adam encouragingly.

"Oh, I can do it," agreed Dick. "I mean there's no difficulty, but why can't you do it yourself?"

"I'm after bigger game," said Adam.

"Bigger game?"

"Yes. This Black isn't the head of the gang. He's a pretty nasty piece of work, but he's just one of the gang. I'm after the kingpin."

"Some people have all the luck!" exclaimed Dick.

"Luck!" echoed Adam.

"Well, all the fun, then," amended Dick. "I've always wanted to track down spies, to pursue them over the hills and catch them and tie them up and all that sort of thing, but I've never even seen a spy, far less caught one. I suppose you couldn't let me in on the racket, could you?"

"You'll see a spy if you go down to the peat hag," replied Adam a trifle shortly for his recent activities had not been such fun as Dick imagined. Fun, thought Adam. Would Dick think it fun to be pursued over the hills (instead of to pursue)? Would it have amused Dick to climb that horrible cliff and to reach the top without an ounce to spare?

"What about letting me in?" Dick was saying. "Isn't there anything I could do?"

"You can fetch my spy and hand him over," Adam replied. "I can't tell you anything more just now, but if there's anything else I'll send you a message . . . Yes, I promise I will."

"What am I to tell the police?" asked Dick. "I mean they'll want to know who caught the fellow and all that. You know what the police are."

They discussed the matter further and Adam gave Dick an expurgated account of the chase over the hills and explained exactly where he had left his captive. He saw that Dick might have some difficulty in explaining matters to the police, but he hoped the police would be so enchanted with the capture of Mr. Black that they would not probe too deeply into the manner in which it had been accomplished.

"You'll have to think of something, that's all," said Adam as he rose to go. "I don't want my name to be dragged into it—I'm not ready yet."

"I *have* thought of something!" cried Dick. "Gosh, it's the simplest thing on earth; I'll go strolling over the hills with my little gun and I'll find the blighter quite by accident——"

"Be careful, won't you," Adam adjured him. "Don't let Black escape whatever you do."

"I'll be careful," Dick promised, as he followed Adam to the door.

They said good-bye and Adam strode off down the road, but the next moment Dick was after him and had caught him by the arm.

"Look here!" cried Dick. "We haven't half arranged things. What am I to say to Evelyn and Uncle John?"

"Say nothing," replied Adam with a smile. "They'll hear all about it in a few days." He shook himself free from Dick's clasp and walked on . . . and presently he looked round and saw Dick disappearing into the Inn.

There was a smell of cooking in the air when Adam reached the cave—a delicious savoury smell—and, as Adam parted the bushes and stepped over the burn, he saw Ebby crouched over the fire stirring something in a pot.

"I said we made a good team," remarked Ebby without turning his head; his ears were so quick that he had heard Adam approaching and had recognised his step.

"You saved my life," declared Adam, standing still and looking down at the small wiry figure with a good deal of affection and respect.

"Maybe I did," agreed Ebby. "You'd do the same for me."

"Where were you, Ebby, and how on earth did you manage to be in the right place at the right moment? I couldn't have run a yard farther to save my life."

"It was lucky," replied Ebby thoughtfully. "It was *very* lucky, really. I was on the hill doctoring a sick sheep and I saw you walking along the river bank with Miss Taylor. I saw Cheller and he saw me for he was watching me with his field-glasses . . . and then I saw the other fellow coming up behind you and I thought you were done for."

"Cheller can run. He was playing with me."

"Yes, cat and mouse . . . and then I played with him so we're quits. It was neat the way you laid out the second fellow. I was away up the hill by that time and I nearly split my sides laughing."

"Laughing!" exclaimed Adam in surprise, for he had not felt in the least amused by the affair.

"Yes, laughing," nodded Ebby. "Oh, I know Cheller's dangerous, but I wasn't afraid of him catching me on my own hills. I was glad when I saw the fellow with the gun was getting his deserts, for I knew, then, that I could amuse myself as much as I liked. I led Cheller a nice dance, sometimes when I thought he was flagging a bit I let him think I was done. I let him come within a few yards of me and then off I went again; it was the best sport I've had for many a day," declared Ebby, chuckling. "I led him up hill and down dale and then I left him floundering up to his waist in a bog. He'll be a tired man when he gets home, will Cheller."

"And an angry man."

"That, too," agreed Ebby, stirring his stew with tender care.

Adam sat down and stretched his legs. He was very tired and he had so much to tell Ebby that he did not know where to begin. He said suddenly: "I think you might call me Adam."

"If you say so," replied Ebby after a pause. "I never thought about it, to tell you the truth."

The words were somewhat ungracious, but Adam was not deceived. He was sure that Ebby was pleased at the idea. "It would sound more friendly," Adam explained.

"Well, if you say so," repeated Ebby.

There was silence for a few moments and then Ebby said: "We were lucky—I don't like depending too much on luck. If I hadn't been on the hill where would you be now?"

"I had to see Miss Taylor."

"You saw her yesterday."

"I know, but you see——"

"Oh well, we were all young once," said Ebby with a sigh.

"I had to see her, Ebby."

Ebby smiled at Adam sideways. "I'm beginning to feel as if I'd like to see the lassie myself," he declared.

The conversation was getting a little too personal for Adam's taste so he decided to change the subject. "I've a lot to tell you," he said. "I found out a great deal yesterday and more to-day. We can get into the castle when we want, or at least you can."

"I can!" exclaimed Ebby, looking up in surprise.

"You and your fishermen," said Adam. "You can climb down the cliff on to the shore and get into the castle quite easily. Miss Taylor is to leave the door unlocked; I've arranged it with her."

"But what about——"

"Then you go up a stone stair," continued Adam in even tones. "It's a very curious staircase, inside the rock, and you come out in the cellars of the castle. I'll make a plan of the castle for you."

"Are you feeling ill?" asked Ebby, looking at Adam with solicitude.

"I can't climb down the cliff," replied Adam shortly.

"But you must be there!" cried Ebby. "We couldn't manage without you. We could get into the castle, I dare say, but we'll need you to deal with Taylor——"

"I've told you——"

"I know, but we could never do it ourselves."

"Why not?"

"Because . . . great snakes, because we couldn't!"

"Then you'll have to get someone else."

Ebby left the matter in abeyance for a few minutes while he set out the supper and ladled the stew into large enamel plates. It was an excellent supper and deserved the full attention of the trenchermen. The stew consisted of mutton and bacon with mushrooms in it, and there were toasted scones and a square of honey and a pot of steaming coffee. Ebby had promised Adam that he would not go hungry if he took up his residence in the cave and he had kept his word—Adam was fed like a fighting cock.

"I don't know how you do it," Adam declared as he helped himself to a chunk of butter and spread it on his scone. "I'm not asking, of course. I'm just wondering."

"Keep on wondering," chuckled Ebby.

There was silence for a few minutes while they ate and then Ebby reopened the subject which they had been discussing.

"It won't do, Adam," he said. "We can't carry the thing through without you. We'll need to find some other way."

"There isn't another way."

"There must be; we'll need to find one."

"No, there isn't." Adam hesitated and then added: "You see, Ebby, cripples have their limitations."

"Cripples!"

"Yes, they aren't much use when it comes to mountaineering. They should stick to Bath-chairs . . ."

Ebby threw back his head and roared with laughter; Adam had never seen him laugh so heartily before. "Will we order a Bath-chair for you?" gasped Ebby. "I'll come and push you up and down the road; it will be a grand job for me in my old age!"

The picture evoked by Ebby's words was so comical that Adam was obliged to laugh too. "All the same I can't do it," he declared. "It was bad enough coming up and it would be worse going down. The mere sight of the place gives me the shudders."

"We might get a rope," said Ebby thoughtfully.

Chapter Six

The day, which had been a long and tiring one for Adam, had been just as long—though perhaps not quite so tiring—for Brenda Taylor. She had returned to Tinal Castle without further adventure and had found her uncle sitting on the terrace reading the paper. She was surprised when she saw him and just a trifle dismayed for it was not like Uncle Roland to change his plans without due notice. He rose when he saw her and came to meet her, waving his hand, and Brenda waved back and hastened her steps.

"You've got home!" she exclaimed, trying to smile naturally. "Did you get your business done sooner than you expected?"

"Yes, I managed to get the night train. Are you pleased to see me?"

"Of course——"

"Where have you been?"

Was it Brenda's fancy that he was scrutinising her with more than ordinary advertence?

"I've been for a walk along the river," Brenda said.

Mr. Taylor put his arm through hers and they strolled up to the house.

"Mr. Southey called," continued Brenda. "He wanted to see you, of course, but he came in and talked to me for a little and had a glass of sherry."

"So young Southey called," said Mr. Taylor but he showed no surprise at the information and Brenda was sure that it was no news to him.

"Last night about six o'clock," said Brenda.

"What did you think of Mr. Southey?"

"He's rather—boring."

"Boring!" echoed her uncle with an easy laugh. "Poor young man, I expect he did his best to entertain you. You're too particular, my dear. We must look about and find someone more exciting for you, mustn't we?"

"You said the Baron was coming," Brenda reminded him.

"So he is," replied Mr. Taylor. "He's in rather a different class from young Southey, isn't he?"

"When is he coming?"

"I don't know exactly—to-morrow or the next day; you had better tell the servants to have his room prepared."

"The best spare room?"

"Of course," said Mr. Taylor. "We must do him well. He's used to comfortable quarters."

"Where are his quarters?"

"He told you, Brenda. He lives in London."

"London is rather a vague address, Uncle Roland."

This seemed to amuse Mr. Taylor for he smiled and said: "You seem very interested in the Baron all of a sudden."

"He's an interesting man."

"You had better ask him what part of London he inhabits."

"I shall," nodded Brenda.

Mr. Taylor hesitated and then he said: "I want you to do something for me, Brenda. I ask it as a favour. It isn't often I ask a favour of you, is it? I know you're feeling a bit under the weather—things haven't been going well lately—but you might make an effort when the Baron comes—an effort to be cheerful." He smiled down at her as he spoke and patted her hand; he was trying to charm her and Brenda knew it.

"I haven't been feeling very cheerful," she said and her voice shook a little in spite of her effort to steady it.

"I know, my dear," said Mr. Taylor. "I've been busy and worried and I've neglected you. I'm so sorry about it, but everything is coming right and we're going to have good times again, you and I. You'll help me, won't you?"

"Help you?"

"Yes, by being nice to Ehrling," said Mr. Taylor, smiling at her in a knowing way. "It may make all the difference, not only to me but to you. In fact it's really for your own sake I ask it."

"That sounds rather—mysterious."

"It's business, my dear," he replied. "You don't know much

about business—and I don't want you to. Why should you bother your pretty head with business matters?"

"But you want me to help you," she pointed out.

"I want Ehrling in a good mood, that's all. You needn't do much —just be your old self, Brenda. Be bright and gay and charming. Nobody can be more charming than you . . ."

Brenda shivered.

"Are you cold, my dear?" he asked.

"A little—cold," she replied.

"You will help me, won't you?"

"Yes, Uncle Roland."

"I knew you would. I knew I could depend on you. . . . Come and see what I've brought you from London."

He was talking to her in the old way, rallying her and charming her and Brenda did her best to respond. She followed him into the library and there she saw a large cardboard dress box lying on the table.

"Open it," he said, putting his penknife into her hand. "Open it and see if you like it." His eyes were shining and his voice had a lilt in it—he was as excited as a boy. This was Uncle Roland at his best, for he loved to surprise people, he adored giving presents.

"I mustn't cut the string," said Brenda, beginning to undo the knot . . . but he could not wait for that, and taking the knife he cut the string in three places.

Brenda opened the box. She found that he had brought her an evening frock of stiff taffeta; it was the colour of primroses, and there were shoes and stockings to match and a little yellow bag embroidered with primroses. It was not only a beautiful gift, but it showed that the donor had taken a good deal of trouble. Everything was in perfect taste and the best that money could buy . . . but this was typical of Roland Taylor who never bungled nor did things by halves.

"How did I manage it!" he exclaimed, laughing delightedly at the sight of Brenda's surprise. "How did I know what size of shoes —why I went to your dressmaker of course. She was a most attractive creature and very helpful. She assured me that everything would fit you and I took her word for it."

Brenda was speechless with the mixture of feelings which warred with each other in her breast. She could not help being grateful to Uncle Roland for his thoughtfulness and for all the trouble he had taken on her behalf . . . and the next moment she felt as if she wanted to throw the box and all it contained into the library fire. The dress was lovely, but how could she wear it when she was plotting Uncle Roland's downfall? He was kind and generous . . . He was a devil in disguise . . .

"Uncle Roland——" began Brenda, and then she choked and could say no more and her eyes filled with tears.

Fortunately Uncle Roland was not a mind reader and put his own construction upon Brenda's emotion. "My dear child!" he said, patting her shoulder. "My dear child, it's nothing at all. Your old uncle is fond of you and enjoys giving you a little present now and then."

"I can't thank you——" Brenda whispered.

"Never mind thanking me," he replied, pinching her cheek in a playful manner. "You like it—that's all that matters—and I shall be thanked enough when I see you wearing it and looking beautiful. We're going to have a good time, you and I. We're nearly out of the wood."

"What do you mean?" asked Brenda. "How can we have a good time until the war is over?"

He did not answer that, but began to talk of something else.

The day wore on. Brenda watched Uncle Roland anxiously; he seemed restless and uneasy, he seemed unable to sit still. Brenda saw him consulting the barometer . . . then he went out on the terrace and gazed at the sky.

"Is there going to be a storm," Brenda inquired.

"A storm!" he cried, turning upon her with sudden anger. "What makes you think that?"

"I just wondered," she replied uncomfortably. The atmosphere had an electric feeling, but she realised that this was probably due to the tension of her own nerves—and Uncle Roland's.

"The barometer is perfectly steady," he declared, tapping it again.

Brenda could not understand why he was anxious about the

weather, but she found reason enough for his restlessness in the fact that Cheller was not at hand. He asked her twice if she had seen Cheller that morning and Brenda replied with perfect truth that he had not been up to the castle.

"He didn't know you were coming home so soon," she pointed out.

"You saw him last night?"

"Yes, I told you about that."

"He didn't leave any message?"

"No."

Teatime came. Sykes laid the table in a sheltered corner of the terrace for the sun was warm, but there was a chill in the breeze.

"Where's Cheller?" asked Mr. Taylor, looking up from the book he was reading and speaking with a good deal of irritation.

"I couldn't say, sir," replied Sykes.

"If you mean you don't know why not say so?"

"Yes, sir," said Sykes with a bewildered air.

Brenda was longing to ask why her uncle was so anxious to see Cheller—it would have been quite a natural question—but she was so afraid of saying too much and betraying herself that she closed her lips firmly and remained dumb.

"I shall have to go down to Yowe Farm," declared Mr. Taylor after a few moments' silence.

"To see Cheller?" asked Brenda.

"Yes, of course."

Presently he took his hat and stick and walked off and Brenda watched him go and wondered if he would find Cheller at the farm and, if so, what they would say to each other. Her mind had been so full of other things that she had not had time to worry very much about Adam, but now that she was alone she began to feel anxious. Had Adam managed to escape from the two men? Perhaps Adam had turned the tables and caught Cheller; perhaps that was why Cheller had not come up to the castle. Brenda was less worried than might have been expected for her faith in Adam was unbounded. He was strong and active and full of resource . . . but all the same she was a trifle uneasy. She wandered about, tidying the place and putting things away. Uncle Roland was untidy; he had left his book lying on the ground beside the tea table, lying on the damp ground. Brenda picked it up and was about to put it away when she noticed that it was a book about South America and this surprised her for as a rule Uncle Roland preferred to read novels or detective stories. South America, thought Brenda, standing on the terrace with the book in her hand. What interest had Uncle Roland in South America?

At dinner Uncle Roland seemed in tremendous spirits. His eyes were bright and he laughed and joked and complimented Brenda on her appearance. He asked if she had tried on the new frock and whether it fitted well, and Brenda replied in the affirmative.

"Did you see Cheller?" Brenda inquired, lifting her eyes suddenly and looking at him.

"No, I didn't go down to the farm after all," replied Mr. Taylor, but his eyes flickered as he spoke and Brenda was sure he was lying.

"You didn't go down to the farm!" she exclaimed. "But I thought you wanted to see Cheller, Uncle Roland."

"I changed my mind," he replied. "I didn't go near the place and I didn't see Cheller. I went for a walk up the river instead. It was a lovely afternoon . . ."

"I thought you wanted to see Cheller," Brenda repeated.

"Yes, but I wasn't going to chase him all over the place. He ought to come here and see me; I shall have something to say to him when he comes."

She was all the more sure that Uncle Roland was lying because he now began to speak of Adam Southey and to speak of him in quite a different way. This morning he had spoken somewhat contemptuously of Adam, but his tone had changed now—and why should it have changed unless Uncle Roland had seen Cheller and heard about this morning's chase over the hills? She was thinking of this and smiling secretly to herself when she suddenly discovered that Uncle Roland was trying to pump her about Adam's movements.

"Did he tell you where he was staying?" asked Mr. Taylor in a casual voice.

"Do you mean Mr. Southey?" asked Brenda innocently. "I thought you said he was staying at Lurg House."

"Not now," replied Mr. Taylor. "But perhaps they would know where he is. You might ring up Miss Brownlee and ask her where he's gone."

"Ring up Miss Brownlee!" exclaimed Brenda in amazement.

"Why not? You can ring her up after dinner——"

"But I scarcely know her," objected Brenda. "She would think it most awfully odd. Why have you suddenly taken such an interest in Mr. Southey?"

"I've heard of a job that might suit him."

That was another lie—she was sure of it. She said: "Oh, there's no need to bother. I expect he will call again and see you quite soon. He said he wanted to ask you about the fishing."

She had closed the subject neatly for Mr. Taylor could not press the point without disclosing the fact that his interest in Adam Southey was acute. He was silent for a few moments and then he changed the subject.

"I can't think what Cheller is up to," said Mr. Taylor seriously. "I can't think why he has not come up to the castle to-day. You say you haven't seen him to-day, Sykes?"

Sykes was handing the pudding. "No, sir," he said. "We 'aven't seen 'im since larst night when 'e came up and saw Miss Taylor in the drawing-room."

"Very strange," declared Mr. Taylor. "I don't know what's come over Cheller lately. He seems unlike himself—you've noticed it, haven't you, Sykes?"

"Oh yes, sir," replied Sykes who made it his business to agree with his master whenever possible.

"A bit depressed, isn't he?" inquired Mr. Taylor in a doubtful voice. "A bit under the weather, wouldn't you say so?"

"Well, sir, I don't know——"

"No," said Mr. Taylor laughing. "I don't know why on earth he should be depressed. That's what you were going to say, wasn't it?"

Brenda was sure that Uncle Roland was wrong. Sykes had been going to say: "I don't know that I should say he was depressed exactly," or words to that effect, but Sykes did not correct the erroneous impression; he left it and retired, somewhat bewildered, to his pantry. Brenda was bewildered too. She was bewildered firstly because Cheller was anything but depressed (he had been uncomfortably bumptious and familiar last night when she had interviewed him in the drawing-room), and secondly because it was most unlike Uncle Roland to speak to Sykes in this way while he was waiting at table. If Brenda had not known Uncle Roland so well, she would have suspected that he had been drinking, but she knew that this explanation of his high spirits and unusual manner was not the true one. What was the explanation? Had Uncle Roland got the plans from Cheller? Brenda felt certain that he had. Brenda felt certain that Uncle Roland had gone down to Yowe Farm and seen Cheller and got the plans. . . . That was why he was so pleased with himself, of course.

The day was over at last. Brenda was thankful to go to bed, but although she was very tired she was too excited and anxious to sleep. Her mind was full of all that had happened and she strove to pierce the veils of the future and to envisage what was going to happen next; she tossed and turned for hours and she was still wide awake when dawn broke and the furniture in her room began to emerge from the gloom and assume its familiar shape. The sea gulls were screaming now, as they always did at the first streak of daylight, and at last Brenda felt that she could lie still no longer so she rose and put on her dressing-gown and leaned out of her window.

The window looked westwards over the sea, so she could not see the sunrise, but she saw the flush of dawn shining upon the waves as they rolled towards her in gentle undulations and broke with little splashes against the reefs. The seagulls were screaming and wheeling and diving into the sea, or floating high up in the sky like pure white snowflakes. Brenda watched and began to feel more peaceful, the fevered thoughts of the night gave place to hope and confidence. The world was so beautiful, it was God's world, and right must triumph over wrong.

Beyond the reefs, about a hundred yards beyond the jagged rocks, Brenda suddenly noticed a curious disturbance in the sea, and at first she thought it must be due to the turn of the tide or to a strong current, a sort of whirlpool. She watched it with interest and saw something dark and glistening rising above the surface of the water. It rose slowly, higher and higher, and the water splashed and glittered round it . . . Brenda held her breath and then gasped with amazement . . . She had never seen a submarine, but she knew she was looking at one now. It was large—so large that when she saw it floating upon the surface she could scarcely believe her eyes—and it was painted dark grey. It was ugly. It was sinister. There was something positively wicked about it. Her eyes were glued to it, she felt as if they were being drawn out of her head, her heart was thumping with excitement. . . . And now Brenda saw little figures appearing from within the bowels of the monstrous thing; she saw them moving about the deck, smartly, busily, as if there was no time to waste . . . and now they had launched a little boat and the boat was leaving the side of the ship and rowing towards the shore.

It was coming here. . . . Yes, it was making straight for Tinal Castle and in another few moments it had reached the rocks and was steering a careful passage between them. It was coming in very slowly, turning this way and then that, skirting the shoals and nosing its way between the reefs . . . So there was a channel, after all, a passage through the rocks that surrounded Tinal Bay!

The boat completed the passage without mishap and now Brenda saw the oars flash as the men rowed across the calm water of the bay. She leaned far out of her window and looked down to the shore below and she saw a man standing there, waiting for the boat to come in, and knew it to be Roland Taylor. He lifted his cap and waved and a figure sitting in the stern of the boat returned the greeting cordially. Then the boat grounded on the shingle—Brenda heard the long-drawn scrape—and the man in the stern of the boat stepped on to the shore . . . Ehrling had arrived.

Brenda was so anxious to see all that was happening down below, and, if possible, to hear what Roland Taylor was saying to his eagerly awaited guest, that she leaned even farther out of her window and craned her neck over the sill, and the morning was so still and windless that she could hear all, and more than she wanted.

"Heil Hitler!" exclaimed Ehrling, standing at attention and giving the Nazi salute.

"Heil Hitler!" echoed Roland Taylor, holding out his hand.

Brenda had seen pictures of the Nazi salute and had formed the impression that there was something slightly ridiculous about it, but now she changed her mind. It was not ridiculous; it was shocking; it was horrible. There was something positively revolting in the sight of these two men standing upon British soil and naming the arch-enemy in reverent tones. . . .

All of a sudden Brenda felt sick and faint, and, sinking on to her knees beside the window she bowed her head in her hands . . . "Oh God, help us!" whispered Brenda struggling with uncontrollable sobs.

Chapter Seven

Baron Ehrling von Brum was in the dining-room when Brenda went down to breakfast; she greeted him cordially with simulated surprise.

"I believe you must have come by aeroplane!" she exclaimed as she shook hands with him.

"By aeroplane!" he said with a laugh. "That is a wonderful idea! Should I land on the roof of Tinal Castle?"

"How did you come?" she asked.

"By train from London in the usual manner."

"I am very glad to see you, anyhow," said Brenda, smiling at him.

"And I am glad to see you," said Ehrling quickly. "I am always glad when I come to Tinal . . . It is a great pleasure to find you looking so well. Your uncle has been telling me that you have not been very well lately."

Mr. Taylor nodded. "Brenda has been feeling a little dull, but you have cured her, my dear Baron."

"I was bored," said Brenda. "We see nobody here—nobody except country bumpkins."

Ehrling looked at Mr. Taylor. "You have not told your niece that you are thinking of leaving Tinal?"

"Going away?" cried Brenda. "Are we really, Uncle Roland?"

"I think we've been here long enough," he said. "You'll be glad to leave Tinal, won't you?"

"Where are we going?" she asked.

"Where do you want to go?"

"To London, of course."

"But what about the bombs?" asked Ehrling with a smile. "The bombs are not very nice, are they? I find them noisy and unpleasant."

"I agree with you heartily," said Mr. Taylor, laughing. "In fact I go a good deal further. The bombs terrify me."

"Where are we going, then?" asked Brenda. "I don't want to go to some other country place; it would be just as dull as Tinal."

She was very anxious to find out their plans but the two men would not be drawn; they began to tease her about her desire to return to London and Brenda played up to them; she assured Uncle Roland that London would be quite safe now and that there would be no more bombs.

"Oh, well, we'll see," said Mr. Taylor kindly. "We'll talk it over with the Baron. He might have some suggestions."

"I should be only too glad to give you any assistance in my power," declared Ehrling solemnly.

She saw a significant look pass between the two men and a shiver of horror ran up her spine . . . For a few moments Brenda had no power of speech nor movement; she felt as if she had been turned to stone. Fortunately her companions had plenty to say to each other for they were both men with wide interests. They discussed the habits of sea birds and especially the habits of the gulls in Tinal Bay. Mr. Taylor informed his guest that a pair of great skuas had nested on the moors and had reared two young birds and his guest appeared very much interested in the circumstances. Brenda, as she listened and toyed half-heartedly with her breakfast, learned that the great skua is rarely seen so far south, that it never lays more than two eggs which are olive brown and about the size of a bantam's egg, and that its habits are cruel and predatory. She might have felt more interest in the great skua if she had not been so apprehensive.

Presently Mr. Taylor rose and took his pipe off the mantelpiece. He said: "So much for the great skua. . . . And now for business, if you are ready, Baron." He turned as he was leaving the room and added in a casual tone: "Oh, Brenda, I think it's about time the servants had their little treat. We'll send them over to Weston to the pictures . . ."

"Not to-night!" exclaimed Brenda. "Not while the Baron is here!"

"Why not?" asked her uncle. "There's a very good film showing at the Regal. The Baron will forgive us if we have a cold supper. He knows that these things must be endured in wartime."

"But of course," nodded Ehrling. "It is understood that the servants must have their annual treat."

"I'll arrange for the village bus to take them over," added Mr. Taylor. "Perhaps we could have soup, or something—you'll see to it, won't you, Brenda?"

Brenda nodded; she could not speak. She was sure that this matter had already been discussed and settled between her uncle and his guest. Something was going to happen to-night and they wanted the servants out of the way. She sat on at the breakfast table after the two men had gone and tried to think what the plan could be. Perhaps the submarine would return to-night and fetch Ehrling and the plans . . . and perhaps Uncle Roland intended to go with Ehrling. Could that be possible? Brenda considered the matter—or tried to consider it—coolly. Did Uncle Roland intend to go with Ehrling and leave her behind? It did not seem likely . . . it seemed more likely that he intended to take her with him. Perhaps this was what he had meant when he said there was "a good time coming" and that they were "nearly out of the wood." It all fitted in, thought Brenda, trying to steady herself and to still the wild fluttering of her heart. It all fitted in so well. She was to "be nice" to Ehrling so that he would agree to take her . . . It was for her own sake that she was to "be nice" to him.

Brenda poured out another cup of coffee and her hand was shaking so that some of it was spilt on the cloth. She looked at the brown stain in dismay . . . "*This won't do*," said Brenda firmly. "You've got to pull yourself together, Brenda Taylor."

When she had drunk the coffee, she felt a good deal better and more able for the fray. After all Uncle Roland was not the only person who was making plans . . . there was Adam . . . they would have to reckon with him. She must send a message to Adam at once, but, before she did so, it might be a good plan to have a look round Ehrling's room.

Brenda rose and went out into the hall; the two men were in the library and it would have been interesting to know what they were saying to each other now that they were alone (they would not be discussing the habits of the great skua); but the library door was firmly shut so there was no chance of overhearing their conversation. She went upstairs and along the passage to the best spare room which had been prepared for Ehrling. The door was slightly ajar. Brenda peeped in and saw his suitcase in the middle of the floor; it was open and some of the garments had been taken out and scattered about the room. Ehrling had started to unpack, but had been interrupted in the middle of his task.

There was nobody about for the servants had not yet come up to make the beds, so Brenda slipped into the room and began to search feverishly amongst Ehrling's belongings. She scarcely knew what she hoped to find . . . papers, perhaps, or German money, something which would prove that Ehrling was a German agent. She looked everywhere; she turned over his clothes and tried to discover a hidden pocket in the lining of his suitcase; she opened his collar box, and the case where he kept his hair brushes; she felt in the pockets of his suits; but Ehrling was too clever, too thorough in his methods to leave anything to chance.

Brenda was about to give up in despair when she saw a small notebook lying on the floor beside the bed (she would have seen it before, but a chair had been moved and the notebook was almost hidden by the cretonne frill). Brenda picked it up and opened it. She found an envelope inside. For a moment she hesitated with the book in her hand. Could she risk taking the notebook, that was the question . . . Would there be a tremendous hue and cry when Ehrling found it was gone? At that moment she heard footsteps outside the door and she realised that it was too late and that she had lost her chance. She thrust the envelope down the neck of her pullover inside her clothes and dropped the notebook on the floor; then she seized the jacket of Ehrling's pyjamas which was lying on the bed and began to fold it up.

"My dear young lady!" exclaimed Ehrling's voice from the doorway.

"I was unpacking for you," said Brenda breathlessly. "We're rather shorthanded at present because the footman was called up and I haven't replaced him—so I do what I can to help . . ."

"But this is dreadful——"

"I like doing things," she babbled, "and the butler is stupid—I knew he wouldn't unpack properly for you—so I thought——"

"But I cannot allow you to do this work for me! I had already started to unpack, and then the breakfast gong was sounded . . .'

"I'm afraid you aren't a very tidy person," said Brenda, shaking out the legs of the pyjamas as she spoke.

He came forward and tried to take them away from her. "No, no," he said earnestly. "This I cannot allow."

Brenda began to laugh. Perhaps her laughter was somewhat hysterical but, if so, Ehrling did not notice for he had begun to laugh too.

"This is a good joke," he declared. "We have a tug of war with my poor pyjamas . . . but truly I cannot let you work for me."

She saw that he was completely deceived and that any suspicions he might have entertained were lulled to rest (it had been a bad few minutes but she was safe now) and because it had been so easy to deceive him she was able to smile.

"Your uncle is waiting," he said regretfully. "I came up to find my notebook—ah, here it is! I wish I could stay and talk to you for a little while. It would be very pleasant indeed."

"Yes," agreed Brenda somewhat doubtfully.

"We understand each other very nicely," continued Ehrling, looking at her with admiring eyes. "It is nice to have jokes together, just you and I."

"But you said Uncle Roland was waiting."

"Yes," he replied with a sigh. "Yes, I must not stay. It is business first and then pleasure afterwards . . . But wait, there was an envelope in my little book!"

"An envelope?" asked Brenda.

"A long thin envelope . . . "

"Is it important?"

"No, not important at all," replied Ehrling, looking about the room with an anxiety that belied his words. "Not important, no, no."

"Perhaps you put it in your pocket."

"No," he said, feeling himself all over. "No, it is not there."

"I'm afraid you're worried about it," said Brenda, and she, too, began to search, pulling out the drawers and looking beneath the piles of clothes which lay on the bed.

"No, I am not worried," he replied. "It is nothing—nothing at all. I must have left it in the—in the train. Yes, that must be it. I had it in my hand . . . it must have blown away . . ."

"How annoying! I hate losing things."

"But this is nothing," Ehrling assured her. "It is of no consequence at all . . . I must not waste any more time looking for it or your good uncle will be getting impatient."

Back in her own bedroom with the door safely locked, Brenda took out the envelope and examined it; she found, inside it, a thin sheet of tracing paper with curious markings which looked like a tracing from a map. There was nothing written on the paper except figures, small neat figures put in with red ink, nor was there anything to show which way up the map—if map it were—should be looked at. Brenda was disappointed with her find for she had hoped to discover something incriminating, something which would be of use to Adam. For a moment she wondered whether this could possibly be the plan of which Adam had spoken, the plan of the fortifications which Cheller had obtained for Uncle Roland . . . but she decided that it was too small and insignificant. There were no guns marked on it, no defences. There were only queer little wavering lines and little red figures. She would send it to Adam, of course, thought Brenda, as she turned the paper this way and that and tried to find some meaning in it, and she must write him a letter, as well, telling him of Ehrling's arrival. Brenda took a sheet of paper and began to write her letter.

Chapter Eight

It was raining now. The rain was soft and misty and it blew across the garden like smoke from a bonfire, shrouding the hills. Brenda opened the front door of the castle and went out. She had put on her waterproof and had tied a scarf over her head so she did not mind the rain; in fact it was rather pleasant to feel the soft moisture on her cheeks and forming into drops of dew upon her eyelashes. She went across the drawbridge and took the river path, and here the atmosphere was even thicker for there was no breeze to blow the mist away. It covered everything; it lay like cotton wool over the river and over the path. The trees loomed up as Brenda approached and faded out again.

Every now and then Brenda stopped and listened . . . just in case someone might be following her. It was Cheller she feared most for she had a feeling that Cheller suspected her. Uncle Roland was fond of her in his own queer selfish way and the Baron could be charmed and wheedled and deceived fairly easily, but Cheller . . . Cheller was sly . . . Cheller hated her. She wondered where Cheller was this morning for usually he came up to the castle directly after breakfast and he had not yet appeared. She heard Uncle Roland asking Sykes about him, talking about him as he had talked last night at dinner— in that same curious way. Brenda felt sure that there was some mystery about Cheller. She was so strung up that every nerve in her body was alive; it was as if her senses were quickened and she could hear and see things which in normal circumstances she would not have noticed, things like the sudden stiffening of muscles beneath the skin of Uncle Roland's face and the slight difference in the tones of his voice when he was lying.

Brenda walked on, she heard nothing and saw nobody and soon she reached the bridge. She was just putting her hand into the crevice to find Adam's cigarette case when a figure appeared at her side . . . it loomed out of the mist in an uncanny sort of way . . . it was so close that she could have touched it.

Brenda was too frightened to scream and she was too frightened to run away for her knees were knocking together, so she stood her ground and looked at the figure which had risen out of the mist and she was somewhat reassured to discover that it was not Cheller, nor anyone she knew. It was a strange little man in a brown tweed suit with sandy hair and freckles; there was nothing alarming in his appearance, in fact he was smiling at her in quite a friendly way.

"What are you doing here?" asked Brenda. "This is private property—you've no business to be here."

"I'm from Mr. Southey," replied the man in a low voice. "I was just putting Mr. Southey's letter in the cache when I heard you coming so I waited."

Brenda looked at him searchingly.

"I'm Ebenezer Ford," he added with a kind of quaint dignity.

So this was Ebby! Brenda had heard quite a lot about Ebby. She smiled at him.

"I didn't mean to frighten you," Ebby continued. "I'm afraid I gave you a bit of a start. I was just waiting to make sure it was really you before I showed myself."

"You frightened me horribly. I thought you were Cheller," she replied.

"Is Cheller somewhere about?" asked Ebby, looking round anxiously. "I don't want to meet Cheller."

Brenda shook her head. "It's rather mysterious," she said. "I haven't seen Cheller since yesterday morning when he ran up the hill after Mr. Southey and disappeared. I wondered whether—but it doesn't matter about Cheller. Tell me about Mr. Southey—is he safe?"

"He's fine," replied Ebby. "He led those two men a grand chase over the hills and managed to catch one of them at the end of it."

"Not Cheller?" she asked.

"No, the other one. It was a fellow called Black. Mr. Southey hid behind a peat stack and leapt out at him and caught him by the knees . . . I guess the fellow got a bit of a surprise," declared Ebby, smiling.

Brenda smiled too. It was nice to hear about Adam's doings. "Did you help him to catch the man?" she asked.

"Not I," replied Ebby. "I was away up the hill by that time. I saw the whole thing. I saw him lay the fellow out in grand style."

"I didn't know what to think when I saw Cheller and Wilson take after him," said Brenda. "I had no idea Wilson was mixed up in all this."

"He said he wasn't—after Mr. Southey tripped him. He said he thought Mr. Southey was a poacher. Mr. Southey knew different, though, and he tied him up and left him by a peat stack. Then he went to the Highland Bull and told Mr. Brownlee's nephew about it all. He took Black—or Wilson—to the police and told them a story that will hold him there until my brother or Dow gets back from Edinburgh on the next van to Lurg and can identify him."

Brenda looked astonished. "But how could they identify him?"

"I forgot," Ebby said, "that you don't know about all that. It's a long story about Mr. Southey and Black in Perth when Mr. Southey and my brother and Dow were driving here from Edinburgh."

"And where was Cheller while Mr. Southey was doing this to Wilson?"

"He was running after me," replied Ebby. "It was a good chase. I've not enjoyed myself so much for years."

"And he's none the worse?" asked Brenda anxiously.

Ebby was aware that Miss Taylor's anxiety was not for Cheller's welfare. He smiled and replied: "He's fine. There's nothing wrong with him at all, Miss Taylor."

"I've been worrying," admitted Brenda with a sigh of relief. "Though, as a matter of fact, so many things have been happening that I haven't had time to worry a great deal. The Baron has arrived, but I've explained all that in my letter."

"Ehrling has arrived!"

"Yes, and Mr. Taylor has got the plans—I'm almost sure of it ... but it's all in the letter," added Brenda, holding it out as she spoke.

Ebby took the letter and gave her one in return. "That's from Mr. Southey," he said as he handed it over. "You'll burn it, won't you, miss? I don't hold with letters, myself, for I've known them to cause a good deal of trouble one way or another."

"I'll burn it," promised Brenda. She raised her eyes as she spoke and saw that Ebby was gazing at her from beneath his shaggy brows with a curiously intent stare.

"What is it?" she asked.

"I was looking at you," said Ebby frankly. "There's a lot been put on your shoulders and they're not very broad."

"I can do what I've undertaken to do," said Brenda in a sober tone.

"Yes, I believe you can."

"I shall unlock the door to-night after dinner and——"

"To-night!" exclaimed Ebby.

"It must be to-night."

"Are you sure, miss?"

"Quite sure. If you don't come to-night it will be too late."

She spoke urgently, and looked at Ebby to see if he appreciated the urgency of the matter . . . but Ebby had gone. Ebby had vanished into the mist in the same manner as he had appeared and without a sound . . . and now she realised why he had disappeared so suddenly for she heard the sound of footsteps approaching. There was somebody coming along the path.

Brenda climbed on to the bridge and waited. She wanted to see who it was, and she could see from the bridge without being seen. It might be Cheller . . . somehow or other Cheller was so much on her mind that it would be relief to see him and to know where he was and what he was doing . . .

It was not Cheller. It was two people. It was Uncle Roland and his guest. Brenda leant over the parapet of the bridge for she wanted to hear what they were saying to each other . . . She could hear the sound of their voices growing louder as they approached.

". . . no, it was on a ledge," Uncle Roland was saying. "It was in a crevice between two rocks. If it were not for this damned mist I could easily take you up and show you where it was."

"The young birds will have flown some time ago," declared Ehrling's deeper voice.

"Oh, yes, but the nest itself is interesting. I found . . ."

Brenda waited till they had passed. She could not help smiling but she was annoyed all the same. Why couldn't they have talked about their plans and given her the information she desired instead of discussing that wretched skua and its nest? As she walked home she thought of Ebby and of all the important things which she should have asked him when she had the chance. She had wasted her time with Ebby for she knew no more now than she had known before she met him. She should have asked how they proposed getting down the cliff and how many men they were bringing and what hour they had fixed for their attempt. She should have had everything cut and dried . . . What a fool she had been!

The rain had stopped when Brenda reached the castle; the mist was rising and dispersing and the sun was shining through, and, over the mountain where Adam's cave was situated there was a rainbow, very faint and delicate, but a perfect arch. Brenda stood and watched it for a few moments . . . It seemed a good omen.

Chapter Nine

Brenda was in her room dressing for dinner. She had put on the new frock of pale yellow silk—it was a picture dress with flounces and a lace fichu and puffed sleeves—and she had put on the sheer silk stockings and the shoes which matched so perfectly. She felt no compunction in wearing the dress that Uncle Roland had given her —none at all; in fact it seemed right that she should wear it. Her feelings towards Roland Taylor had been mixed and confused, but they were mixed no longer, for she had seen the depth of depravity to which he had fallen. The sight of him standing upon the shore and giving the Nazi salute had shocked Brenda and shaken her and cleared her mind. She could go forward with a clear conscience; she could wear the dress he had chosen for her and do her best to bring about his ruin.

He wanted her to wear the dress to-night, and she was wearing it. He wanted her to look her best and Brenda intended to give him his desire. She had taken a good deal of trouble over her toilet; her dark curls were brushed and shining, her nails were carefully manicured and she had put a touch of colour on her lips. There was no doubt about it, Brenda was looking her best (the dress suited her perfectly; it was her colour, it was her style) and Brenda was glad of this for she knew that this would give her confidence and help her to play her role.

Brenda was ready now. She gave a last little pat to her curls . . . yes, they were perfect . . . and then she took up the note that Ebby had given her. There was nothing very much in the note; it was just a few lines to tell her that the writer was thinking of her and that he and Ebby had made their arrangements and would await her signal, but it was Adam's writing—the first scrap of writing she had had from him—and she did not want to burn it. She read it again and marked the firm neat writing, the decisive strokes of the signature . . .

Brenda hesitated with the paper in her hand. It would be quite safe if she slipped it down inside her frock; it could not fall out and nobody would know it was there—nobody except herself. She would know it was there; she would feel it against her breast when she moved and it would give her confidence . . . but she had promised to burn it, she had promised faithfully.

There was no fire in the grate, of course, so she sat down at her dressing-table and put the note in an ash-tray and struck a match. The paper flamed up and sank into charred fragments and she crumbled them into ashes with the match. The mirror reflected her intent face with its delicately chiselled features framed in dark curls. Brenda raised her head and saw the reflection, and looked at it consideringly. Can you do it? she wondered. Are you able to carry through what you have undertaken? What sort of a show are you going to put up? She wondered whether an actress felt like this when she was waiting for her cue at a first-night performance . . . But an actress knew exactly what she had to say, and knew what her fellow actors were going to say. They had practised every movement together, not once but a hundred times.

If things went according to plan it should not be difficult, for all that she had to do was to go down and unlock the door. She would do it directly after dinner while the men were still talking, and the task would be all the easier because the kitchen premises would be empty . . . *if all went well* . . . but supposing something unforeseen occurred and she could not manage it? Supposing they became suspicious and would not let her out of their sight? Adam and Ebby would get as far as the door and find it locked.

Brenda realised to the full the importance of her part in the proceedings. She had shouldered a heavy burden and she must carry it alone, nobody could help her. The fate of thousands—perhaps millions—depended upon the courage and skill with which she played her part.

The dinner gong booming through the house was Brenda's call to action. She hesitated for a moment and then opened a drawer in her dressing-table and took out a little box and a piece of cotton wool . . . She leaned forward to the mirror and applied a touch of colour to her cheeks. The faint rosy tinge seemed to make her eyes shine. Brenda smiled at herself. She seized a handkerchief and the yellow silk bag—which was large enough to hold a little torch—and ran downstairs.

Dinner was a cheerful meal. The conversation was interesting and well sustained and Brenda was able to join in the talk or listen as she felt inclined. She was not frightened now—fear had passed; something outside her had taken charge and she was moving to its command as a puppet moves when the strings are pulled. The two men were in good spirits and seemed pleased with themselves and each other . . . they were pleased with her, too. Uncle Roland was delighted to see her wearing the new frock and looking pretty and gay; he caught her eye and smiled and nodded approvingly. The Baron had begun to pay her compliments (rather stilted little compliments, they were) and his eyes were bright when he looked at her. Once during dinner, the Baron put his hand over Brenda's and gave it a little pat—and this physical contact was almost unendurable. She glanced at Uncle Roland to see if he had noticed and saw that he was smiling to himself as he bent over his plate. Uncle Roland was pleased.

What were his plans? What thoughts and schemes were hidden behind his smooth face? Brenda wished she knew. She was sure that he intended to leave the castle to-night for she had seen a suitcase in his room, half packed and pushed behind the curtain. He was leaving to-night with Ehrling, but what were they going to do with her? Just for a moment Brenda's spirit faltered and she felt that she could not go on. Supposing Adam failed? Supposing Uncle Roland was able to carry out his plans . . . Brenda would find herself on the way to Germany (was that the intention?) with these two unscrupulous men. Ehrling was in love with her; Uncle Roland was using her as a pawn in his game. If Adam failed . . . but Adam would not fail, you could depend on Adam. . . .

Brenda had lost the thread of the conversation now. She was looking across the big dining-room and in the shadows she seemed to see Adam's face smiling at her encouragingly. She remembered every detail of his face, his grey eyes, his strongly marked eyebrows, his broad open brow and his mobile mouth. His face in repose had a strange sadness as if his life had not been happy, but when he spoke his features came alive and his whole expression altered . . . Brenda had noticed that.

"What are you thinking of, Brenda?" asked Uncle Roland.

"Of London," replied Brenda immediately. "We're going to London, aren't we? The only thing you haven't told me is when we are going."

"That's the only thing we haven't told you," agreed Uncle Roland with a serious face.

"Why can't we fix a day?"

"It wouldn't be very polite to ask the Baron when he is leaving us——"

"But he's coming too," she declared. "I thought that was arranged; you're coming with us to London, aren't you?"

"But, yes," agreed Ehrling. "We go together. It is a pleasant thought."

"You must tell me in plenty of time," continued Brenda, simulating anxiety. "You see there's so much to arrange. The silver and linen have to be packed and it all takes time."

"Don't worry, Brenda, I shan't ask you to achieve the impossible."

"I don't like doing things in a hurry," she complained.

"That's where we differ," declared her uncle. "I like doing things at top speed. It amuses me to step into a train when it has started to move."

"Or to be the last person to cross the gangway of a ship," suggested Ehrling.

Roland Taylor laughed and admitted that this had been his ambition for years, but that he had never managed to achieve it. There was always someone a shade later than he had dared to be, someone who was dragged on board at the fifty-ninth minute.

"I shall remember," declared Ehrling solemnly. "It might happen that some day I should find myself in a position to grant this desire of your heart—who can foretell the future?"

Brenda raised her eyes in time to see a glance pass between the two men—a look of secret understanding and amusement—and then she lowered her eyes quickly so that the long lashes swept her cheeks for they must not see that she, too, was amused. It was amusing and exciting—this curious conversation—for there were so many undertones in it, and Brenda, with her acute perception, was aware of more than one cross-current. Her companions seemed in perfect accord on the surface; they were laughing and joking together and were at one in their effort to delude her and give her a false sense of security, but she had a feeling that beneath the surface of perfect accord each man was watching and waiting and playing his own game . . . She, too, was playing her own game and was actually beginning to enjoy it. How easy it was to deceive them, to act the silly dupe! Brenda had never believed herself to be such a convincing actress—her success gave her a feeling of power and confidence—but perhaps this was dangerous, perhaps she was in danger of going too far and overacting her part. She must not allow herself to be carried away by the tide of excitement which was rising within her.

They were talking about the future now, but unfortunately only in a general way.

"One cannot know the future and that is just as well," the Baron was saying somewhat sententiously.

Roland Taylor laughed confidently and replied: "I can't altogether agree with you there. A strong man with a resolute mind can know his future because he makes it himself."

"Ah, yes, of course," said Ehrling quickly.

He had agreed too quickly—or so Brenda fancied—and she fancied there was an odd tone in his voice, but when she looked at him he was smiling at Uncle Roland in the friendliest manner imaginable.

Chapter Ten

"I'm afraid you don't care for that cold pudding, my dear Baron," said Roland Taylor regretfully.

"But it is excellent!" declared Ehrling, seizing his fork and attacking his neglected pudding with determination.

"I don't care for it much," said his host, pushing the plate aside. "I must say I prefer a hot meal."

"If we hadn't sent the servants——" began Brenda.

"I know, I know," he interrupted. "You can't help it, my dear. It's my own fault for sending them to the pictures, but you might make the coffee, now. The coffee will be hot, at any rate."

"Allow me to help!" cried Ehrling, rising and following Brenda to the side table where the coffee percolator stood, "Allow me to help you, Miss Taylor. I am very good at making coffee."

Brenda would much rather have made the coffee herself, but it was impossible to refuse his help so she surrendered the spoon and watched him making it. He made it very well.

"Perhaps you would like to have your coffee in the drawing-room, Brenda," suggested her uncle. "We still have a few tiresome details to arrange—business matters which would not interest you."

Brenda agreed at once, for the suggestion fitted in with her plans, and she was about to leave the room when she found Ehrling was following her.

"I will come too—just for a moment," he said, smiling at her as he spoke.

This was not what she wanted, for the Baron was beginning to get on her nerves, but she forced herself to return his smile and led the way to the drawing-room.

"Ach, it is well I came!" he exclaimed. "Look at the fire—it wants mending. You will allow me to do this little work for you in repayment for the work you did for me this morning."

"Oh, thank you," said Brenda, uncomfortably.

"And here is your chair," he continued, arranging it near the fire.

"You will be warm and comfortable here and later I will come and talk to you."

"Yes, of course," she replied, sitting down and putting her coffee on the little table beside her.

"It is nice?" he asked anxiously. "The coffee is nice? Have I made it as you like it?"

"Very nice," she replied. "Perhaps it's just a trifle too strong for my taste——"

"Ach, I am sorry about that. I will remember the next time I make coffee for Miss Taylor . . . There," he added, arranging a cushion behind her back, "there, that is comfortable. I think you are just a little tired."

"Yes, just a little," agreed Brenda, hoping that he would go.

"What a picture!" he said standing back and looking at her with undisguised admiration. "I think it would inspire a painter to see Miss Taylor in her yellow gown."

Brenda tried to smile but without much success. She said: "My uncle has gone into the library."

"He will not mind waiting a few moments."

"I think you should go."

"I will go," said Ehrling. "Presently I will return and see if you are ready for a little talk. You will not be cross with me?"

"Cross with you?" she asked in surprise.

"Sometimes one has to do something that seems a little unkind," said Ehrling, choosing his words with care, "but all the time one is doing it for the best."

"I don't know what you mean."

He took out a big silk handkerchief and wiped his face. "It does not matter," he declared. "You will understand later. You do not dislike me, Miss Taylor?"

"No, of course not."

"That is nice," he said, smiling at her. "Later, perhaps, you will like me even better. I will go now for there is still some business to be settled and you will rest quietly till I return."

He went away and Brenda was left in peace. It was her chance, now. The moment had come for her to go down and unlock the door. She half rose from her chair and then sat down again for it might be as well to wait a few minutes until Ehrling was safely settled in the library and they had started to talk.

Brenda waited. She watched the fire. Ehrling had mended it thoroughly; he had piled up the coal so that the flames were shooting half-way up the chimney . . . It was very hot . . . She found herself yawning. She lay back in the chair and relaxed her limbs. She was feeling the reaction to her excitement . . . Last night she had not slept at all so it was natural that she should feel a little sleepy . . . Brenda closed her eyes and then opened them widely. How strange they felt, quite stiff and heavy, and her head felt strange, too. It was as if there was something on the top of her head, pressing it down. The feeling was not really unpleasant, she just wanted to rest her head on the cushion and . . . shut her . . . eyes. . . .

"But I can't," said Brenda aloud, sitting up and trying to shake off the lethargy. "I mustn't go to sleep."

She must not sleep until she had unlocked the door . . . the door. . . . Brenda fixed her mind on that. She dragged herself out of the chair by main force and stumbled across the room. Her limbs felt limp and heavy, her eyes were misty.

It was cooler in the hall and the air revived her. She noticed that the door of the library was slightly ajar and she heard the murmur of voices. She went past it quickly and through the kitchen premises and along the passage to the cellar . . . but now she was beginning to feel much worse . . . sick and faint and deathly cold.

Brenda leant against the door at the top of the stairs and tried to steady herself. She knew now what was the matter: they had poisoned her. They could not leave her behind because she knew too much . . . so they had done this. . . . Instead of taking her with them . . they had . . . poisoned her. . . .

Brenda's eyes were growing dim. She rubbed them and opened them widely, but it made no difference. She was blind—or very nearly blind; the shadows were closing in. Her torch was useless; it fell from her limp fingers and rolled down the stairs, clattering on the stone steps and smashing to atoms against the rock.

The noise stirred something in her clouded brain and she remembered what she had to do. The door . . . she must go down and unlock the door. She began to go down the steps, one step at a time, leaning against the wall and feeling her way with her hands. Every now and then there was a roaring sound in her ears and it seemed as if the solid rock were going up and down beneath her feet and she stopped and clung to the wall and leaned her forehead against the cold slimy stone. She had forgotten everything now except the door. She was bemused and dazed and trembling. The door . . . could she reach the door? Down, down, more steps and still more steps. She battled against waves of faintness which threatened to swamp her brain. Adam would be waiting at the door . . . Adam would be waiting . . .

Brenda was talking now, talking aloud, but the words ran together and did not make sense.

More steps and more steps . . . down, down, down. She had been going down these steps for hours now—or so she felt—for hours she had been going down . . . so she must have passed the door . . . but the door was at the bottom, wasn't it? How could she have passed the door? She paused and leant her head against the wall and wondered mistily if she should go back . . . go back and try to find the door . . . but something seemed to drive her on, something outside herself.

One, two, three more steps . . . Adam, where are you? . . . Down another step and then another. . . .

Brenda fell against the door, brushing her shoulder on the handle . . . unconsciousness rolled over her like a flood, but she struggled against it like a swimmer struggling to the surface of the water and she groped for the key, groped for it feebly with both hands. . . .

Chapter Eleven

On the same day in the early part of the afternoon Adam and Ebby took the bus over to Balfinny and walked down the steep street towards the harbour. It was a bright breezy afternoon; the sea and sky were almost unnaturally blue and the sun warm and golden. White sea gulls screamed about the harbour and the jetty and there was a strong smell of fish and tar and seaweed.

"This is it," said Ebby in a quiet voice. "This is Ben's house." He stopped as he spoke and knocked on a green-painted door.

The door opened almost at once and an enormous man appeared, an old man with rugged wind-beaten features and a curly grizzled beard.

"Och, Ebenezer," he exclaimed. "Is it yourself, indeed? Come in, come in, and Mr. Southey, too. The boys are all here. We are just going to have our tea. You could not have chosen a better time."

Adam was ushered into the living-room which was below the level of the street and was very small and dark. It seemed smaller because of its occupants: three men and every one of them outsize ... and every one of them was well over forty years old.

Ben introduced them to Adam with dignified gravity. "These are the boys. That is young Ben and that is Fergus and that is David. They are ready for anything, Mr. Southey."

There was a murmur of agreement from the "boys."

"I was wondering if it would be to-night," said Fergus in a soft sing-song voice. "I was wondering if the people we were after might be something to do with the German submarine. It was Walter saw her when he was line fishing near the Black Rock. He was telling me about it. They were expecting her to shoot them and Walter had taken his rifle and was going to shoot back, but instead of that she dived and disappeared. Walter could not be understanding it at all, but I was wondering if her business was so important that she was taking no risks and had no time to spare for a little fishing boat."

239

"Fergus is the talker of the family," said Ben, turning to Adam and winking slyly.

Two chairs had been found and placed at the table for the two guests, and cups and saucers and plates had been fetched from the cupboard. Adam found himself sitting down and accepting a cup of extremely strong tea from one of Ben's sons and a plate of fried herrings from another. Ben, himself, was cutting thick slices of white bread like doorsteps. . . . Although Adam was far too excited to want food he realised that he would have to accept it for it would have been ungracious to refuse.

While they ate, Ebby explained the plans and produced the map-tracing and laid it on the table, and Ben's eldest son, who was known as young Ben, took up the paper and turned it this way and that and shook his head over it.

"This is a queer thing," he said. "There is no north and south marked and nothing to show what part of the coast it is meant to be."

Old Ben reached across the table and took the paper from his son's hand. "I can tell you what it is," he declared. "Yes, it is a map of the reefs at Tinal and of the channel through the reefs. My father was always saying there was a channel, but it was forgotten and the map of it lost, for nobody wanted to use it. Yes, yes, here is the river and here is the bay, and the soundings are clearly marked. You will be wanting the boat to-night, Ebenezer."

"The boat!" cried Ebby. "You don't mean you could take your boat into the bay!"

"Why not?" said Ben simply. "If other people can do it, so can we."

The little fishing boat with the big brown sail put out from Balfinny harbour with six men in it, but if the sight of this unusually large crew caused any curiosity amongst the other fishermen, their demeanour showed no signs of it. There were about twenty fishermen, lounging about the jetty or leaning against the harbour wall smoking their pipes; they gave Ben and his sons a pleasant "Good evening," and smoked on.

Old Ben took the tiller and held well out to sea, making long tacks against the breeze. The boat pitched a good deal and rolled a little as well and the long green waves followed each other slowly and majestically towards the land. Looking back, Adam saw the little village dwindle in size, he saw the cliffs rising from the sea's edge and behind them rose the moors and the blue mountains. Here and there he saw a break in the cliffs, where a burn flowed into the sea, or a pebbled beach with trees creeping down in gentler slopes. Looking ahead there was nothing to be seen but the sun, dipping towards the sea, and a bank of dark grey clouds with golden edges.

Adam was very contented. He had laid his plans otherwise and had reconciled himself to the idea of being tied to a rope and lowered over the cliff by his companions; it was not a pleasant idea for two reasons: first, it was ignominious and second it was alarming. Adam had not been able to make up his mind which he disliked most, the injury to his pride or the possible injury to his body. Ben's idea was better not only from Adam's personal point of view but for the success of the plan . . . it was much better. They had decided to tack pretty far out to sea and to come back with the wind as dark was falling. It would be dangerous to approach the castle in broad daylight but they would need a little light to find their way through the rocks. Ben seemed confident of finding the channel and his confidence was reflected in the faces of his sons. They were not worrying.

The wind sang in the rigging and the mast squeaked . . . and Adam, who was sitting in the bows on an old tarpaulin coat, felt the boat lift to the swell. His heart lifted, too; everything was going to work out splendidly; Ben was grand and his sons were exactly the sort of fellows he had hoped they would be. They were big men in every sense of the word, big made and big-hearted, with calm eyes and determined chins.

Fergus, the talker of the family, was sitting next to Adam on a coil of rope, mending a net, his large rough hands twisting and knotting the cord with practised skill. He looked up at Adam once or twice, but said nothing until Adam came out of his reverie and smiled at him.

"Will there be fighting, Mr. Southey?" he asked in a low voice and it was obvious that he hoped for an answer in the affirmative.

"I don't know, but we must be prepared for anything," Adam replied, and having reminded himself of the necessity for being prepared he took Mr. Brownlee's revolver out of his pocket and began to load it.

Fergus watched him. "So it is really serious," he said.

"Yes, very serious. They're desperate men."

"It is funny that a gentleman like Mr. Taylor should be mixed up in this business," Fergus said. "He is in the Home Guard. He is a nice gentleman to speak to, free and easy and pleasant."

"Yes, I know," said Adam.

"I did not believe the story that Walter told me, but perhaps it is true after all."

"What was that?"

"It is a queer tale," declared Fergus, shaking his head. "It was Walter's cousin who was here staying with Walter last summer and he saw Mr. Taylor at one of the Home Guard meetings. Walter's cousin said he recognised Mr. Taylor and he was an officer in Walter's cousin's regiment in the last war, but he got into trouble and was sent home from France and dismissed from the service. Walter said his cousin was sure it was the same man though it was twenty-five years ago, but I was not believing the story, myself, for I thought Walter's cousin was making a mistake. I thought it could not be Mr. Taylor, but some other man who was like him."

"Twenty-five years is a long time," said Adam thoughtfully.

"That is just what I said to Walter," agreed Fergus.

"Did your friend say what sort of trouble it was?"

"He said it was cowardice in the face of the enemy," replied Fergus in a low voice. "There was an order to advance and the officer did not do it. Och, it was a dreadful thing! It could not have been Mr. Taylor."

They were silent for a few minutes after that, and then one of the other men raised his hand and pointed, and Adam, following the line of the finger, saw several small specks on the horizon against the sunset clouds.

"Destroyers," said Fergus, nodding. "They have come out to look for Walter's submarine. I wonder if they have found her yet."

"They have not used any depth charges," said young Ben shortly.

"Not yet," agreed Fergus.

"The sea is a big place," said young Ben.

"But the Navy has keen ears," retorted Fergus.

They both laughed at that and old Ben called out and asked what the joke was. It was repeated to him in detail and, although it seemed to Adam that the joke had lost what little humour it possessed by being repeated and explained, old Ben seemed quite pleased with it and chuckled delightedly.

The sun had set by this time and the western sky was aflame, but Ben still held upon his course and it was not until the light had begun to fade that he put over the tiller and made back to land. The waves were behind them now, lifting the boat with a forward motion, but the breeze had died down a little and they seemed to be making less speed. Adam began to worry. It was getting darker, the sky was full of clouds, the moon would not rise until midnight and that would be too late. He began to think that old Ben had misjudged the distance and taken them out too far.

"Fergus," said Adam in a low tone. "It's getting very dark."

"It is going to be a very dark night . . . there will be mist later."

"How do you know?"

"By the smell," replied Fergus with a chuckle.

"How shall we get through the reefs in the dark?" asked Adam anxiously.

Fergus held up a line with a lead attached to it. "I am the one to take the soundings, Mr. Southey, and the soundings are marked in the chart. It is lucky the sea is going down."

"But how will your father see the chart in the dark?" Adam inquired. "Has he got a torch? I could lend him mine if he wants it . . ."

"It is in his head," said Fergus simply.

"In his head?"

"He has made a picture of the chart in his head," explained Fergus patiently. "That is the best way to do it, Mr. Southey."

Adam was silent. He felt he had made himself look foolish by trying to interfere. Old Ben and his sons knew what they were doing, they were experts at this job and he was a novice; he had no doubts at all now of old Ben's ability to get them through the reefs and into the bay. But having set these anxieties at rest Adam began to worry about his own part in the affair. He had not been able to make any definite plans for he did not know what he would find when he entered the castle. He did not know where Taylor and Ehrling would be. Taylor might be packing . . . so might Ehrling for that matter . . . and if so the two men could be taken separately and tied up securely. Then the plans of the ray must be found. On the other hand Taylor and Ehrling might be together and Cheller, too, perhaps. If all three men were together there might be trouble . . . but what was the use of thinking about it and trying to decide what to do? He must leave it to chance and do the best he could when he saw how the land lay.

Adam wrapped the tarpaulin coat round his shoulders and crouched lower in the boat. His spirits were falling and he was cold and cramped. He thought of Brenda and wondered whether she was going down the stairs to unlock the door . . . perhaps she was on her way down now, at this very moment. Poor little Brenda going down those horrible stairs in the dark! He hoped she would not be very frightened. She would never be frightened again, thought Adam, he would see to that. He would take care of her always. Adam had been thinking quite a lot about the future and he had decided to accept Mr. Brownlee's offer to be his secretary. There was no reason, now, why he should not accept it and every reason why he should. It would be a good job, a much better job than schoolmastering for a married man . . . Adam could not help smiling at the idea of himself as a married man.

After a little he heard the sound of surf breaking on the rocks. He raised his head, but he could see very little, only the dark mass of cliffs and the squat towers of Tinal Castle outlined against the sky. He was peering ahead and wondering how near the reefs were when old Ben gave an order, the sails came down with a clatter and were quickly stowed, and young Ben and his brother David got out the oars and began to row.

The oars were muffled and made no noise . . . there was no noise at all save the gurgle of the water beneath the boat and the swish of the waves on the rocks. It was very dark; there was not a star to be seen for the clouds had covered the sky. Adam could scarcely see his hand when he held it in front of his face, but he realised that the fishermen were used to darkness and could probably see a great deal better than he could.

Fergus was right up in the bows and had begun to call out the soundings in his soft sing-song voice and every few minutes old Ben would give a direction and change the course slightly. Presently Adam became aware of dark masses of rock which rose up at each side of the boat as it moved slowly along. The oars dipped when they could, but soon the channel narrowed and the rocks were so close that the oars were shipped and the boat was pushed along by hand . . . and all the time old Ben's voice came through the darkness, clear and confident, and was obeyed instantly by his crew. The boat nosed along, turning this way and that, turning away from an obvious channel where the water looked deep and clear and pushing through long strands of seaweed which made a strange sweeping noise against the hull. There was one place where the seaweed was so thick that it seemed to strangle the boat and it took their united efforts to push her through (even old Ben showed a trace of anxiety here and murmured to Ebby that he doubted the boat from the submarine must have drawn less water than his) and then, quite suddenly, the jagged rocks drew back and the boat was free and floating calmly in the bay; a few swift strokes with the oars brought her into the velvet shadow of the cliff . . . Old Ben had done his part in the night's adventure.

Without a word five men scrambled on to the rocks, and young Ben, who was to stay with the boat and keep open their line of retreat, pulled away into the deeper water and let go the anchor. Adam heard the splash of the anchor as he took his place at the head of the party and led the way up the beach. He had a moment of frightful anxiety now, for supposing they found the door locked? Supposing Brenda had not been able to play her part in the business? She would do her best, he knew, but anything might have happened. Adam was so apprehensive that he hesitated to try the door and it was Ebby who stretched out his hand and opened it.

The door opened easily, it swung back about a foot and then stuck, for there was something behind the door which prevented it from opening farther. As Ebby was much the smallest of the party he took Adam's torch and squeezed through the aperture . . . in another moment the door swung open.

The torch was shining, lighting up the dark cavern of rock, and lying, half on the ground and half on the first steps of the stairs, was Brenda Taylor. Her face was haggard and grey and streaked with dirt; it seemed all the more ghastly with the patches of colour on the cheeks; her yellow silk dress was soiled and bedraggled like a daffodil which has been trampled in the mud; beside her lay a yellow shoe—a tiny shoe stained with water and green slime.

"Oh, heavens, she's dead!" cried Adam, falling on his knees beside her. "She's dead—and I've killed her! Oh, Brenda! Oh, speak to me, Brenda!"

"No, no," said Ebby, taking his arm and shaking it gently. "It's all right, Adam. She's not dead. I've felt her heart and it's beating quite evenly; she's been drugged, I think."

"Drugged?"

"Yes, feel her heart, Adam. Listen to its even beat."

Adam put his ear against her breast and he heard the faint pulsing of her heart and felt the warmth of it. . . .

"She's been drugged," whispered Ebby. "They've drugged her, but they couldn't prevent her from opening the door. She's done her part in the night's business."

Adam realised the implication and he took a grip of himself. (It was not very easy, for the sight of Brenda lying on the stairs had shocked him and shaken him to the core.) He rose to his feet and looked round to see if the men were ready and began to climb the stairs. They left old Ben to look after Brenda and as Adam looked back he saw that Ben had taken off his coat and was wrapping her in it as if she had been a child.

"It's better like this," whispered Ebby's voice at his elbow. "She'll be safe with Ben and we'll not have to think of her safety when we come to grips with the men."

This was true enough, but the burden of responsibility lay heavy upon Adam as he climbed up the stairs . . . if he made a mistake . . . if he bungled it . . . if Ehrling escaped with the plans of the ray in his possession. . . . He could not escape by sea, of course, for that way was closed, but he might have an alternative way of escape.

They climbed on silently. The men were wearing stockings over their boots and Adam had put on tennis shoes so there was no sound except the sound of their breathing and the drip of water from the roof. Presently they reached the top of the stairs, crossed the cellar and found themselves in the deserted kitchen premises.

Adam paused at the green baize door. "Fergus here," he whispered, "and David at the front door." He hesitated and then added: "Hit first and hit hard. Nobody is to get away."

"We understand," said Fergus quietly.

Chapter Twelve

Adam opened the green baize door and stepped into the hall. It was dark except for a glow of shaded light from the library door which was slightly ajar; there were voices to be heard and the sound of Mr. Taylor's cheerful laugh. Remembering the big oak screen which stood just inside the library door, Adam slipped into the room and flattened himself against the wall. He had intended Ebby to remain outside the door but Ebby followed him, for Ebby meant to stick to Adam like a leech.

". . . Oh, yes, plenty of time," Taylor was saying. "I'm all packed and ready and the servants won't be back for another two hours."

"Schrübel will come at midnight," Ehrling replied. "He will get the tide and the moon will have risen. Schrübel does not like your rocks in the dark—in fact he does not like them much at any time."

"He won't have to do it again," said Taylor easily.

"It is a pity," Ehrling said. "It is a great pity that you are what you call 'shutting up shop.' You would not reconsider it?"

"No."

"Even now it is not too late."

"I'm bored with the game. I want to get out while the going's good."

"You are doing valuable work, Taylor."

"I've done enough. I told you this was the last time and you agreed. You promised that if I got the ray for you——"

"I know, but there may be other things. Why do you not carry on with the good work?"

"I've told you I'm sick of it. I'm through. It's damned uncomfortable living on the edge of a volcano. You've got what you wanted, now——"

"And you have got thirty thousand pounds," said Ehrling quietly.

"It's worth it!"

"Why, yes. We should not pay if we were not sure of the value.

. . . We are willing to pay for what you do, and it is easy work for you."

"It isn't as easy as you think," said Taylor with a laugh. "Anyhow I don't intend to go on. I've made all my arrangements to leave to-night with you."

"You want to be taken to Ireland?"

"Yes. I've friends there. Brenda and I will stay with them for a bit and then get a boat to South America. It will be healthier there."

"You are sure that Miss Taylor will not object."

Roland Taylor laughed. "She'll do what she's told," he said. "It's partly for her sake that I want to get out of this country."

"You do not want to be here when we come to invade Britain?"

"No, I don't," said Taylor frankly. "Now that you have got the plans of the ray you should find it pretty easy. I don't want to be caught like a rat in a trap when this damned country gets what it deserves."

"That is the difference between you and me," said Ehrling in thoughtful tones. "We work for the same end, but how different our motives!"

"What do you mean?"

"I wish to see my country great and powerful. You wish to see your country in the dust."

"I don't owe my country much."

"Your country owes you nothing, Taylor," declared Ehrling with a laugh. "You have sold a good many of her secrets from time to time and your house has always been a safe shelter for our agents."

"My country doesn't deserve loyalty," replied Taylor and his voice sounded harsh.

"I remember," Ehrling said. "Yes, I remember you were cashiered—it was in the last war—but I cannot remember the charge."

"I was absolutely innocent. The whole thing was a frame-up. I was the scapegoat——"

"And so you turned traitor," said Ehrling softly.

Taylor laughed. It was not a very pleasant sound. He said: "Surely you're the last person who should complain . . ."

"But you misunderstand me, I was not complaining . . ."

"I wanted to get my own back," Taylor said. "I wanted to be even with them—just for my own satisfaction. I'm satisfied now."

"It is not often that revenge is so lucrative," mused Ehrling.

"Oh, you people aren't stingy; I'll say that for you."

"They pay for good value. You are a clever man and successful. It is a great pity that you refuse to go on."

"It's no use, Ehrling. I've made up my mind—and anyhow I couldn't do much without Cheller."

"Were you wise to—eliminate—Cheller?"

"Wise?"

"Were you not a trifle hasty?"

"I don't do things in haste, Ehrling. I had made up my mind to get rid of Cheller. When I went to Yowe Farm yesterday, he gave me the plans for the ray. Berwick's friend at the works finally got hold of them . . . And then he told me how he and Black had chased Southey over the moors. Black is in the hands of the police. He may talk. And besides that, there are men at the works who can identify him. It's not safe for me to stay here and I couldn't leave Cheller behind. I had to get rid of him."

"May one ask how it was accomplished?"

Taylor laughed. He said: "I see no harm in satisfying your curiosity. It happened in the kitchen at Yowe Farm. The poor fellow shot himself."

"Shot himself?"

"Obviously, since the revolver is lying by his side with his fingerprints on it. The coroner will have no difficulty with the verdict—suicide while temporarily insane, I think that is the usual wording."

"Suicide while temporarily insane," repeated Ehrling thoughtfully. "Yes, that is—clever, but forgive me if I say that I still think it a pity."

"It had to be done," explained Taylor. "The man was dangerous, he knew too much. He had promised to hand over the goods and then at the last moment he stood out for more money."

"You had a quarrel?" suggested Ehrling.

"Not exactly—it was just that he was getting too darned expensive."

"Ah, just so. After a little while people tend to become expensive."

"That sounds a bit enigmatic!"

"No, no," said Ehrling, still in the same quiet tone. "No, no, it is merely a statement of fact. You, yourself, have become too expensive."

There was an exclamation of alarm and dismay from Taylor.

"Yes," said Ehrling evenly. "It is a revolver. Put your hands up above your head, Herr Taylor."

"What nonsense is this?" cried Taylor. "You're trying to double-cross me. You'll regret it. I'm not a man to be trifled with."

"Nobody knows that better than I do. It means that this is the end of the road. You have refused to carry on and I feel it would be criminal to waste my country's money. Thirty thousand pounds is a large sum."

"Stop, you're making a mistake. I've played fair with you. You've got the plans of the ray and you've paid me for them."

"How much better it would be if I had both the plans and the money," Ehrling pointed out.

"I'll go on with the work——" began Taylor.

"It is too late," Ehrling replied. "Yes, it is too late now. A few moments ago it was not too late. . . . Keep your hands above your head."

"What are you going to do?"

"Can you not guess?" asked Ehrling with a surprised inflection in his voice. "You are such a clever man. I could not improve upon your plan for eliminating a tool which has become too expensive. When your servants return from their treat they will find you here alone . . . The coroner will have no difficulty in giving a verdict. Meanwhile your niece and I——"

"No!" cried Taylor. "Can't you see for yourself . . . Brenda won't go with you . . . not without me." He raised his voice and shouted: "Brenda! Brenda!"

"I am afraid Brenda will not come," said Ehrling regretfully. "The fact is I was obliged to put a little powder in her coffee. It is quite a harmless drug, but she will sleep for a long time. She will hear nothing and know nothing. When she awakens she will be in the U-boat—perhaps half-way to Germany—with me. She is a dear sweet girl and I feel sure we shall be very happy together. I felt a little sorry when I put the powder in," confessed Ehrling with a sigh, "but I thought it best to spare her the pain of parting from her good kind uncle——"

"You devil!" Taylor snarled.

"Sit still!" cried Ehrling. "I have nearly finished with you but not quite. It is you who are a devil, not I. I am a patriot, but you are a traitor. I have not enjoyed working with you and eating your food, but I do these dirty things for my country . . . so . . . it will give me a great deal of pleasure to shoot you like the dog you are . . ."

Adam had listened to the conversation, first with interest and excitement and then with growing horror, but now he could bear it no longer. He started forward, grasping the small revolver in his hand.

"Wait!" whispered Ebby, seizing his wrist and pulling him back.

At that moment there was a loud report; it was positively ear-splitting in the confined space of the room, and, for a few seconds Adam was too dazed to move. Then he pushed aside the screen and stepped forward and saw Ehrling bending over the arm-chair in which sprawled the figure of Roland Taylor.

"Hands up!" exclaimed Adam, pointing the revolver at the German's head. He thought as he said the words that they sounded foolish and melodramatic . . .

Ehrling swung round and fired as he swung, without aiming, and Adam felt a sharp blow on his shoulder and a stinging pain. He was so surprised at this sudden move on the part of a man who should have been holding his hands meekly in the air that he pressed the trigger of his own revolver without knowing that he did so. The shot went wide . . .

The next moment Ebby had flung himself straight at the German and bowled him over, and the two of them were rolling on the floor.

Adam recovered his senses. He seized his revolver by the muzzle and, awaiting his opportunity, brought the butt of the weapon down on Ehrling's head with all his force.

The German sank back with a groan and Ebby disengaged himself and rose. He was smiling happily.

"Good," he said. "That was good work, Adam."

"Good work!" cried Adam. "It wasn't good work at all. I messed up the whole thing. I'm the most almighty fool in creation——"

"You're not used to it," said Ebby comfortingly. "You'll do better next time. He's a desperate man, and no coward. Always remember this: if you threaten a desperate man you must be prepared to shoot him."

"But I was——" began Adam.

"No, I don't think so," Ebby replied. "It's not easy to shoot a man in cold blood and Ehrling took the chance."

"Is he—dead?" asked Adam in a lower tone.

"No, no, he's got a crack on the head that'll keep him quiet for a wee while."

"I meant Taylor."

"He's dead all right," replied Ebby with a glance at the sprawling figure in the chair. "I knew he was done for. The German didn't bungle. We'll not waste tears on him."

Adam sat down, rather suddenly, in a chair. He felt a trifle faint and there was a queer warm wet feeling inside his shirt.

"You're not hurt, are you?" inquired Ebby anxiously.

"It's nothing," Adam said.

By this time Fergus and his brother had appeared on the scene, and were bitterly disappointed to find that the battle had been won without their assistance.

Fergus was especially reproachful: ". . . and are they both done for?" he inquired. "Och, and we never had a look-in at all! Why did you not call for us, Mr. Ford? We were ready and waiting and looking forward to the fun, and now it is all over . . ."

Ebby cut short his lamentations and, pointing to the figure of Ehrling which was still lying on the floor, requested Fergus to tie him up securely.

". . . and when I say securely I mean securely," added Ebby in significant tones.

The brothers produced yards of strong cord from their pockets and proceeded with their task while Ebby helped Adam to take off his coat and examined his wounded shoulder.

"It's a clean wound," he declared. "There's little harm done as far as I can see. I'll just make a pad to stop the bleeding until we can get a doctor. Just you sit there quietly. We'll see to everything."

Adam pulled himself together. He knew one thing that he must do—and do without delay. There was a telephone standing upon Mr. Taylor's desk and Adam stretched out his hand, took up the receiver and gave Mr. Brownlee's private number.

Mr. Brownlee's private telephone was switched into his bedroom every night, and Adam, who knew of this arrangement, was not surprised when he heard a very sleepy and irate voice at the other end of the line.

"Adam!" said the voice. "Adam Southey, what have you been doing and why the devil are you ringing me up at this unearthly hour? What have you done with my fishing rod—that's what I want to know. Why haven't you sent us some trout? Why haven't you written to Evelyn?"

Adam did not attempt to stem this flow, he let it run on and said nothing at all until it stopped. Even then he said nothing.

"Are you still there?" asked Mr. Brownlee after a moment's pause.

"Yes, sir," replied Adam.

"What do you want, eh?"

This was what Adam had been waiting for. He told Mr. Brownlee what he wanted and Mr. Brownlee, at first cross and incredulous, gradually realised that this was no hoax but an urgent call to action. He promised to get up at once and come to Tinal Castle himself and bring a doctor, and he added that he would ring up the Chief Constable.

That's done, said Adam to himself as he replaced the receiver. He lay back in his chair and looked round the room. . . . It all seemed vague and like a dream. Ehrling had been lifted and placed in a chair; he was still unconscious and his face had a sickly greenish tinge. Opposite to him in the other chair lay the body of Roland

Taylor; his face was the colour of old ivory, his features pinched and frigid. Fergus had wanted to move the body and lay it out decently, for the Highlander has a great respect for death, but Ebby had warned him off and forbidden him to touch anything until the police came and Adam knew that he was right. All the same it was a strange and horrible sight to see them sitting there opposite to each other in the deep easy-chairs—the spy and the traitor—and Adam turned away his eyes.

On the table lay Ehrling's attaché case containing the blueprints of the ray, and beside it Ehrling's revolver which had been found on the floor and which Ebby had lifted very carefully with the tongs so that the fingerprints should not be obliterated. These things lay on the table on the top of the glossy copies of *The Sphere* and *Punch* and *Country Life* which Adam had coveted so much. . . .

And this was the room he had coveted, the comfortable warm room with its deep chairs and its books. He did not covet it now for it seemed sinister, it seemed full of the foul stench of treachery. How many secrets had been sold in this peaceful room? How many shameful plots had been hatched?

Ebby had been busy with various matters and had left his patient to recover quietly, but now he returned and suggested that if Adam felt better he should move into the drawing-room.

"It will be nicer there," said Ebby with a glance at the two figures sitting before the fire.

Adam was only too ready to move. He was feeling more like himself by this time and was able to walk across the hall without assistance, and, as he did so, the baize door opened and old Ben appeared carrying Brenda carefully in his arms.

"Fergus came and said I was to bring her up the stair," announced Ben. "Fergus said it was all over . . ."

"All but the shouting," replied Ebby. "Bring her into the drawing-room, Ben. There's a good fire there and we want to keep her warm . . . put her down on the couch, Ben. That's the way."

"She's looking a wee bit better," said Ben as he laid his burden on the sofa and covered her with a rug. "There's a wee tinge of colour in her face . . . do you notice it, Ebenezer?"

Adam scarcely heard their voices. He knelt down beside Brenda and took her hand and found it warm and moist. Her breath was coming regularly, her bosom rising and falling slowly . . . she looked like a sleeping child.

"She'll be all right," said Ebby quietly, as he put some more coal on the fire. "There's no need to worry, Adam. The doctor will see her when he comes, but I'm sure she'll be all right. The great thing is to keep her warm . . ."

"She opened the door, Ebby."

"There's plenty of spirit in her," Ebby agreed, and he smiled at Adam somewhat slyly.

Adam smiled back with his crooked mouth. "I think she's wonderful," he said.

"There's more than you thinks it," Ebby replied. "You might go far enough before you found her like."